Explorers

D1367887

ALSO BY GARDNER DOZOIS

ANTHOLOGIES

A Day in the Life
Another World
Best Science Fiction Stories of the Year
    #6–10
The Best of Isaac Asimov's Science
    Fiction Magazine
Time-Travellers from Isaac Asimov's
    Science Fiction Magazine
Transcendental Tales from Isaac
    Asimov's Science Fiction Magazine
Isaac Asimov's Aliens
Isaac Asimov's Mars
Isaac Asimov's SF Lite
Isaac Asimov's War
Isaac Asimov's Planet Earth
    (with Sheila Williams)
Isaac Asimov's Robots
    (with Sheila Williams)
Isaac Asimov's Cyberdreams
    (with Sheila Williams)
Isaac Asimov's Valentines
    (with Sheila Williams)
Isaac Asimov's Skin Deep
    (with Sheila Williams)
Isaac Asimov's Ghosts
    (with Sheila Williams)
Isaac Asimov's Detectives
    (with Sheila Williams)
Isaac Asimov's Vampires
    (with Sheila Williams)
Isaac Asimov's Moons
    (with Sheila Williams)
Isaac Asimov's Christmas
    (with Sheila Williams)
Isaac Asimov's Camelot
    (with Sheila Williams)
Isaac Asimov's Werewolves
    (with Sheila Williams)
Roads Not Taken
    (with Stanley Schmidt)
The Year's Best Science Fiction, #1–15
Future Earths: Under African Skies
    (with Mike Resnick)
Future Earths: Under South American
    Skies (with Mike Resnick)

Slow Dancing Through Time
    (with Jack Dann, Michael Swanwick,
    Susan Casper, and Jack C.
    Haldeman II)
The Peacemaker
Geodesic Dreams (collection)

NONFICTION

The Fiction of James Tiptree, Jr.
Future Power
    (with Jack Dann)
Aliens! (with Jack Dann)
Unicorns! (with Jack Dann)
Magicats! (with Jack Dann)
Magicats 2 (with Jack Dann)
Bestiary! (with Jack Dann)
Mermaids! (with Jack Dann)
Sorcerers! (with Jack Dann)
Demons! (with Jack Dann)
Dogtales! (with Jack Dann)
Ripper! (with Susan Casper)
Seaserpents! (with Jack Dann)
Dinosaurs! (with Jack Dann)
Little People! (with Jack Dann)
Dragons! (with Jack Dann)
Horses! (with Jack Dann)
Unicorns 2 (with Jack Dann)
Invaders! (with Jack Dann)
Angels! (with Jack Dann)
Dinosaurs II (with Jack Dann)
Hackers (with Jack Dann)
Timegates (with Jack Dann)
Clones (with Jack Dann)
Nanotech (with Jack Dann)
Immortals (with Jack Dann)
Armageddons (with Jack Dann)
Modern Classics of Science Fiction
Modern Classic Short Novels of
    Science Fiction
Modern Classics of Fantasy
Killing Me Softly
Dying for It
The Good Old Stuff
The Good New Stuff

FICTION

Strangers
The Visible Man (collection)
Nightmare Blue
    (with George Alec Effinger)

Explorers

SF ADVENTURES TO FAR HORIZONS

Edited by Gardner Dozois

St. Martin's Griffin

New York

Design by Maureen Troy

Library of Congress Cataloging-in-Publication Data

Explorers : SF adventures to far horizons / edited by Gardner
Dozois.—1st St. Martin's Griffin ed.
    p. cm.
  ISBN 0-312-25462-8
  1. Science fiction, American. 2. Explorers—
Fiction. I. Dozois, Gardner R.
PS648.S3 E88 2000
813'.087620835291—dc21   99-087937

First Edition: April 2000

10 9 8 7 6 5 4 3 2 1

Contents

Preface

At one time, all humans were explorers, nomads who wandered ceaselessly over the face of the Earth. And even now, thousands of years later, after the invention of agriculture and towns, when most of us stay at home most of the time, many of us still feel a twinge of restlessness every once in a while, a desire to see what's over the next hill or in the next valley—a desire that we can sublimate and satisfy by listening to the travel tales of those who *don't* stay home, the explorers . . . those brave and reckless and restless enough to venture into unknown, uncharted territory and return to tell us what they've found.

Certainly humans have been telling tales of exploration for millennia—it was a venerable tradition even when Homer was telling his tales of danger-filled voyaging around Bronze Age campfires, and who knows what prehistoric *Odysseys*, now lost and forgotten, were being told around campfires thousands of years before *that*? Not surprisingly, those tales have often contained elements of fantasy, elements that probably crept in on a slow night when the tale-teller noticed that his audience was becoming bored and threw in a dragon or a cockatrice or a hundred-headed monster to spice things up a bit . . . and thus we got stories about the men over the next hill who wore their heads upside down, or the people of a distant country who drank human blood, or the land where the ants were as big as horses and mined gold.

Possibly the more sophisticated members of Homer's fireside audiences recognized these fantasy elements *as* fantasy even then and suspected that there weren't really man-eating Cyclops or sorceresses who turned men into swine out there, but it made for a good story—and besides, who knew for sure that there *weren't* such things, eh? The world was wide. There were many corners of it that no one had ever seen. Who knew *what* could be out there?

This uncertainty as to what was Out There has served authors well ever since, from Herodotus to Sir John Mandeville and Baron Münchausen, and even as late as the nineteenth century was enabling authors to get away with peppering the still largely unexplored (from a European perspective) continents of Africa and Asia with fabulous Lost Cities and Lost Civilizations, chock-full of ugly subhuman Beast-Men and beautiful Caucasian girls in skimpy slave-girl outfits and/or revealingly sheer diaphanous gowns. But by the twentieth century the We-Don't-Know-What's-Out-There alibi was beginning to wear a little thin. Edgar Rice Burroughs littered his Africa with Lost Civilizations, as had H. Rider Haggard before him, but even in the first few decades of the new century, the Dark Continent wasn't quite as dark as it used to be, and it was becoming hard for all except the most determinedly credulous reader to believe that those gleaming alabaster Lost Cities were really *out* there somewhere in the jungle, waiting for Scientific Expeditions consisting of an Absentminded Professor and his Beautiful Daughter to stumble across them in chapter 2. Perhaps this is what motivated Burroughs to set up a competing shop on Mars, where it was harder to check up on him.

In fact, as the twentieth century progressed, as even the remotest and most inaccessible places on Earth—the poles, the Gobi Desert, the Congo, the Matto Grosso—were visited by explorers, and the formerly blank areas on the map began to fill up with tidy countries, or at least with detailed information, it became increasingly obvious that to explore *really* unknown territory, places where *no*body had ever gone before, future explorers, both real and fictional ones, would have to move *off* Earth altogether—and into the depths of space.

Writers of Space Opera had been banging around the solar system since the late twenties or early thirties, of course, and had even launched paper armadas into interstellar space, but as World War II approached, perhaps influenced by visionaries such as Konstantin Tsiolkovsky, Herman Oberth, Robert Goddard (who had himself been influenced by H. G. Wells), Wernher von Braun, Willy Ley, and the founding fathers of the British Interplanetary Society, people who actually wanted to *go* into space, for *real*, and who were carrying out the first crude experiments that might someday make that a possibility (and influenced as well by the Campbellian Revolution in science fiction, circa 1939, when the new editor of *Astounding* magazine, John W. Campbell, began downplaying the melodramatic pulp stuff in favor of more thoughtful material that actually made a stab at rigor and scientific accuracy), we began to get stories that took the idea of space exploration *seriously*, as something that might *actually happen*, as something that could actually be done, in the real world . . . that treated space as a real frontier that one day could be—and *would* be!—explored, rather than just as a setting, a colorful backdrop for chase-and-fight pulp fantasies that wouldn't have been much different in their essentials if the setting had been the Spanish Main rather than the rings of Saturn.

By the fifties, as the science-fiction world began to get into full swing again after the partial interregnum of World War II, new writers such as Arthur C. Clarke, Robert A. Heinlein, Hal Clement, Poul Anderson, and a dozen others had perfected the realistic space exploration story—and, ironically, by so doing, had helped to invoke the very thing they dreamed about, to *call* it into being, as if by incantation, by impressing their dream upon hundreds of young men and women who, inspired, would then go on to become the very scientists and engineers and technicians and astronauts who would make manned space travel a physical reality in the sixties and seventies.

By the mid- and later seventies, though, perhaps because of the prominence of the "New Wave" revolution in science fiction, which concentrated both on introspective, stylistically "experimental" work and work with more immediate sociological and political "relevance" to the tempestuous social scene of the day, perhaps because the space probes of the late sixties and early seventies had "proved" that the solar system was nothing but an "uninteresting" collection of balls of rock and ice, dull as a supermarket parking lot, with no available abodes for life, perhaps because of the feeling that the Space Age was *behind* us, a social aberration fading away into nostalgic memory (a feeling that started in the seventies and grew throughout the eighties as years—and finally decades—went by without a return to the Moon or seemingly any further progress into space), science fiction as a genre would tend to turn away from the Space Exploration tale, with most of the stories published taking place on Earth, often in the near-future, and dealing centrally with the sociological and/ or dystopian problems of society.

But then, in one of those ironic reversals characteristic of the genre, in the late seventies and early eighties a new crew of writers such as John Varley, Gregory Benford, Michael Swanwick, Kim Stanley Robinson, Vernor Vinge, Jack McDevitt, and others began to become interested in exploring the solar system again, began to find the solar system romantic and fascinating *just as it was*, lifeless balls of rock and all, even before the later *Voyager* probes to the Jupiter and Saturn system had proved the solar system to be a lot more complex, contradictory, and surprising place than people thought that it was . . . and by now, by the end of the nineties, the realistic Space Exploration story, reinvented to better fit the aesthetic style and tastes of the day in the hands of writers such as Greg Egan, Stephen Baxter, Allen Steele, Paul J. McAuley, G. David Nordley, Charles Sheffield, Geoffrey A. Landis, Ian McDonald, Alexander Jablokov, and a dozen others, is once again at the artistic center of the field.

This anthology, then, brings you a sampling of some of the best stories about explorers and exploration from almost fifty years of science-fiction writing, from 1950 to 1998. This kind of story has gone out of fashion occasionally during that time and may go out of fashion again, but it always comes back, and I suspect that it will continue to fascinate us as long as we look up at the stars at night and wonder what, or *who*, is Out There, as long as something deep inside us feels that restless itch to know what's over the far horizon—in other words, as long as we remain *human*, as we currently recognize the term.

So sit back and relax—you're about to go on a series of marvelous voyages, to explore strange new worlds and uncharted territories, to face strange new dangers and even stranger wonders, dangers and wonders of a sort that could never be encountered on our familiar, present-day Earth, to learn for *yourself* what's around the bend and over the next hill . . . and all without leaving your chair!

Enjoy.

Explorers

The Sentinel

Arthur C. Clarke is perhaps the most famous modern science-fiction writer in the world, seriously rivaled for that title only by the late Isaac Asimov and Robert A. Heinlein. Clarke is probably most widely known for his work on Stanley Kubrick's film 2001: A Space Odyssey *but is also renowned as a novelist, short-story writer, and a writer of nonfiction, usually on technological subjects such as spaceflight. He has won three Nebula Awards, three Hugo Awards, the British Science Fiction Award, the John W. Campbell Memorial Award, and a Grandmaster Nebula for Life Achievement. His best-known books include the novels* Childhood's End, The City and the Stars, The Deep Range, Rendezvous with Rama, A Fall of Moondust, 2001: A Space Odyssey, 2010: Odyssey Two, 2061: Odyssey Three, Songs of Distant Earth, *and* The Fountains of Paradise *and the collections* The Nine Billion Names of God, Tales of Ten Worlds, *and* The Sentinel. *He has also written many nonfiction books on scientific topics, the best-known of which are probably* Profiles of the Future *and* The Wind from the Sun, *and is generally considered to be the man who first came up with the idea of the communications satellite. His most recent books are the novel* 3001: The Final Odyssey *and the nonfiction collection* Greetings, Carbon-Based Bipeds: Collected Works 1944–1998. *Born in Somerset, England, Clarke now lives in Sri Lanka and was recently knighted*

Clarke may well have written more, and more memorably, about the theme of exploration, particularly space exploration, than any other science-fiction writer, dealing with it with one degree or another of centralness in novels and stories such as Rendezvous with Rama, "A Meeting with Medusa" *(to be found elsewhere in this anthology),* "Before Eden," The Sands of Mars, The City and the Stars, "Rescue Party," "Summertime on Icarus," "Out of the Sun," Songs of Distant Earth, "The Star," "Transit of Earth," *and all of the* Odyssey *novels, as well as in scores of other stories and in dozens of nonfiction articles.*

He's seldom handled the theme better, though, than in the classic story that follows, the inspiration for the later movie 2001: A Space Odyssey, *which I think actually works better than the film in some ways—a near-perfect miniature that captures the odd blend of minutely detailed scientific accuracy and sweeping Stapeldonian mysticism that is the essence of Clark's work and a story still capable of delivering in its last few lines that shiver of mingled fear and wonder that is one of the hallmarks of science fiction at its best.*

The next time you see the full Moon high in the south, look carefully at its right-hand edge and let your eye travel upward along the curve of the disk. Round about two o'clock you will notice a small, dark oval: anyone with normal eyesight can find it quite easily. It is the great walled plain, one of the finest on the Moon, known as the Mare Crisium—the Sea of

Crises. Three hundred miles in diameter, and almost completely surrounded by a ring of magnificent mountains, it had never been explored
until we entered it in the late summer of 1996.

Our expedition was a large one. We had two heavy freighters which
had flown our supplies and equipment from the main lunar base in the
Mare Serenitatis, five hundred miles away. There were also three small
rockets which were intended for short-range transport over regions which
our surface vehicles couldn't cross. Luckily, most of the Mare Crisium is
very flat. There are none of the great crevasses so common and so dangerous elsewhere, and very few craters or mountains of any size. As far
as we could tell, our powerful caterpillar tractors would have no difficulty
in taking us wherever we wished to go.

I was geologist—or selenologist, if you want to be pedantic—in charge
of the group exploring the southern region of the Mare. We had crossed
a hundred miles of it in a week, skirting the foothills of the mountains
along the shore of what was once the ancient sea, some thousand million
years before. When life was beginning on Earth, it was already dying
here. The waters were retreating down the flanks of those stupendous
cliffs, retreating into the empty heart of the Moon. Over the land which
we were crossing, the tideless ocean had once been half a mile deep, and
now the only trace of moisture was the hoarfrost one could sometimes
find in caves which the searing sunlight never penetrated.

We had begun our journey early in the slow lunar dawn, and still had
almost a week of Earth time before nightfall. Half a dozen times a day
we would leave our vehicle and go outside in the space suits to hunt for
interesting minerals, or to place markers for the guidance of future travelers. It was an uneventful routine. There is nothing hazardous or even
particularly exciting about lunar exploration. We could live comfortably
for a month in our pressurized tractors, and if we ran into trouble we
could always radio for help and sit tight until one of the spaceships came
to our rescue.

I said just now that there was nothing exciting about lunar exploration,
but of course that isn't true. One could never grow tired of those incredible mountains, so much more rugged than the gentle hills of Earth. We
never knew, as we rounded the capes and promontories of that vanished
sea, what new splendors would be revealed to us. The whole southern
curve of the Mare Crisium is a vast delta where a score of rivers once
found their way into the ocean, fed perhaps by the torrential rains that
must have lashed the mountains in the brief volcanic age when the Moon
was young. Each of these ancient valleys was an invitation, challenging us
to climb into the unknown uplands beyond. But we had a hundred miles
still to cover, and could only look longingly at the heights which others
must scale.

We kept Earth time aboard the tractor, and precisely at 2200 hours
the final radio message would be sent out to Base and we would close
down for the day. Outside, the rocks would still be burning beneath the
almost vertical sun, but to us it was night until we awoke again eight
hours later. Then one of us would prepare breakfast, there would be a

great buzzing of electric razors, and someone would switch on the short-wave radio from Earth. Indeed, when the smell of frying sausages began to fill the cabin, it was sometimes hard to believe that we were not back on our own world—everything was so normal and homely, apart from the feeling of decreased weight and the unnatural slowness with which objects fell.

It was my turn to prepare breakfast in the corner of the main cabin that served as a galley. I can remember that moment quite vividly after all these years, for the radio had just played one of my favorite melodies, the old Welsh air "David of the White Rock." Our driver was already outside in his space suit, inspecting our caterpillar treads. My assistant, Louis Garnett, was up forward in the control position, making some belated entries in yesterday's log.

As I stood by the frying pan waiting, like any terrestrial housewife, for the sausages to brown, I let my gaze wander idly over the mountain walls which covered the whole of the southern horizon, marching out of sight to east and west below the curve of the Moon. They seemed only a mile or two from the tractor, but I knew that the nearest was twenty miles away. On the Moon, of course, there is no loss of detail with distance—none of that almost imperceptible haziness which softens and sometimes transfigures all far-off things on Earth.

Those mountains were ten thousand feet high, and they climbed steeply out of the plain as if ages ago some subterranean eruption had smashed them skyward through the molten crust. The base of even the nearest was hidden from sight by the steeply curving surface of the plain, for the Moon is a very little world, and from where I was standing the horizon was only two miles away.

I lifted my eyes toward the peaks which no man had ever climbed, the peaks which, before the coming of terrestrial life, had watched the retreating oceans sink sullenly into their graves, taking with them the hope and the morning promise of a world. The sunlight was beating against those ramparts with a glare that hurt the eyes, yet only a little way above them the stars were shining steadily in a sky blacker than a winter midnight on Earth.

I was turning away when my eye caught a metallic glitter high on the ridge of a great promontory thrusting out into the sea thirty miles to the west. It was a dimensionless point of light, as if a star had been clawed from the sky by one of those cruel peaks, and I imagined that some smooth rock surface was catching the sunlight and heliographing it straight into my eyes. Such things were not uncommon. When the Moon is in her second quarter, observers on Earth can sometimes see the great ranges in the Oceanus Procellarum burning with a blue-white iridescence as the sunlight flashes from their slopes and leaps again from world to world. But I was curious to know what kind of rock could be shining so brightly up there, and I climbed into the observation turret and swung our four-inch telescope round to the west.

I could see just enough to tantalize me. Clear and sharp in the field of vision, the mountain peaks seemed only half a mile away, but whatever was catching the sunlight was still too small to be resolved. Yet it seemed to have an elusive symmetry, and the summit upon which it rested was curiously flat. I stared for a long time at that glittering enigma, straining my eyes into space, until presently a smell of burning from the galley told me that our breakfast sausages had made their quarter-million-mile journey in vain.

All that morning we argued our way across the Mare Crisium while the western mountains reared higher in the sky. Even when we were out prospecting in the space suits, the discussion would continue over the radio. It was absolutely certain, my companions argued, that there had never been any form of intelligent life on the Moon. The only living things that had ever existed there were a few primitive plants and their slightly less degenerate ancestors. I knew that as well as anyone, but there are times when a scientist must not be afraid to make a fool of himself.

"Listen," I said at last, "I'm going up there, if only for my own peace of mind. That mountain's less than twelve thousand feet high—that's only two thousand under Earth gravity—and I can make the trip in twenty hours at the outside. I've always wanted to go up into those hills, anyway, and this gives me an excellent excuse."

"If you don't break your neck," said Garnett, "you'll be the laughing-stock of the expedition when we get back to Base. That mountain will probably be called Wilson's Folly from now on."

"I won't break my neck," I said firmly. "Who was the first man to climb Pico and Helicon?"

"But weren't you rather younger in those days?" asked Louis gently.

"That," I said with great dignity, "is as good a reason as any for going."

We went to bed early that night, after driving the tractor to within half a mile of the promontory. Garnett was coming with me in the morning; he was a good climber, and had often been with me on such exploits before. Our driver was only too glad to be left in charge of the machine.

At first sight, those cliffs seemed completely unscalable, but to anyone with a good head for heights, climbing is easy on a world where all weights are only a sixth of their normal value. The real danger in lunar mountaineering lies in overconfidence; a six-hundred-foot drop on the Moon can kill you just as thoroughly as a hundred-foot fall on Earth.

We made our first halt on a wide ledge about four thousand feet above the plain. Climbing had not been very difficult, but my limbs were stiff with the unaccustomed effort, and I was glad of the rest. We could still see the tractor as a tiny metal insect far down at the foot of the cliff, and we reported our progress to the driver before starting on the next ascent.

Inside our suits it was comfortably cool, for the refrigeration units were fighting the fierce sun and carrying away the body heat of our exertions. We seldom spoke to each other, except to pass climbing instructions and to discuss our best plan of ascent. I do not know what Garnett was thinking, probably that this was the craziest goose chase he had ever embarked upon. I more than half agreed with him, but the joy of climbing, the knowledge that no man had ever gone this way before and the exhilaration of the steadily widening landscape gave me all the reward I needed.

I don't think I was particularly excited when I saw in front of us the wall of rock I had first inspected through the telescope from thirty miles away. It would level off about fifty feet above our heads, and there on the plateau would be the thing that had lured me over these barren wastes. It was, almost certainly, nothing more than a boulder splintered ages ago by a falling meteor, and with its cleavage planes still fresh and bright in this incorruptible, unchanging silence.

There were no handholds on the rock face, and we had to use a grapnel. My tired arms seemed to gain new strength as I swung the three-pronged metal anchor round my head and sent it sailing up toward the stars. The first time it broke loose and came falling slowly back when we pulled the rope. On the third attempt, the prongs gripped firmly and our combined weights could not shift it.

Garnett looked at me anxiously. I could tell that he wanted to go first, but I smiled back at him through the glass of my helmet and shook my head. Slowly, taking my time, I began the final ascent.

Even with my space suit, I weighed only forty pounds here, so I pulled myself up hand over hand without bothering to use my feet. At the rim I paused and waved to my companion; then I scrambled over the edge and stood upright, staring ahead of me.

You must understand that until this very moment I had been almost completely convinced that there could be nothing strange or unusual for me to find here. Almost, but not quite; it was that haunting doubt that had driven me forward. Well, it was a doubt no longer, but the haunting had scarcely begun.

I was standing on a plateau perhaps a hundred feet across. It had once been smooth—too smooth to be natural—but falling meteors had pitted and scored its surface through immeasurable eons. It had been leveled to support a glittering, roughly pyramidal structure, twice as high as a man, that was set in the rock like a gigantic many-faceted jewel.

Probably no emotion at all filled my mind in those first few seconds. Then I felt a great lifting of my heart, and a strange, inexpressible joy. For I loved the Moon, and now I knew that the creeping moss of Aristarchus and Eratosthenes was not the only life she had brought forth in her youth. The old, discredited dream of the first explorers was true. There had, after all, been a lunar civilization—and I was the first to find it. That I had come perhaps a hundred million years too late did not distress me; it was enough to have come at all.

My mind was beginning to function normally, to analyze and to ask questions. Was this a building, a shrine—or something for which my language had no name? If a building, then why was it erected in so uniquely inaccessible a spot? I wondered if it might be a temple, and I could picture the adepts of some strange priesthood calling on their gods to preserve them as the life of the Moon ebbed with the dying oceans, and calling on their gods in vain.

I took a dozen steps forward to examine the thing more closely, but some sense of caution kept me from going too near. I knew a little of archaeology, and tried to guess the cultural level of the civilization that must have smoothed this mountain and raised the glittering mirror surfaces that still dazzled my eyes.

The Egyptians could have done it, I thought, if their workmen had possessed whatever strange materials these far more ancient architects had used. Because of the thing's smallness, it did not occur to me that I might be looking at the handiwork of a race more advanced than my own. The idea that the Moon had possessed intelligence at all was still almost too tremendous to grasp, and my pride would not let me take the final, humiliating plunge.

And then I noticed something that set the scalp crawling at the back of my neck—something so trivial and so innocent that many would never have noticed it at all. I have said that the plateau was scarred by meteors; it was also coated inches deep with the cosmic dust that is always filtering down upon the surface of any world where there are no winds to disturb it. Yet the dust and the meteor scratches ended quite abruptly in a wide circle enclosing the little pyramid, as though an invisible wall was protecting it from the ravages of time and the slow but ceaseless bombardment from space.

There was someone shouting in my earphones, and I realized that Garnett had been calling me for some time. I walked unsteadily to the edge of the cliff and signaled him to join me, not trusting myself to speak. Then I went back toward that circle in the dust. I picked up a fragment of splintered rock and tossed it gently toward the shining enigma. If the pebble had vanished at that invisible barrier I should not have been surprised, but it seemed to hit a smooth, hemispherical surface and slide gently to the ground.

I knew then that I was looking at nothing that could be matched in the antiquity of my own race. This was not a building, but a machine, protecting itself with forces that had challenged Eternity. Those forces, whatever they might be, were still operating, and perhaps I had already come too close. I thought of all the radiations man had trapped and tamed in the past century. For all I knew, I might be as irrevocably doomed as if I had stepped into the deadly, silent aura of an unshielded atomic pile.

I remember turning then toward Garnett, who had joined me and was now standing motionless at my side. He seemed quite oblivious to me, so I did not disturb him but walked to the edge of the cliff in an effort to marshal my thoughts. There below me lay the Mare Crisium—Sea of Crises, indeed—strange and weird to most men, but reassuringly familiar to me. I lifted my eyes toward the crescent Earth, lying in her cradle of stars, and I wondered what her clouds had covered when these unknown builders had finished their work. Was it the steaming jungle of the Carboniferous, the bleak shoreline over which the first amphibians must crawl to conquer the land—or, earlier still, the long loneliness before the coming of life?

Do not ask me why I did not guess the truth sooner—the truth that seems so obvious now. In the first excitement of my discovery, I had assumed without question that this crystalline apparition had been built by some race belonging to the Moon's remote past, but suddenly, and with overwhelming force, the belief came to me that it was as alien to the Moon as I myself.

In twenty years we had found no trace of life but a few degenerate plants. No lunar civilization, whatever its doom, could have left but a single token of its existence.

I looked at the shining pyramid again, and the more remote it seemed from anything that had to do with the Moon. And suddenly I felt myself shaking with a foolish, hysterical laughter, brought on by excitement and overexertion: for I had imagined that the little pyramid was speaking to me and was saying: "Sorry, I'm a stranger here myself."

It has taken us twenty years to crack that invisible shield and to reach the machine inside those crystal walls. What we could not understand, we broke at last with the savage might of atomic power and now I have seen the fragments of the lovely, glittering thing I found up there on the mountain.

They are meaningless. The mechanisms—if indeed they are mechanisms—of the pyramid belong to a technology that lies far beyond our horizon, perhaps to the technology of paraphysical forces.

The mystery haunts us all the more now that the other planets have been reached and we know that only Earth has ever been the home of intelligent life in our Universe. Nor could any lost civilization of our own world have built that machine, for the thickness of the meteoric dust on the plateau has enabled us to measure its age. It was set there upon its mountain before life had emerged from the seas of Earth.

When our world was half its present age, *something* from the stars swept through the Solar System, left this token of its passage, and went again upon its way. Until we destroyed it, that machine was still fulfilling the purpose of its builders; and as to that purpose, here is my guess.

Nearly a hundred thousand million stars are turning in the circle of the Milky Way, and long ago other races on the worlds of other suns must have scaled and passed the heights that we have reached. Think of such civilizations, far back in time against the fading afterglow of Creation, masters of a Universe so young that life as yet had come only to a handful of worlds. Theirs would have been a loneliness we cannot imagine, the loneliness of gods looking out across infinity and finding none to share their thoughts.

They must have searched the star clusters as we have searched the planets. Everywhere there would be worlds, but they would be empty or peopled with crawling, mindless things. Such was our own Earth, the smoke of the great volcanoes still staining the skies, when that first ship of the peoples of the dawn came sliding in from the abyss beyond Pluto. It passed the frozen outer worlds, knowing that life could play no part in their destinies. It came to rest among the inner planets, warming themselves around the fire of the Sun and waiting for their stories to begin.

Those wanderers must have looked on Earth, circling safely in the narrow zone between fire and ice, and must have guessed that it was the favorite of the Sun's children. Here, in the distant future, would be intelligence; but there were countless stars before them still, and they might never come this way again.

So they left a sentinel, one of millions they have scattered throughout the Universe, watching over all worlds with the promise of life. It was a beacon that down the ages has been patiently signaling the fact that no one had discovered it.

Perhaps you understand now why that crystal pyramid was set upon the Moon instead of on the Earth. Its builders were not concerned with races still struggling up from savagery. They would be interested in our civilization only if we proved our fitness to survive—by crossing space and so escaping from the Earth, our cradle. That is the challenge that all intelligent races must meet, sooner or later. It is a double challenge, for it depends in turn upon the conquest of atomic energy and the last choice between life and death.

Once we had passed that crisis, it was only a matter of time before we found the pyramid and forced it open. Now its signals have ceased, and those whose duty it is will be turning their minds upon Earth. Perhaps they wish to help our infant civilization. But they must be very, very old, and the old are often insanely jealous of the young.

I can never look now at the Milky Way without wondering from which of those banked clouds of stars the emissaries are coming. If you will pardon so commonplace a simile, we have set off the fire alarm and have nothing to do but to wait.

I do not think we will have to wait for long.

Moonwalk

H . B FYFE

Although H. B. Fyfe sold primarily to Astounding *in the course of his twenty-seven-year career, it was the memorable story that follows, "Moonwalk," published in a second-string pulp magazine called* Space Science Fiction, *that would have the greatest impact on subsequent science fiction. A gritty, hard-edged, and realistic look at one man's struggle to survive in the face of almost overwhelming odds, stranded and alone on the surface of a hostile Moon, with his air running out, "Moonwalk" would inspire—consciously or unconsciously—dozens of similar stories in the years to come, an influence that persists right up to the present day. It remains one of the seminal classics of space exploration.*

H. B. Fyfe sold his first story in 1940. By the time he retired in 1967, he had published more than sixty works of short fiction, most of them in his "Bureau of Slick Tricks" series for Astounding, *and one novel,* D-99, *set in the same series. Fyfe died in 1996 and is survived by his widow, Sonia.*

The radio operator stopped sending out his call and slumped back in the folding chair of canvas and aluminum. Concern showed through the impassivity of his broad, Mexican features.

The footsteps in the corridor outside the radio room pattered lightly because of the Lunar gravity, but with a haste that suggested urgency. Two men entered. Like the operator, they wore dungarees and heavy sweaters, but the gray-haired man had an air of authority.

"Dr. Burney wanted to check with you himself, Mike," said the youth with him.

The operator shrugged.

"Tractor One is okay, Doctor," he reported, "but as Joey must have told you, we've lost Two."

"When was the last time they called in?" asked Burney.

Mike gestured at the map on the side wall, and the elder man stepped over to study it. The area shown was that surrounding the fifty-mile-wide crater of Archimedes.

"The blue line is One and the red is Two," said Mike. "I guess you know the planned routes. Well, the little *x*'s show the positions reported and the times."

Burney glanced briefly at the blue line. From the black square near the northern side of the crater that represented the first major base on Luna, it climbed slantingly over the ringwall. After zigzagging down the broken outer slope and skirting a ridge of vein mountains, the line swept in a wide curve north of Aristillus and Autolycus, the next largest craters of the region, and moved into that subregion of the Mare Imbrium, whimsically christened "Misty Swamp." Thereafter, the blue trail led toward possible passes through the Lunar Apennines to the Mare Serenitatis.

"I could expect to lose One," muttered the operator, "in spite of our tower here. But Two shouldn't be blocked by anything yet."

The red line was more direct. Parting from the blue north of the ringwall of Archimedes, it pushed out across the level plain, avoiding isolated mountain ridges and the seven-mile craters of Kirch and Piazza Smyth. After something like three hundred miles, it passed the towering lonely Mt. Pico and probed a dotted delta of possible routes up the ring-wall of Plato. This route was *x*'ed almost to Pico.

"They were supposed to report before attempting the descent," mused Burney. "Maybe the depression of the Mare Imbrium isn't quite what we estimated. The normal curvature would put a lot of rock between us, in that case. An awful lot of rock."

"Maybe they went over the ringwall in a hurry," suggested Joey.

Burney considered that in a short silence. He ran a hand absently over his balding temple. His lean face became a mask of lines as he puckered up his eyes in thought.

"Number Two has Hansen driving, hasn't it? And Groswald, the mechanic . . . Van Ness, the astronomer . . . and who else?"

"Fernandez from Geology," said Joey.

The entire personnel of the base numbered scarcely fifty. They were just beginning their surface exploration projects after completing the low domes of their buildings. With such scanty resources, Burney was naturally worried about four men and one of the precious tractors.

"They were with us an hour ago," said Mike, fingering his microphone. "Their set must have gone sour."

When no one replied, he hitched around to face his own controls.

"Or else, they're in trouble—"

☙

On the ledge atop the ringwall of Plato, Hansen teetered and tried to maintain his balance by pressing a gauntleted hand against an outcropping of gray Lunar rock. The thermal-eroded surface crumbled slightly beneath the metal-tipped mitten.

In his bulky space suit, he found it difficult to lean very far forward, but he could not bear not seeing. The landslip tumbled down the inner slope of the ringwall with horrible deliberation.

"I told them 'Don't move her till I find a way down!' " Hansen muttered. "I told them, I *told* them!"

He was hardly conscious of speaking aloud. Somewhere in the churning mass was the vacuum tractor in which he had driven from Archimedes. Inside, unless it had already been split open, were Van Ness, Groswald, and Fernandez.

The collection of loose rock and dust passed out of sight for a moment over the edge of a terrace. It reappeared farther down. Once, Hansen thought he saw a glint of bright metal, but the slide almost immediately plunged down another sheer drop.

The phase of Luna being closer to "new" than to "first quarter," the sun was far too low on the horizon to light the floor of the crater, or even the three mountain peaks on the ringwall to Hansen's right front. The light from the gibbous Earth, however, was bright enough for him to see quite clearly the surface around him.

The slide finally reached the bottom, at this point nearly three thousand feet below the man's precarious position. He breathed deeply and tried to straighten the ache from his shoulders.

"Must have taken five minutes," he murmured, realizing that he had frozen in a cramped position as he stared.

It had seemed more like an hour. In the dim shadows of the crater floor, the dust settled rapidly because of the lack of air, but the debris remained heaped at an angle much steeper than would have been possible on Earth. Even the slight vibration Hansen had felt through his boots ceased.

He was alone in the dead silence of a world for eons dead.

He stood there, a spot of color in the chrome yellow of the protective chafing suit. The transparent faceplate of his unpainted helmet revealed a blond young man, perhaps twenty-six, with a lean, square-jawed face. Against the tanned skin, his eyebrows were ludicrously light, but the gray eyes under them were wide with horror.

He was of medium height, but the bulkiness of the suit hid his welterweight trimness; and the pack of oxygen tank and batteries for powering radio, heat pads, and air circulator increased the appearance of stubbiness.

The quiet hiss of the air being circulated through his suit finally aroused him. With painstaking care, he climbed from the ledge to the level terrace on which the tractor was to have remained while he scouted the route down. A hundred yards away, a great bite seemed to have been snapped out of the ridge.

"All the way from Archimedes, and we didn't even get a look at the floor," he whispered.

For a moment, following the raw scar of the slide with his eye, he considered climbing all the way down and venturing out onto the crater floor to examine the ground. For centuries, the floor of Plato had been reported by Earth observers to darken with the rising sun until at noon it was nearly black. Occasionally, there were stories of misty clouds obscuring the surface, and of shifts in the pattern of light streaks and spots.

One of the expedition's first assignments, therefore, had been the investigation of Plato, to check the unlikely possibility that there might be some primitive, airless form of life present. But the present sortie was clearly ended.

"Not one damn chance," Hansen told himself as he squinted downward. "None of them had a suit on when I got out."

On a terrace about a third of the way down lay an object with an oddly regular shape. It gleamed in the blue-green earthlight, and Hansen peered more intently. It looked like one of the spare oxygen cylinders that had been carried on top of the tractor.

Hansen abruptly became sensitive about the supply of his suit tank. Before he did anything, even sitting down to think the situation over, he wanted to get down there and find out if the cylinder was full.

Despite his eagerness, he held back until he thought he had spied a reasonable path. It involved going two or three hundred feet out of his way, but Hansen managed to work his way down to the lower level without serious difficulty. Once or twice, he slithered a few feet when loose rock shaled off under his grip, but even with his suit and equipment, he weighed little over forty pounds. As long as he did not drop very far, he could always stop himself one-handed.

He walked back along the level strip which was about fifty yards wide at this point, until he approached the path of the landslip. Near it, apparently having been scraped off as the tractor rolled, lay the cylinder.

He checked it hurriedly.

"Whew! Well, that's some help, anyway," he told himself, discovering that the tank had not been tapped.

He left the cylinder and walked over to the inner limit of the level band. Scanning the steep slope and the debris of the slide, he thought he could pick out two or three scraps of twisted metal. There was nothing to be done.

"I'd better get back up and think this out," he decided.

He took the broken chain that had held the tank to the tractor and hooked a broken link through it to make a sling. For the time being, he contented himself with using it as a handle to drag the lucky supply of oxygen after him.

☙

After regaining his original position, the going was easier to the top of the ringwall. They had come over one of the several passes crossing the southern part of the cliffs, and Hansen walked through in a few minutes. The thickness of the ringwall here was only a mile or so, although at the base it probably approached ten miles.

He came out onto a little plateau, and the dim plain of the Mare Imbrium spread out before him. Hansen suddenly felt tiny, lost, and insignificant.

"What am I gonna do?" he asked himself.

For the first time, he had admitted his predicament to himself. His gauntlet crept up to his chest where the switch of his radio protruded through the chafing suit.

"Hello Base! Tractor Two to Base! Tractor Two to Base. Over."

He waited several minutes, and repeated the call five or six times. He screwed his eyes shut to throw every ounce of concentration into listening.

No human voice broke into the quiet hissing of the earphones. Hansen sighed.

"Never reach them, of course!" he grumbled. "This set is made to reach about your arm's length."

He remembered that Van Ness had complained about the reception the last time they had called in, and asked Hansen to maneuver to the top of a ridge of vein mountains near the hulking silhouette of Pico. Hansen was higher now, but also much farther from home.

"Mike Ramirez and Joey Friedman aren't the kind to miss a call," he muttered. "It seems to me, Paul E. Hansen, my boy . . . that you are . . . on your own!"

The radio had been but a faint hope, inspired by his height and tales of freak reception. He was not too disappointed. Looking down the rough outer slope of the ringwall, he saw that it was not by any means as steep as the inner, and that fact settled it.

"Guess I'd better see how far I can get," Hansen decided. "When they don't get the regular report over the tractor radio, they'll probably send out another crew to follow the trail. If I can meet them out a way, maybe even as far as Pico, it'll save that much time."

After considerable fumbling, he balanced the large cylinder on his back atop the other equipment with the chain sling across his chest. He started along the series of gentle slopes the tractor had climbed earlier. Deliberately, he pushed to the back of his mind the possibility he would have to face sometime: Base might decide the crew had been too eager to negotiate the ringwall to call back before being blanked out by the mass of rock.

●

He had to restrain a temptation to rush headlong down to the plain across miles of rough grades. Even with his tremendous load of equipment, he might still travel in twenty-foot bounds in Lunar gravity; but he had no desire to plunge all the way to the bottom with one misstep.

"It'll be easy enough going down," he murmured. "And after that, I can judge the direction well enough from Earth."

He looked up at the brightness of the planet. Earth was rather high in the Lunar sky, although not overhead because of his position far north. It would indicate roughly his southerly course toward Archimedes. As he looked, he noticed that much of the eastern coast of North America, which to his view was almost centered on the hemisphere, was blanketed in clouds.

"Wish I was there right now," he sighed. "Rain and all!"

He wondered about the next step as he worked his way around ridges radiating from the sizable minor craterlet in Plato's ringwall. He still had a good view of the gray plain at the foot of the heights. Although reasonably flat—probably leveled by the colossal flow of lava that had formed the Mare Imbrium, filling older craters and melting down or inundating existing mountains until merely their crests showed—it contained many hills and irregularities that would be even more apparent to a man on foot than from the tractor.

He worked past the craterlet, leaving it to his right. Whenever he struck a reasonably level stretch, he moved at a bounding trot. The first time he tried this, he tumbled head over heels and gave himself a fright lest he rupture the space suit on a projecting rock. Thereafter, he was more careful until he got used to being so top-heavy because of the huge oxygen tank.

Finally, scrambling down the last ridges of old debris, he found himself on the level floor of the Sea of Showers, in the region between Plato and the jutting, lonely Mt. Pico. Off to his right, an extension of the ringwall behind him thrust out to point at the group of other peaks known as the Teneriffe Mountains, which were somewhat like a flock of lesser Picos. The ground on which he stood had perhaps once been part of another crater, twin in size to Plato, but now only detectable by faint outlines and vein mountains. In the past, some astronomers had called it Newton, before deciding upon a more worthy landmark for Sir Isaac.

It had taken Hansen nearly half an hour, and he paused now to catch his breath.

"I feel pretty good," he exclaimed with relief. "I'm carrying quite a lot to go at that speed, but I don't seem to get tired." He thought a moment, and warned himself, "You'd better not, either!"

He turned partly to look at the ringwall towering behind him. It loomed grimly, scored with deep shadows of cracks into which the rays of Earth, seventy times brighter than moonlight it received from Luna, could not penetrate.

Hansen turned away hastily. The mountainous mass made him uneasy; he remembered how easily a landslip had started on the inner slope.

"I'd better get moving!"

He struck out at a brisk, bounding pace, a trot on Luna without the effort of a normal trot. The ground was fairly level, and he congratulated himself upon making good time. Once or twice, he staggered a little, having overbalanced; but he soon got into the rhythm of the pace and the load on his back ceased to bother him. He bore slightly to the right, toward the jutting point of the ringwall.

The footing was like powdery gray sand. Alternating extremes of temperature during the two-week Lunar day or night had cracked the rock surface until successive expansions and contractions had affected the crystalline structure of the top layers. When these had flaked off, the powder had formed an insulating layer, but the result as far as Hansen was concerned was that he trotted on a sandy footing. When he looked back, he could see the particles kicked up by his last few steps still above the surface. They fell rather neatly, there being no air to whirl them about.

Gradually, he realized that the unobtrusive noises of his space suit had risen a notch in tone. The clever little machines were laboring to dispel the effects of his faster breathing. He dropped down to an easy walk, which was still a goodly pace in the light gravity.

"Guess I'm sweating more, too," he told himself. "Now that I think of it, my mouth's a little dry."

He twisted his neck until he could get his lips on the thin rubber hose sticking up to the left of his chin. He closed his teeth on the clamp, and sucked up a few swallows of water from his tank. It was not particularly tasty, but at least it was cool. It would have been a lot colder if carried uninsulated, he reflected. The night temperature of Luna was something like minus one-fifty Centigrade, and it dropped like a shot as soon as the surface was shaded from the sun.

Refreshed, he started out again at a bounding run, rejoicing in his strength. He felt as if he were just jogging along, but the ground rolled back under his feet swiftly. Had he been on such a bleak desert on Earth, he knew he would be slogging ankle-deep in sand—if he could move at all. His own weight was between a hundred and fifty and a hundred and sixty pounds. With what he was wearing and carrying, he was probably close to three hundred. It did not bother him here.

"It isn't bad at all," he thought with satisfaction. "Feels like jogging around the track in school, warming up for a race. One . . . two . . . three . . . four—still got pretty good form! Not even breathing hard!"

It occurred to him that it resembled a footrace in one other particular. He was deliberately putting off consideration of the finish while he still felt good.

"Oh, I'll meet them somewhere along the way," he said aloud, despite a momentary doubt that he was talking too much to himself. "Pretty soon, I'll cross the tractor trail. I'll follow it out maybe as far as Pico and wait for them to pick me up. The relief crew can't miss a landmark like that. It's damn near nine thousand feet high, straight up out of the flat plain."

He slowed down somewhat to scrutinize a ridge ahead. It turned out to be an easy grade and he skimmed over it easily. Otherwise, however, he was beginning to lose his recent feeling of satisfaction. Now that he moved out into the flat, empty plain, the essential grimness of Lunar landscape was more apparent than when disguised by the majesty of the view from atop the ringwall. It was a study in gray and black, the powdery sand and the deep shadows groping toward him as he trotted into the earthshine. Above was the deep black of an airless sky, lit by the bright Earth and chilly stars.

Gray, black, green, white—and all of it cold and inhospitable.

"I feel like I'm not wanted here," Hansen thought. "Well, that makes it mutual, I guess!"

He looked back, and was amazed at the distance he had covered. Already, Plato looked more like a range of towering mountains than it did like a barrier of cliffs.

"This won't take so long," he reassured himself. "I must have covered five miles running like this. Maybe almost ten."

He circled a tiny craterlet, or "bead," a few hundred yards across. In the precise center, it had a tiny peak, corresponding to the central mountain masses found in nearly half the craters of Luna. For the first time, Hansen regretted the camera that had gone down with the tractor.

"Too busy driving to take any pix on the way," he growled, "and now that I come across a perfect miniature, I have no camera. A fine spare photographer for an expedition this size!"

He diverted himself for a few minutes by considering what a fool he was to come to Luna in the first place. He had not really wanted to, and he was sure there were plenty of others who would have been better qualified and better pleased at the opportunity. Still, it was strange sometimes how a man would do things he did not want to because someone else was doing them.

He glanced up at Earth, and kept moving southward with the shining globe on his left front.

☞

Mike and Joey sat before their radio, on a folding chair and empty crate respectively, maintaining whenever not directly addressed an almost sullen silence. Their tiny cubicle was becoming entirely too crowded to suit them.

Dr. Burney paced up and down before the wall map of the Mare Imbrium. Opposite him, the lower section of the radiomen's double bunk—canvas and aluminum like their single chair—had collected an overload of three. Dr. Sherman, the chief astronomer, sat between Bucky O'Neil and Emil Wohl. Besides heading the geologists, Wohl was Burney's second in command; and O'Neil was present in case it was decided to send out a rocket to photograph the Plato region.

"Ya'd think they could use their own rooms," Joey whispered into Mike's ear. "All but Bucky got singles. How we gonna catch an incoming call with all this racket?"

The "racket" at the moment consisted mostly of sighs, finger drumming, and a tortured semiwhistle from where Sherman sat staring at the map with his chin cupped in one hand.

"There's little doubt of the general location," repeated Burney, once more reaching a familiar impasse. "But I hate to hold up the other work to send out a crew when we cannot with any certainty agree that something has gone wrong."

"Let's see," said Wohl. "There was some difficulty, was there not, the last time they communicated?"

When no one answered, Mike finally repeated his previous testimony.

"Van Ness said they drove up a sort of mountain to get us. Complained a little about reception. He might've been getting to the limit."

"Then," said Wohl, "there is really no reason for alarm, is there? They could just as well have decided that continuing the mission was more important than running around looking for a good radio position, couldn't they?"

Mike considered that glumly.

"It's funny they didn't back up far enough to make *one* call to let me know they were going out of reach," he grumbled. "The speed they make in that rig, it wouldn'ta taken them long."

"That would have been the proper action," admitted Burney, "but we must not demand perfect adherence to the rules when a group is in the field and may have perfectly good reasons for disregarding them. No, I think we had best—Who's that coming?"

Bucky O'Neil bounded up from the end of the bunk and stuck his head out the door. When he looked around, his freckled face was unhappy.

"Johnny Pierce from the map section," he announced. "He's got Louise with him. I guess you don't need me any more."

He edged out the door as two others of the base staff came in. The one who acted as if he had business there was a lean, bespectacled man who managed to achieve a vaguely scholarly air despite rough clothing.

Trailing him was a girl who looked as if the heating economy that necessitated the standard costume of the base also had the effect of cheating the male personnel of a brightening influence. The shapeless clothing, however, did not lessen the attractiveness of her lightly tanned features or lively black eyes. She wore her dark hair tucked into a knit cap that on Earth probably would have been donned only as a joke.

"We've looked at the photo maps," Pierce reported in a dry, husky voice. "They might very well be out of range. Lots of curvature in that distance, even with the depression caused by a mass of lava like that Mare Imbrium."

Burney accepted this with an expression of relief.

"I heard them talking about the Plato crew," the girl put in. "What's going on?"

Her voice was warm and, like a singer's, stronger than her petite outline would have suggested.

"Oh . . . just checking the radio reception," said Burney. "You can get the details from Mike, I suppose, if you have time off from the observatory. The rest of us are through here."

Mike scowled, and the girl looked puzzled; but Burney, Wohl, and Sherman crowded through the door as if intent upon some new project. Sherman muttered something about the problem of erecting a transparent dome for direct observations, and the voices receded down the corridor. Pierce slipped out after them.

"Did I say something?" inquired Louise. "I only thought there might be news."

"I guess they're just busy, Louise," Mike said. He turned to the radio, unplugged the speaker, and donned a set of earphones. "You know how it is. Why don't you catch Bucky? *He's* got nothing to do for a while."

Louise had started to show her even white teeth in a smile which now faded. Joey picked up his empty crate and busily moved it around to the other side of the radio setup.

"Sorry," said the girl, her dark eyes beginning to smolder. "I'll ask somebody else."

They listened to her footsteps as they faded away in the corridor. Mike looked at Joey and shrugged.

"What was I gonna tell her?" he asked. "That her husband either forgot to call in—or got himself quick-frozen when something in his tractor popped?"

Joey shook his head sympathetically. "Tough on her."

"Dunno why she had to come to Luna in the first place," Mike complained. "I can see a nurse like Jean doin' it, and a typewriter pusher like old Edna oughta be classed expendable. But a babe like Louise!"

"It's her science," said Joey. "She wants to see the stars better."

"We got enough astronomers now. She's a smart girl, all right—can't take that away from her. But if she was *my* woman, she wouldn'ta come up here!"

"If she was mine," countered Joey, "I wouldn'ta taken a second-rate job just to follow her up here either! But you're dreaming about the past, Boss."

"*Uh*-unh," grunted Mike, plugging in the speaker again. "I just believe in equal rights for men. How'd you like to be married to a dame like that and have to trail her to a place where there's three women to forty-eight men?"

"Ask me how I'd like to be married to a dame like that, period!" Joey invited him.

Mike adjusted the shade on the light so as to shadow half the room. He straightened the blanket where the three visitors had sat, appropriated the one from the upper bunk to cover himself, and lay down.

"Your watch," he announced coldly. "Wake me up if anything comes in!"

The rope lacing of the canvas creaked as he settled himself; then Joey was left with only the quiet hiss of the radio. He leaned back in the folding chair and relaxed.

☙

Hansen paused and turned to survey the ground he had covered in the past half hour. The hiss of his air circulator and the whine of the tiny motors within his suit were a comfort in the face of his bleak surroundings.

He had found himself trotting along at such an easy pace that he had kept going past Mt. Pico. Now he wondered if he ought to stop.

"Might as well go on," he muttered. "Now that I've picked up the tractor trail from Archimedes, I can hardly be missed by the relief crew."

He eyed the twin tracks in the gray sand. Flanked by his own wide-spaced footprints, they stretched away into the dim distance. As a sign that man had passed, they did little but accentuate the coldness of the scene.

"Maybe I'll stop at the big triple peak," Hansen planned. "That's about thirty-five or forty miles . . . they ought to be along by then if they started right away."

Careful not to admit to himself that relief might be slow in starting from Archimedes, he took a last look at Pico. Rearing starkly upward, it projected a lonely, menacing grandeur, like a lurking iceberg or an ancient monument half buried in the creeping sands of a desert. In the light of the nearly full Earth, it was a pattern of gray angles and inky black patches—not a hospitable sight.

"Come on, come on!" Hansen reproved himself. "Let's get moving. You want to turn into a monument too?"

He had stopped just before reaching Pico to replenish his suit tank from the big cylinder, and still felt good at having managed the valves without the mishap he had feared. He did not feel like a man who had traveled seventy miles.

"Why, on Earth," he thought, "that would be a good three-day march! I feel it a little, but not to the point of being tired."

He looked up at Earth as he started out again. The cloudy eastern coast of North America had moved around out of sight in the narrow dark portion. Hansen guessed that he had been on the move for at least four or five hours.

"I'd like to see their faces when they meet me way out here," he chuckled.

It occurred to him that he might be more tired than he thought, and as he went on he tried to save himself by holding his pace to a brisk walk. He found that if he got up on his toes a bit, he could still bound along that way.

The gray sand flowed under his feet, relieved occasionally by a stretch of yellowish ground. Hansen kept his eyes on his path and avoided the empty waste. When he did glance into the distance, he felt a twinge of loneliness. It was like the wide plainsland of the western United States, but grimly bare of anything so living as a wheat field.

He tried to remember as he moved along where it was that they had driven the tractor up a mountain ridge. He decided that he would rather avoid the climb, and kept an eye open for the chain of vein mountain beyond Pico.

"It ought to be faster to go around the end of them," he thought. "I can always pick up the tracks again."

When he finally sighted the rise ahead, he bore to his right. He remembered from the maps he had studied that the mountains curved somewhat toward another isolated peak, and he watched for that. As far as he knew, it had no name, but although only half the height of Pico, it was an unmistakable landmark.

The mountains on his left gradually dwindled into ragged hills and sank beneath the layer of lava. Hansen turned toward the last outcroppings as the triple mountain he sought came into sight. He climbed onto a broad rock and started to sit down.

The end of the big cylinder slung across his back clanged on the back of his helmet. Hansen lost his balance and tumbled over the side of the rock. Under his groping hands, the heat-tortured surface of it flaked away, and he bounced once on the ground before sprawling full length.

"Damn!" he grunted. "When'll I learn to watch my balance with this load?"

He picked himself up and unslung the tank. Then, allowing for the normal bulk of his backpack of tank and batteries, he backed against the outcropping until he was resting at a comfortable angle.

"Maybe I ought to relax a few minutes," he told himself. "Give the air circulator time to filter out some of the sweat. Then, too, I don't want to get tired and miss them when they come along."

He idly scanned the arc between the peak toward which he was heading and Mt. Pico, still easily visible off to his right. The northern part of the Mare Imbrium drew his gaze coaxingly into the distance until he felt an insane desire to thrust his head forward. It almost seemed that if he could get beyond the double glass of his insulated faceplate, if he could escape from the restraint of his helmet, he might perceive his bleak surroundings with a better, more real sense of proportion.

There was nothing out there, of course, he forced himself to realize. Except for shadows of craterlets that looked like low mountains, there was nothing to see for fifty miles, and nothing even then more noteworthy than a couple of minor craters.

"Then what are you looking for?" Hansen snapped. "You want it to get on your nerves? And quit talking to yourself!"

He suppressed, however, the sudden urge to spring up and break into a run. Instead, he hitched around to stare along the ridge at whose end he sat.

He was far enough south to be able to see the side lit by earthlight. The ridge climbed higher the farther it went, like the back of some sea monster rising from placid waters. Several miles away, a spur seemed to project out to the south; and Hansen thought he could remember a mile-wide crater on the maps.

☞

He was a bit more comfortable inside his suit by now. He shifted his position to expedite the drying of the coveralls he wore under the space suit. Then he raised his arms and tried to clasp his hands behind his neck, but found that his garb was not that flexible.

"Shouldn't kick, I guess," he thought. "Without plenty of springs in the joints, I wouldn't be able to bend anything, considering the pressure difference."

He spent a minute admiring the construction of the suit that alone stood between him and instant extinction. That led him to think of the marvelous mechanism of the vacuum tractor that had carried him so comfortably—though he had not appreciated it at the time—across the Lunar plain. That, logically, recalled the men who had come with him and now were buried beneath one of Plato's many landslips.

"Talk about borrowed time!" he thought. "I wonder how long I'll stay lucky? Any little thing might do it—"

He had already taken three or four tumbles, or was it more? On any one of them, had he rolled the wrong way perhaps, he might have cracked that faceplate on a projecting rock. It was made as tough as possible, true, but if he ever cracked the outer pane, the insulating sheet of air would spurt out to leave him with a slow leak. The inner plate would lose heat and cloud up from his breath, so that he would end up without even knowing where he was dying.

Or if he had slid over a surface jagged enough to tear through his yellow chafing suit, and then to rip the tough material of the inner suit—

A puncture here would be a real blowout!

He reminded himself to be careful about stepping into shadows, especially if they were more or less straight-edged. He did not remember encountering on the way out any of the canyonlike rills that ran like long cracks straight through all other surface features of Luna—except occasional small craters slammed into the rock after the rill had been formed—but there was always the chance that he might step into some other kind of a hole.

Fortunately, the earthlight shone into his face, so that he should be able to tell a shadow resulting from some elevation ahead of him.

"I'm getting the jitters squatting here," Hansen thought. "It won't do any harm to move on a little way. At least out past that mountain, where I'll have a good view toward Archimedes."

He arose and slung the big cylinder over his back again, jiggling on the toes of his boots to jockey it into place. With one last look over his shoulder at the trail of his footprints splotched in the ashy sand, he started off.

He was surprised to discover that the rest had stiffened him slightly, but that soon worked out. As soon as he was warmed up, he moved out in a brisk walk which on Luna sent him bounding along with fifteen-foot strides. Swinging his arms to keep his balance, he concentrated upon the footing ahead of him. Once more he was alone with the hissing and humming of his suit and the sound of his own breathing, undisturbed by either memory or anticipation.

◠

Mike Ramirez stirred on his bunk with the change of the quiet hissing of the radio. Something more than the occasional crackle or creak of Joey's chair or footfall in the corridor brought him up with eyes still half closed. To his sleep-drugged mind, it seemed that nothing had existed until a second ago, when a faint, dreamlike voice had started to speak.

He started to push back his blanket—Joey's blanket—and said, "Joey! You got a call!"

". . . to Archimedes Base. Hello Base! Over."

"I hear him!" snarled Joey. "Go back to sleep!"

He pushed his switch and the rushing noise that had partly muffled the weak voice gave way before the surge of his own transmitter.

"Archimedes Base to Tractor One!" Joey answered, and Mike leaned back on one elbow and sighed.

He did not listen while Joey took the message, but swung his feet to the floor and sat up. Wiggling his toes uncomfortably, he wished he had taken off his shoes; but he had expected to lie down only half an hour or so. Until the call came in, he had been sound asleep.

Joey acknowledged the message and turned to Mike after dropping his pencil.

"The Serenitatis bunch," he said. "They left two of them at Linné to take photos and poke around while the other pair brought the tractor back through between the Apennines and Caucasus to call in."

"Everything okay?"

"Yeah, they're on the way back already, but they say Linné didn't look as if it was ever a volcano after all."

"Very true if interesting," said Mike. "Okay, take it to Burney. I'll bend an ear a while."

He tossed the blanket back onto the upper bunk and walked over to the chair. He stretched, and sat down as Joey's footsteps departed down the corridor.

He sat there, staring moodily at the softly lighted dials of the radio, wishing he had a cigarette. That was one habit he had had to cut off short when joining the expedition.

"I think I'm getting over it some," he congratulated himself. He looked up at the sound in the corridor, thinking that Joey had made good time to Burney's compartment and back. He raised an eyebrow as Louise entered.

"I just saw Joey go by," she announced hastily. "Did some news come in?"

"Tractor One reported—just routine. What are you doing, picketing this dive?"

"I—I just happened to be passing the Junction, and I saw the paper in Joey's hand."

"Uh-huh," grunted Mike.

●

What the members of the expedition had come to call the Junction was an intermediate dome equipped with the main airlock. The other buildings connected with it through safety doors so as to localize any danger of air loss in the event of a rupture in one of the domes. It was, in effect, the front hall of the whole base.

And if you stand there long enough, thought Mike, *everyone you know on Luna will pass by, and you'll find out everything that's going on.*

"Where is number Two now?" demanded Louise quietly.

Scared, thought Mike, noting the overcontrolled tenseness of her voice.

"I don't know for sure," he answered, not looking at her. "It's time they were inside Plato, and we can't expect to hear them from in there."

Louise walked jerkily to the bunk and sat on the foot of the lower section. She crossed her legs. Seeing the nervous manner in which she twitched her foot, Mike turned to his radio.

After a moment, she spoke again, and his shoulders quivered at the agonized harshness of her tone.

"Don't string me along, Mike! I want to know! You were worried about them hours ago, weren't you?"

Mike licked his lips.

"That don't mean anything," he muttered.

"The others backtracked to report, didn't they? To call in, I mean. Something happened to number Two, didn't it?"

"Now, take it easy, Louise!" Mike squirmed in his chair, then forced himself to sit still. It was not the sort of furniture that would stand much squirming. "Burney kinda considered that as a possibility, but in the end they decided things were probably okay."

"Then why did they have Bucky in here?" she demanded.

"Just in case they thought it worth the trouble of scouting the Plato region. Nothing special."

Louise bounced up from the bunk. She stood beside it, stiff, with her little fists clenched tightly at her sides.

"They wouldn't let this long a time go by without calling in and you know it!" she declared. "Even if they did, there ought to be a tractor on the way to check."

"You might have a point there," admitted Mike.

"It could always be called back."

"It's probably been thought of," said Mike. "Look, Louise, why don't you calm down and let the worryin' get done by the people supposed to do it?"

She did not look at him. The darkness of her eyes surprised him, and he realized how she had paled beneath her tan.

"I can't help it," she said. "It's my fault, in a way. He only came along because I got so excited about the expedition I couldn't stay down on Earth. He didn't want to come, and now he's out there—"

Mike rose and shoved his chair aside with his foot. He thought the girl was going to faint. Watching her narrowly, he reached out to put his hand on her arm.

He sighed with relief as he heard Joey whistling outside. Louise straightened and moved away from his hand as the younger operator entered.

"Why don't you go see Burney?" suggested Mike. "He'll explain how he figures the odds; or if you want to argue, it's more sense to do it with him than me. I got nothing to do with it."

The girl pulled herself together with a visible effort.

"I know, Mike. Thanks for listening, anyway."

"Joey, go along with her to Burney's quarters!"

"That's all right," said Louise. "I can find my way farther than that."

They watched her leave.

Once more, Joey took the chair before the set and the pair of them sat in glum silence. The ventilation system came to life in one of its efforts to homogenize the base atmosphere, and its sigh partly drowned out the hiss of the radio.

"You know something, Joey?" grunted Mike.

"What?"

"I got a feelin' we're not gonna see those guys again."

"Hope you're wrong," said Joey. "It's awful tough digging around here, after the first few inches."

➤

Hansen trotted along steadily with the four-thousand-foot mountain rising in a sheer sweep out of the lava "sea" over to his right. There were three distinct peaks, he knew, but they ran in a line away from him so that the whole thing appeared one towering mass to him. Most of it, from his position, was black with the deepness of Lunar shadows, although he was gradually reaching a location where he could see the splashes of earth-light on the tortured rocks.

"Pretty soon I'll be out in the real flat, with nothing but a scattering of little craters to steer by," he reflected. "If I don't want to stop, how had I better head?"

Just in case the problem should arise, he began to estimate the direction he should take and the sort of ground he would find.

The first thing would be to bear slightly left until he picked up the trail of the tractor once more. Then he could expect a region of fairly frequent craterlets, leading up to Kirch, a modest but respectable seven miles in diameter. If he passed to the right of Kirch, he would be kept from wandering aimlessly out into the Mare Imbrium by a range of vein mountains. He might go farther astray by passing Kirch to the left, but there the going would probably be easier.

"Then what?" he murmured, trying to recall the map and the journey in the tractor.

There was another open area, he seemed to remember, and then the forty-mile string of peaks called the Kirch Mountains, bordered on the right by an even longer ridge of vein mountains which might once have been part of the range.

And then, another thirty miles or so would bring him to the ringwall of Archimedes!

Hansen shook his head.

"That would be going a little too far," he muttered.

His voice sounded husky to his own ears, and he paused to suck up a few swallows of water through the hose. He must have been half hypnotized by the steady streaming of the gray surface under his feet, for he suddenly realized that he had gone considerably beyond the triple peak.

Without his steady forward speed, he found it difficult for a moment to stand erect. He braced against the movement of the big tank on his back, and turned around to look back.

He stared at the dark, earthlit ground over which he had been trotting. With the looming mountain in the foreground, and the upthrust ringwalls of smaller craterlets here and there above the level, aseptic frigidity of the plain, it was a scene of complete desolation. It was more naked of life or any kind of softness than any desert on Earth; yet to Hansen, it did not really seem like a desert. There was some further overtone plucking at the fringe of his consciousness.

Then it came to him.

"It's like an *ocean!*" he exclaimed. "There's something about it that's like . . . like a cold, gray, winter sea smashing in on a rocky coast!"

There was the same monstrous, chilling power, the same effect upon the beholder that here was a massive, half-sentient entity against whose callous strength and cruelty nothing human could stand. It was a *thing* to observe from a safe distance, to cower from lest it somehow become aware of the puny structure of bone, blood, and flesh spying upon it. Then there would be no escape, no withstanding the crushing force of its malice. But he was on no safe cliff. He was down in the sea.

He looked around. Gray everywhere, mottled with inky shadows. Gray ash underfoot, gray-and-black lumps thrusting up from the surface like colossal vertebrae, gray distance in all directions.

"Been going for hours," he thought, "and there's no sign, really, that I'll ever get anywhere! I might as well be in the middle of the far side of Pluto!"

The huge mountain towered behind him, like a hulking beast from some alien world stalking the only object in all its frozen world that dared to move. Hansen suddenly could not bear to have his back turned to it. He faced it and edged clumsily away. The helmet that reduced his field of vision was his prison. If that black-shadowed mass of rock chose to topple over, it would easily reach him, and more. He would be ground under countless tons of weight, mangled and frozen in one instant—

Hansen whirled about and bolted.

On his first stride, he caught the toe of his right foot in the sand and sprawled forward with flailing arms. He plowed into the ground, throwing up spurts of sand like a speedboat tossing spray.

Somehow, he was up immediately, running in long, wobbling, forty-foot bounds. His eyes bulged and the breath rasped between his lips as he strove desperately to keep his balance.

It was like running in a dream, the nightmare come true. More than once, until he adapted to the pace, he found himself churning two or three steps at the zenith of his trajectory, too impatient to wait for the touch of boot on sand. There was sudden, dynamic power in his tiring muscles. All his joints felt loose.

His chest began to labor and he stumbled slightly. With a quick spasm, he blew his lungs and sucked in a deeper breath. After a few repetitions, he felt a trifle easier. In a minute he began to get his second wind. All this came like a half-perceived process of instinct, while he concentrated narrowly upon speeding ahead.

He flew up a slight grade and took off in a soaring leap to the next crest of an undulating stretch of pale yellow ash. The next thing he knew, he was rushing upon a long shadow that barred his path.

A hasty glance each way warned him there was no use trying to skirt it, for the shadow or hole or whatever it was ran for hundreds of yards right and left. Hansen stamped hard at the near edge and kicked off for at least sixty feet. Something seemed to snap in his right knee, but he came down all right and kept running, well clear of the shadow.

How long he ran, dodging this way and that to avoid hills and shadows obstructing his path, he did not know. In the end, the tiny motors of his suit fell behind the rate at which he consumed oxygen and gave off carbon dioxide and copious moisture.

●

When he began to feel like an underwater swimmer reaching his limit with writhing chest, Hansen gave up. He stopped.

That felt worse. He moved on at a gentle walk, accomplishing it mostly by motion from the ankles down. Amid the stifling warmth and stickiness inside his space suit, it was borne in upon him how badly he had lost his head.

He looked back, panting. Where was the mountain? Then, following the trail of isolated scars on the surface beyond where they faded into the gray distance, he saw a small knob of gray against the star-dotted black of the horizon.

"I guess . . . I've . . . really been traveling!" he panted. "Twenty minutes or half an hour—wonder how fast I went to put a mountain out of sight? Of course . . . I was well past when I started."

That reminded him of his bolt, and he closed his eyes in a paroxysm of shame.

The sweat beading his forehead began to trickle down his cheekbones or nose. Now and then, a drop rolled into his eyes, despite efforts to shake his head inside the confines of the helmet. It stung, but he was too blown to get excited over that.

"Why did I have to go and do that?" he groaned inwardly.

He remembered how levelheaded he had been in the first minutes of the catastrophe. Calmly, he had judged the odds of there being any survivors; calmly, he had climbed down for the prime requisite, the tank of oxygen; calmly, he had started off by a well-chosen route that led him accurately to landmarks so plain that they could be spotted from Earth with a good pair of field glasses.

He had intended to go only as far as Pico, or perhaps the triple peak. Or had he?

Somewhere back there, he remembered, he had begun planning a further march. There could be no reason for that except—

Except that he was secretly aware that he could count upon no help to reach him in time!

"Why should they send anybody out yet?" he asked himself. "For all they know, we're still inside Plato, camping on the nice level lava floor. I *must* have been thinking that, underneath, when I was figuring which side to pass Kirch."

He had been skating on thin ice and should have expected a crack-up. For a moment, he considered the possibility that it would have been better had he broken down on the spot. But then he might have quit while still on the ringwall of the great crater.

"As it is," he said aloud, "I'll at least get the most possible mileage out of this suit. If I live long enough, I might even walk in on them at base, for a surprise."

He grinned a bit as he considered that pleasant fantasy:

"Hi, Paul; where you been?"

"Oh, just out for a little walk on the moon."

"And where did you go on your little moon walk?"

"Took a turn around Plato. Pretty boring but 'toujours gai, whatthehell whatthehell!'"

He managed a deeper breath as his equipment caught up somewhat to his physical needs. The half grin on his lean features faded, and he stepped up his plodding pace.

"Why kid myself?" he snorted. "I'm just about scared senseless! And I've got a right to be!"

☙

Bucky O'Neil, as the pilot who was to take the scouting rocket, occupied the only extra chair in Dr. Burney's headquarters room. Burney sat across from him at the folding table and circled the proposed search area continuously with the butt of his pencil. Both men eyed the map reflectively. Burney looked as if he were trying to guess the precise location of his tractor crew. O'Neil, tracing his route with a blunt forefinger, was obviously attempting to estimate where he would have to punch his flare release in order to have his camera working by the time he whipped across Plato.

"Just to save us the wait," said Burney, leaning back in the silent, crowded room, "report by radio as soon as you loop back. Have you checked your set with Mike?"

The radio operator, standing to the rear of the little group, spoke up, "Joey's checking with the field now."

"Good!" approved Burney. "Does anyone have anything to add?"

He looked about. Sherman whistled quietly and tonelessly. Wohl shook his head. Johnny Pierce hovered, waiting to get his hands on his photomap again. Louise leaned against one wall near the door, worrying a pencil end between her white teeth.

"All right, then," said Burney, "you can get into your suit, Bucky. Good luck!"

The gathering broke up. Burney signaled for Wohl and Dr. Sherman to stay behind, and forestalled Johnny's move to reappropriate the map.

"We may want to consider further," he offered as an excuse, and Pierce left with Mike.

Outside, they watched Louise follow Bucky in the opposite direction.

"Wonder how it feels to have her man out there and maybe not coming back?" murmured Johnny.

His long face looked sad.

"What do you think their chances are?" he persisted after a brief pause as they turned a corner in the corridor.

Mike shrugged.

"Tractor One is starting back already," he said simply.

Hurrying along the other end of the corridor, Bucky was unable to shake off the following footsteps without putting on an obvious burst of speed. It sounded like Louise, and he wanted to think about his flight plan.

Finally, as he passed through the safety door—a double mounting that could be used in an emergency as an airlock—he had to pause long enough to acknowledge her presence.

"Do you mind if I ask you something, Bucky?" Louise inquired.

"Of course not, but I have to—"

"I know; I won't take more than a minute. The thing I don't like is that they just want you to photograph Plato."

Bucky released the door which swung shut automatically. He looked puzzled.

"Don't you think it's worth doing?" he asked.

"Oh, yes! Yes, I do. But how about all the other places?"

The pilot fidgeted.

"I can't take shots of the whole Mare Imbrium, Louise."

"You might take a few of the section this side of Plato, though. How do we know they ever reached the crater? If tracks show up on your pictures, we'll know how far they got."

"That's a good point," admitted Bucky, scratching his head. "But why didn't you bring it up in the meeting?"

Louise looked away. She shrugged slightly.

"Well, maybe Burney would have talked you out of it," Bucky conceded. "We all know you're worried."

"I know what everybody thinks," Louise replied. "I'm getting excited because one of the four happens to be my husband. I'm not thinking calmly about what's best for the base as a whole, whether it's worth taking people off other jobs to play hide-and-seek out on the surface. I probably shouldn't have come to Luna in the first place."

Bucky looked around, but there was no one passing through the Junction. Louise stepped closer and put a trembling hand on his arm.

"All right, Bucky, it's true enough. I'm frightened. I wish I'd never thought of coming here and making Paul feel he had to trail along! Are you married, Bucky, or engaged?"

"Well, there's a little blonde waiting down there for me—I hope. She'd better wait."

"How would you like it if *she* were out there?"

"Ummm," murmured the pilot. "I see what you mean."

He saw more than that. He saw how close she was to losing her grip, how she was keeping back the tears with an effort, trying to use every ounce of self-discipline so as to keep from being ignored as hysterical. Getting a few little things done, like influencing him to take extra photos, was all she could do at the moment to look out for her man. He remembered hearing from Pierce that Burney had refused her offer to take out a tractor herself.

"Well . . ." he yielded, "I'll see if I have a chance. I figure to cover the approaches to the ringwall anyway; maybe I can get a shot out around Pico, or thereabouts."

She did not thank him, but hid her face against his shoulder for a second. Bucky looked around again, touched her lightly on the head with one big, freckled hand, and disengaged himself gently.

When he glanced back over his shoulder, Louise was opening the safety door to go back.

"Heading for Mike and the radio, I bet," he thought. "Wonder when she slept last?"

He reminded himself that he had a job to do which involved delicate judgments at high speed, and he had no business going into it with hindering worries on his mind. If that girl did not watch herself, she would wind up under the care of Jean and "M.D." McLeod.

"I'm liable to, myself," he muttered, "if I don't snap out of it now! I wonder who'll pick me up if I zig out there when I ought to zag?"

He stopped at a phone connection and called the field control dome to learn if they were ready for him.

☙

Dazzling glints of light flashed here and there from that part of the Pacific Ocean still in bright sunlight as Hansen came in sight of Kirch. The coast of California had faded into the darkness and Asia was partly in view. He estimated that he had been moving for nearly eight hours.

His pace was still a rhythmic lope, but the feeling of having vigorous reserves of strength had worn off. Hansen knew that he must rest soon. In traversing the flat, crater-speckled plain since his panic, he had paused only once when he took a few minutes to recharge the oxygen tank of his suit.

"But I'm due for a good half hour off my feet," he decided.

His legs, he noticed, had lost some of their snap, so that his bounding trot was less exuberant. On the other hand, this resulted in his getting slightly better control of his stride; he no longer broke his rhythm by bouncing too high. The thing that bothered him most was the growing ache across the small of his back.

He skirted the ringwall of the last of a series of small craters and saw the shadowed side of the seven-mile wall. He was approaching the left curve of it, for he had hours ago decided to abandon the tractor tracks when he had crossed them again.

"No use running up the right and getting into the Kirch Mountains," he had muttered. "I'd have to zig-zag through them and I doubt I'll feel like making any extra distance by then."

His guess now, from the angle of Earth in the starry sky, was that he was heading a shade left of his generally southerly route. He reminded himself that he must change after rounding Kirch.

"I'll keep going till I'm past," he promised himself. "Then I'll sit down and relax a while."

He could not see much point in making another few miles out into the empty wasteland beyond Kirch. The crater was a natural goal to mark a section of his journey. About halfway between Plato and Archimedes, it was farther than he had dreamed of going. Even now, after he had seen how fast he could travel in the light gravity, it struck him as almost unbelievable that he could have covered such a distance. It was nearly a hundred and fifty miles.

Yet here he was, not in bad shape at all. He glanced at the outer slope of the ringwall on his right, and mentally cataloged his various irritations. There was, of course, the general clamminess that resulted from spending hours in a space suit, plus the fact that his bladder was beginning to bother him and there was nothing he could do about it. The overheating due to his exertions had been partially adjusted when he had discovered during his last halt that he could regulate the heating unit by a small dial in his battery pack, which discovery left him slightly aggrieved at not having had the finer points of the care and handling of space suits more exhaustively explained to him.

"But then," he reflected, "I was probably expected to spend a lot of time in the darkroom as a spare photographer."

He could not say he was hungry, although he supposed that sooner or later he would discover feelings of weakness. His suit seemed to be functioning as well as could be expected, except for something that had given way in the right knee on that one leap. He wondered if a spring was working loose.

"That could end up giving me a beautiful limp," he thought. "With fourteen pounds inside, and no air at all outside, it'd be tough to bend a joint without some mechanical help."

By now he could see light-streaks along the ring-wall, and knew that he was rounding it. The lighting gradually increased as he continued, until when he began to move out into the open plain some time later, the walls were mostly gray with earthlight. Kirch had a "new" appearance, as craters went. Its floor was not lava-filled, nor its ringwall seemingly as long exposed to thermal erosion, so that the probability was that it had been formed after the "sea" around it.

Hansen began to keep an eye out for a suitable place to sit down. Presently, he located a rock the size of an auto.

"Time for a drink, and then I'll pick out a good spot," he sighed.

The second he stopped to grope with his lips for the little hose, he knew he was really tired.

The water, cool from being only partly surrounded by heating coils to protect it from the exterior cold, refreshed him but slightly. The running had left a thick taste in his mouth.

Hansen unslung the big cylinder he had carried on his back and set it down beside a comfortable indentation in the rock. He then unfastened his backpack of tank and batteries. The metal-covered connection protecting the hose and wires was long enough to permit the pack to be set at his side.

He lowered himself to the fine sand and leaned his back against the rock with a sigh of relief. He squirmed into a more comfortable position.

"Wish I hadn't drunk all that water," he growled.

He leaned the back of his neck against the neck-piece of his suit. It was not uncomfortable except that he found himself staring directly into the light of Earth.

"I'm getting used to it all right, if I think that's too bright," he thought. "Bet my pupils are big as a cat's now."

Ironically, his feet had not started to hurt until his weight was off them. It felt as if he were developing blisters. The coveralls he wore under the space suit, moreover, had begun to chafe in a few places—around the armpits as he swung his arms, behind his right knee, on the inside of his thighs.

He also was reminded of the sweat that had trickled around or into his eyes, for the lids felt sore.

"I want a different view," he grunted, picking himself up. "Facing the other way, maybe I can rest my eyes."

Carrying his backpack, he started around the rock, then prudently went back for his big oxygen cylinder. He could think of no good reason for dragging this with him, but he somehow felt more comfortable with it beside him.

☙

The other face of the rock was blackly shadowed, and he was forced to find a convenient spot by groping about. With a sigh, he settled down, squirmed again into an easy position, and found himself contemplating the ringwall of Kirch a few miles away. The regular sough of air through his suit and the quiet hum of the mechanisms that were keeping him alive were so familiar by now that he hardly noticed them. It was the cessation of movement, not any diminishment of the normal sounds, that lent an impression of quiet to the scene.

He looked at the ringwall, squinting against the sting in his eyes that caused them to water occasionally. The left extremity was dim in the distance, but to the right, he could clearly see the slope of the wall as it curved to meet the plain. There was no feeling of a towering, insecurely balanced mass like that of the mountain.

"Although a crater at a distance does look like a mountain range," he thought. "Not so close as this; it goes up too steeply."

In a way, it was almost like looking at the skyscrapers of a big city, like looking at Manhattan from across the Hudson River. Except that there were no lights.

He closed his eyes for a moment and tried to visualize the sharp peak a little to his left atop the wall as it might look with a thousand lighted windows gleaming white and yellow.

It was hard to do. The stark fact was that there was only Lunar dimness, relieved by earthlight but tending to be uniform in intensity without the rays of the sun. If the silhouette of Kirch was like that of a city, the metropolis it resembled was a dead one.

A dead city in the midst of a cold, frozen sea of lava. A ghost city that had never lived, yet rose up from the gray sea over which no ship had sailed and whispered and whined ghostly warnings. "Stay with me, Man! I am dry and lonely. There are no people to warm me with light and sound. . . . There is none to see my massive strength and, by seeing, make it into reality. . . . Stay where you are, Man!"

"But it's dead," thought Hansen. "More than dead—sterile!"

"But you, Man, you too are dead. You are already turning cold. You will slowly congeal . . . become solid . . . a monument . . . a symbol of the tribute brought by folly and life to the sea of coldness and gray death—No, do not shake your head. . . . It is too late. . . . My shadows are about you. . . . You have no light. . . . All your prayers and wishes will not turn on a single light. The shadows reach you . . . touch you. . . . The pain in your leg is the cold of space. . . . You will sit there forever . . . drowned in the gray sea of frozen lava . . . imagining lights for me in the blackness . . . imagining life in me in the noon glare. . . . But now there is no light unless you have the force to see it . . . but you are cold . . . cold . . . cold . . . cold. . . ."

The sky flared with flickering light. It turned black while the image of light still remained in Hansen's eyes. Then a new light, tinier and higher streaked overhead. Hansen awoke with the hairs tingling on his neck and leaped to his feet with a hoarse shout.

"A rocket!"

☙

In the stillness of the radio room, the incoming call from Bucky's rocket made Mike jump in his chair before the set. Hastily, he turned down the volume he had kept up in hope of picking up faint calls from Plato.

When he had answered and relayed the message by phone to the landing area, he turned to the others in the room.

Joey had been sleeping in the upper bunk. Louise had asked to stay and Mike had offered his bunk for her to sit on. She had not slept, as far as he knew; but he had turned to the radio and maintained a lengthy silence.

"Maybe I ought to talk to her," he thought, "but what is there to say? Four good guys; but they're awful late checking in."

But when he looked around, they were both watching him; and he had to tell them.

"Bucky's coming in," he said.

"Did he find anything?" demanded Louise.

"Don't know yet," Mike told her. "He said he took a snap of Plato coming and going and three more on the way back."

Louise moved toward the door.

"Thanks a lot, Mike," she said.

Joey slipped down from the bunk as she disappeared into the corridor.

"Never mind," advised Mike. "With Louise and Bucky in that hole they call a darkroom, dodging the photographer's elbow every time he breathes in, they won't have any place for you but up on a shelf."

"I just thought I'd—"

"We'll get told. Now, stay with me, kid, an' make sure *I* don't go wanderin' off to have a look too!"

☙

Hansen stood stiffly by the rock and painfully tried his neck muscles. He searched the sky, but nothing moved among the stars.

"Now, *did* I see something?" he asked himself slowly. "Or was I still dreaming?"

He grimaced, and raised a hand to the back of his head before he remembered that he was still in his space suit. His neck was stiff and sore from lying across the rigid neckpiece of his suit, and he was chilled to the bone.

"Must have been asleep quite a while," he thought. "Maybe I ought to turn up the heating again—or should I just warm up as I walk?"

He paused a moment to stare in open-mouthed amazement at the ringwall of Kirch, rearing up three thousand feet toward the stars.

"When am I going to do something right?" he asked. "Why couldn't I stay where I was, facing Earth, and go to sleep dreaming I was home?"

He went on to wish that he had not gone to sleep at all. The aches that were irritations when he was warm from walking were now centers of agony.

He was sure he had blisters, and the chafed places under the suit jabbed little warnings of tenderness as he tried to move. Reaching for his battery pack, he nearly toppled over because his right leg was asleep. Even after he recovered and took a few steps to restore the circulation, the knee did not feel right.

"I wonder if I pulled a muscle?" he mused. "Or is it in the suit?"

He looked up at Earth. India was moving into the arc of shadow, but he could see Africa, the Mediterranean, and Europe.

When he realized he must have been out for three or perhaps four hours, he immediately checked his oxygen. It was none too soon. He refilled his suit tank and examined the pressure of the big cylinder. He guessed that he could do the trick once more.

"I wonder how long a man can live in a space suit?" he muttered. "Hansen, why aren't you dead?"

Groaning with stiffness, he adjusted his battery pack and tank and slung the cylinder atop the load. Although he seemed as wet as ever, he sucked up a drink of water while he listened to the hiss of his air circulator.

"Wish I wasn't so thirsty," he said. "I'll have to watch it. Beginning to feel lack of food, too."

He started off, moving mincingly to favor his sore muscles, and immediately felt the weakness brought on by hunger. It was hard to believe that a nightmare could last so long, but he remembered that it was almost a full day since he had eaten a sandwich in the tractor.

Gradually, as he moved along, marching away from Kirch into the open wasteland, he began to warm up. The stiffness left his muscles, although the chafing remained annoying. His feet felt sticky in the thick socks, suggesting that he would have trouble. He thought they might be bleeding.

What the hell was the matter with that knee? he wondered.

He thought of stopping to examine it, but the likelihood of his falling over on his face if he bent to feel the joint deterred him. He kept on. In half an hour, it became clear that a spring had snapped.

Not only was the knee harder to bend than it should have been, but something began to dig through his coveralls behind the knee.

"That's not so good," he told himself, but there was nothing he could think of to do.

He finally mustered the ambition to get up on his toes and bound along at a fairly brisk pace. The miles again floated under his feet, but he found that he could not maintain the trot the way he had earlier. Then, he had congratulated himself on his freshness, but he had come a long way since those few hours of immunity to fatigue.

The end of an hour found him moving at a moderate walk. One more, and he stopped noticing the pace particularly. There were few landmarks about him. He did not even strain ahead to catch a glimpse of the Kirch Mountains.

Finally, the nagging pain behind his knee became bad enough to make him stop.

"This is damn silly!" he growled. "I can't go along until that point of metal saws through a vein or something! Must be something I can do about it."

He thought it over, but it seemed that there simply was nothing he *could* do. The broken bit of metal was beyond his reach; he could not even feel it through the thickness of the space suit and the protective yellow chafing suit. Even if he should remove the latter by some weird contortion, the knee joint, as an obvious trouble spot, was reinforced by a bulge of metal. He would not be able to pinch or prod through that.

"Of course," he muttered, "I might take it off entirely. That would make things easy right away. A lot easier than just sitting down to wait for my air to run out."

He shook that out of mind with a jerk of his head, and struck out across the plain once more.

He had come to a stretch of gently rolling rises, and he tried to get most of his upward push from his left leg. Coming down the slopes, he hopped stiff-legged on his right. It was not too long before this became more tiring than it was worth.

"To hell with it!" he growled, and grimly drove onward with a more normal gait despite the sharp dig . . . dig . . . dig into his flesh at every stride.

☙

Burney and Bucky again sat across the table in the former's room. Instead of the map they had consulted earlier, they gazed down at the new photographs. The room, as before, was crowded with others who had edged in to watch silently. Even "M.D." McLeod, so nicknamed to distinguish him from all the doctors of philosophy and doctors of science among the expedition, lingered with his stethoscope dangling after giving Bucky a routine, postflight check.

Johnny Pierce stood lankily behind Burney's shoulder, holding a spare magnifying glass and squinting down at the photos. Sherman, Wohl, and Joey stood around the table with the photographers who had developed and enlarged the pictures. Louise watched from behind Bucky, resting her hands on his shoulders.

Burney nodded slowly, examining the picture of the interior of Plato through his lens.

"I very much fear," he said, tapping a forefinger on the half-lit heap of material at the foot on the ringwall, "that there is only one conclusion. That is a new slide, is it not?"

"It is," said Dr. Sherman, gesturing slightly with an older photograph of the region.

"And it is quite clear that they reached the crater," Burney continued. "These are excellent pictures, and the trail of the tractor treads shows very definitely."

"How about this one, Dr. Burney?" asked Bucky, pushing across another photo.

It showed the region around Mt. Pico, and had been enlarged until tracks of the tractor could be clearly seen. Burney frowned when he looked at it.

"To be perfectly frank," he murmured, "I do not know what to make of it. Those marks accompanying the trail *could* be footprints, I suppose, as has been suggested. But why . . . or how?"

"A man running could make marks that far apart in this gravity," said Bucky. "I know Johnny estimates those little dots are twenty and thirty feet apart, but it's possible."

"It is also possible that they are nothing of the sort. You notice that they leave the trail after a time."

Louise spoke up.

"That at least rules out one interpretation," she said. "They certainly aren't footprints made by someone on the surface on the way *to* Plato. Anybody walking beside the tractor would have left a trail starting and ending at the tread tracks."

There was silence. Some of the men looked at her with pity, others stared very hard at the photographs on the table.

Burney prodded another picture with his finger.

"Bucky took this where the tracks passed Kirch," he reminded them. "There are none of these so-called footprints there. I regret to point out the obvious conclusion—"

"But can't you do something to make sure?" Louise burst out. "You aren't just going to leave them out there. You couldn't!"

"Of course not," said Burney, biting his lip uncomfortably. "As soon as the Serenitatis crew get a few hours' rest, I shall send them out to recover . . . ah . . . to check. But the time element has already become such—that—Well, my dear, there is simply no use in rushing things. Either there is no need, or it is already too late."

There was not much doubt as to which possibility seemed the more likely. The meeting began to break up in unhappy silence.

⟐

Hansen trudged along with his chin on the neckpiece of the suit. Every so often, when he lurched in the shifting sand, his forehead bumped against the face-plate of his helmet.

"And that's not so easy to do," he thought foolishly. "Takes a supple neck to accomplish it."

He concentrated for perhaps a hundred paces, and slowly arrived at the corollary.

"Takes a pretty soft and supple head to get out here in the first place. Shoulda stood at home in bed. Should've stayed on Plato and tried to build some kind of a marker. Base'll send out somebody . . . wonder if that was a rocket I saw? Maybe I'd be dead . . . but I'm gonna be dead anyway. Why don't I just sit down and wait? At least, it won't hurt anymore. And, I'll be easy."

No arguments to the contrary occurred to him, but some deep impulse refused to let him quit.

He had to pause again; his stops for rest were becoming frequent. He did not sit down.

Never get up again, he realized.

He planted his feet wide apart and stood there, panting and letting his hands hang limply at his sides. His face felt stiff as he bared his teeth against the throb of the cut behind his knee. By now, he was so used to the wetness of the leg that he could not be sure the blood trickled down any faster.

He saw that he was standing on ground lighter than usual, and tinted pale yellow. Remembering passing several such areas, he slowly realized that they must be rays from Aristillus, traces of vaporized minerals blown out across the surrounding territory when the crater had been formed. It meant, for what it might be worth, that he was getting near Archimedes. Some of the rays of Aristillus reached the larger crater.

He gritted his teeth and took the first step forward. A glance to his right assured him that the jagged peaks of the Kirch Mountains were where they should be. Once, as he walked along half awake, he had discovered himself turning away on a course that would have sent him circling back into the Mare Imbrium.

"Sea of Showers," he thought. "I wish there were some. I wish I even had a glass of water to pour over my head. Just a glass of water to rinse out these eyes. I wouldn't even care about a shave."

He began to notice his footsteps, besides the hiss of the air circulator and the laboring of the suit's motors. Through his boots, they had a distant, swishing sound that insidiously lowered his puffed eyelids little by little. His head bumped against the faceplate again.

Hansen jerked upright with a start. Clumsily, he turned to look back. His tracks were long, dragging gashes in the sandy surface.

"Hell! Going to sleep again," he croaked.

With the effort of speaking aloud—it was getting difficult to think clearly otherwise—the corner of his lower lip cracked. He opened his dry mouth, making a face at the morning-after taste, and gently touched the tip of his tongue to the spot. It stung.

No harm in taking a little water, he decided, though he knew it would offer only a fleeting relief. But he needed that.

He turned his head to the left and got the thin rubber tube between his teeth. The cracked lip stung as he sucked on the tube.

The water was cool. His tired eyes closed with the sheer pleasure of the sensation.

On the third swallow, it stopped flowing.

"Oh, no!" Hansen groaned.

He drew harder on the hose and eked out another mouthful. That was all. The tank was empty. It was supposed to be partly replenished by moisture removed from the air in the suit, but he had apparently reached the limit. The suit was not designed to be worn for twenty hours. It was a wonder that nothing had yet broken down.

He held the last mouthful without swallowing, letting it roll slowly about his mouth.

"Come on!" he thought. "That's all there is. What are you waiting for?"

He knew it was silly to feel angry at this latest pinprick. His growing rage was a sign of exhaustion, and some part of his mind recognized that fact; but he deliberately let his temper go . . . and drew extra strength from it.

The swallow of water gradually slipped down as he surged forward. With the stiff right knee, he staggered once and came so near falling flat that he skidded on all fours under him again.

"Dammit!" he raged. "What are they doing at base? Waiting for a weather report? Anybody with an ounce of brain would know by now things went sour!"

He lurched down a gentle slope and charged the next rise.

"I'll show them!" he grunted. "I don't need them, if they're too chicken to come out for me. I'll get there. . . . I don't know how I'll get up the goddamned wall . . . but I'll get *to* it! I'll get there!"

Mike sat before his radio and looked at the other three in the room.

Pierce looked thoughtful, Joey was frankly excited, and Louise Hansen paced nervously back and forth.

"The crew from Tractor One say they saw no tracks of any kind," he said, "but that doesn't prove a thing. They came nowheres near the line between Plato and Archimedes."

"Then you think we're justified in not waiting for the same crew?" asked Louise.

"Sure," said Mike. "I don't like to sound like I'm egging you on to something I wouldn't do myself, but—"

"Of course, Mike, of course," interrupted Johnny. "One of you has to stay on the radio, or we couldn't call back. We could get Bucky to take Joey's place, I guess, but why wake him up?"

"He did his share," Joey put in quickly.

Mike looked from face to face.

"Well, Joey can say I gave him permission," he said. "I don't know what you will say, but it'd be better if you got going and figured that out on the way back."

The shadowed ringwall loomed up before the yellow speck on the plain. Just enough earthlight reached this face to show where the seven-mile-wide outer slope was terraced by gentle inclines. Several of these led upward toward the pass used by the scouting expedition. Against the black sky, Hansen could not see the radio tower that had been erected, but he was no longer interested in that. He had jettisoned his radio batteries back on the plain to be rid of their weight as he tackled the long slope leading to Archimedes.

"There you are . . . there you are!" he mumbled. "Eureka, eureka! Damn near three hundred miles . . . maybe more the way I came. That's navigating, ain't it?"

The ringwall stood passively before him.

"Well, ain't it?" snarled Hansen thickly. "All right, here we go!"

He lurched forward. Despite having abandoned every bit of excess gear—the empty oxygen cylinder lay back beside the last craterlet he had passed—he could walk no faster than if he had been on Earth. It probably meant that on Earth he would have long since collapsed, but he was beyond thinking of that.

He found he could not climb the first seven-foot ledge he came to, and had to walk along it to a lower spot.

"No time, no time," he muttered against the delay. "You're on your last tankful now . . . in fact, well into it. You get up there . . . now . . . or not ever."

He found a long lateral slope and followed it up several hundred yards. He was cold and sluggish, and it seemed that his heating batteries were close to exhausted.

The ache across his back seemed normal. Even the dull misery of his legs, chafed, cut, rubbed raw, and the sogginess of his bleeding feet had come to be merely part of his general limpness.

He found himself finishing the last few yards of the slope on hands and knees.

"Funny," he croaked. "Don't remember fallin'."

He reached out for an outcropping of rock to pull himself up. The broken spring twisted in the mangled spot on the back of his thigh as he tried to rise. Getting both hands on the rock, he inched upward little by little.

It took him all of five minutes before he was on his feet again. At first, he thought he was dreaming again. The rock seemed to move under him.

Then he saw, peering blearily upward, that it was part of an old landslide. One slip on his part now might set it off again, and send him crashing down to the bottom of the ringwall again. Hansen groaned and stepped away as carefully as he could.

He was faced by a forty-five degree slope. If he could negotiate it for about thirty feet, he would reach another ramp. He looked down, and wondered if it would be easier to slide down to a lower terrace which would eventually lead higher than his present position.

"No time," he said dazedly.

He began to scrabble his way up the incline, not one too difficult to climb on Luna. The sun-powered rock flaked off beneath his hands, elbows, knees, and feet. He slid back about as fast as he climbed.

With a sob, he lunged for a projection the size of a man's head and got one mitten on it. The rock cracked off and he slid to the foot of the incline.

"*Oh, God! It's too much!*"

His face twisted up and he expected to feel tears running down his face. Apparently, however, he was too dried out for that.

◆

He sat there dully, staring at the lower ramp and trying to tell himself he could always try that.

He knew better.

"This is the end of the line," he told himself. "Last stop. . . . You're done."

Even his conscience did not twitch at his surrender. He only wished he could see Earth and look at North America again where it was centered on the globe once more.

It was too much effort to turn around.

"Wonder if they'll find me," he mumbled. "Dunno if I want to get buried or not. . . ."

Something moved to his left. A light.

"I'm seeing things," he muttered. "Not long now."

But the light swung up and down, it lit the slope below him, and it kept moving.

Nothing looked like that but a tractor.

But it would pass a hundred yards below him. The driver would have his eyes glued to the ground ahead, watching for holes or cracks.

Hansen started to laugh and managed to catch himself.

"The chance after the last chance!" he thought he said aloud, although his lips barely moved.

The effort of pulling himself to his knees brought out sweat he did not know he had left.

He waited for the tractor to reach a point below him. Waited . . . lifting the head-sized rock in both hands.

The tiny weight tired him, and he lowered the stone to his knees. The tractor lumbered along, heading down the slope into the plain.

Hansen swayed where he knelt, but concentrated everything upon estimating the distance.

With a grunt, he raised the rock and thrust it away from his chest, outward over the slope on which he sprawled with the motion.

He raised himself on his elbows and looked to see what happened. The tractor had slid to an abrupt halt.

Dimly, he could see the shattered pieces of his missile bouncing in and out of patches of earthlight below the vehicle. The driver could not have missed it crossing his path.

"Gotta get up . . . up!" Hansen thought desperately.

He did not realize that his air was turning foul, but the simple feat of getting his feet under him left his heart pounding wildly.

He planted his feet somehow until the light swept up the slope as those in the tractor searched for a possible slide.

Brightness filled his helmet. He was dazzled, and felt himself falling.

◆

"Paul, try to help!"

"Paul, can't you get some grip when I shove you in? I can't keep you from sliding out the airlock. Paul!"

The voice was young and desperate.

When the other man backed away, parting the contact of their helmets, Hansen saw the features of Joey, the radio operator, through the other faceplate.

He stirred feebly.

"That's it, Paul," said the faraway voice as Joey bent to lift him again. "Just a little bit of help till I get you inside the airlock."

Something clanged, leaving him in blackness.

The next thing he knew, he was gulping in sobbing breaths of fresh, oxygen-rich air. His head ached, but he felt better.

Someone was mopping his sweaty face with a wet handkerchief. The handkerchief dripped, and the drops were salty.

He could not see Louise, because she held his head cradled against her breast, but Joey was looking at him wide-eyed over the back of another seat.

"How long ago did you start?" asked someone else, and Hansen saw that Johnny Pierce was driving.

"Right after we got to Plato," said Hansen. "Everything but me and a tank of oxygen went down in a slide."

"Musta been nearly twenty-four hours ago!" exclaimed Joey.

"Gol-darn!" said Pierce primly. "Three hundred miles, give or take a few!"

"You ain't human, Paul!" said Joey.

"Do you want your suit off now?" asked Louise. "We could only get your helmet loose in this space."

Without seeing her face, he could tell that she had been crying.

"Just leave it on," said Hansen. "Wait till we're in, and I can go right from the suit to a bath."

"We're coming over the crest," announced Johnny. "Louise, you better hold him in case I hit a few bumps."

Hansen relaxed with a sigh as he felt her hands tighten against him.

"Hold tight, honey!" he whispered as he closed his eyes against the lights in the tractor. "I . . . I'm a little tired."

Grandpa

JAMES H. SCHMITZ

James H. Schmitz made his first sale in 1943, to Unknown. *He served in the U. S. Air Force during World War II and, after the war quickly established himself as one of the mainstays of the postwar* Astounding, *a role he would fill all through the fifties and sixties. Schmitz's action-packed space opera, especially stories such as his* Vega *series, later collected as* Agent of Vega, *holds up well for verve, imagination, and headlong pacing against the work of his contemporaries, although it's less intense, paranoid, ornate, and rabidly xenophobic than A. E. van Vogt's stuff, for instance. Unlike most of his peers, Schmitz even occasionally shows sympathy for the alien monsters his characters battle, who are sometimes seen in the end not to be monsters at all, but rather creatures with agendas and priorities and points of view of their own, from which perspectives their actions are justified and sometimes even admirable. Even more extreme, and unlike almost anyone else in the business at that time, Schmitz frequently used women as the heroes in swashbuckling tales of interplanetary adventure (sacrilege!) and portrayed them as the total equal of the male characters, every bit as competent and brave and smart (and ruthless, when need be) as the men.*

*Although he did write a few novels—*The Witches of Karres *is usually thought of as Schmitz's best novel and perhaps is his best work—Schmitz was also unlike his peers in that he did most of his best work at short lengths, most of it for* Astounding *(and later for* Analog, *after the magazine had changed its name) and for* Galaxy, *including such memorable stories as "Balanced Ecology," "Lion Loose . . . ," "Trouble Tide," "Greenface," "The Searcher," "The Winds of Time," "The Custodians," and dozens of others, plus a large number of stories about the adventures of a PSI-powered teenager, Telzey Amberdon. Schmitz's stories have been collected in* A Nice Day For Screaming and Other Tales of the Hub, A Pride of Monsters, *the aforementioned* Agent of Vega, *and, most recently, the posthumous collection* The Best of James H. Schmitz; *the "Telzey Amberdon" stories have been collected in* The Universe against Her *and* The Telzey Toy. *Schmitz's other books include* The Demon Breed, A Tale of Two Clocks, *and* The Eternal Frontiers.

Schmitz was also known for his aliens, and especially for the construction of intricate and inventive alien ecosystems, with all the interlocking details of the biosphere carefully worked out. (He may have been one of the first authors, in fact, to use the word ecology *in a story.) The alien ecosystem he describes here is particularly ingenious and well thought out, as he takes us along for a hair-raising lesson in why explorers should never take* anything *for granted—even things they think they already know.*

Most of Schmitz's work is out-of-print, although an occasional copy of The Witches of Karres *still shows up in used-book stores. Your best choice of sampling his work would probably be his most recent book, published in 1991,* The Best of James H. Schmitz, *which does contain several of his best stories. You could try ordering it from the publisher, NESFA Press (NESFA Press, PO Box 809, Framingham, MA 97101-0203), although I have no idea whether they have any left in stock or not; the price was $18.95, but you'd better write first and ask for information.*

A green-winged, downy thing as big as a hen fluttered along the hillside to a point directly above Cord's head and hovered there, twenty feet above him. Cord, a fifteen-year-old human being, leaned back against a skipboat parked on the equator of a world that had known human beings for only the past four Earth years, and eyed the thing speculatively. The thing was, in the free and easy terminology of the Sutang Colonial Team, a swamp bug. Concealed in the downy fur back of the bug's head was a second, smaller, semiparastical thing, classed as a bug rider.

The bug itself looked like a new species to Cord. Its parasite might or might not turn out to be another unknown. Cord was a natural research man; his first glimpse of the odd flying team had sent endless curiosities thrilling through him. How did that particular phenomenon tick, and why? What fascinating things, once you'd learned about it, could you get it to do?

Normally, he was hampered by circumstances in carrying out any such investigation. The Colonial Team was a practical, hardworking outfit—two thousand people who'd been given twenty years to size up and tame down the brand-new world of Sutang to the point where a hundred thousand colonists could be settled on it, in reasonable safety and comfort. Even junior colonial students like Cord were expected to confine their curiosity to the pattern of research set up by the station to which they were attached. Cord's inclination toward independent experiments had got him into disfavor with his immediate superiors before this.

He sent a casual glance in the direction of the Yoger Bay Colonial Station behind him. No signs of human activity about that low, fortress-like bulk in the hill. Its central lock was still closed. In fifteen minutes, it was scheduled to be opened to let out the Planetary Regent, who was inspecting the Yoger Bay Station and its principal activities today.

Fifteen minutes was time enough to find out something about the new bug, Cord decided.

But he'd have to collect it first.

He slid out one of the two handguns holstered at his side. This one was his own property: a Vanadian projectile weapon. Cord thumbed it to position for anesthetic small-game missiles and brought the hovering swamp bug down, drilled neatly and microscopically through the head.

As the bug hit the ground, the rider left its back. A tiny scarlet demon, round and bouncy as a rubber ball, it shot toward Cord in three long hops, mouth wide to sink home inch-long, venom-dripping fangs. Rather breathlessly, Cord triggered the gun again and knocked it out in midleap. A new species, all right! Most bug riders were harmless plant-eaters, mere suckers of vegetable juice—

"*Cord!*" A feminine voice.

Cord swore softly. He hadn't heard the central lock click open. She must have come around from the other side of the station.

"Hi, Grayan!" he shouted innocently without looking around. "Come see what I got! New species!"

Grayan Mahoney, a slender, black-haired girl two years older than himself, came trotting down the hillside toward him. She was Sutang's star colonial student, and the station manager, Nirmond, indicated from time to time that she was a fine example for Cord to pattern his own behavior on. In spite of that, she and Cord were good friends, but she bossed him around considerably.

"Cord, you dope!" she scowled as she came up. "Quit acting like a collector! If the Regent came out now, you'd be sunk. Nirmond's been telling her about you!"

"Telling her what?" Cord asked, startled.

"For one," Grayan reported, "that you don't keep up on your assigned work. Two, that you sneak off on one-man expeditions of your own at least once a month and have to be rescued—"

"Nobody," Cord interrupted hotly, "has had to rescue me yet!"

"How's Nirmond to know you're alive and healthy when you just drop out of sight for a week?" Grayan countered. "Three," she resumed checking the items off on slim fingertips, "he complained that you keep private zoological gardens of unidentified and possibly deadly vermin in the woods back of the station. And four . . . well, Nirmond simply doesn't want the responsibility for you any more!" She held up the four fingers significantly.

"Golly!" gulped Cord, dismayed. Summed up tersely like that, his record *didn't* look too good.

"Golly is right! I keep warning you! Now Nirmond wants the Regent to send you back to Vanadia—and there's a starship coming in to New Venus forty-eight hours from now!" New Venus was the Colonial Team's main settlement on the opposite side of Sutang.

"What'll I do?"

"Start acting like you had good sense mainly." Grayan grinned suddenly. "I talked to the Regent, too—Nirmond isn't rid of you yet! But if you louse up on our tour of the Bay Farms today, you'll be off the Team for good!"

She turned to go. "You might as well put the skipboat back; we're not using it. Nirmond's driving us down to the edge of the Bay in a treadcar, and we'll take a raft from there. Don't let them know I warned you!"

Cord looked after her, slightly stunned. He hadn't realized his reputation had become as bad as all that! To Grayan, whose family had served on Colonial Teams for the past four generations, nothing worse was imaginable than to be dismissed and sent back ignominiously to one's own homeworld. Much to his surprise, Cord was discovering now that he felt exactly the same way about it!

Leaving his newly bagged specimens to revive by themselves and flutter off again, he hurriedly flew the skipboat around the station and rolled it back into its stall.

✦

Three rafts lay moored just offshore in the marshy cove, at the edge of which Nirmond had stopped the treadcar. They looked somewhat like exceptionally broad-brimmed, well-worn sugarloaf hats floating out there, green and leathery. Or like lily pads twenty-five feet across, with the upper section of a big, gray-green pineapple growing from the center of each. Plant animals of some sort. Sutang was too new to have had its phyla sorted out into anything remotely like an orderly classification. The rafts were a local oddity which had been investigated and could be regarded as harmless and moderately useful. Their usefulness lay in the fact that they were employed as a rather slow means of transportation about the shallow, swampy waters of the Yoger Bay. That was as far as the Team's interest in them went at present.

The Regent had stood up from the back seat of the car, where she was sitting next to Cord. There were only four in the party; Grayan was up front with Nirmond.

"Are those our vehicles?" The Regent sounded amused.

Nirmond grinned, a little sourly. "Don't underestimate them, Dane! They could become an important economic factor in this region in time. But, as a matter of fact, these three are smaller than I like to use." He was peering about the reedy edges of the cove. "There's a regular monster parked here usually—"

Grayan turned to Cord. "Maybe Cord knows where Grandpa is hiding."

It was well-meant, but Cord had been hoping nobody would ask him about Grandpa. Now they all looked at him.

"Oh, you want Grandpa?" he said, somewhat flustered. "Well, I left him . . . I mean I saw him a couple of weeks ago about a mile south from here—"

Grayan sighed. Nirmond grunted and told the Regent, "The rafts tend to stay wherever they're left, providing it's shallow and muddy. They use a hair-root system to draw chemicals and microscopic nourishment directly from the bottom of the bay. Well—Grayan, would you like to drive us there?"

Cord settled back unhappily as the treadcar lurched into motion. Nirmond suspected he'd used Grandpa for one of his unauthorized tours of the area, and Nirmond was quite right.

"I understand you're an expert with these rafts, Cord," Dane said from beside him. "Grayan told me we couldn't find a better steersman, or pilot, or whatever you call it, for our trip today."

"I can handle them," Cord said, perspiring. "They don't give you any trouble!" He didn't feel he'd made a good impression on the Regent so far. Dane was a young, handsome-looking woman with an easy way of talking and laughing, but she wasn't the head of the Sutang Colonial Team for nothing. She looked quite capable of shipping out anybody whose record wasn't up to par.

"There's one big advantage our beasties have over a skipboat, too," Nirmond remarked from the front seat. "You don't have to worry about a snapper trying to climb on board with you!" He went on to describe the stinging ribbon-tentacles the rafts spread around them under water to discourage creatures that might make a meal off their tender under-parts. The snappers and two or three other active and aggressive species of the Bay hadn't yet learned it was foolish to attack armed human beings in a boat, but they would skitter hurriedly out of the path of a leisurely perambulating raft.

Cord was happy to be ignored for the moment. The Regent, Nirmond and Grayan were all Earth people, which was true of most of the members of the Team; and Earth people made him uncomfortable, particularly in groups. Vanadia, his own homeworld, had barely graduated from the status of Earth colony itself, which might explain the difference. All the Earth people he'd met so far seemed dedicated to what Grayan Mahoney called the Big Picture, while Nirmond usually spoke of it as "Our Purpose Here." They acted strictly in accordance with their Team Regulations—sometimes, in Cord's opinion, quite insanely. Because now and then the Regulations didn't quite cover a new situation and then somebody was likely to get killed. In which case, the Regulations would be modified promptly, but Earth people didn't seem otherwise disturbed by such events.

Grayan had tried to explain it to Cord:

"We can't really ever *know* in advance what a new world is going to be like! And once we're there, there's too much to do, in the time we've got, to study it inch by inch. You get your job done, and you take a chance. But if you stick by the Regulations you've got the best chances of surviving anybody's been able to figure out for you—"

Cord felt he preferred to just use good sense and not let Regulations or the job get him into a situation he couldn't figure out for himself.

To which Grayan replied impatiently that he hadn't yet got the Big Picture—

The treadcar swung around and stopped, and Grayan stood up in the front seat, pointing. "That's Grandpa, over there!"

Dane also stood up and whistled softly, apparently impressed by Grandpa's fifty-foot spread. Cord looked around in surprise. He was pretty sure this was several hundred yards from the spot where he'd left the big raft two weeks ago; and as Nirmond said, they didn't usually move about by themselves.

Puzzled, he followed the others down a narrow path to the water, hemmed in by tree-sized reeds. Now and then he got a glimpse of Grandpa's swimming platform, the rim of which just touched the shore. Then the path opened out, and he saw the whole raft lying in sunlit, shallow water; and he stooped short, startled.

Nirmond was about to step up on the platform, ahead of Dane.

"Wait!" Cord shouted. His voice sounded squeaky with alarm. "Stop!" He came running forward.

They had frozen where they stood, looked around swiftly. Then glanced back at Cord coming up. They were well trained.

"What's the matter, Cord?" Nirmond's voice was quiet and urgent.

"Don't get on that raft—it's changed!" Cord's voice sounded wobbly, even to himself. "Maybe it's not even Grandpa—"

He saw he was wrong on the last point before he'd finished the sentence. Scattered along the rim of the raft were discolored spots left by a variety of heat-guns, one of which had been his own. It was the way you goaded the sluggish and mindless things into motion. Cord pointed at the cone-shaped central projection. "There—his head! He's sprouting!"

"Sprouting?" the station manager repeated uncomprehendingly. Grandpa's head, as befitted his girth, was almost twelve feet high and equally wide. It was armor-plated like the back of a saurian to keep off plant-suckers, but two weeks ago it had been an otherwise featureless knob, like those on all other rafts. Now scores of long, kinky, leafless vines had grown out from all surfaces of the cone, like green wires. Some were drawn up like tightly coiled springs, others trailed limply to the platform and over it. The top of the cone was dotted with angry red buds, rather like pimples, which hadn't been there before either. Grandpa looked unhealthy.

"Well," Nirmond said, "so it is. Sprouting!" Grayan made a choked sound. Nirmond glanced at Cord as if puzzled. "Is that all that was bothering you, Cord?"

"Well, sure!" Cord began excitedly. He hadn't caught the significance of the word "all"; his hackles were still up, and he was shaking. "None of them ever—"

Then he stopped. He could tell by their faces that they hadn't got it. Or rather, that they'd got it all right but simply weren't going to let it change their plans. The rafts were classified as harmless, according to the Regulations. Until proved otherwise, they would continue to be regarded as harmless. You didn't waste time quibbling with the Regulations—apparently even if you were the Planetary Regent. You didn't feel you had the time to waste.

He tried again. "Look—" he began. What he wanted to tell them was that Grandpa with one unknown factor added wasn't Grandpa any more. He was an unpredictable, oversized lifeform, to be investigated with cautious thoroughness till you knew what the unknown factor meant.

But it was no use. They knew all that. He stared at them helplessly. "I—"

Dane turned to Nirmond. "Perhaps you'd better check," she said. She didn't add, "—to reassure the boy!" but that was what she meant.

Cord felt himself flushing terribly. They thought he was scared—which he was—and they were feeling sorry for him, which they had no right to do. But there was nothing he could say or do now except watch Nirmond walk steadily across the platform. Grandpa shivered slightly a few times, but the rafts always did that when someone first stepped on them. The station manager stopped before one of the kinky sprouts, touched it and then gave it a tug. He reached up and poked at the lowest of the budlike growths. "Odd-looking things!" he called back. He gave Cord another glance. "Well, everything seems harmless enough, Cord. Coming aboard, everyone?"

It was like dreaming a dream in which you yelled and yelled at people and couldn't make them hear you! Cord stepped up stiff-legged on the platform behind Dane and Grayan. He knew exactly what would have happened if he'd hesitated even a moment. One of them would have said in a friendly voice, careful not to let it sound too contemptuous: "You don't have to come along if you don't want to, Cord!"

Grayan had unholstered her heat-gun and was ready to start Grandpa moving out into the channels of the Yoger Bay.

Cord hauled out his own heat-gun and said roughly, "I was to do that!"

"All right, Cord." She gave him a brief, impersonal smile, as if he were someone she'd met for the first time that day, and stood aside.

They were so infuriatingly polite! He was, Cord decided, as good as on his way back to Vanadia right now.

For a while, Cord almost hoped that something awesome and catastrophic would happen promptly to teach the Team people a lesson. But nothing did. As always, Grandpa shook himself vaguely and experimentally when he felt the heat on one edge of the platform and then decided to withdraw from it, all of which was standard procedure. Under the water, out of sight, were the raft's working sections: short, thick leaf-structures shaped like paddles and designed to work as such, along with the slimy nettle-streamers which kept the vegetarians of the Yoger Bay away, and a jungle of hair roots through which Grandpa sucked nourishments from the mud and the sluggish waters of the Bay, and with which he also anchored himself.

The paddles started churning, the platform quivered, the hair roots were hauled out of the mud; and Grandpa was on his ponderous way.

Cord switched off the heat, reholstered his gun, and stood up. Once in motion, the rafts tended to keep traveling unhurriedly for quite a while. To stop them, you gave them a touch of heat along their leading edge; and they could be turned in any direction by using the gun lightly on the opposite side of the platform.

It was simple enough. Cord didn't look at the others. He was still burning inside. He watched the reed beds move past and open out, giving him glimpses of the misty, yellow and green and blue expanse of the brackish Bay ahead. Behind the mist, to the west, were the Yoger Straits, tricky and ugly water when the tides were running; and beyond the Straits lay the open sea, the great Zlanti Deep, which was another world entirely and one of which he hadn't seen much as yet.

Suddenly he was sick with the full realization that he wasn't likely to see any more of it now! Vanadia was a pleasant enough planet; but the wildness and strangeness were long gone from it. It wasn't Sutang.

Grayan called from beside Dane, "What's the best route from here into the farms, Cord?"

"The big channel to the right," he answered. He added somewhat sullenly, "We're headed for it!"

Grayan came over to him. "The Regent doesn't want to see all of it," she said, lowering her voice. "The algae and plankton beds first. Then as much of the mutated grains as we can show her in about three hours.

Steer for the ones that have been doing best, and you'll keep Nirmond happy!"

She gave him a conspiratorial wink. Cord looked after her uncertainly. You couldn't tell from her behavior that anything was wrong. Maybe—

He had a flare of hope. It was hard not to like the Team people, even when they were being rock-headed about their Regulations. Perhaps it was that purpose that gave them their vitality and drive, even though it made them remorseless about themselves and everyone else. Anyway, the day wasn't over yet. He might still redeem himself in the Regent's opinion. Something might happen—

Cord had a sudden cheerful, if improbable, vision of some Bay monster plunging up on the raft with snapping jaws, and of himself alertly blowing out what passed for the monster's brains before anyone else—Nirmond, in particular—was even aware of the threat. The Bay monsters shunned Grandpa, of course, but there might be ways of tempting one of them.

So far, Cord realized, he'd been letting his feelings control him. It was time to start thinking!

Grandpa first. So he'd sprouted—green vines and red buds, purpose unknown, but with no change observable in his behavior-patterns otherwise. He was the biggest raft in this end of the Bay, though all of them had been growing steadily in the two years since Cord had first seen one. Sutang's seasons changed slowly; its year was somewhat more than five Earth years long. The first Team members to land here hadn't yet seen a full year pass.

Grandpa then was showing a seasonal change. The other rafts, not quite so far developed, would be reacting similarly a little later. Plant animals—they might be blossoming, preparing to propagate.

"Grayan," he called, "how do the rafts get started? When they're small, I mean."

Grayan looked pleased; and Cord's hopes went up a little more. Grayan was on his side again anyway!

"Nobody knows yet," she said. "We were just talking about it. About half of the coastal marsh-fauna of the continent seems to go through a preliminary larval stage in the sea." She nodded at the red buds on the raft's cone. "It *looks* as if Grandpa is going to produce flowers and let the wind or ride take the seeds out through the Straits."

It made sense. It also knocked out Cord's still half-held hope that the change in Grandpa might turn out to be drastic enough, in some way, to justify his reluctance to get on board. Cord studied Grandpa's armored head carefully once more—unwilling to give up that hope entirely. There were a series of vertical gummy black slits between the armor plates, which hadn't been in evidence two weeks ago either. It looked as if Grandpa were beginning to come apart at the seams. Which might indicate that the rafts, big as they grew to be, didn't outlive a full seasonal cycle, but came to flower at about this time of Sutang's year and died. However, it was a safe bet that Grandpa wasn't going to collapse into senile decay before they completed their trip today.

Cord gave up on Grandpa. The other notion returned to him—per-

haps he could coax an obliging Bay monster into action that would show
the Regent he was no sissy!

Because the monsters were there, all right.

Kneeling at the edge of the platform and peering down into the wine-
colored, clear water of the deep channel they were moving through, Cord
could see a fair selection of them at almost any moment.

Some five or six snappers, for one thing. Like big, flattened crayfish,
chocolate-brown mostly, with green and red spots on their carapaced
backs. In some areas they were so thick you'd wonder what they found
to live on, except that they ate almost anything, down to chewing up
the mud in which they squatted. However, they preferred their food in
large chunks and alive, which was one reason you didn't go swimming
in the Bay. They would attack a boat on occasion; but the excited manner in which the ones he saw were scuttling off toward the edges of the
channel showed they wanted to have nothing to do with a big moving
raft.

Dotted across the bottom were two-foot round holes which looked
vacant at the moment. Normally, Cord knew, there would be a head
filling each of those holes. The heads consisted mainly of triple sets of
jaws, held open patiently like so many traps to grab at anything that came
within range of the long, wormlike bodies behind the heads. But
Grandpa's passage, waving his stingers like transparent pennants through
the water, had scared the worms out of sight, too.

Otherwise, mostly schools of small stuff—and then a flash of wicked
scarlet, off to the left behind the raft, darting out from the reeds! Turning
its needle-nose into their wake.

Cord watched it without moving. He knew that creature, though it was
rare in the Bay and hadn't been classified. Swift, vicious—alert enough
to snap swamp bugs out of the air as they fluttered across the surface.
And he'd tantalized one with fishing tackle once into leaping up on a
moored raft, where it had flung itself about furiously until he was able to
shoot it.

No fishing tackle. A handkerchief might just do it, if he cared to risk
an arm—

"What fantastic creatures!" Dane's voice just behind him.

"Yellowheads," said Nirmond. "They've got a high utility rating. Keep
down the bugs."

Cord stood up casually. It was no time for tricks! The reed bed to their
right was thick with yellowheads, a colony of them. Vaguely froggy
things, man-sized and better. Of all the creatures he'd discovered in the
Bay, Cord liked them least. The flabby, sacklike bodies clung with four
thin limbs to the upper sections of the twenty-foot reeds that lined the
channel. They hardly ever moved, but their huge, bulging eyes seemed
to take in everything that went on about them. Every so often, a downy
swamp bug came close enough; and a yellowhead would open its vertical,
enormous, tooth-lined slash of a mouth, extend the whole front of its face
like a bellows in a flashing strike; and the bug would be gone. They might
be useful, but Cord hated them.

"Ten years from now we should know what the cycle of coastal life is like," Nirmond said. "When we set up the Yoger Bay Station there were no yellowheads here. They came the following year. Still with traces of the oceanic larval form; but the metamorphosis was almost complete. About twelve inches long—"

Dane remarked that the same pattern was duplicated endlessly elsewhere. The Regent was inspecting the yellowhead colony with field glasses; she put them down now, looked at Cord and smiled. "How far to the farms?"

"About twenty minutes."

"The key," Nirmond said, "seems to be the Zlanti Basin. It must be almost a soup of life in spring."

"It is," nodded Dane, who had been here in Sutang's spring, four Earth years ago. "It's beginning to look as if the Basin alone might justify colonization. The question is still—", she gestured towards the yellowheads—"how do creatures like that get there?"

They walked off toward the other side of the raft, arguing about ocean currents. Cord might have followed. But something splashed back of them, off to the left and not too far back. He stayed, watching.

After a moment, he saw the big yellowhead. It had slipped down from its reedy perch, which was what had caused the splash. Almost submerged at the water line, it stared after the raft with huge pale-green eyes. To Cord, it seemed to look directly at him. In that moment, he knew for the first time why he didn't like yellowheads. There was something very like intelligence in that look, an alien calculation. In creatures like that, intelligence seemed out of place. What use could they have for it?

A little shiver went over him when it sank completely under the water and he realized it intended to swim after the raft. But it was mostly excitement. He had never seen a yellowhead come down out of the reeds before. The obliging monster he'd been looking for might be presenting itself in an unexpected way.

Half a minute later, he watched it again, swimming awkwardly far down. It had no immediate intention of boarding at any rate. Cord saw it come into the area of the raft's trailing stingers. It maneuvered its way between them with curiously human swimming motions, and went out of sight under the platform.

He stood up, wondering what it meant. The yellowhead had appeared to know about the stingers; there had been an air of purpose in every move of its approach. He was tempted to tell the others about it, but there was the moment of triumph he could have if it suddenly came slobbering up over the edge of the platform and he nailed it before their eyes.

It was almost time anyway to turn the raft in toward the farms. If nothing happened before then—

He watched. Almost five minutes, but no sign of the yellowhead. Still wondering, a little uneasy, he gave Grandpa a calculated needling of heat.

After a moment, he repeated it. Then he drew a deep breath and forgot all about the yellowhead.

"Nirmond!" he called sharply.

The three of them were standing near the center of the platform, next to the big armored cone, looking ahead at the farms. They glanced around.

"What's the matter now, Cord?"

Cord couldn't say it for a moment. He was suddenly, terribly scared again. Something had gone wrong!

"The raft won't turn!" he told them.

"Give it a real burn this time!" Nirmond said.

Cord glanced up at him. Nirmond, standing a few steps in front of Dane and Grayan as if he wanted to protect them, had begun to look a little strained, and no wonder. Cord already had pressed the gun to three different points on the platform; but Grandpa appeared to have developed a sudden anesthesia for heat. They kept moving out steadily toward the center of the Bay.

Now Cord held his breath, switched the heat on full and let Grandpa have it. A six-inch patch on the platform blistered up instantly, turned brown, then black—

Grandpa stopped dead. Just like that.

"That's right! Keep burn—" Nirmond didn't finish his order.

A giant shudder. Cord staggered back toward the water. Then the whole edge of the raft came curling up behind him and went down again, smacking the Bay with a sound like a cannon shot. He flew forward off his feet, hit the platform face down and flattened himself against it. It swelled up beneath him. Two more enormous slaps and joltings. Then quiet. He looked round for the others.

He lay within twelve feet of the central cone. Some twenty or thirty of the mysterious new vines the cone had spouted were stretched out stiffly toward him now, like so many thin green fingers. They couldn't quite reach him. The nearest tip was still ten inches from his shoes.

But Grandpa had caught the others, all three of them. They were tumbled together at the foot of the cone, wrapped in a stiff network of green vegetable ropes, and they didn't move.

Cord drew his feet up cautiously, prepared for another earthquake reaction. But nothing happened. Then he discovered that Grandpa was back in motion on his previous course. The heatgun had vanished. Gently, he took out the Vanadian gun.

"Cord? It didn't get you?" It was the Regent.

"No," he said, keeping his voice low. He realized suddenly he'd simply assumed they were all dead. Now he felt sick and shaky.

"What are you doing?"

Cord looked at Grandpa's big armor-plated head with a certain hunger. The cones were hollowed out inside; the station's lab had decided their chief function was to keep enough air trapped under the rafts to float them. But in that central section was also the organ that controlled Grandpa's overall reactions.

He said softly, "I got a gun and twelve heavy-duty explosive bullets. Two of them will blow that cone apart."

"No good, Cord!" the pain-racked voice told him. "If the thing sinks, we'll die anyway. You have anesthetic charges for that gun of yours?"

He stared at her back. "Yes."

"Give Nirmond and the girl a shot each, before you do anything else. Directly into the spine, if you can. But don't come any closer—"

Somehow, Cord couldn't argue with that voice. He stood up carefully. The gun made two soft spitting sounds.

"All right," he said hoarsely. "What do I do now?"

Dane was silent a moment. "I'm sorry, Cord. I can't tell you that. I'll tell you what I can—"

She paused for some seconds again. "This thing didn't try to kill us, Cord. It could have easily. It's incredibly strong. I saw it break Nirmond's legs. But as soon as we stopped moving, it just held us. They were both unconscious then—"

"You've got that to go on. It was trying to pitch you within reach of its vines or tendrils, or whatever they are, wasn't it?"

"I think so," Cord said shakily. That was what had happened, of course; and at any moment Grandpa might try again.

"Now it's feeding us some sort of anesthetic of its own through those vines. Tiny thorns. A sort of numbness—" Dane's voice trailed off a moment. Then she said clearly, "Look, Cord—it seems we're food it's storing up! You get that?"

"Yes," he said.

"Seeding time for the rafts. There are analogues. Live food for its seed probably; not for the raft. One couldn't have counted on that. Cord?"

"Yes. I'm here."

"I want," said Dane, "to stay awake as long as I can. But there's really just one other thing—this raft's going somewhere. To some particularly favorable location. And that might be very near shore. You might make it in then; otherwise it's up to you. But keep your head and wait for a chance. No heroics, understand?"

"Sure, I understand," Cord told her. He realized then that he was talking reassuringly, as if it weren't the Planetary Regent but someone like Grayan.

"Nirmond's the worst," Dane said. "The girl was knocked unconscious at once. If it weren't for my arm—But, if we can get help in five hours or so, everything should be all right. Let me know if anything happens, Cord."

"I will," Cord said gently again. Then he sighted his gun carefully at a point between Dane's shoulder blades, and the anesthetic chamber made its soft, spitting sound once more. Dane's taut body relaxed slowly, and that was all.

There was no point Cord could see in letting her stay awake; because they weren't going anywhere near shore.

The reed beds and the channels were already behind them, and Grandpa hadn't changed direction by the fraction of a degree. He was moving out into the open Bay—and he was picking up company!

So far, Cord could count seven big rafts within two miles of them; and on the three that were closest he could make out a sprouting of new green vines. All of them were traveling in a straight direction; and the common point they were all headed for appeared to be the roaring center of the Yoger Straits, now some three miles away!

Behind the Straits, the cold Zlanti Deep—the rolling fogs, and the open sea! It might be seeding time for the rafts, but it looked as if they weren't going to distribute their seeds in the Bay—

For a human being, Cord was a fine swimmer. He had a gun and he had a knife, in spite of what Dane had said; he might have stood a chance among the killers of the Bay. But it would be a very small chance, at best. And it wasn't, he thought, as if there weren't still other possibilities. He was going to keep his head.

Except by accident, of course, nobody was going to come looking for them in time to do any good. If anyone did look, it would be around the Bay Farms. There were a number of rafts moored there; and it would be assumed they'd used one of them. Now and then something unexpected happened and somebody simply vanished—by the time it was figured out just what had happened on this occasion, it would be much too late.

Neither was anybody likely to notice within the next few hours that the rafts had started migrating out of the swamps through the Yoger Straits. There was a small weather station a little inland, on the north side of the Straits, which used a helicopter occasionally. It was about as improbable, Cord decided dismally, that they'd use it in the right spot just now as it would be for a jet transport to happen to come in low enough to spot them.

The fact that it was up to him, as the Regent had said, sank in a little more after that! Cord had never felt so lonely.

Simply because he was going to try it sooner or later, he carried out an experiment next that he knew couldn't work. He opened the gun's anesthetic chamber and counted out fifty pellets—rather hurriedly because he didn't particularly want to think of what he might be using them for eventually. There were around three hundred charges left in the chamber then; and in the next few minutes Cord carefully planted a third of them in Grandpa's head.

He stopped after that. A whale might have showed signs of somnolence under a lesser load. Grandpa paddled on undisturbed. Perhaps he had become a little numb in spots, but his cells weren't equipped to distribute the soporific effect of that type of drug.

There wasn't anything else Cord could think of doing before they reached the Straits. At the rate they were moving, he calculated that would happen in something less than an hour; and if they did pass through the Straits, he was going to risk a swim. He didn't think Dane would have disapproved, under the circumstances. If the raft simply carried them all out into the foggy vastness of the Zlanti Deep, there would be no practical chance of survival left at all.

Meanwhile, Grandpa was definitely picking up speed. And there were other changes going on—minor ones, but still a little awe-inspiring to Cord. The pimply-looking red buds that dotted the upper part of the cone were opening out gradually. From the center of most of them protruded now something like a thin, wet, scarlet worm: a worm that twisted weakly, extended itself by an inch or so, rested and twisted again, and stretched up a little farther, groping into the air. The vertical black slits between the armor plates looked somehow deeper and wider than they had been even some minutes ago; a dark, thick liquid dripped slowly from several of them.

Under other circumstances Cord knew he would have been fascinated by these developments in Grandpa. As it was, they drew his suspicious attention only because he didn't know what they meant.

Then something quite horrible happened suddenly. Grayan started moaning loudly and terribly and twisted almost completely around. Afterwards, Cord knew it hadn't been a second before he stopped her struggles and the sounds together with another anesthetic pellet; but the vines had tightened their grip on her first, not flexibly but like the digging, bony green talons of some monstrous bird of prey. If Dane hadn't warned him—

White and sweating, Cord put his gun down slowly while the vines relaxed again. Grayan didn't seem to have suffered any additional harm; and she would certainly have been the first to point out that his murderous rage might have been as intelligently directed against a machine. But for some moments Cord continued to luxuriate furiously in the thought that, at any instant he chose, he could still turn the raft very quickly into a ripped and exploded mess of sinking vegetation.

Instead, and more sensibly, he gave both Dane and Nirmond another shot, to prevent a similar occurrence with them. The contents of two such pellets, he knew, would keep any human being torpid for at least four hours. Five shots—

Cord withdrew his mind hastily from the direction it was turning into; but it wouldn't stay withdrawn. The thought kept coming up again; until at last he had to recognize it:

Five shots would leave the three of them completely unconscious, whatever else might happen to them, until they either died from other causes or were given a counteracting agent.

Shocked, he told himself he couldn't do it. It was exactly like killing them.

But then, quite steadily, he found himself raising the gun once more, to bring the total charge for each of the three Team people up to five. And if it was the first time in the last four years Cord had felt like crying, it also seemed to him that he had begun to understand what was meant by using your head—along with other things.

Barely thirty minutes later, he watched a raft as big as the one he rode go sliding into the foaming white waters of the Straits a few hundred yards ahead, and dart off abruptly at an angle, caught by one of the swirling currents. It pitched and spun, made some headway, and was swept aside again. And then it righted itself once more. Not like some blindly animated vegetable, Cord thought, but like a creature that struggled with intelligent purpose to maintain its chosen direction.

At least, they seemed practically unsinkable—

Knife in hand, he flattened himself against the platform as the Straits roared just ahead. When the platform jolted and tilted up beneath him, he rammed the knife all the way into it and hung on. Cold water rushed suddenly over him, and Grandpa shuddered like a laboring engine. In the middle of it all, Cord had the horrified notion that the raft might release its unconscious human prisoners in its struggle with the Straits. But he underestimated Grandpa in that. Grandpa also hung on.

Abruptly, it was over. They were riding a long swell, and there were three other rafts not far away. The Straits had swept them together, but they seemed to have no interest in one another's company. As Cord stood up shakily and began to strip off his clothes, they were visibly drawing apart again. The platform of one of them was half-submerged; it must have lost too much of the air that held it afloat and, like a small ship, it was foundering.

From this point, it was only a two-mile swim to the shore north of the Straits, and another mile inland from there to the Straits Head Station. He didn't know about the current; but the distance didn't seem too much, and he couldn't bring himself to leave knife and gun behind. The Bay creatures loved warmth and mud, they didn't venture beyond the Straits. But Zlanti Deep bred its own killers, though they weren't often observed so close to shore.

Things were beginning to look rather hopeful.

Thin, crying voices drifted overhead, like the voices of curious cats, as Cord knotted his clothes into a tight bundle, shoes inside. He looked up. There were four of them circling there; magnified seagoing swamp bugs, each carrying an unseen rider. Probably harmless scavengers—but the ten-foot wingspread was impressive. Uneasily, Cord remembered the venomously carnivorous rider he'd left lying beside the station.

One of them dipped lazily and came sliding down toward him. It soared overhead and came back, to hover about the raft's cone.

The bug rider that directed the mindless flier hadn't been interested in him at all! Grandpa was baiting it!

Cord stared in fascination. The top of the cone was alive now with a softly wriggling mass of the scarlet, wormlike extrusions that had started sprouting before the raft left the Bay. Presumably, they looked enticingly edible to the bug rider.

The flier settled with an airy fluttering and touched the cone. Like a trap springing shut, the green vines flashed up and around it, crumpling the brittle wings, almost vanishing into the long soft body—

Barely a second later, Grandpa made another catch, this one from the sea itself. Cord had a fleeting glimpse of something like a small, rubbery seal that flung itself out of the water upon the edge of the raft, with a suggestion of desperate haste—and was flipped on instantly against the cone where the vines clamped it down beside the flier's body.

It wasn't the enormous ease with which the unexpected kill was accomplished that left Cord standing there, completely shocked. It was the shattering of his hopes to swim to shore from here. Fifty yards away, the

creature from which the rubbery thing had been fleeing showed briefly
on the surface, as it turned away from the raft; and the glance was all he
needed. The ivory-white body and gaping jaws were similar enough to
those of the sharks of Earth to indicate the pursuer's nature. The important difference was that, wherever the white hunters of the Zlanti Deep
went, they went by the thousands.

Stunned by that incredible piece of bad luck, still clutching his bundled
clothes, Cord stared toward shore. Knowing what to look for, he could
spot the telltale roilings of the surface now—the long, ivory gleams that
flashed through the swells and vanished again. Shoals of smaller things
burst into the air in sprays of glittering desperation and fell back.

He would have been snapped up like a drowning fly before he'd covered a twentieth of that distance!

But almost another full minute passed before the realization of the
finality of his defeat really sank in.

Grandpa was beginning to eat!

Each of the dark slits down the sides of the cone was a mouth. So far
only one of them was in operating condition, and the raft wasn't able to
open that one very wide as yet. The first morsel had been fed into, however: the bug rider the vines had plucked out of the flier's downy neck
fur. It took Grandpa several minutes to work it out of sight, small as it
was. But it was a start.

Cord didn't feel quite sane any more. He sat there, clutching his bundle of clothes and only vaguely aware of the fact that he was shivering
steadily under the cold spray that touched him now and then, while he
followed Grandpa's activities attentively. He decided it would be at least
some hours before one of that black set of mouths grew flexible and
vigorous enough to dispose of a human being. Under the circumstances,
it couldn't make much difference to the other human beings here; but
the moment Grandpa reached for the first of them would also be the
moment he finally blew the raft to pieces. The white hunters were cleaner
eaters, at any rate; and that was about the extent to which he could still
control what was going to happen.

Meanwhile, there was the very faint chance that the weather station's
helicopter might spot them—

Meanwhile also, in a weary and horrified fascination, he kept debating
the mystery of what could have produced such a nightmarish change in
the rafts. He could guess where they were going by now; there were
scattered strings of them stretching back to the Straits or roughly parallel
to their own course, and the direction was that of the plankton-swarming
pool of the Zlanti Basin, a thousand miles to the north. Given time, even
mobile lily pads like the rafts had been could make that trip for the benefit
of their seedlings. But nothing in their structure explained the sudden
change into alert and capable carnivores.

He watched the rubbery little seal-thing being hauled up to a mouth
next. The vines broke its neck; and the mouth took it in up to the shoulders and then went on working patiently at what was still a trifle too large
a bite. Meanwhile, there were more thin cat cries overhead; and a few

minutes later, two more sea bugs were trapped almost simultaneously and added to the larder. Grandpa dropped the dead seal-thing and fed himself another bug rider. The second rider left its mount with a sudden hop, sank its teeth viciously into one of the vines that caught it again, and was promptly battered to death against the platform.

Cord felt a resurge of unreasoning hatred against Grandpa. Killing a bug was about equal to cutting a branch from a tree; they had almost no life-awareness. But the rider had aroused his partisanship because of its appearance of intelligent action—and it was in fact closer to the human scale in that feature than to the monstrous life-form that had, mechanically, but quite successfully, trapped both it and the human beings. Then his thoughts had drifted again; and he found himself. Speculating vaguely on the curious symbiosis in which the nerve systems of two creatures as dissimilar as the bugs and their riders could be linked so closely that they functioned as one organism.

Suddenly an expression of vast and stunned surprise appeared on his face.

Why—now he knew!

Cord stood up hurriedly, shaking with excitement, the whole plan complete in his mind. And a dozen long vines snaked instantly in the direction of his sudden motion, and groped for him, taut and stretching. They couldn't reach him, but their savagely alert reaction froze Cord briefly where he was. The platform was shuddering under his feet, as if in irritation at his inaccessibility; but it couldn't be tilted up suddenly here to throw him within the grasp of the vines, as it could around the edges.

Still, it was a warning! Cord sidled gingerly around the cone till he had gained the position he wanted, which was on the forward half of the raft. And then he waited. Waited long minutes, quite motionless, until his heart stopped pounding and the irregular angry shivering of the surface of the raft-thing died away, and the last vine tendril had stopped its blind groping. It might help a lot if, for a second or two after he next started moving, Grandpa wasn't too aware of his exact whereabouts

He looked back once to check how far they had gone by now beyond the Straits Head Station. It couldn't, he decided, be even an hour behind them. Which was close enough, by the most pessimistic count—if everything else worked out all right! He didn't try to think out in detail what that "everything else" could include, because there were factors that simply couldn't be calculated in advance. And he had an uneasy feeling that speculating too vividly about them might make him almost incapable of carrying out his plan.

At last, moving carefully, Cord took the knife in his left hand but left the gun holstered. He raised the tightly knotted bundle of clothes slowly over his head, balanced in his right hand. With a long, smooth motion he tossed the bundle back across the cone, almost to the opposite edge of the platform.

It hit with a soggy thump. Almost immediately, the whole far edge of the raft buckled and flapped up to toss the strange object to the reaching vines.

Simultaneously, Cord was racing forward. For a moment, his attempt to divert Grandpa's attention seemed completely successful—then he was pitched to his knees as the platform came up.

He was within eight feet of the edge. As it slapped down again, he threw himself desperately forward.

An instant later, he was knifing down through cold, clear water, just ahead of the raft, then twisting and coming up again.

The raft was passing over him. Clouds of tiny sea creatures scattered through its dark jungle of feeding roots. Cord jerked back from a broad, wavering streak of glassy greenness, which was a stinger, and felt a burning jolt on his side, which meant he'd been touched lightly by another. He bumped on blindly through the slimy black tangles of hair roots that covered the bottom of the raft; then green half-light passed over him, and he burst up into the central bubble under the cone.

Half-light and foul, hot air. Water slapped around him, dragging him away again—nothing to hang on to here! Then above him, to his right, molded against the interior curve of the cone as if it had grown there from the start, the froglike, man-sized shape of the yellowhead.

The raft rider—

Cord reached up and caught Grandpa's symbiotic partner and guide by a flabby hind leg, pulled himself half out of the water and struck twice with the knife, fast while the pale-green eyes were still opening.

He'd thought the yellowhead might need a second or so to detach itself from its host, as the bug riders usually did, before it tried to defend itself. This one merely turned its head; the mouth slashed down and clamped on Cord's left arm above the elbow. His right hand sank the knife through one staring eye, and the yellowhead jerked away, pulling the knife from his grasp.

Sliding down, he wrapped both hands around the slimy leg and hauled with all his weight. For a moment more, the yellowhead hung on. Then the countless neural extensions that connected it now with the raft came free in a succession of sucking, tearing sounds; and Cord and the yellowhead splashed into the water together.

Black tangle of roots again—and two more electric burns suddenly across his back and legs! Strangling, Cord let go. Below him, for a moment, a body was turning over and over with oddly human motions; then a solid wall of water thrust him up and aside, as something big and white struck the turning body and went on.

Cord broke the surface twelve feet behind the raft. And that would have been that, if Grandpa hadn't already been slowing down.

After two tries, he floundered back up on the platform and lay there gasping and coughing awhile. There were no indications that his presence was resented now. A few vine tips twitched uneasily, as if trying to remember previous functions, when he came limping up presently to make sure his three companions were still breathing; but Cord never noticed that.

They were still breathing; and he knew better than to waste time trying to help them himself. He took Grayan's heat-gun from its holster. Grandpa had come to a full stop.

Cord hadn't had time to become completely sane again, or he might have worried now whether Grandpa, violently sundered from his controlling partner, was still capable of motion on his own. Instead, he determined the approximate direction of the Straits Head Station, selected a corresponding spot on the platform and gave Grandpa a light tap of heat.

Nothing happened immediately. Cord sighed patiently and stepped up the heat a little.

Grandpa shuddered gently. Cord stood up.

Slowly and hesitatingly at first, then with steadfast—though now again brainless—purpose, Grandpa began paddling back toward the Straits Head Station.

The Red Hills of Summer

EDGAR PANGBORN

The late Edgar Pangborn is almost forgotten these days and is rarely ever mentioned even in historical surveys of the fifties and sixties . . . which is a pity, since he had a depth and breadth of humanity that have rarely been matched inside the field or out. Although he was never a particularly prolific writer (five science-fiction novels, one or two mainstream novels, and a baker's dozen or so of short pieces) he was nevertheless one of that select crew of underappreciated authors (one thinks of Cordwainer Smith, Fritz Leiber, Jack Vance, Avram Davidson, and Richard McKenna) who have had an enormous underground effect on the field simply by impressing the hell out of other writers and numerous authors-in-the-egg. Pangborn wrote about "little people" for the most part, only rarely focusing on the famous and powerful. He was one of only a handful of science-fiction writers capable of writing about small-town or rural people with insight and sympathy (most science fiction is urban in orientation, written by city people about city people—or, when it is written by people from small towns, they are frequently kids who couldn't wait to get out of those small towns and off to the bright lights of the big city . . . which often amounts to the same thing, as far as sympathies are concerned), and he was also one of the few who could get inside the minds of both the very young and the very old with equal ease and compassion.

Pangborn's masterpiece was Davy, which, in spite of a somewhat weak ending (or, at least, a final third that doesn't quite live up to the two-thirds that came before it), may well be the finest postholocaust novel ever written—in my opinion, it is seriously rivaled only by Walter M. Miller's A Canticle for Leibowitz and John Wyndham's Re-Birth. In any fair world, Davy alone ought to be enough to guarantee Pangborn a distinguished place in the history of the genre, but there were also novels like A Mirror for Observers—his International Fantasy Award winner, somewhat dated now, but still powerful, in which alien observers from two opposing philosophical camps vie for the soul of a brilliant human boy—and West of the Sun, an underrated novel about the efforts of human castaways to survive on an alien world, as well as beautifully crafted short work such as "A Master of Babylon," "Longtooth," "The World Is a Sphere," and "Angel's Egg." Edgar Pangborn's other works include The Judgment of Eve and The Company of Glory, the mainstream novel The Trial of Castilla Blake, the collection Good Neighbors and Other Strangers, and the posthumously published collection Still I Persist in Wondering.

The story that follows, "The Red Hills of Summer," which was later expanded into West of the Sun, paints a vivid picture, both hardheadedly realistic and beautifully evocative, of humankind's first attempt to explore an alien world, and the landing party's discovery that no matter how far away you go, you can't outrun the monsters that dwell within your own heart. . . .

I

Miranda caught my hand, her own soft small hands gone hard with tension. Captain Madison on the speaker's platform had mentioned the pilot mission, and possible lethal elements on the shining dot below us—bacteria, viruses, qualities of the lower atmosphere not discoverable from orbit. It had not dawned on me till then that my troubled Miranda might be desiring the pilot mission for herself and me. For the last year she had been in the shadow of private unhappiness, often remote even when she was in my arms.

Below us. For the first time in fifteen years that word *below* was more than a reference to the place where your feet happened to be. It possessed a meaning in relation to the ship, to me as a unit of living matter, to black-haired Miranda.

Madison's square face recaptured my attention. I had first glimpsed it at the beginning of the voyage, when I came aboard with the unsparing eyes of a boy of twelve. That year he was thirty-five. Now at fifty he looked little changed—more tired, hair grayer, voice flatter. Who wouldn't be tired, after the job of bringing our enormous sphere into a safe orbit? My own healthy red-haired carcass felt exhausted too, from the excitement that had churned in all of us since the planet was sighted and we knew we must decide whether to risk a descent. We were in the meeting-room now, all three hundred, to make that decision.

I, David Leroy, am not a scientist nor a technician. Miranda and I were Randies—chosen like most of the kids for good health and what the Builders' Directives solemnly call Random Talents. There's a pride in it. You discover the virtues of comprehensive wide-ranging ignorance.

Captain Rupert Madison was saying: "If we go on, I don't suppose any of you, even children born in space, would live to see the end of the journey. The distances are too vast, Earth-type planets too far apart. The chance of finding another as promising as this one, within our lifetime, is small. The other choice is to go down—and stay."

It was that simple. A huge frail sphere like ours, built to transport a colony for generations if necessary, doesn't land anywhere. You don't take it into atmosphere. Compartmented and honeycombed, spheres within spheres down to the core where the computer hummed its mathematical daydreams, the ship *Galileo* was designed for one purpose only: to bear our splinter fragment of humanity away from a world that humanity had apparently ruined, away to some cleaner place where the sickness in our germ plasm might work itself out—perhaps, always perhaps, and only after many generations. That errand performed, the emptied shell of *Galileo* would shine on as a satellite, a golden moon circling a second-chance world.

When you live in close awareness of it for fifteen years, even the new curse of Cain can become a commonplace. But I had been obliged to learn it was not so for Miranda. Her trouble was there, a sense of futility forced on her by the radiation sickness of Earth: for what, her heart said, is the point of a million years of human evolution if it must end not even with a bang, only with the whimper of babies born armless, distorted, blind? She had grown terrified of the times when she couldn't *care* about anything. "Not even about you, Davy..."

Captain Madison was hammering home the truth of no return, speaking of what it requires—in terms of industry, labor, raw materials—to build just one launching center like the twelve that toiled eight years to send the bits and pieces of this vessel out of Earth's gravity. Earth had bled herself white for her children, after men once and for all faced the probability of racial extinction. They would build another *Galileo*, and another; would go on doggedly building, all else subordinated, so long as any courage and equipment remained. "The gravity of that planet down there is a bit greater than the gravity of Earth. Launching centers!" Madison said. "I remember. That was my life, you know, from teens into thirties, beginning as a grease monkey at Canaveral... Well, you know the arithmetic: three hundred colonists don't reproduce a technology that was based on a population of three billion.

"The know-how? We have it all, in the microfilm library. Raw materials, yes—down there we'll find the same minerals, same general chemical pattern. But the building of launching centers, new ships, the reconquest of space if you want that inflated language—let's say it just might be an enterprise of our great-great-grand-children, if we have any, if enough of them are healthy and active human beings, and if space travel happens to be what they want most, at any cost, in their own far-off time."

Nobody sighed or fidgeted, as many would have done if this had been another pep-talk by our Psychometric Coordinator Cecil Dorman, known to Miranda and me and others of the irreverent as Cecil Psycho.

"The planet is habitable," said Captain Madison, "so far as we know from orbit study." Miranda felt my look but would not return it; her hands grasping mine were cold. "So far as we know," he repeated, "in advance of the pilot mission—which will consist of two men and two women who will go down, maintain radio contact at least four weeks, and make the final tests we can't make up here. Your only vote in this meeting, I suppose, will be to decide whether the pilot mission starts at all—remembering that whatever they find, those four volunteers can't come back."

◆

Behind me, I heard the suave voice of Andrea del Sentiero—fifty-eight, the only colonist older than Madison. His official title was Historian. "Does anything in the latest studies suggest a civilization?"

"Nothing, sir. Forest, savannah, large lakes, marshes, deserts, mountain ranges running generally north and south, a few of the summits snow-capped." He was talking for all of us, who had had only brief chances at the telescopes; the view-plate in the panel behind him gave a low magnification, the planet a blur of blue and reddish green. "Six continental land masses paired north and south, three main oceans, polar caps small and broken up. Bound to be dense tropics near the equator, the rest subtropical, with narrow temperate zones. No roads in the open areas, nothing like cities. No vessels on the seas, river mouths surrounded by the same vegetation that covers most of the land. The reddish green deepens on the seaward slopes of the hills, but that suggests—Dr. Bunuan agrees—a result of rainfall, not intelligent agriculture. Dr. Bunuan thinks we may find something like Earth in the time of dinosaurs. He calls that a half-educated guess."

"Quarter-educated," the biologist's mellow voice corrected him.

Captain Madison grinned. "If you insist, José. No, Andrea, if there's life at the social, technological level it would have to be hidden under forest cover—unlikely."

"Yes," said del Sentiero. "I have no other questions."

"Maybe something to add?"

"Only two things," said the Historian. "One, that my vote will be for going down and making the best of it. Two, that the pilot mission ought to be a privilege of the old."

Captain Madison winced. "You mean, why risk the young?"

Del Sentiero said nothing. I knew, without seeing, the stoical Latin shrug, the dark eyes contemplating eternity, the mild outward motion of eloquent hands.

"Anyone may volunteer for it," said Madison heavily, and he shut his eyes, his face freezing into difficult calm. "Responsibility for choosing the four is on me, Andrea, nowhere else." His eyes flew open, probing here and there. "Questions? Discussion?"

I had expected that Paul Cutter would seize this moment to sound off on the revision of the model constitution, which could not even begin to function until after a landing. The constitution was an attempt of the Builders to suggest the framework of such government as a colony of 300 might be expected to need. Mirthless and lonely Paul Cutter had grappled with it, conceiving amendment after amendment, identifying his unhappy self with each improvement to the point of monomania. He ate and drank the constitution, slept and got up with it. At any time his blaring monologue might nail you to the wall explaining how it *must* be amended or the whole expedition would Betray the Human Heritage.

Paul was younger than Miranda and myself, a boy of ten at the start of the voyage. Some hereditary slant made him grow from a normal-looking child into a small bandy-legged man, gnarled, not misshapen but seeming so, a bulging head connected by a weak neck to a tight barrel of torso. A bore, comical and ugly through no fault of his own. He had chosen psychology as his field of specialization, becoming a noisy satellite of Cecil Dorman. Unfortunately for Paul's ambitions, not Dorman but the learned, humorous and peaceful Dr. Carey was boss of the Psychology Department. (*Galileo* was certainly in its way a college; I still think of it so.) Paul Cutter never earned a title: a Randy still, the fact no source of pride to him but an ingrowing pain.

I saw Cutter in the front row, big head alertly cocked. Nothing happened. No fresh amendment, no bray of earnest argument. Maybe Cecil Dorman had persuaded him to let the constitution wait a minute or two . . .

We were voting, by a simple show of hands. No opposition. No one could bear the thought of another fifteen years, or another generation, or another century, in space. But I remember that when my own hand went up I was not thinking of that, but of red-green seaward hills, and of the sound of ocean that might resemble what I had heard when I was a boy at Martha's Vineyard watching the loud hurry and change of waves under the sudden winds of September.

I believe this was the only unanimous decision ever taken by the colonists of the planet Demeter.

➤

Madison was speaking evenly: "The pilot mission. You know the Builders' Directives. You know the necessity. We can't take down the whole colony to be destroyed by something not discoverable from orbit. We haven't the means to break out of gravity and come back. Directives recommend the mission consist of two men and two women. Partly to avoid trusting the judgment of one volunteer. Partly because one sex might be immune to a lethal factor that would kill the other. Partly on the chance that the four might pull through with their survival equipment, and multiply, even if they had to tell the rest of us to stay away. So I want four guinea-pigs. Whoever they are, they'll be four individuals whom we love and can't spare. I am now calling for them."

This was the way it came, like all great questions, not with trumpets but plainly spoken and quiet as morning. I thought at first there was also a question in Miranda's brown-eyed gaze, one not weighted toward yes or no. Then I understood she was not asking me: *Are you going to stand up?* She was silently saying: *I must do this, I'm driven from within. Whether you stand up or not, Davy, I must and I will.*

I took her hand again and I was on my feet.

Five or six other couples were standing, and a surprising number, ten or a dozen, stood up alone. I heard a murmuring, voices here and there attempting the unsayable, as Rupert Madison looked us over through his captain's mask.

I supposed he would choose the volunteers from among the Randies. Breezy Arthur Clay for instance, standing alone two rows ahead of us, solemn as I had never seen him. Or Joe and Miriam Somers, solidly married with the formalities Miranda had never quite wanted for us, decent, unexciting Joe and Miriam who rather thought they'd like to be farmers if we ever landed. Or Laurette Vieuxtemps, a housewife temperament but not committed to any man, religious, reservedly sweet.

Madison told a few of them—all specialists—to sit down. Then he appeared to have reached a private impasse, brooding in his loneliness. Fussy and dapper Cecil Dorman, on the platform with him, leaned forward suggesting something, and shriveled in Madison's glare. Madison would not be saying again, in words, where responsibility lay, but the Psychometric Coordinator was just the one guy who wouldn't understand it unless he got his nose rubbed in it twice. Madison sighed and spoke names.

Just names. No request to sit down.

"Paul Cutter." I was unready to understand. I had not noticed till then that Paul Cutter had risen; his squat form had been hidden by Art Clay. "Laurette Vieuxtemps . . ." Miranda's fingers gripped tightly. I did understand. "Miranda Klein . . . David Leroy."

II

David Leroy, pilot. I had a title . . .

I don't recall much about the entry into atmosphere. I remember a tight-sealed pocket of heat skimming interminably above a world that gradually expanded in the viewplates above my controls. I remember fear, doubt of my own skill based on nothing but years of theoretical drill without experience. Most clearly, I recall Captain Madison's voice, linked to me by the tenuous nerve of radio, a true part of me, the one part that remained unshaken.

I had known there would be breaks in communication—static interference, other difficulties—and there was one when Madison was on the other side of the planet. No foreknowledge can prepare you for such a loneliness. Yet I'd always been lonely, like Miranda, like everyone else, a single human planet in the galaxy of the human race.

Then Madison, remote and *above*, in an orbit become incredibly *swift* relative to my *slow*, was speaking again. I was able to give him a much lower temperature reading, a respectably diminished altitude. He said: "You're past the worst. How do you feel?"

"Fine, dandy and lonesome." I glanced in the mirror that gave me the cabin. "Others in good shape. Colonizing with no pain."

"You'll be over that plateau in six minutes, then test your power. Better not use it much till you're down to say 90,000—but that's up to you, Davy. From here on you play it by the seat of your pants."

"I'll do that, Captain."

"We won't try calling from the blind side again. Reestablish contact 0940 hours *Galileo* time." Then with some dry noise that might have been static: "See you, boy."

Below me, ocean and red-green land, an infinity of brooding day. I found the 40-mile oval of my target, and tested the power in a long cautious turn—no trouble. Trust the Builders for that.

The Builders? There was no one, no one at all to trust except Miranda Klein, Laurette Vieuxtemps, Paul Cutter and myself. The Builders were finished with us, had done their magnificent best fifteen years ago, and by now many of them would be dead, and, groping somewhere through the unthinkable reaches, there might be a *Galileo II*, even a *Galileo III*. I would not think now about the Builders, who had known they could have no reward except consciousness of a piece of good work completed . . .

Our chosen landing spot was a roughly oval plateau, 40 miles at the greatest length, on one of the three continents of the southern hemisphere. It had been selected by the Council of *Galileo*—del Sentiero presiding, we four volunteers awkwardly attending. The choice had to be partly arbitrary, for the photographic map showed little to suggest that any one spot in the temperate belts would be better than another. I favored the notion of an island, but kept my Randy mouth shut. Del Sentiero suggested the same thing and was overruled: aircraft fuel would give out before our technology could replace it, the building of ships might be difficult, we might even find no suitable timber. And a plateau is, in a way, an island.

My turn carried us out over the sea, then inland, miles above the white summits of a mountain range that rose to the west of our plateau. I cut the power and we drifted soundless in the thickening air.

The plateau lay 30 miles in from the sea. Vegetation covered most of it, but reddish-white patches suggested open ground, possibly sand. We had noticed the same pinkish tinge on many of the ocean beaches. Easy for landing (I hoped) and an easy mark for *Galileo* to hold in observation. Westward for 500 miles spread the random masses of the mountains, our plateau a midget among their numberless foothills.

Prevailing winds in the southern hemisphere blew westward as on Earth; Dr. Bunuan was surely right in assuming plentiful rainfall on the seaward slopes. The region west of the range was no desert, however, but deep forest, 800 miles of it, divided by the silver furrow of a river flowing south. That forest ended at another, narrower range, following the continent's western shore. Our plateau stood at the 45th parallel south, where the continent dwindled in a triangular pattern rather like South America. No land bridge to the continent in the northern hemisphere, and no continental mass at the south polar region, but a myriad scattered islands, and drift ice, and occasional stretches of blue sea all the way to the pole.

"Handling right?" I had known Paul Cutter would be the first and only one to forget Madison's order about letting me alone on this job. I didn't mind the distraction; the little ship was gliding with almost no need of attention. I did mind the jitters in Paul's crashing voice.

I said: "Yes. You people happy back there?"

"Happy as three ticks on a dog—you're the dog." The voice I wanted, Miranda's. It went on, cool but not too sharp: "Let's keep a cork in it, Paul—the man's busy."

Wounded to the core, Paul boomed: "Sorry! Sorry!"

Two birds, or creatures in the shape of birds, were circling between me and the plateau, as a hawk soars, with unmoving wings. Frightened perhaps by our descending gleam, they sped away downwind—at least I thought, from the gust of speed without wing-motion, that they were heading downwind, and I tried to remember the games of seagulls over Martha's Vineyard. Only the color returned to me and the sense of an airy freedom, the taste of salt wind, the brown ghost of a Portuguese boy who used to play with me.

The smooth course of the ship told me nothing—maybe no wind at all was blowing. Maybe it was blowing some other way at a lower altitude. I saw no wind-motion of the forest, but I was still too high to be certain.

And too low to look down any longer on the mountain-tops. They were above me and would remain above me.

The spot of open ground I had selected for landing was the only one beginning at an edge of the plateau. If the wind was right—where *was* the wind?—I would circle out beyond the edge, come in slightly above it, and still have two miles clear for a landing. With this trim vessel, Madison said, I could manage with less than a thousand yards. But where was the wind?

The time to swing out beyond the plateau was now, right now. The plane made the turn in graceful ease—and dropped, hideously.

I think I yelled it was just an air pocket. But when I lurched out of it we were bound straight for the sullen wall of the plateau. In panic I somehow slammed the power on in time, and ran scared up a channel of hell like a dragonfly on fire. We cleared the cliff by a yard and shot a thousand feet up before I had the wits to level off and cut the jets. Paul was howling: "God Almighty, you almost—"

Miranda's voice came small and cold: "Have a tranquillizer, Paul, it's on the house. Have you noticed, by the way, we're all right?"

I began talking myself, though, when I realized I'd forgotten to lower the landing gear. The talk did me good. I got the gear down. I soared out further beyond the plateau, came in higher, ready for the air pocket, hitting it again and coming out happy, skittering over half a mile of reddish white and touching down in a landing soft as a baby's kiss. Miranda said: "Davy, when you get around to it, explain me some of those nouns and adjectives, huh? I thought I knew em all."

⟶

We equalized the pressure, a difference too small to bother the eardrums, and breathed the unknown atmosphere—nothing to gain by delaying. It was wild, warm, the freshness wholly sweet. I could have sat there half an hour doing nothing but breathe the air of Demeter—and wondering whether in a few weeks we would be voting on that name, a poetic whim of Andrea del Sentiero.

The stuff outside was mostly sand, sparse red grains mingled with the white. Miranda whispered: "Be first to set your foot on it." It seemed unimportant, a thing I might do to please her—until I had done it. Then absurd pride startled me, and I held up my arms for her.

Laurette and Paul emerged, Laurette moving away from us, looking toward the mountains in the west—praying I think, or merely wanting a small time of solitude. She had talked with the chaplain during most of our last hour on *Galileo*. Miranda and I had spent that time with the half dozen friends who had been closest to us through the voyage—not saying goodbye; they all wanted to take it for granted they would rejoin us in four weeks. Paul Cutter had employed the hour furiously writing in a corner of the common room—some intense document which he delivered into Madison's keeping. "Not to be opened," he blared for all of us to hear, "except in the event that *Galileo* must proceed without us." Captain Madison took it gravely, probably with no smothered impulse to laugh, and shook hands with the hero.

Impossible that I could ever have looked down on those mountain peaks. Yet I had done so. I would remember it.

Miranda kicked off her right shoe, pressed her bare foot in the reddish sand, drew it away, gazed curiously at the dainty human imprint. I asked: "Are you caring now?"

She held my shoulder, putting back the shoe; watched me a while with midnight eyes; said: "I think I am . . . Let's walk off a way."

We approached the somber edge of the woods. "You'd know it," I said, "wouldn't you, dear? You wouldn't just think."

"Maybe." She was frowning gravely at the sand, not wanting to touch me or be touched. "You've felt it yourself, Davy, that emptiness. Impulse to give up because nothing can make much difference."

"Sometimes. I found I could push it away by studying something new—holing up in the library—talking to del Sentiero."

"I couldn't. Not the last year anyway. It was partly the ship, the monotony. Suspended animation." She looked about rather blindly into the depth of morning. "We're—home, aren't we?"

"Yes."

"It wasn't only the ship. I kept thinking, even if we can have a baby, there'll be—ah, what do the damn Directives call it?—70 per cent chance of normal birth. I remember hearing my father say that even the 70 per cent was a sort of statistician's lie. The dice are loaded, Davy. . . . I loved Earth. You did too. I know. Inside me somewhere I've got every word you ever said about Martha's Vineyard. . . . Davy, it's just barely possible I'm pregnant. I can't be sure, hasn't been time, quite." She wanted nearness then, twisting her fingers in my shirt, clinging, suddenly crying. "Let it be true, Davy! Let it be right, not a—not a 30-per-center. I'd care— I'd care *then!*"

It meant nothing to Paul Cutter that she was crying in my arms. I felt his tap on my shoulder, his brazen voice exploding: "Who is leader?"

Miranda laughed; looked past me at the little man and laughed, with brimming eyes—which puzzled the hell out of him. Simply Paul's way. He was incapable of understanding other people's urgencies.

I straightened my face, suggesting that for the moment we hardly needed leadership: we all knew what work was to be done, maybe we'd already done the biggest part by breathing the air and continuing to live. I looked at my watch. "*Galileo* will be calling in fifteen minutes. Until then why don't we just look around? Only we'd better break out some armament, I suppose."

I should have thought of that sooner, too. The bland quiet here made the idea of guns downright obscene. Nothing was stirring. Two bird-like things soared high overhead, maybe curious at the alien brightness of our plane. The lack of vegetation at this landing spot puzzled me. In places the ground was clay instead of sand; small stones resembling the granites and composites of Earth lay here and there. Nothing suggested animal life. In a spot higher than the rest of the open land, I noticed a boulder thrusting from the ground and a wraith of vapor rising from it to dissolve in the still air. A geyser, perhaps, that periodically flooded the area, killing plant life. The trees, and the rim of very dark grass between them and the open ground, looked rich and healthy.

The trees were in the pattern of Earth, but I saw no such complex of a thousand species as in forests of the old world. One type was completely dominant, a broad-leaf tree averaging fifty feet in height, thick-trunked, spreading only at the top, the young leaves and twigs red as maple buds, the mature leaves a hemlock green with wide red veining. The grass was like Earth's except for its darkness, shading almost to a cobalt blue; it grew hardly a foot high, dense as carpet-pile. We had seen that color solid in most of the open areas of the plateau, and it was the characteristic hue of the savannahs elsewhere on the planet.

We opened a storage compartment of the plane. Paul and I slung light carbines; Miranda strapped on a .32 automatic. The bullets for all three were designed to fragment on impact, releasing an anesthetic poison that would stop anything if the wound failed to—anything with an Earth-type bloodstream. Laurette Vieuxtemps, when I called her, smiled and shook her head.

"Will you stand by the radio then, Laurette, till they call in?"

"Yes." She was good with instruments, deft and careful; delicate tests on soil and plants would be part of her work. She returned to the plane, after a last glance at the hills, their red-green mystery, cloud-trailing spires brilliant with snow.

I said: "I don't like carrying this thing either, Laurette. But just at first I don't want any of us wandering out here unarmed."

Laurette nodded amiably. And Paul Cutter said with some clang of bitterness: "Well, Dave, you've answered my question."

"I'm not leader unless you all three agree to it."

I think I spoke with friendliness. I meant to; we had need of it. His face, turned toward me in the mild heat of the sun of Demeter, had gone opaque. Miranda's arm slid around me; she studied the ground, perhaps waiting. Paul said politely, with none of his normal stridency: "Four weeks, they said. I agree you should be leader, for four weeks."

III

At the close of the second day we imagined we knew a little about that plateau. I had hedge-hopped over it twice, beginning to enjoy the plane, except for the always rugged instant of landing.

I flew alone both times—no sense risking two lives with an inexperienced pilot. In the first one I proved that the only part of the plateau safe for the larger landing ships of *Galileo* was the one I had first chosen. Then I indulged myself in a 30-mile flight to the sea above the course of a small river that skirted the northern base of the plateau and wound down through the piedmont past rolling land, meadow and forest, meeting the ocean at a harbor a mile wide. Madison wanted to know more about that harbor.

A small hilly island stood twenty miles out to sea from it, hazy and purple in the sun. It pulled me, called me. I was thinking, I know, of Martha's Vineyard. I thought also of fuel, danger, the need of my people for this plane and for me too; and I did not go.

On my flight to the harbor I noticed a few tawny deerlike animals bounding into the woods away from the shadow of the plane, and some flying creatures, none very close. On the way back something different showed itself, night-black, lizard-shaped, basking in a sunny meadow. I circled down for a better look. Hugely unconcerned, it did not retreat when I skimmed over it sixty feet up. Not dead, for I saw the great triangle of the head moving, and a twitch of a saurian tail. I shot up then; the sudden clamor of the jets did not disturb it. I guessed the length at twenty-five feet.

We slept in the plane on the first night. My second flight, next day, was for study of a smaller open area two miles from our landing site, that looked reasonable for a camp. It was a clearing of level dark grass half a mile square with a brook slipping across the northern side, widening to a pond near the edge of the woods. I landed and explored.

The pond-water shone deep ruby, reflecting red-leaved bushes. I found the banks pockmarked with prints of small divided hoofs, and noticed one set of tracks with pads and claw-marks, not frighteningly large. Mammals or something like them lived in this land, knew fear, ate each other, bred, died. I remembered my black lizard, his vastness curved rather like a question-mark.

The forms would be new to me. The forms themselves would change, must already have done so through millions of years in the manner of Earth. So far as I knew, so far as I know today, the meaning, if there was one, would be the same.

I was bothered by the absence of anything like humanly edible plants. Maybe the forest would take care of that. Here I found only the short grass and a few of the red-leaved bushes that grew by the pond. I brought a shovel from the plane and drove it into the sod. The loosened earth displayed brown worms, legless grubs, nothing like ants or beetles. In any such region on Earth I would have encountered a hundred forms of insect life. Grasshoppers would have shot up around my feet; bees and flies would have buzzed near me; beetles would have scampered away from the shovel. The grassblades should have been scarred by the nibbling of tiny mouths; butterflies ought to have been drifting and fluttering in innocent splendor.

No bugs. I supposed I could do without them . . .

The earth under the grass was dark, rich-looking, with a pleasing aromatic smell. We must learn what it could do. I collected a sample of pond water for testing and returned to the others. That was near noon of the second day.

By evening we had moved to that clearing and set up our camp around a light dome shelter—astonishingly large, strong against storms, capable of lasting indefinitely under any conditions the Builders could imagine for a planet that was bound to be much like their own.

We set out a wire-covered pen for a pair of rabbits, potential food. Those, and a few mice and rats for experiment, were the only animals that shared the pilot mission. From *Galileo* would come sheep, chickens, a few precious cattle of a recently developed breed hardly bigger than goats. Other animals would arrive (if anything arrived to join us) in the form of frozen ova and sperm that our skill might or might not be able to bring to maturity—still a rudimentary art when we left Earth.

These outside bunnies were pilot bunnies. Our three other pairs must get along on *Galileo* rations until we were sure the first pair was thriving. Laurette set up her miniature laboratory for soil and water tests. Paul Cutter dug magnificently until the light began to fail. I felt now a kind of permanency and sense of achievement, and Miranda felt it too, working like a little dynamo at whatever came to hand.

Toward sundown I roved the whole clearing again, with the carbine, not wanting it until I noticed the sun of Demeter slipping beyond the mountains, then pleased enough to be carrying that slim bit of functional wickedness. Once or twice I heard small life scuttering away in the grass, but if Demeter was blessed with field mice I didn't see them. We had set our camp not too near the pond; we wanted the wild things to continue using it if they would. As I approached it now, I thought I glimpsed some of those "deer" slipping into the shadows. Later we must shoot a few, for science if not for food. I felt no fear, only pleasure and curiosity, when a night flier, like a bat or bird, hurried over me and flickered into evening light above the trees. . . .

And before dawn on the third day, Miranda was ill.

◆

She woke me before sunrise, during Paul's tour of guard duty. I could barely see her face. She was speaking soberly, carefully, as if describing someone else's trouble—pain in the right leg, in the right foot a numbness that had started as an itching, and now the beginning of fever, headache, nausea.

Under the light of my lantern, the sole of her right foot looked inflamed, but at that time I found no break in the skin; the leg was reddened up to the knee. She said she was afraid of blacking out, and her voice was blurring—but it was Miranda who had the wits to remember how she had made that barefoot imprint on the sand of our landing place.

By mid-morning, near the time of our next radio contact with *Galileo*, she was unconscious. No signs of pain or delirium. She was unreachable, breathing too rapidly in a fevered sleep.

We had given her MH-12, for lack of anything better, and because it's the most generally useful and safe of the antibiotics developed on Earth. Then Laurette had searched the medical information in our "library"— *Galileo's* great microfilm library cut to the essentials. We could expect no precise help there, since the diseases of Earth would not be paralleled closely enough for proper guidance, but what Laurette found concerning Earth's tropical fevers did give me the idea of searching Miranda's foot with a hand-lens. I discovered a puncture so small that without the lens I had missed it completely. It seemed to be a true eschar with a definite center. It could have been made by an infinitesimal wood or mineral sliver, admitting some poison latent in the ground, or it could have been the bite of an organism hidden under the sand or too tiny to see. For what it was worth, and so far as I could endure it, I might then consider the scrub typhus that was endemic in some regions of Earth's tropics, a rickettsial disease carried by a mite no bigger than a grain of pepper.

I remembered my black lizard in the meadow. I would take him on any time in preference to this. No man is born with any skill at fighting shadows. You have to learn it, and always the hard way.

I could not look at the implications. I could only stand by and wait for Miranda to come back to me; to bring back, if it might be so, the meaning and the purpose I knew I was losing. It was not a case of thinking how I loved her: that was deep-down, bloodstream knowledge requiring no thought, and to think of it then would have made me even more useless in trying to help her.

I was with her—needing to fight, and no antagonist; needing to talk with her, and she could not know it—when I heard the noise of Paul Cutter, subdued because it came from within the plane. Laurette had just rejoined me by Miranda's cot in the shelter; Paul would be talking to *Galileo*, and a black uneasiness vaguely telepathic nudged me to rise. "Stay with her, Laurette," I said, and hurried for the plane.

I saw him at the radio, the prominent, somehow pathetic cords at the back of his neck, his heavy head wobbling a little, his voice attempting a casualness denied by that tremor and by his sweating hands. He was saying: "Yes, the rabbits go for the grass and they're thriving. What? . . . Oh sure, everyone's fine. We—"

He jumped a foot when my fingers dug at his shoulder. I nodded at the transmitter, and he croaked: "Here's Leroy—wants to talk to you." He lurched away, but an animal warning of danger reached me—perhaps he made some half-completed motion. I drew the automatic I was carrying and held it aimed at his heart while I talked to the Captain.

Paul slumped to his haunches and dropped his face on his knees. I told Madison as quickly as I could about Miranda, and he said: "I'll switch you to Dr. Dana, he's right here—then I want to talk to you again, Dave."

Dr. Dana helped me—just the voice and the manner. I could imagine I was in touch with the three thousand years of his tradition; out of space, that was Hippocrates talking. He questioned me, approving what we had done, suggesting other supportive measures. He admitted no other important measures were possible, since we knew nothing of the disease, hence nothing of the prognosis. He agreed it might be similar in some ways to Earth's tropical fevers, though when I mentioned scrub typhus he roared at me to forget that. But then he mentioned methods of searching the dead sand area for a guilty organism if there was one, and warned against letting Demeter's earth come in contact with our skins; so he would be reviewing his knowledge of the rickettsial diseases, and the snarling statistics of mortality. Well, Paul and I in our digging had both shoved our hands in the dirt several times. It flickered through my mind that Paul himself might be ill. He was sick enough, avoiding the cold eye of the .32, but not with fever.

Madison was back. "Dave, why did Paul say everyone was fine?"

"Oh—didn't realize the seriousness. It's all new this morning, Captain.

Laurette and I have been caring for her, while Paul was getting on with the work."

I suppose Madison knew I was lying, and knew Paul Cutter had to be my problem. Paul flashed me a sick and haunted thank-you-for-nothing glare. I gave Madison the rest of the report—water pure, test animals in good shape, no time yet for much aerial reconnaissance outside the plateau. At the close Madison said: "Dave, if you possibly can, be on hand yourself when we're due to call in."

"I'll do that, Captain."

"Soon as Miranda wakes up, give her my love. See you, Davy."

I closed the transmitter; studied the man suffering beyond the gun-sights, and holstered the automatic. "Why, Paul?"

He was on his feet and swaying. "Why don't you shoot?"

"No cause, now. You were ready to jump me till I made the report. That was in your face . . . Why?"

"I'm ashamed," he said. "Is that enough?"

"Look: you knew I'd be reporting next time, if not now."

The tremor of his head ceased, his mouth steadied to tightness. A man of twenty-five, he looked forty. "Maybe I thought by that time you'd—understand."

"Or maybe you only saw them leaving, abandoning us, and didn't think."

"Have it your way."

"Paul, while there's any chance at all, they'll never abandon us."

"You're wrong there." He knotted his hands, white-knuckled. "They'll go. Dr. Carey will influence them. Dr. God-Almighty Carey will see to that if no one else does." I scolded myself for failing to recognize the paranoid pattern sooner; or maybe I was wrong now, and seeing spooks. I made a note that I must talk to Carey at the next contact. "Dave—I've said, I'm ashamed. I was afraid and foolish, and I admit it. Isn't that enough?"

"I suppose it is." It was true—he was sick with shame, and other inward disasters; but did shame fit the pattern? I thought, the hell with patterns—the poor devil was human; leave it at that. Of course he was also profoundly hating me. Because I had seen him in an act of dishonesty and betrayal, he would always hate me. I said: "Let's get on with the work."

He stumbled out of the cabin and resumed digging away sod for our test plot in open ground. Attacking it rather—driving the bright blade into the green face of an enemy.

Late in the morning of our fourth day on Demeter, Miranda recovered consciousness. Her fever had risen to a peak of 106° during an intermi-nable night, when the green-white moon of Demeter was to me no longer enchanting, only sickly and baleful. Then, about dawn, the fever rapidly subsided. Miranda came back to me. I could forget about scrub typhus. I could sweep away all the horrors, because I saw memory and understand-ing and awareness of my kiss.

"How long, Davy? What's the time?"

"You've been out for one day of twenty-six hours. The computer up-stairs has dreamed up a calendar for us—got it yesterday. This is Friday morning—sorry fresh out of fish."

"They know of course?"

"Yes, and since you're recovering it won't make any difference."

"So what's the man crying about?"

"Stardust up my nose—itches. How about your foot—does that itch now?"

"Little bit. No numbness. Feels about all right." Under the lens, the puncture spot looked healed, like any tiny injury.

"You got a bite. I'm going after the beast soon as you're up and around—earth samples, and so on. We'll run down the little devil." She couldn't smile much, but she was trying. "He won't stop anything."

"That's right, Bud—we'll rise above bugs and stuff." She was trying, but then her eyes dilated, she winced and turned her face away from me. "Ask Laurette to come, will you please?"

"Yes—what is it?"

"Oh, damn everything!"

"What is it, Miranda?"

"Don't you know?" I suppose I did. "My baby—it was going to be my—my—Demeter's killed my baby."

IV

Saturday morning Miranda was able to sit up without help, and eat. She said she felt nothing wrong except exhaustion. She blamed that on the gravity of Demeter, but I think it was the after-effect of fever; we other three had adjusted to the gravity with almost no effort. Then after a decent meal, an hour of her old love Sibelius on the tapes, and another hour of just sitting with me in the temperate sunlight, Miranda let me talk to her, and suggest that she had not been pregnant at all. Rejecting the idea at first in despair, she presently came around to accepting it, and I felt she was at least half convinced that Demeter had nothing to do with our disappointment. Just before she fell asleep beside me in the sunshine, she murmured: "False-alarm Miranda. From here on out I'm going to try to behave like a rational mammal. But it's uphill work—you know? . . ."

Sunday morning Miranda climbed into the cabin of the plane, wanting to do it without the help of my arm, and talked to Captain Madison and Dr. Dana, rejoining me with a new quiet resembling cheerfulness.

Paul Cutter was speaking to me only when necessary, and with an intense politeness that affected me like a split fingernail. He made a point of asking, in private, for "official" permission to carry his carbine. There was no danger in him for the present. My leadership had become an immediate fact; I knew Paul felt terror at the thought of having to assume responsibility if anything happened to me. Actually he wouldn't have had to: Laurette would have stood aloof while Miranda assumed it, and Caliban-as-hero would have minded the chores.

When Miranda promised to loaf and rest, I took off that Sunday morning to blaze a trail alone through the woods to the dead-sand area. Miranda's recovery and her new calm had brought the kind of joy where recklessness bubbles near the surface. It had brought me too a burgeoning love for this one planet among all the stars. In such a mood the foot can slip—mine didn't. I went slowly, mindful of my blazes on the wood of these ancient trees.

The forest was all one hush, cool under the thickness of the canopy. I walked on a carpet formed from the rotted wood and leaves of centuries. Almost no undergrowth. At one place, a tree had fallen from old age; here a hundred saplings of the same species had already shot up high at the touch of the sun. Therefore they grew from seed; therefore the trees ought to bear *some* kind of fruit in their season, whenever that was.

Rarely and far apart, I noticed trees with holes high off the ground— natural holes left by the fall of dead branches and rotting of the sapwood. They were occupied. The corner of my eye caught a squirrely character popping into one of them, and I was aware of the scrutiny of harmless eyes.

After the first mile my ears told me of something larger following. I tried quick turns but learned nothing—once, maybe, a hint of motion retiring behind the reddish column of a tree-trunk. Anyhow not a twenty-five-foot lizard.

I was humming for a while—Schubert's *Die Forelle* I think it was, or some other memory of Earth equally light and happy.

Observing Dr. Dana's instructions, I was covered except for my face, and I took care not to let that be brushed by branches, though I was fairly sure the enemy I hunted lived under the sand. Close-fitting leggings, shirt tucked in, gloves. I carried a shovel, carbine, hand-ax, a sack with several small bags that could be tightly sealed, and a cage with four white mice.

Not much of a load. I supposed I could drop everything but the carbine, fast, but though I caught a few more dim sounds, nothing bothered me. If whatever followed me possessed anything like my kind of wits, it would know I was aware of its presence.

I came out on the dead sand near that vapor column idly rising from the fissured rock. The vapor gave off a slight sulfur smell. It drifted up with no pulsation, no force. Some age-old dirty business in the gut of Demeter, a planet that never asked for us. Yet I loved her.

Apologetically I set the wire-bottom cage of mice out on a patch of sand, with a cloth to shade them from the sun. Poor little rascals, as martyrs to science they even had their bellies shaved, to make it easier for our enemy to bite them—if it would, if there was such an enemy. I filled the small bags with samples of the sand, the clay patches, the good-seeming earth near the woods, the sod, the forest mold itself. One bag still empty, I searched for Miranda's barefoot print. It had been blurred by a breeze that must have stirred the sand at the edges without obliterating it. No rain had fallen since we landed. Nothing had made tracks out on this desolate ground. The ruts of our plane, our shoe-prints, patches where the jets had blasted sand hollows in take-off—all still plain to read.

For reasons of sentiment or superstition I took my final sample from a spot as near Miranda's footprint as I could set the shovel without destroying the mark—bad science, no excuse offered.

Nothing had followed me out here. If anything watched from the edge of the woods I caught no sense of it.

I had been away from the unfortunate mice for twenty minutes. As I removed the cloth they looked fair enough, but when I raised the cage a midget drop of blood splashed on the sand. I held the cage above the level of my eyes. Two of the mice flitted about in natural nervousness. The others were sluggish, and on the shaved belly of one of them I saw another blood-drop form and fall. No sign of normal coagulation.

I spread the cloth, drove in the shovel where the cage had rested, and spilled out the sand with care. That's where I found the thing, a worm two inches long gorged with blood. With a gloved fingertip I stirred the sand and found another, not distended, thin as a fine hair and barely visible, the same pinkish-white color as the sand. Exposed, the things moved feebly, obscene head ends lifting and blindly searching, mouth parts apparent as specks of black.

I drew the cloth into the form of a bag, tied it tightly for my collection and started home.

☙

On the way back through the woods I tried to puzzle it out. If nothing ventured on that sand, where did the worms find their natural food supply? Subterranean maybe—burrowing animals, grubs, other worms. I could leave all that to Dr. Bunuan, but it teased my curiosity, reminding me how mystery is always with us. I could not live long enough to see our colony (if there was to be a colony) become more than a trifling spot of intrusion on a most ancient planet. If we had grandchildren to the seventh generation, this world would remain imperfectly explored—and yet some of them would certainly hunger for space flight.

We never really learned much about the beautiful planet Earth.

Twice I stopped to search the forest mold for more of the hair-worms. I found none, but did find more of the stocky brown worms than in the sod of our clearing. They were active, burrowing, wriggling, hunting. I saw one attack a grub. Grasping organs shot out from either side of the worm's head and squeezed the grub helpless while the mouth consumed it. Maybe these brown fellows ate the poison hair-worms.

I glanced up from the vanishing grub, and saw what was lying flat along a branch that overhung my trail.

That clawed track by the pond had deceived me about the size of its maker. The paws were disproportionately large, the animal itself lean as an ocelot, not much bigger. The claws, hooked for efficient climbing and piercing, were relatively immense, partly retractile, though less so than a cat's. The creature was hairless, with a reddish-brown skin obscure against the color of the branch. I saw a narrow-nosed head, like a fox's except that the external ears were mere flaps of skin close to the skull. It had the wonderful deep eyes of a beast that must be mainly nocturnal.

I could bypass that part of the trail and circle around. I said aloud: "Would that sit all right with you, Jackson?"

Jackson winced at the sound of my voice—he shouldn't have, after hearing my no-account baritone murder *Die Forelle*—and flattened himself, or herself, close to the branch. I took up the carbine, seeing the narrow head begin a measuring motion from side to side. The hindquarters quivered, the motion of the head ceased in a frozen readiness. Not happy about that, I said: "Look, I'm not a deer. I'm not even a darling."

After all, I suppose Jackson could hardly have forgiven that. He was fifteen feet above the ground, six yards from the muzzle of the carbine. He could jump it with no strain and evidently had it in mind. The mouth opened and closed on interesting daggers of orange teeth. My sights steadied on the thin neck. I said: "Sorry, Jackson!" and fired.

Beginner's luck. Jackson shuddered, dropped and lay twitching, orange-red blood gushing from the shattered neck. I turned the body over with my foot. Not ugly nor beautiful, just strange. The sex organs puzzled me—female I thought, but peculiar. I tied the body to my sack, finding it curiously light. We learned later that the bones are partly hollow, and most of the viscera lighter than the corresponding tissues of Earth animals.

Dissection and observation in the next few days also demonstrated that Jackson, the timid and stupid creatures resembling deer, and the mouselike animals nesting in the grass, are mammals, in the sense that they bear their young alive and nurse them. And they are functional hermaphrodites. Demeter hasn't arranged for boy to meet girl. Well, we're here to fix that.

The brains, even to my uneducated eye, look primitively smooth. Maybe we can fix that too . . .

We found poison hair-worms in all the samples of sand and clay from the open ground, none at all in the sod or forest mold. The two lively mice from my cage remained lively—not bitten, apparently. Of the other two, one went into stupor the following day, and died. The one that had been bleeding did not die. Its wound clotted normally soon after my return to camp, and after a period of sluggishness the mouse recovered with no observable after-effects.

We repeated the experiment with other mice—couldn't spare many— and hair-worms from my samples. The results were the same. Under Laurette's guidance Miranda gladly introduced a brown worm to a hairworm, with delightful results. In sixty seconds, no hair-worm, the brown guy acting as contented as I do after a mince pie.

Conclusion, given me over the radio by Dr. Bunuan: "You've got a lovely little thing there, boy. Apparently the poison is, or is associated with, an anti-coagulant that probably helps the worm to feed. If the bite is interrupted, likely the poison stays in the wound, enters the bloodstream, generates some kind of systemic toxin. But if your trichinoid critter finishes the drink, I suggest he sucks back most of the poison with the blood and everybody's happy. And let me say, Davy, you people have put through a handsome little preliminary study." O my Miranda, burning that night with a fever of 106° and far away! But there was a sweet healthiness in the biologist's way of speaking; he had not forgotten the pain and terror any more than I had. I reserve judgment on physicists, but I'll drink beer with a biologist any day of the week—if we can make beer on Demeter. "Very handsome, Davy. I wish I was there."

I transmitted his remarks to Paul Cutter. Paul was alone in the clearing outside the shelter, with nothing much to do. We had dug as large a test plot as we needed, the seeds from Earth had been planted—in fact it was almost time for the radishes, rye-grass and other quick-sprouting plants to show themselves if they were going to. I passed on Dr. Bunuan's comment mostly for something pleasant to say. Paul had shown a polite interest in our study of the worms, saying that he had no talent himself for technician's work.

Paul faced me gravely, listened with bent head to my recital of Dr. Bunuan's words, nodded amiably, and replied: "The fundamental error is in the very first clause—as I tried so many times to make plain. If the colony is to be defined as a *republic*, in that opening clause, you bypass and throw away the entire experience of the 19th and 20th Centuries of Earth history, which is absurd. May I remind you that at the time of the founding of the United States of America, the word 'democracy' was a *bad* word, a term of *opprobrium*?" He smacked his fist into his palm; the tawny grazers could have heard his voice and quivered to the vibration half a mile away in the woods. "Now manifestly I am no Marxian. The Russian experiment, for all its important achievements, was ethically and politically a dead end. And why? Because dictatorship supervened. Because in Russia the essence of social democracy was never in effect, once more the cause of the common man was *lost*. Now in the very first amendment I proposed, or I should say *tried* to propose—"

I heard him out . . .

V

Rain fell heavily all through our sixteenth day on Demeter; warm rain without a wind; we huddled miserably in the shelter. Laurette put in the time mending some of our clothes. Paul read, glued to the scanner—politics I guess, or psychology. Miranda played chess with me, and listened to Sibelius.

Our seeds from Earth had rotted. The day before we had dug up a few—squash, corn, garden pea, bean seeds, all sodden pulp without life. But here and there a wheat kernel showed a feeble sprout. Even the busy grubs in Demeter's earth had not wanted them.

Of course, one can get along on a carnivorous diet. If our rabbits could flourish on Demeter's grass, probably the sheep and cattle from *Galileo* could do the same. I had shot two of the deer-like animals. We tried the meat on the white rats and then ate of it without harm—muttony and rank, but not impossible.

The rain stopped after sunrise of the seventeenth day. I took off for a wider reconnaissance. Captain Madison had suggested this after learning of the failure of our seeds. Somewhere in the meadows or hills there ought to be edible plants worth a try. Captain Madison had also made it plain that nothing so far reported had discouraged him; his intention was to bring the whole colony down at the end of our four weeks. "Keep in your calculations, Davy, that we'll bring machines and three hundred pairs of hands."

It didn't sound like talk for my morale. And I wondered, I think for the first time, what the mere fact of the pilot mission might be doing to those who remained on the ship. . . .

I left the plateau behind me and flew north, a broadening morning on my right hand. The world glittered from the rain, the forest a field of diamonds. At five thousand feet, I saw that island twenty miles out from the river mouth shining like dawn made tangible.

Del Sentiero's suggestion of an island for the colony had been over-ruled; but shouldn't I at least go and look? Wasn't I playing it by the seat of my pants, accepted leader of the pilot mission?

Accepted anyway by Miranda and partly by Laurette Vieuxtemps. Paul Cutter was still at his brittle play-acting, ludicrously deferring to me, contriving each time to drop a hint that my "glory" would end. He seemed unworried about a bloody nose—may have craved one.

With Laurette, the question of leadership hardly arose, for she was sensible, hard-working; given another year on *Galileo* she would have earned a title. There hadn't been more than two or three occasions when it was up to me to tell her what to do, and those unimportant. She was inevitably remote from us in her religious faith, which answered a need in her mind not present in my own. Unlike our kind, perpetually worried chaplain, Laurette paid Miranda and me the rare courtesy of not trying to change our agnosticism. She may have been privately sorry for us, but we were spared hearing about it. We were friends; we got along in the limited area of mental contact.

Again I did not go to look at my island. Perhaps I was afraid that its summoning beauty was an effect of haze, distance, memory and irrelevant dreams . . . Some of the time as I flew north I was reliving a moment of the day before, when Miranda grinned at me across the shambles of the chessboard and said: "The things that happen when your knights break loose are pitiful, that's all. I find myself caring deeply about that butchered pawn, Captain Leroy." Caring—she wasn't talking about chess. She proved that in the night, when the rain tapped on the roof of our shelter, and she was whispering we'd try again, maybe our child would be the first to be conceived on the planet Demeter. . . .

The seaward slopes of the foothills had changed color after the rain. From an even, reddish green they had become a riot of tomato-scarlet splashes. I supposed—and I was wrong—that the downpour must have brought some plant into sudden blossoming.

I skimmed past the hills searching for a level place to land. Not so easy; the terrain was nearly all sloping, vegetation thick. The radio was with me: I had thought it safer to leave it installed in the plane, on the chance we might have to take off from the plateau in a hurry. Now I could picture myself abandoning a wrecked plane and the only means of communicating with *Galileo*. I could observe a lost human fool groping back twenty-odd miles through unknown forest, no armament except the .32 at my hip, no assurance that I could scale the walls of the plateau if I reached it. Even snug in the perfectly functioning plane, wasn't I a very naked creature in a lonely place? But I think any planet is a lonely place.

At four hundred feet I learned it was no blooming of flowers down there. The brilliance was that of scarlet fruit, on great tangles of low-growing bushes unlike any we had found on the plateau.

Evidently, while it grows, the fruit of those bushes wears a dull powdery bloom. The samples I later secured carried traces of it. It must be that in the final ripening the bloom loosens, washed away by the rain, so that when the hills break out in a sudden gleaming it's time for harvest.

The lizards were at it.

On every hillside where the fruit was shining, a dozen or more of those monsters writhed and scampered on short saurian legs. They paid no heed to the plane, nor to the hundreds of small bird-like creatures that darted about sharing the meal. It was hot holiday for the lizards in the genial sun; their black enormous jaws munched and slobbered, dripping scarlet. Here and there about the slopes, gorged pairs were breeding. When I cut the jets for brief glides I could hear the bellowing and roaring, smashing of bushes and the monstrous slap of black primordial flesh against flesh.

Just hungry and lusty hermaphrodite vegetarians having themselves a Mesozoic ball. But not too good for a little thin-hided foreign mammal who hadn't been invited. I climbed back to a thousand feet and began to get mad. They were first comers by several million years, had a right to the red lush stuff and needed it. But so did I.

A few miles further on I located a small valley in a pocket of the hills, with enough level ground for landing. The eastern of the two slopes closing it in bore the red splashes; the lizards were present there too, but not so numerously. I noticed only five or six as I circled down. If I dared climb that slope on foot for a hundred yards, I would be at the edge of the area where the bushes grew.

It became a thing that had to be done. I don't believe I was trying to prove anything. I haven't much patience with heroes. I'm afraid many of them have been in the pattern of Paul Cutter, ridden by the devil of one idea, and legend has supplied the pleasing part of the picture after silence took them. I'm simply a Randy who loves the idea of staying alive. I just wanted some of that fruit for my people and me.

The clamor of the beasts surged up to me as soon as I shut off the jets. Only a few, they made uproar enough for a convention. I lit nicely, coming to rest in the shadow of a tall solitary tree, and knew I must start at once, or hesitation would demoralize me. I took a sack for the fruit, and my .32, which might at least make me look like a hero later if one of the boys happened to step on me.

I was counting on the dullness of a primitive brain in a saurian hulk, too dim even for curiosity about the plane. I forgot that while the lizards were enjoying rich food and love, something else might be planning to enjoy the lizards. And, yes, there was a slight error of a few million years, for which I had no excuse after shooting mammals on the plateau. If Demeter's evolution has paralleled Earth's as closely as I think, those "lizards" are a survival from long ago. I was mistaking pseudo-Cenozoic for quasi-Mesozoic—Dr. Bunuan wouldn't have liked that.

At the base of that eastern slope the grass admitted some vegetation different from any I had so far seen. Many individual plants—call them weeds—were bushy, some taller than my head. This tall growth thickened as I climbed. For several yards I glimpsed no more of the revels up yonder, only heard the sodden gurgling and the roaring.

In the thicket I won a good look at one of the small flying animals clinging to a tall weed. It let me blunder within ten feet and then sailed off swift and airy. Not a bird; furry, with small teeth; the size of a big robin. The triangular wings are anchored, not to the hind foot like a bat's, but to the animal's side just below a rather large rib-cage. The free hind legs pull up in flight and vanish in the belly-fur. It seemed to me that two of the modified phalanges were projecting beyond the upper angle of the wing, but I couldn't be sure. Maybe they hang themselves up to sleep, like bats.

At the upper limit of the thicket I halted to watch through the leaves. The nearest of the red-fruited bushes were still at some distance. I would have to step out in the open—not nice, but better than scuttling back from the riot empty-handed and licked. I told myself those jolly black nightmares were not aggressive. Their enormous grappling—just sex, Demeter style. I'd heard of sex.

◆

The lizards' vision might be dim; maybe that was why they had ignored the plane. Really there was nothing terrible about them except their size. They wouldn't smell me—a light breeze blew toward me down the slope, bringing me their musky reek.

I crawfished into the sunlight holding open the mouth of my sack, and snatched at the red pear-shaped fruit, a little thieving mammal making off with whatever wasn't nailed down. The fruit, big and firm, separated readily from the stems, warm with sunshine, aromatic like muskmelon, smooth and delightful in the hand.

The lizards paid no attention, though the bushes where I was pilfering their steak and potatoes stood hardly twenty yards from the spot where the nearest one of them lurched about alone. And when the other beast crashed out of deep bushes up there on my left, the only lizard that acted aware of the attack was that nearest one—when he was knocked flat by the rushing impact, stricken in the belly by orange fangs.

Earth-born, I thought of it as a bear—shaggy block of body, massive head, thick long-clawed legs. The color was dull cinnamon. It was more than half the length of the lizard it assaulted, and taller—I suppose about the size of the brown Kodiak bear of Alaska. Now, being still alive, I peacefully remember, from boyhood reading, someone's statement that if a Kodiak bear stood upright inside an ordinary house his head would poke well into the second story—so it wouldn't do you much good to hightail into the bathroom and slam the door.

That killer was majestically casual, rearing over the lizard, driving down both forepaws as a bear might grab a log, twitching the black monster over on its back with impudent ease and tearing open the pale belly with a swipe of orange tusks. Then I think it sheared the muscles of the hind legs, the stabbing bites too swift for my eyes to follow. The lizard's legs quit threshing; they twitched without effect or purpose. I saw no teeth in the howling cavern of the lizard's mouth. And while the bear began to feed on the slow-dying thing, the other lizards up the slope continued gorging and mating.

I'm not sure a small mammal from Earth's 21st Century should have witnessed that kind of death. No more significant than other kinds, but at this moment of writing I tend to remember it too much: the gaudy mess of it, the other lizards' unconcern, the mindless cruelty that was not cruelty at all but only single-minded hunger. For a second or two there in the sun I myself was lizard and bear, killer and killed, knowing down in the gut how it was for both of them.

After all, in the home cave of one of my great-grandfathers, Homo Pekinensis, there was a rather messy assortment of human bones, well gnawed; difficult to hush up that kind of family history.

I backed slowly into the thicket, once more Homo Quasi-sapiens. I had my peewee .32 out; my left hand clung to the sack with its couple of dozen lumps of scarlet treasure. Some noise I made must have caused the bear's head to swing. It saw me and stood quiet, measuring me with little wicked orange-veined eyes. A chunk of the lizard's liver hung dripping from its under jaw.

No use trying to freeze; it knew I was alive and interesting. It turned unhurriedly to study me. The piece of liver, bigger than my head, dropped to the ground. Not losing sight of me, the bear snuffed it, swallowed it in a gulp, and walked toward me, head swaying from side to side. Under stress one still observes: for the record, the pair of upper teeth that would be called canine in an Earth animal are about ten inches long, and slant outward; I believe the ends thrusting down beyond the under jaw have a slicing edge on the inner side.

I fired twice, trying for the eyes. Then I was in the thicket, reeling to one side as the crazed roaring mass plunged for the spot where I had been, and shuddered past me down the hill. It fell, rose on its hind legs to an impossible height, fell again rolling, scrabbling pitiably at its head with both paws, as a human being might clutch at a mortal wound. It should have been dead or helpless from the anesthetic poison in those bullets. But it would not die.

I followed. My body was sick and shaking. When the beast fell the second time, I managed to control my right hand and place more shots. One of them pierced the spine, for the bear plainly could not rise. But since it could not even then die, I must suppose the poison of those bullets has no rapid effect in the bloodstream of the animals of Demeter. The deerlike things, and the ocelot-like thing, I had shot on the plateau received heart or head wounds severe enough to account for the way they toppled over without a struggle. That bear was still trying to crawl toward me, hauling with vast forelegs, when I stepped close and put him out with a bullet that shattered the skull.

My wits came back, too gradually. I knew I was hearing something besides the commotion of the lizards up the hill. I pawed at the sweat dribbling into my eyes. Well, of course—that shrill imperious buzz could only be our radio in the plane. *Galileo* calling, report overdue.

My left hand was locked in a grip on that sack or I might have lost it. I remembered it as I reached the plane and flung it in ahead of me. I croaked: "Leroy to *Galileo*, over."

"Where the *hell* were you?" Madison was shouting. "You all right?

"Yes. Recon, away from plane, sorry, ran into bit of delay."

"All right."

"Sure. I just—"

He cut in sharply: "Where are you? Where's the plane?"

"I'm about thirty miles north of the plateau. Went to look for edible plants, found 'em too I think. I—"

"Alone?"

"Yes."

"What's the fog, Davy? We can't even find the plateau."

"Fog?" I was panting, sick and stupid. "Fog, on the plateau?"

VI

Madison said carefully: "There are several areas of thick fog over the region of the plateau and south of there. They were still developing when we got your territory in the sights ten minutes ago. Now they seem to have stopped spreading. I'm watching a white blur the same size and shape as the plateau. I can see five other fog areas along the foothills to the south, none up where you must be. Over."

"I'm taking off." I did, my hands thinking for me. The jets roared and I was climbing.

"I think I see you—sun on the wings. In a valley, weren't you?"

"Yes."

"You'll see the fog from six or seven thousand, then save your fuel. And don't get nerved up—it looks like ordinary fog, milky white. I don't see how it could be smoke, starting in so many different places at once . . . What about that geyser you reported? Are there others like it on the plateau?"

I had seen none; there could have been. A few of the open areas on the plateau were blank sand instead of grass. There could have been fissures with no vapor columns to reveal them. I remembered and mentioned the rain of the day before. "Could that have touched off something?"

Madison said: "Dr. Matsumoto thought of it when we saw the fog.

He's sweating it out—I'm no geologist, Davy. He says it's reasonable—if a heavy seepage of water reached something hot underground, you might get a vapor cover like that. If it's just water vapor, it ought to dissipate fairly soon in this sunlight. Is there any wind?"

"Hardly any."

Now I could see it in the south, a horror of sluggishly heaving white where I had left my people at work and cheerful in a sparkling morning. And once again I glimpsed my island, far to the left, twenty miles out to sea. No fog there. A fringe of beach was peacefully gleaming; the low hills stood tranquil under the sun.

"You've reported there's never much wind."

"Only day before yesterday, wind and some overcast, the day before the rain. Inshore and offshore breezes night and morning, but at the camp we've hardly noticed them; the trees shut them away. . . . I'm at eight thousand and going down. I've got the landmarks beyond the plateau that show me where the camp is."

"You can't try to land till it clears—hell, what am I saying? You don't need to be told."

I didn't need to be told, but I wanted his voice, or failing that, my own. I reported on the morning's flight, the bushes on the hills, the shift to scarlet and the reason for it. I told him of the lizards' festival, the thing I had killed, the fruit, with me in the plane cabin.

"There'll be food," he said, "and ways of growing more. Ways of doing without most of the things we knew on Earth."

"Including war."

"Including war, I hope, though not the causes of it, which were bound to travel with us, Davy. Look, I must say again, I must make sure you understand—there's been nothing in the reports to change my mind. And this fog doesn't, no matter what the reason for it is. This is our planet and we must take it, never mind your damn dinosaurs and cave bears and hair-worms—that's all duck soup. Don't worry about it." He sounded tired, and hoarse. "Where are you now?"

"About five miles to go. It looks like—just fog."

"What matters," he said, "is our people. The ways of living we must find. New problems. What to do about the—30-per-centers. A lot of things not in the Builders' Directives, Davy."

"We make our own, don't we?"

"Of course. And the Builders knew that. All they could give us were sketches—history. You know, Davy, I'm rather ashamed, how ignorant of history I was until three or four years ago, when Andrea began to get through my engineer's crust. Well . . . With this world we must somehow do better." Then when I most needed to hear him, his voice was cut short by a cough. He spoke two or three more words, blurred as if he had turned his face away from the transmitter. I caught the meaningless hum of other voices near him.

Confusion and then silence from the control room of *Galileo*. Seething below me, a white nothing of fog.

◆

Down in that sea of blindness, Miranda and the others—I couldn't think. I climbed high with full power and drifted down again. If they were alive they would hear the jets. Why shouldn't they be alive? It was only fog— only fog. If it meant some upheaval from underground, that would have happened before, at other rains—but animals and plants lived on the plateau. Why shouldn't my people be alive?

Meanwhile *Galileo* was slipping away to the blind side of the world. I called them a few times. Then at last: "*Galileo* to Leroy." I knew that voice.

"Receiving."

"Del Sentiero, David. The Captain was called away. One of the patches of fog south of you is clearing. Can you find anything yet?"

"Not yet. Thought I saw treetops, but can't be sure. I'm climbing again, to try it from six thousand."

"David, consider this an order, as if Captain Madison were transmitting it. When the fog clears, if you find the worst has happened and the others are lost—though there's no reason I can see to expect it—you will then do everything possible to keep your own self alive, and you will assist the rest of the colony in coming down. . . . Are you hearing me?"

"Yes. The rest of the—"

"We're coming down. Tomorrow or the day after."

"But—"

"Forget the four weeks. I can't give you details—no time, we'll soon be out of range. See anything yet?"

"Treetops—yes—it can't be anything else—yes!" I was babbling. The plane had gone dangerously low. I shot up away from the white confusion, but the spots of darkness I had seen could only be treetops.

Del Sentiero was saying: "You'll find them. Just fog. One place south of you looks almost normal. Did a minute ago, I mean. We're out of sight now." His voice was smooth but faint. I lost some other words in a crackle of static. They would be slipping to the other side, presently watching the depth of Demeter's night.

I rechecked the outer landmarks. The tallest trees near our clearing grew by the pond. I saw those tops rising from the swirl of fog and recognized them, dripping, steaming with a thinner vapor in the sun.

Then at the top of the tallest tree-motion, a flutter of white and blue. Why, on all the world of Demeter I don't suppose there's more than one such bit of color, and that one is a blouse Miranda wears. I was shouting like an idiot as I dipped the plane to let her know I had seen it. Then I swept around and rose—not high this time, no need.

Cottony white smothered the clearing still, but it was dwindling. Soon I made out the upper half of our dome shelter. I could find time now to fret about *Galileo*, and Captain Madison. He couldn't have been called away by trouble with the ship, could he? My ignorant mind pecked at the notion of an error in the orbit—then I was going down into a rolling ground-fog, knowing that the fog was no more than four or five feet thick on the landing strip. I touched down, and stepped into vapor barely waist-high, walked through it over the invisible grass.

Miranda was still waving her blouse like a flag as we ran to each other in the mist, speaking the same stumbling words and not by chance: "What am I without you?"

➤

The damp air carried a faint reek of sulfur and something unidentifiable; not a sharp irritant, merely unpleasant. Some fog swirled to my nostrils; I breathed it with no apparent harm, as Miranda talked in a roughened, uncomfortable voice.

"The others must be all right. I breathed it, I'm alive. I think they're still in the shelter. I'd gone to the pond for drinking water when it began. I thought, just evaporation from wet ground, then it came thicker, I couldn't see my way back to the shelter. Couldn't see a foot ahead, eyes watered." I saw they were still slightly inflamed; her cute nose was reddened; but she was alive. "I called, I guess they didn't hear—it choked me some, couldn't make much noise. People can't live here, Davy, if this happens."

"No, but I've found a place where they can. Our island—wait till you see—no fog there." I couldn't talk well either.

She was rubbing her face in my shirt. "Couldn't think of anything but that tree."

"Good thinking."

"At the top, it was all around me still, but I knew you'd be coming back. I just hung on—"

I said: "How else would we ever win Demeter . . . ?"

Laurette was in the shelter, in her "room"—we used that word for the plastic-walled compartments that gave us a bit of privacy—and she was alone. I shouted for Paul and heard no answer. Laurette was red-eyed, red-nosed, from the vapor I think, and not from tears. As Miranda hurried in, Laurette looked up from the table where she sat, indifferently, almost as if puzzled by Miranda's urgency.

"Laurette, come out of this! It's clearing outside. Davy's got back." Laurette blinked; Miranda shook her. "What's the matter? Come out into the air, it's much cleaner outside."

Laurette stood up then drowsily and left the shelter with us. She gazed about the clearing, where now the fog was no more than a heaving, milky blur over the grass. She said: "We go on living a while?"

"Laurette, what's happened?"

"Why, nothing, Miranda." She was not speaking impatiently. "I understand it now, that's all. We weren't meant to come here."

"Not meant"—for once in my life I saw Miranda angry. She started once or twice to speak, then only said, with too much restraint: "Forgive me if I don't think you're that much wiser than the rest of us."

"Nothing to forgive." Laurette spoke gently, and with the note of forgiveness. "I'm not, dear, it's not *my* wisdom. You see, we've all been very stupid. The radiation sickness back on Earth—that was the judgment. We should have understood then."

Miranda's brown eyes went incandescent, then quiet. "Well," she said, "maybe you'd still better forgive me, for understanding my own little speck of life rather differently."

I noticed a table outside the shelter, part of Laurette's laboratory equipment, overturned, solutions spilled, glassware broken. No great damage except the loss of several hours of good work. I asked: "Did Paul do that? Where is he, Laurette?"

"No," she said remotely, "I did it. I'm sorry—I guess I got a bit emotional: silly of me. I know you don't look at these things the way I do. Paul—I don't know. He went off somewhere, into the fog." She shrugged, turning more matter-of-fact, more like the girl we had known. "I won't disgrace you again. I can see we're nothing but naughty children fighting against the will of God, but since we're still alive—well, that must be His will too—somehow. I won't say any more about it—you can't see it my way, you don't understand. . . . I couldn't see for sure, David, but I think Paul went—that way." She pointed toward the pond.

"You two stay together while I find him. That's an order . . ."

I found him soon, by the noise of his footsteps, a small man blundering toward me through misty tree-shadows, halting when he saw me, frowning with folded arms but letting me approach, too unhappy to be absurd. His mouth was tight, his inflamed eyes steady on me and aloof. "Leroy— did Captain Madison order you to go on that flight this morning?"

"Order me?" I was stupidly puzzled. "No. He suggested it. How do you feel?"

"As you can see, I am still alive." He tapped a foot on the ground, brooding, watching me. "He suggested it—I suppose after a conference with Dr. Matsumoto?"

"What are you talking about?"

"I know—I'm not supposed to be able to figure things out . . . I dare say, as soon as you reported that vapor coming out of the rock, Matsumoto guessed what might happen after a rain. Then he, and Carey of course, and Madison—oh well, let it go. You're just a sort of—innocent tool, Leroy. You know that, don't you?"

In a way, I blame Paul's paranoid state at that time partly on the fog. I don't know its chemical qualities—I suppose our experts will study it when the colony comes down—but I do know one true name for the thing that rode that mist: Fear. Laurette had retreated, in her fashion. Paul had retreated, into this. Miranda—just hung on. And I was by force of circumstances a pilot. With a Randy's scattered knowledge of everything in general and nothing in particular, I groped after what I ought to do here and now. I said: "Paul, the colony is coming down tomorrow or the day after. Del Sentiero just told me so."

"Del Sentiero!" Something blazed up cleanly in him—courage or hope or common sense—and a great deal of the misery and sour suspicion drained away. I take no credit for it; I hadn't remembered that del Sentiero was one of the few he admired and, more important, trusted. "Well—that's different! Tomorrow? They're not waiting?"

"No. The ship went out of range before del Sentiero could explain it, but I got that much for sure. And I've found a place where there's no fog, an island. We're going there now, soon as we can pack up—let's get going."

"An island." He liked that too. He rubbed his face, and smiled, and delivered the greatest understatement so far made on the planet Demeter: "I suppose my judgment isn't always too good, Dave, and I've been under a—sort of strain."

"Sure," I said. "Let's move." I bumped his shoulder, and we walked peacefully back to the plane, damn near friends.

◆

Today is the 21st of June, and the sound of ocean beyond our shelter is the music I remember from childhood.

It is not the month of June on the planet Earth. Andrea del Sentiero (whom I shall see tomorrow) suggested we might give that name to our first month here, because in the old world June was a month of beauty and beginnings, an end to the troubling dangerous time of spring.

The orbit of Demeter and the phases of the green moon give us a year of fourteen four-week months. We can name the others as we please, when June is over. Next year, if the bushes grow that quickly from the seed I took, the hills of this island will redden with the harvest of early summer. But this is the 21st of June in the Year One.

The island is quiet. I miss the morning and evening music of the birds I remember. I miss the butterflies and moths, the dragonflies. We shall gradually learn about other creatures of Demeter, and our children—if we can have them—will feel no such nostalgia.

A firm beach two miles long faces the mainland, and two promontories like the horns of a crescent create a bay there; it would be a good harbor for boats of shallow draft. I landed on the beach. The larger landing ships from *Galileo* can touch down on the water and ride in easily. East of the crescent, the island is an oval block of about thirty square miles, the only level land in small mountain valleys of the interior. I noticed lakes and streams, one large enough to be called a river. No red fruit grows on the slopes. I believe it will.

We flew low over every part of the island before landing. Miranda spotted a few "deer." No larger forms; no lizards. The bears could be living here—if they are they'll have to go the hard way. We have searched samples of the beach sand for hair-worms and found none. They may be here but didn't Captain Madison himself call that sort of thing duck soup?

We had the shelter up, under tree cover at the edge of the beach, when *Galileo* called in again. It was Andrea del Sentiero. Even that early, I could honestly give him a good report of the island, and he told me once more that the colony would come down without waiting for the four weeks. I asked for three or four days to explore and make sure and he agreed—I may have spent too much of that time in writing up this sketchy personal account. But we know the island is good. As for shortening the pilot mission—well, those people up there voted so.

In a sense, they voted against the Builders' Directives, or at least against the logic of the pilot mission, which so far as I can see is still perfectly unanswerable—as logic. Against it, our people mount the equally unanswerable logic of love. They said in effect that since we four had come down, they could do nothing but follow.

Del Sentiero said: "David, with regard to Captain Madison . . ."

The silence hurt. I said: "What?"

"I'm sorry, I was hunting for words, but there are none of the kind I need. I suggest you remember the legend of Moses. It happened very quickly, David. A coronary—he'd been getting warnings; no one else knew of it except Dr. Dana. After that coughing spell—I guess you heard it—he turned to us and said: 'Davy's going down, but the fog is clearing.' Then I think his eyes troubled him, because he stood up and tried to move nearer the viewplate. I reached him before he fell. He said: 'We'll do better—we must.'

"That was all, David—but I think he was satisfied that we would. . . . You agree?"

"Yes."

And I do. Laurette may see us as the naughty rebellious children of God. Paul may spin visions of a perfect state that can never exist except inside the sanctuary of a lonely mind. Miranda will just hang on. And I think we shall be able to deal with each other in charity, more or less, and mind our campfires.

The Longest Voyage

POUL ANDERSON

One of the best-known writers in science fiction, Poul Anderson made his first sale in 1947, while he was still in college, and in the course of his subsequent fifty-plus-year career has published almost a hundred books (in several different fields, as Anderson has written historical novels, fantasies, and mysteries, in addition to science fiction), sold hundreds of short pieces to every conceivable market, and won seven Hugo Awards, three Nebula Awards, the Grandmaster Nebula, and the Tolkien Memorial Award for life achievement.

Anderson had trained to be a scientist, taking a degree in physics from the University of Minnesota, but the writing life proved to be more seductive, and he never did get around to working in his original field of choice. Instead, the sales mounted steadily, until by the late fifties and early sixties he may have been one of the most prolific writers in the genre.

In spite of his high output of fiction, he somehow managed to maintain an amazingly high standard of literary quality as well, and by the early-to-mid sixties was also on his way to becoming one of the most honored and respected writers in the genre. At one point during this period (in addition to nonrelated work and lesser series such as the "Hoka" stories he was writing in collaboration with Gordon R. Dickson), Anderson was running three of the most popular and prestigious series in science fiction all at the same time: the Technic History series detailing the numerous exploits of the wily trader Nicholas Van Rijn (which includes novels such as The Man Who Counts, The Trouble Twisters, Satan's World, Mirkheim, and The People of the Wind and collections such as Trader to the Stars and The Earth Book of Stormgate); the extremely popular series relating the adventures of interstellar secret agent Dominic Flandry, probably the most successful attempt to cross science fiction with the spy thriller, next to Jack Vance's Demon Princes novels (the Flandry series includes novels such as A Circus of Hells, The Rebel Worlds, The Day of Their Return, Flandry of Terra, A Knight of Ghosts and Shadows, A Stone in Heaven, and The Game of Empire and collections such as Agent of the Terran Empire); and, my own personal favorite, a series that took us along on assignment with the agents of the Time Patrol (including the collections The Guardians of Time, Time Patrolman, The Shield of Time, and The Time Patrol).

When you add to this amazing collection of memorable titles the impact of the best of Anderson's nonseries novels, work such as Brain Wave, Three Hearts and Three Lions, The Night Face, The Enemy Stars, and The High Crusade, all of which were being published in addition to the series books, it becomes clear that Anderson dominated the late fifties and the pre–New Wave sixties in a way that only Robert A. Heinlein, Isaac Asimov, and Arthur C. Clarke could rival. And, like them, he remained an active and dominant figure right through the seventies and *eighties. He is* still *producing strong new work and turning up on best-seller lists at the end of the decade of the nineties as well.*

Explorers and exploration of all sorts have long fascinated Anderson, and several different stories by him would have fit into this anthology perfectly well, but "The Longest Voyage" details the meeting of two different *explorers from two different worlds and is his purest examination of the restless, questing spirit of those who are driven to seek out the farthest horizon they can possibly reach— and then long for horizons farther still. It won him a Hugo Award in 1960, and for its lyricism, compassion, subtlety, thoughtfulness, and, above all, the relish it takes in the bristling strangeness and wonder of the world it still goes nearly unmatched in the field.*

Anderson's other books (among many *others) include:* The Broken Sword, Tau Zero, A Midsummer Tempest, Orion Shall Rise, *and* The Boat of a Million Years. *His short work has been collected in* The Queen of Air and Darkness and Other Stories, Fantasy, The Unicorn Trade *(with Karen Anderson),* Past Times, The Best of Poul Anderson, *and* Explorations. *His most recent books are the novels* Harvest of Stars, The Fleet of Stars, Starfarers, *and* Operation Luna *and the retrospective collection* All One Universe. *Upcoming is a new novel,* Genesis. *Anderson lives in Orinda, California, with his wife (and fellow writer) Karen.*

When first we heard of the sky ship, we were on an island whose name, as nearly as Montalirian tongues can wrap themselves about so barbarous a noise, was Yarzik. That was almost a year after the *Golden Leaper* sailed from Lavre Town, and we judged we had come halfway round the world. So befouled was our poor caravel with weeds and shells that all sail could scarce drag her across the sea. What drinking water remained in the butts was turned green and evil, the biscuit was full of worms, and the first signs of scurvy had appeared on certain crewmen.

"Hazard or no," decreed Captain Rovic, "we must land somewhere." A gleam I remembered appeared in his eyes. He stroked his red beard and murmured, "Besides, it's long since we asked for the Aureate Cities. Perhaps this time they'll have intelligence of the place."

Steering by that ogre planet which climbed daily higher as we bore westward, we crossed such an emptiness that mutinous talk broke out afresh. In my heart I could not blame the crew. Imagine, my lords. Day upon day upon day when we saw naught but blue waters, white foam, high clouds in a tropic sky; heard only the wind, *whoosh* of waves, creak of timbers, sometimes at night the huge sucking and rushing as a sea monster breached. These were terrible enough to common sailors, unlettered men who still thought the world must be flat. But then to have Tambur hang forever above the bowsprit, and climb, so we could see we must eventually pass directly beneath the brooding thing . . . and what upbore it? the crew mumbled in the forecastle. Would an angered God not let it fall down on us?

At last a deputation waited on Captain Rovic. Very timid and respectful they were, those rough burly men, as they asked him to turn about. But their comrades massed below, muscled sun-blackened bodies taut in the ragged kilts, daggers and belaying pins ready to hand. We officers on the quarterdeck had swords and pistols, true. But we numbered a mere six, including that frightened boy who was myself, and aged Froad the astrologue, whose robe and white beard were reverend to see but of small use in a fight.

Rovic stood mute for a long while after the spokesman had voiced this demand. The stillness grew, until the empty shriek of wind in our shrouds, the empty glitter of ocean out to the world's rim, became all there was. Most splendid our master looked, for he had donned scarlet hose and bell-tipped shoon when he knew the deputation was coming, as well as helmet and corselet polished to mirror brightness. The plumes blew around that blinding steel head and the diamonds on his fingers flashed against the rubies in his sword hilt. Yet when he spoke, it was not as a knight of the Queen's court, but in the broad Anday of his fisher boyhood.

"So 'tis back ye'd wend, lads? Wi' a fair wind an' a warm sun, liefer ye'd come about an' beat half round the globe? How ye're changed from yere fathers! Ken ye nay the legend, that once everything did as man commanded, an' 'twas an Andayman's lazy fault that now we must work? For see ye, 'twas nay too much that he told his ax to cut down a tree for him, an' told the faggots to walk home, but when he told 'em to carry him, then God was wroth an' took the power away. Though to be sure, as recompense God gave Andaymen sea-luck, dice-luck, an' love-luck. What more d'ye ask for, lads?"

Bewildered at this response, the spokesman wrung his hands, flushed, looked at the deck, and stammered that we'd perish miserably . . . starve, or thirst, or drown, or be crushed under that horrible moon, or sail off the world's edge . . . the *Golden Leaper* had come farther than ship had sailed since the Fall of Man, and if we returned at once, our fame would live forever.

"But can ye eat fame, Etien?" asked Rovic, still mild and smiling. "We've had fights an' storms, aye, an' merry carouses too; but devil an Aureate City we've seen, though well ye ken they lie out here someplace, stuffed wi' treasure for the first bold gang who'll come plunder 'em. What ails yere gutworks, lad? Is't nay an easy cruise? What would the foreigners say? How will yon arrogant cavaliers o' Sathayn, yon grubby chapmen o' Wondland, laugh—nay alone at us, but at all Montalir—did we turn back!"

Thus he jollied them. Only once did he touch his sword, half drawing it, as if absentmindedly, when he recalled how we had weathered the hurricane off Xingu. But they remembered the mutiny that followed then, and how that same sword had pierced three armed sailors who attacked him together. His dialect told them he would let bygones lie forgotten, if they would. His bawdy promises of sport among lascivious heathen tribes yet to be discovered, his recital of treasure legends, his appeal to their pride as seamen and Montalirians, soothed fear. And then in the end, when he saw them malleable, he dropped the provincial speech. He stood forth on the quarterdeck in burning casque and tossing plumes, and the flag of Montalir blew its sea-faded colors above him, and he said as the knights of the Queen say:

"Now you know I do not propose to turn back until the great globe has been rounded and we bring to Her Majesty that gift which is most peculiarly ours to give. The which is not gold or slaves, nor even that lore of far places that she and her most excellent Company of Merchant Adventures desire. No, what we shall lift in our hands to give her, on that day when again we lie by the long docks of Lavre, shall be our achievement: that we did this thing which no men have dared in all the world ere now, and did it to her glory."

A while longer he stood, through a silence full of the sea's noise. Then he said quietly, "Dismissed," turned on his heel and went back into his cabin.

☙

So we continued for some days more, the men subdued but not uncheerful, the officers taking care to hide their doubts. I found myself busied, less with the clerical duties for which I was paid or the study of captaincy for which I was apprenticed—both these amounting to little by now—than with assisting Froad the astrologue. In these balmy airs he could carry on his work even on shipboard. To him it scarce mattered whether we sank or swam; he had lived more than a common span of years already. But the knowledge of the heavens to be gained here, that was something else. At night, standing on the foredeck amidst quadrant, astrolabe, and telescope, drenched in the radiance from above, he resembled some frosty-bearded saint in the windows of Provien Minster.

"See there, Zhean." His thin hand pointed above waves that glowed and rippled with light, past the purple sky and the few stars still daring to show themselves, toward Tambur. Huge it was in full phase, sprawling over seven degrees of sky, a shield or barry of soft vert and azure, splotched with angry sable that could be seen to move across its face. The firefly moon we had named Siett twinkled near the hazy edge of the giant. Balant, espied rarely and low on the horizon in our part of the world, here stood high: a crescent, but the dark part of its disk tinged by luminous Tambur.

"Observe," declared Froad, "there's no doubt left; one can *see* how the globe rotates on an axis, and how storms boil up in its air. Tambur is no longer the dimmest of frightened legends, nor a dreadful apparition seen to rise as we entered unknown waters; Tambur is real. A world like our own. Immensely bigger, certes, but still a spheroid in space, around which our own world moves, always turning the same hemisphere to her monarch. The conjectures of the ancients are triumphantly confirmed. Not merely that our world is round—*pouf*, that's obvious to anyone—but that we move, about a greater center, which in turn has an annual path about the sun. But, then, how big is the sun?"

"Siett and Balant are inner satellites of Tambur," I rehearsed, struggling for comprehension. "Vieng, Darou, and the other moons commonly seen at home have paths outside our own world's. Aye. But what holds it all up?"

"That I don't know. Mayhap the crystal sphere containing the stars exerts an inward pressure. The same pressure, maybe, that hurled mankind down onto the earth, at the time of the Fall From Heaven."

The night was warm, but I shivered, as if those had been winter stars. "Then," I breathed, "there may also be men on . . . Siett, Balant, Vieng . . . even on Tambur?"

"Who knows? We'll need many lifetimes to find out. And what lifetimes they'll be! Thank the good God, Zhean, that you were born in this dawn of the coming age."

Froad returned to making measurements. A dull business, the other officers thought; but by now I had learned enough of the mathematic arts to understand that from these endless tabulations might come the true size of the earth, of Tambur, of sun and moons and stars, the paths they took through space and the direction of Paradise. So the common sailors, who muttered and made signs against evil as they passed our instruments, were closer to fact than Rovic's gentlemen, for indeed Froad practiced a most potent gramarye.

◆

At length we saw weeds floating on the sea, birds, towering cloud masses, the signs of land. Three days later we raised an island. It was an intense green under those calm skies. Surf, still more violent than in our hemisphere, flung against high cliffs, burst in a smother of foam and roared back down again. We coasted carefully, the palomers aloft to seek an approach, the gunners standing by our cannon with lighted matches. For not only were there unknown currents and shoals—familiar hazards—but we had had brushes with canoe-sailing cannibals in the past. Especially did we fear the eclipses. My lords can visualize how in that hemisphere the sun each day must go behind Tambur. In our longitude the occurrence was about midafternoon and lasted nearly ten minutes. An awesome sight: the primary planet—for so Froad now called it, a planet akin to Diell or Coint, with our own world humbled to a mere satellite thereof!— became a black disk bordered red, up in a sky suddenly full of stars. A cold wind blew across the sea, and even the breakers seemed hushed. Yet so impudent is the soul of man that we continued about our duties, stopping only for the briefest prayer as the sun disappeared, thinking more about the chance of shipwreck in the gloom than of God's Majesty.

So bright is Tambur that we continued to work our way around the island at night. From sunup to sunup, twelve mortal hours, we kept the *Golden Leaper* slowly moving. Toward the second noon, Captain Rovic's persistence was rewarded. An opening in the cliffs revealed a long fjord. Swampy shores overgrown with saltwater trees told us that while the tides rose high in that bay, it was not one of those bores dreaded by mariners. The wind being against us, we furled sail and lowered the boats, towing in our caravel by the power of oars. This was a vulnerable moment, especially since we had perceived a village within the fjord. "Should we not stand out, master, and let them come first to us?" I ventured.

Rovic spat over the rail. "I've found it best never to show doubt," said he. "If a canoe fleet should assail us, we'll give 'em a whiff of grapeshot and trust to break their nerve. But I think, thus showing ourselves fearless of them from the very first, we're less likely to meet treacherous ambuscade later."

He proved right.

In the course of time, we learned we had come upon the eastern end of a large archipelago. The inhabitants were mighty seafarers, considering that they had only outrigger dugouts to travel in. These, though, were often a hundred feet long. With forty paddles, or with three bast-sailed masts, such a vessel could almost match our best speed, and was more maneuverable. However, the small cargo space limited their range of travel.

Albeit they lived in houses of wood and thatch, possessing only stone tools, the natives were cultivated folk. They farmed as well as fished; their priests had an alphabet. Tall and vigorous, somewhat darker and less hairy than we, they were impressive to behold, whether nude, as was common, or in full panoply of cloth and feathers and shell ornaments. They had formed a loose empire throughout the archipelago, raided islands lying farther north, and carried on a brisk trade within their own borders. Their whole nation they called the Hisagazi, and the island on which we had chanced was Yarzik.

This we learned slowly, as we mastered somewhat their tongue. For we were several weeks at that town. The duke of the island, Guzan, made us welcome, supplying us food, shelter, and helpers as we required. For our part, we pleased them with glassware, bolts of Wondish cloth, and suchlike trade goods. Nonetheless we encountered many difficulties. The shore above highwater mark being too swampy for beaching a vessel as heavy as ours, we must build a drydock before we could careen. Numerous of us took a flux from some disease, though all recovered in time, and this slowed us further.

"Yet I think our troubles will prove a blessing," Rovic told me one night. As had become his habit, once he learned I was a discreet amanuensis, he confided certain thoughts in me. The captain is ever a lonely man; and Rovic, fisher lad, freebooter, self-taught navigator, victor over the Grand Fleet of Sathayn and ennobled by the Queen herself, must have found the keeping of that necessary aloofness harder than would a gentleman born.

I waited silent, there in the grass hut they had given him. A soapstone lamp threw wavering light and enormous shadows over us; something rustled the thatch. Outside, the damp ground sloped past houses on stilts and murmurous fronded trees, to the fjord where it shimmered under Tambur. Faintly I heard drums throb, a chant and stamping of feet around a sacrificial fire. Indeed, the cool hills of Montalir seemed far.

Rovic leaned back his muscular form, clad in a mere seaman's kilt in this heat. He had had them fetch him a civilized chair from the ship. "For see you, young fellow," he continued, "at other times we'd have established just enough communication to ask about gold. Well, we might also try to get a few sailing directions. But all in all, we'd hear little except the old story—'aye, foreign lord, indeed there's a kingdom where the very streets are paved with gold . . . a hundred miles west'—anything to get rid of us, eh? But in this prolonged stay, I've asked out the duke and the idolater priests more subtly. I've been so coy about whence we came and what we already know, that they've let slip a gobbet of knowledge they'd not otherwise have disgorged on the rack itself."

"The Aureate Cities?" I cried.

"Hush! I'd not have the crew get excited and out of hand. Not yet."

His leathery, hook-nosed face turned strange with thought. "I've always believed those cities an old wives' tale," he said. My shock must have been mirrored to his gaze, for he grinned and went on, "A useful one. Like a lodestone on a stick, it's dragging us around the world." His mirth faded. Again he got that look, which was not unlike the look of Froad considering the heavens. "Aye, of course I want gold, too. But if we find none on this voyage, I'll not care. I'll capture a few ships of Eralia or Sathayn when we're back in home waters, and pay for the voyage thus. I spoke God's truth that day on the quarterdeck, Zhean, that this journey was its own goal, until I can give it to Queen Odela, who once gave me the kiss of ennoblement."

He shook himself out of his reverie and said in a brisk tone: "Having led him to believe I already knew the most of it, I teased from Duke Guzan the admission that on the main island of this Hisagazi empire is something I scarce dare think about. A ship of the gods, he says, and an actual live god who came from the stars therein. Any of the natives will tell you that much. The secret reserved to the noble folk is that this is no legend or mummery, but sober fact. Or so Guzan claims. I know not what to think. But . . . he took me to a holy cave and showed me an object from that ship. It was some kind of clockwork mechanism, I believe. What, I know not. But of a shining silvery metal such as I've never seen before. The priest challenged me to break it. The metal was not heavy, must have been thin. But it blunted my sword, splintered a rock I pounded with, and my diamond ring would not scratch it."

I made signs against evil. A chill went along me, spine and skin and scalp, until I prickled all over. For the drums were muttering in a jungle dark, and the waters lay like quicksilver beneath gibbous Tambur, and each afternoon that planet ate the sun. Oh, the bells of Provien, heard across windswept Anday downs!

➤

When the *Golden Leaper* was seaworthy again, Rovic had no trouble gaining permission to visit the Hisagazian emperor on the main island. He would, indeed, have found difficulty in not doing so. By now the canoes had borne word of us from one end of the realm to another, and the great lords were agog to see these blue-eyed strangers. Sleek and content once more, we disentangled ourselves from the arms of tawny wenches and embarked. Up anchor, up sail, chanties whose echoes sent sea birds whirling above the steeps, and we stood out to sea. This time we were escorted. Guzan himself was our pilot, a big middle-aged man whose handsomeness was not much injured by the livid green tattoos his folk affected on face and body. Several of his sons spread their pallets on our decks, while a swarm of warriors paddled alongside.

Rovic summoned Etien the boatswain to him in his cabin. "You're a man of some wit," he said. "I give you charge of keeping our crew alert, weapons ready, however peaceful this may look."

"Why, master!" The scarred brown face sagged with near dismay. "Think you the natives plot a treachery?"

"Who can tell?" answered Rovic. "Now, say naught to the crew. They've no skill in dissembling. Did greed or fear rise among 'em, the natives would sense as much, and grow uneasy—which would worsen the attitude of our own men, until none but God's Daughter could tell what'd happen. Only see to it, as casually as you're able, that our arms are ever close by and that our folk stay together."

Etien collected himself, bowed, and left the cabin. I made bold to ask what Rovic had in mind.

"Nothing, yet," said he. "However, I did hold in these fists a piece of clockwork such as the Grand Ban of Giair never imagined; and yarns were spun me of a Ship which flew down from heaven, bearing a god or a prophet. Guzan thinks I know more than I do, and hopes we'll be a new, disturbing element in the balance of things, by which he may further his private ambitions. He did not take those many fighting men along by accident. As for me . . . I intend to learn more about this."

He sat awhile at his table, staring at a sunbeam which sickled up and down the wainscot as the ship rocked. Finally: "Scripture tells us man dwelt beyond the stars before the Fall. The astrologues of the past generation or two have told us the planets are corporeal bodies like this earth. A traveler from Paradise—"

I left with my head in a roar.

We made an easy passage among scores of islands. After several days we raised the main one, Ulas-Erkila. It is about a hundred miles long, forty miles across at the widest, rising steep and green toward central mountains dominated by a volcanic cone. The Hisagazi worship two sorts of gods, watery and fiery, and believe this Mount Ulas houses the latter. When I saw that snowpeak afloat in the sky above emerald ridges, staining the blue with smoke, I could feel what the pagans did. The holiest act a man can perform among them is to cast himself into the burning crater of Ulas, and often an aged warrior is carried up the mountain that he may do so. Women are not allowed on the slopes.

Nikum, the royal seat, is situated at the head of a fjord, like the village where we had been staying. But Nikum is rich and extensive, being about the size of Roann. Many houses are made from timber rather than thatch; there is also a massive basalt temple atop a cliff, overlooking the city, with orchards, jungle, and mountains at its back. So great are the tree trunks available to them for pilings, the Hisagazi have built here a regular set of docks like those at Lavre—instead of moorings and floats that can rise or fall with the tides, such as most harbors use throughout the world. We were offered a berth of honor at the central wharf, but Rovic made the excuse that our ship was awkward to handle and got us tied at the far end.

"In the middle, we'd have the watchtower straight above us," he muttered to me. "And they may not have discovered the bow here, but their javelin throwers are good. Furthermore, they'd have an easy approach to our ship, plus a clutter of moored canoes between us and the bay mouth. Here, though, a few of us could hold the pier whilst the others ready for quick departure."

"But have we anything to fear, master?" I asked.

He gnawed his mustache. "I know not. Much depends on what they really believe about this god-ship of theirs . . . as well as what the truth is. But come all death and hell against us, we'll not return without that truth for Queen Odela."

❧

Drums rolled and feathered spearmen leaped as our officers disembarked. A royal catwalk stretched above highwater level. (Common townsfolk in this realm swim from house to house when the tide laps their thresholds, or take a coracle if they have burdens to carry.) Across the graceful span of vines and canes lay the palace, which was a long building made from logs, the roof pillars carved into fantastic god-shapes.

Iskilip, Priest-Emperor of the Hisagazi, was an old and corpulent man. A soaring headdress of plumes, a feather robe, a wooden scepter topped with a human skull, his facial tattoos, his motionlessness, all made him seem unhuman. He sat on a dais, under sweet-smelling torches. His sons sat crosslegged at his feet, his courtiers on either side. Down the long walls were ranged his guardsmen. They had not our custom of standing to attention; but they were big, supple young men, bearing shields and corselets of scaly sea-monster leather, flint axes and obsidian spears that could kill as easily as iron. Their heads were shaven, which made them look the fiercer.

Iskilip greeted us well, called for refreshment, bade us be seated on a bench little lower than his dais. He asked many perceptive questions. Wide ranging, the Hisagazi knew of islands far beyond their own chain. They could even point the direction and tell us roughly the distance of a many-castled country they named Yurakadak, though none of them had traveled that far himself. Judging by their third-hand description, what could this be but Giair, which the Wondish adventurer Hanas Tolasson had reached overland? It blazed in me that we were indeed rounding the world. Only after that glory had faded a little did I again heed the talk.

"As I told Guzan," Rovic was saying, "another thing which drew us hither was the tale that you were blessed with a Ship from Heaven. And he showed me this was true."

A hissing went down the hall. The princes grew stiff, the courtiers blanked their countenances, the guardsmen stirred and muttered. Remotely through the walls I heard the rumbling, nearing tide. When Iskilip spoke, through the mask of himself, his voice had gone whetted: "Have you forgotten that these things are not for the uninitiated to see, Guzan?"

"No, Holy One," said the duke. Sweat sprang forth among the devils on his face, though not the sweat of fear. "However, this captain knew. His people also . . . as nearly as I could learn . . . he still has trouble speaking so I can understand . . . his people are initiate too. The claim seems reasonable, Holy One. Look at the marvels they brought. The hard, shining stone-which-is-not-stone, as in this long knife I was given—is that not like the stuff of which the Ship is built? The tubes which make distant things look close at hand, such as he has given you, Holy One—is this not akin to the far-seer the Messenger possesses?"

Iskilip leaned forward, toward Rovic. His scepter hand trembled till the pegged jaws of the skull clattered together. "Did the Star People themselves teach you to make all this?" he cried. "I never imagined. . . . The Messenger never spoke of any others—"

Rovic held up both palms. "Not so fast, Holy One, I pray you," said he. "We are poorly versed in your tongue. I couldn't recognize a word just now."

This was his deceit. His officers had been ordered to feign a knowledge of Hisagazi less than they really possessed. (We had improved our command of it by secret practicing with each other.) Thus he had an unimpeachable device for equivocation.

"Best we talk in private, Holy One," suggested Guzan, with a glance at the courtiers. They returned him a jealous glare.

Iskilip slouched in his gorgeous regalia. His words fell blunt, but in the weak tone of an old, uncertain man. "I know not. If these strangers are already initiate, certes we can show them what we have. But otherwise—if profane ears heard the Messenger's own tale—"

Guzan raised a dominator's hand. Bold and ambitious, long thwarted in his petty province, he had taken fire today. "Holy One," he said, "why has the full story been withheld these many years? In part to keep the commoners obedient, aye. But also, did you and your councillors not fear the whole world might swarm hither, greedy for knowledge, if it knew, and we then be overwhelmed? Well, if we let the blue-eyed men go home with curiosity unsatisfied, I think they are sure to return in strength. Thus we have naught to lose by revealing the truth to them. If they have never had a Messenger of their own, if they can be of no real use to us, time enough to kill them. But if they have indeed been visited like us, what might we and they not do together!"

This was spoken fast and softly, lest we Montalirians understand. And, indeed, our gentlemen failed to. I, having young ears, got the gist; and Rovic preserved such a fatuous smile of incomprehension that I knew he was seizing every word.

In the end they decided to take our leader—and my insignificant self, for no Hisagazian magnate goes anywhere quite unattended—to the temple. Iskilip led the way in person, Guzan and two brawny princes behind. A dozen spearmen brought up the rear. I thought Rovic's blade would be scant use if trouble came, but set my lips firmly together and made myself walk beside him. He looked as eager as a child on Thanksday Morning, teeth agleam in the pointed beard, a plumed bonnet slanted rakish over his brow. None would have thought him aware of any peril.

We left about sundown; in Tambur's hemisphere, folk make less distinction between day and night than our people must. Having observed Siett and Balant in high tide position, I was not surprised that Nikum lay nearly drowned. And yet, as we climbed the cliff trail toward the temple, methought I had never seen a view more alien.

Below us lay a sheet of water, on which the long grass roofs of the city appeared to float; the crowded docks, where our own ship's masts and spars raked above heathen figureheads; the fjord, winding between precipices toward its mouth, where the surf broke white and terrible on the skerries. The heights above us seemed altogether black, against a fire-colored sunset that filled nigh half the sky and bloodied the waters. Wan through those clouds I glimpsed the thick crescent of Tambur, banded in a heraldry no man could read. A basalt column chipped into the shape of a head loomed in outline athwart the planet. Right and left of the path grew sawtoothed turf, summer dry. The sky was pale at the zenith, dark purple in the east, where the first few stars had appeared. Tonight I found no comfort in the stars. We walked silent. The bare native feet made no noise. My shoes went pad-pad and the bells on Rovic's toes raised a tiny jingle.

The temple was a bold piece of work. Within a quadrangle of basalt walls guarded by tall stone heads lay several buildings of the same material. Only the fresh-cut fronds that roofed them were alive. Iskilip leading us, we brushed past acolytes and priests to a wooden cabin behind the sanctum. Two guardsmen stood watch at its door. They knelt for him. The emperor rapped with his curious scepter.

My mouth was dry and my heart thunderous. I expected almost any being hideous or radiant to stand in the doorway as it was opened. Astonishing, then, to see just a man, and of no great stature. By lamplight within I discerned his room, clean, austere, but not uncomfortable; this could have been an ordinary Hisagazian dwelling. He himself wore a simple bast skirt. The legs beneath were bent and thin, old man's shanks. His body was likewise thin, but still erect, the white head proudly carried. In complexion he was darker than a Montalirian, lighter than a Hisagazian, with brown eyes and sparse beard. His visage differed subtly, in nose and lips and slope of jaw, from any other race I had ever encountered. But he was human.

Naught else.

We entered the cabin, shutting out the spearmen. Iskilip doddered through a half-religious ceremony of introduction. I saw Guzan and the princes shift their stance, restless and unawed. Their class had long been party to this. Rovic's face was unreadable. He bowed in courtly wise to Val Nira, Messenger of Heaven, and explained our presence in a few words. But as he spoke, their eyes met and I saw him take the star man's measure.

"Aye, this is my home," said Val Nira. Habit spoke for him; he had given the same account to so many young nobles that the edges were worn off it. As yet he had not observed our metallic instruments, or else had not grasped their significance to him. "For . . . forty-three years, is that right, Iskilip? I have been treated as well as might be. If at times I was near screaming from loneliness, that is what an oracle must expect."

The emperor stirred, uneasy in his robe. "His demon left him," he explained. "Now he is simple human flesh. That's the real secret we keep. It was not ever thus. I remember when he first came. He prophesied immense things, and the people wailed and went on their faces. But sithence his demon has gone back to the stars, and the once-potent weapon he bore has equally been emptied of its force. The people would not believe this, however, so we will still pretend otherwise, or there would be unrest among them."

"Affecting your own privileges," said Val Nira. His tone was tired and sardonic. "Iskilip was young then," he added to Rovic, "and the imperial succession was in doubt. I gave him my influence. He promised in return to do certain things for me."

"I tried, Messenger," said the monarch. "Ask all the sunken canoes and drowned men if I did not try. But the will of the gods was otherwise."

"Evidently." Val Nira shrugged. "These islands have few ores, Captain Rovic, and no person capable of recognizing those I required. It's too far to the mainland for Hisagazian canoes. But I don't deny you tried, Iskilip . . . then." He cocked an eyebrow back at us. "This is the first time foreigners have been taken deeply into the imperial confidence, my friends. Are you certain you can get back out again, alive?"

"Why, why, why, they're our guests!" blustered Iskilip and Guzan, almost in each other's mouths.

"Besides," smiled Rovic, "I had most of the secret already. My country has secrets of its own, to set against this. Yes, I think we might well do business, Holy One."

The emperor trembled. His voice cracked across. "Have you indeed a Messenger too?"

"What?" For a numbed moment Val Nira stared at us. Red and white pursued each other across his countenance. Then he sat down on the bench and began to weep.

"Well, not precisely." Rovic laid a hand on the shaking shoulder. "I confess no heavenly vessel has docked at Montalir. But we've certain other secrets, belike equally valuable." Only I, who knew his moods somewhat, could sense the tautness in him. He locked eyes with Guzan and stared the duke down as a wild animal tamer does. And meanwhile, motherly gentle, he spoke with Val Nira. "I take it, friend, your Ship was wrecked on these shores, but could be repaired if you had certain materials?"

"Yes . . . yes . . . listen—" Stammering and gulping at the thought he might see his home again ere he died, Val Nira tried to explain.

◆

The doctrinal implications of what he said are so astounding, even dangerous, that I feel sure my lords would not wish me to repeat much. However, I do not believe they are false. If the stars are indeed suns like our own, each attended by planets like our own, this demolishes the crystal-sphere theory. But Froad, when he was told later, did not think that matters to the true religion. Scriptures have never said that Paradise lies directly above the birthplace of God's Daughter; this was merely assumed, during those centuries when the earth was believed to be flat. Why should Paradise not be those planets of distant suns, where men dwell in magnificence, who possess the ancient arts and flit from star to star as casually as we might go from Lavre to West Alayn?

Val Nira believed our ancestors had been cast away on this world, several thousand years ago. They must have been fleeing the consequences of some crime or heresy, to come so far from any human domain. Somehow their ship was wrecked, the survivors went back to savagery, and only by degrees have their descendants regained a little knowledge. I cannot see where this explanation contradicts the dogma of the Fall. Rather, it amplifies it. The Fall was not the portion of all mankind but only a few—our own tainted blood—while the others continued to dwell prosperous and content in the heavens.

Our world still lies far off the trade lanes of the Paradise folk. Very few of them nowadays have any interest in seeking new realms. Val Nira, though, was such a one. He traveled at hazard for months until he chanced upon our earth. Then the curse seized him, too. Something went wrong. He descended upon Ulas-Erkila, and the Ship would fly no more.

"I know what the damage is," he said ardently. "I've not forgotten. How could I? No day has passed throughout these years that I didn't recite to myself what must be done. A certain subtle engine in the Ship requires quicksilver." (He and Rovic must spend some time talking ere they deduced this must be what he meant by the word he used.) "When the engine failed, I landed so hard that its tanks burst. All the quicksilver, what I had in reserve as well as what I was employing, poured forth. That much, in a hot enclosed space, would have poisoned me. I fled outside, forgetting to close the doorway. The deck being canted, the quicksilver ran after me. By the time I had recovered from blind panic, a tropical rainstorm had carried off the fluid metal. A series of unlikely accidents, yes, that's what's condemned me to a life's exile. It really would have made more sense to perish outright!"

He clutched Rovic's hand, staring up from his seat at the captain who stood over him. "Can you actually get quicksilver?" he begged. "I need no more than the volume of a man's head. Only that, and a few repairs easily made with tools in the Ship. When this cult grew up around me, I must needs release certain things I possessed, that each provincial temple might have a relic. But I took care never to give away anything important. Whatever I need is waiting there. A gallon of quicksilver, and—oh, God, my wife may even be alive, on Terra!"

Guzan, at least, had begun to understand the situation. He gestured to the princes, who hefted their axes and stepped a little closer. The door was shut on the cabin. Rovic looked from Val Nira to Guzan, whose face was grown ugly with tension. My captain laid hand on hilt. In no other way did he seem to feel any nearness of trouble.

"I take it, milord," he said lightly, "you're willing that the Heaven Ship be made to fly again."

Guzan was jarred. He had never expected this. "Why, of course," he exclaimed. "Why not?"

"Your tame god would depart you. What then becomes of your power in Hisagazia?"

"I—I'd not thought of that," Iskilip stuttered.

Val Nira's eyes shuttled among us, as if watching a game of paddleball. His thin body shook. "No," he whispered. "You can't. You can't keep me!"

Guzan nodded. "In a few more years," he said, not unkindly, "you would depart in death's canoe anyhow. If meanwhile we held you against your will, you might not speak the right oracles for us. Nay, be at ease; we'll get your flowing stone." With a slitted glance at Rovic: "Who shall fetch it?"

"My folk," said the knight. "Our ship can readily reach Giair, where there are civilized nations who surely have the quicksilver. We could return within a year, I think."

"Accompanied by a fleet of adventurers, to help you seize the sacred vessel?" asked Guzan bluntly. "Or, once out of our islands, you might not proceed to Yurakadak at all. You might continue the whole way home, and tell your Queen, and return with the power she commands."

Rovic lounged against a roof post, like a big pounce-cat at its ease in ruffles and hose and scarlet cape. His right hand continued to rest on his sword pommel. "None save Val Nira could make that Ship go, I suppose," he drawled. "Does it matter who aids him in making repairs? Surely you don't think either of our nations could conquer Paradise!"

"The ship is very easy to operate," chattered Val Nira. "Anyone can fly it in air. I showed many nobles what levers to use. It's navigating among the stars which is more difficult. No nation on this world could even reach my people unaided—let alone fight them—but why should you think of fighting? I've told you a thousand times, Iskilip, the dwellers in the Milky Way are dangerous to nobody. They have so much wealth they're hard put to find a use for most of it. Gladly would they spend large amounts to help the peoples of this world become civilized again." With an anxious, half-hysterical look at Rovic: "Fully civilized, I mean. We'll teach you our arts. We'll give you engines, automata, homunculi, that do all the toilsome work; and boats that fly through the air; and regular passenger service on those ships that ply between the stars—"

"These things you have promised for forty years," said Iskilip. "We've naught but your word."

"And, finally, a chance to confirm his word," I blurted.

Guzan said with calculated grimness: "Matters are not that simple, Holy One. I've watched these men from across the ocean for weeks, while they lived on Yarzik. Even on their best behavior, they're a fierce and greedy lot. I trust them no further than my eyes reach. This very night I see how they've befooled us. They know our language better than they ever admitted. And they misled us to believe they might have some inkling of a Messenger. If the Ship were indeed made to fly again, them in possession, who knows what they might choose to do?"

Rovic's tone softened still further. "What do you propose, Guzan?"

"We can discuss that another time."

I saw knuckles tighten around stone axes. For a moment, only Val Nira's unsteady breathing was heard. Guzan stood heavy in the lamplight, rubbing his chin, the small black eyes turned downward in thoughtfulness. At last he shook himself. "Perhaps," he said crisply, "a crew mainly Hisagazian could sail your ship, Rovic, and fetch the flowing stone. A few of your men could go along to instruct ours. The rest could remain here as hostages."

My captain made no reply. Val Nira groaned, "You don't understand! You're squabbling over nothing! When my people come here, there'll be no more war, no more oppression. They'll cure you of every disease. They'll show friendship to all and favor to none. I beg you—"

"Enough," said Iskilip. His own words fell ragged. "We shall sleep on this. If anyone can sleep after so much strangeness."

Rovic looked past the emperor's plumes, into the face of Guzan. "Before we decide anything . . ." His fingers tightened on the sword hilt till the nails turned white. Some thought had sprung up within him. But he kept his tone even. "First I want to see that Ship. Can we go there tomorrow?"

Iskilip was the Holy One, but he stood huddled in his feather robe. Guzan nodded agreement.

◆

We bade our good-nights and went forth under Tambur. The planet was waxing toward full, flooding the courtyard with cold luminance, but the hut was shadowed by the temple. It remained a black outline, a narrow lamplight rectangle of doorway in the middle. There was etched the frail body of Val Nira, who had come from the stars. He watched us till we had gone out of sight.

On the way down the path, Guzan and Rovic bargained in curt words. The Ship lay two days' march inland, on the slopes of Mount Ulas. We would go in a joint party to inspect it, but a mere dozen Montalirians were allowed. Afterward we would debate our course of action.

Lanthorns glowed yellow at our caravel's poop. Refusing Iskilip's hospitality, Rovic and I returned thither for the night. A pikeman on guard at the gangway inquired what I had learned. "Ask me tomorrow," I said feebly. "My head's in too much of a whirl."

"Come into my cabin, lad, for a stoup ere we retire," the captain invited me.

God knows I needed wine. We entered the low room, crowded with nautical instruments, books, and printed charts that looked quaint to me now I had seen a little of those spaces where the cartographer drew mermaids and windsprites. Rovic sat down behind his table, gestured me to a chair opposite, and poured from a carafe into two goblets of Quaynish crystal. Then I knew he had momentous thoughts in his head—far more than the problem of saving our lives.

We sipped a while, unspeaking. I heard the lap-lap of wavelets on our hull, the tramp of men on watch, the rustle of distant surf—otherwise nothing. At last Rovic leaned back, staring at the ruby wine on the table. I could not read his expression.

"Well, lad," said he, "what do you think?"

"I know not what to think, master."

"You and Froad are a trifle prepared for this idea that the stars are other suns. You're educated. As for me, I've seen sufficient eldritch in my day that this seems quite believable. The rest of our people, though . . ."

"An irony that barbarians like Guzan should long have been familiar with the concept, having had the old man from the sky to preach it privily to their class for more than forty years. Is he indeed a prophet, master?"

"He denies it. He plays prophet because he must, but it's evident that the dukes and earls of this realm know it's a trick. Iskilip is senile, more than half converted to his own artificial creed. He was mumbling about prophecies Val Nira made long ago, true prophecies. Bah! Tricks of memory and wishfulness. Val Nira is as human and fallible as I am. We Montalirians are the same flesh as these Hisagazi, even if we have learned the use of metal before they did. Val Nira's people know more in turn than us; they're still mortals, by Heaven. I must remember that they are."

"Guzan remembers."

"Bravo, lad!" Rovic's mouth bent upward, one-sidedly. "He's a clever one, and bold. When he came, he saw his chance to stop stagnating as the petty lord of an outlying island. He'll not let that chance slip without a fight. Like many a double-dealer before him, he accuses us of plotting the very things he hopes to do."

"But what does he hope for?"

"My guess would be, he wants the Ship for himself. Val Nira said it was easy to fly. Navigation between the stars would be too difficult for anyone save him; nor could any man in his right mind hope to play pirate along the Milky Way. However . . . if the Ship stayed right here, on this earth, rising no higher than a mile above ground . . . the warlord who used it might conquer more widely than Lame Darveth himself."

I was aghast. "Do you mean Guzan would not even try to seek out Paradise?"

Rovic scowled so blackly at his wine that I saw he wanted solitude. I stole off to my bunk in the poop.

➤

The captain was awake before dawn, readying our folk. Plainly he he had reached some decision, and it was not pleasant. But once he set a course, he seldom veered. He was long in conference with Etien, who came out of the cabin looking frightened. As if to reassure himself, the boatswain ordered the men about harshly.

Our allowed dozen were to be Rovic, Froad, myself, Etien, and eight crewmen. We were issued helmets and corselets, muskets and edged weapons. Since Guzan had told us there was a beaten path to the Ship, we assembled a supply cart on the dock. Etien supervised its landing. I was astonished to see that nearly all it carried, till the axles groaned, was barrels of gunpowder. "But we're not taking cannon!" I protested.

"Skipper's orders," rapped Etien. He turned his back on me. After a glance at Rovic's face, nobody ventured to ask him the reason. I remembered we would be going up a mountainside. A wagonful of powder, with lit fuse, set rolling down toward a hostile army, might win a battle. But did Rovic anticipate open conflict?

Certes his orders to the men and officers remaining behind suggested as much. They were to stay aboard the *Golden Leaper*, holding her ready for instant fight or flight.

As the sun rose, we said our morning prayers to God's Daughter and marched down the docks. The wood banged hollow under our boots. A few thin mists drifted on the bay; Tambur's crescent hung wan above. Nikum town lay hushed as we passed through.

Guzan met us at the temple. A son of Iskilip was supposedly in charge, but the duke ignored that youth as much as we did. They had a hundred guardsmen along, scaly-coated, shaven-headed, tattooed with storms and dragons. The early sunlight gleamed off obsidian spearheads. Our approach was watched in silence. But when we halted before those disorderly ranks, Guzan trod forth. He was also y-clad in leather, and carried the sword Rovic had given him on Yarzik. The dew shimmered on his feather cloak. "What have you in that wagon?" he demanded.

"Supplies," Rovic answered.

"For four days?"

"Send home all but ten of your men," said Rovic coolly, "and I'll send back this cart."

Their eyes clashed, until Guzan turned and gave his orders. We started off, a few Montalirians surrounded by pagan warriors. The jungle lay ahead of us, a deep and burning green, rising halfway up the slope of Ulas. Then the mountain became naked black, to the snow that edged its smoking crater.

Val Nira walked between Rovic and Guzan. Strange, I thought, that the instrument of God's will for us was so shriveled. He ought to have walked tall and haughty, a star on his brow.

During the day, at night when we made camp, and again the next day, Rovic and Froad questioned him eagerly about his home. Of course, their talk was in fragments. Nor did I hear everything, since I must take my turn at pulling our wagon along that narrow, steep, damnable trail. The Hisagazi have no draft animals, therefore they make slight use of the wheel and have no proper roads. But what I did hear kept me long awake.

Ah, greater marvels than the poets have imagined for Elf Land! Entire cities built in a single tower half a mile high. The sky made to glow so that there is no true darkness after sunset. Food not grown in the earth, but manufactured in alchemical elaboratories. The lowest peasant owning a score of machines which serve him more subtly and humbly than might a thousand slaves; owning an aerial carriage which can fly him around his world in less than a day; owning a crystal window on which theatrical images appear, to beguile his abundant leisure. Argosies between suns, stuffed with the wealth of a thousand planets; yet every ship unarmed and unescorted, for there are no pirates and this realm is on such good terms with the other starfaring nations that war has also ceased. (These foreign countries, it seems, are more akin to the supernatural than Val Nira's, in that the races composing them are not human, though able to speak and reason.) In this happy land is little crime. When it does occur, the criminal is soon captured by the arts of the provost corps; yet he is not hanged, nor even transported overseas. Instead, his mind is cured of the wish to violate any law. He returns home to live as an especially honored citizen, since folk know he is now completely trustworthy. As for the government—but here I lost the thread of discourse. I believe it is in form a republic, but in practice a devoted fellowship of men, chosen by examination, who see to the welfare of everyone else.

Surely, I thought, this was Paradise!

Our sailors listened agape. Rovic's mien was reserved, but he gnawed his mustaches incessantly. Guzan, to whom this was an old tale, grew rough of manner. Plain to see, he disliked our intimacy with Val Nira, and the ease wherewith we grasped ideas that were spoken.

But, then, we came of a nation which has long encouraged natural philosophy and improvement of the mechanic arts. I myself, in my short lifetime, had witnessed the replacement of the waterwheel in regions where there are few streams by the modern form of windmill. The pendulum clock was invented the year before I was born. I had read many romances about the flying machines which no few men have tried to devise. Living at such a dizzy pace of progress, we Montalirians were all prepared to entertain still vaster concepts.

At night, sitting with Froad and Etien around a campfire, I spoke somewhat of this to the savant. "Ah," he crooned, "today Truth stood unveiled before me. Did you hear what the starman said? The three laws of planetary motion about a sun, and the one great law of attraction which explains them? Dear saints, that law can be put in a single short sentence, and yet the development will keep mathematicians busy for three hundred years!"

He stared past the flames, and the other fires around which the heathen slept, and jungle gloom, and angry volcanic glow in heaven. I started to query him. "Leave be, lad," grunted Etien. "Can ye nay tell when a man's in love?"

I shifted a little closer to the boatswain's stolid, comforting bulk. "What do you think of this?" I asked, softly, for the jungle whispered and croaked on every side.

"Me, I stopped thinking a while back," he said. "After yon day on the quarterdeck, when the skipper jested us into sailing wi' him though we went off the world's edge an' tumbled down in foam amongst the nether stars . . . well, I'm but a poor sailor man, an' my one chance o' regaining home is to follow the skipper."

"Even beyond the sky?"

"Less hazard to that, maybe, than sailing on around the world. The little man swore his vessel was safe, an' no storms blow between the suns."

"Can you trust his word?"

"Oh, aye. Even a knocked-about old palomer like me has seen enough o' men to ken when a one's too timid an' eagersome to stand by a lie. I fear not the folk in Paradise, nor does the skipper. Except in some way . . ." Etien rubbed his bearded jaw, scowling. "In some way I can nay wholly grasp, they affright Rovic. He fears nay they'll come hither wi' torch an' sword; but there's somewhat else about 'em that frets him."

I felt the ground shudder the least bit. Ulas had cleared his throat. "It does seem we'd be daring God's anger—"

"That's nay what gnaws on the skipper's mind. He was never an overpious man." Etien scratched himself, yawned, and climbed to his feet. "Glad I am to be nay the skipper. Let him think over what's best to do. Time ye an' me was asleep."

But I slept little that night.

Rovic, I think, rested well. Yet as the next day wore on, I could see haggardness on him. I wondered why. Did he think the Hisagazi would turn on us? If so, why had he come? As the slope steepened, the wagon grew so toilsome to push and drag that my fears died for lack of breath.

Yet when we came upon the Ship, toward evening, I forgot my weariness. And after an amazed volley of oaths, our mariners rested silent on their pikes. The Hisagazi, never talkative, crouched low in token of awe. Only Guzan remained erect among them. I glimpsed his expression as he stared at the marvel. It was a look of lust.

Wild was that place. We had gone above timberline. The land was a green sea below us, edged with silvery ocean. Here we stood among tumbled black boulders, cinders and spongy tufa underfoot. The mountain rose in steeps and scarps and ravines, on to snows and smoke, which rose another mile into a pale chilly sky. And here stood the Ship.

And the Ship was beauty.

I remember. In length—height, rather, since it stood on its tail—it was about equal to our caravel, in form not unlike a lance head, in color a shining white, untarnished after forty years. That was all. But words are paltry, my lords. What can they show of clean soaring curves, of iridescence on burnished metal, of a thing which was proud and lovely and in its very shape aquiver to be off? How can I conjure back the glamour which hazed that Ship whose keel had cloven starlight?

We stood there a long time. My vision blurred. I wiped my eyes, angry to be seen thus affected, until I noticed a tear glisten in Rovic's red beard. But the captain's visage was quite blank. When he spoke, he said merely, in a flat voice, "Come, let's make camp."

The Hisagazian guardsmen dared approach no closer than these several hundred yards to as potent an idol as the Ship had become. Our mariners were glad to maintain the same distance. But after dark, when everything else was in order, Val Nira led Rovic, Froad, Guzan, and myself to the vessel.

As we approached, a double door in the side swung noiselessly open and a metal gangplank descended therefrom. Glowing in Tambur's light, and in the dull clotted red reflected off the smoke clouds, the Ship was already as strange as I could endure. When it thus beckoned me, as if a ghost stood guard, I whimpered and fled. The cinders crunched beneath my boots; I caught a whiff of sulfurous air.

But at the edge of camp I rallied myself enough to look again. The dark ground blotted up light, so that the Ship appeared alone with its grandeur. Presently I went back.

The interior was lit by luminous panels, cool to the touch. Val Nira explained that the great engine which drove it—as if the troll of folklore were put on a treadmill—was intact, and would furnish power at the flick of a lever. As nearly as I could understand what he said, this was done by changing the metallic part of salt into light . . . thus I do not understand after all. The quicksilver was required for a part of the controls, which channeled power from the engine into another mechanism that hurtled the Ship skyward. We inspected the broken container. Enormous indeed had been the impact of landing, to twist and bend that thick alloy. And yet Val Nira had been shielded by invisible forces, and the rest of the Ship had not suffered important damage. He fetched some tools, which flamed and hummed and whirled, and demonstrated a few repair operations on the broken part. Obviously he would have no trouble completing the work—and then he need only pour in a gallon of quicksilver, to bring his vessel alive again.

Much else did he show us that night. I shall say naught of it, for I cannot even remember such strangeness very clearly, let alone find words. Suffice that Rovic, Froad, and Zhean spent a few hours in Elf Hill.

So, too, did Guzan. Though he had been taken here before, as part of his initiation, he had never been shown this much ere now. Watching him, however, I saw less marveling in him than greed.

No doubt Rovic observed the same. There was little which Rovic did not observe. When we departed the Ship, his silence was not stunned like Froad's or mine. At the time, I thought in a vague fashion that he fretted over the trouble Guzan was certain to make. Now, looking back, I believe his mood was sadness.

Sure it is that long after we others were in our bedrolls, he stood by himself, looking at the planet-lit Ship.

●

Early in a cold dawn, Etien shook me awake. "Up, lad, we've work to do. Load yere pistols an' belt on yere dirk."

"What? What's to happen?" I fumbled with a hoar-frosted blanket. Last night seemed a dream.

"The skipper's nay said, but plainly he awaits a fight. Report to the wagon an' help us move into yon flying tower." Etien's thick form heel-squatted a moment longer beside me. Then, slowly: "Methinks Guzan has some idea o' murdering us here on the mountain. One officer an' a few crewmen can be made to sail the *Golden Leaper* for him, to Giair an' back. The rest o' us would be less trouble to him wi' our weasands slit."

I crawled forth, teeth clattering in my head. After arming myself, I snatched some food from the common store. The Hisagazi on the march carry dried fish and a sort of bread made from a powdered weed. The saints alone knew when I'd next get a chance to eat. I was the last to join Rovic at the cart. The natives were drifting sullenly toward us, unsure what we intended.

"Let's go, lads," said Rovic. He gave his orders. Four men started manhandling the wagon across the rocky trail toward the Ship, where this gleamed among mists. We others stood by, weapons ready. Guzan hastened toward us, Val Nira toiled in his wake.

Anger darkened his countenance. "What are you doing?" he barked.

Rovic gave him a calm stare. "Why, milord, as we may be here for some time, inspecting the wonders aboard the Ship—"

"What?" exclaimed Guzan. "What do you mean? Have you not seen ample for a first visit? We must get home again, and prepare to sail after the flowing stone."

"Go if you wish," said Rovic. "I choose to linger. And since you don't trust me, I reciprocate the feeling. My folk will stay in the Ship, which can be defended if necessary."

Guzan stormed and raged, but Rovic ignored him. Our men continued hauling the cart over the uneven ground. Guzan signaled his spearmen, who approached in a disordered but alert mass. Etien spoke a command. We fell into line. Pikes slanted forward, muskets took aim.

Guzan stepped back. We had demonstrated firearms for him at his home island. Doubtless he could overwhelm us with sheer numbers, were he determined, but the cost would be heavy. "No reason to fight, is there?" purred Rovic. "I am only taking a sensible precaution. The Ship is a most valuable prize. It could bring Paradise for all . . . or dominion over this earth for a few. There are those who'd prefer the latter. I've not accused you of being among them. However, in prudence I'd liefer keep the Ship for my hostage and my fortress, as long as it pleases me to remain here."

I think then I was convinced of Guzan's real intentions, not as a surmise of ours but as plain fact. Had he truly wished to attain the stars, his single concern would have been to keep the Ship safe. He would not have reached out, snatched little Val Nira in his powerful hands, and dragged the starman backward like a shield against our fire. Not that his intent matters, save to my own conscience. Wrath distorted his patterned visage. He screamed at us, "Then I'll keep a hostage too! And much good may your shelter do you!"

The Hisagazi milled about, muttering, hefting their spears and axes, but not prepared to follow us. We grunted our way across the black mountainside. The sun strengthened. Froad twisted his beard. "Dear me, master captain," he said, "think you they'll lay siege to us?"

"I'd not advise anyone to venture forth alone," said Rovic dryly.

"But without Val Nira to explain things, what use for us to stay at the Ship? Best we go back. I've mathematic texts to consult. My head's aspin with the law that binds the turning planets. I must ask the man from Paradise what he knows of—"

Rovic interrupted with a gruff order to three men, that they help lift a wheel wedged between two stones. He was in a savage temper. I confess his action seemed mad to me. If Guzan intended treachery, we had gained little by immobilizing ourselves in the Ship, where he could starve us. Better to let him attack in the open, where we would have a chance of fighting our way through. And if Guzan did not plan to fall on us in the jungle—or any other time—then this was senseless provocation on our part. But I dared not question.

➼

When we had brought our wagon to the Ship, its gangplank again descended for us. The sailors started and cursed. Rovic forced himself out of his bitterness, to speak soothing words. "Easy, lads. I've been aboard already, ye ken. Naught harmful within. Now we must tote our powder thither, an' stow it as I've planned."

Being slight of frame, I was not set to carrying the heavy casks, but put at the foot of the gangplank to watch the Hisagazi. Although we were too far away to distinguish words, I saw how Guzan stood on a boulder and harangued them. They shook their weapons at us and whooped. They did not venture to attack. I wondered wretchedly what this was all about. If Rovic had foreseen us besieged, that would explain why he brought the powder along. . . . No, it would not, for there was more than a dozen men could shoot off in weeks of musketry, even if we had enough bullets . . . and we had almost no food! I looked past the poisonous volcano clouds, to Tambur where storms raged that could engulf our whole earth, and wondered what demons lurked here to possess men.

I sprang to alertness at an indignant shout from within. Froad! Almost, I ran up the gangway, then remembered my duty. I heard Rovic roar him down and order the crewfolk to carry on. Froad and Rovic must have gone by themselves into the pilot's compartment and talked for an hour or more. When the old man emerged, he protested no longer. But as he walked down the gangway, he wept.

Rovic followed, grimmer of countenance than I had ever seen ere now. The sailors filed after, some looking appalled, some relieved, but chiefly watching the Hisagazian camp. They were simply mariners; the Ship was little to them save a weird and disquieting object. Last came Etien, walking backward down the metal plank as he uncoiled a long string.

"Form square!" barked Rovic. The men snapped into position. "Get at the middle, Zhean and Froad," said the captain. "You can better carry extra ammunition than fight." He placed himself in the van.

I tugged Froad's sleeve. "Please, I beg you, master, what's happening?" He sobbed too much to answer.

Etien crouched, flint and steel in his hands. He heard me—for otherwise we were deathly silent—and said in a hard voice: "We placed casks o' powder throughout this hull, lad, wi' powder trains to join 'em. Here's the fuse to the whole."

I could not speak, could not even think, so monstrous was this. As if from immensely far away, I heard the click of stone on metal in Etien's fingers, heard him blow on the spark and add: "A good idea, methinks. I said t'other eventide, I'd follow the skipper wi'out fear o' God's curse— but let's not tempt Him overmuch."

"Forward march!" Rovic's sword blazed clear of the scabbard.

Our feet scrunched loud and horrible on the mountain as we quick-stepped away. I did not look back. I could not. I was still fumbling in a nightmare. Since Guzan would have moved to intercept us anyhow, we proceeded straight toward his band. He stepped forth as we halted at the camp's edge. Val Nira slunk shivering after him. I heard the words dimly.

"Well, Rovic, what now? Are you ready to go home?"

"Yes," said the captain. His voice was dull. "All the way home."

Guzan squinted in rising suspiciousness. "Why did you abandon your wagon? What did you leave behind?"

"Supplies. Come, let's march."

Val Nira stared at the cruel shapes of our pikes. He must wet his lips a few times ere he could quaver, "What are you talking about? There's no reason to leave food there. It would spoil in the time until . . . until—" He faltered as he looked into Rovic's eyes. The blood drained from him.

"What have you done?" he whispered.

Suddenly Rovic's free hand arose, to cover his face. "What I must," he said thickly. "Daughter of God, forgive me."

The starman regarded us an instant more. Then he turned and ran. Past the astonished warriors he burst, out onto the cindery slope, toward his Ship.

"Come back!" bellowed Rovic. "You fool, you'll never—"

He swallowed hard. As he looked after that small, stumbling, lonely shape, hurrying across a fire mountain toward the Beautiful One, the sword sank in his grasp. "Perhaps it's best," he said, like a benediction.

Guzan raised his own sword. In scaly coat and blowing feathers, he was a figure as impressive as steel-clad Rovic. "Tell me what you've done," he snarled, "or I'll kill you this moment!"

He paid our muskets no heed. He, too, had had dreams.

He, too, saw them end, when the Ship exploded.

Even that adamantine hull could not withstand a wagonload of care-fully placed gunpowder, set off at the same time. A crash knocked me to my knees, and the hull cracked open. White-hot chunks of metal screamed across the slopes. I saw one of them strike a boulder and split it in twain. Val Nira vanished, destroyed too quickly to have seen what happened; thus, in the ultimate, God was merciful to him. Through the flames and smokes and doomsday noise which followed, I saw the Ship fall. It rolled down the slope, strewing its mangled guts behind. Then the mountainside grumbled and slid in pursuit, and buried it, and dust hid the sky.

More than this, I have no heart to remember.

The Hisagazi shrieked and fled. They must have thought hell was come to earth. Guzan stood his ground. As the dust enveloped us, hiding the grave of the Ship and the white volcano crater, turning the sun red, he sprang at Rovic. A musketeer raised his weapon. Etien slapped it down. We stood and watched those two men fight, up and over the shaken cinder land, and knew in our private darkness that this was their right.

Sparks flew where the blades clamored together. At last Rovic's skill prevailed. He took his foe in the throat.

We gave Guzan decent burial and went down through the jungle.

That night the guardsmen rallied their courage to attack us. We were aided by our muskets, but must chiefly use sword and pike. We hewed our way through them because we had no place else to go than the sea.

They retreated, but carried word ahead of us. When we reached Nikum, all the forces Iskilip could raise were besieging the *Golden Leaper* and waiting to oppose Rovic's entry. We formed a square again, and no matter how many thousands they had, only a score or so could reach us at any time. Nonetheless, we left six good men in the crimsoned mud of those streets. When our people on the caravel realized Rovic was coming back, they bombarded the town. This ignited the thatch roofs and distracted the enemy enough that a sortie from the ship was able to effect a juncture with us. We chopped our way to the pier, got aboard, and manned the capstan.

Outraged and very brave, the Hisagazi paddled their canoes up to our hull, where our cannon could not be brought to bear. They stood on each other's shoulders to reach our rail. One band forced itself aboard, and the fight was fierce which cleared them from the decks. That was when I got the shattered collarbone which plagues me to this day.

But in the end, we came out of the fjord. A fresh east wind was blowing. Sail aloft, we outran the foe. We counted our dead, bound our wounds, and slept.

☞

Next dawning, awakened by the pain of my wound and the worse pain within, I mounted the quarterdeck. The sky was overcast. The wind had stiffened; the sea ran cold and green, whitecaps out to a cloudy-gray horizon. Timbers groaned and rigging thrummed. I stood an hour facing aft, into the chill wind that numbs pain.

When I heard boots behind me, I did not turn around. I knew they were Rovic's. He stood beside me a long while, bareheaded. I noticed that he was starting to turn gray.

Finally, not yet regarding me, still squinting into the air that lashed tears from our eyes, he said: "I had a chance to talk Froad over, that day. He was grieved, but owned I was right. Has he spoken to you about it?"

"No," I said.

"None of us are ever likely to speak of it much," said Rovic.

After another time: "I was not afraid Guzan or anyone else would seize the Ship and try to turn conqueror. We men of Montalir should well be able to deal with any such rogues. Nor was I afraid of the Paradise dwellers. That poor little man could only have been telling truth. They would never have harmed us . . . willingly. They would have brought precious gifts, and taught us their esoteric arts, and let us visit their stars."

"Then why?" I got out.

"Someday Froad's successors will solve the riddles of the universe," he said. "Someday our descendants will build their own Ship, and go forth to whatever destiny they wish."

Spume blew around us until our hair was wet. I tasted the salt on my lips.

"Meanwhile," said Rovic, "we'll sail the seas of this earth, and walk its mountains, and chart and subdue and come to understand it. Do you see, Zhean? That is what the Ship would have taken from us."

Then I was also made able to weep. He laid his hand on my uninjured shoulder and stood with me while the *Golden Leaper*, all sail set, proceeded westward.

Hot Planet

HAL CLEMENT

Hal Clement—the writing name of longtime science teacher Harry Clement Stubbs—made his first sale in 1942, to Astounding, and became one of the mainstays of that magazine throughout the fifties and sixties, with much of his best short work appearing there. Clement's most famous novel is Mission of Gravity, which in retrospect still holds up as one of the best science-fiction books of the sixties, although I am also fond of the underrated Cycle of Fire. Clement's influence on later writers such as G. David Nordley, Stephen Baxter, Harry Turtledove, Janet Kagan, and others is clear and unmistakable. His other books include the novels Star Light (the sequel to Mission of Gravity), Needle, Close to Critical, Iceworld, Ocean on Top, and The Nitrogen Fix and the collections Small Changes, Natives of Space, and The Best of Hal Clement.

Although known as one of the most scrupulously accurate of the "hard science" writers, someone careful to always get the scientific details right, Clement also has a rich and lively imagination, especially when it comes to alien lifeforms, and he has created some of the most memorable alien characters in science fiction. His major contribution to the theme of exploration happens also to be the book that features his most intriguing alien characters, Mission of Gravity, in which two different parties of explorers, one human and one native, find they must work together in order to succeed in a mission on the surface of the bizarre high-gravity world Mesklin, where the gravity varies from 3g at the equator to 700g at the poles, one of the strangest alien worlds ever explored in print.

There are no aliens in the taut, suspenseful tale that follows, but it remains one of the classic stories of space exploration and a reminder of how humans exploring hostile environments must somehow be prepared even for the totally unexpected—or else! (Note: It's an irony in the face of Clement's reputation for rigorous hard science that almost everything he says here about the planet Mercury is wrong, but it's not his fault that later, fuller information led scientists to change their minds; at the time, in 1963, the story stuck scrupulously to the "facts" about Mercury as they were known—or thought to be known. This is one of the dangers of hard science writing—no matter how much research you do the facts themselves can always change tomorrow, undoing all your hard work. You still ought to get points for trying, though!)

Clement's most recent books are a new novel, Half Life, and an omnibus reprint of three of his previous novels (Needle, Iceworld, and Close to Critical), bound together as The Essential Hal Clement, Volume 1: Trio for Slide Rule and Typewriter (NESFA Press, PO Box 809, Framingham, MA 01701—$25 plus $2 postage). Keep an eye out for the next volume in this series, as it's bringing a lot of Clement's long-unavailable work back into print.

I

The wind which had nearly turned the *Albireo*'s landing into a disaster instead of a mathematical exercise was still playing tunes about the fins and landing legs as Schlossberg made his way down to Deck Five.

The noise didn't bother him particularly, though the endless seismic tremors made him dislike the ladders. But just now he was able to ignore both. He was curious—though not hopeful. "Is there anything at all obvious on the last set of tapes, Joe?"

Mardikian, the geophysicist, shrugged. "Just what you'd expect . . . on a planet which has at least one quake in each fifty-mile-square area every five minutes. You know yourself we had a nice seismic programme set up, but when we touched down we found we couldn't carry it out. We've done our best with the natural tremors—incidentally stealing most of the record tapes the other projects would have used. We have a lot of nice information for the computers back home; but it will take all of them to make any sense out of it."

Schlossberg nodded; the words had not been necessary. His astronomical programme had been one of those sabotaged by the transfer of tapes to the seismic survey.

"I just hoped," he said. "We each have an idea why Mercury developed an atmosphere during the last few decades, but I guess the high school kids on Earth will know whether it's right before we do. I'm resigned to living in a chess-type universe—few and simple rules, but infinite combinations of them. But it would be nice to know an answer sometime."

"So it would. As a matter of fact, I need to know a couple right now. From you. How close to finished are the other programmes—or what's left of them?"

"I'm all set," replied Schlossberg. "I have a couple of instruments still monitoring the sun just in case, but everything in the revised programme is on tape."

"Good. Tom, any use asking you?"

The biologist grimaced. "I've been shown two hundred and sixteen different samples of rock and dust. I have examined in detail twelve crystal growths which looked vaguely like vegetation. Nothing was alive or contained living things by any standards I could conscientiously set."

Mardikian's gesture might have meant sympathy.

"Camille?"

"I may as well stop now as any time. I'll never be through. Tape didn't make much difference to me, but I wish I knew what weight of specimens I could take home."

"Eileen?" Mardikian's glance at the stratigrapher took the place of the actual question.

"Cam speaks for me, except that I could have used any more tape you could have spared. What I have is gone."

"All right, that leaves me, the tape-thief. The last spools are in the seismographs now, and will start running out in seventeen hours. The tractors will start out on their last rounds in sixteen, and should be back in roughly a week. Will, does that give you enough to figure the weights we rockhounds can have on the return trip?"

The *Albireo*'s captain nodded. "Close enough. There really hasn't been much question since it became evident we'd find nothing for the mass tanks here. I'll have a really precise check in an hour, but I can tell right now that you have about one and a half metric tons to split up among the three of you.

"Ideal departure time is three hundred and ten hours away, as you all know. We can stay here until then, or go into a parking-and-survey orbit at almost any time before then. You have all the survey you need, I should think, from the other time. But suit yourselves."

"I'd just as soon be space-sick as seasick," remarked Camille Burkett. "I still hate to think that the entire planet is as shivery as the spot we picked."

Willard Rowson smiled. "You researchers told me where to land after ten days in orbit mapping this rockball. I set you just where you asked. If you'd found even five tons of juice we could use in the reaction tanks I could still take you to another one—if you could agree which one. I hate to say 'Don't blame me,' but I can't think of anything else that fits."

"So we sit until the last of the tractors is back with the precious seismo tapes, playing battleship while our back teeth are being shaken out by earthquakes—excuse the word. What a thrill! Glorious adventure!" Zaino, the communications specialist who had been out of a job almost constantly since the landing, spoke sourly. The captain was the only one who saw fit to answer.

"If you want adventure, you made a mistake exploring space. The only space adventures I've heard of are second-hand stories built on guesswork; the people who really had them weren't around to tell about it. Unless Dr. Marini discovers a set of Mercurian monsters at the last minute and they invade the ship or cut off one of the tractors, I'm afraid you'll have to do without adventures." Zaino grimaced.

"That sounds funny coming from a spaceman, Captain. I didn't really mean adventure, though; all I want is something to do besides betting whether the next quake will come in one minute or five. I haven't even had to fix a suit-radio since we touched down. How about my going out with one of the tractors on this last trip, at least?"

"It's all right with me," replied Rowson, "but Dr. Mardikian runs the professional part of this operation. I require that Spurr, Trackman, Hargedon and Aiello go as drivers, since without them even a minor mechanical problem would be more than an adventure. As I recall it, Dr. Harmon, Dr. Schlossberg, Dr. Marini and Dr. Mardikian are scheduled to go; but if any one of them is willing to let you take his or her place, I certainly don't mind."

The radioman looked around hopefully. The geologists and the biologist shook their heads negatively, firmly and unanimously; but the astronomer pondered for a moment. Zaino watched tensely.

"It may be all right," Schlossberg said at last. "What I want to get is a set of wind, gas pressure, gas temperature and gas composition measures around the route. I didn't expect to be more meteorologist than astronomer when we left Earth, and didn't have exactly the right equipment. Hargedon and Aiello helped me improvise some, and this is the first chance to use it on the Darkside. If you can learn what has to be done with it before starting time, though, you are welcome to my place."

The communicator got to his feet fast enough to leave the deck in Mercury's feeble gravity.

"Lead me to it, Doc. I guess I can learn to read a home-made weathervane!"

"Is that merely bragging, or a challenge?" drawled a voice which had not previously joined the discussion. Zaino flushed a bit.

"Sorry, Luigi," he said hastily. "I didn't mean it just that way. But I still think I can run the stuff."

"Likely enough," Aiello replied. "Remember though, it wasn't made just for talking into." Schlossberg, now on his feet, cut in quickly.

"Come on, Arnie. We'll have to suit up to see the equipment; it's outside."

He shepherded the radioman to the hatch at one side of the deck and shooed him down towards the engine and air lock levels. Both were silent for some moments; but, safely out of earshot of Deck Five, the younger man looked up and spoke.

"You needn't push, Doc. I wasn't going to make anything of it. Luigi was right, and I asked for it." The astronomer slowed a bit in his descent.

"I wasn't really worried," he replied, "but we have several months yet before we can get away from each other, and I don't like talk that could set up grudges. Matter of fact, I'm even a little uneasy about having the girls along, though I'm no misogynist."

"Girls? They're not—"

"There goes your foot again. Even Harmon is about ten years older than you, I suppose. But they're girls to me. What's more important, they no doubt think of themselves as girls."

"Even Dr. Burkett? That is—I mean—"

"Even Dr. Burkett. Here, get into your suit. And maybe you'd better take out the mike. It'll be enough if you can listen for the next hour or two." Zaino made no answer, suspecting with some justice that anything he said would be wrong.

Each made final check on the other's suit; then they descended one more level to the air lock. This occupied part of the same deck as the fusion plants, below the wings and reaction mass tanks but above the main engine. Its outer door was just barely big enough to admit a spacesuited person. Even with the low air pressure carried by spaceships, a large door area meant large total force on jamb, hinges and locks. It opened on to a small balcony from which a ladder led to the ground. The two men paused on the balcony to look over the landscape.

This hadn't changed noticeably since the last time either had been out, though there might have been some small difference in the volcanic cones a couple of miles away to the north-east. The furrows down the sides of these, which looked as though they had been cut by water but were actually bone-dry ash slides, were always undergoing alteration as gas from below kept blowing fresh scoria fragments out of the craters.

The spines—steep, jagged fragments of rock which thrust upward from the plain beyond and to both sides of the cones—seemed dead as ever.

The level surface between the *Albireo* and the cones was more interesting. Mardikian and Schlossberg believed it to be a lava sheet dating from early in Mercury's history, when more volatile substances still existed in the surface rocks to cut down their viscosity when molten. They supposed that much—perhaps most—of the surface around the "twilight" belt had been flooded by this very liquid lava, which had cooled to a smoother surface than most Earthly lava flows.

How long it had stayed cool they didn't guess. But both men felt sure that Mercury must have periodic upheavals as heat accumulated inside it—heat coming not from radioactivity but from tidal energy. Mercury's orbit is highly eccentric. At perihelion, tidal force tries to pull it apart along the planet-to-sun line, while at aphelion the tidal force is less and the little world's own gravity tries to bring it back to a spherical shape. The real change in form is not great, but a large force working through even a small amount of distance can mean a good deal of energy.

If the energy can't leak out—and Mercury's rocks conduct heat no better than those of Earth—the temperature must rise.

Sooner or later, the men argued, deeply buried rock must fuse to magma. Its liquefaction would let the bulk of the planet give farther under tidal stress, so heat would be generated even faster. Eventually a girdle of magma would have to form far below the crust all around the twilight strip, where the tidal strain would be greatest. Sooner or later this would melt its way to the surface, giving the zone a period of intense volcanic activity and, incidentally, giving the planet a temporary atmosphere.

The idea was reasonable. It had, the astronomer admitted, been suggested long before to account for supposed vulcanism on the moon. It justified the careful examination that Schlossberg and Zaino gave the plain before they descended the ladder; for it made reasonable the occasional changes which were observed to occur in the pattern of cracks weaving over its surface.

No one was certain just how permanent the local surface was—though no one could really justify feeling safer on board the *Albireo* than outside on the lava. If anything really drastic happened, the ship would be no protection.

The sun, hanging just above the horizon slightly to the watcher's right, cast long shadows which made the cracks stand out clearly; as far as either man could see, nothing had changed recently. They descended the ladder carefully—even the best designed spacesuits are somewhat vulnerable—and made their way to the spot where the tractors were parked.

A sheet-metal fence a dozen feet high and four times as long provided shade, which was more than a luxury this close to the sun. The tractors were parked in this shadow, and beside and between them were piles of equipment and specimens. The apparatus Schlossberg had devised was beside the tractor at the north end of the line, just inside the shaded area.

It was still just inside the shade when they finished, four hours later. Hargedon had joined them during the final hour and helped pack the equipment in the tractor he was to drive. Zaino had had no trouble in learning to make the observations Schlossberg wanted, and the youngster was almost unbearably cocky. Schlossberg hoped, as they returned to the *Albireo*, that no one would murder the communications expert in the next twelve hours. There would be nothing to worry about after the trip started; Hargedon was quite able to keep anyone in his place without being nasty about it. If Zaino had been going with Aiello or Harmon— but he wasn't, and it was pointless to dream up trouble.

And no trouble developed all by itself.

II

Zaino was not only still alive but still reasonably popular when the first of the tractors set out, carrying Eileen Harmon and Eric Trackman, the *Albireo*'s nuclear engineer.

It started more than an hour before the others, since the stratigrapher's drilling programme, "done" or not, took extra time. The tractor hummed off to the south, since both Darkside routes required a long detour to pass the chasm to the west. Routes had been worked out from the stereophotos taken during the orbital survey. Even Darkside had been covered fairly well with Uniquantum film under Venus light.

The Harmon-Trackman vehicle was well out of sight when Mardikian and Aiello started out on one of the Brightside routes, and a few minutes later Marini set out on the other with the spacesuit technician, Mary Spurr, driving.

Both vehicles disappeared quickly into a valley to the northeast, between the ash cones and a thousand-foot spine which rose just south of them. All the tractors were in good radio contact; Zaino made sure of that before he abandoned the radio watch to Rowson, suited up and joined Hargedon at the remaining one. They climbed in, and Hargedon set it in motion.

At about the same time, the first tractor came into view again, now travelling north on the farther side of the chasm. Hargedon took this as evidence that the route thus far was unchanged, and kicked in highest speed.

The cabin was pretty cramped, even though some of the equipment had been attached outside. The men could not expect much comfort for the next week.

Hargedon was used to the trips, however. He disapproved on principle of people who complained about minor inconveniences such as having to sleep in spacesuits; fortunately, Zaino's interest and excitement overrode any thought he might have had about discomfort.

This lasted through the time they spent doubling the vast crack in Mercury's crust, driving on a little to the north of the ship on the other side and then turning west towards the dark hemisphere. The route was identical to that of Harmon's machine for some time, though no trace of its passage showed on the hard surface. Then Hargedon angled off towards the southwest. He had driven this run often enough to know it well even without the markers which had been set out with the seismographs. The photographic maps were also aboard. With them, even Zaino had no trouble keeping track of their progress while they remained in sunlight.

However, the sun sank as they travelled west. In two hours its lower rim would have been on the horizon, had they been able to see the horizon; as it was, more of the "sea level" lava plain was in the shadow than not, even near the ship, and their route now lay in semi-darkness.

The light came from peaks projecting into the sunlight, from scattered sky-light which was growing rapidly fainter and from the brighter celestial objects such as Earth. Even with the tractor's lights it was getting harder to spot crevasses and seismometer markers. Zaino quickly found the fun wearing off . . . though his pride made him cover this fact as best he could.

If Hargedon saw this, he said nothing. He set Zaino to picking up every other instrument, as any partner would have, making no allowance for the work the youngster was doing for Schlossberg. This might, of course, have had the purpose of keeping the radioman too busy to think about discomfort. Or it might merely have been Hargedon's idea of normal procedure.

Whatever the cause, Zaino got little chance to use the radio once they had driven into the darkness. He managed only one or two brief talks with those left at the ship.

The talks might have helped his morale, since they certainly must have given the impression that nothing was going on in the ship while at least he had something to do in the tractor. However, this state of affairs did not last. Before the vehicle was four hours out of sight of the *Albireo*, a broadcast by Camille Burkett reached them.

The mineralogist's voice contained at least as much professional enthusiasm as alarm, but everyone listening must have thought promptly of the dubious stability of Mercury's crust. The call was intended for her fellow geologists Mardikian and Harmon. But it interested Zaino at least as much.

"Joe! Eileen! There's a column of what looks like black smoke rising over Northeast Spur. It can't be a real fire, of course; I can't see its point of origin, but if it's the convection current it seems to be the source must be pretty hot. It's the closest thing to a genuine volcano I've seen since we arrived; it's certainly not another of those ash mounds. I should think you'd still be close enough to make it out, Joe. Can you see anything?"

The reply from Mardikian's tractor was inaudible to Zaino and Hargedon, but Burkett's answer made its general tenor plain.

"I hadn't thought of that. Yes, I'd say it was pretty close to the Brightside route. It wouldn't be practical for you to stop your run now to come back to see. You couldn't do much about it anyway. I could go out to have a look and then report to you. If the way back is blocked there'll be plenty of time to work out another." Hargedon and Zaino passed questioning glances at each other during the shorter pause that followed.

"I know there aren't," the voice then went on, responding to the words they could not hear, "but it's only two or three miles, I'd say. Two to the spur and not much farther to where I could see the other side. Enough of the way is in shade so I could make it in a suit easily enough. I can't see calling back either of the Darkside tractors. Their work is just as important as the rest—anyway, Eileen is probably out of range. She hasn't answered yet." Another pause.

"That's true. Still, it would mean sacrificing that set of seismic records—no, wait. We could go out later for those. And Mel could take his own weather measures on the later trip. There's plenty of time!" Pause, longer this time.

"You're right, of course. I just wanted to get an early look at this volcano, if it is one. We'll let the others finish their runs, and when you get back you can check the thing from the other side yourself. If it is blocking your way there's time to find an alternate route. We could be doing that from the maps in the meantime, just in case."

Zaino looked again at his companion.

"Isn't that just my luck!" he exclaimed. "I jump at the first chance to get away from being bored to death. The minute I'm safely away, the only interesting thing of the whole operation happens—back at the ship!"

"Who asked to come on this trip?"

"Oh, I'm not blaming anyone but myself. If I'd stayed back there the volcano would have popped out here somewhere, or else waited until we were gone."

"If it is a volcano. Dr. Burkett didn't seem quite sure."

"No, and I'll bet a nickel she's suiting up right now to go out and see. I hope she comes back with something while we're still near enough to hear about it."

Hargedon shrugged. "I suppose it was also just your luck that sent you on a Darkside trip? You know the radio stuff. You knew we couldn't reach as far this way with the radios. Didn't you think of that in advance?"

"I didn't think of it, any more than you would have. It was bad luck, but I'm not grousing about it. Let's get on with this job." Hargedon nodded with approval, and possibly with some surprise, and the tractor hummed on its way.

The darkness deepened around the patches of lava shown by the driving lights; the sky darkened towards a midnight hue, with stars showing ever brighter through it; and radio reception from the *Albireo* began to get spotty. Gas density at the ion layer was high enough so that recombination of molecules with their radiation-freed electrons was rapid. Only occasional streamers of ionised gas reached far over Darkside. As these thinned out, so did radio reception. Camille Burkett's next broadcast came through very poorly.

There was enough in it, however, to seize the attention of the two men in the tractor.

She was saying: ". . . real all right, and dangerous. It's the . . . thing I ever saw . . . kinds of lava from what looks like . . . same vent. There's high viscosity stuff building a spatter cone to end all spatter cones, and some very thin fluid from somewhere at the bottom. The flow has already blocked the valley used by the Brightside routes and is coming along it. A new return route will have to be found for the tractors that . . . was spreading fast when I saw it. I can't tell how much will come. But unless it stops there's nothing at all to keep the flow away from the ship. It isn't coming fast, but it's coming. I'd advise all tractors to turn back. Captain Rowson reminds me that only one take-off is possible. If we leave this site, we're committed to leaving Mercury. Arnie and Ren, do you hear me?"

Zaino responded at once. "We got most of it, Doctor. Do you really think the ship is in danger?"

"I don't know. I can only say that *if* this flow continues the ship will have to leave, because this area will sooner or later be covered. I can't guess how likely . . . check further to get some sort of estimate. It's different from any Earthly lava source—maybe you heard—should try to get Eileen and Eric back, too. I can't raise them. I suppose they're well out from under the ion layer by now. Maybe you're close enough to them to catch them with diffracted waves. Try, anyway. Whether you can raise them or not you'd better start back yourself."

Hargedon cut in at this point. "What does Dr. Mardikian say about that? We still have most of the seismometers on this route to visit."

"I think Captain Rowson has the deciding word here, but if it helps your decision Dr. Mardikian has already started back. He hasn't finished his route, either. So hop back here, Ren. And Arnie, put that technical skill you haven't had to use yet to work raising Eileen and Eric."

"What I can do, I will," replied Zaino, "but you'd better tape a recall message and keep it going out on. Let's see—band F."

"All right. I'll be ready to check the volcano as soon as you get back. How long?"

"Seven hours—maybe six and a half," replied Hargedon. "We have to be careful."

"Very well. Stay outside when you arrive; I'll want to go right out in the tractor to get a closer look." She cut off.

"And *that* came through clearly enough!" remarked Hargedon as he swung the tractor around. "I've been awake for fourteen hours, driving off and on for ten or them; I'm about to drive for another six; and then I'm to stand by for more."

"Would you like me to do some of the driving?" asked Zaino.

"I guess you'll have to, whether I like it or not," was the rather lukewarm reply. "I'll keep on for a while, though—until we're back in better light. You get at your radio job."

III

Zaino tried. Hour after hour he juggled from one band to another. Once he had Hargedon stop while he went out to attach a makeshift antenna which, he hoped, would change his output from broadcast to some sort of beam; after this he kept probing the sky with the "beam," first listening to the *Albireo*'s broadcast in an effort to find projecting wisps of iono-sphere and then, whenever he thought he had one, switching on his trans-mitter and driving his own message at it.

Not once did he complain about lack of equipment or remark how much better he could do once he was back at the ship.

Hargedon's silence began to carry an undercurrent of approval not usual in people who spent much time with Zaino. The technician made no further reference to the suggestion of switching drivers. They came in sight of the *Albireo* and doubled the chasm with Hargedon still at the wheel, Zaino still at his radio and both of them still uncertain whether any of the calls had got through.

Both had to admit, even before they could see the ship, that Burkett had had a right to be impressed.

The smoke column showed starkly against the sky, blowing back over the tractor and blocking the sunlight which would otherwise have glared into the driver's eyes. Fine particles fell from it in a steady shower; looking back, the men could see tracks left by their vehicle in the deposit which had already fallen.

As they approached the ship the dark pillar grew denser and narrower, while the particles raining from it became coarser. In some places the ash was drifting into fairly deep piles, giving Hargedon some anxiety about possible concealed cracks. The last part of the trip, along the edge of the great chasm and around its end, was really dangerous; cracks running from its sides were definitely spreading. The two men reached the *Albireo* later than Hargedon had promised, and found Burkett waiting impatiently with a pile of apparatus beside her.

She didn't wait for them to get out before starting to organise.

"There isn't much here. We'll take off just enough of what you're carrying to make room for this. No—wait. I'll have to check some of your equipment; I'm going to need one of Milt Schlossberg's gadgets, I think, so leave that on. We'll take—"

"Excuse me, Doctor," cut in Hargedon. "Our suits need servicing, or at least mine will if you want me to drive you. Perhaps Arnie can help you load for a while, if you don't think it's too important for him to get at the radio—"

"Of course. Excuse me. I should have had someone out here to help me with this. You two go on in. Ren, please get back as soon as you can. I can do the work here; none of this stuff is very heavy."

Zaino hesitated as he swung out of the cab. True, there wasn't too much to be moved, and it wasn't very heavy in Mercury's gravity, and he really should be at the radio; but the thirty-nine-year-old mineralogist was a middle-aged lady by his standards, and shouldn't be allowed to carry heavy packages . . .

"Get along, Arnie!" the middle-aged lady interrupted this train of thought. "Eric and Eileen are getting farther away and harder to reach every second you dawdle!"

He got, though he couldn't help looking north-east as he went rather than where he was going.

The towering menace in that direction would have claimed anyone's attention. The pillar of sable ash was rising straighter, as though the wind were having less effect on it. An equally black cone had risen into sight beyond Northeast Spur—a cone that must have grown to some two thousand feet in roughly ten hours. It had far steeper sides than the cinder mounds near it; it couldn't be made of the same loose ash. Perhaps it consisted of half-melted particles which were fusing together as they fell—that might be what Burkett had meant by "spatter-cone." Still, if that were the case, the material fountaining from the cone's top should be lighting the plain with its incandescence rather than casting an inky shadow for its entire height.

Well, that was a problem for the geologists; Zaino climbed aboard and settled to his task.

The trouble was that he could do very little more here than he could in the tractor. He could have improvised longer-wave transmitting coils whose radiations would have diffracted a little more effectively beyond the horizon, but the receiver on the missing vehicle would not have detected them. He had more power at his disposal, but could only beam it into empty space with his better antennae. He had better equipment for locating any projecting wisps of charged gas which might reflect his waves, but he was already located under a solid roof of the stuff—the *Albireo* was technically on Brightside. Bouncing his beam from this layer still didn't give him the range he needed, as he had found both by calculation and trial.

What he really needed was a relay satellite. The target was simply too far around Mercury's sharp curve by now for anything less.

Zaino's final gesture was to set his transmission beam on the lowest frequency the tractor would pick up, aim it as close to the vehicle's direction as he could calculate from map and itinerary and set the recorded return message going. He told Rowson as much.

"Can't think of anything else?" the captain asked. "Well, neither can I, but of course it's not my field. I'd give a year's pay if I could. How long before they should be back in range?"

"About four days. A hundred hours, give or take a few. They'll be heading back anyway by that time."

"Of course. Well, keep trying."

"I am—or rather, the equipment is. I don't see what else I can do unless a really bright idea should suddenly sprout. Is there anywhere else I could be useful? I'm as likely to have ideas working as just sitting."

"We can keep you busy, all right. But how about taking a transmitter up one of those mountains? That would get your wave farther."

"Not as far as it's going already. I'm bouncing it off the ion layer, which is higher than any mountain we've seen on Mercury even if it's nowhere near as high as Earth's."

"Hmph. All right."

"I could help Ren and Dr. Burkett. I could hang on outside the tractor—"

"They've already gone. You'd better call them, though, and keep a log of what they do."

"All right." Zaino turned back to his board and with no trouble raised the tractor carrying Hargedon and the mineralogist. The latter had been trying to call the *Albireo* and had some acid comments about radio operators who slept on the job.

"There's only one of me, and I've been trying to get the Darkside team," he pointed out. "Have you found anything new about this lava flood?"

"Flow, not flood," corrected the professional automatically. "We're not in sight of it yet. We've just rounded the corner that takes us out of your sight. It's over a mile yet, and a couple of more corners, before we get to the spot where I left it. Of course, it will be closer than that by now. It was spreading at perhaps a hundred yards an hour then. That's one figure we must refine . . . Of course, I'll try to get samples, too. I wish there were some way to get samples of the central cone. The whole thing is the queerest volcano I've ever heard of. Have you got Eileen started back?"

"Not as far as I can tell. As with your cone samples, there are practical difficulties," replied Zaino. "I haven't quit yet, though."

"I should think not. If some of us were paid by the idea we'd be pretty poor, but the perspiration part of genius is open to all of us."

"You mean I should charge a bonus for getting this call through?" retorted the operator.

Whatever Burkett's reply to this might have been was never learned; her attention was diverted at that point.

"We've just come in sight of the flow. It's about five hundred yards ahead. We'll get as close as seems safe, and I'll try to make sure whether it's really lava or just mud."

"Mud? Is that possible? I thought there wasn't—couldn't be—any water on this planet!"

"It is, and there probably isn't. The liquid phase of mud doesn't have to be water, even though it usually is on Earth. Here, for example, it might conceivably be sulphur."

"But if it's just mud, it wouldn't hurt the ship, would it?"

"Probably not."

"Then why all this fuss about getting the tractors back in a hurry?"

The voice which answered reminded him of another lady in his past, who had kept him after school for drawing pictures in maths class.

"Because in my judgment the flow is far more likely to be lava than mud, and if I must be wrong I'd rather my error were one that left us alive. I have no time at the moment to explain the basis of my judgment. I will be reporting our activities quite steadily from now on, and would prefer that you not interrupt unless a serious emergency demands it, or you get a call from Eileen.

"We are about three hundred yards away now. The front is moving about as fast as before, which suggests that the flow is coming only along this valley. It's only three or four feet high, so viscosity is very low or density very high. Probably the former, considering where we are. It's as black as the smoke column."

"Not glowing?" cut in Zaino thoughtlessly.

"*Black*, I said. Temperature will be easier to measure when we get closer. The front is nearly straight across the valley, with just a few lobes projecting ten or twelve yards and one notch where a small spine is being surrounded. By the way, I trust you're taping all this?" Again Zaino was reminded of the afternoon after school.

"Yes, Ma'am," he replied. "On my one and only monitor tape."

"Very well. We're stopping near the middle of the valley one hundred yards from the front. I am getting out, and will walk as close as I can with a sampler and a radiometer. I assume that the radio equipment will continue to relay my suit broadcast back to you." Zaino cringed a little, certain as he was that the tractor's electronic apparatus was in perfect order.

It struck him that Dr. Burkett was being more snappish than usual. It never crossed his mind that the woman might be afraid.

"Ren, don't get any closer with the tractor unless I call. I'll get a set of temperature readings as soon as I'm close enough. Then I'll try to get a sample. Then I'll come back with that to the tractor, leave it and the radiometer and get the markers to set out."

"Couldn't I be putting out the markers while you get the sample, Doctor?"

"You could, but I'd rather you stayed at the wheel." Hargedon made no answer, and Burkett resumed her description for the record.

"I'm walking towards the front, a good deal faster than it's flowing towards me. I am now about twenty yards away, and am going to take a set of radiation-temperature measures." A brief pause. "Readings coming. Nine sixty. Nine eighty. Nine ninety—that's from the bottom edge near the spine that's being surrounded. Nine eighty-five—" The voice droned on until about two dozen readings had been taped. Then, "I'm going closer now. The sampler is just a ladle on a twelve-foot handle we improvised, so I'll have to get that close. The stuff is moving slowly; there should be no trouble. I'm in reach now. The lava is very liquid; there's no trouble getting the sampler in—or out again—it's not very dense, either. I'm heading back towards the tractor now. No, Ren, don't come to meet me."

There was a minute of silence, while Zaino pictured the spacesuited figure, with its awkwardly long burden, walking away from the creeping menace to the relative safety of the tractor. "It's frozen solid already; we needn't worry about spilling. The temperature is about—five eighty. Give me the markers, please."

Another pause, shorter this time. Zaino wondered how much of that could be laid to a faster walk without the ladle and how much to the lessening distance between flow and tractor. "I'm tossing the first marker close to the edge—it's landed less than a foot from the lava. They're all on a light cord at ten-foot intervals; I'm paying out the cord as I go back to the tractor. Now we'll stand by and time the arrival at each marker as well as we can."

"How close are you to the main cone?" asked Zaino.

"Not close enough to see its base, I'm afraid. Or to get a sample of it, which is worse. We—goodness, what was that?"

Zaino had just time to ask, "What was what?" when he found out.

IV

For a moment, he thought that the *Albireo* had been flung bodily into the air. Then he decided that the great metal pillar had merely fallen over. Finally he realised that the ship was still erect, but the ground under it had just tried to leave.

Everyone in the group had become so used to the almost perpetual ground tremors that they had ceased to notice them; but this one demanded attention. Rowson, using language which suggested that his career might not have been completely free of adventure after all, flashed through the communication level on his way down to the power section. Schlossberg and Babineau followed, the medic pausing to ask Zaino if he were all right. The radioman merely nodded affirmatively; his attention was already back at his job. Burkett was speaking a good deal faster than before.

"Never mind if the sample isn't lashed tight yet—if it falls off there'll be plenty more. There isn't time! Arnie, get in touch with Dr. Mardikian and Dr. Marini. Tell them that this volcano is explosive, that all estimates of what the flow may do are off until we can make more measures, and in any case the whole situation is unpredictable. Everyone should get back as soon as possible. Remember, we decided that those big craters Eileen checked were not meteor pits. I don't know whether this thing will let go in the next hour, the next year, or at all. Maybe what's happening now will act as a safety valve—but let's get out. Ren, that flow is speeding up and getting higher, and the ash rain is getting a lot worse. Can you see to drive?"

She fell silent. Zaino, in spite of her orders, left his set long enough to leap to the nearest port for a look at the volcano.

He never regretted it.

Across the riven plain, whose cracks were now nearly hidden under the new ash, the black cone towered above the nearer elevations. It was visibly taller than it had been only a few hours before. The fountain from its top was thicker, now jetting straight up as though wind no longer meant a thing to the fiercely driven column of gas and dust. The darkness was not so complete; patches of red and yellow incandescence showed briefly in the pillar, and glowing sparks rather than black cinders rained back on the steep slopes. Far above, a ring of smoke rolled and spread about the column, forming an ever-broadening blanket of opaque cloud above a landscape which had never before been shaded from the sun. Streamers of lightning leaped between cloud and pillar, pillar and mountain, even cloud and ground. Any thunder there might have been was drowned in the howl of the escaping gas, a roar which seemed to combine every possible note from the shrillest possible whistle to a bass felt by the chest rather than heard by the ears. Rowson's language had become inaudible almost before he had disappeared down the hatch.

For long moments the radioman watched the spreading cloud, and wondered whether the *Albireo* could escape being struck by the flickering, ceaseless lightning. Far above the widening ring of cloud the smoke fountain drove, spreading slowly in the thinning atmosphere and beyond it. Zaino had had enough space experience to tell at a glance whether a smoke or dust cloud was in air or not. This wasn't, at least at the upper extremity . . .

And then, quite calmly, he turned back to his desk, aimed the antenna straight up, and called Eileen Harmon. She answered promptly.

The stratigrapher listened without interruption to his report and the order to return. She conferred briefly with her companion, replied "We'll be back in twelve hours," and signed off. And that was that.

Zaino settled back with a sigh, and wondered whether it would be tactful to remind Rowson of his offer of a year's pay.

All four vehicles were now homeward bound; all one had to worry about was whether any of them would make it. Hargedon and Burkett were fighting their way through an ever-increasing ash rain a scant two miles away—ash which not only cut visibility but threatened to block the way with drifts too deep to negotiate. The wind, now blowing fiercely towards the volcano, blasted the gritty stuff against their front window as though it would erode through; and the lava flow, moving far faster than the gentle ooze they had never quite measured, surged—and glowed— grimly behind.

A hundred miles or more to the east, the tractors containing Mardikian, Marini and their drivers headed south-west along the alternate route their maps had suggested; but Mardikian, some three hours in the lead, reported that he could see four other smoke columns in that general direction.

Mercury seemed to be entering a new phase. The maps might well be out of date.

Harmon and Trackman were having no trouble at the moment, but they would have to pass the great chasm. This had been shooting out daughter cracks when Zaino and Hargedon passed it hours before. No one could say what it might be like now, and no one was going out to make sure.

"We can see you!" Burkett's voice came through suddenly. "Half a mile to go, and we're way ahead of the flow."

"But it's coming?" Rowson asked tensely. He had returned from the power level at Zaino's phoned report of success.

"It's coming."

"How fast? When will it get here? Do you know whether the ship can stand contact with it?"

"I don't know the speed exactly. There may be two hours, maybe five or six. The ship can't take it. Even the temperature measures I got were above the softening point of the alloys, and it's hotter and much deeper now. Anyway, if the others aren't back before the flow reaches the ship they won't get through. The tractor wheels would char away, and I doubt that the bodies would float. You certainly can't wade through the stuff in a spacesuit, either."

"And you think there can't be more than five or six hours before the flow arrives?"

"I'd say that was a very optimistic guess. I'll stop and get a better speed estimate if you want, but won't swear to it."

Rowson thought for a moment.

"No," he said finally, "don't bother. Get back here as soon as you can. We need the tractor and human muscles more than we need even expert guesses." He turned to the operator.

"Zaino, tell all the tractors there'll be no answer from the ship for a while, because no one will be aboard. Then suit up and come outside." He was gone.

◆

Ten minutes later, six human beings and a tractor were assembled in the flame-lit near-darkness outside the ship. The cloud had spread to the horizon, and the sun was gone. Burkett and Hargedon had arrived, but Rowson wasted no time on congratulations.

"We have work to do. It will be easy enough to keep the lava from the ship, since there seems to be a foot or more of ash on the ground and a touch of main drive would push it into a ringwall around us, but that's not the main problem. We have to keep it from reaching the chasm anywhere south of us, since that's the way the others will be coming. If they're cut off, they're dead. It will be brute work. We'll use the tractor any way we can think of. Unfortunately it has no plough attachment, and I can't think of anything aboard which could be turned into one. You have shovels, such as they are. The ash is light, especially here, but there's a mile and a half of dam to be built. I don't see how it can possibly be done . . . but it's going to be."

"Come on, Arnie! You're young and strong," came the voice of the mineralogist. "You should be able to lift as much of this stuff as I can. I understand you were lucky enough to get hold of Eileen—have you asked for the bonus yet?—but your work isn't done."

"It wasn't luck," Zaino retorted. Burkett, in spite of her voice, seemed much less of a schoolmistress when encased in a spacesuit and carrying a shovel, so he was able to talk back to her. "I was simply alert enough to make use of existing conditions, which I had to observe for myself in spite of all the scientists around. I'm charging the achievement to my regular salary. I saw—"

He stopped suddenly, both with tongue and shovel. Then, "Captain!"

"What is it?"

"The only reason we're starting this wall here is to keep well ahead of the flow so we can work as long as possible, isn't it?"

"Yes, I suppose so. I never thought of trying anywhere else. The valley would mean a much shorter dam, but if the flow isn't through it by now it would be before we could get there—oh! Wait a minute!"

"Yes, sir. You can put the main switch anywhere in a D.C. circuit. Where are the seismology stores we never had to use?"

Four minutes later the tractor set out from the *Albireo*, carrying Rowson and Zaino. Six minutes after that it stopped at the base of the ash cone which formed the north side of the valley from which the lava was coming. They parked a quarter of the way around the cone's base from the emerging flood and started to climb on foot, both carrying burdens.

Forty-seven minutes later they returned empty-handed to the vehicle, to find that it had been engulfed by the spreading liquid.

With noticeable haste they floundered through the loose ash a few yards above the base until they had outdistanced the glowing menace, descended and started back across the plain to where they knew the ship to be, though she was invisible through the falling detritus. Once they had to detour around a crack. Once they encountered one which widened towards the chasm on their right, and they knew a detour would be impossible. Leaping it seemed impossible, too, but they did it. Thirty seconds after this, forty minutes after finding the tractor destroyed, the landscape was bathed in a magnesium-white glare as the two one-and-a-half kiloton charges planted just inside the crater rim let go.

"Should we go back and see if it worked?" asked Zaino.

"What's the use? The only other charges we had were in the tractor. Thank goodness they were nuclear instead of H.E. If it didn't work we'd have more trouble to get back than we're having now."

"If it didn't work, is there any point in going back?"

"Stop quibbling and keep walking. Dr. Burkett, are you listening?"

"Yes, Captain."

"We're fresh out of tractors, but if you want to try it on foot you might start a set of flow measures on the lava. Arnie wants to know whether our landslide slid properly."

However, the two were able to tell for themselves before getting back to the *Albireo*.

The flow didn't stop all at once, of course; but with the valley feeding it blocked off by a pile of volcanic ash four hundred feet high on one side, nearly fifty on the other and more than a quarter of a mile long, its enthusiasm quickly subsided. It was thin, fluid stuff, as Burkett had noted; but as it spread it cooled, and as it cooled it thickened.

Six hours after the blast it had stopped with its nearest lobe almost a mile from the ship, less than two feet thick at the edge.

When Markidian's tractor arrived, Burkett was happily trying to analyse samples of the flow, and less happily speculating on how long it would be before the entire area would be blown off the planet. When Marini's and Harmon's vehicles arrived, almost together, the specimens had been loaded and everything stowed for acceleration. Sixty seconds after the last person was aboard, the *Albireo* left Mercury's surface at two gravities.

The haste, it turned out, wasn't really necessary. She had been in parking orbit nearly forty-five hours before the first of the giant volcanoes reached its climax, and the one beside their former site was not the first. It was the fourth.

"And that seems to be that," said Camille Burkett rather tritely as they drifted a hundred miles above the little world's surface. "Just a belt of white-hot calderas all around the planet. Pretty, if you like symmetry."

"I like being able to see it from this distance," replied Zaino, floating weightless beside her. "By the way, how much bonus should I ask for getting that idea of putting the seismic charges to use after all?"

"I wouldn't mention it. Any one of us might have thought of that. We all knew about them."

"Anyone *might* have. Let's speculate on how long it would have been before anyone *did*."

"It's still not like the other idea, which involved your own specialty. I still don't see what made you suppose that the gas pillar from the volcano would be heavily charged enough to reflect your radio beam. How did that idea strike you?"

Zaino thought back, and smiled a little as the picture of lightning blazing around pillar, cloud and mountain rose before his eyes.

"You're not quite right," he said. "I was worried about it for a while, but it didn't actually strike me."

It fell rather flat; Camille Burkett, Ph.D., had to have it explained to her.

Drunkboat

CORDWAINER SMITH

The late Cordwainer Smith—in "real" life Dr. Paul M. A. Linebarger, scholar, statesman, and author of the definitive text (still taught from today) on the art of psychological warfare—was a writer of enormous talents who, from 1948 until his untimely death in 1966, produced a double handful of some of the best short fiction this genre has ever seen: "Alpha Ralpha Boulevard," "A Planet Named Shayol," "On the Storm Planet," "The Ballad of Lost C'Mell," "The Dead Lady of Clown Town," "The Game of Rat and Dragon," "The Lady Who Sailed The Soul," *"Under Old Earth," and "Scanners Live in Vain," as well as a large number of lesser, but still fascinating, stories, all twisted and blended and woven into an interrelated tapestry of incredible lushness and intricacy. Smith created a baroque cosmology unrivaled even today for its scope and complexity: a millennia-spanning Future History, logically outlandish and elegantly strange, set against a vivid, richly colored, mythically intense universe where animals assume the shape of men, vast planoform ships whisper through multidimensional space, immense sick sheep are the most valuable objects in the universe, immortality can be bought, and the mysterious Lords of the Instrumentality rule a hunted Earth too old for history. . . .*

It is a cosmology that looks as evocative and bizarre today in the 1990s as it did in the 1960s—certainly for sheer sweep and daring of conceptualization in its vision of how different and strange *the future will be it rivals any contemporary vision conjured up by Young Turks such as Bruce Sterling and Greg Bear, and I suspect that it is timeless.*

In the bizarre and dazzling story that follows, decades ahead of its time both stylistically and conceptually (I suspect that it would still be considered cutting-edge even here at the brink of a new century, in fact), Smith sends an explorer off on a voyage unlike anyone has ever made before, in a vessel unlike any explorer has ever used—his own naked flesh and blood and bone.

Cordwainer Smith's books include the novel Norstrilia *and the collections* Space Lords—*one of the landmark collections of the genre—*The Best of Cordwainer Smith, Quest of the Three Worlds, Stardreamer, You Will Never Be the Same, *and* The Instrumentality of Mankind. *As Felix C. Forrest, he wrote two mainstream novels,* Ria *and* Carola, *and as Carmichael Smith he wrote the thriller* Atomsk.

His most recent book is the posthumous collection The Rediscovery of Man: The Complete Short Science Fiction of Cordwainer Smith *(NESFA Press, P.O. Box 809, Framingham, MA 07101-0203), a huge book that collects almost all of his short fiction and will certainly stand as one of the very best collections of the decade—and a book that belongs in every good science-fiction collection.*

Perhaps it is the saddest, maddest, wildest story in the whole long history of space. It is true that no one else had ever done anything like it before, to travel at such a distance, and at such speeds, and by such means. The hero looked like such an ordinary man—when people looked at him for the first time. The second time, ah! that was different.

And the heroine. Small she was, and ash-blonde, intelligent, perky, and hurt. Hurt—yes, that's the right word. She looked as though she needed comforting or helping, even when she was perfectly all right. Men felt more like men when she was near. Her name was Elizabeth.

Who would have thought that her name would ring loud and clear in the wild vomiting nothing which made up space[3]?

He took an old, old rocket, of an ancient design. With it he outflew, outfled, outjumped all the machines which had ever existed before. You might almost think that he went so fast that he shocked the great vaults of the sky, so that the ancient poem might have been written for him alone. "All the stars threw down their spears and watered heaven with their tears."

Go he did, so fast, so far that people simply did not believe it at first. They thought it was a joke told by men, a farce spun forth by rumor, a wild story to while away the summer afternoon.

We know his name now.

And our children and their children will know it for always.

Rambo. Artyr Rambo of Earth Four.

But he followed his Elizabeth where no space was. He went where men could not go, had not been, did not dare, would not think.

He did all this of his own free will.

Of course people thought it was a joke at first, and got to making up silly songs about the reported trip.

"Dig me a hole for that reeling feeling . . . !" sang one.

"Push me the call for the umber number . . . !" sang another.

"Where is the ship of the ochre joker . . . ?" sang a third.

Then people everywhere found it was true. Some stood stock still and got gooseflesh. Others turned quickly to everyday things. Space[3] had been found, and it had been pierced. Their world would never be the same again. The solid rock had become an open door.

Space itself, so clean, so empty, so tidy, now looked like a million million light-years of tapioca pudding—gummy, mushy, sticky, not fit to breathe, not fit to swim in.

How did it happen?

Everybody took the credit, each in his own different way.

I

"He came for me," said Elizabeth. "I died and he came for me because the machines were making a mess of my life when they tried to heal my terrible, useless death."

II

"I went myself," said Rambo. "They tricked me and lied to me and fooled me, but I took the boat and I became the boat and I got there. Nobody made me do it. I was angry, but I went. And I came back, didn't I?"

He too was right, even when he twisted and whined on the green grass of earth, his ship lost in a space so terribly far and strange that it might have been beneath his living hand, or might have been half a galaxy away.

How can anybody tell, with space-three?

It was Rambo who got back, looking for his Elizabeth. He loved her. So the trip was his, and the credit his.

III

But the Lord Crudelta said, many years later, when he spoke in a soft voice and talked confidentially among friends, "The experiment was mine. I designed it. I picked Rambo. I drove the selectors mad, trying to find a man who would meet those specifications. And I had that rocket built to the old, old plans. It was the sort of thing which human beings first used when they jumped out of the air a little bit, leaping like flying fish from one wave to the next and already thinking that they were eagles. If I had used one of the regular planoform ships, it would have disappeared with a sort of reverse gurgle, leaving space milky for a little bit while it faded into nastiness and obliteration. But I did not risk that. I put the rocket on a launching pad. *And the launching pad itself was an interstellar ship!* Since we were using an ancient rocket, we did it up right, with the old, old writing, mysterious letters printed all over the machine. We even had the name of our Organization—I and O and M—for 'the Instrumentality of Mankind' written on it good and sharp.

"How would I know," went on the Lord Crudelta, "that we would succeed more than we wanted to succeed, that Rambo would tear space itself loose from its hinges and leave that ship behind, just because he loved Elizabeth so sharply much, so fiercely much?"

Crudelta sighed.

"I know it and I don't know it. I'm like that ancient man who tried to take a water boat the wrong way around the planet Earth and found a new world instead. Columbus, he was called. And the land, that was Australia or America or something like that. That's what I did. I sent Rambo out in that ancient rocket and he found a way through space[3]. Now none of us will ever know who might come bulking through the floor or take shape out of the air in front of us."

Crudelta added, almost wistfully: "What's the use of telling the story? Everybody knows it, anyhow. My part in it isn't very glorious. Now the end of it, that's pretty. The bungalow by the waterfall and all the wonderful children that other people gave to them, you could write a poem about that. But the next to the end, how he showed up at the hospital helpless and insane, looking for his own Elizabeth. That was sad and eerie, that was frightening. I'm glad it all came to the happy ending with the bungalow by the waterfall, but it took a crashing long time to get there. And there are parts of it that we will never quite understand, the naked skin against naked space, the eyeballs riding something much faster than light ever was. Do you know what an *aoudad* is? It's an ancient sheep that used to live on Old Earth, and here we are, thousands of years later, with a children's nonsense rhyme about it. The animals are gone but the rhyme remains. It'll be like that with Rambo someday. Everybody will know his name and all about his drunkboat, but they will forget the scientific milestone that he crossed, hunting for Elizabeth in an ancient rocket that couldn't fly from peetle to pootle.... Oh, the rhyme? Don't you know that? It's a silly thing. It goes,

> Point your gun at a murky lurky.
> (*Now you're talking ham or turkey!*)
> Shoot a shot at a dying aoudad.
> (*Don't ask the lady why or how, dad!*)

Don't ask me what 'ham' and 'turkey' are. Probably parts of ancient animals, like beefsteak or sirloin. But the children still say the words. They'll do that with Rambo and his drunken boat some day. They may even tell the story of Elizabeth. But they will never tell the part about how he got to the hospital. That part is too terrible, too real, too sad and wonderful at the end. They found him on the grass. Mind you, naked on the grass, and nobody knew where he had come from!"

IV

They found him naked on the grass and nobody knew where he had come from. They did not even know about the ancient rocket which the Lord Crudelta had sent beyond the end of nowhere with the letters, I, O and M written on it. They did not know that this was Rambo, who had gone through space-three. The robots noticed him first and brought him in, photographing everything that they did. They had been programmed that way, to make sure that anything unusual was kept in the records.

Then the nurses found him in an outside room.

They assumed that he was alive, since he was not dead, but they could not prove that he was alive, either.

That heightened the puzzle.

The doctors were called in. Real doctors, not machines. They were very important men. Citizen Doctor Timofeyev, Citizen Doctor Grosbeck and the director himself, Sir and Doctor Vomact. They took the case.

(*Over on the other side of the hospital Elizabeth waited, unconscious, and nobody knew it at all. Elizabeth, for whom he had jumped space, and pierced the stars, but nobody knew it yet!*)

The young man could not speak. When they ran eyeprints and fingerprints through the Population Machine, they found that he had been bred on earth itself, but had been shipped out as a frozen and unborn baby to Earth Four. At tremendous cost, they queried Earth Four with an "instant message," only to discover that the young man who lay before them in the hospital had been lost from an experimental ship on an intergalactic trip.

Lost.

No ship and no sign of ship.

And here he was.

They stood at the edge of space, and did not know what they were looking at. They were doctors and it was their business to repair or rebuild people, not to ship them around. How should such men know about space^3 when they did not even know about space^2 except for the fact that people got on the planoform ships and made trips through it? They were looking for sickness when their eyes saw engineering. They treated him when he was well.

All he needed was time, to get over the shock of the most tremendous trip ever made by a human being, but the doctors did not know that and they tried to rush his recovery.

When they put clothes on him, he moved from coma to a kind of mechanical spasm and tore the clothing off. Once again stripped, he lay himself roughly on the floor and refused food or speech.

They fed him with needles while the whole energy of space, had they only known it, was radiating out of his body in new forms.

They put him all by himself in a locked room and watched him through the peephole.

He was a nice-looking young man, even though his mind was blank and his body was rigid and unconscious. His hair was very fair and his eyes were light blue but his face showed character—a square chin; a handsome, resolute, sullen mouth; old lines in the face which looked as though, when conscious, he must have lived many days or months on the edge of rage.

When they studied him the third day in the hospital, their patient had not changed at all.

He had torn off his pajamas again and lay naked, face down, on the floor.

His body was as immobile and tense as it had been on the day before.

(One year later, this room was going to be a museum with a bronze sign reading, "Here lay Rambo after he left the Old Rocket for Space Three," but the doctors still had no idea of what they were dealing with.)

His face was turned so sharply to the left that the neck muscles showed. His right arm stuck out straight from the body. The left arm formed an exact right angle from the body, with the left forearm and hand pointing rigidly upward at 90° from the upper arm. The legs were in the grotesque parody of a running position.

Doctor Grosbeck said, "It looks to me like he's swimming. Let's drop him in a tank of water and see if he moves." Grosbeck sometimes went in for drastic solutions to problems.

Timofeyev took his place at the peephole. "Spasm, still," he murmured.

"I hope the poor fellow is not feeling pain when his cortical defenses are down. How can a man fight pain if he does not even know what he is experiencing?"

"And you, Sir and Doctor," and Grosbeck to Vomact, "what do you see?"

Vomact did not need to look. He had come early and had looked long and quietly at the patient through the peephole before the other doctors arrived. Vomact was a wise man, with good insight and rich intuitions. He could guess in an hour more than a machine could diagnose in a year; he was already beginning to understand that this was a sickness which no man had ever had before. Still, there were remedies waiting.

The three doctors tried them.

They tried hypnosis, electrotherapy, message, subsonics, atropine, surgital, a whole family of the digitalinids, and some quasi-narcotic viruses which had been grown in orbit where they mutated fast. They got the beginning of a response when they tried gas hypnosis combined with an electronically amplified telepath; this showed that something still went on inside the patient's mind. Otherwise the brain might have seemed to be mere fatty tissue, without a nerve in it. The other attempts had shown nothing. The gas showed a faint stirring away from fear and pain. The telepath reported glimpses of unknown skies. (The doctors turned the telepath over to the Space Police promptly, so they could try to code the star patterns which he had seen in the patient's mind, but the patterns did not fit. The telepath, though a keen-witted man, could not remember them in enough detail for them to be scanned against the samples of piloting sheets.)

The doctors went back to their drugs and tried ancient, simple remedies—morphine and caffeine to counteract each other, and a rough massage to make him dream again, so that the telepath could pick it up.

There was no further result that day, or the next.

◆

Meanwhile the Earth authorities were getting restless. They thought, quite rightly, that the hospital had done a good job of proving that the patient had not been on Earth until a few moments before the robots found him on the grass. How had he gotten on the grass?

The airspace of earth reported no intrusion at all, no vehicle marking a blazing arc of air incandescing against metal, no whisper of the great forces which drove a planoform ship through space[2].

(*Crudelta, using faster-than-light ships, was creeping slow as a snail back toward Earth, racing his best to see if Rambo had gotten there first.*)

On the fifth day, there was the beginning of a breakthrough.

V

Elizabeth had passed.

This was found out only much later, by a careful check of the hospital records.

The doctors only knew this much:

Patients had been moved down the corridor, sheet-covered figures immobile on wheeled beds.

Suddenly the beds stopped rolling.

A nurse screamed.

The heavy steel-and-plastic wall was bending inward. Some slow, silent force was pushing the wall into the corridor itself.

The wall ripped.

A human hand emerged.

One of the quick-witted nurses screamed,

"*Push* those beds! *Push* them out of the way."

The nurses and robots obeyed.

The beds rocked like a group of boats crossing a wave when they came to the place where the floor, bonded to the wall, had bent upward to meet the wall as it tore inward. The peach-colored glow of the lights flicked. Robots appeared.

A second human hand came through the wall. Pushing in opposite directions, the hands tore the wall as though it had been wet paper.

The patient from the grass put his head through.

He looked blindly up and down the corridor, his eyes not quite focusing, his skin glowing a strange red-brown from the burns of open space.

"No," he said. Just that one word.

But that "No" was heard. Though the volume was not loud, it carried through the hospital. The internal telecommunications system relayed it. Every switch in the place went negative. Frantic nurses and robots, with even the doctors helping them, rushed to turn all the machines back on—the pumps, the ventilators, the artificial kidneys, the brain re-recorders, even the simple air engines which kept the atmosphere clean.

Far overhead an aircraft spun giddily. Its "off" switch, surrounded by triple safeguards, had suddenly been thrown into the negative position. Fortunately the robot-pilot got it going again before crashing into earth.

The patient did not seem to know that his word had this effect.

(*Later the world knew that this was part of the "drunkboat effect." The man himself had developed the capacity for using his neurophysical system as a machine control.*)

In the corridor, the machine robot who served as policeman arrived. He wore sterile, padded velvet gloves with a grip of sixty metric tons inside his hands. He approached the patient. The robot had been carefully trained to recognize all kinds of danger from delirious or psychotic humans; later he reported that he had an input of "danger, extreme" on every band of sensation. He had been expecting to seize the prisoner with irreversible firmness and to return him to his bed, but with this kind of danger sizzling in the air, the robot took no chances. His wrist itself contained a hypodermic pistol which operated on compressed argon.

He reached out toward the unknown, naked man who stood in the big torn gap of the wall. The wrist-weapon hissed and a sizeable injection of condamine, the most powerful narcotic in the known universe, spat its way through the skin of Rambo's neck. The patient collapsed.

The robot picked him up gently and tenderly, lifted him through the torn wall, pushed the door open with a kick which broke the lock and put the patient back on his bed. The robot could hear doctors coming, so he used his enormous hands to pat the steel wall back into its proper shape. Work-robots or underpeople could finish the job later, but meanwhile it looked better to have that part of the building set at right angles again.

Doctor Vomact arrived, followed closely by Grosbeck.

"What happened?" he yelled, shaken out of a lifelong calm. The robot pointed at the ripped wall.

"He tore it open. I put it back," said the robot.

The doctors turned to look at the patient. He had crawled off his bed again and was on the floor, but his breathing was light and natural.

"What did you give him?" cried Vomact to the robot.

"Condamine," said the robot, "according to rule 47-B. The drug is not to be mentioned outside the hospital."

"I know that," said Vomact absent-mindedly and a little crossly. "You can go along now. Thank you."

"It is not usual to thank robots," said the robot, "but you can read a commendation into my record if you want to."

"Get the blazes out of here!" shouted Vomact at the officious robot.

The robot blinked. "There are no blazes but I have the impression you mean me. I shall leave, with your permission." He jumped with odd gracefulness around the two doctors, fingered the broken doorlock absentmindedly, as though he might have wished to repair it, and then, seeing Vomact glare at him, left the room completely.

A moment later soft muted thuds began. Both doctors listened a moment and then gave up. The robot was out in the corridor, gently patting the steel floor back into shape. He was a tidy robot, probably animated by an amplified chicken-brain, and when he got tidy he became obstinate.

"Two questions, Grosbeck," said the Sir and Doctor Vomact.

"Your service, sir!"

"Where was the patient standing when he pushed the wall into the corridor, and how did he get the leverage to do it?"

Grosbeck narrowed his eyes in puzzlement. "Now that you mention it, I have no idea of how he did it. In fact, he could not have done it. But he has. And the other question?"

"What do you think of condamine?"

"Dangerous, of course, as always. Addiction can—"

"Can you have addiction with no cortical activity?" interrupted Vomact.

"Of course," said Grosbeck promptly. "Tissue addiction."

"Look for it, then," said Vomact.

Grosbeck knelt beside the patient and felt with his fingertips for the muscle endings. He felt where they knotted themselves into the base of the skull, the tips of the shoulders, the striped area of the back.

When he stood up there was a look of puzzlement on his face. "I never felt a human body like this one before. I am not even sure that it *is* human any longer."

Vomact said nothing. The two doctors confronted one another. Grosbeck fidgeted under the calm stare of the senior man. Finally he blurted out,

"Sir and Doctor, I know what we *could* do."

"And that," said Vomact levelly, without the faintest hint of encouragement or of warning, "is what?"

"It wouldn't be the first time that it's been done in a hospital."

"What?" said Vomact, his eyes—those dreaded eyes!—making Grosbeck say what he did not want to say.

Grosbeck flushed. He leaned toward Vomact so as to whisper, even though there was no one standing near them. His words, when they came, had the hasty indecency of a lover's improper suggestion,

"Kill the patient, Sir and Doctor. Kill him. We have plenty of records of him. We can get a cadaver out of the basement and make it into a good simulacrum. Who knows what we will turn loose among mankind if we let him get well?"

"Who knows?" said Vomact without tone or quality to his voice. "But citizen and doctor, what is the twelfth duty of a physician?"

" 'Not to take the law into his own hands, keeping healing for the healers and giving to the state or the Instrumentality whatever properly belongs to the state or the Instrumentality.' " Grosbeck sighed as he retracted his own suggestion. "Sir and Doctor, I take it back. It wasn't medicine which I was talking about. It was government and politics which were really in my mind."

"And now . . . ?" asked Vomact.

"Heal him, or let him be until he heals himself."

"And which would you do?"

"I'd try to heal him."

"How?" said Vomact.

"Sir and Doctor," cried Grosbeck, "do not ride my weaknesses in this case! I know that you like me because I am a bold, confident sort of man. Do not ask me to be myself when we do not even know where this body came from. If I were bold as usual, I would give him typhoid and condamine, stationing telepaths nearby. But this is something new in the history of man. We are people and perhaps he is not a person any more. Perhaps he represents the combination of people with some kind of a new force. How did he get here from the far side of nowhere? How many million times has he been enlarged or reduced? We do not know what he is or what has happened to him. How can we treat a man when we are treating the cold of space, the heat of suns, the frigidity of distance? We know what to do with flesh, but this is not quite flesh any more. Feel him yourself, Sir and Doctor! You will touch something which nobody has ever touched before."

"I have," Vomact declared, "already felt him. You are right. We will try typhoid and condamine for half a day. Twelve hours from now let us meet each other at this place. I will tell the nurses and the robots what to do in the interim."

They both gave the red-tanned spread-eagled figure on the floor a parting glance. Grosbeck looked at the the body with something like distaste mingled with fear; Vomact was expressionless, save for a wry wan smile of pity.

At the door the head nurse awaited them. Grosbeck was surprised at his chief's orders.

"Ma'am and nurse, do you have a weapon-proof vault in this hospital?"

"Yes, sir," she said. "We used to keep our records in it until we tele-metered all our records into Computer Orbit. Now it is dirty and empty."

"Clean it out. Run a ventilator tube into it. Who is your military pro-tector?"

"My what?" she cried, in surprise.

"Everyone on Earth has military protection. Where are the forces, the soldiers, who protect this hospital of yours?"

"My Sir and Doctor!" she called out, "my Sir and Doctor! I'm an old woman and I have been allowed to work here for three hundred years. But I never thought of that idea before. Why would I need soldiers?"

"Find who they are and ask them to stand by. They are specialists too, with a different kind of art from ours. Let them stand by. They may be needed before this day is out. Give my name as authority to their lieu-tenant or sergeant. Now here is the medication which I want you to apply to this patient."

Her eyes widened as he went on talking, but she was a disciplined woman and she nodded as she heard him out, point by point. Her eyes looked very sad and weary at the end but she was a trained expert herself and she had enormous respect for the skill and wisdom of the Sir and Doctor Vomact. She also had a warm, feminine pity for the motionless young male figure on the floor, swimming forever on the heavy floor, swimming between archipelagoes which no man living had ever dreamed before.

VI

Crisis came that night.

The patient had worn handprints into the inner wall of the vault, but he had not escaped.

The soldiers, looking oddly alert with their weapons gleaming in the bright corridor of the hospital, were really very bored, as soldiers always become when they are on duty with no action.

Their lieutenant was keyed up. The wirepoint in his hand buzzed like a dangerous insect. Sir and Doctor Vomact, who knew more about weap-ons than the soldiers thought he knew, saw that the wirepoint was set to HIGH, with a capacity of paralyzing people five stories up, five stories down or a kilometer sideways. He said nothing. He merely thanked the lieutenant and entered the vault, closely followed by Grosbeck and Ti-mofeyev.

The patient swam here too.

He had changed to an arm-over-arm motion, kicking his legs against the floor. It was as though he had swum on the other floor with the sole purpose of staying afloat, and had now discovered some direction in which to go, albeit very slowly. His motions were deliberate, tense, rigid, and so reduced in time that it seemed as though he hardly moved at all. The ripped pajamas lay on the floor beside him.

Vomact glanced around, wondering what forces the man could have used to make those handprints on the steel wall. He remembered Grosbeck's warning that the patient should die, rather than subject all mankind to new and unthought risks, but though he shared the feeling, he could not condone the recommendation.

Almost irritably, the great doctor thought to himself—where could the man be going?

(*To Elizabeth, the truth was, to Elizabeth, now only sixty meters away. Not till much later did people understand what Rambo had been trying to do— crossing sixty mere meters to reach his Elizabeth when he had already jumped an un-count of light-years to return to her. To his own, his dear, his well-beloved who needed him!*)

The condamine did not leave its characteristic mark of deep lassitude and glowing skin: perhaps the typhoid was successfully contradicting it. Rambo did seem more lively than before. The name had come through on the regular message system, but it still did not mean anything to the Sir and Doctor Vomact. It would. It would.

Meanwhile the other two doctors, briefed ahead of time, got busy with the apparatus which the robots and the nurses had installed.

Vomact murmured to the others. "I think he's better off. Looser all around. I'll try shouting."

So busy were they that they just nodded.

Vomact screamed at the patient, "Who are you? What are you? Where do you come from?"

The sad blue eyes of the man on the floor glanced at him with a surprisingly quick glance, but there was no other real sign of communication. The limbs kept up their swim against the rough concrete floor of the vault. Two of the bandages which the hospital staff had put on him had worn off again. The right knee, scraped and bruised, deposited a sixty-centimeter trail of blood—some old and black and coagulated, some fresh, new and liquid—on the floor as it moved back and forth.

Vomact stood up and spoke to Grosbeck and Timofeyev. "Now," he said, "let us see what happens when we apply the pain."

The two stepped back without being told to do so.

Timofeyev waved his hand at a small white-enamelled orderly-robot who stood in the doorway.

The pain net, a fragile cage of wires, dropped down from the ceiling.

It was Vomact's duty, as senior doctor, to take the greatest risk. The patient was wholly encased by the net of wires, but Vomact dropped to his hands and knees, lifted the net at one corner with his right hand, thrust his own head into it next to the head of the patient. Doctor Vomact's robe trailed on the clean concrete, touching the black old stains of blood left from the patient's "swim" throughout the night.

Now Vomact's mouth was centimeters from the patient's ear.

Said Vomact, "Oh."

The net hummed.

The patient stopped his slow motion, arched his back, looked steadfastly at the doctor.

Doctors Grosbeck and Timofeyev could see Vomact's face go white with the impact of the pain machine, but Vomact kept his voice under control and said evenly and loudly to the patient,

"Who-are-you?"

The patient said flatly, "Elizabeth."

The answer was foolish but the tone was rational.

Vomact pulled his head out from under the net, shouting again at the patient, *"Who—are—you?"*

The naked man replied speaking very clearly:

"Chwinkle, chwinkle, little chweeble,
I am feeling very feeble!"

Vomact frowned and murmured to the robot, "More pain. Turn it up to pain ultimate."

The body threshed under the net, trying to resume its swim on the concrete.

A loud wild braying cry came from the victim under the net. It sounded like a screamed distortion of the name Elizabeth, echoing out from endless remoteness.

It did not make sense.

Vomact screamed back, *"Who—are-you?"*

With unexpected clarity and resonance, the voice came back to the three doctors from the twisting body under the net of pain:

"I'm the shipped man, the ripped man, the gypped man, the dipped man, the hipped man, the tripped man, the tipped man, the slipped man, the flipped man, the nipped man, the ripped man, the clipped man— aah!" His voice choked off with a cry and he went back to swimming on the floor, despite the intensity of the pain net immediately above him.

The doctor lifted his hand. The pain net stopped buzzing and lifted high into the air.

He felt the patient's pulse. It was quick. He lifted an eyelid. The reactions were much closer to normal.

"Stand back," he said to the others.

"Pain on both of us," he said to the robot.

The net came down on the two of them.

"Who are you?" shrieked Vomact, right into the patient's ear, holding the man halfway off the floor and not quite knowing whether the body which tore steel walls might not, somehow, tear both of them apart as they stood.

The man babbled back at him: "I'm the most man, the post man, the host man, the ghost man, the coast man, the boast man, the dosed man, the grossed man, the toast man, the roast man, no! no! no!"

He struggled in Vomact's arms. Grosbeck and Timofeyev stepped forward to rescue their chief when the patient added, very calmly and clearly,

"Your procedure is all right, doctor, whoever you are. More fever, please. More pain, please. Some of that dope to fight the pain. You're pulling me back. I know I am on Earth. Elizabeth is near. For the love of God, get me Elizabeth! But don't rush me. I need days and days to get well."

The rationality was so startling that Grosbeck, without waiting for orders from Vomact, as chief doctor, ordered the pain net lifted.

The patient began babbling again: "I'm the three man, the he man, the tree man, the me man, the three man, the three man . . ." His voice faded and he slumped unconscious.

Vomact walked out of the vault. He was a little unsteady.

His colleagues took him by the elbows.

He smiled wanly at them: "I wish it were lawful. . . . I could use some of that condamine myself. No wonder the pain nets wake the patients up and even make dead people do twitches! Get me some liquor. My heart is old."

Grosbeck sat him down while Timofeyev ran down the corridor in search of medicinal liquor.

Vomact murmured, "How are we going to find *his* Elizabeth? There must be millions of them. And he's from Earth Four too."

"Sir and Doctor, you have worked wonders," said Grosbeck. "To go under the net. To take those chances. To bring him to speech. I will never see anything like it again. It's enough for any one lifetime, to have seen this day."

"But what do we do next?" asked Vomact wearily, almost in confusion.

That particular question needed no answer.

VII

The Lord Crudelta had reached Earth.

His pilot landed the craft and fainted at the controls with sheer exhaustion.

Of the escort cats, who had ridden alongside the space craft in the miniature space-ships, three were dead, one was comatose and the fifth was spitting and raving.

When the port authorities tried to slow the Lord Crudelta down to ascertain his authority, he invoked Top Emergency, took over the command of troops in the name of the Instrumentality, arrested everyone in sight but the troop commander, and requisitioned the troop commander to take him to the hospital. The computers at the port had told him that one Rambo, "sans origine," had arrived mysteriously on the grass of a designated hospital.

Outside the hospital, the Lord Crudelta invoked Top Emergency again, placed all armed men under his own command, ordered a recording monitor to cover all his actions if he should later be channeled into a court-martial, and arrested everyone in sight.

The tramp of heavily armed men, marching in combat order, overtook Timofeyev as he hurried back to Vomact with a drink. The men were jogging along on the double. All of them had live helmets and their wire-points were buzzing.

Nurses ran forward to drive the intruders out, ran backward when the sting of the stun-rays brushed cruelly over them. The whole hospital was in an uproar.

The Lord Crudelta later admitted that he had made a serious mistake. The Two Minutes' War broke out immediately.

You have to understand the pattern of the Instrumentality to see how it happened. The Instrumentality was a self-perpetuating body of men with enormous powers and a strict code. Each was a plenum of the low, the middle and the high justice. Each could do anything he found necessary or proper to maintain the Instrumentality and to keep the peace between the worlds. But if he made a mistake or committed a wrong— ah, then, it was suddenly different. Any Lord could put another Lord to death in an emergency, but he was assured of death and disgrace himself if he assumed this responsibility. The only difference between ratification and repudiation came in the fact that Lords who killed in an emergency and were proved wrong were marked down on a very shameful list, while those who killed other Lords rightly (as later examination might prove) were listed on a very honorable list, but still killed.

With three Lords, the situation was different. Three Lords made an emergency court; if they acted together, acted in good faith, and reported to the computers of the Instrumentality, they were exempt from punishment, though not from blame or even reduction to citizen status. Seven Lords, or all the Lords on a given planet at a given moment, were beyond any criticism except that of a dignified reversal of their actions should a later ruling prove them wrong.

This was all the business of the Instrumentality. The Instrumentality had the perpetual slogan: "Watch, but do not govern; stop war but do not wage it; protect, but do not control; and first, survive!"

The Lord Crudelta had seized the troops—not his troops, but the light regular troops of Manhome Government—because he feared that the greatest danger in the history of man might come from the person whom he himself had sent through space.

He never expected that the troops would be plucked out from his command—an overriding power reinforced by robotic telepathy and the incomparable communications net, both open and secret, reinforced by thousands of years in trickery, defeat, secrecy, victory, and sheer experience, which the Instrumentality had perfected since it emerged from the Ancient Wars.

Overriding, overridden!

These were the commands which the Instrumentality had used before recorded time began. Sometimes they suspended their antagonists on points of law, sometimes by the deft and deadly insertion of weapons, most often by cutting in on other peoples' mechanical and social controls and doing their will, only to drop the controls as suddenly as they had taken them.

But not Crudelta's hastily-called troops.

VIII

The war broke out with a change of pace.

Two squads of men were moving into that part of the hospital where Elizabeth lay, waiting the endless returns to the jelly-baths which would rebuild her poor ruined body.

The squads changed pace.

The survivors could not account for what happened.

They all admitted to great mental confusion—afterward.

At the time it seemed that they had received a clear, logical command to turn and to defend the women's section by counterattacking their own main battalion right in their rear.

The hospital was a very strong building. Otherwise it would have melted to the ground or shot up in flame.

The leading soldiers suddenly turned around, dropped for cover and blazed their wirepoints at the comrades who followed them. The wirepoints were cued to organic material, though fairly harmless to inorganic. They were powered by the power relays which every soldier wore on his back.

In the first ten seconds of the turnaround, twenty-seven soldiers, two nurses, three patients and one orderly were killed. One hundred and nine other people were wounded in that first exchange of fire.

The troop commander had never seen battle, but he had been well trained. He immediately deployed his reserves around the external exits of the building and sent his favorite squad, commanded by a Sergeant Lansdale whom he trusted well, down into the basement, so that it could rise vertically from the basement into the women's quarters and find out who the enemy was.

As yet, he had no idea that it was his own leading troops turning and fighting their comrades.

He testified later, at the trial, that he personally had no sensations of eerie interference with his own mind. He merely knew that his men had unexpectedly come upon armed resistance from antagonists—identity unknown!—who had weapons identical with theirs. Since the Lord Crudelta had brought them along in case there might be a fight with unspecified antagonists, he felt right in assuming that a Lord of the Instrumentality knew what he was doing. This was the enemy all right.

In less than a minute, the two sides had balanced out. The line of fire had moved right into his own force. The lead men, some of whom were wounded, simply turned around and began defending themselves against the men immediately behind them. It was as though an invisible line, moving rapidly, had parted the two sections of the military force.

The oily black smoke of dissolving bodies began to glut the ventilators.

Patients were screaming, doctors cursing, robots stamping around and nurses trying to call each other.

The war ended when the troop commander saw Sergeant Lansdale, whom he himself had sent upstairs, leading a charge out of the women's quarters—directly at his own commander!

The officer kept his head.

He dropped to the floor and rolled sidewise as the air chittered at him, the emanations of Lansdale's wirepoint killing all the tiny bacteria in the air. On his helmet phone he pushed the manual controls to TOP VOLUME and to NON-COMS ONLY and he commanded, with a sudden flash of brilliant mother-wit,

"Good job, Lansdale!"

Lansdale's voice came back as weak as if it had been off-planet, "We'll keep them out of this section yet, sir!"

The troop commander called back very loudly but calmly, not letting on that he thought his sergeant was psychotic.

"Easy now. Hold on. I'll be with you."

He changed to the other channel and said to his nearby men, "Cease fire. Take cover and wait."

A wild scream came to him from the phones.

It was Lansdale. "Sir! Sir! I'm fighting *you*, sir. I just caught on. It's getting me again. Watch out."

The buzz and burr of the weapons suddenly stopped.

The wild human uproar of the hospital continued.

A tall doctor, with the insignia of high seniority, came gently to the troop commander and said,

"You can stand up and take your soldiers out now, young fellow. The fight was a mistake."

"I'm not under your orders," snapped the young officer. "I'm under the Lord Crudelta. He requisitioned this force from the Manhome Government. Who are you?"

"You may salute me, captain," said the doctor, "I am Colonel General Vomact of the Earth Medical Reserve. But you had better not wait for the Lord Crudelta."

"But *where* is he?"

"In my bed," said Vomact.

"Your *bed?*" cried the young officer in complete amazement.

"In bed. Doped the to the teeth. I fixed him up. He was excited. Take your men out. We'll treat the wounded on the lawn. You can see the dead in the refrigerators downstairs in a few minutes, except for the ones that went smoky from direct hits."

"But the fight . . . ?"

"A mistake, young man, or else—"

"Or else what?" shouted the young officer, horrified at the utter mess of his own combat experience.

"Or else a weapon no man has ever seen before. Your troops fought each other. Your command was intercepted."

"I could see that," snapped the officer, "as soon as I saw Lansdale coming at me."

"But do you know what took him over?" said Vomact gently, while taking the officer by the arm and beginning to lead him out of the hospital. The captain went willingly, not noticing where he was going, so eagerly did he watch for the other man's words.

"I think I know," said Vomact. "Another man's dreams. Dreams which have learned how to turn themselves into electricity or plastic or stone. Or anything else. Dreams coming to us out of space three."

The young officer nodded dumbly. This was too much. "Space three?" he murmured. It was like being told that the really alien invaders, whom men had been expecting for fourteen thousand years and had never met, were waiting for him on the grass. Until now space three had been a mathematical idea, a romancer's day-dream, but not a fact.

❧

The sir and doctor Vomact did not even ask the young officer. He brushed the young man gently at the nape of the neck and shot him through with tranquilizer. Vomact then led him out to the grass. The young captain stood alone and whistled happily at the stars in the sky. Behind him, his sergeants and corporals were sorting out the survivors and getting treatment for the wounded.

The Two Minutes' War was over.

Rambo had stopped dreaming that his Elizabeth was in danger. He had recognized, even in his deep sick sleep, that the tramping in the corridor was the movement of armed men. His mind had set up defenses to protect Elizabeth. He took over command of the forward troops and set them to stopping the main body. The powers which space^3 had worked into him made this easy for him to do, even though he did not know that he was doing it.

IX

"How many dead?" said Vomact to Grosbeck and Timofeyev.

"About two hundred."

"And how many irrecoverable dead?"

"The ones that got turned into smoke. A dozen, maybe fourteen. The other dead can be fixed up, but most of them will have to get new personality prints."

"Do you know what happened?" asked Vomact.

"No, Sir and Doctor," they both chorused.

"I do. I think I do. No, *I know* I do. It's the wildest story in the history of man. Our patient did it—Rambo. He took over the troops and set them against each other. That Lord of the Instrumentality who came charging in—Crudelta. I've known him for a long long time. He's behind this case. He thought that troops would help, not sensing that troops would invite attack upon themselves. And there is something else."

"Yes?" they said, in unison.

"Rambo's woman—the one he's looking for. She must be here."

"Why?" said Timofeyev.

"Because *he's* here."

"You're assuming that he came here because of his own will, Sir and Doctor."

Vomact smiled the wise crafty smile of his family; it was almost a trademark of the Vomact house.

"I am assuming all the things which I cannot otherwise prove.

"First, I assume that he came here naked out of space itself, driven by some kind of force which we cannot even guess.

"Second, I assume he came *here* because he wanted something. A woman named Elizabeth, who must already be here. In a moment we can go inventory all our Elizabeths.

"Third, I assume that the Lord Crudelta knew something about it. He has led troops into the building. He began raving when he saw me. I know hysterical fatigue, as do you, my brothers, so I condamined him for a night's sleep.

"Fourth, let's leave our man alone. There'll be hearings and trials enough, Space knows, when all these events get scrambled out."

☙

Vomact was right.

He usually was.

Trials did follow.

☙

It was lucky that Old Earth no longer permitted newspapers or television news. The population would have been frothed up to riot and terror if they had ever found out what happened at the Old Main Hospital just to the west of Meeya Meefla.

X

Twenty-one days later, Vomact, Timofeyev and Grosbeck were summoned to the trial of the Lord Crudelta. A full panel of seven Lords of the Instrumentality was there to give Crudelta an ample hearing and, if required, a sudden death. The doctors were present both as doctors for Elizabeth and Rambo and as witnesses for the Investigating Lord.

Elizabeth, fresh up from being dead, was as beautiful as a newborn baby in exquisite, adult feminine form. Rambo could not take his eyes off her, but a look of bewilderment went over his face every time she gave him a friendly, calm, remote little smile. (She had been told that she was his girl, and she was prepared to believe it, but she had no memory of him or of anything else more than sixty hours back, when speech had been reinstalled in her mind; and he, for his part, was still thick of speech and subject to strains which the doctors could not quite figure out.)

The investigating Lord was a man named Starmount.

He asked the panel to rise.

They did so.

He faced the Lord Crudelta with great solemnity, "You are obliged, my Lord Crudelta, to speak quickly and clearly to this court."

"Yes, my Lord," he answered.

"We have the summary power."

"You have the summary power. I recognize it."

"You will tell the truth or else you will lie."

"I shall tell the truth or I will lie."

"You may lie, if you wish, about matters of fact and opinion, but you will in no case lie about human relationships. If you do lie, nevertheless, you will ask that your name be entered in the Roster of Dishonor."

"I understand the panel and the rights of this panel. I will lie if I wish— though I don't think I will need to do so—" and here Crudelta flashed a weary intelligent smile at all of them—"but I will not lie about matters of relationship. If I do, I will ask for dishonor."

"You have yourself been well trained as a Lord of the Instrumentality?"

"I have been so trained and I love the Instrumentality well. In fact, I am myself the Instrumentality, as are you, and as are the honorable Lords beside you. I shall behave well, for as long as I live this afternoon."

"Do you credit him, my Lords?" asked Starmount.

The members of the panel nodded their mitred heads. They had dressed ceremonially for the occasion.

"Do you have a relationship to the woman Elizabeth?"

The members of the trial panel caught their breath as they saw Crudelta turn white: "My Lords!" he cried, and answered no further.

"It is the custom," said Starmount firmly, "that you answer promptly or that you die."

The Lord Crudelta got control of himself. "I am answering. I did not know who she was, except for the fact that Rambo loved her. I sent her to Earth from Earth Four, where I then was. Then I told Rambo that she had been murdered and hung desperately at the edge of death, wanting only his help to return to the green fields of life."

Said Starmount: "Was that the truth?"

"My Lord and Lords, it was a lie."

"Why did you tell it?"

"To induce rage in Rambo and to give him an overriding reason for wanting to come to Earth faster than any man has ever come before."

"A-a-ah! A-a-ah!" Two wild cries came from Rambo, more like the call of an animal than like the sound of a man.

Vomact looked at his patient, felt himself beginning to growl with a deep internal rage. Rambo's powers, generated in the depths of space[3], had begun to operate again. Vomact made a sign. The robot behind Rambo had been coded to keep Rambo calm. Though the robot had been enamelled to look like a white gleaming hospital orderly, he was actually a police-robot of high powers, built up with an electronic cortex based on the frozen midbrain of an old wolf. (A wolf was a rare animal, something like a dog.) The robot touched Rambo, who dropped off to sleep. Doctor Vomact felt the anger in his own mind fade away. He lifted his hand gently; the robot caught the signal and stopped applying the narcoleptic radiation. Rambo slept normally; Elizabeth looked worriedly at the man whom she had been told was her own.

The Lords turned back from the glances at Rambo.

Said Starmount, icily: "And why did you do that?"

"Because I wanted him to travel through space-three."

"Why?"

"To show it could be done."

"And do you, my Lord Crudelta, affirm that this man has in fact travelled through space-three?"

"I do."

"Are you lying?"

"I have the right to lie, but I have no wish to do so. In the name of the Instrumentality itself, I tell you that this is the truth."

The panel members gasped. Now there was no way out. Either the Lord Crudelta was telling the truth, *which meant that all former times had come to an end and that a new age had begun for all the kinds of mankind,* or else he was lying in the face of the most powerful form of affirmation which any of them knew.

Even Starmount himself took a different tone. His teasing, restless, intelligent voice took on a new timbre of kindness.

"You do therefore assert that this man has come back from outside our galaxy with nothing more than his own natural skin to cover him? No instruments? No power?"

"I did not say that," said Crudelta. "Other people have begun to pretend I used such words. I tell you, my Lords, that I planoformed for twelve consecutive Earth Days and nights. Some of you may remember where Outpost Baiter Gator is. Well, I had a good Go-captain, and he took me four long jumps beyond there, out into intergalactic space. I left this man there. When I reached Earth, he had been here twelve days, more or less. I have assumed, therefore, that his trip was more or less instantaneous. I was on my way back to Baiter Gator, counting by Earth time, when the doctor here found this man on the grass outside the hospital."

Vomact raised his hand. The Lord Starmount gave him the right to speak, "My Sirs and Lords, we did not find this man on the grass. The robots did, and made a record. But even the robots did not see or photograph his arrival."

"We know that," said Starmount angrily, "and we know that we have been told that nothing came to Earth by any means whatever, in that particular quarter hour. Go on, my Lord Crudelta. What relation are you to Rambo?"

"He is my victim."

"Explain yourself!"

"I computed him out. I asked the machines where I would be most apt to find a man with a tremendous lot of rage in him, and was informed that on Earth Four the rage level had been left high because that particular planet had a considerable need for explorers and adventurers, in whom rage was a strong survival trait. When I got to Earth Four, I commanded the authorities to find out which border cases had exceeded the limits of allowable rage. They gave me four men. One was much too large. Two were old. This man was the only candidate for my experiment. I chose him."

"What did you tell him?"

"Tell him? I told him his sweetheart was dead or dying."

"No, no," said Starmount. "Not at the moment of crisis. What did you tell him to make him cooperate in the first place?"

"I told him," said the Lord Crudelta evenly, "that I was myself a Lord of the Instrumentality and that I would kill him myself if he did not obey, and obey promptly."

"And under what custom or law did you act?"

"Reserved material," said the Lord Crudelta promptly. "There are telepaths here who are not a part of the Instrumentality. I beg leave to defer until we have a shielded place."

Several members of the panel nodded and Starmount agreed with them. He changed the line of questioning.

"You forced this man, therefore, to do something which he did not wish to do?"

"That is right," said the Lord Crudelta.

"Why didn't you go yourself, if it is that dangerous?"

"My Lords and honorables, it was the nature of the experiment that the experimenter himself should not be expended in the first try. Artyr Rambo has indeed travelled through space-three. I shall follow him myself, in due course." (How the Lord Crudelta did do so is another tale, told about another time.) "If I had gone and if I had been lost, that would have been the end of the space-three trials. At least for our time."

"Tell us the exact circumstances under which you last saw Artyr Rambo before you met after the battle in the old Main Hospital."

"We had put him in a rocket of the most ancient style. We also wrote writing on the outside of it, just the way the Ancients did when they first ventured into space. Ah, that was a beautiful piece of engineering and archeology! We copied everything right down to the correct models of fifteen thousand years ago, when the Paroskii and Murkins were racing each other into space. The rocket was white, with a red and white gantry beside it. The letters IOM were on the rocket, not that the words mattered. The rocket has gone into nowhere, but the passenger sits here. It rose on a stool of fire. The stool became a column. Then the landing field disappeared."

"And the landing field," said Starmount quietly, "what was that?"

"A modified planoform ship. We have had ships go milky in space because they faded molecule by molecule. We have had others disappear utterly. The engineers had changed this around. We took out all the machinery needed for circumnavigation, for survival or for comfort. The landing field was to last three or four seconds, no more. Instead, we put in fourteen planoform devices, all operating in tandem, so that the ship would do what other ships do when they planoform—namely, drop one of our familiar dimensions and pick up a new dimension from some unknown category of space—but do it with such force as to get out of what people call space-two and move over into space-three."

"And space-three, what did you expect of that?"

"I thought that it was universal and instantaneous, in relation to our universe. That everything was equally distant from everything else. That Rambo, wanting to see his girl again, would move in a thousandth of a second from the empty space beyond Outpost Baiter Gator into the hospital where she was."

"And, my Lord Crudelta, what made you think so?"

"A hunch, my Lord, for which you are welcome to kill me."

Starmount turned to the panel. "I suspect, my Lord, that you are more likely to doom him to long life, great responsibility, immense rewards, and the fatigue of being his own difficult and complicated self."

The mitres moved gently and the members of the panel rose.

"You, my Lord Crudelta, will sleep till the trial is finished."

A robot stroked him and he fell asleep.

"Next witness," said the Lord Starmount, "in five minutes."

XI

Vomact tried to keep Rambo from being heard as a witness. He argued fiercely with the Lord Starmount in the intermission. "You Lords have shot up my hospital, abducted two of my patients and now you are going to torment both Rambo and Elizabeth. Can't you leave them alone? Rambo is in no condition to give coherent answers and Elizabeth may be damaged if she sees him suffer."

The Lord Starmount said to him, "You have your rules, doctor, and we have ours. This trial is being recorded, inch by inch and moment by moment. Nothing is going to be done to Rambo unless we find that he has planet-killing powers. If that is true, of course, we will ask you to take him back to the hospital and to put him to death very pleasantly. But I don't think it will happen. We want his story so that we can judge my colleague Crudelta. Do you think that the Instrumentality would survive if it did not have fierce internal discipline?"

Vomact nodded sadly; he went back to Grosbeck and Timofeyev, murmuring sadly to them, "Rambo's in for it. There's nothing we could do."

The panel reassembled. They put on their judicial mitres. The lights of the room darkened and the weird blue light of justice was turned on.

The robot orderly helped Rambo to the witness chair.

"You are obliged," said Starmount, "to speak quickly and clearly to this court."

"You're not Elizabeth," said Rambo.

"I am the Lord Starmount," said the investigating Lord, quickly deciding to dispense with the formalities. "Do you know me?"

"No," said Rambo.

"Do you know where you are?"

"Earth," said Rambo.

"Do you wish to lie or to tell the truth?"

"A lie," said Rambo, "is the only truth which men can share with each other, so I will tell you lies, the way we always do."

"Can you report your trip?"

"No."

"Why not, citizen Rambo?"

"Words won't describe it."

"Do you remember your trip?"

"Do you remember your pulse of two minutes ago?" countered Rambo.

"I am not playing with you," said Starmount. "We think you have been in space-three and we want you to testify about the Lord Crudelta?"

"Oh!" said Rambo. "I don't like him. I never did like him."

"Will you nevertheless try to tell us what happened also to you?"

"Should I, Elizabeth?" asked Rambo of the girl, who sat in the audience.

She did not stammer. "Yes," she said, in a clear voice which rang through the big room. "Tell them, so that we can find our lives again."

"I will tell you," said Rambo.

"When did you last see the Lord Crudelta?"

"When I was stripped and fitted to the rocket, four jumps out beyond Outpost Baiter Gator. He was on the ground. He waved good-by to me."

"And then what happened?"

"The rocket rose. It felt very strange, like no craft I had ever been in before. I weighed many, many gravities."

"And then?"

"The engines went on. I was thrown out of space itself."

"What did it seem like?"

"Behind me I left the working ships, the cloth and the food which goes through space. I went down rivers which did not exist. I felt people around me though I could not see them, red people shooting arrows at live bodies."

"*Where* were you?" asked a panel member.

"In the winter time where there is no summer. In an emptiness like a child's mind. In peninsulas which had torn loose from the land. And I *was* the ship."

"You were what?" asked the same panel member.

"The rocket nose. The cone. The boat. I was drunk. It was drunk. I was the drunkboat myself," said Rambo.

"And where did you go?" resumed Starmount.

"Where crazy lanterns stared with idiot eyes. Where the waves washed back and forth with the dead of all the ages. Where the stars became a pool and I swam in it. Where blue turns to liquor, stronger than alcohol, wilder than music, fermented with the *red red reds* of love. I saw all the things that men have ever thought they saw, but it was me who really saw them. I've heard phosphorescence singing and tides that seemed like crazy cattle clawing their way out of the ocean, their hooves beating the reefs. You will not believe me, but I found Floridas wilder than this, where the flowers had human skins and eyes like big cats."

"What are you talking about?" asked the Lord Starmount.

"What I found in space³," snapped Artyr Rambo. "Believe it or not. This is what I now remember. Maybe it's a dream, but it's all I have. It was years and years and it was the blink of an eye. I dreamed green nights. I felt places where the whole horizon became one big waterfall. The boat that was me met children and I showed them El Dorado, where the gold men live. The people drowned in space washed gently past me. I was a boat where all the lost space ships lay ruined and still. Seahorses which were not real ran beside me. The summer month came and hammered down the sun. I went past archipelagoes of stars, where the delirious skies opened up for wanderers. I cried for me. I wept for man. I wanted to be the drunkboat sinking. I sank. I fell. It seemed to me that the grass was a lake, where a sad child, on hands and knees, sailed a toy boat as fragile as a butterfly in spring. I can't forget the pride of unremembered flags, the arrogance of prisons which I suspected, the swimming of the businessmen! Then I was on the grass."

"This may have scientific value," said the Lord Starmount, "but it is not of judicial importance. Do you have any comment on what you did during the battle in the hospital?"

Rambo was quick and looked sane: "What I did, I did not do. What I did not do, I cannot tell. Let me go, because I am tired of you and space, big men and big things. Let me sleep and let me get well."

Starmount lifted his hand for silence.

The panel members stared at him.

Only the few telepaths present knew that they had all said, "*Aye. Let the man go. Let the girl go. Let the doctors go. But bring back the Lord Crudelta later on. He has many troubles ahead of him, and we wish to add to them.*"

XII

Between the Instrumentality, the Manhome Government and the authorities at the Old Main Hospital, everyone wished to give Rambo and Elizabeth happiness.

As Rambo got well, much of his Earth Four memory returned. The trip faded from his mind.

When he came to know Elizabeth, he hated the girl.

This was not his girl—his bold, saucy, Elizabeth of the markets and the valleys, of the snowy hills and the long boat rides. This was somebody meek, sweet, sad and hopelessly loving.

Vomact cured that.

He sent Rambo to the Pleasure City of the Herperides, where bold and talkative women pursued him because he was rich and famous.

In a few weeks—a very few indeed—he wanted *his* Elizabeth, this strange shy girl who had been cooked back from the dead while he rode space with his own fragile bones.

"Tell the truth, darling." He spoke to her once gravely and seriously. "The Lord Crudelta did not arrange the accident which killed you?"

"They say he wasn't there," said Elizabeth. "They say it was an actual accident. I don't know. I will never know."

"It doesn't matter now," said Rambo. "Crudelta's off among the stars, looking for trouble and finding it. We have our bungalow, and our waterfall, and each other."

"Yes, my darling," she said, "each other. And no fantastic Floridas for us."

He blinked at this reference to the past, but he said nothing. A man who has been through space[3] needs very little in life, outside of *not* going back to space[3]. Sometimes he dreamed he was the rocket again, the old rocket taking off on an impossible trip. Let other men follow! he thought, let other men go! I have Elizabeth and I am here.

Becalmed in Hell

LARRY NIVEN

Larry Niven made his first sale to Worlds of If *magazine in 1964 and soon estab-*
lished himself as one of the best new writers of "hard" science fiction since Robert
Heinlein. By the end of the seventies, Niven had won several Hugo and Nebula
Awards, published Ringworld, *one of the most acclaimed technological novels of*
its decade, and written several best-selling novels in collaboration with Jerry Pour-
nelle, including The Mote in God's Eye. *Niven's influence can clearly be seen on*
many of the new writers of the seventies, eighties, and nineties, including authors
such as John Varley, Gregory Benford, Stephen Baxter, Paul J. McAuley, G. David
Nordley, Geoffrey A. Landis, and many others. Niven's other books include the
novels Protector, World of Ptavvs, A Gift from Earth-Ringworld Engineers, Smoke
Ring, *and* Destiny's Road *and the collections* Tales of Known Space, Inconstant
Moon, Neutron Star, N-Space, *and* Playground of the Mind. *His most recent book*
is an omnibus novel/collection, Rainbow Mars.

Niven has explored many exotic locales, including the aforementioned Ring-
world, the core of the galaxy, and the heart of a neutron star. Here he visits a pair
of explorers stranded in the sullen atmosphere of Venus, hot and poisonous
enough to put Hell itself to shame, for a lesson in how believing can sometimes
make it so—whether you want *it to or not!*

I could feel the heat hovering outside. In the cabin it was bright and dry
and cool, almost too cool, like a modern office building in the dead of
the summer. Beyond the two small windows it was as black as it ever gets
in the solar system, and hot enough to melt lead, at a pressure equivalent
to three hundred feet beneath the ocean.

"There goes a fish," I said, just to break the monotony.

"So how's it cooked?"

"Can't tell. It seems to be leaving a trail of breadcrumbs. Fried? Imagine that, Eric! A fried jellyfish."

Eric sighed noisily. "Do I have to?"

"You have to. Only way you'll see anything worthwhile in this—this—"
Soup? Fog? Boiling maple syrup?

"Searing black calm."

"Right."

"Someone dreamed up that phrase when I was a kid, just after the news
of the Mariner II probe. An eternal searing black calm, hot as a kiln,
under an atmosphere thick enough to keep any light or any breath of
wind from ever reaching the surface."

I shivered. "What's the outside temperature now?"

"You'd rather not know. You've always had too much imagination, Howie."

"I can take it, Doc."

"Six hundred and twelve degrees."

"I can't take it, Doc!"

This was Venus, Planet of Love, favorite of the science-fiction writers of three decades ago. Our ship hung below the Earth-to-Venus hydrogen fuel tank, twenty miles up and all but motionless in the syrupy air. The tank, nearly empty now, made an excellent blimp. It would keep us aloft as long as the internal pressure matched the external. That was Eric's job, to regulate the tank's pressure by regulating the temperature of the hydrogen gas. We had collected air samples after each ten mile drop from three hundred miles on down, and temperature readings for shorter intervals, and we had dropped the small probe. The data we had gotten from the surface merely confirmed in detail our previous knowledge of the hottest world in the solar system.

"Temperature just went up to six-thirteen," said Eric. "Look, are you through bitching?"

"For the moment."

"Good. Strap down. We're taking off."

"Oh frabjous day!" I started untangling the crash webbing over my couch.

"We've done everything we came to do. Haven't we?"

"Am I arguing? Look, I'm strapped down."

"Yeah."

I knew why he was reluctant to leave. I felt a touch of it myself. We'd spent four months getting to Venus in order to spend a week circling her and less than two days in her upper atmosphere, and it seemed a terrible waste of time.

But he was taking too long. "What's the trouble, Eric?"

"You'd rather not know."

He meant it. His voice was a mechanical, inhuman monotone; he wasn't making the extra effort to get human expression out of his "prosthetic" vocal apparatus. Only a severe shock would affect him that way.

"I can take it," I said.

"Okay. I can't feel anything in the ramjet controls. Feels like I've just had a spinal anaesthetic."

The cold in the cabin drained into me, all of it. "See if you can send motor impulses the other way. You could run the rams by guess-and-hope even if you can't feel them."

"Okay." One split second later, "They don't. Nothing happens. Good thinking though."

I tried to think of something to say while I untied myself from the couch. What came out was, "It's been a pleasure knowing you, Eric. I've liked being half of this team, and I still do."

"Get maudlin later. Right now, start checking my attachments. Carefully."

I swallowed my comments and went to open the access door in the cabin's forward wall. The floor swayed ever so gently beneath my feet.

Beyond the four-foot-square access door was Eric. Eric's central nervous system, with the brain perched at the top and the spinal cord coiled in a loose spiral to fit more compactly into the transparent glass-and-sponge-plastic housing. Hundreds of wires from all over the ship led to the glass walls, where they were joined to selected nerves which spread like an electrical network from the central coil of nervous tissue and fatty protective membrane.

Space leaves no cripples; and don't call Eric a cripple, because he doesn't like it. In a way he's the ideal spaceman. His life support system weighs only half of what mine does, and takes up a twelfth as much room. But his other prosthetic aids take up most of the ship. The ramjets were hooked into the last pair of nerve trunks, the nerves which once moved his legs, and dozens of finer nerves in those trunks sensed and regulated fuel feed, ram temperature, differential acceleration, intake aperture dilation, and spark pulse.

These connections were intact. I checked them four different ways without finding the slightest reason why they shouldn't be working.

"Test the others," said Eric.

It took a good two hours to check every trunk nerve connection. They were all solid. The blood pump was chugging along, and the fluid was rich enough, which killed the idea that the ram nerves might have "gone to sleep" from lack of nutrients or oxygen. Since the lab is one of his prosthetic aids, I let Eric analyse his own blood sugar, hoping that the "liver" had goofed and was producing some other form of sugar. The conclusions were appalling. There was nothing wrong with Eric—inside the cabin.

"Eric, you're healthier than I am."

"I could tell. You looked worried, son, and I don't blame you. Now you'll have to go outside."

"I know. Let's dig out the suit."

It was in the emergency tools locker, the Venus suit that was never supposed to be used. NASA had designed it for use at Venusian ground level. Then they had refused to okay the ship below twenty miles until they knew more about the planet. The suit was a segmented armor job. I had watched it being tested in the heat-and-pressure box at Cal Tech, and I knew that the joints stopped moving after five hours, and wouldn't start again until they had been cooled. Now I opened the locker and pulled the suit out by the shoulders and held it in front of me. It seemed to be staring back.

"You still can't feel anything in the ramjets?"

"Not a twinge."

I started to put on the suit, piece by piece like medieval armor. Then I thought of something else. "We're twenty miles up. Are you going to ask me to do a balancing act on the hull?"

"No! Wouldn't think of it. We'll just have to go down."

The lift from the blimp tank was supposed to be constant until takeoff. When the time came Eric could get extra lift by heating the hydrogen to higher pressure, then cracking a valve to let the excess out. Of course he'd have to be very careful that the pressure was higher in the tank, or we'd get Venusian air coming in, and the ship would fall instead of rising. Naturally that would be disastrous.

So Eric lowered the tank temperature and cracked the valve, and down we went.

"Of course there's a catch," said Eric.

"I know."

"The ship stood the pressure twenty miles up. At ground level it'll be six times that."

"I know."

We fell fast, with the cabin tilted forward by the drag on our tailfins. The temperature rose gradually. The pressure went up fast. I sat at the window and saw nothing, nothing but black, but I sat there anyway and waited for the window to crack. NASA had refused to okay the ship below twenty miles . . .

Eric said, "The blimp tank's okay, and so's the ship, I think. But will the cabin stand up to it?"

"I wouldn't know."

"Ten miles."

Five hundred miles above us, unreachable, was the atomic ion engine that was to take us home. We couldn't get to it on the chemical rocket alone. The rocket was for use after the air became too thin for the ramjets.

"Four miles. Have to crack the valve again."

The ship dropped.

"I can see ground," said Eric.

I couldn't. Eric caught me straining my eyes and said, "Forget it. I'm using deep infrared, and getting no detail."

"No vast, misty swamps with weird, terrifying monsters and man-eating plants?"

"All I see is hot, bare dirt."

But we were almost down, and there were no cracks in the cabin wall. My neck and shoulder muscles loosened. I turned away from the window. Hours had passed while we dropped through the poisoned, thickening air. I already had most of my suit on. Now I screwed on my helmet and three-finger gantlets.

"Strap down," said Eric. I did.

We bumped gently. The ship tilted a little, swayed back, bumped again. And again, with my teeth rattling and my armor-plated body rolling against the crash webbing. "Damn," Eric muttered. I heard the hiss from above. Eric said, "I don't know how we'll get back up."

Neither did I. The ship bumped hard and stayed down, and I got up and went to the airlock.

"Good luck," said Eric. "Don't stay out too long." I waved at his cabin camera. The outside temperature was seven hundred and thirty.

The outer door opened. My suit refrigerating unit set up a complaining whine. With an empty bucket in each hand, and with my headlamp blazing a way through the black murk, I stepped out onto the right wing.

My suit creaked and settled under the pressure, and I stood on the wing and waited for it to stop. It was almost like being under water. My headlamp beam went out thick enough to be solid, penetrating no more than a hundred feet. The air couldn't have been that opaque, no matter how dense. It must have been full of dust, or tiny droplets of some fluid.

The wing ran back like a knife-edged running board, widening toward the tail until it spread into a tailfin. The two tailfins met back of the fuselage. At the tailfin tip was the ram, a big sculptured cylinder with an atomic engine inside. It wouldn't be hot because it hadn't been used yet, but I had my counter anyway.

I fastened a line to the wing and slid to the ground. As long as we were *here* . . . The ground turned out to be a dry, reddish dirt, crumbly, and so porous that it was almost spongy. Lava etched by chemicals? Almost anything would be corrosive at this pressure and temperature. I scooped one pailful from the surface and another from underneath the first, then climbed up the line and left the buckets on the wing.

The wing was terribly slippery. I had to wear magnetic sandals to stay on. I walked up and back along the two hundred foot length of the ship, making a casual inspection. Neither wing nor fuselage showed damage. Why not? If a meteor or something had cut Eric's contact with his sensors in the rams, there should have been evidence of a break in the surface.

Then, almost suddenly, I realized that there was an alternative.

It was too vague a suspicion to put into words yet, and I still had to finish the inspection. Telling Eric would be very difficult if I was right.

Four inspection panels were set into the wing, well protected from the reentry heat. One was halfway back on the fuselage, below the lower edge of the blimp tank, which was molded to the fuselage in such a way that from the front the ship looked like a dolphin. Two more were in the trailing edge of the tailfin, and the fourth was in the ram itself. All opened, with powered screwdriver on recessed screws, on junctions of the ship's electrical system.

There was nothing out of place under any of the panels. By making and breaking contacts and getting Eric's reactions, I found that his sensation ended somewhere between the second and third inspection panels. It was the same story on the left wing. No external damage, nothing wrong at the junctions. I climbed back to ground and walked slowly beneath the length of each wing, my headlamp tilted up. No damage underneath.

I collected my buckets and went back inside.

◆

"A bone to pick?" Eric was puzzled. "Isn't this a strange time to start an argument? Save it for space. We'll have four months with nothing else to do."

"This can't wait. First of all, did you notice anything I didn't?" He'd been watching everything I saw and did through the peeper in my helmet.

"No. I'd have yelled."

"Okay. Now get this.

"The break in your circuits isn't inside, because you get sensation up to the second wing inspection panels. It isn't outside because there's no evidence of damage, not even corrosion spots. That leaves only one place for the flaw."

"Go on."

"We also have the puzzle of why you're paralyzed in both rams. Why should they both go wrong at the same time? There's only one place in the ship where the circuits join."

"What? Oh, yes, I see. They join through me."

"Now let's assume for the moment that you're the piece with the flaw in it. You're not a piece of machinery, Eric. If something's wrong with you it isn't medical. That was the first thing we covered. But it could be psychological."

"It's nice to know you think I'm human. So I've slipped a cam, have I?"

"Slightly. I think you've got a case of what used to be called trigger anaesthesia. A soldier who kills too often sometimes finds that his right index finger or even his whole hand has gone numb, as if it were no longer a part of him. Your comment about not being a machine is important, Eric. I think that's the whole problem. You've never really believed that any part of the ship is a part of *you*. That's intelligent, because it's true. Every time the ship is redesigned you get a new set of parts, and it's right to avoid thinking of a change of model as a series of amputations." I'd been rehearsing this speech, trying to put it so that Eric would have no choice but to believe me. Now I know that it must have sounded phony. "But now you've gone too far. Subconsciously you've stopped believing that the rams can *feel* like a part of you, which they were designed to do. So you've persuaded yourself that you don't feel anything."

With my prepared speech done, and nothing left to say, I stopped talking and waited for the explosion.

"You make good sense," said Eric.

I was staggered. "You agree?"

"I didn't say that. You spin an elegant theory, but I want time to think about it. What do we do if it's true?"

"Why . . . I don't know. You'll just have to cure yourself."

"Okay. Now here's *my* idea. I propose that you thought up this theory to relieve yourself of a responsibility for getting us home alive. It puts the whole problem in my lap, metaphorically speaking."

"Oh, for—"

"Shut up. I haven't said you're wrong. That would be an ad hominem argument. We need time to think about this."

❧

It was lights-out, four hours later, before Eric would return to the subject.

"Howie, do me a favor. Assume for awhile that something mechanical is causing all our trouble. I'll assume it's psychosomatic."

"Seems reasonable."

"It is reasonable. What can you do if I've gone psychosomatic? What can I do if it's mechanical? I can't go around inspecting myself. We'd each better stick to what we know."

"It's a deal." I turned him off for the night and went to bed.

But not to sleep.

With the lights off it was just like outside. I turned them back on. It wouldn't wake Eric. Eric never sleeps normally, since his blood doesn't accumulate fatigue poisons, and he'd go mad from being awake all the time if he didn't have a Russian sleep inducer plate near his cortex. The ship could implode without waking Eric when his sleep inducer's on. But I felt foolish being afraid of the dark.

While the dark stayed outside it was all right.

But it wouldn't stay there. It had invaded my partner's mind. Because his chemical checks guard him against chemical insanities like schizophrenia, we'd assumed he was permanently sane. But how could any prosthetic device protect him from his own imagination, his own misplaced common sense?

I couldn't keep my bargain. I knew I was right. But what could I do about it?

Hindsight is wonderful. I could see exactly what our mistake had been, Eric's and mine and the hundreds of men who had built his life support after the crash. There was nothing left of Eric then except the intact central nervous system, and no glands except the pituitary. "We'll regulate his blood composition," they said, "and he'll always be cool, calm, and collected. No panic reactions from Eric!"

I know a girl whose father had an accident when he was forty-five or so. He was out with his brother, the girl's uncle, on a fishing trip. They were blind drunk when they started home and the guy was riding on the hood while the brother drove. Then the brother made a sudden stop. Our hero left two important glands on the hood ornament.

The only change in his sex life was that his wife stopped worrying about late pregnancy. His *habits* were developed.

Eric doesn't need adrenal glands to be afraid of death. His emotional patterns were fixed long before the day he tried to land a moonship without radar. He'd grab any excuse to believe that I'd fixed whatever was wrong with the ram connections.

But he was counting on me to do it.

The atmosphere leaned on the windows. Not wanting to, I reached out to touch the quartz with my fingertips. I couldn't feel the pressure. But it was there, inexorable as the tide smashing a rock into sand grains. How long would the cabin hold it back?

If some broken part were holding us here, how could I have missed finding it? Perhaps it had left no break in the surface of either wing. But how?

That was the angle.

Two cigarettes later I got up to get the sample buckets. They were empty, the alien dirt safely stored away. I filled them with water and put them in the cooler, set the cooler for 40° Absolute, then turned off the lights and went to bed.

●

The morning was blacker than the inside of a smoker's lungs. What Venus really needs, I decided, philosophizing on my back, is to lose ninety-nine percent of her air. That would give her a bit more than half as much air as Earth, which would lower the greenhouse effect enough to make the temperature livable. Drop Venus' gravity to near zero for a few weeks and the work would do itself.

The whole damn universe is waiting for us to discover antigravity.

"Morning," said Eric. "Thought of anything?"

"Yes." I rolled out of bed. "Now don't bug me with questions, I'll explain everything as I go."

"No breakfast?"

"Not yet."

Piece by piece I put my suit on, just like one of King Arthur's gentlemen, and went for the buckets only after the gauntlets were on. The ice, in the cold section, was in the chilly neighborhood of absolute zero. "This is two buckets of ordinary ice," I said, holding them up. "Now let me out."

"I should keep you here till you talk," Eric groused. But the doors opened and I went out onto the wing. I started talking while I unscrewed the number two right panel.

"Eric, think a moment about the tests they run on a manned ship before they'll let a man walk into the lifesystem. They test every part separately and in conjunction with other parts. Yet if something isn't working, either it's damaged or it wasn't tested right. Right?"

"Reasonable." He wasn't giving away anything.

"Well, nothing caused any damage. Not only is there no break in the ship's skin, but no coincidence could have made both rams go haywire at the same time. So something wasn't tested right."

I had the panel off. In the buckets the ice boiled gently where it touched the surfaces of the glass buckets. The blue ice cakes had cracked under their own internal pressure. I dumped one bucket into the maze of wiring and contacts and relays, and the ice shattered, giving me room to close the panel.

"So I thought of something last night, something that wasn't tested. Every part of the ship must have been in the heat-and-pressure box, exposed to artificial Venus conditions, but the ship as a whole, a unit, couldn't have been. It's too big." I'd circled around to the left wing and was opening the number three panel in the trailing edge. My remaining ice was half water and half small chips; I sloshed these in and fastened the panel. "What cut your circuits must have been the heat or the pressure or both. I can't help the pressure, but I'm cooling these relays with ice. Let me know which ram gets its sensation back first, and we'll know which inspection panel is the right one."

"Howie. Has it occurred to you what the cold water might do to those hot metals?"

"It could crack them. Then you'd lose all control over the ramjets, which is what's wrong right now."

"Uh. Your point, partner. But I still can't feel anything."

I went back to the airlock with my empty buckets swinging, wondering if they'd get hot enough to melt. They might have, but I wasn't out that long. I had my suit off and was refilling the buckets when Eric said, "I can feel the right ram."

"How extensive? Full control?"

"No. I can't feel the temperature. Oh, here it comes. We're all set, Howie."

My sigh of relief was sincere.

I put the buckets in the freezer again. We'd certainly want to take off with the relays cold. The water had been chilling for perhaps twenty minutes when Eric reported, "Sensation's going."

"What?"

"Sensation's going. No temperature, and I'm losing fuel feed control. It doesn't stay cold long enough."

"Ouch! Now what?"

"I hate to tell you. I'd almost rather let you figure it out for yourself."

I had. "We go as high as we can on the blimp tank, then I go out on the wing with a bucket of ice in each hand—"

We had to raise the blimp tank temperature to almost eight hundred degrees to get pressure, but from then on we went up in good shape. To sixteen miles. It took three hours.

"That's as high as we go," said Eric. "You ready?"

I went to get the ice. Eric could see me, he didn't need an answer. He opened the airlock for me.

Fear I might have felt, or panic, or determination or self-sacrifice—but there was nothing. I went out feeling like a used zombie.

My magnets were on full. It felt like I was walking through shallow tar. The air was thick, though not as heavy as it had been down there. I followed my headlamp to the number two panel, opened it, poured ice in, and threw the bucket high and far. The ice was in one cake. I couldn't close the panel. I left it open and hurried around to the other wing. The second bucket was filled with exploded chips; I sloshed them in and locked the number two left panel and came back with both hands free. It still looked like limbo in all directions, except where the headlamp cut a tunnel through the darkness, and—my feet were getting hot. I closed the right panel on boiling water and sidled back along the hull into the airlock.

"Come in and strap down," said Eric. "Hurry!"

"Gotta get my suit off." My hands had started to shake from reaction. I couldn't work the clamps.

"No you don't. If we start right now we may get home. Leave the suit on and come in."

I did. As I pulled my webbing shut, the rams roared. The ship shuddered a little, then pushed forward as we dropped from under the blimp tank. Pressure mounted as the rams reached operating speed. Eric was giving it all he had. It would have been uncomfortable even without the metal suit around me. With the suit on it was torture. My couch was afire from the suit, but I couldn't get breath to say so. We were going almost straight up.

We had gone twenty minutes when the ship jerked like a galvanized frog. "Ram's out," Eric said calmly. "I'll use the other." Another lurch as we dropped the dead one. The ship flew on like a wounded penguin, but still accelerating.

One minute . . . two . . .

The other ram quit. It was as if we'd run into molasses. Eric blew off the ram and the pressure eased. I could talk.

"Eric."

"What?"

"Got any marshmallows?"

"*What?* Oh, I see. Is your suit tight?"

"Sure."

"Live with it. We'll flush the smoke out later. I'm going to coast above some of this stuff, but when I use the rocket it'll be savage. No mercy."

"Will we make it?"

"I think so. It'll be close."

The relief came first, icy cold. Then the anger. "No more inexplicable numbnesses?" I asked.

"No. Why?"

"If any come up you'll be sure and tell me, won't you?"

"Are you getting at something?"

"Skip it." I wasn't angry any more.

"I'll be damned if I do. You know perfectly well it was mechanical trouble, you fool. You fixed it yourself!"

"No. I convinced you I must have fixed it. You needed to believe the rams *should* be working again. I gave you a miracle cure, Eric. I just hope I don't have to keep dreaming up new placebos for you all the way home."

"You thought that, but you went out on the wing sixteen miles up?" Eric's machinery snorted. "You've got guts where you need brains, Shorty."

I didn't answer.

"Five thousand says the trouble was mechanical. We let the mechanics decide after we land."

"You're on."

"Here comes the rocket. Two, one—"

It came, pushing me down into my metal suit. Sooty flames licked past my ears, writing black on the green metal ceiling, but the rosy mist before my eyes was not fire.

The man with the thick glasses spread a diagram of the Venus ship and jabbed a stubby finger at the trailing edge of the wing. "Right around here," he said. "The pressure from outside compressed the wiring channel a little, just enough so there was no room for the wire to bend. It had to act as if it were rigid, see? Then when the heat expanded the metal these contacts pushed past each other."

"I suppose it's the same design on both wings?"

He gave me a queer look. "Well, naturally."

I left my check for $5000 in a pile of Eric's mail and hopped a plane for Brasilia. How he found me I'll never know, but the telegram arrived this morning

HOWIE COME HOME ALL IS FORGIVEN
DONOVANS BRAIN

I guess I'll have to.

Nine Hundred Grandmothers

R. A. LAFFERTY

R. A. Lafferty started writing in 1960, at the relatively advanced age (for a new writer, anyway) of forty-six, and in the years before his retirement in 1987 published some of the freshest and funniest short stories ever written, almost all of them dancing on the borderlines between fantasy, science fiction, and the tall tale, that most boisterous and quintessentially American of forms.

Lafferty has published memorable novels that stand up quite well today—among the best of them are Past Master, The Devil Is Dead, The Reefs of Earth, *the historical novel* Okla Hannali, *and the totally unclassifiable (a fantasy novel disguised as* a nonfiction historical study, perhaps?) The Fall of Rome—*but it was the prolific stream of short stories he began publishing in 1960 that would eventually establish his reputation. Stories like "Slow Tuesday Night," "Thus We Frustrate Charlemagne, "Hog-Belly Honey," "The Hole on the Corner," "All Pieces of a River Shore," "Among the Hairy Earthmen," "Seven Day Terror," "Continued on Next Rock," "All But the Words," and many others, all clearly demonstrating Lafferty's characteristic virtues: folksy exuberance, a singing lyricism of surprising depth and power, outlandish imagination, a store of offbeat erudition matched only by Avram Davidson, and a strong, shaggy sense of humor unrivaled by anyone.*

Lafferty's short work has been gathered in the landmark collection Nine Hundred Grandmothers, *as well as in* Strange Doings, Does Anyone Else Have Something Further to Add?, *Golden Gate and Other Stories, and* Ringing Changes. *Much of his later work is available only in small-press editions—like the very strange novel* Archipelago *and* My Heart Leaps Up, *which was serialized as a sequence of chapbooks—but his other novels available in trade editions (although many of them are long out-of-print) include* Fourth Mansions, Arrive at Easterwine, Space Chantey, *and* The Flame Is Green. *Lafferty won the Hugo Award in 1973 for his story "Eurema's Dam" and in 1990 received the prestigious World Fantasy Life Achievement Award. His most recent books are the collections* Lafferty In Orbit *and* Iron Tears. *He lives in Oklahoma.*

It's hardly surprising that Lafferty would have his own unique and quirky take on the theme of space exploration, just as he did on just about every other conceivable concept. In the razor-sharp and very funny story that follows, he takes us along on a journey of discovery with an intrepid and persistent (if perhaps not terribly wise) explorer who is about to discover that, gee, maybe there are things that Man Was Not Meant to Know, after all!

Ceran Swicegood was a promising young Special Aspects Man. But, like all Special Aspects, he had one irritating habit. He was forever asking the question: How Did It All Begin?

They all had tough names except Ceran. Manbreaker Crag, Heave Huckle, Blast Berg, George Blood, Move Manion (when Move says "Move," you move), Trouble Trent. They were supposed to be tough, and they had taken tough names at the naming. Only Ceran kept his own—to the disgust of his commander, Manbreaker.

"Nobody can be a hero with a name like Ceran Swicegood!" Manbreaker would thunder. "Why don't you take Storm Shannon? That's good. Or Gutboy Barrelhouse or Slash Slagle or Nevel Knife? You barely glanced at the suggested list."

"I'll keep my own," Ceran always said, and that is where he made his mistake. A new name will sometimes bring out a new personality. It had done so for George Blood. Though the hair on George's chest was a graft job, yet that and his new name had turned him from a boy into a man. Had Ceran assumed the heroic name of Gutboy Barrelhouse he might have been capable of rousing endeavors and man-sized angers rather than his tittering indecisions and flouncy furies.

They were down on the big asteroid Proavitus—a sphere that almost tinkled with the potential profit that might be shaken out of it. And the tough men of the Expedition knew their business. They signed big contracts on the native velvet-like bark scrolls and on their own parallel tapes. They impressed, inveigled and somewhat cowed the slight people of Proavitus. Here was a solid two-way market, enough to make them slaver. And there was a whole world of oddities that could lend themselves to the luxury trade.

"Everybody's hit it big but you," Manbreaker crackled in kindly thunder to Ceran after three days there. "But even Special Aspects is supposed to pay its way. Our charter compels us to carry one of your sort to give a cultural twist to the thing, but it needn't be restricted to that. What we go out for every time, Ceran, is to cut a big fat hog in the rump—we make no secret of that. But if the hog's tail can be shown to have a cultural twist to it, that will solve a requirement. And if that twist in the tail can turn us a profit, then we become mighty happy about the whole thing. Have you been able to find out anything about the living dolls, for instance? They might have both a cultural aspect and a market value."

"The living dolls seem a part of something much deeper," Ceran said. "There's a whole complex of things to be unraveled. The key may be the statement of the Proavitoi that they do not die."

"I think they die pretty young, Ceran. All those out and about are young, and those I have met who do not leave their houses are only middling old."

"Then where are their cemeteries?"

"Likely they cremate the old folks when they die."

"Where are the crematories?"

"They might just toss the ashes out or vaporize the entire remains. Probably they have no reverence for ancestors."

"Other evidence shows their entire culture to be based on an exaggerated reverence for ancestors."

"You find out, Ceran. You're Special Aspects Man."

➤

Ceran talked to Nokoma, his Proavitoi counterpart as translator. Both were expert, and they could meet each other halfway in talk. Nokoma was likely feminine. There was a certain softness about both the sexes of the Proavitoi, but the men of the Expedition believed that they had them straight now.

"Do you mind if I ask some straight questions?" Ceran greeted her today.

"Sure is not. How else I learn the talk well but by talking?"

"Some of the Proavitoi say that they do not die, Nokoma. Is this true?"

"How is not be true? If they die, they not be here to say they do not die. Oh, I joke, I joke. No, we do not die. It is a foolish alien custom which we see no reason to imitate. On Proavitus, only the low creatures die."

"None of you does?"

"Why, no. Why should one want to be an exception in this?"

"But what do you do when you get very old?"

"We do less and less then. We come to a deficiency of energy. Is it not the same with you?"

"Of course. But where do you go when you become exceedingly old?"

"Nowhere. We stay at home then. Travel is for the young and those of the active years."

"Let's try it from the other end," Ceran said. "Where are your father and mother, Nokoma?"

"Out and about. They aren't really old."

"And your grandfathers and grandmothers?"

"A few of them still get out. The older ones stay home."

"Let's try it this way. How many grandmothers do you have, Nokoma?"

"I think I have nine hundred grandmothers in my house. Oh, I know that isn't many, but we are the young branch of a family. Some of our clan have very great numbers of ancestors in their houses."

"And all these ancestors are alive?"

"What else? Who would keep things not alive? How would such be ancestors?"

Ceran began to hop around in his excitement.

"Could I see them?" he twittered.

"It might not be wise for you to see the older of them," Nokoma cautioned. "It could be an unsettling thing for strangers, and we guard it. A few tens of them you can see, of course."

Then it came to Ceran that he might be onto what he had looked for all his life. He went into a panic of expectation.

"Nokoma, it would be finding the key!" he fluted. "If none of you has ever died, then your entire race would still be alive!"

"Sure. Is like you count fruit. You take none away, you still have them all."

"But if the first of them are still alive, then they might know their origin! They would know how it began! Do they? Do you?"

"Oh, not I. I am too young for the Ritual."

"But who knows? Doesn't someone know?"

"Oh, yes, All the old ones know how it began."

"How old? How many generations back from you till they know?"

"Ten, no more. When I have ten generations of children, then I will also go to the Ritual."

"The Ritual, what is it?"

"Once a year, the old people go to the very old people. They wake them up and ask them how it all began. The very old people tell them the beginning. It is a high time. Oh, how they hottle and laugh! Then the very old people go back to sleep for another year. So it is passed down to the generations. That is the Ritual."

◆

The Proavitoi were not humanoid. Still less were they "monkey-faces," though that name was now set in the explorers' lingo. They were upright and robed and swathed, and were assumed to be two-legged under their garments. Though, as Manbreaker said, "They might go on wheels, for all we know."

They had remarkable flowing hands that might be called everywhere-digited. They could handle tools, or employ their hands as if they were the most intricate tools.

George Blood was of the opinion that the Proavitoi were always masked, and that the men of the Expedition had never seen their faces. He said that those apparent faces were ritual masks, and that no part of the Proavitoi had ever been seen by the men except for those remarkable hands, which perhaps were their real faces.

The men reacted with cruel hilarity when Ceran tried to explain to them just what a great discovery he was verging on.

"Little Ceran is still on the how-did-it-begin-jag," Manbreaker jeered. "Ceran, will you never give off asking which came first, the chicken or the egg?"

"I will have that answer very soon," Ceran sang. "I have the unique opportunity. When I find how the Proavitoi began, I may have the clue to how everything began. All of the Proavitoi are still alive, the very first generation of them."

"It passes belief that you can be so simpleminded," Manbreaker moaned. "They say that one has finally mellowed when he can suffer fools gracefully. By God, I hope I never come to that."

But two days later, it was Manbreaker who sought out Ceran Swicegood on nearly the same subject. Manbreaker had been doing a little thinking and discovering of his own.

"You are Special Aspects Man, Ceran," he said, "and you have been running off after the wrong aspect."

"What is that?"

"It don't make a damn how it began. What is important is that it may not have to end."

"It is the beginning that I intend to discover," said Ceran.

"You fool, can't you understand anything? What do the Proavitoi possess so uniquely that we don't know whether they have it by science or by their nature or by fool luck?"

"Ah, their chemistry, I suppose."

"Sure. Organic chemistry has come of age here. The Proavitoi have every kind of nexus and inhibitor and stimulant. They can grow and shrink and telescope and prolong what they will. These creatures seem stupid to me; it is as if they had these things by instinct. But they have them, that is what is important. With these things, we can become the patent medicine kings of the universes, for the Proavitoi do not travel or make many outside contacts. These things can do anything or undo anything. I suspect that the Proavitoi can shrink cells, and I suspect that they can do something else."

"No, they couldn't shrink cells. It is you who talk nonsense now, Manbreaker."

"Never mind. Their things already make nonsense of conventional chemistry. With the pharmacopoeia that one could pick up here, a man need never die. That's the stick horse you've been riding, isn't it? But you've been riding it backward with your head to the tail. The Proavitoi say that they never die."

"They seem pretty sure that they don't. If they did, they would be the first to know it, as Nokoma says."

"What? Have these creatures humor?"

"Some."

"But, Ceran, you don't understand how big this is."

"I'm the only one who understands it so far. It means that if the Proavitoi have always been immortal, as they maintain, then the oldest of them are still alive. From them I may be able to learn how their species—and perhaps every species—began."

Manbreaker went into his dying buffalo act then. He tore his hair and nearly pulled out his ears by the roots. He stomped and pawed and went off bull-bellowing: "It don't make a damn how it began, you fool! It might not have to end!" so loud that the hills echoed back: "It don't make a damn—you fool."

Ceran Swicegood went to the house of Nokoma, but not with her on her invitation. He went without her when he knew that she was away from home. It was a sneaky thing to do, but the men of the Expedition were trained in sneakery.

He would find out better without a mentor about the nine hundred grandmothers, about the rumored living dolls. He would find out what the old people did do if they didn't die, and find if they knew how they were first born. For his intrusion, he counted on the innate politeness of the Proavitoi.

The house of Nokoma, of all the people, was in the cluster on top of the large flat hill, the Acropolis of Proavitus. They were earthen houses, though finely done, and they had the appearance of growing out of and being a part of the hill itself.

Ceran went up the winding, ascending flagstone paths, and entered the house which Nokoma had once pointed out to him. He entered furtively, and encountered one of the nine hundred grandmothers—one with whom nobody need be furtive.

The grandmother was seated and small and smiling at him. They talked without real difficulty, though it was not as easy as with Nokoma, who could meet Ceran halfway in his own language. At her call, there came a grandfather who likewise smiled at Ceran. These two ancients were somewhat smaller than the Proavitoi of active years. They were kind and serene. There was an atmosphere about the scene that barely missed being an odor—not unpleasant, sleepy, reminiscent of something, almost sad.

"Are there those here older than you?" Ceran asked earnestly.

"So many, so many, who could know how many?" said the grandmother. She called in other grandmothers and grandfathers older and smaller than herself, these no more than half the size of the active Proavitoi—small, sleepy, smiling.

Ceran knew now that the Proavitoi were not masked. The older they were, the more character and interest there was in their faces. It was only of the immature active Proavitoi that there could have been a doubt. No masks could show such calm and smiling old age as this. The queer textured stuff was their real faces.

So old and friendly, so weak and sleepy, there must have been a dozen generations of them there back to the oldest and smallest.

"How old are the oldest?" Ceran asked the first grandmother.

"We say that all are the same age since all are perpetual," the grandmother told him. "It is not true that all are the same age, but it is indelicate to ask how old."

"You do not know what a lobster is," Ceran said to them, trembling, "but it is a creature that will boil happily if the water on him is heated slowly. He takes no alarm, for he does not know at what point the heat is dangerous. It is that gradual here with me. I slide from one degree to another with you and my credulity is not alarmed. I am in danger of believing anything about you if it comes in small doses, and it will. I believe that you are here and as you are for no other reason than that I see and touch you. Well, I'll be boiled for a lobster, then, before I turn back from it. Are there those here even older than the ones present?"

The first grandmother motioned Ceran to follow her. They went down a ramp through the floor into the older part of the house, which must have been under ground.

Living dolls! They were here in rows on the shelves, and sitting in small chairs in their niches. Doll-sized indeed, and several hundred of them.

Many had wakened at the intrusion. Others came awake when spoken to or touched. They were incredibly ancient, but they were cognizant in their glances and recognition. They smiled and stretched sleepily, not as humans would, but as very old puppies might. Ceran spoke to them, and they understood each other surprisingly.

Lobster, lobster, said Ceran to himself, *the water has passed the danger point! And it hardly feels different. If you believe your senses in this, then you will be boiled alive in your credulity.*

He knew now that the living dolls were real and that they were the living ancestors of the Proavitoi.

Many of the little creatures began to fall asleep again. Their waking moments were short, but their sleeps seemed to be likewise. Several of the living mummies woke a second time while Ceran was still in the room, woke refreshed from very short sleeps and were anxious to talk again.

"You are incredible!" Ceran cried out, and all the small and smaller and still smaller creatures smiled and laughed their assent. Of course they were. All good creatures everywhere are incredible, and were there ever so many assembled in one place? But Ceran was greedy. A roomful of miracles wasn't enough.

"I have to take this back as far as it will go!" he cried avidly. "Where are the even older ones?"

"There are older ones and yet older and again older," said the first grandmother, "and thrice-over older ones, but perhaps it would be wise not to seek to be too wise. You have seen enough. The old people are sleepy. Let us go up again."

Go up again, out of this? Ceran would not. He saw passages and descending ramps, down into the heart of the great hill itself. There were whole worlds of rooms about him and under his feet. Ceran went on and down, and who was to stop him? Not dolls and creatures much smaller than dolls.

Manbreaker had once called himself an old pirate who reveled in the stream of his riches. But Ceran was the Young Alchemist who was about to find the Stone itself.

He walked down the ramps through centuries and millennia. The atmosphere he had noticed on the upper levels was a clear odor now— sleepy, half-remembered, smiling, sad and quite strong. That is the way Time smells.

"Are there those here even older than you?" Ceran asked a small grandmother whom he held in the palm of his hand.

"So old and so small that I could hold in my hand," said the grandmother in what Ceran knew from Nokoma to be the older uncompounded form of the Proavitus language.

Smaller and older the creatures had been getting as Ceran went through the rooms. He was boiled lobster now for sure. He had to believe it all: he saw and felt it. The wren-sized grandmother talked and laughed and nodded that there were those far older than herself, and in doing so she nodded herself back to sleep. Ceran returned her to her niche in the hive-like wall where there were thousands of others, miniaturized generations.

Of course he was not in the house of Nokoma now. He was in the heart of the hill that underlay all the houses of Proavitus, and these were the ancestors of everybody on the asteroid.

"Are there those here even older than you?" Ceran asked a small grandmother whom he held on the tip of his finger.

"Older and smaller," she said, "but you come near the end."

She was asleep, and he put her back in her place. The older they were, the more they slept.

He was down to solid rock under the roots of the hill. He was into the passages that were cut out of that solid rock, but they could not be many or deep. He had a sudden fear that the creatures would become so small that he could not see them or talk to them, and so he would miss the secret of the beginning.

But had not Nokoma said that all the old people knew the secret? Of course. But he wanted to hear it from the oldest of them. He would have it now, one way or the other.

"Who is the oldest? Is this the end of it? Is this the beginning? Wake up! Wake up!" he called when he was sure he was in the lowest and oldest room.

"Is it Ritual?" asked some who woke up. Smaller than mice they were, no bigger than bees, maybe older than both.

"It is a special Ritual," Ceran told them. "Relate to me how it was in the beginning."

What was that sound—too slight, too scattered to be a noise? It was like a billion microbes laughing. It was the hilarity of little things waking up to a high time.

"Who is the oldest of all?" Ceran demanded, for their laughter bothered him. "Who is the oldest and first?"

"I am the oldest, the ultimate grandmother," one said gaily. "All the others are my children. Are you also of my children?"

"Of course," said Ceran, and the small laughter of unbelief flittered out from the whole multitude of them.

"Then you must be the ultimate child, for you are like no other. If you be, then it is as funny at the end as it was in the beginning."

"How was it in the beginning?" Ceran bleated. "You are the first. Do you know how you came to be?"

"Oh, yes, yes," laughed the ultimate grandmother, and the hilarity of the small things became a real noise now.

"How did it begin?" demanded Ceran, and he was hopping and skipping about in his excitement.

"Oh, it was so funny a joke the way things began that you would not believe it," chittered the grandmother. "A joke, a joke!"

"Tell me the joke, then. If a joke generated your species, then tell me that cosmic joke."

"Tell yourself," tinkled the grandmother. "You are a part of the joke if you are of my children. Oh, it is too funny to believe. How good to wake up and laugh and go to sleep again."

Blazing green frustration! To be so close and to be balked by a giggling bee!

"Don't go to sleep again! Tell me at once how it began!" Ceran shrilled, and he had the ultimate grandmother between thumb and finger.

"This is not Ritual," the grandmother protested. "Ritual is that you guess what it was for three days, and we laugh and say 'No, no, no, it was something nine times as wild as that. Guess some more.' "

"I will *not* guess for three days! Tell me at once or I will crush you," Ceran threatened in a quivering voice.

"I look at you, you look at me, I wonder if you will do it," the ultimate grandmother said calmly.

Any of the tough men of the Expedition would have done it—would have crushed her, and then another and another and another of the creatures till the secret was told. If Ceran had taken on a tough personality and a tough name he'd have done it. If he'd been Gutboy Barrelhouse he'd have done it without a qualm. But Ceran Swicegood couldn't do it.

"Tell me," he pleaded in agony. "All my life I've tried to find out how it began, how anything began. And you know!"

"We know. Oh, it was so funny how it began. So joke! So fool, so clown, so grotesque thing! Nobody could guess, nobody could believe."

"Tell me! Tell me!" Ceran was ashen and hysterical.

"No, no, you are no child of mine," chortled the ultimate grandmother. "Is too joke a joke to tell a stranger. We could not insult a stranger to tell so funny, so unbelieve. Strangers can die. Shall I have it on conscience that a stranger died laughing?"

"Tell me! Insult me! Let me die laughing!" But Ceran nearly died crying from the frustration that ate him up as a million bee-sized things laughed and hooted and giggled:

"Oh, it was so funny the way it began!"

And they laughed. And laughed. And went on laughing . . . until Ceran Swicegood wept and laughed together, and crept away, and returned to the ship still laughing. On his next voyage he changed his name to Blaze Bolt and ruled for ninety-seven days as king of a sweet sea island in M-81, but that is another and much more unpleasant story.

The Keys to December

ROGER ZELAZNY

Like a number of other writers, the late Roger Zelazny began publishing in 1962 in the pages of Cele Goldsmith's Amazing. This was the so-called Class of '62, whose membership also included Thomas M. Disch, Keith Laumer, and Ursula K. Le Guin. Everyone in that "class" would eventually achieve prominence, but some of them would achieve it faster than others, and Zelazny's subsequent career was one of the most meteoric in the history of science fiction. The first Zelazny story to attract wide notice was "A Rose for Ecclesiastes," published in 1963. (It was later selected by vote of the SFWA membership as one of the best science-fiction stories of all time.) By the end of that decade, he had won two Nebula Awards and two Hugo Awards and was widely regarded as one of the two most important American science-fiction writers of the sixties. (The other was Samuel R. Delany). By the end of the seventies, although Zelazny's critical acceptance as an important science-fiction writer had dimmed, his long series of novels about the enchanted land of Amber—beginning with Nine Princes in Amber—had made him one of the most popular and best-selling fantasy writers of our time and inspired the founding of worldwide fan clubs and fanzines.

Zelazny's early novels were, on the whole, well received (This Immortal won a Hugo, as did his most famous novel, Lord of Light), but it was the strong and stylish short work he published in magazines like F&SF and Amazing and Worlds of If throughout the middle years of the decade that electrified the genre, and it was these early stories—stories like "This Moment of the Storm," "The Doors of His Face, the Lamps of His Mouth," "The Graveyard Heart," "He Who Shapes," "For a Breath I Tarry," and "This Mortal Mountain"—that established Zelazny as a giant of the field, and that many still consider to be his best work. These stories are still amazing for their invention and elegance and verve, for their good-natured effrontery and easy ostentation, for the risks Zelazny took in pursuit of eloquence without ruffling a hair, the grace and nerve he displayed as he switched from high-flown pseudo-Spenserian, to wisecracking Chandlerian slang, to vivid prose poetry, to Hemingwayesque starkness in the course of only a few lines—and for the way he made it all look easy and effortless, the same kind of illusion Fred Astaire used to generate when he danced.

Here's one of those eloquent and elegant stories, written by Zelazny at the top of his form, demonstrating that if you can't find the kind of world you're looking for out there in the galaxy somewhere, you may have to create it yourself—but that even then, exploring that world may turn up dangers and wonders that you never planned on, unexpected things that you now have to deal with, no matter what the consequences may be. . . .

Zelazny won another Nebula and Hugo Award in 1976 for his novella Home Is the Hangman, a Hugo in 1982 for "Unicorn Variation," another Hugo in 1986 for his novella 24 Views of Mt. Fuji, by Hokusai, and a final Hugo in 1987 for his story *"Permafrost." His other books include, in addition to the multivolume* Amber *series, the novels* This Immortal, The Dream Master, Isle of the Dead, Jack of Shadows, Eye of Cat, Doorways in the Sand, Today We Choose Faces, Bridge of Ashes, To Die in Italbar, *and* Roadmarks *and the collections* Four for Tomorrow, The Doors of His Face, the Lamps of His Mouth and Other Stories, The Last Defender of Camelot, *and* Frost and Fire. *Among his last books are two collaborative novels,* A Farce to Be Reckoned With, *with Robert Sheckley, and* Wilderness, *with Gerald Hausman, and, as editor, two anthologies,* Wheel of Fortune *and* Warriors of Blood and Dream. *Zelazny died in 1995. Since his death, several posthumous collaborative novels have been published, including* Psychoshop, *with the late Alfred Bester, and* Donnerjack *and* Lord Demon, *both with Jane Lindskold. A tribute anthology to Zelazny, featuring stories by authors who had been inspired by his work,* Lord of the Fantastic, *was published in 1998.*

Born of man and woman, in accordance with Catform Y7 requirements, Coldworld Class (modified per Alyonal), 3.2E, G.M.I. option, Jarry Dark was not suited for existence anywhere in the universe which had guaranteed him a niche. This was either a blessing or a curse, depending on how you looked at it.

So look at it however you would, here is the story:

🔊

It is likely that his parents could have afforded the temperature control unit, but not much more than that. (Jarry required a temperature of at least −50°C. to be comfortable.)

It is unlikely that his parents could have provided for the air pressure control and gas mixture equipment required to maintain his life.

Nothing could be done in the way of 3.2-E grav-simulation, so daily medication and physiotherapy were required. It is unlikely that his parents could have provided for this.

The much-maligned option took care of him, however. It safeguarded his health. It provided for his education. It assured his economic welfare and physical well-being.

It might be argued that Jarry Dark would not have been a homeless Coldworld Catform (modified per Alyonal) had it not been for General Mining, Incorporated, which had held the option. But then it must be borne in mind that no one could have foreseen the nova which destroyed Alyonal.

When his parents had presented themselves at the Public Health Planned Parenthood Center and requested advice and medication pending offspring, they had been informed as to the available worlds and the body-form requirements for them. They had selected Alyonal, which had recently been purchased by General Mining for purposes of mineral exploitation. Wisely, they had elected the option; that is to say, they had signed a contract on behalf of their anticipated offspring, who would be eminently qualified to inhabit that world, agreeing that he would work as an employee of General Mining until he achieved his majority, at which time he would be free to depart and seek employment wherever he might choose (though his choices would admittedly be limited). In return for this guarantee, General Mining agreed to assure his health, education and continuing welfare for so long as he remained in their employ.

When Alyonal caught fire and went away, those Coldworld Catforms covered by the option who were scattered about the crowded galaxy were, by virtue of the agreement, wards of General Mining.

This is why Jarry grew up in a hermetically sealed room containing temperature and atmosphere controls, and why he received a first-class closed circuit education, along with his physiotherapy and medicine. This is also why Jarry bore some resemblance to a large gray ocelot without a tail, had webbing between his fingers and could not go outside to watch the traffic unless he wore a pressurized refrigeration suit and took extra medication.

All over the swarming galaxy, people took the advice of Public Health Planned Parenthood Centers, and many others had chosen as had Jarry's parents. Twenty-eight thousand, five hundred sixty-six of them, to be exact. In any group of over twenty-eight thousand five hundred sixty, there are bound to be a few talented individuals. Jarry was one of them. He had a knack for making money. Most of his General Mining pension check was invested in well-chosen stocks of a speculative nature. (In fact, after a time he came to own considerable stock in General Mining.)

When the man from the Galactic Civil Liberties Union had come around, expressing concern over the pre-birth contracts involved in the option and explaining that the Alyonal Catforms would make a good test case (especially since Jarry's parents lived within jurisdiction of the 877th Circuit, where they would be assured a favorable courtroom atmosphere), Jarry's parents had demurred, for fear of jeopardizing the General Mining pension. Later on, Jarry himself dismissed the notion also. A favorable decision could not make him an E-world Normform, and what else mattered? He was not vindictive. Also, he owned considerable stock in G.M. by then.

He loafed in his methane tank and purred, which meant that he was thinking. He operated his cryo-computer as he purred and thought. He was computing the total net worth of all the Catforms in the recently organized December Club.

He stopped purring and considered a sub-total, stretched, shook his head slowly. Then he returned to his calculations.

When he had finished, he dictated a message into his speech-tube, to Sanza Barati, President of December and his betrothed:

"Dearest Sanza—The funds available, as I suspected, leave much to be desired. All the more reason to begin immediately. Kindly submit the proposal to the business committee, outline my qualifications and seek immediate endorsement. I've finished drafting the general statement to the membership. (Copy attached.) From these figures, it will take me between five and ten years, if at least eighty percent of the membership backs me. So push hard, beloved. I'd like to meet you someday, in a place where the sky is purple. Yours, always, Jarry Dark, Treasurer. P.S. I'm pleased you were pleased with the ring."

Two years later, Jarry had doubled the net worth of December Incorporated.

A year and a half after that, he had doubled it again.

When he received the following letter from Sanza, he leapt onto his trampoline, bounded into the air, landed upon his feet at the opposite end of his quarters, returned to his viewer and replayed it:

Dear Jarry,

Attached are specifications and prices for five more worlds. The research staff likes the last one. So do I. What do you think? Alyonal II? If so, how about the price? When could we afford that much? The staff also says that an hundred Worldchange units could alter it to what we want in 5-6 centuries. Will forward costs of this machinery shortly.

Come live with me and be my love, in a place where there are no walls. . . .

Sanza

"One year," he replied, "and I'll buy you a world! Hurry up with the costs of machinery and transport . . ."

⬯

When the figures arrived Jarry wept icy tears. One hundred machines, capable of altering the environment of a world, plus twenty-eight thousand coldsleep bunkers, plus transportation costs for the machinery and his people, plus . . . Too high! He did a rapid calculation.

He spoke into the speech-tube:

". . . Fifteen additional years is too long to wait, Pussycat. Have them figure the time-span if we were to purchase only twenty Worldchange units. Love and kisses, Jarry."

During the days which followed, he stalked above his chamber, erect at first, then on all fours as his mood deepened.

"Approximately three thousand years," came the reply. "May your coat be ever shiny—Sanza."

"Let's put it to a vote, Greeneyes," he said.

⬯

Quick, a world in 300 words or less! Picture this. . . .

One land mass, really, containing three black and brackish looking seas; gray plains and yellow plains and skies the color of dry sand; shallow forests with trees like mushrooms which have been swabbed with iodine; no mountains, just hills brown, yellow, white, lavender; green birds with wings like parachutes, bills like sickles, feathers like oak leaves, an inside-out umbrella behind; six very distant moons, like spots before the eyes in daytime, snowflakes at night, drops of blood at dusk and dawn; grass like mustard in the moister valleys; mists like white fire on windless mornings, albino serpents when the air's astir; radiating chasms, like fractures in frosted windowpanes; hidden caverns, like chains of dark bubbles; seventeen known dangerous predators, ranging from one to six meters in length, excessively furred and fanged; sudden hailstorms, like hurled hammerheads from a clear sky; an icecap like a blue beret at either flattened pole; nervous bipeds a meter and a half in height, short on cerebrum, which wander the shallow forests and prey upon the giant caterpillar's larva, as well as the giant caterpillar, the green bird, the blind burrower, and the offal-eating murk-beast; seventeen mighty rivers; clouds like pregnant purple cows, which quickly cross the land to lie-in beyond the visible east; stands of windblasted stones like frozen music; nights like soot, to obscure the lesser stars; valleys which flow like the torsos of women or instruments of music; perpetual frost in places of shadow; sounds in the morning like the cracking of ice, the trembling of tin, the snapping of steel strands. . . .

They knew they would turn it to heaven.

✦

The vanguard arrived, decked out in refrigeration suits, installed ten Worldchange units in either hemisphere, began setting up cold-sleep bunkers in several of the larger caverns.

Then came the members of December down from the sand-colored sky.

They came and they saw, decided it was almost heaven, then entered their caverns and slept. Over twenty-eight thousand Coldworld Catforms (modified per Alyonal) came into their own world to sleep for a season in silence the sleep of ice and of stone, to inherit the new Alyonal. There is no dreaming in that sleep. But had there been, their dreams might have been as the thoughts of those yet awake.

"It is bitter, Sanza."

"Yes, but only for a time—"

". . . To have each other and our own world, and still to go forth like divers at the bottom of the sea. To have to crawl when you want to leap . . ."

"It is only for a short time, Jarry, as the senses will reckon it."

"But it is really three thousand years! An ice age will come to pass as we doze. Our former worlds will change so that we would not know them were we to go back for a visit—and none will remember us."

"Visit what? Our former cells? Let the rest of the worlds go by! Let us be forgotten in the lands of our birth! We are a people apart and we have found our home. What else matters?"

"True. . . . It will be but a few years, and we shall stand our tours of wakefulness and watching together."

"When is the first?"

"Two and a half centuries from now—three months of wakefulness."

"What will it be like then?"

"I don't know. Less warm . . ."

"Then let us return and sleep. Tomorrow will be a better day."

"Yes."

"Oh! See the green bird! It drifts like a dream . . ." When they awakened that first time, they stayed within the World-change installation at the place called Deadland. The world was already colder and the edges of the sky were tinted with pink. The metal walls of the great installation were black and rimed with frost. The atmosphere was still lethal and the temperature far too high. They remained within their special chambers for most of the time, venturing outside mainly to make necessary tests and to inspect the structure of their home.

Deadland. . . . Rocks and sand. No trees, no marks of life at all.

The time of terrible winds was still upon the land, as the world fought back against the fields of the machines. At night great clouds of real estate smoothed and sculpted the stands of stone, and when the winds departed the desert would shimmer as if fresh-painted and the stones would stand like flames within the morning and its singing. After the sun came up into the sky and hung there for a time, the winds would begin again and a dun-colored fog would curtain the day. When the morning winds departed, Jarry and Sanza would stare out across Deadland through the east window of the installation, for that was their favorite—the one on the third floor—where the stone that looked like a gnarly Normform waved to them, and they would lie upon the green couch they had moved up from the first floor, and would sometimes make love as they listened for the winds to rise again, or Sanza would sing and Jarry would write in the log or read back through it, the scribblings of friends and unknowns through the centuries, and they would purr often but never laugh, because they did not know how.

One morning, as they watched, they saw one of the biped creatures of the iodine forests moving across the land. It fell several times, picked itself up, continued, fell once more, lay still.

"What is it doing this far from its home?" asked Sanza.

"Dying," said Jarry. "Let's go outside."

They crossed a catwalk, descended to the first floor, donned their protective suits and departed the installation.

The creature had risen to its feet and was staggering once again. It was covered with a reddish down, had dark eyes and a long wide nose, lacked a true forehead. It had four brief digits, clawed, upon each hand and foot.

When it saw them emerge from the Worldchange unit, it stopped and stared at them. Then it fell.

They moved to its side and studied it where it lay.

It continued to stare at them, its dark eyes wide, as it lay there shivering.

"It will die if we leave it here," said Sanza.

". . . And it will die if we take it inside," said Jarry.

It raised a forelimb toward them, let it fall again. Its eyes narrowed, then closed.

Jarry reached out and touched it with the toe of his boot. There was no response.

"It's dead," he said.

"What will we do?"

"Leave it here. The sands will cover it."

They returned to the installation, and Jarry entered the event in the log.

During their last month of duty, Sanza asked him, "Will everything die here but us? The green birds and the big eaters of flesh? The funny little trees and the hairy caterpillars?"

"I hope not," said Jarry. "I've been reading back through the biologists' notes. I think life might adapt. Once it gets a start anywhere, it'll do anything it can to keep going. It's probably better for the creatures of this planet that we could afford only twenty Worldchangers. That way they have three millennia to grow more hair and learn to breathe our air and drink our water. With a hundred units we might have wiped them out and had to import coldworld creatures or breed them. This way, the ones who live here might be able to make it."

"It's funny," she said, "but the thought just occurred to me that we're doing here what was done to us. They made us for Alyonal, and a nova took it away . . . These creatures came to life in this place, and we're taking it away. We're turning all of life on this planet into what we were on our former worlds—misfits."

"The difference, however, is that we are taking our time," said Jarry, "and giving them a chance to get used to the new conditions."

"Still, I feel that all that—outside there"—she gestured toward the window—"is what this world is becoming: one big Deadland."

"Deadland was here before we came. We haven't created new deserts."

"All the animals are moving south. The trees are dying. When they get as far south as they can go and still the temperature drops, and the air continues to burn in their lungs—then it will be all over for them."

"By then they might have adapted. The trees are spreading, are developing thicker barks. Life will make it."

"I wonder . . ."

"Would you prefer to sleep until it's all over?"

"No; I want to be by your side, always."

"Then you must reconcile yourself to the fact that something is always hurt by any change. If you do this, you will not be hurt yourself."

Then they listened for the winds to rise.

Three days later, in the still of sundown, between the winds of day and the winds of night, she called him to the window. He climbed to the third floor and moved to her side. Her breasts were rose in the sundown light and the places beneath them silver and dark. The fur of her shoulders and haunches was like an aura of smoke. Her face was expressionless and her wide, green eyes were not turned toward him.

He looked out.

The first big flakes were falling, blue, through the pink light. They drifted past the stone and gnarly Normform; some stuck to the thick quartz windowpane; they fell upon the desert and lay there like blossoms of cyanide; they swirled as more of them came down and were caught by the first puffs of the terrible winds. Dark clouds had mustered overhead and from them, now, great cables and nets of blue descended. Now the flakes flashed past the window like butterflies, and the outline of Deadland flickered on and off. The pink vanished and there was only blue, blue and darkening blue, as the first great sigh of evening came into their ears and the billows suddenly moved sidewise rather than downwards, becoming indigo as they raced by.

⬦

"The machine is never silent," Jarry wrote. "Sometimes I fancy I can hear voices in its constant humming, its occasional growling, its crackles of power. I am alone here at the Deadland station. Five centuries have passed since our arrival. I thought it better to let Sanza sleep out this tour of duty, lest the prospect be too bleak. (It is.) She will doubtless be angry. As I lay half-awake this morning, I thought I heard my parents' voices in the next room. No words. Just the sounds of their voices as I used to hear them over my old intercom. They must be dead by now, despite all geriatrics. I wonder if they thought of me much after I left? I couldn't even shake my father's hand without my gauntlet, or kiss my mother goodbye. It is strange, the feeling, to be this alone, with only the throb of the machinery about me as it rearranges the molecules of the atmosphere, refrigerates the world, here in the middle of the blue place. Deadland. This, despite the fact that I grew up in a steel cave. I call the other nineteen stations every afternoon. I am afraid I am becoming something of a nuisance. I won't call them tomorrow, or perhaps the next day.

"I went outside without my refrig-pack this morning, for a few moments. It is still deadly hot. I gulped a mouthful of air and choked. Our day is still far off. But I can notice the difference from the last time I tried it, two and a half hundred years ago. I wonder what it will be like when we have finished?—And I, an economist! What will my function be in our new Alyonal? Whatever, so long as Sanza is happy. . . .

"The Worldchanger stutters and groans. All the land is blue for so far as I can see. The stones still, but their shapes are changed from what they were. The sky is entirely pink now, and it becomes almost maroon in the morning and the evening. I guess it's really a wine-color, but I've never seen wine, so I can't say for certain. The trees have not died. They've grown hardier. Their barks are thicker, their leaves are darker and larger. They grow much taller now, I've been told. There are no trees in Deadland.

"The caterpillars still live. They seem much larger, I understand, but it is actually because they have become woolier than they used to be. It seems that most of the animals have heavier pelts these days. Some apparently have taken to hibernating. A strange thing: Station Seven reported that they had thought the bipeds were growing heavier coats. There seem to be quite a few of them in that area, and they often see them off in the distance. They looked to be shaggier. Closer observation, however, revealed that some of them were either carrying or were wrapped in the skins of dead animals! Could it be that they are more intelligent than we have given them credit for? This hardly seems possible, since they were tested quite thoroughly by the Bio Team before we set the machines in operation. Yet, it is very strange.

"The winds are still severe. Occasionally, they darken the sky with ash. There has been considerable vulcanism southwest of here. Station Four was relocated because of this. I hear Sanza singing now, within the sounds of the machine. I will let her be awakened the next time. Things should be more settled by then. No, that is not true. It is self-ishness. I want her here beside me. I feel as if I were the only living thing in the whole world. The voices on the radio are ghosts. The clock ticks loudly and the silences between the ticks are filled with the humming of the machine, which is a kind of silence, too, because it is constant. Sometimes I think it is not there; I listen for it, I strain my ears, and I do not know whether there is a humming or not. I check the indicators then, and they assure me that the machine is functioning. Or perhaps there is something wrong with the indicators. But they seem to be all right. No. It is me. And the blue of Deadland is a kind of visual silence. In the morning even the rocks are covered with blue frost. It is beautiful or ugly? There is no response within me. It is a part of the great silence, that's all. Perhaps I shall become a mystic. Perhaps I shall develop occult powers to achieve something bright and liberating as I sit here at the center of the great silence. Perhaps I shall see visions. Already I hear voices. Are there ghosts in Deadland? No, there was never anything here to be ghosted. Except perhaps for the little biped. Why did it cross Deadland, I wonder? Why did it head for the center of destruction rather than away, as its fellows did? I shall never know. Unless perhaps I have a vision. I think it is time to suit up and take a walk. The polar icecaps are heavier. The glaciation has be-gun. Soon, soon things will be better. Soon the silence will end, I hope. I wonder, though, whether silence is not the true state of affairs in the universe, our little noises serving only to accentuate it, like a speck of black on a field of blue. Everything was once silence and will be so again—is now, perhaps. Will I ever hear real sounds, or only sounds out of the silence? Sanza is singing again. I wish I could wake her up now, to walk with me, out there. It is beginning to snow."

◆

Jarry awakened again on the eve of the millennium.

Sanza smiled and took his hand in hers and stroked it, as he explained why he had let her sleep, as he apologized.

"Of course I'm not angry," she said, "considering I did the same thing to you last cycle."

Jarry stared up at her and felt the understanding begin.

"I'll not do it again," she said, "and I know you couldn't. The aloneness is almost unbearable."

"Yes," he replied.

"They warmed us both alive last time. I came around first and told them to put you back to sleep. I was angry then, when I found out what you had done. But I got over it quickly, so often did I wish you were there."

"We will stay together," said Jarry.

"Yes, always."

They took a flier from the cavern of sleep to the World-change installation at Deadland, where they relieved the other attendants and moved the new couch up to the third floor.

The air of Deadland, while sultry, could now be breathed for short periods of time, though a headache invariably followed such experiments. The heat was still oppressive. The rock, once like an old Normform waving, had lost its distinctive outline. The winds were no longer so severe.

On the fourth day, they found some animal tracks which seemed to belong to one of the larger predators. This cheered Sanza, but another, later occurrence produced only puzzlement.

One morning they went forth to walk in Deadland.

Less than a hundred paces from the installation, they came upon three of the giant caterpillars, dead. They were stiff, as though dried out rather than frozen, and they were surrounded by rows of markings within the snow. The footprints which led to the scene and away from it were rough of outline, obscure.

"What does it mean?" she asked.

"I don't know, but I think we had better photograph this," said Jarry.

They did. When Jarry spoke to Station Eleven that afternoon, he learned that similar occurrences had occasionally been noted by attendants of other installations. These were not too frequent, however.

"I don't understand," said Sanza.

"I don't want to," said Jarry.

It did not happen again during their tour of duty. Jarry entered it into the log and wrote a report. Then they abandoned themselves to lovemaking, monitoring, and occasional nights of drunkenness. Two hundred years previously, a biochemist had devoted his tour of duty to experimenting with compounds which would produce the same reactions in Catforms as the legendary whiskey did in Normforms. He had been successful, had spent four weeks on a colossal binge, neglected his duty and been relieved of it, was then retired to his coldbunk for the balance of the Wait. His basically simple formula had circulated, however, and Jarry and Sanza found a well-stocked bar in the storeroom and a hand-written manual explaining its use and a variety of drinks which might be compounded. The author of the document had expressed the hope that each tour of attendance might result in the discovery of a new mixture, so that when he returned for his next cycle the manual would have grown to a size proportionate to his desire. Jarry and Sanza worked at it conscientiously, and satisfied the request with a Snowflower Punch which warmed their bellies and made their purring turn into giggles, so that they discovered laughter also. They celebrated the millennium with an entire bowl of it, and Sanza insisted on calling all the other installations and giving them the formula, right then, on the graveyard watch, so that everyone could share in their joy. It is quite possible that everyone did, for the recipe was well-received. And always, even after that bowl was but a memory, they kept the laughter. Thus are the first simple lines of tradition sometimes sketched.

◆

"The green birds are dying," said Sanza, putting aside a report she had been reading.

"Oh?" said Jarry.

"Apparently they've done all the adapting they're able to," she told him.

"Pity," said Jarry.

"It seems less than a year since we came here. Actually, it's a thousand."

"Time flies," said Jarry.

"I'm afraid," she said.

"Of what?"

"I don't know. Just afraid."

"Why?"

"Living the way we've been living, I guess. Leaving little pieces of ourselves in different centuries. Just a few months ago, as my memory works, this place was a desert. Now it's an ice field. Chasms open and close. Canyons appear and disappear. Rivers dry up and new ones spring forth. Everything seems so very transitory. Things look solid, but I'm getting afraid to touch things now. They might go away. They might turn into smoke, and my hand will keep on reaching through the smoke and touch—something . . . God, maybe. Or worse yet, maybe not. No one really knows what it will be like here when we've finished. We're traveling toward an unknown land and it's too late to go back. We're moving through a dream, heading toward an idea. . . . Sometimes I miss my cell . . . and all the little machines that took care of me there. Maybe *I* can't adapt. Maybe I'm like the green bird . . ."

"No, Sanza. You're not. We're real. No matter what happens out there, *we* will last. Everything is changing because we want it to change. We're stronger than the world, and we'll squeeze it and paint it and poke holes in it until we've made it exactly the way we want it. Then we'll take it and cover it with cities and children. You want to see God? Go look in the mirror. God has pointed ears and green eyes. He is covered with soft gray fur. When He raises His hand there is webbing between His fingers."

"It is good that you are strong, Jarry."

"Let's get out the power sled and go for a ride."

"All right."

Up and down, that day, they drove through Deadland, where the dark stones stood like clouds in another sky.

☞

It was twelve and a half hundred years.

Now they could breathe without respirators, for a short time.

Now they could bear the temperature, for a short time.

Now all the green birds were dead.

Now a strange and troubling thing began.

The bipeds came by night, made markings upon the snow, left dead animals in the midst of them. This happened now with much more frequency than it had in the past. They came long distances to do it, many of them with fur which was not their own upon their shoulders.

Jarry searched through the history files for all the reports on the creatures.

"This one speaks of lights in the forest," he said. "Station Seven."

"What . . . ?"

"Fire," he said. "What if they've discovered fire?"

"Then they're not really beasts!"

"But they were!"

"They wear clothing now. They make some sort of sacrifice to our machines. They're not beasts any longer."

"How could it have happened?"

"How do you think? *We* did it. Perhaps they would have remained stupid—animals—if we had not come along and forced them to get smart in order to go on living. We've accelerated their evolution. They had to adapt or die, and they adapted."

"D'you think it would have happened if we hadn't come along?" he asked.

"Maybe—some day. Maybe not, too."

Jarry moved to the window, stared out across Deadland.

"I have to find out," he said. "If they are intelligent, if they are—human, like us," he said, then laughed, "then we must consider their ways."

"What do you propose?"

"Locate some of the creatures. See whether we can communicate with them."

"Hasn't it been tried?"

"Yes."

"What were the results?"

"Mixed. Some claim they have considerable understanding. Others place them far below the threshold where humanity begins."

"We may be doing a terrible thing," she said. "Creating men, then destroying them. Once, when I was feeling low, you told me that we were the gods of this world, that ours was the power to shape and to break. Ours is the power to shape and break, but I don't feel especially divine. What can we do? They have come this far, but do you think they can bear the change that will take us the rest of the way? What if they are like the green birds? What if they've adapted as fast and as far as they can and it is not sufficient? What would a god do?"

"Whatever he wished," said Jarry.

That day, they cruised over Deadland in the flier, but the only signs of life they saw were each other. They continued to search in the days that followed, but they did not meet with success.

Under the purple morning, however, two weeks later, it happened.

"They've been here," said Sanza.

Jarry moved to the front of the installation and stared out.

The snow was broken in several places, inscribed with the lines he had seen before, about the form of a small, dead beast.

"They can't have gone very far," he said.

"No."

"We'll search in the sled."

Now over the snow and out, across the land called Dead they went, Sanza driving and Jarry peering at the lines of footmarks in the blue.

They cruised through the occurring morning, hinting of fire and violet, and the wind went past them like a river, and all about them there came sounds like the cracking of ice, the trembling of tin, the snapping of steel strands. The bluefrosted stones stood like frozen music, and the long shadow of their sled, black as ink, raced on ahead of them. A shower of hailstones drumming upon the roof of their vehicle like a sudden visitation of demon dancers, as suddenly was gone. Deadland sloped downward, slanted up again.

Jarry placed his hand upon Sanza's shoulder.

"Ahead!"

She nodded, began to brake the sled.

They had it at bay. They were using clubs and long poles which looked to have fire-hardened points. They threw stones. They threw pieces of ice.

Then they backed away and it killed them as they went.

The Catforms had called it a bear because it was big and shaggy and could rise up onto its hind legs. . . .

This one was about three and a half meters in length, was covered with bluish fur and had a thin, hairless snout like the business end of a pair of pliers.

Five of the little creatures lay still in the snow. Each time that it swung a paw and connected, another one fell.

Jarry removed the pistol from its compartment and checked the charge.

"Cruise by slowly," he told her. "I'm going to try to burn it about the head."

His first shot missed, scoring the boulder at its back. His second singed the fur of its neck. He leapt down from the sled then, as they came abreast of the beast, thumbed the power control up to maximum, and fired the entire charge into its breast, point-blank.

The bear stiffened, swayed, fell, a gaping wound upon it, front to back.

Jarry turned and regarded the little creatures. They stared up at him.

"Hello," he said. "My name is Jarry. I dub thee Redforms—"

He was knocked from his feet by a blow from behind.

He rolled across the snow, lights dancing before his eyes, his left arm and shoulder afire with pain.

A second bear had emerged from the forest of stone.

He drew his long hunting knife with his right hand and climbed back to his feet.

As the creature lunged, he moved with the catspeed of his kind, thrusting upward, burying his knife to the hilt in its throat.

A shudder ran through it, but it cuffed him and he fell once again, the blade torn from his grasp.

The Redforms threw more stones, rushed toward it with their pointed sticks.

Then there was a thud and a crunching sound, and it rose up into the air and came down on top of him.

He awakened.

He lay on his back, hurting, and everything he looked at seemed to be pulsing, as if about to explode.

How much time had passed, he did not know.

Either he or the bear had been moved.

The little creatures crouched, watching.

Some watched the bear. Some watched him.

Some watched the broken sled. . . .

The broken sled. . . .

He struggled to his feet.

The Redforms drew back.

He crossed to the sled and looked inside.

He knew she was dead when he saw the angle of her neck. But he did all the things a person does to be sure, anyway, before he would let himself believe it.

She had delivered the deathblow, crashing the sled into the creature, breaking its back. It had broken the sled. Herself, also.

He leaned against the wreckage, composed his first prayer, then removed her body.

The Redforms watched.

He lifted her in his arms and began walking, back toward the installation, across Deadland.

The Redforms continued to watch as he went, except for the one with the strangely high brow-ridge, who studied instead the knife that protruded from the shaggy and steaming throat of the beast.

⟡

Jarry asked the awakened executives of December: "What should we do?"

"She is the first of our race to die on this world," said Yan Turl, Vice President.

"There is no tradition," said Selda Kein, Secretary. "Shall we establish one?"

"I don't know," said Jarry. "I don't know what is right to do."

"Burial or cremation seem to be the main choices. Which would you prefer?"

"I don't—No, not the ground. Give her back to me. Give me a large flier . . . I'll burn her."

"Then let us construct a chapel."

"No. It is a thing I must do in my own way. I'd rather do it alone."

"As you wish. Draw what equipment you need, and be about it."

"Please send someone else to keep the Deadland installation. I wish to sleep again when I have finished this thing—until the next cycle."

"Very well, Jarry. We are sorry."

"Yes—we are."

Jarry nodded, gestured, turned, departed.

Thus are the heavier lines of life sometimes drawn.

●

At the southeastern edge of Deadland there was a blue mountain. It stood to slightly over three thousand meters in height. When approached from the northwest, it gave the appearance of being a frozen wave in a sea too vast to imagine. Purple clouds rent themselves upon its peak. No living thing was to be found on its slopes. It had no name, save that which Jarry Dark gave it.

He anchored the flier.

He carried her body to the highest point to which a body might be carried.

He placed her there, dressed in her finest garments, a wide scarf concealing the angle of her neck, a dark veil covering her emptied features.

He was about to try a prayer when the hail began to fall. Like thrown rocks, the chunks of blue ice came down upon him, upon her.

"God damn you!" he cried and he raced back to the flier.

He climbed into the air, circled.

Her garments were flapping in the wind. The hail was a blue, beaded curtain that separated them from all but these final caresses: fire aflow from ice to ice, from clay aflow immortally through guns.

He squeezed the trigger and a doorway into the sun opened in the side of the mountain that had been nameless. She vanished within it, and he widened the doorway until he had lowered the mountain.

Then he climbed upward into the cloud, attacking the storm until his guns were empty.

He circled then above the molten mesa, there at the southeastern edge of Deadland.

He circled above the first pyre this world had seen.

Then he departed, to sleep for a season in silence the sleep of ice and of stone, to inherit the new Alyonal. There is no dreaming in that sleep.

●

Fifteen centuries. Almost half the Wait. Two hundred words or less. . . . Picture—

. . . Nineteen mighty rivers flowing, but the black seas rippling violet now.

. . . No shallow iodine-colored forests. Mighty shag-barked barrel trees instead, orange and lime and black and tall across the land.

. . . Great ranges of mountains in the place of hills brown, yellow, white, lavender. Black corkscrews of smoke unwinding from smoldering cones.

. . . Flowers, whose roots explore the soil twenty meters beneath their mustard petals, unfolded amidst the blue frost and the stones.

. . . Blind burrowers burrowing deeper; offal-eating murk-beasts now showing formidable incisors and great rows of ridged molars; giant caterpillars growing smaller but looking larger because of increasing coats.

. . . The contours of valleys still like the torsos of women, flowing and rolling, or perhaps like instruments of music.

. . . Gone much windblasted stone, but ever the frost.

. . . Sounds in the morning as always, harsh, brittle, metallic.

They were sure they were halfway to heaven.

Picture that.

The Deadland log told him as much as he really needed to know. But he read back through the old reports, also.

Then he mixed himself a drink and stared out the third floor window.

". . . Will die," he said, then finished his drink, outfitted himself, and abandoned his post.

It was three days before he found a camp.

He landed the flier at a distance and approached on foot. He was far to the south of Deadland, where the air was warmer and caused him to feel constantly short of breath.

They were wearing animal skins—skins which had been cut for a better fit and greater protection, skins which were tied about them. He counted sixteen lean-to arrangements and three campfires. He flinched as he regarded the fires, but he continued to advance.

When they saw him, all their little noises stopped, a brief cry went up, and then there was silence.

He entered the camp.

The creatures stood unmoving about him. He heard some bustling within the large lean-to at the end of the clearing.

He walked about the camp.

A slab of dried meat hung from the center of a tripod of poles. Several long spears stood before each dwelling place. He advanced and studied one. A stone which had been flaked into a leaf-shaped spearhead was affixed to its end.

There was the outline of a cat carved upon a block of wood. . . .

He heard a footfall and turned.

One of the Redforms moved slowly toward him. It appeared older than the others. Its shoulders sloped; as it opened its mouth to make a series of popping noises, he saw that some of its teeth were missing; its hair was grizzled and thin. It bore something in its hands, but Jarry's attention was drawn to the hands themselves.

Each hand bore an opposing digit.

He looked about him quickly, studying the hands of the others. All of them seemed to have thumbs. He studied their appearance more closely.

They now had foreheads.

He returned his attention to the old Redform.

It placed something at his feet, and then it backed away from him.

He looked down.

A chunk of dried meat and a piece of fruit lay upon a broad leaf.

He picked up the meat, closed his eyes, bit off a piece, chewed and swallowed. He wrapped the rest in the leaf and placed it in the side pocket of his pack.

He extended his hand and the Redform drew back.

He lowered his hand, unrolled the blanket he had carried with him and spread it upon the ground. He seated himself, pointed to the Redform, then indicated a position across from him at the other end of the blanket.

The creature hesitated, then advanced and seated itself.

"We are going to learn to talk with one another," he said slowly. Then he placed his hand upon his breast and said, "Jarry."

◆

Jarry stood before the reawakened executives of December.

"They are intelligent," he told them. "It's all in my report."

"So?" asked Yan Turl.

"I don't think they will be able to adapt. They have come very far, very rapidly. But I don't think they can go much further. I don't think they can make it all the way."

"Are you a biologist, an ecologist, a chemist?"

"No."

"Then on what do you base your opinion?"

"I observed them at close range for six weeks."

"Then it's only a feeling you have . . . ?"

"You know there are no experts on a thing like this. It's never happened before."

"Granting their intelligence—granting even that what you have said concerning their adaptability is correct—what do you suggest we do about it?"

"Slow down the change. Give them a better chance. If they can't make it the rest of the way, then stop short of our goal. It's already livable here. *We* can adapt the rest of the way."

"Slow it down? How much?"

"Supposing we took another seven or eight thousand years?"

"Impossible!"

"Entirely!"

"Too much!"

"Why?"

"Because everyone stands a three-month watch every two hundred fifty years. That's one year of personal time for every thousand. You're asking too much of everyone's time."

"But the life of an entire race may be at stake!"

"You do not know for certain."

"No, I don't. But do you feel it is something to take a chance with?"

"Do you want to put it to an executive vote?"

"No—I can see that I'll lose. I want to put it before the entire membership."

"Impossible. They're all asleep."

"Then wake them up."

"That would be quite a project."

"Don't you think that the fate of a race is worth the effort? Especially since we're the ones who forced intelligence upon them? We're the ones who made them evolve, cursed them with intellect."

"Enough! They were right at the threshhold. They might have become intelligent had we *not* come along—"

"But you can't say for certain! You don't really know! And it doesn't really matter how it happened. They're here and we're here, and they think we're gods—maybe because we do nothing for them but make them miserable. We have some responsibility to an intelligent race though. At least to the extent of not murdering it."

"Perhaps we could do a long-range study . . ."

"They could be dead by then. I formally move, in my capacity as Treasurer, that we awaken the full membership and put the matter to a vote."

"I don't hear any second to your motion."

"Selda?" he said.

She looked away.

"Tarebell? Clond? Bondici?"

There was silence in the cavern that was high and wide about him.

"All right. I can see when I'm beaten. We will be our own serpents when we come into our Eden. I'm going now, back to Deadland, to finish my tour of duty."

"You don't have to. In fact, it might be better if you sleep the whole thing out . . ."

"No. If it's going to be this way, the guilt will be mine also. I want to watch, share it fully."

"So be it," said Turl.

⟟

Two weeks later, when Installation Nineteen tried to raise the Deadland Station on the radio, there was no response.

After a time, a flier was dispatched.

The Deadland Station was a shapeless lump of melted metal.

Jarry Dark was nowhere to be found.

Later that afternoon, Installation Eight went dead.

A flier was immediately dispatched.

Installation Eight no longer existed. Its attendants were found several miles away, walking. They told how Jarry Dark had forced them from the station at gunpoint. Then he burnt it to the ground, with the firecannons mounted upon his flier.

At about the time they were telling this story, Installation Six became silent.

The order went out: MAINTAIN CONTINUOUS RADIO CONTACT WITH TWO OTHER STATIONS AT ALL TIMES.

The other order went out: GO ARMED AT ALL TIMES. TAKE ANY VISITOR PRISONER.

⟟

Jarry waited. At the bottom of a chasm, parked beneath a shelf of rock, Jarry waited. An opened bottle stood upon the control board of his flier. Next to it was a small case of white metal.

Jarry took a long, last drink from the bottle as he waited for the broadcast he knew would come.

When it did, he stretched out on the seat and took a nap.

When he awakened, the light of day was waning.

The broadcast was still going on. . . .

". . . Jarry. They will be awakened and a referendum will be held. Come back to the main cavern. This is Yan Turl. Please do not destroy any

more installations. This action is not necessary. We agree with your proposal that a vote be held. Please contact us immediately. We are waiting
for your reply, Jarry . . ."

He tossed the empty bottle through the window and raised the flier
out of the purple shadow into the air and up.

●

When he descended upon the landing stage within the main cavern, of
course they were waiting for him. A dozen rifles were trained upon him
as he stepped from the flier.

"Remove your weapons, Jarry," came the voice of Yan Turl.

"I'm not wearing any weapons," said Jarry. "Neither is my flier," he
added; and this was true, for the fire-cannons no longer rested within
their mountings.

Yan Turl approached, looked up at him.

"Then you may step down."

"Thank you, but I like it right where I am."

"You are a prisoner."

"What do you intend to do with me?"

"Put you back to sleep until the end of the Wait. Come down here!"

"No. And don't try shooting—or using a stun charge or gas, either. If
you do, we're all of us dead the second it hits."

"What do you mean?" asked Turl, gesturing gently to the riflemen.

"My flier," said Jarry, "is a bomb, and I'm holding the fuse in my right
hand." He raised the white metal box. "So long as I keep the lever on
the side of this box depressed, we live. If my grip relaxes, even for an
instant, the explosion which ensues will doubless destroy this entire cavern."

"I think you're bluffing."

"You know how you can find out for certain."

"You'll die too, Jarry."

"At the moment, I don't really care. Don't try burning my hand off
either, to destroy the fuse," he cautioned, "because it doesn't really matter.
Even if you should succeed, it will cost you at least two installations."

"Why is that?"

"What do you think I did with the fire-cannons? I taught the Redforms
how to use them. At the moment, these weapons are manned by Redforms
and aimed at two installations. If I do not personally visit my gunners by
dawn, they will open fire. After destroying their objectives, they will move
on and try for two more."

"You trusted those beasts with laser projectors?"

"That is correct. Now, will you begin awakening the others for the
voting?"

Turl crouched as if to spring at him, appeared to think better of it,
relaxed.

"Why did you do it, Jarry?" he asked. "What are they to you that you
would make your own people suffer for them?"

"Since you do not feel as I feel," said Jarry, "my reasons would mean
nothing to you. After all, they are only based upon my feelings, which

are different than your own—for mine are based upon sorrow and lone-liness. Try this one, though: I am their god. My form is to be found in their every camp. I am the Slayer of Bears from the Desert of the Dead. They have told my story for two and a half centuries, and I have been changed by it. I am powerful and wise and good, so far as they are con-cerned. In this capacity, I owe them some consideration. If I do not give them their lives, who will there be to honor me in snow and chant my story around the fires and cut for me the best portions of the woolly caterpillar? None, Turl. And these things are all that my life is worth now. Awaken the others. You have no choice."

"Very well," said Turl. "And if their decision should go against you?"

"Then I'll retire, and you can be god," said Jarry.

●

Now every day when the sun goes down out of the purple sky, Jarry Dark watches it in its passing, for he shall sleep no more the sleep of ice and of stone, wherein there is no dreaming. He has elected to live out the span of his days in a tiny instant of the Wait, never to look upon the New Alyonal of his people. Every morning, at the new Deadland instal-lation, he is awakened by sounds like the cracking of ice, the trembling of tin, the snapping of steel strands, before they come to him with their offerings, singing and making marks upon the snow. They praise him and he smiles upon them. Sometimes he coughs.

Born of man and woman, in accordance with Catform Y7 require-ments, Coldworld Class, Jarry Dark was not suited for existence anywhere in the universe which had guaranteed him a niche. This was either a blessing or a curse, depending on how you looked at it. So look at it however you would, that was the story. Thus does life repay those who would serve her fully.

Vaster than Empires and More Slow

URSULA K. LE GUIN

Like Roger Zelazny, Ursula K. Le Guin started publishing in 1962 in the pages of Cele Goldsmith's Amazing, but her career would rise in a less meteoric way, even if, in the end, its arc would take her even higher. Her first novel, Rocannon's World, published in 1966 at the bottom of the novel market as half of a garishly covered Ace Double, was resolutely ignored by almost every critic in the field. Her next few novels, the excellent and still-underrated Planet of Exile and the complex, van Vogtian City of Illusions, were also mostly overlooked and would only be discovered retrospectively by most readers (in the same fashion as was Samuel R. Delany's early work), after her plunge into wide public notice was accomplished by the publication of her most famous and acclaimed novel, The Left Hand of Darkness, in 1969, as part of Terry Carr's new Ace Specials line. Rarely has a novel had as sharp and sudden an impact or been accepted as widely as a modem masterpiece.

Here at the end of the nineties, thirty years further on, it's probably fair to say that Le Guin is one of the best-known and most universally respected science-fiction writers in the world today, and one of the few living science-fiction writers widely known and accepted outside the boundaries of genre. The Left Hand of Darkness may have been the most influential science-fiction novel of its decade and shows every sign of becoming one of the enduring classics of the genre— even ignoring the rest of Le Guin's work, the impact of this one novel alone on future science-fiction and future science-fiction writers would be incalculably strong. (Her 1968 fantasy novel, A Wizard of Earthsea, would be almost as influential on future generations of High Fantasy writers.) The Left Hand of Darkness won both the Hugo and Nebula Awards, as did Le Guin's monumental novel The Dispossessed a few years later. Her novel Tehanu won her another Nebula in 1990, and she has also won three other Hugo Awards and a Nebula Award for her short fiction, as well as the National Book Award for Children's Literature for her novel The Farthest Shore, part of her acclaimed Earthsea trilogy. Her other novels include The Lathe of Heaven, The Beginning Place, A Wizard of Earthsea, The Tombs of Atuan, Tehanu, Searoad, and the controversial multimedia novel Always Coming Home. She has had six collections: The Wind's Twelve Quarters, Orsinian Tales, The Compass Rose, Buffalo Gals and Other Animal Presences, A Fisherman of the Inland Sea, and her most recent book, Four Ways to Forgiveness. Upcoming is a new novel, The Telling, and a collection of fantasy stories set in the Earthsea universe.

Most of Le Guin's science-fiction novels and stories share a common background, the star-spanning, interstellar community known as the Ekumen. Since the many races of the Ekumen (including Terran humans) were seeded by a race

of explorers, the Hainish, thousands of years ago, exploration themes are funda-
mental to the background of all the Ekumen stories, but occasionally Le Guin
focuses more directly on explorers in the foreground action as well, as she does
in The Left Hand of Darkness *and* City of Illusion *and in the recent sequence of*
stories, such as "Another World," "The Shobbies's Story," and "Dancing to
Ganam," that document the development of a method of instantaneous travel
called churten. *Rarely, though, has she concentrated on the lives and journeys*
of explorers more closely or with greater effect than in the story that follows, which
shows us that explorers are often a special breed of people—in fact, that may be
the problem!

It was only during the earliest decades of the League that the Earth sent
ships out on the enormously long voyages, beyond the pale, over the stars
and far away. They were seeking for worlds which had not been seeded
or settled by the Founders on Hain, truly alien worlds. All the Known
Worlds went back to the Hainish Origin, and the Terrans, having been
not only founded but salvaged by the Hainish, resented this. They wanted
to get away from the family. They wanted to find somebody new. The
Hainish, like tiresomely understanding parents, supported their explorations, and contributed ships and volunteers, as did several other worlds
of the League.

All these volunteers to the Extreme Survey crews shared one peculi-
arity: they were of unsound mind.

What sane person, after all, would go out to collect information that
would not be received for five or ten centuries? Cosmic mass interference
had not yet been eliminated from the operation of the ansible, and so
instantaneous communication was reliable only within a range of 120
lightyears. The explorers would be quite isolated. And of course they had
no idea what they might come back to, if they came back. No normal
human being who had experienced time-slippage of even a few decades
between League worlds would volunteer for a round trip of centuries.
The Surveyors were escapists, misfits. They were nuts.

Ten of them climbed aboard the ferry at Smeming Port, and made vary-
ingly inept attempts to get to know one another during the three days the
ferry took getting to their ship, *Gum*. Gum is a Cetian nickname, on the order of Baby or Pet. There were two Cetians on the team, two Hainishmen,
one Beldene, and five Terrans; the Cetian-built ship was chartered by the
Government of Earth. Her motley crew came aboard wriggling through
the coupling tube one by one like apprehensive spermatozoa trying to fer-
tilize the universe. The ferry left, and the navigator put *Gum* underway. She
flittered for some hours on the edge of space a few hundred million miles
from Smeming Port, and then abruptly vanished.

When, after 10 hours 29 minutes, or 256 years, *Gum* reappeared in
normal space, she was supposed to be in the vicinity of Star KG-E-96651.
Sure enough, there was the gold pinhead of the star. Somewhere within
a four-hundred-million-kilometer sphere there was also a greenish planet,
World 4470, as charted by a Cetian mapmaker. The ship now had to find

the planet. This was not quite so easy as it might sound, given a four-hundred-million-kilometer haystack. And *Gum* couldn't bat about in planetary space at near lightspeed; if she did, she and Star KG-F-96651 and World 4470 might all end up going bang. She had to creep, using rocket propulsion, at a few hundred thousand miles an hour. The Mathematician/Navigator, Asnanifoil, knew pretty well where the planet ought to be, and thought they might raise it within ten E-days. Meanwhile the members of the Survey team got to know one another still better.

"I can't stand him," said Porlock, the Hard Scientist (chemistry, plus physics, astronomy, geology, etc.), and little blobs of spittle appeared on his mustache. "The man is insane. I can't imagine why he was passed as fit to join a Survey team, unless this is a deliberate experiment in noncompatibility, planned by the Authority, with us as guinea pigs."

"We generally use hamsters and Hainish gholes," said Mannon, the Soft Scientist (psychology, plus psychiatry, anthropology, ecology, etc.), politely; he was one of the Hainishmen. "Instead of guinea pigs. Well, you know, Mr. Osden is really a very rare case. In fact, he's the first fully cured case of Render's Syndrome—a variety of infantile autism which was thought to be incurable. The great Terran analyst Hammergeld reasoned that the cause of the autistic condition in this case is a supernormal empathic capacity, and developed an appropriate treatment. Mr. Osden is the first patient to undergo that treatment, in fact he lived with Dr. Hammergeld until he was eighteen. The therapy was completely successful."

"Successful?"

"Why, yes. He certainly is not autistic."

"No, he's intolerable!"

"Well, you see," said Mannon, gazing mildly at the saliva-flecks on Porlock's mustache, "the normal defensive-aggressive reaction between strangers meeting—let's say you and Mr. Osden just for example—is something you're scarcely aware of; habit, manners, inattention get you past it; you've learned to ignore it, to the point where you might even deny it exists. However, Mr. Osden, being an empath, feels it. Feels his feelings, and yours, and is hard put to say which is which. Let's say that there's a normal element of hostility towards any stranger in your emotional reaction to him when you meet him, plus a spontaneous dislike of his looks, or clothes, or handshake—it doesn't matter what. He feels that dislike. As his autistic defense has been unlearned, he resorts to an aggressive-defense mechanism, a response in kind to the aggression which you have unwittingly projected onto him." Mannon went on for quite a long time.

"Nothing gives a man the right to be such a bastard," Porlock said.

"He can't tune us out?" asked Harfex, the Biologist, another Hainishman.

"It's like hearing," said Olleroo, Assistant Hard Scientist, stooping over to paint her toenails with fluorescent lacquer. "No eyelids on your ears. No Off switch on empathy. He hears our feelings whether he wants to or not."

"Does he know what we're *thinking?*" asked Eskwana, the Engineer, looking round at the others in real dread.

"No," Porlock snapped. "Empathy's not telepathy! Nobody's got telepathy."

"Yet," said Mannon, with his little smile. "Just before I left Hain there was a most interesting report in from one of the recently rediscovered worlds, a hilfer named Rocannon reporting what appears to be a teachable telepathic technique existent among a mutated hominid race; I only saw a synopsis in the HILF Bulletin, but—" He went on. The others had learned that they could talk while Mannon went on talking; he did not seem to mind, nor even to miss much of what they said.

"Then why does he hate us?" Eskwana said.

"Nobody hates you, Ander honey," said Olleroo, daubing Eskwana's left thumbnail with fluorescent pink. The engineer flushed and smiled vaguely.

"He acts as if he hated us," said Haito, the Coordinator. She was a delicate-looking woman of pure Asian descent, with a surprising voice, husky, deep, and soft, like a young bullfrog. "Why, if he suffers from our hostility, does he increase it by constant attacks and insults? I can't say I think much of Dr. Hammergeld's cure, really, Mannon; autism might be preferable. . . ."

She stopped. Osden had come into the main cabin.

He looked flayed. His skin was unnaturally white and thin, showing the channels of his blood like a faded road map in red and blue. His Adam's apple, the muscles that circled his mouth, the bones and ligaments of his wrists and hands, all stood out distinctly as if displayed for an anatomy lesson. His hair was pale rust, like long-dried blood. He had eyebrows and lashes, but they were visible only in certain lights; what one saw was the bones of the eye sockets, the veining of the lids, and the colorless eyes. They were not red eyes, for he was not really an albino, but they were not blue or grey; colors had cancelled out in Osden's eyes, leaving a cold water-like clarity, infinitely penetrable. He never looked directly at one. His face lacked expression, like an anatomical drawing, or a skinned face.

"I agree," he said in a high, harsh tenor, "that even autistic withdrawal might be preferable to the smog of cheap secondhand emotions with which you people surround me. What are you sweating hate for now, Porlock? Can't stand the sight of me? Go practice some auto-eroticism the way you were doing last night, it improves your vibes. Who the devil moved my tapes, here? Don't touch my things, any of you. I won't have it."

"Osden," said Asnanifoil in his large slow voice, "why *are* you such a bastard?"

Ander Eskwana cowered and put his hands in front of his face. Contention frightened him. Olleroo looked up with a vacant yet eager expression, the eternal spectator.

"Why shouldn't I be?" said Osden. He was not looking at Asnanifoil, and was keeping physically as far away from all of them as he could in the crowded cabin. "None of you constitute, in yourselves, any reason for my changing my behavior."

Harfex, a reserved and patient man, said, "The reason is that we shall be spending several years together. Life will be better for all of us if—"

"Can't you understand that I don't give a damn for all of you?" Osden said, took up his microtapes, and went out. Eskwana had suddenly gone to sleep. Asnanifoil was drawing slipstreams in the air with his finger and muttering the Ritual Primes. "You cannot explain his presence on the team except as a plot on the part of the Terran Authority. I saw this almost at once. This mission is meant to fail," Harfex whispered to the Coordinator, glancing over his shoulder. Porlock was fumbling with his fly-button; there were tears in his eyes. I did tell you they were all crazy, but you thought I was exaggerating.

All the same, they were not unjustified. Extreme Surveyors expected to find their fellow team members intelligent, well-trained, unstable, and personally sympathetic. They had to work together in close quarters and nasty places, and could expect one another's paranoias, depressions, manias, phobias and compulsions to be mild enough to admit of good personal relationships, at least most of the time. Osden might be intelligent, but his training was sketchy and his personality was disastrous. He had been sent only on account of his singular gift, the power of empathy: properly speaking, of wide-range bioempathic receptivity. His talent wasn't species-specific; he could pick up emotion or sentience from anything that felt. He could share lust with a white rat, pain with a squashed cockroach, and phototropy with a moth. On an alien world, the Authority had decided, it would be useful to know if anything nearby is sentient, and if so, what its feelings towards you are. Osden's title was a new one: he was the team's Sensor.

"What is emotion, Osden?" Haito Tomiko asked him one day in the main cabin, trying to make some rapport with him for once. "What is it, exactly, that you pick up with your empathic sensitivity?"

"Muck," the man answered in his high, exasperated voice. "The psychic excreta of the animal kingdom. I wade through your faeces."

"I was trying," she said, "to learn some facts." She thought her tone was admirably calm.

"You weren't after facts. You were trying to get at me. With some fear, some curiosity, and a great deal of distaste. The way you might poke a dead dog, to see the maggots crawl. Will you understand once and for all that I don't want to be got at, that I want to be left alone?" His skin was mottled with red and violet, his voice had risen. "Go roll in your own dung, you yellow bitch!" he shouted at her silence.

"Calm down," she said, still quietly, but she left him at once and went to her cabin. Of course he had been right about her motives; her question had been largely a pretext, a mere effort to interest him. But what harm in that? Did not that effort imply respect for the other? At the moment of asking the question she had felt at most a slight distrust of him; she had mostly felt sorry for him, the poor arrogant venomous bastard, Mr.

No-Skin as Olleroo called him. What did he expect, the way he acted? Love?

"I guess he can't stand anybody feeling sorry for him," said Olleroo, lying on the lower bunk, gilding her nipples.

"Then he can't form any human relationship. All his Dr. Hammergeld did was turn an autism inside out. . . ."

"Poor frot," said Olleroo. "Tomiko, you don't mind if Harfex comes in for a while tonight, do you?"

"Can't you go to his cabin? I'm sick of always having to sit in Main with that damned peeled turnip."

"You do hate him, don't you? I guess he feels that. But I slept with Harfex last night too, and Asnanifoil might get jealous, since they share the cabin. It would be nicer here."

"Service them both," Tomiko said with the coarseness of offended modesty. Her Terran subculture, the East Asian, was a puritanical one; she had been brought up chaste.

"I only like one a night," Olleroo replied with innocent serenity. Beldene, the Garden Planet, had never discovered chastity, or the wheel.

"Try Osden, then," Tomiko said. Her personal instability was seldom so plain as now: a profound self-distrust manifesting itself as destructivism. She had volunteered for this job because there was, in all probability, no use in doing it.

The little Beldene looked up, paintbrush in hand, eyes wide. "Tomiko, that was a dirty thing to say."

"Why?"

"It would be vile! I'm not attracted to Osden!"

"I didn't know it mattered to you," Tomiko said indifferently, though she did know. She got some papers together and left the cabin, remarking, "I hope you and Harfex or whoever it is finish by last bell; I'm tired."

Olleroo was crying, tears dripping on her little gilded nipples. She wept easily. Tomiko had not wept since she was ten years old.

It was not a happy ship; but it took a turn for the better when Asnanifoil and his computers raised World 4470. There it lay, a dark-green jewel, like truth at the bottom of a gravity well. As they watched the jade disc grow, a sense of mutuality grew among them. Osden's selfishness, his accurate cruelty, served now to draw the others together. "Perhaps," Mannon said, "he was sent as a beating gron. What Terrans call a scapegoat. Perhaps his influence will be good after all." And no one, so careful were they to be kind to one another, disagreed.

They came into orbit. There were no lights on nightside, on the continents none of the lines and clots made by animals who build.

"No men," Harfex murmured.

"Of course not," snapped Osden, who had a viewscreen to himself, and his head inside a polythene bag. He claimed that the plastic cut down on the empathic noise he received from the others. "We're two lightcenturies past the limit of the Hainish Expansion, and outside that there are no men. Anywhere. You don't think Creation would have made the same hideous mistake twice?"

No one was paying him much heed; they were looking with affection at that jade immensity below them, where there was life, but not human life. They were misfits among men, and what they saw there was not desolation, but peace. Even Osden did not look quite so expressionless as usual; he was frowning.

Descent in fire on the sea; air reconnaissance; landing. A plain of something like grass, thick, green, bowing stalks, surrounded the ship, brushed against extended viewcameras, smeared the lenses with a fine pollen.

"It looks like a pure phytosphere," Harfex said. "Osden, do you pick up anything sentient?"

They all turned to the Sensor. He had left the screen and was pouring himself a cup of tea. He did not answer. He seldom answered spoken questions.

The chitinous rigidity of military discipline was quite inapplicable to these teams of mad scientists; their chain of command lay somewhere between parliamentary procedure and peck-order, and would have driven a regular service officer out of his mind. By the inscrutable decision of the Authority, however, Dr. Haito Tomiko had been given the title of Coordinator, and she now exercised her prerogative for the first time. "Mr. Sensor Osden," she said, "please answer Mr. Harfex."

"How could I 'pick up' anything from outside," Osden said without turning, "with the emotions of nine neurotic hominids pullulating around me like worms in a can? When I have anything to tell you, I'll tell you. I'm aware of my responsibility as Sensor. If you presume to give me an order again, however, Coordinator Haito, I'll consider my responsibility void."

"Very well, Mr. Sensor. I trust no orders will be needed henceforth." Tomiko's bullfrog voice was calm, but Osden seemed to flinch slightly as he stood with his back to her, as if the surge of her suppressed rancor had struck him with physical force.

The biologist's hunch proved correct. When they began field analyses they found no animals even among the microbiota. Nobody here ate anybody else. All life-forms were photosynthesizing or saprophagous, living off light or death, not off life. Plants: infinite plants, not one species known to the visitors from the house of Man. Infinite shades and intensities of green, violet, purple, brown, red. Infinite silences. Only the wind moved, swaying leaves and fronds, a warm soughing wind laden with spores and pollens, blowing the sweet pale-green dust over prairies of great grasses, heaths that bore no heather, flowerless forests where no foot had ever walked, no eye had ever looked. A warm, sad world, sad and serene. The Surveyors, wandering like picnickers over sunny plains of violet filicaliformes, spoke softly to each other. They knew their voices broke a silence of a thousand million years, the silence of wind and leaves, leaves and wind, blowing and ceasing and blowing again. They talked softly; but being human, they talked.

"Poor old Osden," said Jenny Chong, Bio and Tech, as she piloted a helijet on the North Polar Quadrating run. "All that fancy hi-fi stuff in his brain and nothing to receive. What a bust."

"He told me he hates plants," Olleroo said with a giggle.

"You'd think he'd like them, since they don't bother him like we do."

"Can't say I much like these plants myself," said Porlock, looking down at the purple undulations of the North Circumpolar Forest. "All the same. No mind. No change. A man alone in it would go right off his head."

"But it's all alive," Jenny Chong said. "And if it lives, Osden hates it."

"He's not really so bad," Olleroo said, magnanimous. Porlock looked at her sidelong and asked, "You ever slept with him, Olleroo?"

Olleroo burst into tears and cried, "You Terrans are obscene!"

"No she hasn't," Jenny Chong said, prompt to defend. "Have you, Porlock?"

The chemist laughed uneasily: ha, ha, ha. Flecks of spittle appeared on his mustache.

"Osden can't bear to be touched," Olleroo said shakily. "I just brushed against him once by accident and he knocked me off like I was some sort of dirty . . . thing. We're all just things, to him."

"He's evil," Porlock said in a strained voice, startling the two women. "He'll end up shattering this team, sabotaging it, one way or another. Mark my words. He's not fit to live with other people!"

They landed on the North Pole. A midnight sun smouldered over low hills. Short, dry, greenish-pink bryoform grasses stretched away in every direction, which was all one direction, south. Subdued by the incredible silence, the three Surveyors set up their instruments and set to work, three viruses twitching minutely on the hide of an unmoving giant.

Nobody asked Osden along on runs as pilot or photographer or recorder, and he never volunteered, so he seldom left base camp. He ran Harfex's botanical taxonomic data through the onship computers, and served as assistant to Eskwana, whose job here was mainly repair and maintenance. Eskwana had begun to sleep a great deal, twenty-five hours or more out of the thirty-two-hour day, dropping off in the middle of repairing a radio or checking the guidance circuits of a helijet. The Coordinator stayed at base one day to observe. No one else was home except Poswet To, who was subject to epileptic fits; Mannon had plugged her into a therapy-circuit today in a state of preventive catatonia. Tomiko spoke reports into the storage banks, and kept an eye on Osden and Eskwana. Two hours passed.

"You might want to use the 860 microwaldoes in sealing that connection," Eskwana said in his soft, hesitant voice.

"Obviously!"

"Sorry. I just saw you had the 840's there—"

"And will replace them when I take the 860's out. When I don't know how to proceed, Engineer, I'll ask your advice."

After a minute Tomiko looked round. Sure enough, there was Eskwana sound asleep, head on the table, thumb in his mouth.

"Osden."

The white face did not turn, he did not speak, but conveyed impatiently that he was listening.

"You can't be unaware of Eskwana's vulnerability."

"I am not responsible for his psychopathic reactions."

"But you are responsible for your own. Eskwana is essential to our work here, and you're not. If you can't control your hostility, you must avoid him altogether."

Osden put down his tools and stood up. "With pleasure!" he said in his vindictive, scraping voice. "You could not possibly imagine what it's like to experience Eskwana's irrational terrors. To have to share his horrible cowardice, to have to cringe with him at everything!"

"Are you trying to justify your cruelty towards him? I thought you had more self-respect." Tomiko found herself shaking with spite. "If your empathic power really makes you share Ander's misery, why does it never induce the least compassion in you?"

"Compassion," Osden said. "Compassion. What do you know about compassion?"

She stared at him, but he would not look at her.

"Would you like me to verbalize your present emotional affect regarding myself?" he said. "I can do so more precisely than you can. I'm trained to analyze such responses as I receive them. And I do receive them."

"But how can you expect me to feel kindly towards you when you behave as you do?"

"What does it matter how I *behave*, you stupid sow, do you think it makes any difference? Do you think the average human is a well of loving-kindness? My choice is to be hated or to be despised. Not being a woman or a coward, I prefer to be hated."

"That's rot. Self-pity. Every man has—"

"But I am not a man," Osden said. "There are all of you. And there is myself. I am *one*."

Awed by that glimpse of abysmal solipsism, she kept silent a while; finally she said with neither spite nor pity, clinically, "You could kill yourself, Osden."

"That's your way, Haito," he jeered. "I'm not depressive, and *seppuku* isn't my bit. What do you want me to do here?"

"Leave. Spare yourself and us. Take the aircar and a data-feeder and go do a species count. In the forest; Harfex hasn't even started the forests yet. Take a hundred-square-meter forested area, anywhere inside radio range. But outside empathy range. Report in at 8 and 24 o'clock daily."

Osden went, and nothing was heard from him for five days but laconic all-well signals twice daily. The mood at base camp changed like a stage-set. Eskwana stayed awake up to eighteen hours a day. Poswet To got out her stellar lute and chanted the celestial harmonies (music had driven Osden into a frenzy). Mannon, Harfex, Jenny Chong, and Tomiko all went off tranquillizers. Porlock distilled something in his laboratory and drank it all by himself. He had a hangover. Asnanifoil and Poswet To held an all-night Numerical Epiphany, that mystical orgy of higher mathematics which is the chief pleasure of the religious Cetian soul. Olleroo slept with everybody. Work went well.

The Hard Scientist came towards base at a run, laboring through the high, fleshy stalks of the graminiformes. "Something—in the forest—" His eyes bulged, he panted, his mustache and fingers trembled. "Something big. Moving, behind me. I was putting in a benchmark, bending down. It came at me. As if it was swinging down out of the trees. Behind me." He stared at the others with the opaque eyes of terror or exhaustion.

"Sit down, Porlock. Take it easy. Now wait, go through this again. You *saw* something—"

"Not clearly. Just the movement. Purposive. A—an—I don't know what it could have been. Something self-moving. In the trees, the arboriformes, whatever you call 'em. At the edge of the woods."

Harfex looked grim. "There is nothing here that could attack you, Porlock. There are not even microzoa. There *could not* be a large animal."

"Could you possibly have seen an epiphyte drop suddenly, a vine come loose behind you?"

"No," Porlock said. "It was coming down at me, through the branches, fast. When I turned it took off again, away and upward. It made a noise, a sort of crashing. If it wasn't an animal, God knows what it could have been! It was big—as big as a man, at least. Maybe a reddish color. I couldn't see, I'm not sure."

"It was Osden," said Jenny Chong, "doing a Tarzan act." She giggled nervously, and Tomiko repressed a wild feckless laugh. But Harfex was not smiling.

"One gets uneasy under the arboriformes," he said in his polite, repressed voice. "I've noticed that. Indeed that may be why I've put off working in the forests. There's a hypnotic quality in the colors and spacing of the stems and branches, especially the helically-arranged ones; and the spore-throwers grow so regularly spaced that it seems unnatural. I find it quite disagreeable, subjectively speaking. I wonder if a stronger effect of that sort mightn't have produced a hallucination . . . ?"

Porlock shook his head. He wet his lips. "It was there," he said. "Something. Moving with purpose. Trying to attack me from behind."

When Osden called in, punctual as always, at 24 o'clock that night, Harfex told him Porlock's report. "Have you come on anything at all, Mr. Osden, that could substantiate Mr. Porlock's impression of a motile, sentient life-form, in the forest?"

Ssss, the radio said sardonically. "No. Bullshit," said Osden's unpleasant voice.

"You've been actually inside the forest longer than any of us," Harfex said with unmitigable politeness. "Do you agree with my impression that the forest ambiance has a rather troubling and possibly hallucinogenic effect on the perceptions?"

Ssss. "I'll agree that Porlock's perceptions are easily troubled. Keep him in his lab, he'll do less harm. Anything else?"

"Not at present," Harfex said, and Osden cut off.

Nobody could credit Porlock's story, and nobody could discredit it. He was positive that something, something big, had tried to attack him by surprise. It was hard to deny this, for they were on an alien world, and everyone who had entered the forest had felt a certain chill and foreboding under the "trees." ("Call them trees, certainly," Harfex had said. "They really are the same thing, only, of course, altogether different.") They agreed that they had felt uneasy, or had had the sense that something was watching them from behind.

"We've got to clear this up," Porlock said, and he asked to be sent as a temporary Biologist's Aide, like Osden, into the forest to explore and observe. Olleroo and Jenny Chong volunteered if they could go as a pair. Harfex sent them all off into the forest near which they were encamped, a vast tract covering four-fifths of Continent D. He forbade side-arms. They were not to go outside a fifty-mile half-circle, which included Osden's current site. They all reported in twice daily, for three days. Porlock reported a glimpse of what seemed to be a large semi-erect shape moving through the trees across the river; Olleroo was sure she had heard something moving near the tent, the second night.

"There are no animals on this planet," Harfex said, dogged.

Then Osden missed his morning call.

Tomiko waited less than an hour, then flew with Harfex to the area where Osden had reported himself the night before. But as the helijet hovered over the sea of purplish leaves, illimitable, impenetrable, she felt a panic despair. "How can we find him in this?"

"He reported landing on the riverbank. Find the aircar; he'll be camped near it, and he can't have gone far from his camp. Species-counting is slow work. There's the river."

"There's his car," Tomiko said, catching the bright foreign glint among the vegetable colors and shadows. "Here goes, then."

She put the ship in hover and pitched out the ladder. She and Harfex descended. The sea of life closed over their heads.

As her feet touched the forest floor, she unsnapped the flap of her holster; then glancing at Harfex, who was unarmed, she left the gun untouched. But her hand kept coming back up to it. There was no sound at all, as soon as they were a few meters away from the slow, brown river, and the light was dim. Great boles stood well apart, almost regularly, almost alike; they were soft-skinned, some appearing smooth and others spongy, grey or greenish-brown or brown, twined with cable-like creepers and festooned with epiphytes, extending rigid, entangled armfuls of big, saucer-shaped, dark leaves that formed a roof-layer twenty to thirty meters thick. The ground underfoot was springy as a mattress, every inch of it knotted with roots and peppered with small, fleshy-leaved growths.

"Here's his tent," Tomiko said, cowed at the sound of her voice in that huge community of the voiceless. In the tent was Osden's sleeping bag, a couple of books, a box of rations. We should be calling, shouting for him, she thought, but did not even suggest it; nor did Harfex. They circled out from the tent, careful to keep each other in sight through the thick-standing presences, the crowding gloom. She stumbled over Osden's body, not thirty meters from the tent, led to it by the whitish gleam of a dropped notebook. He lay face down between two huge-rooted trees. His head and hands were covered with blood, some dried, some still oozing red.

Harfex appeared beside her, his pale Hainish complexion quite green in the dusk. "Dead?"

"No. He's been struck. Beaten. From behind." Tomiko's fingers felt over the bloody skull and temples and nape. "A weapon or a tool . . . I don't find a fracture."

As she turned Osden's body over so they could lift him, his eyes opened. She was holding him, bending close to his face. His pale lips writhed. A deathly fear came into her. She screamed aloud two or three times and tried to run away, shambling and stumbling into the terrible dusk. Harfex caught her, and at his touch and the sound of his voice, her panic decreased. "What is it? What is it?" he was saying.

"I don't know," she sobbed. Her heartbeat still shook her, and she could not see clearly. "The fear—the . . . I panicked. When I saw his eyes."

"We're both nervous. I don't understand this—"

"I'm all right now, come on, we've got to get him under care."

Both working with senseless haste, they lugged Osden to the riverside and hauled him up on a rope under his armpits; he dangled like a sack, twisting a little, over the glutinous dark sea of leaves. They pulled him into the helijet and took off. Within a minute they were over open prairie. Tomiko locked onto the homing beam. She drew a deep breath, and her eyes met Harfex's.

"I was so terrified I almost fainted. I have never done that."

"I was . . . unreasonably frightened also," said the Hainishman, and indeed he looked aged and shaken. "Not so badly as you. But as unreasonably."

"It was when I was in contact with him, holding him. He seemed to be conscious for a moment."

"Empathy? . . . I hope he can tell us what attacked him."

Osden, like a broken dummy covered with blood and mud, half lay as they had bundled him into the rear seats in their frantic urgency to get out of the forest.

More panic met their arrival at base. The ineffective brutality of the assault was sinister and bewildering. Since Harfex stubbornly denied any possibility of animal life they began speculating about sentient plants, vegetable monsters, psychic projections. Jenny Chong's latent phobia reasserted itself and she could talk about nothing except the Dark Egos which followed people around behind their backs. She and Olleroo and Porlock had been summoned back to base; and nobody was much inclined to go outside.

Osden had lost a good deal of blood during the three or four hours he had lain alone, and concussion and severe contusions had put him in shock and semi-coma. As he came out of this and began running a low fever he called several times for "Doctor," in a plaintive voice: "Doctor Hammergeld . . ." When he regained full consciousness, two of those long days later, Tomiko called Harfex into his cubicle.

"Osden: can you tell us what attacked you?"

The pale eyes flickered past Harfex's face.

"You were attacked," Tomiko said gently. The shifty gaze was hatefully familiar, but she was a physician, protective of the hurt. "You may not remember it yet. Something attacked you. You were in the forest—"

"Ah!" he cried out, his eyes growing bright and his features contorting. "The forest—in the forest—"

"What's in the forest?"

He gasped for breath. A look of clearer consciousness came into his face. After a while he said, "I don't know."

"Did you see what attacked you?" Harfex asked.

"I don't know."

"You remember it now."

"I don't know."

"All our lives may depend on this. You must tell us what you saw!"

"I don't know," Osden said, sobbing with weakness. He was too weak to hide the fact that he was hiding the answer, yet he would not say it. Porlock, nearby, was chewing his pepper-colored mustache as he tried to hear what was going on in the cubicle. Harfex leaned over Osden and said, "You *will* tell us—" Tomiko had to interfere bodily.

Harfex controlled himself with an effort that was painful to see. He went off silently to his cubicle, where no doubt he took a double or triple dose of tranquillizers. The other men and women, scattered about the big frail building, a long main hall and ten sleeping-cubicles, said nothing, but looked depressed and edgy. Osden, as always, even now, had them all at his mercy. Tomiko looked down at him with a rush of hatred that burned in her throat like bile. This monstrous egotism that fed itself on others' emotions, this absolute selfishness, was worse than any hideous deformity of the flesh. Like a congenital monster, he should not have lived. Should not be alive. Should have died. Why had his head not been split open?

As he lay flat and white, his hands helpless at his sides, his colorless eyes were wide open, and there were tears running from the corners. He tried to flinch away. "Don't," he said in a weak hoarse voice, and tried to raise his hands to protect his head. "Don't!"

She sat down on the folding-stool beside the cot, and after a while put her hand on his. He tried to pull away, but lacked the strength.

A long silence fell between them.

"Osden," she murmured, "I'm sorry. I'm very sorry. I will you well. Let me will you well, Osden. I don't want to hurt you. Listen, I do see now. It was one of us. That's right, isn't it. No, don't answer, only tell me if I'm wrong; but I'm not . . . Of course there are animals on this planet. Ten of them. I don't care who it was. It doesn't matter, does it. It could have been me, just now. I realize that. I didn't understand how it is, Osden. You can't see how difficult it is for us to understand. . . . But listen. If it were love, instead of hate and fear . . . Is it never love?"

"No."

"Why not? Why should it never be? Are human beings all so weak? That is terrible. Never mind, never mind, don't worry. Keep still. At least right now it isn't hate, is it? Sympathy at least, concern, well-wishing. You do feel that, Osden? Is it what you feel?"

"Among . . . other things," he said, almost inaudibly.

"Noise from my subconscious, I suppose. And everybody else in the room . . . Listen, when we found you there in the forest, when I tried to turn you over, you partly wakened, and I felt a horror of you. I was insane with fear for a minute. Was that your fear of me I felt?"

"No."

Her hand was still on his, and he was quite relaxed, sinking towards sleep, like a man in pain who has been given relief from pain. "The forest," he muttered; she could barely understand him. "Afraid."

She pressed him no further, but kept her hand on his and watched him go to sleep. She knew what she felt, and what therefore he must feel. She was confident of it: there is only one emotion, or state of being, that can thus wholly reverse itself, polarize, within one moment. In Great Hainish indeed there is one word, *ontá*, for love and for hate. She was not in love with Osden, of course, that was another kettle of fish. What she felt for him was *ontá*, polarized hate. She held his hand and the current flowed between them, the tremendous electricity of touch, which he had always dreaded. As he slept the ring of anatomy-chart muscles around his mouth relaxed, and Tomiko saw on his face what none of them had ever seen, very faint, a smile. It faded. He slept on.

He was tough; next day he was sitting up, and hungry. Harfex wished to interrogate him, but Tomiko put him off. She hung a sheet of polythene over the cubicle door, as Osden himself had often done. "Does it actually cut down your empathic reception?" she asked, and he replied, in the dry, cautious tone they were now using to each other, "No."

"Just a warning, then."

"Partly. More faith-healing. Dr. Hammergeld thought it worked. . . . Maybe it does, a little."

There had been love, once. A terrified child, suffocating in the tidal rush and battering of the huge emotions of adults, a drowning child, saved by one man. Taught to breathe, to live, by one man. Given everything, all protection and love, by one man. Father/Mother/God: no other. "Is he still alive?" Tomiko asked, thinking of Osden's incredible loneliness, and the strange cruelty of the great doctors. She was shocked when she heard his forced, tinny laugh. "He died at least two and a half centuries ago," Osden said. "Do you forget where we are, Coordinator? We've all left our little families behind. . . ."

Outside the polythene curtain the eight other human beings on World 4470 moved vaguely. Their voices were low and strained. Eskwana slept; Poswet To was in therapy; Jenny Chong was trying to rig lights in her cubicle so that she wouldn't cast a shadow.

"They're all scared," Tomiko said, scared. "They've all got these ideas about what attacked you. A sort of ape-potato, a giant fanged spinach, I don't know. . . . Even Harfex. You may be right not to force them to see. That would be worse, to lose confidence in one another. But why are we all so shaky, unable to face the fact, going to pieces so easily? Are we really all insane?"

"We'll soon be more so."

"Why?"

"There *is* something." He closed his mouth, the muscles of his lips stood out rigid.

"Something sentient?"

"A sentience."

"In the forest?"

He nodded.

"What is it, then—?"

"The fear." He began to look strained again, and moved restlessly. "When I fell, there, you know, I didn't lose consciousness at once. Or I kept regaining it. I don't know. It was more like being paralyzed."

"You were."

"I was on the ground. I couldn't get up. My face was in the dirt, in that soft leaf mold. It was in my nostrils and eyes. I couldn't move. Couldn't see. As if I was in the ground. Sunk into it, part of it. I knew I was between two trees even though I never saw them. I suppose I could feel the roots. Below me in the ground, down under the ground. My hands were bloody, I could feel that, and the blood made the dirt around my face sticky. I felt the fear. It kept growing. As if they'd finally known I was there, lying on them there, under them, among them, the thing they feared, and yet part of their fear itself. I couldn't stop sending the fear back, and it kept growing, and I couldn't get away. I would pass out, I think, and then the fear would bring me to again, and I still couldn't move. Any more than they can."

Tomiko felt the cold stirring of her hair, the readying of the apparatus of terror. "They: who are they, Osden?"

"They, it—I don't know. The fear."

"What is he talking about?" Harfex demanded when Tomiko reported this conversation. She would not let Harfex question Osden yet, feeling that she must protect Osden from the onslaught of the Hainishman's powerful, over-repressed emotions. Unfortunately this fueled the slow fire of paranoid anxiety that burned in poor Harfex, and he thought she and Osden were in league, hiding some fact of great importance or peril from the rest of the team.

"It's like the blind man trying to describe the elephant. Osden hasn't seen or heard the . . . the sentience, any more than we have."

"But he's felt it, my dear Haito," Harfex said with just-suppressed rage. "Not empathically. On his skull. It came and knocked him down and beat him with a blunt instrument. Did he not catch *one* glimpse of it?"

"What would he have seen, Harfex?" Tomiko asked, but he would not hear her meaningful tone; even he had blocked out that comprehension. What one fears is alien. The murderer is an outsider, a foreigner, not one of us. The evil is not in me!

"The first blow knocked him pretty well out," Tomiko said a little wearily, "he didn't see anything. But when he came to again, alone in the forest, he felt a great fear. Not his own fear, an empathic effect. He is certain of that. And certain it was nothing picked up from any of us. So that evidently the native life-forms are not all insentient."

Harfex looked at her a moment, grim. "You're trying to frighten me, Haito. I do not understand your motives." He got up and went off to his laboratory table, walking slowly and stiffly, like a man of eighty not of forty.

She looked round at the others. She felt some desperation. Her new, fragile, and profound interdependence with Osden gave her, she was well aware, some added strength. But if even Harfex could not keep his head, who of the others would? Porlock and Eskwana were shut in their cubicles, the others were all working or busy with something. There was something queer about their positions. For a while the Coordinator could not tell what it was, then she saw that they were all sitting facing the nearby forest. Playing chess with Asnanifoil, Olleroo had edged her chair around until it was almost beside his.

She went to Mannon, who was dissecting a tangle of spidery brown roots, and told him to look for the pattern-puzzle. He saw it at once, and said with unusual brevity, "Keeping an eye on the enemy."

"What enemy? What do *you* feel, Mannon?" She had a sudden hope in him as a psychologist, on this obscure ground of hints and empathies where biologists went astray.

"I feel a strong anxiety with a specific spatial orientation. But I am not an empath. Therefore the anxiety is explicable in terms of the particular stress-situation, that is, the attack on a team member in the forest, and also in terms of the total stress-situation, that is, my presence in a totally alien environment, for which the archetypical connotations of the word 'forest' provide an inevitable metaphor."

Hours later Tomiko woke to hear Osden screaming in nightmare; Mannon was calming him, and she sank back into her own dark-branching pathless dreams. In the morning Eskwana did not wake. He could not be roused with stimulant drugs. He clung to his sleep, slipping farther and farther back, mumbling softly now and then until, wholly regressed, he lay curled on his side, thumb at his lips, gone.

"Two days; two down. Ten little Indians, nine little Indians . . ." That was Porlock.

"And you're the next little Indian," Jenny Chong snapped. "Go analyze your urine, Porlock!"

"He is driving us all insane," Porlock said, getting up and waving his left arm. "Can't you feel it? For God's sake, are you all deaf and blind? Can't you feel what he's doing, the emanations? It all comes from him—from his room there—from his mind. He is driving us all insane with fear!"

"Who is?" said Asnanifoil, looming precipitous and hairy over the little Terran.

"Do I have to say his name? Osden, then. Osden! Osden! Why do you think I tried to kill him? In self-defense! To save all of us! Because you won't see what he's doing to us. He's sabotaged the mission by making us quarrel, and now he's going to drive us all insane by projecting fear at us so that we can't sleep or think, like a huge radio that doesn't make any sound, but it broadcasts all the time, and you can't sleep, and you can't think. Haito and Harfex are already under his control but the rest of you can be saved. I had to do it!"

"You didn't do it very well," Osden said, standing half-naked, all rib and bandage, at the door of his cubicle. "I could have hit myself harder. Hell, it isn't me that's scaring you blind, Porlock, it's out there—there, in the woods!"

Porlock made an ineffectual attempt to assault Osden; Asnanifoil held him back, and continued to hold him effortlessly while Mannon gave him a sedative shot. He was put away shouting about giant radios. In a minute the sedative took effect, and he joined a peaceful silence to Eskwana's.

"All right," said Harfex. "Now, Osden, you'll tell us what you know and all you know."

Osden said, "I don't know anything."

He looked battered and faint. Tomiko made him sit down before he talked.

"After I'd been three days in the forest, I thought I was occasionally receiving some kind of affect."

"Why didn't you report it?"

"Thought I was going spla, like the rest of you."

"That, equally, should have been reported."

"You'd have called me back to base. I couldn't take it. You realize that my inclusion in the mission was a bad mistake. I'm not able to coexist with nine other neurotic personalities at close quarters. I was wrong to volunteer for Extreme Survey, and the Authority was wrong to accept me."

No one spoke; but Tomiko saw, with certainty this time, the flinch in Osden's shoulders and the tightening of his facial muscles, as he registered their bitter agreement.

"Anyhow, I didn't want to come back to base because I was curious. Even going psycho, how could I pick up empathic affects when there was no creature to emit them? They weren't bad, then. Very vague. Queer. Like a draft in a closed room, a flicker in the corner of your eye. Nothing really."

For a moment he had been borne up on their listening: they heard, so he spoke. He was wholly at their mercy. If they disliked him he had to be hateful; if they mocked him he became grotesque; if they listened to him he was the storyteller. He was helplessly obedient to the de-mands of their emotions, reactions, moods. And there were seven of them, too many to cope with, so that he must be constantly knocked about from one to another's whim. He could not find coherence. Even as he spoke and held them, somebody's attention would wander: Olle-roo perhaps was thinking that he wasn't unattractive, Harfex was seek-ing the ulterior motive of his words, Asnanifoil's mind, which could not be long held by the concrete, was roaming off towards the eternal peace of number, and Tomiko was distracted by pity, by fear. Osden's voice faltered. He lost the thread. "I . . . I thought it must be the trees," he said, and stopped.

"It's not the trees," Harfex said. "They have no more nervous system than do plants of the Hainish Descent on Earth. None."

"You're not seeing the forest for the trees, as they say on Earth," Mannon put in, smiling elfinly; Harfex stared at him. "What about those root-nodes we've been puzzling about for twenty days—eh?"

"What about them?"

"They are, indubitably, connections. Connections among the trees. Right? Now let's just suppose, most improbably, that you knew nothing of animal brain-structure. And you were given one axon, or one detached glial cell, to examine. Would you be likely to discover what it was? Would you see that the cell was capable of sentience?"

"No. Because it isn't. A single cell is capable of mechanical response to stimulus. No more. Are you hypothesizing that individual arboriformes are 'cells' in a kind of brain, Mannon?"

"Not exactly. I'm merely pointing out that they are all interconnected, both by the root-node linkage and by your green epiphytes in the branches. A linkage of incredible complexity and physical extent. Why, even the prairie grass-forms have those root-connectors, don't they? I know that sentience or intelligence isn't a thing, you can't find it in, or analyze it out from, the cells of a brain. It's a function of the connected cells. It is, in a sense, the connection: the connectedness. It doesn't exist. I'm not trying to say it exists. I'm only guessing that Osden might be able to describe it."

And Osden took him up, speaking as if in trance. "Sentience without senses. Blind, deaf, nerveless, moveless. Some irritability, response to touch. Response to sun, to light, to water, and chemicals in the earth around the roots. Nothing comprehensible to an animal mind. Presence without mind. Awareness of being, without object or subject. Nirvana."

"Then why do you receive fear?" Tomiko asked in a low voice.

"I don't know. I can't see how awareness of objects, of others, could arise: an unperceiving response . . . But there was an uneasiness, for days. And then when I lay between the two trees and my blood was on their roots—" Osden's face glittered with sweat. "It became fear," he said shrilly, "only fear."

"If such a function existed," Harfex said, "it would not be capable of conceiving of a self-moving, material entity, or responding to one. It could no more become aware of us than we can 'become aware' of Infinity."

" 'The silence of those infinite expanses terrifies me,' " muttered Tomiko. "Pascal was aware of Infinity. By way of fear."

"To a forest," Mannon said, "we might appear as forest fires. Hurricanes. Dangers. What moves quickly is dangerous, to a plant. The rootless would be alien, terrible. And if it is mind, it seems only too probable that it might become aware of Osden, whose own mind is open to connection with all others so long as he's conscious, and who was lying in pain and afraid within it, actually inside it. No wonder it was afraid—"

"Not 'it,' " Harfex said. "There is no being, no huge creature, no person! There could at most be only a function—"

"There is only a fear," Osden said.

They were all still a while, and heard the stillness outside.

"Is that what I feel all the time coming up behind me?" Jenny Chong asked, subdued.

Osden nodded. "You all feel it, deaf as you are. Eskwana's the worst off, because he actually has some empathic capacity. He could send if he learned how, but he's too weak, never will be anything but a medium."

"Listen, Osden," Tomiko said, "you can send. Then send to it—the forest, the fear out there—tell it that we won't hurt it. Since it has, or is, some sort of affect that translates into what we feel as emotion, can't you translate back? Send out a message, We are harmless, we are friendly."

"You must know that nobody can emit a false empathic message, Haito. You can't send something that doesn't exist."

"But we don't intend harm, we are friendly."

"Are we? In the forest, when you picked me up, did you feel friendly?"

"No. Terrified. But that's—it, the forest, the plants, not my own fear, isn't it?"

"What's the difference? It's all you felt. Can't you see," and Osden's voice rose in exasperation, "why I dislike you and you dislike me, all of you? Can't you see that I retransmit every negative or aggressive affect you've felt towards me since we first met? I return your hostility, with thanks. I do it in self-defense. Like Porlock. It is self-defense, though; it's the only technique I developed to replace my original defense of total withdrawal from others. Unfortunately it creates a closed circuit, self-sustaining and self-reinforcing. Your initial reaction to me was the instinctive antipathy to a cripple; by now of course it's hatred. Can you fail to see my point? The forest-mind out there transmits only terror, now, and the only message I can send it is terror, because when exposed to it I can feel nothing except terror!"

"What must we do, then?" said Tomiko, and Mannon replied promptly, "Move camp. To another continent. If there are plant-minds there, they'll be slow to notice us, as this one was; maybe they won't notice us at all."

"It would be a considerable relief," Osden observed stiffly. The others had been watching him with a new curiosity. He had revealed himself, they had seen him as he was, a helpless man in a trap. Perhaps, like Tomiko, they had seen that the trap itself, his crass and cruel egotism, was their own construction, not his. They had built the cage and locked him in it, and like a caged ape he threw filth out through the bars. If, meeting him, they had offered trust, if they had been strong enough to offer him love, how might he have appeared to them?

None of them could have done so, and it was too late now. Given time, given solitude, Tomiko might have built up with him a slow resonance of feeling, a consonance of trust, a harmony; but there was no time, their job must be done. There was not room enough for the cultivation of so great a thing, and they must make do with sympathy, with pity, the small change of love. Even that much had given her strength, but it was nowhere near enough for him. She could see in his flayed face now his savage resentment of their curiosity, even of her pity.

"Go lie down, that gash is bleeding again," she said, and he obeyed her.

Next morning they packed up, melted down the sprayform hangar and living quarters, lifted *Gum* on mechanical drive and took her halfway round World 4470, over the red and green lands, the many warm green seas. They had picked out a likely spot on Continent G: a prairie, twenty thousand square kilos of windswept graminiformes. No forest was within a hundred kilos of the site, and there were no lone trees or groves on the plain. The plant-forms occurred only in large species-colonies, never intermingled, except for certain tiny ubiquitous saprophytes and spore-bearers. The team sprayed holomeld over structure forms, and by evening of the thirty-two-hour day were settled in to the new camp. Eskwana was still asleep and Porlock still sedated, but everyone else was cheerful. "You can breathe here!" they kept saying.

Osden got on his feet and went shakily to the doorway; leaning there he looked through twilight over the dim reaches of the swaying grass that was not grass. There was a faint, sweet odor of pollen on the wind; no sound but the soft, vast sibilance of wind. His bandaged head cocked a little, the empath stood motionless for a long time. Darkness came, and the stars, lights in the windows of the distant house of Man. The wind had ceased, there was no sound. He listened.

In the long night Haito Tomiko listened. She lay still and heard the blood in her arteries, the breathing of sleepers, the wind blowing, the dark veins running, the dreams advancing, the vast static of stars increasing as the universe died slowly, the sound of death walking. She struggled out of her bed, fled the tiny solitude of her cubicle. Eskwana alone slept. Porlock lay straitjacketed, raving softly in his obscure native tongue. Olleroo and Jenny Chong were playing cards, grim-faced. Poswet To was in the therapy niche, plugged in. Asnanifoil was drawing a mandala, the Third Pattern of the Primes. Mannon and Harfex were sitting up with Osden.

She changed the bandages on Osden's head. His lank, reddish hair, where she had not had to shave it, looked strange. It was salted with white, now. Her hands shook as she worked. Nobody had yet said anything.

"How can the fear be here too?" she said, and her voice rang flat and false in the terrific silence.

"It's not just the trees; the grasses too . . ."

"But we're twelve thousand kilos from where we were this morning, we left it on the other side of the planet."

"It's all one," Osden said. "One big green thought. How long does it take a thought to get from one side of your brain to the other?"

"It doesn't think. It isn't thinking," Harfex said, lifelessly. "It's merely a network of processes. The branches, the epiphytic growths, the roots with those nodal junctures between individuals: they must all be capable of transmitting electrochemical impulses. There are no individual plants, then, properly speaking. Even the pollen is part of the linkage, no doubt, a sort of windborne sentience, connecting overseas. But it is not conceivable. That all the biosphere of a planet should be one network of communications, sensitive, irrational, immortal, isolated. . . ."

"Isolated," said Osden. "That's it! That's the fear. It isn't that we're motile, or destructive. It's just that we are. We are other. There has never been any other."

"You're right," Mannon said, almost whispering. "It has no peers. No enemies. No relationship with anything but itself. One alone forever."

"Then what's the function of its intelligence in species-survival?"

"None, maybe," Osden said. "Why are you getting teleological, Harfex? Aren't you a Hainishman? Isn't the measure of complexity the measure of the eternal joy?"

Harfex did not take the bait. He looked ill. "We should leave this world," he said.

"Now you know why I always want to get out, get away from you," Osden said with a kind of morbid geniality. "It isn't pleasant, is it—the other's fear . . . ? If only it were an animal intelligence. I can get through to animals. I get along with cobras and tigers; superior intelligence gives one the advantage. I should have been used in a zoo, not on a human team. . . . If I could get through to the damned stupid potato! If it wasn't so overwhelming . . . I still pick up more than the fear, you know. And before it panicked it had a—there was a serenity. I couldn't take it in, then, I didn't realize how big it was. To know the whole daylight, after all, the whole night. All the winds and lulls together. The winter stars and the summer stars at the same time. To have roots, and no enemies. To be entire. Do you see? No invasion. No others. To be whole . . ."

He had never spoken before, Tomiko thought.

"You are defenseless against it, Osden," she said. "Your personality has changed already. You're vulnerable to it. We may not all go mad, but you will, if we don't leave."

He hesitated, then he looked up at Tomiko, the first time he had ever met her eyes, a long, still look, clear as water.

"What's sanity ever done for me?" he said, mocking. "But you have a point, Haito. You have something there."

"We should get away," Harfex muttered.

"If I gave in to it," Osden mused, "could I communicate?"

"By 'give in,' " Mannon said in a rapid, nervous voice, "I assume that you mean, stop sending back the empathic information which you receive from the plant-entity: stop rejecting the fear, and absorb it. That will either kill you at once, or drive you back into total psychological withdrawal, autism."

"Why?" said Osden. "Its message is *rejection*. But my salvation is rejection. It's not intelligent. But I am."

"The scale is wrong. What can a single human brain achieve against something so vast?"

"A single human brain can perceive pattern on the scale of stars and galaxies," Tomiko said, "and interpret it as Love."

Mannon looked from one to the other of them; Harfex was silent.

"It'd be easier in the forest," Osden said. "Which of you will fly me over?"

"When?"

"Now. Before you all crack up or go violent."

"I will," Tomiko said.

"None of us will," Harfex said.

"I can't," Mannon said. "I . . . I am too frightened. I'd crash the jet."

"Bring Eskwana along. If I can pull this off, he might serve as a medium."

"Are you accepting the Sensor's plan, Coordinator?" Harfex asked formally.

"Yes."

"I disapprove. I will come with you, however."

"I think we're compelled, Harfex," Tomiko said, looking at Osden's face, the ugly white mask transfigured, eager as a lover's face.

Olleroo and Jenny Chong, playing cards to keep their thoughts from their haunted beds, their mounting dread, chattered like scared children. "This thing, it's in the forest, it'll get you—"

"Scared of the dark?" Osden jeered.

"But look at Eskwana, and Porlock, and even Asnanifoil—"

"It can't hurt you. It's an impulse passing through synapses, a wind passing through branches. It is only a nightmare."

They took off in a helijet, Eskwana curled up still sound asleep in the rear compartment, Tomiko piloting, Harfex and Osden silent, watching ahead for the dark line of forest across the vague grey miles of starlit plain.

They neared the black line, crossed it; now under them was darkness.

She sought a landing place, flying low, though she had to fight her frantic wish to fly high, to get out, get away. The huge vitality of the plant-world was far stronger here in the forest, and its panic beat in immense dark waves. There was a pale patch ahead, a bare knoll-top a little higher than the tallest of the black shapes around it; the not-trees; the rooted; the parts of the whole. She set the helijet down in the glade, a bad landing. Her hands on the stick were slippery, as if she had rubbed them with cold soap.

About them now stood the forest, black in darkness.

Tomiko cowered and shut her eyes. Eskwana moaned in his sleep. Harfex's breath came short and loud, and he sat rigid, even when Osden reached across him and slid the door open.

Osden stood up; his back and bandaged head were just visible in the dim glow of the control panel as he paused stooping in the doorway.

Tomiko was shaking. She could not raise her head. "No, no, no, no, no, no, no," she said in a whisper. "No. No. No."

Osden moved suddenly and quietly, swinging out of the doorway, down into the dark. He was gone.

I am coming! said a great voice that made no sound.

Tomiko screamed. Harfex coughed; he seemed to be trying to stand up, but did not do so.

Tomiko drew in upon herself, all centered in the blind eye in her belly, in the center of her being; and outside that there was nothing but the fear.

It ceased.

She raised her head; slowly unclenched her hands. She sat up straight. The night was dark, and stars shone over the forest. There was nothing else.

"Osden," she said, but her voice would not come. She spoke again, louder, a lone bullfrog croak. There was no reply.

She began to realize that something had gone wrong with Harfex. She was trying to find his head in the darkness, for he had slipped down from the seat, when all at once, in the dead quiet, in the dark rear compartment of the craft, a voice spoke. "Good," it said.

It was Eskwana's voice. She snapped on the interior lights and saw the engineer lying curled up asleep, his hand half over his mouth.

The mouth opened and spoke. "All well," it said.

"Osden—"

"All well," said the soft voice from Eskwana's mouth.

"Where are you?"

Silence.

"Come back."

A wind was rising. "I'll stay here," the soft voice said.

"You can't stay—"

Silence.

"You'd be alone, Osden!"

"Listen." The voice was fainter, slurred, as if lost in the sound of wind. "Listen. I will you well."

She called his name after that, but there was no answer. Eskwana lay still. Harfex lay stiller.

"Osden!" she cried, leaning out the doorway into the dark, windshaken silence of the forest of being. "I will come back. I must get Harfex to the base. I will come back, Osden!"

Silence and wind in leaves.

●

They finished the prescribed survey of World 4470, the eight of them; it took them forty-one days more. Asnanifoil and one or another of the women went into the forest daily at first, searching for Osden in the region around the bare knoll, though Tomiko was not in her heart sure which bare knoll they had landed on that night in the very heart and vortex of terror. They left piles of supplies for Osden, food enough for fifty years, clothing, tents, tools. They did not go on searching; there was no way to find a man alone, hiding, if he wanted to hide, in those unending labyrinths and dim corridors vine-entangled, root-floored. They might have passed within arm's reach of him and never seen him.

But he was there; for there was no fear any more.

Rational, and valuing reason more highly after an intolerable experience of the immortal mindless, Tomiko tried to understand rationally what Osden had done. But the words escaped her control. He had taken the fear into himself, and, accepting, had transcended it. He had given up his self to the alien, an unreserved surrender, that left no place for evil. He had learned the love of the Other, and thereby had been given his whole self.—But this is not the vocabulary of reason.

The people of the Survey team walked under the trees, through the vast colonies of life, surrounded by a dreaming silence, a brooding calm that was half aware of them and wholly indifferent to them. There were no hours. Distance was no matter. Had we but world enough and time ... The planet turned between the sunlight and the great dark; winds of winter and summer blew fine, pale pollen across the quiet seas.

Gum returned after many surveys, years, and lightyears, to what had several centuries ago been Smeming Port. There were still men there, to receive (incredulously) the team's reports, and to record its losses: Biologist Harfex, dead of fear, and Sensor Osden, left as a colonist.

A Meeting with Medusa

ARTHUR C. CLARKE

*Here's another seminal story by Arthur C. Clarke, whose "The Sentinel" appeared
earlier in this anthology. In this one, he takes us on a terrifying plunge into the
hellish interior of the immense, banded gas-giant, Jupiter, where storms rage
large enough to swallow the entire Earth and a lone explorer in a frail little craft
will need every bit of skill and courage and determination he possesses to steer
his way out again—if he can keep himself from being distracted by some very big
surprises he runs into along the way. . . .*

1. A DAY TO REMEMBER

The *Queen Elizabeth* was over three miles above the Grand Canyon, daw-
dling along at a comfortable hundred and eighty, when Howard Falcon
spotted the camera platform closing in from the right. He had been expecting it—nothing else was cleared to fly at this altitude—but he was
not too happy to have company. Although he welcomed any signs of
public interest, he also wanted as much empty sky as he could get. After
all, he was the first man in history to navigate a ship three-tenths of a
mile long. . . .

So far, this first test flight had gone perfectly; ironically enough, the
only problem had been the century-old aircraft carrier *Chairman Mao*,
borrowed from the San Diego Naval Museum for support operations.
Only one of *Mao*'s four nuclear reactors was still operating, and the old
battlewagon's top speed was barely thirty knots. Luckily, wind speed at
sea level had been less than half this, so it had not been too difficult to
maintain still air on the flight deck. Though there had been a few anxious
moments during gusts, when the mooring lines had been dropped, the
great dirigible had risen smoothly, straight up into the sky, as if on an
invisible elevator. If all went well, *Queen Elizabeth IV* would not meet
Chairman Mao again for another week.

Everything was under control; all test instruments gave normal readings. Commander Falcon decided to go upstairs and watch the rendezvous. He handed over to his second officer, and walked out into the
transparent tubeway that led through the heart of the ship. There, as
always, he was overwhelmed by the spectacle of the largest single space
ever enclosed by man.

The ten spherical gas cells, each more than a hundred feet across, were
ranged one behind the other like a line of gigantic soap bubbles. The
tough plastic was so clear that he could see through the whole length of
the array, and make out details of the elevator mechanism, more than a

third of a mile from his vantage point. All around him, like a three-dimensional maze, was the structural framework of the ship—the great longitudinal girders running from nose to tail, the fifteen hoops that were the circular ribs of this skyborne colossus, and whose varying sizes defined its graceful, streamlined profile.

At this low speed, there was little sound—merely the soft rush of wind over the envelope and an occasional creak of metal as the pattern of stresses changed. The shadowless light from the rows of lamps far overhead gave the whole scene a curiously submarine quality, and to Falcon this was enhanced by the spectacle of the translucent gasbags. He had once encountered a squadron of large but harmless jellyfish, pulsing their mindless way above a shallow tropical reef, and the plastic bubbles that gave *Queen Elizabeth* her lift often reminded him of these—especially when changing pressures made them crinkle and scatter new patterns of reflected light.

He walked down the axis of the ship until he came to the forward elevator, between gas cells one and two. Riding up to the Observation Deck, he noticed that it was uncomfortably hot, and dictated a brief memo to himself on his pocket recorder. The *Queen* obtained almost a quarter of her buoyancy from the unlimited amounts of waste heat produced by her fusion power plant. On this lightly loaded flight, indeed, only six of the ten gas cells contained helium; the remaining four were full of air. Yet she still carried two hundred tons of water as ballast. However, running the cells at high temperatures did produce problems in refrigerating the access ways; it was obvious that a little more work would have to be done there.

A refreshing blast of cooler air hit him in the face when he stepped out onto the Observation Deck and into the dazzling sunlight streaming through the Plexiglas roof. Half a dozen workmen, with an equal number of superchimp assistants, were busily laying the partly completed dance floor, while others were installing electric wiring and fixing furniture. It was a scene of controlled chaos, and Falcon found it hard to believe that everything would be ready for the maiden voyage, only four weeks ahead. Well, that was not *his* problem, thank goodness. He was merely the Captain, not the Cruise Director.

The human workers waved to him, and the "simps" flashed toothy smiles, as he walked through the confusion, into the already completed Skylounge. This was his favorite place in the whole ship, and he knew that once she was operating he would never again have it all to himself. He would allow himself just five minutes of private enjoyment.

He called the bridge, checked that everything was still in order, and relaxed into one of the comfortable swivel chairs. Below, in a curve that delighted the eye, was the unbroken silver sweep of the ship's envelope. He was perched at the highest point, surveying the whole immensity of the largest vehicle ever built. And when he had tired of that—all the way out to the horizon was the fantastic wilderness carved by the Colorado River in half a billion years of time.

Apart from the camera platform (it had now fallen back and was filming from amidships), he had the sky to himself. It was blue and empty, clear down to the horizon. In his grandfather's day, Falcon knew, it would have been streaked with vapor trails and stained with smoke. Both had gone: the aerial garbage had vanished with the primitive technologies that spawned it, and the long-distance transportation of this age arced too far beyond the stratosphere for any sight or sound of it to reach Earth. Once again, the lower atmosphere belonged to the birds and the clouds—and now to *Queen Elizabeth IV*.

It was true, as the old pioneers had said at the beginning of the twentieth century: this was the only way to travel—in silence and luxury, breathing the air around you and not cut off from it, near enough to the surface to watch the everchanging beauty of land and sea. The subsonic jets of the 1980s, packed with hundreds of passengers seated ten abreast, could not even begin to match such comfort and spaciousness.

Of course, the *Queen* would never be an economic proposition, and even if her projected sister ships were built, only a few of the world's quarter of a billion inhabitants would ever enjoy this silent gliding through the sky. But a secure and prosperous global society could afford such follies and indeed needed them for their novelty and entertainment. There were at least a million men on Earth whose discretionary income exceeded a thousand new dollars a year, so the *Queen* would not lack for passengers.

Falcon's pocket communicator beeped. The copilot was calling from the bridge.

"O.K. for rendezvous, Captain? We've got all the data we need from this run, and the TV people are getting impatient."

Falcon glanced at the camera platform, now matching his speed a tenth of a mile away.

"O.K.," he replied. "Proceed as arranged. I'll watch from here."

He walked back through the busy chaos of the Observation Deck so that he could have a better view amidships. As he did so, he could feel the change of vibration underfoot; by the time he had reached the rear of the lounge, the ship had come to rest. Using his master key, he let himself out onto the small external platform flaring from the end of the deck; half a dozen people could stand here, with only low guardrails separating them from the vast sweep of the envelope—and from the ground, thousands of feet below. It was an exciting place to be, and perfectly safe even when the ship was traveling at speed, for it was in the dead air behind the huge dorsal blister of the Observation Deck. Nevertheless, it was not intended that the passengers would have access to it; the view was a little too vertiginous.

The covers of the forward cargo hatch had already opened like giant trap doors, and the camera platform was hovering above them, preparing to descend. Along this route, in the years to come, would travel thousands of passengers and tons of supplies. Only on rare occasions would the *Queen* drop down to sea level and dock with her floating base.

A sudden gust of cross wind slapped Falcon's cheek, and he tightened his grip on the guardrail. The Grand Canyon was a bad place for turbulence, though he did not expect much at this altitude. Without any real anxiety, he focused his attention on the descending platform, now about 150 feet above the ship. He knew that the highly skilled operator who was flying the remotely controlled vehicle had performed this simple maneuver a dozen times already; it was inconceivable that he would have any difficulties.

Yet he seemed to be reacting rather sluggishly. That last gust had drifted the platform almost to the edge of the open hatchway. Surely the pilot could have corrected before this. . . . Did he have a control problem? It was very unlikely; these remotes had multiple redundancy, fail-safe takeovers, and any number of backup systems. Accidents were almost unheard of.

But there he went again, off to the left. Could the pilot be *drunk*? Improbable though that seemed, Falcon considered it seriously for a moment. Then he reached for his microphone switch.

Once again, without warning, he was slapped violently in the face. He hardly felt it, for he was staring in horror at the camera platform. The distant operator was fighting for control, trying to balance the craft on its jets—but he was only making matters worse. The oscillations increased—twenty degrees, forty, sixty, ninety. . . .

"Switch to automatic, you fool!" Falcon shouted uselessly into his microphone. "Your manual control's not working!"

The platform flipped over on its back. The jets no longer supported it, but drove it swiftly downward. They had suddenly become allies of the gravity they had fought until this moment.

Falcon never heard the crash, though he felt it; he was already inside the Observation Deck, racing for the elevator that would take him down to the bridge. Workmen shouted at him anxiously, asking what had happened. It would be many months before he knew the answer to that question.

Just as he was stepping into the elevator cage, he changed his mind. What if there was a power failure? Better be on the safe side, even if it took longer and time was the essence. He began to run down the spiral stairway enclosing the shaft.

Halfway down he paused for a second to inspect the damage. That damned platform had gone clear through the ship, rupturing two of the gas cells as it did so. They were still collapsing slowly, in great falling veils of plastic. He was not worried about the loss of lift—the ballast could easily take care of that, as long as eight cells remained intact. Far more serious was the possibility of structural damage. Already he could hear the great latticework around him groaning and protesting under its abnormal loads. It was not enough to have sufficient lift; unless it was properly distributed, the ship would break her back.

He was just resuming his descent when a superchimp, shrieking with fright, came racing down the elevator shaft, moving with incredible speed, hand over hand, along the *outside* of the latticework. In its terror, the poor beast had torn off its company uniform, perhaps in an unconscious attempt to regain the freedom of its ancestors.

Falcon, still descending as swiftly as he could, watched its approach with some alarm. A distraught simp was a powerful and potentially dangerous animal, especially if fear overcame its conditioning. As it overtook him, it started to call out a string of words, but they were all jumbled together, and the only one he could recognize was a plaintive, frequently repeated "boss." Even now, Falcon realized, it looked toward humans for guidance. He felt sorry for the creature, involved in a man-made disaster beyond its comprehension, and for which it bore no responsibility.

It stopped opposite him, on the other side of the lattice; there was nothing to prevent it from coming through the open framework if it wished. Now its face was only inches from his, and he was looking straight into the terrified eyes. Never before had he been so close to a simp, and able to study its features in such detail. He felt that strange mingling of kinship and discomfort that all men experience when they gaze thus into the mirror of time.

His presence seemed to have calmed the creature. Falcon pointed up the shaft, back toward the Observation Deck, and said very clearly and precisely: "Boss—boss—*go*." To his relief, the simp understood; it gave him a grimace that might have been a smile, and at once started to race back the way it had come. Falcon had given it the best advice he could. If any safety remained aboard the *Queen*, it was in that direction. But his duty lay in the other.

He had almost completed his descent when, with a sound of rending metal, the vessel pitched nose down, and the lights went out. But he could still see quite well, for a shaft of sunlight streamed through the open hatch and the huge tear in the envelope. Many years ago he had stood in a great cathedral nave watching the light pouring through the stained-glass windows, forming pools of multicolored radiance on the ancient flagstones. The dazzling shaft of sunlight through the ruined fabric high above reminded him of that moment. He was in a cathedral of metal, falling down the sky.

When he reached the bridge, and was able for the first time to look outside, he was horrified to see how close the ship was to the ground. Only three thousand feet below were the beautiful and deadly pinnacles of rock and the red rivers of mud that were still carving their way down into the past. There was no level area anywhere in sight where a ship as large as the *Queen* could come to rest on an even keel.

A glance at the display board told him that all the ballast had gone. However, rate of descent had been reduced to a few yards a second; they still had a fighting chance.

Without a word, Falcon eased himself into the pilot's seat and took over such control as still remained. The instrument board showed him everything he wished to know; speech was superfluous. In the background, he could hear the Communications Officer giving a running report over the radio. By this time, all the news channels of Earth would have been preempted, and he could imagine the utter frustration of the program controllers. One of the most spectacular wrecks in history was occurring—without a single camera to record it. The last moments of the

Queen would never fill millions with awe and terror, as had those of the *Hindenburg*, a century and a half before.

Now the ground was only about 1,700 feet away, still coming up slowly. Though he had full thrust, he had not dared to use it, lest the weakened structure collapse; but now he realized that he had no choice. The wind was taking them toward a fork in the canyon, where the river was split by a wedge of rock like the prow of some gigantic, fossilized ship of stone. If she continued on her present course, the *Queen* would straddle that triangular plateau and come to rest with at least a third of her length jutting out over nothingness; she would snap like a rotten stick.

Far away, above the sound of straining metal and escaping gas, came the familiar whistle of the jets as Falcon opened up the lateral thrusters. The ship staggered, and began to slew to port. The shriek of tearing metal was now almost continuous—and the rate of descent had started to increase ominously. A glance at the damage-control board showed that cell number five had just gone.

The ground was only yards away. Even now, he could not tell whether his maneuver would succeed or fail. He switched the thrust vectors over to vertical, giving maximum lift to reduce the force of impact.

The crash seemed to last forever. It was not violent—merely prolonged, and irresistible. It seemed that the whole universe was falling about them.

The sound of crunching metal came nearer, as if some great beast were eating its way through the dying ship.

Then floor and ceiling closed upon him like a vise.

2. "BECAUSE IT'S THERE"

"Why do you want to go to Jupiter?"

"As Springer said when he lifted for Pluto—'because it's there.' "

"Thanks. Now we've got that out of the way—the real reason."

Howard Falcon smiled, though only those who knew him well could have interpreted the slight, leathery grimace. Webster was one of them; for more than twenty years they had been involved in each other's projects. They had shared triumphs and disasters—including the greatest disaster of all.

"Well, Springer's cliché is still valid. We've landed on all the terrestrial planets, but none of the gas giants. They are the only real challenge left in the solar system."

"An expensive one. Have you worked out the cost?"

"As well as I can; here are the estimates. Remember, though—this isn't a one-shot mission, but a transportation system. Once it's proved out, it can be used over and over again. And it will open up not merely Jupiter, but all the giants."

Webster looked at the figures, and whistled.

"Why not start with an easier planet—Uranus, for example? Half the gravity, and less than half the escape velocity. Quieter weather, too—if that's the right word for it."

Webster had certainly done his homework. But that, of course, was why he was head of Long-Range Planning.

"There's very little saving—when you allow for the extra distance and the logistics problems. For Jupiter, we can use the facilities of Ganymede. Beyond Saturn, we'd have to establish a new supply base."

Logical, thought Webster; but he was sure that it was not the important reason. Jupiter was lord of the solar system; Falcon would be interested in no lesser challenge.

"Besides," Falcon continued, "Jupiter is a major scientific scandal. It's more than a hundred years since its radio storms were discovered, but we still don't know what causes them—and the Great Red Spot is as big a mystery as ever. That's why I can get matching funds from the Bureau of Astronautics. Do you know how many probes they have dropped into that atmosphere?"

"A couple of hundred, I believe."

"*Three* hundred and twenty-six, over the last fifty years—about a quarter of them total failures. Of course, they've learned a hell of a lot, but they've barely scratched the planet. Do you realize how *big* it is?"

"More than ten times the size of Earth."

"Yes, yes—but do you know what that really means?"

Falcon pointed to the large globe in the corner of Webster's office.

"Look at India—how small it seems. Well, if you skinned Earth and spread it out on the surface of Jupiter, it would look about as big as India does here."

There was a long silence while Webster contemplated the equation: Jupiter is to Earth as Earth is to India. Falcon had—deliberately, of course—chosen the best possible example. . . .

Was it already ten years ago? Yes, it must have been. The crash lay seven years in the past (that date was engraved on his heart), and those initial tests had taken place three years before the first and last flight of the *Queen Elizabeth*.

Ten years ago, then, Commander (no, Lieutenant) Falcon had invited him to a preview—a three-day drift across the northern plains of India, within sight of the Himalayas. "Perfectly safe," he had promised. "It will get you away from the office—and will teach you what this whole thing is about."

Webster had not been disappointed. Next to his first journey to the Moon, it had been the most memorable experience of his life. And yet, as Falcon had assured him, it had been perfectly safe, and quite uneventful.

They had taken off from Srinagar just before dawn, with the huge silver bubble of the balloon already catching the first light of the Sun. The ascent had been made in total silence; there were none of the roaring propane burners that had lifted the hot-air balloons of an earlier age. All the heat they needed came from the little pulsed-fusion reactor, weighing only about 220 pounds, hanging in the open mouth of the envelope. While they were climbing, its laser was zapping ten times a second, igniting the merest whiff of deuterium fuel. Once they had reached altitude, it would fire only a few times a minute, making up for the heat lost through the great gasbag overhead.

And so, even while they were almost a mile above the ground, they could hear dogs barking, people shouting, bells ringing. Slowly the vast, Sun-smitten landscape expanded around them. Two hours later, they had leveled out at three miles and were taking frequent draughts of oxygen. They could relax and admire the scenery; the on-board instrumentation was doing all the work—gathering the information that would be required by the designers of the still-unnamed liner of the skies.

It was a perfect day. The southwest monsoon would not break for another month, and there was hardly a cloud in the sky. Time seemed to have come to a stop; they resented the hourly radio reports, which interrupted their reverie. And all around, to the horizon and far beyond, was that infinite, ancient landscape, drenched with history—a patchwork of villages, fields, temples, lakes, irrigation canals. . . .

With a real effort, Webster broke the hypnotic spell of that ten-year-old memory. It had converted him to lighter-than-air flight—and it had made him realize the enormous size of India, even in a world that could be circled within ninety minutes. And yet, he repeated to himself, Jupiter is to Earth as Earth is to India. . . .

"Granted your argument," he said, "and supposing the funds are available, there's another question you have to answer. Why should you do better than the—what is it—326 robot probes that have already made the trip?"

"I am better qualified than they were—as an observer, and as a pilot. *Especially* as a pilot. Don't forget—I've more experience of lighter-than-air flight than anyone in the world."

"You could still serve as controller, and sit safely on Ganymede."

"*But that's just the point!* They've already done that. Don't you remember what killed the *Queen*?"

Webster knew perfectly well; but he merely answered: "Go on."

"*Time lag—time lag!* That idiot of a platform controller thought he was using a local radio circuit. But he'd been accidentally switched through a satellite—oh, maybe it wasn't his fault, but he should have noticed. That's a half-second time lag for the round trip. Even then it wouldn't have mattered flying in calm air. It was the turbulence over the Grand Canyon that did it. When the platform tipped, and he corrected for that—it had already tipped the other way. Ever tried to drive a car over a bumpy road with a half-second delay in the steering?"

"No, and I don't intend to try. But I can imagine it."

"Well, Ganymede is a million kilometers from Jupiter. That means a round-trip delay of six seconds. No, you need a controller on the spot—to handle emergencies in real time. Let me show you something. Mind if I use this?"

"Go ahead."

Falcon picked up a postcard that was lying on Webster's desk; they were almost obsolete on Earth, but this one showed a 3-D view of a Martian landscape, and was decorated with exotic and expensive stamps. He held it so that it dangled vertically.

"This is an old trick, but helps to make my point. Place your thumb and finger on either side, not quite touching. That's right."

Webster put out his hand, almost but not quite gripping the card.

"Now catch it."

Falcon waited for a few seconds; then, without warning, he let go of the card. Webster's thumb and finger closed on empty air.

"I'll do it again, just to show there's no deception. You see?"

Once again, the falling card had slipped through Webster's fingers.

"Now you try it on me."

This time, Webster grasped the card and dropped it without warning. It had scarcely moved before Falcon had caught it. Webster almost imagined he could hear a click, so swift was the other's reaction.

"When they put me together again," Falcon remarked in an expressionless voice, "the surgeons made some improvements. This is one of them—and there are others. I want to make the most of them. Jupiter is the place where I can do it."

Webster stared for long seconds at the fallen card, absorbing the improbable colors of the Trivium Charontis Escarpment. Then he said quietly: "I understand. How long do you think it will take?"

"With your help, plus the Bureau, plus all the science foundations we can drag in—oh, three years. Then a year for trials—we'll have to send in at least two test models. So, with luck—five years."

"That's about what I thought. I hope you get your luck; you've earned it. But there's one thing I won't do."

"What's that?"

"Next time you go ballooning, don't expect *me* as passenger."

3. THE WORLD OF THE GODS

The fall from Jupiter V to Jupiter itself takes only three and a half hours. Few men could have slept on so awesome a journey. Sleep was a weakness that Howard Falcon hated, and the little he still required brought dreams that time had not yet been able to exorcise. But he could expect no rest in the three days that lay ahead, and must seize what he could during the long fall down into that ocean of clouds, some sixty thousand miles below.

As soon as *Kon-Tiki* had entered her transfer orbit and all the computer checks were satisfactory, he prepared for the last sleep he might ever know. It seemed appropriate that at almost the same moment Jupiter eclipsed the bright and tiny Sun as he swept into the monstrous shadow of the planet. For a few minutes a strange golden twilight enveloped the ship; then a quarter of the sky became an utterly black hole in space, while the rest was a blaze of stars. No matter how far one traveled across the solar system, *they* never changed; these same constellations now shone on Earth, millions of miles away. The only novelties here were the small, pale crescents of Callisto and Ganymede; doubtless there were a dozen other moons up there in the sky, but they were all much too tiny, and too distant, for the unaided eye to pick them out.

"Closing down for two hours," he reported to the mother ship, hanging almost a thousand miles above the desolate rocks of Jupiter V, in the radiation shadow of the tiny satellite. If it never served any other useful purpose, Jupiter V was a cosmic bulldozer perpetually sweeping up the charged particles that made it unhealthy to linger close to Jupiter. Its wake was almost free of radiation, and there a ship could park in perfect safety, while death sleeted invisibly all around.

Falcon switched on the sleep inducer, and consciousness faded swiftly out as the electric pulses surged gently through his brain. While *Kon-Tiki* fell toward Jupiter, gaining speed second by second in that enormous gravitational field, he slept without dreams. They always came when he awoke; and he had brought his nightmares with him from Earth.

Yet he never dreamed of the crash itself, though he often found himself again face to face with that terrified superchimp, as he descended the spiral stairway between the collapsing gasbags. None of the simps had survived; those that were not killed outright were so badly injured that they had been painlessly "euthed." He sometimes wondered why he dreamed only of this doomed creature—which he had never met before the last minutes of its life—and not of the friends and colleagues he had lost aboard the dying *Queen*.

The dreams he feared most always began with his first return to consciousness. There had been little physical pain; in fact, there had been no sensation of any kind. He was in darkness and silence, and did not even seem to be breathing. And—strangest of all—he could not locate his limbs. He could move neither his hands nor his feet, because he did not know where they were.

The silence had been the first to yield. After hours, or days, he had become aware of a faint throbbing, and eventually, after long thought, he deduced that this was the beating of his own heart. That was the first of his many mistakes.

Then there had been faint pinpricks, sparkles of light, ghosts of pressures upon still-unresponsive limbs. One by one his senses had returned, and pain had come with them. He had had to learn everything anew, recapitulating infancy and babyhood. Though his memory was unaffected, and he could understand words that were spoken to him, it was months before he was able to answer except by the flicker of an eyelid. He could remember the moments of triumph when he had spoken the first word, turned the page of a book—and, finally, learned to move under his own power. *That* was a victory indeed, and it had taken him almost two years to prepare for it. A hundred times he had envied that dead superchimp, but *he* had been given no choice. The doctors had made their decision—and now, twelve years later, he was where no human being had ever traveled before, and moving faster than any man in history.

Kon-Tiki was just emerging from shadow, and the Jovian dawn bridged the sky ahead in a titanic bow of light, when the persistent buzz of the alarm dragged Falcon up from sleep. The inevitable nightmares (he had been trying to summon a nurse, but did not even have the strength to push the button) swiftly faded from consciousness. The greatest—and perhaps last—adventure of his life was before him.

He called Mission Control, now almost sixty thousand miles away and falling swiftly below the curve of Jupiter, to report that everything was in order. His velocity had just passed thirty-one miles a second (that was one for the books) and in half an hour Kon-Tiki would hit the outer fringes of the atmosphere, as he started on the most difficult reentry in the entire solar system. Although scores of probes had survived this flaming ordeal, they had been tough, solidly packed masses of instrumentation, able to withstand several hundred gravities of drag. Kon-Tiki would hit peaks of thirty g's, and would average more than ten, before she came to rest in the upper reaches of the Jovian atmosphere. Very carefully and thoroughly, Falcon began to attach the elaborate system of restraints that would anchor him to the walls of the cabin. When he had finished, he was virtually a part of the ship's structure.

The clock was counting backward; one hundred seconds to reentry. For better or worse, he was committed. In a minute and a half, he would graze the Jovian atmosphere, and would be caught irrevocably in the grip of the giant.

The countdown was three seconds late—not at all bad, considering the unknowns involved. From beyond the walls of the capsule came a ghostly sighing, which rose steadily to a high-pitched, screaming roar. The noise was quite different from that of a reentry on Earth or Mars; in this thin atmosphere of hydrogen and helium, all sounds were transformed a couple of octaves upward. On Jupiter, even thunder would have falsetto overtones.

With the rising scream came mounting weight; within seconds, he was completely immobilized. His field of vision contracted until it embraced only the clock and the accelerometer; fifteen g, and 480 seconds to go. . . .

He never lost consciousness; but then, he had not expected to. Kon-Tiki's trail through the Jovian atmosphere must be really spectacular—by this time, thousands of miles long. Five hundred seconds after entry, the drag began to taper off: ten g, five g, two. . . . Then weight vanished almost completely. He was falling free, all his enormous orbital velocity destroyed.

There was a sudden jolt as the incandescent remnants of the heat shield were jettisoned. It had done its work and would not be needed again; Jupiter could have it now. He released all but two of the restraining buckles, and waited for the automatic sequencer to start the next, and most critical, series of events.

He did not see the first drogue parachute pop out, but he could feel the slight jerk, and the rate of fall diminished immediately. Kon-Tiki had lost all her horizontal speed and was going straight down at almost a thousand miles an hour. Everything depended on what happened in the next sixty seconds.

There went the second drogue. He looked up through the overhead window and saw, to his immense relief, that clouds of glittering foil were billowing out behind the falling ship. Like a great flower unfurling, the thousands of cubic yards of the balloon spread out across the sky, scooping up the thin gas until it was fully inflated. *Kon-Tiki's* rate of fall dropped to a few miles an hour and remained constant. Now there was plenty of time; it would take him days to fall all the way down to the surface of Jupiter.

But he would get there eventually, even if he did nothing about it. The balloon overhead was merely acting as an efficient parachute. It was providing no lift; nor could it do so, while the gas inside and out was the same.

With its characteristic and rather disconcerting crack the fusion reactor started up, pouring torrents of heat into the envelope overhead. Within five minutes, the rate of fall had become zero; within six, the ship had started to rise. According to the radar altimeter, it had leveled out at about 267 miles above the surface—or whatever passed for a surface on Jupiter.

Only one kind of balloon will work in an atmosphere of hydrogen, which is the lightest of all gases—and that is a hot-hydrogen balloon. As long as the fuser kept ticking over, Falcon could remain aloft, drifting across a world that could hold a hundred Pacifics. After traveling over 300,000,000 miles, *Kon-Tiki* had at last begun to justify her name. She was an aerial raft, adrift upon the currents of the Jovian atmosphere.

➤

Though a whole new world was lying around him, it was more than an hour before Falcon could examine the view. First he had to check all the capsule's systems and test its response to the controls. He had to learn how much extra heat was necessary to produce a desired rate of ascent, and how much gas he must vent in order to descend. Above all, there was the question of stability. He must adjust the length of the cables attaching his capsule to the huge, pear-shaped balloon, to damp out vibrations and get the smoothest possible ride. Thus far, he was lucky; at this level, the wind was steady, and the Doppler reading on the invisible surface gave him a ground speed of 217.5 miles an hour. For Jupiter, that was modest; winds of up to a thousand had been observed. But mere speed was, of course, unimportant; the real danger was turbulence. If he ran into that, only skill and experience and swift reaction could save him—and these were not matters that could yet be programmed into a computer.

Not until he was satisfied that he had got the feel of his strange craft did Falcon pay any attention to Mission Control's pleadings. Then he deployed the booms carrying the instrumentation and the atmospheric samplers. The capsule now resembled a rather untidy Christmas tree, but still rode smoothly down the Jovian winds while it radioed its torrents of information to the recorders on the ship miles above. And now, at last, he could look around. . . .

His first impression was unexpected, and even a little disappointing. As far as the scale of things was concerned, he might have been ballooning over an ordinary cloudscape on Earth. The horizon seemed at a normal distance; there was no feeling at all that he was on a world eleven times the diameter of his own. Then he looked at the infrared radar, sounding the layers of atmosphere beneath him—and knew how badly his eyes had been deceived.

That layer of clouds apparently about three miles away was really more than thirty-seven miles below. And the horizon, whose distance he would have guessed at about 125, was actually 1,800 miles from the ship.

The crystalline clarity of the hydrohelium atmosphere and the enormous curvature of the planet had fooled him completely. It was even harder to judge distances here than on the Moon; everything he saw must be multiplied by at least ten.

It was a simple matter, and he should have been prepared for it. Yet somehow, it disturbed him profoundly. He did not feel that Jupiter was huge, but that *he* had shrunk—to a tenth of his normal size. Perhaps, with time, he would grow accustomed to the inhuman scale of this world; yet as he stared toward that unbelievably distant horizon, he felt as if a wind colder than the atmosphere around him was blowing through his soul. Despite all his arguments, this might never be a place for man. He could well be both the first and the last to descend through the clouds of Jupiter.

The sky above was almost black, except for a few wisps of ammonia cirrus perhaps twelve miles overhead. It was cold up there, on the fringes of space, but both pressure and temperature increased rapidly with depth. At the level where *Kon-Tiki* was drifting now, it was fifty below zero, and the pressure was five atmospheres. Sixty-five miles farther down, it would be as warm as equatorial Earth, and the pressure about the same as at the bottom of one of the shallower seas. Ideal conditions for life . . .

A quarter of the brief Jovian day had already gone; the sun was halfway up the sky, but the light on the unbroken cloudscape below had a curious mellow quality. That extra three hundred million miles had robbed the Sun of all its power. Though the sky was clear, Falcon found himself continually thinking that it was a heavily overcast day. When night fell, the onset of darkness would be swift indeed; though it was still morning, there was a sense of autumnal twilight in the air. But autumn, of course, was something that never came to Jupiter. There were no seasons here.

Kon-Tiki had come down in the exact center of the equatorial zone— the least colorful part of the planet. The sea of clouds that stretched out to the horizon was tinted a pale salmon; there were none of the yellows and pinks and even reds that banded Jupiter at higher altitudes. The Great Red Spot itself—most spectacular of all of the planet's features—lay thousands of miles to the south. It had been a temptation to descend there, but the south tropical disturbance was unusually active, with currents reaching over nine hundred miles an hour. It would have been asking for trouble to head into that maelstrom of unknown forces. The Great Red Spot and its mysteries would have to wait for future expeditions.

The Sun, moving across the sky twice as swiftly as it did on Earth, was now nearing the zenith and had become eclipsed by the great silver canopy of the balloon. *Kon-Tiki* was still drifting swiftly and smoothly westward at a steady 217.5, but only the radar gave any indication of this. Was it always as calm here? Falcon asked himself. The scientists who had talked learnedly of the Jovian doldrums, and had predicted that the equator would be the quietest place, seemed to know what they were talking about, after all. He had been profoundly skeptical of all such forecasts, and had agreed with one unusually modest researcher who had told him bluntly: "There are *no* experts on Jupiter." Well, there would be at least one by the end of this day.

If he managed to survive until then.

4. THE VOICES OF THE DEEP

That first day, the Father of the Gods smiled upon him. It was as calm and peaceful here on Jupiter as it had been, years ago, when he was drifting with Webster across the plains of northern India. Falcon had time to master his new skills, until *Kon-Tiki* seemed an extension of his own body. Such luck was more than he had dared to hope for, and he began to wonder what price he might have to pay for it.

The five hours of daylight were almost over; the clouds below were full of shadows, which gave them a massive solidity they had not possessed when the Sun was higher. Color was swiftly draining from the sky, except in the west itself, where a band of deepening purple lay along the horizon. Above this band was the thin crescent of a closer moon, pale and bleached against the utter blackness beyond.

With a speed perceptible to the eye, the Sun went straight down over the edge of Jupiter, over 1,800 miles away. The stars came out in their legions—and there was the beautiful evening star of Earth, on the very frontier of twilight, reminding him how far he was from home. It followed the Sun down into the west. Man's first night on Jupiter had begun.

With the onset of darkness, *Kon-Tiki* started to sink. The balloon was no longer heated by the feeble sunlight and was losing a small part of its buoyancy. Falcon did nothing to increase lift; he had expected this and was planning to descend.

The invisible cloud deck was still over thirty miles below, and he would reach it about midnight. It showed up clearly on the infrared radar, which also reported that it contained a vast array of complex carbon compounds, as well as the usual hydrogen, helium, and ammonia. The chemists were dying for samples of that fluffy, pinkish stuff; though some atmospheric probes had already gathered a few grams, that had only whetted their appetites. Half the basic molecules of life were here, floating high above the surface of Jupiter. And where there was food, could life be far away? That was the question that, after more than a hundred years, no one had been able to answer.

The infrared was blocked by the clouds, but the microwave radar sliced right through and showed layer after layer, all the way down to the hidden surface almost 250 miles below. That was barred to him by enormous pressures and temperatures; not even robot probes had ever reached it intact. It lay in tantalizing inaccessibility at the bottom of the radar screen, slightly fuzzy, and showing a curious granular structure that his equipment could not resolve.

An hour after sunset, he dropped his first probe. It fell swiftly for about sixty miles, then began to float in the denser atmosphere, sending back torrents of radio signals, which he relayed to Mission Control. Then there was nothing else to do until sunrise, except to keep an eye on the rate of descent, monitor the instruments, and answer occasional queries. While she was drifting in this steady current, *Kon-Tiki* could look after herself.

Just before midnight, a woman controller came on watch and introduced herself with the usual pleasantries. Ten minutes later she called again, her voice at once serious and excited.

"Howard! Listen in on channel forty-six—high gain."

Channel forty-six? There were so many telemetering circuits that he knew the numbers of only those that were critical; but as soon as he threw the switch, he recognized this one. He was plugged in to the microphone on the probe, floating more than eighty miles below him in an atmosphere now almost as dense as water.

At first, there was only a soft hiss of whatever strange winds stirred down in the darkness of that unimaginable world. And then, out of the background noise, there slowly emerged a booming vibration that grew louder and louder, like the beating of a gigantic drum. It was so low that it was felt as much as heard, and the beats steadily increased their tempo, though the pitch never changed. Now it was a swift, almost infrasonic throbbing. Then, suddenly, in mid-vibration, it stopped—so abruptly that the mind could not accept the silence, but memory continued to manufacture a ghostly echo in the deepest caverns of the brain.

It was the most extraordinary sound that Falcon had ever heard, even among the multitudinous noises of Earth. He could think of no natural phenomenon that could have caused it; nor was it like the cry of any animal, not even one of the great whales. . . .

It came again, following exactly the same pattern. Now that he was prepared for it, he estimated the length of the sequence; from first faint throb to final crescendo, it lasted just over ten seconds.

And this time there was a real echo, very faint and far away. Perhaps it came from one of the many reflecting layers, deeper in this stratified atmosphere; perhaps it was another, more distant source. Falcon waited for a second echo, but it never came.

Mission Control reacted quickly and asked him to drop another probe at once. With two microphones operating, it would be possible to find the approximate location of the sources. Oddly enough, none of *Kon-Tiki's* own external mikes could detect anything except wind noises. The boomings, whatever they were, must have been trapped and channeled beneath an atmospheric reflecting layer far below.

They were coming, it was soon discovered, from a cluster of sources about 1,200 miles away. The distance gave no indication of their power; in Earth's oceans, quite feeble sounds could travel equally far. And as for the obvious assumption that living creatures were responsible, the Chief Exobiologist quickly ruled that out.

"I'll be very disappointed," said Dr. Brenner, "if there are no microorganisms or plants there. But nothing like animals, because there's no free oxygen. All biochemical reactions on Jupiter must be low-energy ones—there's just no way an active creature could generate enough power to function."

Falcon wondered if this was true; he had heard the argument before, and reserved judgment.

"In any case," continued Brenner, "some of those sound waves are a hundred yards long! Even an animal as big as a whale couldn't produce them. They *must* have a natural origin."

Yes, that seemed plausible, and probably the physicists would be able to come up with an explanation. What would a blind alien make, Falcon wondered, of the sounds he might hear when standing beside a stormy sea, or a geyser, or a volcano, or a waterfall? He might well attribute them to some huge beast.

About an hour before sunrise the voices of the deep died away, and Falcon began to busy himself with preparation for the dawn of his second day. *Kon-Tiki* was now only three miles above the nearest cloud layer; the external pressure had risen to ten atmospheres, and the temperature was a tropical thirty degrees. A man could be comfortable here with no more equipment than a breathing mask and the right grade of heliox mixture.

"We've some good news for you," Mission Control reported, soon after dawn. "The cloud layer's breaking up. You'll have partial clearing in an hour—but watch out for turbulence."

"I've already noticed some," Falcon answered. "How far down will I be able to see?"

"At least twelve miles, down to the second thermocline. *That* cloud deck is solid—it never breaks."

And it's out of my reach, Falcon told himself; the temperature down there must be over a hundred degrees. This was the first time that any balloonist had ever had to worry, not about his ceiling, but about his basement!

Ten minutes later he could see what Mission Control had already observed from its superior vantage point. There was a change in color near the horizon, and the cloud layer had become ragged and humpy, as if something had torn it open. He turned up his little nuclear furnace and gave *Kon-Tiki* another three miles of altitude, so that he could get a better view.

The sky below was clearing rapidly, completely, as if something was dissolving the solid overcast. An abyss was opening before his eyes. A moment later he sailed out over the edge of a cloud canyon about twelve miles deep and six hundred miles wide.

A new world lay spread beneath him; Jupiter had stripped away one of its many veils. The second layer of clouds, unattainably far below, was much darker in color than the first. It was almost salmon pink, and curiously mottled with little islands of brick red. They were all oval-shaped, with their long axes pointing east-west, in the direction of the prevailing wind. There were hundreds of them, all about the same size, and they reminded Falcon of puffy little cumulus clouds in the terrestrial sky.

He reduced buoyancy, and *Kon-Tiki* began to drop down the face of the dissolving cliff. It was then that he noticed the snow.

White flakes were forming in the air and drifting slowly downward. Yet it was much too warm for snow—and, in any event, there was scarcely a trace of water at this altitude. Moreover, there was no glitter or sparkle about these flakes as they went cascading down into the depths. When, presently, a few landed on an instrument boom outside the main viewing port, he saw that they were a dull, opaque white—not crystalline at all— and quite large—several inches across. They looked like wax, and Falcon guessed that this was precisely what they were. Some chemical reaction was taking place in the atmosphere around him, condensing out the hydrocarbons floating in the Jovian air.

About sixty miles ahead, a disturbance was taking place in the cloud layer. The little red ovals were being jostled around, and were beginning to form a spiral—the familiar cyclonic pattern so common in the meteorology of Earth. The vortex was emerging with astonishing speed; if that was a storm ahead, Falcon told himself, he was in big trouble.

And then his concern changed to wonder—and to fear. What was developing in his line of flight was not a storm at all. Something enormous—something scores of miles across—was rising through the clouds.

The reassuring thought that it, too, might be a cloud—a thunderhead boiling up from the lower levels of the atmosphere—lasted only a few seconds. No; this was *solid*. It shouldered its way through the pink-and-salmon overcast like an iceberg rising from the deeps.

An *iceberg* floating on hydrogen? That was impossible, of course; but perhaps it was not too remote an analogy. As soon as he focused the telescope upon the enigma, Falcon saw that it was a whitish, crystalline mass, threaded with streaks of red and brown. It must be, he decided, the same stuff as the "snowflakes" falling around him—a mountain range of wax. And it was not, he soon realized, as solid as he had thought; around the edges it was continually crumbling and re-forming. . . .

"I know what it is," he radioed Mission Control, which for the last few minutes had been asking anxious questions. "It's a mass of bubbles—some kind of foam. Hydrocarbon froth. Get the chemists working on . . . *Just a minute!*"

"What is it?" called Mission Control. "What is it?"

He ignored the frantic pleas from space and concentrated all his mind upon the image in the telescope field. He had to be sure; if he made a mistake, he would be the laughing stock of the solar system.

Then he relaxed, glanced at the clock, and switched off the nagging voice from Jupiter V.

"Hello, Mission Control," he said, very formally. "This is Howard Falcon aboard *Kon-Tiki*. Ephemeris Time nineteen hours twenty-one minutes fifteen seconds. Latitude zero degrees five minutes North. Longitude 105 degrees forty-two minutes, System One.

"Tell Dr. Brenner that there is life on Jupiter. And it's *big*. . . ."

5. THE WHEELS OF POSEIDON

"I'm very happy to be proved wrong," Dr. Brenner radioed back cheerfully. "Nature always has something up her sleeve. Keep the long-focus camera on target and give us the steadiest pictures you can."

The things moving up and down those waxen slopes were still too far away for Falcon to make out many details, and they must have been very large to be visible at all at such a distance. Almost black, and shaped like arrowheads, they maneuvered by slow undulations of their entire bodies, so that they looked rather like giant manta rays, swimming above some tropical reef.

Perhaps they were skyborne cattle, browsing on the cloud pastures of Jupiter, for they seemed to be feeding along the dark, red-brown streaks that ran like dried-up river beds down the flanks of the floating cliffs. Occasionally, one of them would dive headlong into the mountain of foam and disappear completely from sight.

Kon-Tiki was moving only slowly with respect to the cloud layer below; it would be at least three hours before she was above those ephemeral hills. She was in a race with the Sun. Falcon hoped that darkness would not fall before he could get a good view of the mantas, as he had christened them, as well as the fragile landscape over which they flapped their way.

It was a long three hours. During the whole time, he kept the external microphones on full gain, wondering if here was the source of that booming in the night. The mantas were certainly large enough to have produced it; when he could get an accurate measurement, he discovered that they were almost a hundred yards across the wings. That was three times the length of the largest whale—though he doubted if they could weigh more than a few tons.

Half an hour before sunset, *Kon-Tiki* was almost above the "mountains."

"No," said Falcon, answering Mission Control's repeated questions about the mantas, "they're still showing no reaction to me. I don't think they're intelligent—they look like harmless vegetarians. And even if they try to chase me, I'm sure they can't reach my altitude."

Yet he was a little disappointed when the mantas showed not the slightest interest in him as he sailed high above their feeding ground. Perhaps they had no way of detecting his presence. When he examined and photographed them through the telescope, he could see no signs of any sense organs. The creatures were simply huge black deltas, rippling over hills and valleys that, in reality, were little more substantial than the clouds of Earth. Though they looked solid, Falcon knew that anyone who stepped on those white mountains would go crashing through them as if they were made of tissue paper.

At close quarters he could see the myriads of cellules or bubbles from which they were formed. Some of these were quite large—a yard or so in diameter—and Falcon wondered in what witches' cauldron of hydrocarbons they had been brewed. There must be enough petrochemicals deep down in the atmosphere of Jupiter to supply all Earth's needs for a million years.

The short day had almost gone when he passed over the crest of the waxen hills, and the light was fading rapidly along their lower slopes. There were no mantas on this western side, and for some reason the topography was very different. The foam was sculptured into long, level terraces, like the interior of a lunar crater. He could almost imagine that they were gigantic steps leading down to the hidden surface of the planet.

And on the lowest of those steps, just clear of the swirling clouds that the mountain had displaced when it came surging skyward, was a roughly oval mass, one or two miles across. It was difficult to see, since it was only a little darker than the gray-white foam on which it rested. Falcon's first thought was that he was looking at a forest of pallid trees, like giant mushrooms that had never seen the Sun.

Yes, it must be a forest—he could see hundreds of thin trunks, springing from the white waxy froth in which they were rooted. But the trees were packed astonishingly close together; there was scarcely any space between them. Perhaps it was not a forest, after all, but a single enormous tree—like one of the giant multitrunked banyans of the East. Once he had seen a banyan tree in Java that was over 650 yards across; this monster was at least ten times that size.

The light had almost gone. The cloudscape had turned purple with refracted sunlight, and in a few seconds that, too, would have vanished. In the last light of his second day on Jupiter, Howard Falcon saw—or thought he saw—something that cast the gravest doubts on his interpretation of the white oval.

Unless the dim light had totally deceived him, those hundreds of thin trunks were beating back and forth, in perfect synchronism, like fronds of kelp rocking in the surge.

And the tree was no longer in the place where he had first seen it.

☞

"Sorry about this," said Mission Control, soon after sunset, "but we think Source Beta is going to blow within the next hour. Probability 70 percent."

Falcon glanced quickly at the chart. Beta—Jupiter latitude 140 degrees—was over 18,600 miles away and well below his horizon. Even though major eruptions ran as high as ten megatons, he was much too far away for the shock wave to be a serious danger. The radio storm that it would trigger was, however, quite a different matter.

The decameter outbursts that sometimes made Jupiter the most powerful radio source in the whole sky had been discovered back in the 1950s, to the utter astonishment of the astronomers. Now, more than a century later, their real cause was still a mystery. Only the symptoms were understood; the explanation was completely unknown.

The "volcano" theory had best stood the test of time, although no one imagined that this word had the same meaning on Jupiter as on Earth. At frequent intervals—often several times a day—titanic eruptions occurred in the lower depths of the atmosphere, probably on the hidden surface of the planet itself. A great column of gas, more than six hundred miles high, would start boiling upward as if determined to escape into space.

Against the most powerful gravitational field of all the planets, it had no chance. Yet some traces—a mere few million tons—usually managed to reach the Jovian ionosphere; and when they did, all hell broke loose.

The radiation belts surrounding Jupiter completely dwarf the feeble Van Allen belts of Earth. When they are short-circuited by an ascending column of gas, the result is an electrical discharge millions of times more powerful than any terrestrial flash of lightning; it sends a colossal thunderclap of radio noise flooding across the entire solar system and on out to the stars.

It had been discovered that these radio outbursts came from four main areas of the planet. Perhaps there were weaknesses there that allowed the fires of the interior to break out from time to time. The scientists on Ganymede, largest of Jupiter's many moons, now thought that they could predict the onset of a decameter storm; their accuracy was about as good as a weather forecaster's of the early 1900s.

Falcon did not know whether to welcome or to fear a radio storm; it would certainly add to the value of the mission—if he survived it. His course had been planned to keep as far as possible from the main centers of disturbance, especially the most active one, Source Alpha. As luck would have it, the threatening Beta was the closest to him. He hoped that the distance, almost three-fourths the circumference of Earth, was safe enough.

"Probability 90 percent," said Mission Control with a distinct note of urgency. "And forget that hour. Ganymede says it may be any moment."

The radio had scarcely fallen silent when the reading on the magnetic field-strength meter started to shoot upward. Before it could go off scale, it reversed and began to drop as rapidly as it had risen. Far away and thousands of miles below, something had given the planet's molten core a titanic jolt.

"There she blows!" called Mission Control.

"Thanks, I already know. When will the storm hit me?"

"You can expect onset in five minutes. Peak in ten."

Far around the curve of Jupiter, a funnel of gas as wide as the Pacific Ocean was climbing spaceward at thousands of miles an hour. Already, the thunderstorms of the lower atmosphere would be raging around it— but they were nothing compared with the fury that would explode when the radiation belt was reached and began dumping its surplus electrons onto the planet. Falcon began to retract all the instrument booms that were extended out from the capsule. There were no other precautions he could take. It would be four hours before the atmospheric shock wave reached him—but the radio blast, traveling at the speed of light, would be here in a tenth of a second, once the discharge had been triggered.

The radio monitor, scanning back and forth across the spectrum, still showed nothing unusual, just the normal mush of background static. Then Falcon noticed that the noise level was slowly creeping upward. The explosion was gathering its strength.

At such a distance he had never expected to *see* anything. But suddenly a flicker as of far-off heat lightning danced along the eastern horizon. Simultaneously, half the circuit breakers jumped out of the main switchboard, the lights failed, and all communications channels went dead.

He tried to move, but was completely unable to do so. The paralysis that gripped him was not merely psychological; he seemed to have lost all control of his limbs and could feel a painful tingling sensation over his entire body. It was impossible that the electric field could have penetrated this shielded cabin. Yet there was a flickering glow over the instrument board, and he could hear the unmistakable crackle of a brush discharge.

With a series of sharp bangs, the emergency systems went into operation, and the overloads reset themselves. The lights flickered on again. And Falcon's paralysis disappeared as swiftly as it had come.

After glancing at the board to make sure that all circuits were back to normal, he moved quickly to the viewing ports.

There was no need to switch on the inspection lamps—the cables supporting the capsule seemed to be on fire. Lines of light glowing an electric blue against the darkness stretched upward from the main lift ring to the equator of the giant balloon; and rolling slowly along several of them were dazzling balls of fire.

The sight was so strange and so beautiful that it was hard to read any menace in it. Few people, Falcon knew, had ever seen ball lightning from such close quarters—and certainly none had survived if they were riding a hydrogen-filled balloon back in the atmosphere of Earth. He remembered the flaming death of the *Hindenburg*, destroyed by a stray spark when she docked at Lakehurst in 1937; as it had done so often in the past, the horrifying old newsreel film flashed through his mind. But at least that could not happen here, though there was more hydrogen above his head than had ever filled the last of the Zeppelins. It would be a few billion years yet, before anyone could light a fire in the atmosphere of Jupiter.

With a sound like briskly frying bacon, the speech circuit came back to life.

"Hello, *Kon-Tiki*—are you receiving? Are you receiving?"

The words were chopped and badly distorted, but intelligible. Falcon's spirits lifted; he had resumed contact with the world of men.

"I receive you," he said. "Quite an electrical display, but no damage—so far."

"Thanks—thought we'd lost you. Please check telemetry channels three, seven, twenty-six. Also gain on camera two. And we don't quite believe the readings on the external ionization probes. . . ."

Reluctantly Falcon tore his gaze away from the fascinating pyrotechnic display around *Kon-Tiki*, though from time to time he kept glancing out of the windows. The ball lightning disappeared first, the fiery globes slowly expanding until they reached a critical size, at which they vanished in a gentle explosion. But even an hour later, there were still faint glows around all the exposed metal on the outside of the capsule; and the radio circuits remained noisy until well after midnight.

The remaining hours of darkness were completely uneventful—until just before dawn. Because it came from the east, Falcon assumed that he was seeing the first faint hint of sunrise. Then he realized that it was twenty minutes too early for this—and the glow that had appeared along the horizon was moving toward him even as he watched. It swiftly detached itself from the arch of stars that marked the invisible edge of the planet, and he saw that it was a relatively narrow band, quite sharply defined. The beam of an enormous searchlight appeared to be swinging beneath the clouds.

Perhaps sixty miles behind the first racing bar of light came another, parallel to it and moving at the same speed. And beyond that another, and another—until all the sky flickered with alternating sheets of sheets of light and darkness.

By this time, Falcon thought, he had been inured to wonders, and it seemed impossible that this display of pure, soundless luminosity could present the slightest danger. But it was so astonishing, and so inexplicable, that he felt cold, naked fear gnawing at his self-control. No man could look upon such a sight without feeling like a helpless pygmy in the presence of forces beyond his comprehension. Was it possible that, after all, Jupiter carried not only life but also intelligence? And, perhaps, an intelligence that only now was beginning to react to his alien presence?

"Yes, we see it," said Mission Control, in a voice that echoed his own awe. "We've no idea what it is. Stand by, we're calling Ganymede."

The display was slowly fading; the bands racing in from the far horizon were much fainter, as if the energies that powered them were becoming exhausted. In five minutes it was all over; the last faint pulse of light flickered along the western sky and then was gone. Its passing left Falcon with an overwhelming sense of relief. The sight was so hypnotic, and so disturbing, that it was not good for any man's peace of mind to contemplate it too long.

He was more shaken than he cared to admit. The electrical storm was something that he could understand; but *this* was totally incomprehensible.

Mission Control was still silent. He knew that the information banks up on Ganymede were now being searched as men and computers turned their minds to the problem. If no answer could be found there, it would be necessary to call Earth; that would mean a delay of almost an hour. The possibility that even Earth might be unable to help was one that Falcon did not care to contemplate.

He had never before been so glad to hear the voice of Mission Control as when Dr. Brenner finally came on the circuit. The biologist sounded relieved, yet subdued—like a man who has just come through some great intellectual crisis.

"Hello, *Kon-Tiki*. We've solved your problem, but we can still hardly believe it.

"What you've been seeing is bioluminescence, very similar to that produced by microorganisms in the tropical seas of Earth. Here they're in the atmosphere, not the ocean, but the principle is the same."

"But the pattern," protested Falcon, "was so regular—so *artificial*. And it was hundreds of miles across!"

"It was even larger than you imagine; you observed only a small part of it. The whole pattern was over three thousand miles wide and looked like a revolving wheel. You merely saw the spokes, sweeping past at you at about six-tenths of a mile a second. . . ."

"A *second*!" Falcon could not help interjecting. "No animals could move that fast!"

"Of course not. Let me explain. What you saw was triggered by the shock wave from Source Beta, moving at the speed of sound."

"But what about the pattern?" Falcon insisted.

"That's the surprising part. It's a very rare phenomenon, but identical wheels of light—except that they're a thousand times smaller—have been observed in the Persian Gulf and the Indian Ocean. Listen to this: British India Company's *Patna*, Persian Gulf, May 1880, 11:30 P.M.—'an enormous luminous wheel, whirling round, the spokes of which appeared to brush the ship along. The spokes were two hundred or three hundred yards long . . . each wheel contained about sixteen spokes. . . .' And here's one from the Gulf of Omar, dated May 23, 1906: 'The intensely bright luminescence approached us rapidly, shooting sharply defined light rays to the west in rapid succession, like the beam from the searchlight of a warship. . . . To the left of us, a gigantic fiery wheel formed itself, with spokes that reached as far as one could see. The whole wheel whirled around for two or three minutes. . . .' The archive computer on Ganymede dug up about five hundred cases. It would have printed out the lot if we hadn't stopped it in time."

"I'm convinced—but still baffled."

"I don't blame you. The full explanation wasn't worked out until late in the twentieth century. It seems that these luminous wheels are the results of submarine earthquakes, and always occur in shallow waters where the shock waves can be reflected and cause standing wave patterns. Sometimes bars, sometimes rotating wheels—the 'Wheels of Poseidon,' they've been called. The theory was finally proved by making underwater explosions and photographing the results from a satellite. No wonder sailors used to be superstitious. Who would have believed a thing like *this*?"

So that was it, Falcon told himself. When Source Beta blew its top, it must have sent shock waves in all directions—through the compressed gas of the lower atmosphere, through the solid body of Jupiter itself. Meeting and crisscrossing, those waves must have canceled here, reinforced there; the whole planet must have rung like a bell.

Yet the explanation did not destroy the sense of wonder and awe; he would never be able to forget those flickering bands of light, racing through the unattainable depths of the Jovian atmosphere. He felt that he was not merely on a strange planet, but in some magical realm between myth and reality.

This was a world where absolutely *anything* could happen, and no man could possibly guess what the future would bring.

And he still had a whole day to go.

6. MEDUSA

When the true dawn finally arrived, it brought a sudden change of weather. *Kon-Tiki* was moving through a blizzard; waxen snowflakes were falling so thickly that visibility was reduced to zero. Falcon began to worry about the weight that might be accumulating on the envelope. Then he noticed that any flakes settling outside the windows quickly disappeared; *Kon-Tiki's* continual outpouring of heat was evaporating them as swiftly as they arrived.

If he had been ballooning on Earth, he would also have worried about the possibility of collision. At least that was no danger here; any Jovian mountains were several hundred miles below him. And as for the floating islands of foam, hitting them would probably be like plowing into slightly hardened soap bubbles.

Nevertheless, he switched on the horizontal radar, which until now had been completely useless; only the vertical beam, giving his distance from the invisible surface, had thus far been of any value. Then he had another surprise.

Scattered across a huge sector of the sky ahead were dozens of large and brilliant echoes. They were completely isolated from one another and apparently hung unsupported in space. Falcon remembered a phrase the earliest aviators had used to describe one of the hazards of their profession: "clouds stuffed with rocks." That was a perfect description of what seemed to lie in the track of *Kon-Tiki*.

It was a disconcerting sight; then Falcon again reminded himself that nothing *really* solid could possibly hover in this atmosphere. Perhaps it was some strange meteorological phenomenon. In any case, the nearest echo was about 125 miles.

He reported to Mission Control, which could provide no explanation. But it gave the welcome news that he would be clear of the blizzard in another thirty minutes.

It did not warn him, however, of the violent cross wind that abruptly grabbed *Kon-Tiki* and swept it almost at right angles to its previous track. Falcon needed all his skill and the maximum use of what little control he had over his ungainly vehicle to prevent it from being capsized. Within minutes he was racing northward at over three hundred miles an hour. Then, as suddenly as it had started, the turbulence ceased; he was still moving at high speed, but in smooth air. He wondered if he had been caught in the Jovian equivalent of a jet stream.

The snow storm dissolved; and he saw what Jupiter had been preparing for him.

Kon-Tiki had entered the funnel of a gigantic whirlpool, some six hundred miles across. The balloon was being swept along a curving wall of cloud. Overhead, the sun was shining in a clear sky; but far beneath, this great hole in the atmosphere drilled down to unknown depths until it reached a misty floor where lightning flickered almost continuously.

Though the vessel was being dragged downward so slowly that it was in no immediate danger, Falcon increased the flow of heat into the envelope until *Kon-Tiki* hovered at a constant altitude. Not until then did he abandon the fantastic spectacle outside and consider again the problem of the radar.

The nearest echo was now only about twenty-five miles away. All of them, he quickly realized, were distributed along the wall of the vortex, and were moving with it, apparently caught in the whirlpool like *Kon-Tiki* itself. He aimed the telescope along the radar bearing and found himself looking at a curious mottled cloud that almost filled the field of view.

It was not easy to see, being only a little darker than the whirling wall of mist that formed its background. Not until he had been staring for several minutes did Falcon realize that he had met it once before.

The first time it had been crawling across the drifting mountains of foam, and he had mistaken it for a giant, many-trunked tree. Now at last he could appreciate its real size and complexity and could give it a better name to fix its image in his mind. It did not resemble a tree at all, but a jellyfish—a medusa, such as might be met trailing its tentacles as it drifted along the warm eddies of the Gulf Stream.

This medusa was more than a mile across and its scores of dangling tentacles were hundreds of feet long. They swayed slowly back and forth in perfect unison, taking more than a minute for each complete undulation—almost as if the creature was clumsily rowing itself through the sky.

The other echoes were more distant medusae. Falcon focused the telescope on half a dozen and could see no variations in shape or size. They all seemed to be of the same species, and he wondered just why they were drifting lazily around in this six-hundred-mile orbit. Perhaps they were feeding upon the aerial plankton sucked in by the whirlpool, as *Kon-Tiki* itself had been.

"Do you realize, Howard," said Dr. Brenner, when he had recovered from his initial astonishment, "that this thing is about a hundred thousand times as large as the biggest whale? And even if it's only a gasbag, it must still weigh a million tons! I can't even guess at its metabolism. It must generate megawatts of heat to maintain its buoyancy."

"But if it's just a gasbag, why is it such a damn good radar reflector?"

"I haven't the faintest idea. Can you get any closer?"

Brenner's question was not an idle one. If he changed altitude to take advantage of the differing wind velocities, Falcon could approach the medusa as closely as he wished. At the moment, however, he preferred his present twenty-five miles and said so, firmly.

"I see what you mean," Brenner answered, a little reluctantly. "Let's stay where we are for the present." That "we" gave Falcon a certain wry amusement; an extra sixty thousand miles made a considerable difference in one's point of view.

For the next two hours *Kon-Tiki* drifted uneventfully in the gyre of the great whirlpool, while Falcon experimented with filters and camera contrast, trying to get a clear view of the medusa. He began to wonder if its elusive coloration was some kind of camouflage; perhaps, like many animals of Earth, it was trying to lose itself against its background. That was a trick used by both hunters and hunted.

In which category was the medusa? That was a question he could hardly expect to have answered in the short time that was left to him. Yet just before noon, without the slightest warning, the answer came. . . .

Like a squadron of antique jet fighters, five mantas came sweeping through the wall of mist that formed the funnel of the vortex. They were flying in a V formation directly toward the pallid gray cloud of the medusa; and there was no doubt, in Falcon's mind, that they were on the attack. He had been quite wrong to assume that they were harmless vegetarians.

Yet everything happened at such a leisurely pace that it was like watching a slow-motion film. The mantas undulated along at perhaps thirty miles an hour; it seemed ages before they reached the medusa, which continued to paddle imperturbably along at an even slower speed. Huge though they were, the mantas looked tiny beside the monster they were approaching. When they flapped down on its back, they appeared about as large as birds landing on a whale.

Could the medusa defend itself, Falcon wondered. He did not see how the attacking mantas could be in danger as long as they avoided those huge clumsy tentacles. And perhaps their host was not even aware of them; they could be insignificant parasites, tolerated as are fleas upon a dog.

But now it was obvious that the medusa was in distress. With agonizing slowness, it began to tip over like a capsizing ship. After ten minutes it had tilted forty-five degrees; it was also rapidly losing altitude. It was impossible not to feel a sense of pity for the beleaguered monster, and to Falcon the sight brought bitter memories. In a grotesque way, the fall of the medusa was almost a parody of the dying *Queen's* last moments.

Yet he knew that his sympathies were on the wrong side. High intelligence could develop only among predators—not among the drifting browsers of either sea or air. The mantas were far closer to him than was this monstrous bag of gas. And anyway, who could *really* sympathize with a creature a hundred thousand times larger than a whale?

Then he noticed that the medusa's tactics seemed to be having some effect. The mantas had been disturbed by its slow roll and were flapping heavily away from its back—like gorged vultures interrupted at mealtime. But they did not move very far, continuing to hover a few yards from the still-capsizing monster.

There was a sudden, blinding flash of light synchronized with a crash of static over the radio. One of the mantas, slowly twisting end over end, was plummeting straight downward. As it fell, a plume of black smoke trailed behind it. The resemblance to an aircraft going down in flames was quite uncanny.

In unison, the remaining mantas dived steeply away from the medusa, gaining speed by losing altitude. They had, within minutes, vanished back into the wall of cloud from which they had emerged. And the medusa, no longer falling, began to roll back toward the horizontal. Soon it was sailing along once more on an even keel, as if nothing had happened.

"Beautiful!" said Dr. Brenner, after a moment of stunned silence. "It's developed electric defenses, like some of our eels and rays. But that must have been about a million volts! Can you see any organs that might produce the discharge? Anything looking like electrodes?"

"No," Falcon answered, after switching to the highest power of the telescope. "But here's something odd. Do you see this pattern? Check back on the earlier images. I'm sure it wasn't there before."

A broad, mottled band had appeared along the side of the medusa. It formed a startlingly regular checkerboard, each square of which was itself speckled in a complex subpattern of short horizontal lines. They were spaced at equal distances in a geometrically perfect array of rows and columns.

"You're right," said Dr. Brenner, with something very much like awe in his voice. "That's just appeared. And I'm afraid to tell you what I think it is."

"Well, I have no reputation to lose—at least as a biologist. Shall I give my guess?"

"Go ahead."

"That's a large meter-band radio array. The sort of thing they used back at the beginning of the twentieth century."

"I was afraid you'd say that. Now we know why it gave such a massive echo."

"But why has it just appeared?"

"Probably an aftereffect of the discharge."

"I've just had another thought," said Falcon, rather slowly. "Do you suppose it's *listening* to us?"

"On this frequency? I doubt it. Those are meter—no, *decameter* antennas—judging by their size. Hmm . . . that's an idea!"

Dr. Brenner fell silent, obviously contemplating some new line of thought. Presently he continued: "I bet they're tuned to the radio outbursts! That's something nature never got around to doing on Earth. . . . We have animals with sonar and even electric senses, but nothing ever developed a radio sense. Why bother where there was so much light?"

"But it's different here. Jupiter is *drenched* with radio energy. It's worthwhile using it—maybe even tapping it. That thing could be a floating power plant!"

A new voice cut into the conversation.

"Mission Commander here. This is all very interesting, but there's a much more important matter to settle. *Is it intelligent?* If so, we've got to consider the First Contact directives."

"Until I came here," said Dr. Brenner, somewhat ruefully, "I would have sworn that anything that could make a short-wave antenna system *must* be intelligent. Now, I'm not sure. This could have evolved naturally. I suppose it's no more fantastic than the human eye."

"Then we have to play safe and assume intelligence. For the present, therefore, this expedition comes under all the clauses of the Prime directive."

There was a long silence while everyone on the radio circuit absorbed the implications of this. For the first time in the history of space flight, the rules that had been established through more than a century of argument might have to be applied. Man had—it was hoped—profited from his mistakes on Earth. Not only moral considerations, but also his own self-interest demanded that he should not repeat them among the planets. It could be disastrous to treat a superior intelligence as the American settlers had treated the Indians, or as almost everyone had treated the Africans. . . .

The first rule was: keep your distance. Make no attempt to approach, or even to communicate, until "they" have had plenty of time to study you. Exactly what was meant by "plenty of time," no one had ever been able to decide. It was left to the discretion of the man on the spot.

A responsibility of which he had never dreamed had descended upon Howard Falcon. In the few hours that remained to him on Jupiter, he might become the first ambassador of the human race.

And *that* was an irony so delicious that he almost wished the surgeons had restored to him the power of laughter.

7. PRIME DIRECTIVE

It was growing darker, but Falcon scarcely noticed as he strained his eyes toward that living cloud in the field of the telescope. The wind that was steadily sweeping *Kon-Tiki* around the funnel of the great whirlpool had now brought him within twelve miles of the creature. If he got much closer than six, he would take evasive action. Though he felt certain that the medusa's electric weapons were short-ranged, he did not wish to put the matter to the test. That would be a problem for future explorers, and he wished them luck.

Now it was quite dark in the capsule. That was strange, because sunset was still hours away. Automatically, he glanced at the horizontally scanning radar, as he had done every few minutes. Apart from the medusa he was studying, there was no other object within about sixty miles of him.

Suddenly, with startling power, he heard the sound that had come booming out of the Jovian night—the throbbing beat that grew more and more rapid, then stopped in mid-crescendo. The whole capsule vibrated with it like a pea in a kettledrum.

Falcon realized two things almost simultaneously during the sudden, aching silence. *This* time the sound was not coming from thousands of miles away, over a radio circuit. It was in the very atmosphere around him.

The second thought was even more disturbing. He had quite forgotten—it was inexcusable, but there had been other apparently more important things on his mind—that most of the sky above him was completely blanked out by *Kon-Tiki's* gasbag. Being lightly silvered to conserve its heat, the great balloon was an effective shield both to radar and to vision.

He had known this, of course; it had been a minor defect of the design, tolerated because it did not appear important. It seemed very important to Howard Falcon now—as he saw that fence of gigantic tentacles, thicker than the trunks of any tree, descending all around the capsule.

He heard Brenner yelling: "Remember the Prime directive! Don't alarm it!" Before he could make an appropriate answer that overwhelming drumbeat started again and drowned all other sounds.

The sign of a really skilled test pilot is how he reacts not to foreseeable emergencies, but to ones that nobody could have anticipated. Falcon did not hesitate for more than a second to analyze the situation. In a lightning-swift movement, he pulled the rip cord.

That word was an archaic survival from the days of the first hydrogen balloons; on *Kon-Tiki*, the rip cord did not tear open the gasbag, but merely operated a set of louvers around the upper curve of the envelope. At once the hot gas started to rush out; *Kon-Tiki*, deprived of her lift, began to fall swiftly in this gravity field two and a half times as strong as Earth's.

Falcon had a momentary glimpse of great tentacles whipping upward and away. He had just time to note that they were studded with large bladders or sacs, presumably to give them buoyancy, and that they ended in multitudes of thin feelers like the roots of a plant. He half expected a bolt of lightning—but nothing happened.

His precipitous rate of descent was slackening as the atmosphere thickened and the deflated envelope acted as a parachute. When *Kon-Tiki* had dropped about two miles, he felt that it was safe to close the louvers again. By the time he had restored buoyancy and was in equilibrium once more, he had lost another mile of altitude and was getting dangerously near his safety limit.

He peered anxiously through the overhead windows, though he did not expect to see anything except the obscuring bulk of the balloon. But he had sideslipped during his descent, and part of the medusa was just visible a couple of miles above him. It was much closer than he expected—and it was still coming down, faster than he would have believed possible.

Mission Control was calling anxiously. He shouted: "I'm O.K.—but it's still coming after me. I can't go any deeper."

That was not quite true. He could go a lot deeper—about 180 miles. But it would be a one-way trip, and most of the journey would be of little interest to him.

Then, to his great relief, he saw that the medusa was leveling off, not quite a mile above him. Perhaps it had decided to approach this strange intruder with caution; or perhaps it, too, found this deeper layer uncomfortably hot. The temperature was over fifty degrees centigrade, and Falcon wondered how much longer his life-support system could handle matters.

Dr. Brenner was back on the circuit, still worrying about the Prime directive.

"Remember—it may only be inquisitive!" he cried, without much conviction. "Try not to frighten it!"

Falcon was getting rather tired of this advice and recalled a TV discussion he had once seen between a space lawyer and an astronaut. After the full implications of the Prime directive had been carefully spelled out, the incredulous spacer had exclaimed: "Then if there was no alternative, I must sit still and let myself be eaten?" The lawyer had not even cracked a smile when he answered: "That's an *excellent* summing up."

It had seemed funny at the time; it was not at all amusing now.

And then Falcon saw something that made him even more unhappy. The medusa was still hovering about a mile above him—but one of its tentacles was becoming incredibly elongated, and was stretching down toward *Kon-Tiki*, thinning out at the same time. As a boy he had once seen the funnel of a tornado descending from a storm cloud over the Kansas plains. The thing coming toward him now evoked vivid memories of that black, twisting snake in the sky.

"I'm rapidly running out of options," he reported to Mission Control. "I now have only a choice between frightening it—and giving it a bad stomach ache. I don't think it will find *Kon-Tiki* very digestible, if that's what it has in mind."

He waited for comments from Brenner, but the biologist remained silent.

"Very well. It's twenty-seven minutes ahead of time, but I'm starting the ignition sequencer. I hope I'll have enough reserve to correct my orbit later."

He could no longer see the medusa; once more it was directly overhead. But he knew that the descending tentacle must now be very close to the balloon. It would take almost five minutes to bring the reactor up to full thrust. . . .

The fusor was primed. The orbit computer had not rejected the situation as wholly impossible. The air scoops were open, ready to gulp in tons of the surrounding hydrohelium on demand. Even under optimum conditions, this would have been the moment of truth—for there had been no way of testing how a nuclear ramjet would really work in the strange atmosphere of Jupiter.

Very gently something rocked *Kon-Tiki*. Falcon tried to ignore it.

Ignition had been planned at six miles higher, in an atmosphere of less than a quarter of the density and thirty degrees cooler. Too bad.

What was the shallowest dive he could get away with, for the air scoops to work? When the ram ignited, he'd be heading toward Jupiter with two and a half g's to help him get there. Could he possibly pull out in time?

A large, heavy hand patted the balloon. The whole vessel bobbed up and down, like one of the Yo-yo's that had just become the craze on Earth.

Of course, Brenner *might* be perfectly right. Perhaps it was just trying to be friendly. Maybe he should try to talk to it over the radio. Which should it be: "Pretty pussy"? "Down, Fido"? Or "Take me to your leader"?

The tritium-deuterium ratio was correct. He was ready to light the candle, with a hundred-million-degree match.

The thin tip of the tentacle came slithering around the edge of the balloon some sixty yards away. It was about the size of an elephant's trunk, and by the delicate way it was moving appeared to be almost as sensitive. There were little palps at its end, like questing mouths. He was sure that Dr. Brenner would be fascinated.

This seemed about as good a time as any. He gave a swift scan of the entire control board, started the final four-second ignition count, broke the safety seal, and pressed the Jettison switch.

There was a sharp explosion and an instant loss of weight. *Kon-Tiki* was falling freely, nose down. Overhead, the discarded balloon was racing upward, dragging the inquisitive tentacle with it. Falcon had no time to see if the gasbag actually hit the medusa, because at that moment the ramjet fired and he had other matters to think about.

A roaring column of hot hydrohelium was pouring out of the reactor nozzles, swiftly building up thrust—but *toward* Jupiter, not away from it. He could not pull out yet, for vector control was too sluggish. Unless he could gain complete control and achieve horizontal flight within the next five seconds, the vehicle would dive too deeply into the atmosphere and would be destroyed.

With agonizing slowness—those five seconds seemed like fifty—he managed to flatten out, then pull the nose upward. He glanced back only once and caught a final glimpse of the medusa, many miles away. *Kon-Tiki's* discarded gasbag had apparently escaped from its grasp, for he could see no sign of it.

Now he was master once more—no longer drifting helplessly on the winds of Jupiter, but riding his own column of atomic fire back to the stars. He was confident that the ramjet would steadily give him velocity and altitude until he had reached near-orbital speed at the fringes of the atmosphere. Then, with a brief burst of pure rocket power, he would regain the freedom of space.

Halfway to orbit, he looked south and saw the tremendous enigma of the Great Red Spot—that floating island twice the size of Earth—coming up over the horizon. He stared into its mysterious beauty until the computer warned him that conversion to rocket thrust was only sixty seconds ahead. He tore his gaze reluctantly away.

"Some other time," he murmured.

"What's that?" said Mission Control. "What did you say?"

"It doesn't matter," he replied.

8. BETWEEN TWO WORLDS

"You're a hero now, Howard," said Webster, "not just a celebrity. You've given them something to think about—injected some excitement into their lives. Not one in a million will actually travel to the Outer Giants, but the whole human race will go in imagination. And that's what counts."

"I'm glad to have made your job a little easier."

Webster was too old a friend to take offense at the note of irony. Yet it surprised him. And this was not the first change in Howard that he had noticed since the return from Jupiter.

The Administrator pointed to the famous sign on his desk, borrowed from an impresario of an earlier age: ASTONISH ME!

"I'm not ashamed of my job. New knowledge, new resources—they're all very well. But men also need novelty and excitement. Space travel has become routine; you've made it a great adventure once more. It will be a long, long time before we get Jupiter pigeonholed. And maybe longer still before we understand those medusae. I still think that one *knew* where your blind spot was. Anyway, have you decided on your next move? Saturn, Uranus, Neptune—you name it."

"I don't know. I've thought about Saturn, but I'm not really needed there. It's only one gravity, not two and a half like Jupiter. So men can handle it."

Men, thought Webster. He said "men." He's never done that before. And when did I last hear him use the word "we"? He's changing, slipping away from us. . . .

"Well," he said aloud, rising from his chair to conceal his slight uneasiness, "let's get the conference started. The cameras are all set up and everyone's waiting. You'll meet a lot of old friends."

He stressed the last word, but Howard showed no response. The leathery mask of his face was becoming more and more difficult to read. Instead, he rolled back from the Administrator's desk, unlocked his undercarriage so that it no longer formed a chair, and rose on his hydraulics to his full seven feet of height. It had been good psychology on the part of the surgeons to give him that extra twelve inches, to compensate somewhat for all that he had lost when the *Queen* had crashed.

Falcon waited until Webster had opened the door, then pivoted neatly on his balloon tires and headed for it at a smooth and silent twenty miles an hour. The display of speed and precision was not flaunted arrogantly; rather, it had become quite unconscious.

Howard Falcon, who had once been a man and could still pass for one over a voice circuit, felt a calm sense of achievement—and, for the first time in years, something like peace of mind. Since his return from Jupiter, the nightmares had ceased. He had found his role at last.

He now knew why he had dreamed about that superchimp aboard the doomed *Queen Elizabeth*. Neither man nor beast, it was between two worlds; and so was he.

He alone could travel unprotected on the lunar surface. The life-support system inside the metal cylinder that had replaced his fragile body functioned equally well in space or under water. Gravity fields ten times that of Earth were an inconvenience, but nothing more. And no gravity was best of all. . . .

The human race was becoming more remote, the ties of kinship more tenuous. Perhaps these air-breathing, radiation-sensitive bundles of unstable carbon compounds had no right beyond the atmosphere; they should stick to their natural homes—Earth, Moon, Mars.

Some day the real masters of space would be machines, not men—and he was neither. Already conscious of his destiny, he took a somber pride in his unique loneliness—the first immortal midway between two orders of creation.

He would, after all, be an ambassador; between the old and the new—between the creatures of carbon and the creatures of metal who must one day supersede them.

Both would have need of him in the troubled centuries that lay ahead.

The Man Who Walked Home

JAMES TIPTREE, JR.

As most of you probably know by now, multiple Hugo and Nebula–winning author James Tiptree, Jr.—at one time a figure reclusive and mysterious enough to be regarded as the B. Traven of science fiction—was actually the pseudonym of the late Dr. Alice Sheldon, a semiretired experimental psychologist who also wrote occasionally under the name of Raccoona Sheldon. Dr. Sheldon's tragic death in 1987 put an end to "both" authors' careers, but, before that, she had won two Nebula and two Hugo Awards as Tiptree, won another Nebula Award as Raccoona Sheldon, and established herself, under whatever name, as one of the best writers in science fiction.

*Although "Tiptree" published two reasonably well received novels—*Up the Walls of the World *and* Brightness Falls from the Air*—she was, like Damon Knight and Theodore Sturgeon (two writers she aesthetically resembled and by whom she was strongly influenced) more comfortable with the short story and more effective with it. She wrote some of the very best short stories of the seventies: "The Screwfly Solution," "The Girl Who Was Plugged In," "The Women Men Don't See," "Beam Us Home," "And I Awoke and Found Me Here on the Cold Hill's Side," "I'm Too Big but I Love to Play," "Slow Music," and "His Smoke Rose Up Forever." Already it's clear that these are stories that will last. They—and a dozen others almost as good—show that Alice Sheldon was simply one of the best short-story writers to work in the genre in our times.*

Exploration played an important part in Sheldon's work, although, ironically, often what her explorers were obsessively searching for was a way to get home *again—a theme she never expressed more clearly than in the vivid and compelling story that follows, which takes us home by the longest way imaginable and shows us although home may only be a step away, sometimes that step can be very hard to take. . . .*

As James Tiptree, Jr., Alice Sheldon also published nine short-story collections: Ten Thousand Light Years from Home, Warm Worlds and Otherwise, Starsongs of an Old Primate, Out of the Everywhere, Tales of the Quintana Roo, Byte Beautiful, The Starry Rift, *the posthumously published* Crown of Stars, *and the retrospective collection* Her Smoke Rose Up Forever.

Transgression! Terror! And he thrust and lost there—punched into impossibility, abandoned, never to be known how, the wrong man in the most wrong of all wrong places in that unimaginable collapse of never-to-be-reimagined mechanism—he stranded, undone, his lifeline severed, he in that nanosecond knowing his only tether parting, going away, the longest line to life withdrawing, winking out, disappearing forever beyond his grasp—telescoping away from him into the closing vortex beyond which lay his home, his life, his only possibility of being;

seeing it sucked back into the deepest maw, melting, leaving him orphaned on what never-to-be-known shore of total wrongness—of beauty beyond joy, perhaps? Of horror? Of nothingness? Of profound otherness only, certainly whatever it was, that place into which he transgressed, certainly it could not support his life there, his violent and violating aberrance; and he, fierce, brave, crazy—clenched into one total protest, one body-fist of utter repudiation of himself there in that place, forsaken there—what did he do? Rejected, exiled, hungering homeward more desperate than any lost beast driving for its unreachable home, his home, his—HOME—and no way, no transport, no vehicle, means, machinery, no force but his intolerable resolve aimed homeward along that vanishing vector, that last and only lifeline—he did, what?

    He walked.

    Home.

    Precisely what hashed up in the work of the major industrial lessee of the Bonneville Particle Acceleration Facility in Idaho was never known. Or rather, all those who might have been able to diagnose the original malfunction were themselves obliterated almost at once in the greater catastrophe which followed.

    The nature of this second cataclysm was not at first understood either. All that was ever certain was that at 1153.6 of May 2, 1989 Old Style, the Bonneville laboratories and all their personnel were transformed into an intimately disrupted form of matter resembling a high-energy plasma, which became rapidly airborne to the accompaniment of radiating seismic and atmospheric events.

    The disturbed area unfortunately included an operational MIRV Watchdog bomb.

    In the confusions of the next hours the Earth's population was substantially reduced, the biosphere was altered, and the Earth itself was marked with numbers of more conventional craters. For some years thereafter the survivors were existentially preoccupied and the peculiar dust bowl at Bonneville was left to weather by itself in the changing climatic cycles.

    It was not a large crater; just over a kilometer in width and lacking the usual displacement lip. Its surface was covered with a finely divided substance which dried into dust. Before the rains began it was almost perfectly flat. Only in certain lights, had anyone been there to inspect it, a small surface marking or abraded place could be detected almost exactly at the center.

    Two decades after the disaster a party of short brown people appeared from the south, together with a flock of somewhat atypical sheep. The crater at this time appeared as a wide shallow basin in which the grass did not grow well, doubtless from the almost complete lack of soil microorganisms. Neither this nor the surrounding vigorous grass were found to harm the sheep. A few crude hogans went up at the southern edge and a faint path began to be traced across the crater itself, passing by the central by the bare spot.

    One spring morning two children who had been driving sheep across the crater came screaming back to camp. A monster had burst out of the ground before them, a huge flat animal making a dreadful roar. It vanished in a flash and a shaking of the earth, leaving an evil smell. The sheep had run away.

Since this last was visibly true, some elders investigated. Finding no sign of the monster and no place in which it could hide, they settled for beating the children, who settled for making a detour around the monster-spot, and nothing more occurred for a while.

The following spring the episode was repeated. This time an older girl was present but she could add only that the monster seemed to be rushing flat out along the ground without moving at all. And there was a scraped place in the dirt. Again nothing was found; an evil-ward in a cleft stick was placed at the spot.

When the same thing happened for the third time a year later, the detour was extended and other charm-wands were added. But since no harm seemed to come of it and the brown people had seen far worse, sheep-tending resumed as before. A few more instantaneous apparitions of the monster were noted, each time in the spring.

At the end of the third decade of the new era a tall old man limped down the hills from the south, pushing his pack upon a bicycle wheel. He camped on the far side of the crater, and soon found the monster-site. He attempted to question people about it, but no one understood him, so he traded a knife for some meat. Although he was obviously feeble, something about him dissuaded them from killing him, and this proved wise because he later assisted the women to treat several sick children.

He spent much time around the place of the apparition and was nearby when it made its next appearance. This excited him very much, and he did several inexplicable but apparently harmless things, including moving his camp into the crater by the trail. He stayed on for a full year watching the site and was close by for its next manifestation. After this he spent a few days making a charmstone for the spot and then left, northward, hobbling, as he had come.

More decades passed. The crater eroded and a rain-gully became an intermittent steamlet across one edge of the basin. The brown people and their sheep were attacked by a band of grizzled men, after which the survivors went away eastward. The winters of what had been Idaho were now frost-free; aspen and eucalyptus sprouted in the moist plain. Still the crater remained treeless, visible as a flat bowl of grass, and the bare place at the center remained. The skies cleared somewhat.

After another three decades a larger band of black people with ox-drawn carts appeared and stayed for a time, but left again when they too saw the thunderclap-monster. A few other vagrants straggled by.

Five decades later a small permanent settlement had grown up on the nearest range of hills, from which men riding on small ponies with dark stripes down their spines herded humped cattle near the crater. A herdsman hut was built by the steamlet, which in time became the habitation of an oliveskinned, red-haired family. In due course one of this clan again observed the monster-flash, but these people did not depart. The stone the tall man had placed was noted and left undisturbed.

The homestead at the crater's edge grew into a group of three and was joined by others, and the trail across it became a cartroad with a log bridge over the stream. At the center of the still-faintly-discernible crater the cartroad made a bend, leaving a grassy place which bore on its center about a square meter of curiously impacted bare earth and a deeply-etched sandstone rock.

The apparition of the monster was now known to occur regularly each spring on a certain morning in this place, and the children of the community dared each other to approach the spot. It was referred to in a phrase that could be translated as "the Old Dragon." The Old Dragon's appearance was always the same: a brief, violent thunderburst which began and cut off abruptly, in the midst of which a dragon-like creature was seen apparently in furious motion on the earth although it never actually moved. Afterward there was a bad smell and the earth smoked. People who saw it from close by spoke of a shivering sensation.

Early in the second century two young men rode into town from the north. Their ponies were shaggier than the local breed and the equipment they carried included two boxlike objects which the young men set up at the monster-site. They stayed in the area a full year, observing two materializations of the Old Dragon, and they provided much news and maps of roads and trading-towns in the cooler regions to the north. They built a windmill which was accepted by the community and offered to build a lighting machine, which was refused. Then they departed with their boxes after unsuccessfully attempting to persuade a local boy to learn to operate one.

In the course of the next decades other travelers stopped by and marveled at the monster, and there was sporadic fighting over the mountains to the south. One of the armed bands made a cattle-raid into the crater hamlet. It was repulsed, but the raiders left a spotted sickness which killed many. For all this time the bare place at the crater's center remained, and the monster made his regular appearances, observed or not.

The hill-town grew and changed and the crater hamlet grew to be a town. Roads widened and linked into networks. There were gray-green conifers in the hills now, spreading down into the plain, and chirruping lizards lived in their branches.

At century's end a shabby band of skin-clad squatters with stunted milk-beasts erupted out of the west and were eventually killed or driven away, but not before the local herds had contracted a vicious parasite. Veterinaries were fetched from the market-city up north, but little could be done. The families near the crater left, and for some decades the area was empty. Finally cattle of a new strain reappeared in the plain and the crater hamlet was reoccupied. Still the bare center continued annually to manifest the monster and he became an accepted phenomenon of the area. On several occasions parties came from the distant Northwest Authority to observe it.

The crater hamlet flourished and grew into the fields where cattle had grazed and part of the old crater became the town park. A small seasonal tourist industry based on the monstersite developed. The townspeople rented rooms for the appearances and many more-or-less authentic monster-relics were on display in the local taverns.

Several cults now grew up around the monster. Some held that it was a devil or damned soul forced to appear on Earth in torment to expiate the catastrophe of two centuries back. Others believed that it, or he, was some kind of messenger whose roar portended either doom or hope according to the believer. One very vocal sect taught that the apparition registered the moral conduct of the townspeople over the past year, and scrutinized the annual apparition for changes which could be interpreted for good or ill. It was considered lucky, or dangerous, to be touched by some of the dust raised by the monster. In every generation at least one small boy would try to hit the monster with a stick, usually acquiring a broken arm and a lifelong tavern tale. Pelting the monster with stones or other objects was a popular sport, and for some years people systematically flung prayers and flowers at it. Once a party tried to net it and were left with strings and vapor. The area itself had long since been fenced off at the center of the park.

Through all this the monster made his violently enigmatic annual appearance, sprawled furiously motionless, unreachably roaring.

Only as the fourth century of the new era went by was it apparent that the monster had been changing slightly. He was now no longer on the earth but had an arm and a leg thrust upward in a kicking or flailing gesture. As the years passed he began to change more quickly until at the end of the century he had risen to a contorted crouching pose, arms outflung as if frozen in gyration. His roar, too, seemed somewhat differently pitched and the earth after him smoked more and more.

It was then widely felt that the man-monster was about to do something, to make some definitive manifestation, and a series of natural disasters and marvels gave support to a vigorous cult teaching this doctrine. Several religious leaders journeyed to the town to observe the apparitions.

However, the decades passed and the man-monster did nothing more than turn slowly in place, so that he now appeared to be in the act of sliding or staggering while pushing himself backward like a creature blown before a gale. No wind, of course, could be felt, and presently the general climate quieted and nothing came of it all.

Early in the fifth century New Calendar three survey parties from the North Central Authority came through the area and stopped to observe the monster. A permanent recording device was set up at the site, after assurances to the townfolk that no hardscience was involved. A local boy was trained to operate it; he quit when his girl left him but another volunteered. At this time nearly everyone believed that the apparition was a man, or the ghost of one. The record-machine boy and a few others, including the school mechanics teacher, referred to him as The Man John. In the next decades the roads were greatly improved; all forms of travel increased and there was talk of building a canal to what had been the Snake River.

One May morning at the end of Century Five a young couple in a smart green mule-trap came jogging up the highroad from the Sandreas Rift Range to the southwest. The girl was golden-skinned and chatted with her young husband in a language unlike that ever heard by the Man John either at the end or the beginning of his life. What she said to him has, however, been heard in every age and tongue.

"Oh Serli, I'm so glad we're taking this trip now! Next summer I'll be so busy with baby."

To which Serli replied as young husbands often have, and so they trotted up to the town's inn. Here they left trap and bags and went in search of her uncle who was expecting them there. The morrow was the day of the Man John's annual appearance, and her Uncle Laban had come from the MacKenzie History Museum to observe it and to make certain arrangements.

They found him with the town school instructor of mechanics, who was also the recorder at the monster-site. Presently Uncle Laban took them all with him to the town mayor's office to meet with various religious personages. The mayor was not unaware of tourist values, but he took Uncle Laban's part in securing the cultists' grudging assent to the MacKenzie authorities' secular interpretation of the "monster," which was made easier by the fact that they disagreed among themselves. Then, seeing how pretty the niece was, the mayor took them all home to dinner.

When they returned to the inn for the night it was abrawl with holiday makers.

"Whew," said Uncle Laban. "I've talked myself dry, sister's daughter. What a weight of holy nonsense is that Morsha female! Serli, my lad, I know you have questions. Let me hand you this to read; it's the guide book we're giving 'em to sell. Tomorrow I'll answer for it all." And he disappeared into the crowded tavern.

So Serli and his bride took the pamphlet upstairs to bed with them, but it was not until the next morning at breakfast that they found time to read it.

" 'All that is known of John Delgano,' " read Serli with his mouth full, " 'comes from two documents left by his brother Carl Delgano in the archives of the MacKenzie Group in the early years after the holocaust.' Put some honey on this cake, Mira my dove. 'Verbatim transcript follows; this is Carl Delgano speaking.

" 'I'm not an engineer or an astronaut like John. I ran an electronics repair shop in Salt Lake City. John was only trained as a spaceman, he never got to space, the slump wiped all that out. So he tied up with this commercial group who were leasing part of Bonneville. They wanted a man for some kind of hard vacuum tests; that's all I knew about it. John and his wife moved to Bonneville, but we all got together several times a year, our wives were like sisters. John had two kids, Clara and Paul.

" 'The tests were all supposed to be secret, but John told me confidentially they were trying for an anti-gravity chamber. I don't know if it ever worked. That was the year before.

" 'Then that winter they came down for Christmas and John said they had something new. He was really excited. A temporal displacement, he called it; some kind of time effect. He said the chief honcho was like a real mad scientist. Big ideas. He kept adding more angles every time some other project would quit and leave equipment he could lease. No, I don't know who the top company was—maybe an insurance conglomerate, they had all the cash, didn't they? I guess they'd pay to catch a look at the future; that figures. Anyway, John was go, go, go. Katharine was scared; that's natural. She pictured him like, you know, H. G. Wells—walking around in some future world. John told her it wasn't like that at all. All they'd get would be this kind of flicker, like a second or two. All kinds of complications'—Yes, yes, my greedy piglet, some brew for me too. This is thirsty work!

"So . . . 'I remember I asked him, what about the Earth moving? I mean, you could come back in a different place, right? He said they had that all figured. A spatial trajectory. Katherine was so scared we dropped it. John told her, don't worry, I'll come home. But he didn't. Not that it makes any difference, of course; everything was wiped out. Salt Lake too. The only reason I'm here is that I went up by Calgary to see Mom, April twenty-ninth. May second it all blew. I didn't find you folks at MacKenzie until July. I guess I may as well stay. That's all I know about John, except that he was an all-right guy. If that accident started all this it wasn't his fault.

" 'The second document'—In the name of love, little mother, do I have to read all this! Oh very well; but you will kiss me first, madam. Must you look so ineffable? . . . 'The second document. Dated in the year eighteen, New Style, writter by Carl'—see the old handwriting, my plump pigeon. Oh, very well, very well.

" 'Written at Bonneville Crater. I have seen my brother John Delgano. When I knew I had the rad sickness I came down here to look around. Salt Lake's still hot. So I hiked up here by Bonneville. You can see the crater where the labs were; it's grassed over. It's different, it's not radioactive, my film's OK. There's a bare place in the middle. Some Indios here told me a monster shows up here every year in the spring. I saw it myself a couple of days after I got here but I was too far away to see much, except I was sure it's a man. In a vacuum suit. There was a lot of noise and dust, took me by surprise. It was all over in a second. I figure it's pretty close to the day, I mean, May second, old.

" 'So I hung around a year and he showed up again yesterday. I was on the face side and I could see his face through the faceplate. It's John all right. He's hurt. I saw blood on his mouth and his suit is frayed some. He's lying on the ground. He didn't move while I could see him but the dust boiled up, like a man sliding onto base without moving. His eyes are open like he was looking. I don't understand it anyway, but I know it's John, not a ghost. He was in exactly the same position each time and there's a loud crack like thunder and another sound like a siren, very fast. And an ozone smell, and smoke. I felt a kind of shudder.

" 'I know it's John there and I think he's alive. I have to leave here now to take this back while I can still walk. I think somebody should come here and see. Maybe you can help John. Signed, Carl Delgano.

" 'These records were kept by the MacKenzie Group but it was not for several years—' Etcetera, first light-print, etcetera, archives, analysts, etcetera—very good! Now it is time to meet your uncle, my edible one, after we go upstairs for just a moment."

"No, Serli, I will wait for you downstairs," said Mira prudently.

➤

When they came into the town park Uncle Laban was directing the installation of a large durite slab in front of the enclosure around the Man John's appearance-spot. The slab was wrapped in a curtain to await the official unveiling. Townspeople and tourists and children thronged the walks and a Ride-For-Good choir was singing in the bandshell. The morning was warming up fast. Vendors hawked ices and straw toys of the monster and flowers and good-luck confetti to throw at him. Another religious group stood by in dark robes; they belonged to the Repentance church beyond the park. Their pastor was directing somber glares at the crowd in general and Mira's uncle in particular.

Three official-looking strangers who had been at the inn came up and introduced themselves to Uncle Laban as observers from Alberta Central. They went on into the tent which had been erected over the enclosure, carrying with them several pieces of equipment which the town-folk eyed suspiciously.

The mechanics teacher finished organizing a squad of students to protect the slab's curtain, and Mira and Serli and Laban went on into the tent. It was much hotter inside. Benches were set in rings around a railed enclosure about twenty feet in diameter. Inside the railing the earth was bare and scuffed. Several bunches of flowers and blooming poinciana branches leaned against the rail. The only thing inside the rail was a rough sandstone rock with markings etched on it.

Just as they came in a small girl raced across the open center and was yelled at by everybody. The officials from Alberta were busy at one side of the rail, where the light-print box was mounted.

"Oh, no," muttered Mira's uncle, as one of the officials leaned over to set up a tripod stand inside the rails. He adjusted it and a huge horsetail of fine feathery filaments blossomed out and eddied through the center of the space.

"Oh, no," Laban said again. "Why can't they let it be?"

"They're trying to pick up dust from his suit, is that right?" Serli asked.

"Yes, insane. Did you get time to read?"

"Oh yes," said Serli.

"Sort of," added Mira.

"Then you know. He's falling. Trying to check his—well, call it velocity. Trying to slow down. He must have slipped or stumbled. We're getting pretty close to when he lost his footing and started to fall. What did it? Did somebody trip him?" Laban looked from Mira to Serli, dead serious now. "How would you like to be the one who made John Delgano fall?"

"Ooh," said Mira in quick sympathy. Then she said, "Oh."

"You mean," asked Serli, "whoever made him fall caused all the, caused—"

"Possible," said Laban.

"Wait a minute," Serli frowned. "He did fall. So somebody had to do it—I mean, he has to trip or whatever. If he doesn't fall the past would all be changed, wouldn't it? No war, no—"

"Possible," Laban repeated. "God knows. All *I* know is that John Delgano and the space around him is the most unstable, improbable, highly charged area ever known on Earth and I'm damned if I think anybody should go poking sticks in it."

"Oh come now, Laban!" One of the Alberta men joined them, smiling. "Our dust-mop couldn't trip a gnat. It's just vitreous monofilaments."

"Dust from the future," grumbled Laban. "What's it going to tell you? That the future has dust in it?"

"If we could only get a trace from that thing in his hand."

"In his hand?" asked Mira. Serli started leafing hurriedly through the pamphlet.

"We've had a recording analyzer aimed at it," the Albertan lowered his voice, glancing around. "A spectroscope. We know there's something there, or was. Can't get a decent reading. It's severely deteriorated."

"People poking at him, grabbing at him," Laban muttered. "You—"

"*Ten minutes!*" shouted a man with a megaphone. "Take your places, friends and strangers."

The Repentance people were filing in at one side, intoning an ancient incantation, "mi-seri-cordia, ora pro nobis!"

The atmosphere suddenly took on tension. It was now very close and hot in the big tent. A boy from the mayor's office wiggled through the crowd, beckoning Laban's party to come and sit in the guest chairs on the second level on the "face" side. In front of them at the rail one of the Repentance ministers was arguing with an Albertan official over his right to occupy the space taken by a recorder, it being his special duty to look into the Man John's eyes.

"Can he really see us?" Mira asked her uncle.

"Blink your eyes," Laban told her. "A new scene every blink, that's what he sees. Phantasmagoria. Blink-blink-blink—for god knows how long."

"Mi-sere-re, pec-cavi," chanted the penitentials. A soprano neighed "May the red of sin pa-aa-ass from us!"

"They believe his oxygen tab went red because of the state of their souls." Laban chuckled. "Their souls are going to have to stay damned a while; John Delgano has been on oxygen reserve for five centuries—or rather, he *will be* low for five centuries more. At a half-second per year his time, that's fifteen minutes. We know from the audio trace he's still breathing more or less normally and the reserve was good for twenty minutes. So they should have their salvation about the year seven hundred, if they last that long."

"*Five minutes!* Take your seats, folks. Please sit down so everyone can see. Sit down, folks."

"It says we'll hear his voice through his suit speaker," Serli whispered. "Do you know what he's saying?"

"You get mostly a twenty-cycle howl," Laban whispered back. "The recorders have spliced up something like *ayt*, part of an old word. Take centuries to get enough to translate."

"Is it a message?"

"Who knows? Could be his word for 'date' or 'hate.' 'Too late,' maybe. Anything."

The tent was quieting. A fat child by the railing started to cry and was pulled back onto a lap. There was a subdued mumble of praying. The Holy Joy faction on the far side rustled their flowers.

"Why don't we set our clocks by him?"

"It's changing. He's on sidereal time."

"*One minute.*"

In the hush the praying voices rose slightly. From outside a chicken cackled. The bare center space looked absolutely ordinary. Over it the recorder's silvery filaments eddied gently in the breath from a hundred lungs. Another recorder could be heard ticking faintly.

For long seconds nothing happened.

The air developed a tiny hum. At the same moment Mira caught a movement at the railing on her left.

The hum developed a beat and vanished into a peculiar silence and suddenly everything happened at once.

Sound burst on them, raced shockingly up the audible scale. The air cracked as something rolled and tumbled in the space. There was a grinding, wailing roar and—

He was there.

Solid, huge—a huge man in a monster suit, his head was a dull bronze transparent globe holding a human face, dark smear of open mouth. His position was impossible, legs strained forward thrusting himself back, his arms frozen in a whirlwind swing. Although he seemed to be in a frantic forward motion nothing moved, only one of his legs buckled or sagged slightly—

—And then he was gone, utterly and completely gone in a thunderclap, leaving only the incredible afterimage in a hundred pairs of staring eyes. Air boomed, shuddering, dust roiled out mixed with smoke.

"Oh, oh my God," gasped Mira, unheard, clinging to Serli. Voices were crying out, choking. "He saw me, he saw me!" a woman shrieked. A few people dazedly threw their confetti into the empty dust-cloud; most had failed to throw at all. Children began to howl. "He *saw* me!" the woman screamed hysterically. "Red, Oh Lord have mercy!" a deep male voice intoned.

Mira heard Laban swearing furiously and looked again into the space. As the dust settled she could see that the recorder's tripod had tipped over into the center. There was a dusty mound lying against it—flowers. Most of the end of the stand seemed to have disappeared or been melted. Of the filaments nothing could be seen.

"Some damn fool pitched flowers into it. Come on, let's get out."

"Was it under, did it trip him?" asked Mira, squeezed in the crowd.

"It was still red, his oxygen thing," Serli said over her head. "No mercy this trip, eh, Laban?"

"Shsh!" Mira caught the Repentance pastor's dark glance. They jostled through the enclosure gate and were out in the sunlit park, voices exclaiming, chattering loudly in excitement and relief.

"It was terrible," Mira cried softly. "Oh, I never thought it was a real live man. There he is, he's *there*. Why can't we help him? Did we trip him?"

"I don't know; I don't think so," her uncle grunted. They sat down near the new monument, fanning themselves. The curtain was still in place.

"Did we change the past?" Serli laughed, looked lovingly at his little wife. He wondered for a moment why she was wearing such odd earrings. Then he remembered he had given them to her at that Indian pueblo they'd passed.

"But it wasn't just those Alberta people," said Mira. She seemed obsessed with the idea. "It was the flowers really." She wiped at her forehead.

"Mechanics or superstition," chuckled Serli. "Which is the culprit, love or science?"

"Shsh." Mira looked about nervously. "The flowers were love, I guess . . . I feel so strange. It's hot. Oh, thank you." Uncle Laban had succeeded in attracting the attention of the iced-drink vendor.

People were chatting normally now and the choir struck into a cheerful song. At one side of the park a line of people were waiting to sign their names in the visitors' book. The mayor appeared at the park gate, leading a party up the bougainvillea alley for the unveiling of the monument.

"What did it say on that stone by his foot?" Mira asked. Serli showed her the guidebook picture of Carl's rock with the inscription translated below: WELCOME HOME JOHN.

"I wonder if he can see it."

The mayor was about to begin his speech.

Much later when the crowd had gone away the monument stood alone in the dark, displaying to the moon the inscription in the language of that time and place:

ON THIS SPOT THERE APPEARS ANNUALLY THE FORM OF MAJOR JOHN DELGANO, THE FIRST AND ONLY MAN TO TRAVEL IN TIME.

MAJOR DELGANO WAS SENT INTO THE FUTURE SOME HOURS BEFORE THE HOLOCAUST OF DAY ZERO. ALL KNOWLEDGE OF THE MEANS BY WHICH HE WAS SENT IS LOST, PERHAPS FOREVER. IT IS BELIEVED THAT AN ACCIDENT OCCURRED WHICH SENT HIM MUCH FARTHER THAN WAS INTENDED. SOME ANALYSTS SPECULATE THAT HE MAY HAVE GONE AS FAR AS FIFTY THOUSAND YEARS AHEAD. HAVING REACHED THIS UN-

KNOWN POINT MAJOR DELGANO APPARENTLY WAS RECALLED, OR AT-
TEMPTED TO RETURN, ALONG THE COURSE IN SPACE AND TIME
THROUGH WHICH HE WAS SENT. HIS TRAJECTORY IS THOUGHT TO
START AT THE POINT WHICH OUR SOLAR SYSTEM WILL OCCUPY AT A
FUTURE TIME AND IS TANGENT TO THE COMPLEX HELIX WHICH OUR
EARTH DESCRIBES AROUND THE SUN.

HE APPEARS ON THIS SPOT IN THE ANNUAL INSTANTS IN WHICH
HIS COURSE INTERSECTS OUR PLANET'S ORBIT AND HE IS APPARENTLY
ABLE TO TOUCH THE GROUND IN THOSE INSTANTS. SINCE NO TRACE
OF HIS PASSAGE INTO THE FUTURE HAS BEEN MANIFESTED, IT IS BE-
LIEVED THAT HE IS RETURNING BY A DIFFERENT MEANS THAN HE WENT
FORWARD. HE IS ALIVE IN OUR PRESENT. OUR PAST IS HIS FUTURE AND
OUR FUTURE IS HIS PAST. THE TIME OF HIS APPEARANCES IS SHIFTING
GRADUALLY IN SOLAR TIME TO CONVERGE ON THE MOMENT OF 1153.6
ON MAY 2ND 1989 OLD STYLE, OR DAY ZERO.

THE EXPLOSION WHICH ACCOMPANIED HIS RETURN TO HIS OWN
TIME AND PLACE MAY HAVE OCCURRED WHEN SOME ELEMENTS OF THE
PAST INSTANTS OF HIS COURSE WERE CARRIED WITH HIM INTO THEIR
OWN PRIOR EXISTENCE. IT IS CERTAIN THAT THIS EXPLOSION PRECIPI-
TATED THE WORLDWIDE HOLOCAUST WHICH ENDED FOREVER THE AGE
OF HARDSCIENCE.

*—He was falling, losing control, failing in his fight against the terrible mo-
mentum he had gained, fighting with his human legs shaking in the inhuman
stiffness of his armor, his soles charred, not gripping well now, not enough trac-
tion to brake, battling, thrusting as the flashes came, the punishing alternation
of light, dark, light, dark, which he had borne so long, the claps of air thickening
and thinning against his armor as he skidded through space which was time,
desperately braking as the flickers of earth hammered against his feet—only his
feet mattered now, only to slow and stay on course—and the pull, the beacon was
getting slacker; as he came near home it was fanning out, hard to stay centered:
he was becoming, he supposed, more probable; the wound he had punched in time
was healing itself. In the beginning it had been so tight—a single ray in a closing
tunnel—he had hurled himself after it like an electron flying to the anode, aimed
surely along that exquisitely complex single vector of possibility of life, shot and
been shot like a squeezed pip into the last chink in that rejecting and rejected
nowhere through which he, John Delgano, could conceivably continue to exist,
the hole leading to home—had pounded down it across time, across space, pumping with his human legs as the real Earth of that unreal time came under him,
his course as certain as the twisting dash of an animal down its burrow, he a
cosmic mouse on an interstellar, intertemporal race for his nest with the wrongness of everything closing round the rightness of that one course, the atoms of his
heart, his blood, his every well crying Home—HOME!—as he drove himself
after that fading breath-hole, each step faster, surer, stronger, until he raced
with invincible momentum upon the rolling flickers of Earth as a man might
race a rolling log in a torrent! Only the stars stayed constant around him from
flash to flash, he looked down past his feet at a million strobes of Crux, of
Triangulum; once at the height of his stride he had risked a century's glance*

upward and seen the Bears weirdly strung out from Polaris—But a Polaris not the Pole Star now, he realized, jerking his eyes back to his racing feet, thinking, I am walking home to Polaris, home to the strobing beat. He had ceased to remember where he had been, the beings, people or aliens or things he had glimpsed in the impossible moment of being where he could not be; had ceased to see the flashes of worlds around him, each flash different, the jumble of bodies, walls, landscapes, shapes, and colors beyond deciphering—some lasting a breath, some changing pell-mell—the faces, limbs, things poking at him; the nights he had pounded through, dark or lit by strange lamps; roofed or unroofed; the days flashing sunlight, gales, dust, snow, interiors innumerable, strobe after strobe into night again; he was in daylight now, a hall of some kind; *I am getting closer at last,* he thought, *the feel is changing*—but he had to slow down, to check; and that stone near his feet, it had stayed there some time now, he wanted to risk a look but he did not dare, he was so tired, and he was sliding, was going out of control, fighting to kill the merciless velocity that would not let him slow down; he was hurt, too, something had hit him back there, they had done something, he didn't know what back somewhere in the kaleidoscope of faces, arms, hooks, beams, centuries of creatures grabbing at him—and his oxygen was going, never mind, it would last—it had to last, he was going home, home! And he had forgotten now the message he had tried to shout, hoping it could be picked up somehow, the important thing he had repeated; and the thing he had carried, it was gone now, his camera was gone too, something had torn it away—but he was coming home! Home! If only he could kill this momentum, could stay on the failing course, could slip, scramble, slide, somehow ride this avalanche down to home, to home—and his throat said *Home!*—said *Kate, Kate!* And his heart shouted, his lungs almost gone now, as his legs fought, fought and failed, as his feet gripped and skidded and held and slid, as he pitched, flailed, pushed, strove in the gale of timerush across space, across time, at the end of the longest path ever: the path of John Delgano, coming home.

Long Shot

VERNOR VINGE

Born in Waukesha, Wisconsin, Vernor Vinge now lives in San Diego, California, where he is an associate professor of math sciences at San Diego State University. He sold his first story, "Apartness," to New Worlds *in 1965; it immediately attracted a good deal of attention, was picked up for Donald A. Wollheim and Terry Carr's collaborative* World's Best Science Fiction *anthology the following year, and still strikes me as one of the strongest stories of that entire period, holding up well even in comparison with more-famous stories also reprinted in that same anthology, such as Clarke's "Sunjammer" or Ellison's " 'Repent, Harlequin!' Said the Ticktockman." Since this impressive debut, Vinge has become a frequent contributor to* Analog; *he has also sold to* Orbit, Far Frontiers, If, Stellar, *and other markets. His novella "True Names" was a finalist for both the Nebula and Hugo Awards in 1981 and is famous in Internet circles and among computer enthusiasts well outside the usual limits of the genre, cited by some as having been the real progenitor of cyberpunk rather than William Gibson's "Burning Chrome" or* Neuromancer. *Vinge's novel* A Fire upon the Deep, *one of the most epic and sweeping of modern Space Operas, won him a Hugo Award in 1993, and these days he is regarded as one of the best of the new breed of American hard science writers, along with people such as Charles Sheffield and Greg Bear.*

In the poignant story that follows, Vinge takes us to the outer reaches of the galaxy in company with a most unusual sort of explorer. . . .

Vinge's other books include Tatja Grimm's World *and* The Witling, *two Hugo finalists,* The Peace War *and* Marooned in Realtime, *which have been released in an omnibus volume as* Across Realtime, *and two short-story collections,* True Names and Other Dangers *and* Threats and Other Promises. *His most recent book is a major new novel,* A Deepness in the Sky, *a sequel to* A Fire upon the Deep. *Coming up is* True Names and the Opening of the Cyberspace Frontier, *an anthology of essays edited by James Frenkel related to Vinge's story "True Names."*

They named her Ilse, and of all Earth's creatures, she was to be the longest lived—and perhaps the last. A prudent tortoise might survive three hundred years and a bristle-cone pine six thousand, but Ilse's designed span exceeded one hundred centuries. And though her brain was iron and germanium doped with arsenic, and her heart was a tiny cloud of hydrogen plasma, Ilse *was*—in the beginning—one of Earth's creatures: she could feel, she could question, and—as she discovered during the dark centuries before her fiery end—she could also forget.

Ilse's earliest memory was a fragment, amounting to less than fifteen seconds. Someone, perhaps inadvertently, brought her to consciousness as she sat atop her S-5N booster. It was night, but their launch was imminent and the booster stood white and silver in the light of a dozen spotlights. Ilse's sharp eye scanned rapidly around the horizon, untroubled by the glare from below. Stretching away from her to the north was a line of thirty launch pads. Several had their own boosters, though none were lit up as Ilse's was. Three thousand meters to the west were more lights, and the occasional sparkle of an automatic rifle. To the east, surf marched in phosphorescent ranks against the Merrit Island shore.

There the fragment ended: she was not conscious during the launch. But that scene remained forever her most vivid and incomprehensible memory.

When next she woke, Ilse was in low Earth orbit. Her single eye had been fitted to a one hundred and fifty centimeter reflecting telescope so that now she could distinguish stars set less than a tenth of an arcsecond apart, or, if she looked straight down, count the birds in a flock of geese two hundred kilometers below. For more than a year Ilse remained in this same orbit. She was not idle. Her makers had allotted this period for testing. A small manned station orbited with her, and from it came an endless sequence of radioed instructions and exercises.

Most of the problems were ballistic: hyperbolic encounters, transfer ellipses, and the like. But it was often required that Ilse use her own telescope and spectrometer to discover the parameters of the problems. A typical exercise: determine the orbits of Venus and Mercury; compute a minimum energy flyby of both planets. Another: determine the orbit of Mars; analyze its atmospheric; plan a hyperbolic entry subject to constraints. Many observational problems dealt with Earth: determine atmospheric pressure and composition; perform multispectrum analysis of vegetation. Usually she was required to solve organic analysis problems in less than thirty seconds. And in these last problems, the rules were often changed even while the game was played. Her orientation jets would be caused to malfunction. Critical portions of her mind and senses would be degraded.

One of the first things Ilse learned was that in addition to her private memories, she had a programmed memory, a "library" of procedures and facts. As with most libraries, the programmed memory was not as accessible as Ilse's own recollections, but the information contained there was much more complete and precise. The solution program for almost any ballistic, or chemical, problem could be lifted from this "library," used for seconds, or hours, as an integral part of Ilse's mind, and then returned to the "library." The real trick was to select the proper program on the basis of incomplete information, and then to modify that program to meet various combinations of power and equipment failure. Though she did poorly at first, Ilse eventually surpassed her design specifications. At this point her training stopped and for the first—but not the last—time, Ilse was left to her own devices.

Though she had yet to wonder on her ultimate purpose, still she wanted to see as much of her world as possible. She spent most of each daylight pass looking straight down, trying to see some order in the jumble of blue and green and white. She could easily follow the supply rockets as they climbed up from Merritt Island and Baikonur to rendezvous with her. In the end, more than a hundred of the rockets were floating about her. As the weeks passed, the squat white cylinders were fitted together on a spidery frame.

Now her ten-meter-long body was lost in the webwork of cylinders and girders that stretched out two hundred meters behind her. Her programmed memory told her that the entire assembly massed 22,563.901 tons—more than most ocean-going ships—and a little experimenting with her attitude control jets convinced her that this figure was correct.

Soon her makers connected Ilse's senses to the mammoth's control mechanisms. It was as if she had been given a new body, for she could feel, and see, and use each of the hundred propellant tanks and each of the fifteen fusion reactors that made up the assembly. She realized that now she had the power to perform some of the maneuvers she had planned during her training.

◆

Finally the great moment arrived. Course directions came over the maser link with the manned satellite. Ilse quickly computed the trajectory that would result from these directions. The answer she obtained was correct, but it revealed only the smallest part of what was in store for her.

In her orbit two hundred kilometers up, Ilse coasted smoothly toward high noon over the Pacific. Her eye was pointed forward, so that on the fuzzy blue horizon she could see the edge of the North American continent. Nearer, the granulated cloud cover obscured the ocean itself. The command to begin the burn came from the manned satellite, but Ilse was following the clock herself, and she had determined to take over the launch if any mistakes were made. Two hundred meters behind her, deep in the maze of tanks and beryllium girders, Ilse felt magnetic fields establish themselves, felt hydrogen plasma form, felt fusion commence. Another signal from the station, and propellant flowed around each of ten reactors.

Ilse and her twenty-thousand-ton booster were on their way.

Acceleration rose smoothly to one gravity. Behind her, vidicons on the booster's superstructure showed the Earth shrinking. For half an hour the burn continued, monitored by Ilse, and the manned station now fallen far behind. Then Ilse was alone with her booster, coasting away from Earth and her creators at better than twenty kilometers a second.

So Ilse began her fall toward the sun. For eleven weeks she fell. During this time, there was little to do: monitor the propellants, keep the booster's sunshade properly oriented, relay data to Earth. Compared to much of her later life, however, it was a time of hectic activity.

A fall of eleven weeks toward a body as massive as the sun can result in only one thing: speed. In those last hours, Ilse hurtled downward at better than two hundred and fifty kilometers per second—an Earth to Moon distance every half hour. Forty-five minutes before her closest approach to the sun—perihelion—Ilse jettisoned the empty first stage and its sunshade. Now she was left with the two-thousand-ton second stage, whose insulation consisted of a bright coat of white paint. She felt the pressure in the propellant tanks begin to rise.

Though her telescope was pointed directly away from the sun, the vidicons on the second stage gave her an awesome view of the solar fire-ball. She was moving so fast now that the sun's incandescent prominences changed perspective even as she watched.

Seventeen minutes to perihelion. From somewhere beyond the flames, Ilse got the expected maser communication. She pitched herself and her booster over so that she looked along the line of her trajectory. Now her own body was exposed to the direct glare of the sun. Through her tele-scope she could see luminous tracery within the solar corona. The booster's fuel tanks were perilously close to bursting, and Ilse was having trouble keeping her own body at its proper temperature.

Fifteen minutes to perihelion. The command came from Earth to be-gin the burn. Ilse considered her own trajectory data, and concluded that the command was thirteen seconds premature. Consultation with Earth would cost at least sixteen minutes, and her decision must be made in the next four seconds. Any of Man's earlier, less sophisticated creations would have accepted the error and taken the mission on to catastrophe, but independence was the essence of Ilse's nature: she overrode the maser command, and delayed ignition till the instant she thought correct.

The sun's northern hemisphere passed below her, less than three solar diameters away.

Ignition, and Ilse was accelerated at nearly two gravities. As she swung toward what was to have been perihelion, her booster lifted her out of elliptic orbit and into a hyperbolic one. Half an hour later she shot out from the sun into the spaces south of the ecliptic at three hundred and twenty kilometers per second—about one solar diameter every hour. The booster's now empty propellant tanks were between her and the sun, and her body slowly cooled.

Shortly after burnout, Earth offhandedly acknowledged the navigation error. This is not to say that Ilse's makers were without contrition for their mistake, or without praise for Ilse. In fact, several men lost what little there remained to confiscate for jeopardizing this mission, and Man's last hope. It was simply that Ilse's makers did not believe that she could appreciate apologies or praise.

Now Ilse fled up out of the solar gravity well. It had taken her eleven weeks to fall from Earth to Sol, but in less than two weeks she had re-gained this altitude, and still she plunged outward at more than one hun-dred kilometers per second. That velocity remained her inheritance from the sun. Without the gravity well maneuver, her booster would have had to be five hundred times as large, or her voyage three times as long. It had been the very best that men could do for her, considering the time remaining to them.

So began the voyage of one hundred centuries. Ilse parted with the empty booster and floated on alone: a squat cylinder, twelve meters wide, five meters long, with a large telescope sticking from one end. Four light-years below her in the well of the night she saw Alpha Centauri, her destination. To the naked human eye, it appears a single bright star, but with her telescope Ilse could clearly see two stars, one slightly fainter and redder than the other. She carefully measured their position and her own, and concluded that her aim had been so perfect that a midcourse correction would not be necessary for a thousand years.

For many months, Earth maintained maser contact—to pose problems and ask after her health. It was almost pathetic, for if anything went wrong now, or in the centuries to follow, there was very little Earth could do to help. The problems were interesting, though. Ilse was asked to chart the nonluminous bodies in the Solar System. She became quite skilled at this and eventually discovered all nine planets, most of their moons, and several asteroids and comets.

In less than two years, Ilse was farther from the sun than any known planet, than any previous terrestrial probe. The sun itself was no more than a very bright star behind her, and Ilse had no trouble keeping her frigid innards at their proper temperature. But now it took sixteen hours to ask a question of Earth and obtain an answer.

A strange thing happened. Over a period of three weeks, the sun became steadily brighter until it gleamed ten times as luminously as before. The change was not really a great one. It was far short of what Earth's astronomers would have called a nova. Nevertheless, Ilse puzzled over the event, in her own way, for many months, since it was at this time that she lost maser contact with Earth. That contact was never regained.

Now Ilse changed herself to meet the empty centuries. As her designers had planned, she split her mind into three co-equal entities. Theoretically each of these minds could handle the entire mission alone, but for any important decision, Ilse required the agreement of at least two of the minds. In this fractionated state, Ilse was neither as bright nor as quick-thinking as she had been at launch. But scarcely anything happened in interstellar space, the chief danger being senile decay. Her three minds spent as much time checking each other as they did overseeing the various subsystems.

The one thing they did not regularly check was the programmed memory, since Ilse's designers had—mistakenly—judged that such checks were a greater danger to the memories than the passage of time.

Even with her mentality diminished, and in spite of the caretaker tasks assigned her, Ilse spent much of her time contemplating the universe that spread out forever around her. She discovered binary star systems, then watched the tiny lights swing back and forth around each other as the decades and centuries passed. To her the universe became a moving, almost a living, thing. Several of the nearer stars drifted almost a degree every century, while the great galaxy in Andromeda shifted less than a second of arc in a thousand years.

Occasionally, she turned about to look at Sol. Even ten centuries out she could still distinguish Jupiter and Saturn. These were auspicious observations.

Finally it was time for the midcourse correction. She had spent the

preceding century refining her alignment and her navigational observations. The burn was to be only one hundred meters per second, so accurate had been her perihelion impulse. Nevertheless, without that
correction she would miss the Centauran system entirely. When the second arrived and her alignment was perfect, Ilse lit her tiny rocket—and
discovered that she could obtain at most only three-quarters of the rated
thrust. She had to make two burns before she was satisfied with the new
course.

For the next fifty years, Ilse studied the problem. She tested the
rocket's electrical system hundreds of times, and even fired the rocket in
microsecond bursts. She never discovered how the centuries had robbed
her, but extrapolating from her observations, Ilse realized that by the time
she entered the Centauran system, she would have only a thousand meters
per second left in her rocket—less than half its designed capability. Even
so it was possible that, without further complications, she would be able
to survey the planets of both stars in the system.

But before she finished her study of the propulsion problem, Ilse discovered another breakdown—the most serious she was to face:

She had forgotten her mission. Over the centuries the pattern of magnetic fields on her programmed memory had slowly disappeared—the
least used programs going first. When Ilse recalled those programs to
discover how her reduced maneuverability affected the mission, she discovered that she no longer had any record of her ultimate purpose. The
memories ended with badly faded programs for biochemical reconnaissance and planetary entry, and Ilse guessed that there was something crucial left to do after a successful landing on a suitable planet.

Ilse was a patient sort—especially in her cruise configuration—and she
didn't worry about her ultimate purpose, so far away in the future. But
she did do her best to preserve what programs were left. She played each
program into her own memory and then back to the programmed memory. If the process were repeated every seventy years, she found that she
could keep the programmed memories from fading. On the other hand,
she had no way of knowing how many errors this endless repetition was
introducing. For this reason she had each of her subminds perform the
process separately, and she frequently checked the ballistic and astronomical programs by doing problems with them.

Ilse went further: she studied her own body for clues as to its purpose.
Much of her body was filled with a substance she must keep within a few
degrees of absolute zero. Several leads disappeared into this mass. Except
for her thermometers, however, she had no feeling in this part of her
body. Now she raised the temperature in this section a few thousandths
of a degree, a change well within design specifications, but large enough
for her to sense. Comparing her observations and the section's mass with
her chemical analysis programs, Ilse concluded that the mysterious area
was a relatively homogeneous body of frozen water, doped with various
impurities. It was interesting information, but no matter how she compared it with her memories she could not see any significance to it.

Ilse floated on—and on. The period of time between the midcourse maneuver and the next important event on her schedule was longer than Man's experience with agriculture had been on Earth.

As the centuries passed, the two closely set stars that were her destination became brighter until, a thousand years from Alpha Centauri, she decided to begin her search for planets in the system. Ilse turned her telescope on the brighter of the two stars . . . call it Able. She was still thirty-five thousand times as far from Able—and the smaller star . . . call it Baker—as Earth is from Sol. Even to her sharp eye, Able didn't show as a disk but rather as a diffraction pattern: a round blob of light—many times larger than the star's true disk—surrounded by a ring of light. The faint gleam of any planets would be lost in the diffraction pattern. For five years Ilse watched the pattern, analyzed it with one of her most subtle programs. Occasionally she slid occulting plates into the telescope and studied the resulting, distorted, pattern. After five years she had found suggestive anomalies in the diffraction pattern, but no definite signs of planets.

No matter. Patient Ilse turned her telescope a tiny fraction of a degree, and during the next five years she watched Baker. Then she switched back to Able. Fifteen times Ilse repeated this cycle. While she watched, Baker completed two revolutions about Able, and the stars' maximum mutual separation increased to nearly a tenth of a degree. Finally Ilse was certain: she had discovered a planet orbiting Baker, and perhaps another orbiting Able. Most likely they were both gas giants. No matter: she knew that any small, inner planets would still be lost in the glare of Able and Baker.

There remained less than nine hundred years before she coasted through the Centauran system.

Ilse persisted in her observations. Eventually she could see the gas giants as tiny spots of light—not merely as statistical correlations in her carefully collected diffraction data. Four hundred years out, she decided that the remaining anomalies in Able's diffraction pattern must be another planet, this one at about the same distance from Able as Earth is from Sol. Fifteen years later she made a similar discovery for Baker.

If she were to investigate both of these planets she would have to plan very carefully. According to her design specifications, she had scarcely the maneuvering capability left to investigate one system. But Ilse's navigation system had survived the centuries better than expected, and she estimated that a survey of both planets might still be possible.

Three hundred and fifty years out, Ilse made a relatively large course correction, better than two hundred meters per second. This change was essentially a matter of pacing: it would delay her arrival by four months. Thus she would pass near the planet she wished to investigate and, if no landing were attempted, her path would be precisely bent by Able's gravitational field and she would be cast into Baker's planetary system.

Now Ilse had less than eight hundred meters per second left in her rocket—less than one percent of her velocity relative to Able and Baker. If she could be at the right place at the right time, that would be enough, but otherwise . . .

⬥

Ilse plotted the orbits of the bodies she had detected more and more accurately. Eventually she discovered several more planets: a total of three for Able, and four for Baker. But only her two prime candidates—call them Able II and Baker II—were at the proper distance from their suns.

Eighteen months out, Ilse sighted moons around Able II. This was good news. Now she could accurately determine the planet's mass, and so refine her course even more. Ilse was now less than fifty astronomical units from Able, and eighty from Baker. She had no trouble making spectroscopic observations of the planets. Her prime candidates had plenty of oxygen in their atmosphere—though the farther one, Baker II, seemed deficient in water vapor. On the other hand, Able II had complex carbon compounds in its atmosphere, and its net color was blue-green. According to Ilse's damaged memory, these last were desirable features.

The centuries had shrunk to decades, then to years, and finally to days. Ilse was within the orbit of Able's gas giant. Ten million kilometers ahead her target swept along a nearly circular path about its sun, Able. Twenty-seven astronomical units beyond Able gleamed Baker.

But Ilse kept her attention on that target, Able II. Now she could make out its gross continental outlines. She selected a landing site, and performed a two hundred meter per second burn. If she chose to land, she would come down in a greenish, beclouded area.

Twelve hours to contact. Ilse checked each of her subminds one last time. She deleted all malfunctioning circuits, and reassembled herself as a single mind out of what remained. Over the centuries, one third of all her electrical components had failed, so that besides her lost memories, she was not nearly as bright as she had been when launched. Nevertheless, with her subminds combined she was much cleverer than she had been during the cruise. She needed this greater alertness, because in the hours and minutes preceding her encounter with Able II, she would do more analysis and make more decisions than ever before.

One hour to contact. Ilse was within the orbit of her target's outer moon. Ahead loomed the tentative destination, a blue and white crescent two degrees across. Her landing area was around the planet's horizon. No matter. The important task for these last moments was a biochemical survey—at least that's what her surviving programs told her. She scanned the crescent, looking for traces of green through the clouds. She found a large island in a Pacific sized ocean, and began the exquisitely complex analysis necessary to determine the orientation of amino acids. Every fifth second, she took one second to reestimate the atmospheric densities. The problems seemed even more complicated than her training exercises back in Earth orbit.

Five minutes to contact. She was less than forty thousand kilometers out, and the planet's hazy limb filled her sky. In the next ten seconds she must decide whether or not to land on Able II. Her ten-thousand-year mission was at stake here. For once Ilse landed, she knew that she would never fly again. Without the immense booster that had pushed her out along this journey, she was nothing but a brain and an entry shield and a chunk of frozen water. If she decided to bypass Able II, she must now use a large portion of her remaining propellants to accelerate at right angles to her trajectory. This would cause her to miss the upper edge of the planet's atmosphere, and she would go hurtling out of Able's planetary system. Thirteen months later she would arrive in the vicinity of Baker, perhaps with enough left in her rocket to guide herself into Baker II's atmosphere. But, if that planet should be inhospitable, there would be no turning back: she would have to land there, or else coast on into interstellar darkness.

Ilse weighed the matter for three seconds and concluded that Able II satisfied every criterion she could recall, while Baker II seemed a bit too yellow, a bit too dry.

Ilse turned ninety degrees and jettisoned the small rocket that had given her so much trouble. At the same time she ejected the telescope which had served her so well. She floated indivisible, a white biconvex disk, twelve meters in diameter, fifteen tons in mass.

She turned ninety degrees more to look directly back along her trajectory. There was not much to see now that she had lost her scope, but she recognized the point of light that was Earth's sun and wondered again what had been on all those programs that she had forgotten.

Five seconds. Ilse closed her eye and waited.

Contact began as a barely perceptible acceleration. In less than two seconds that acceleration built to two hundred and five gravities. This was beyond Ilse's experience, but she was built to take it: her body contained no moving parts and—except for her fusion reactor—no empty spaces. The really difficult thing was to keep her body from turning edgewise and burning up. Though she didn't know it, Ilse was repeating—on a grand scale—the landing technique that men had used so long ago. But Ilse had to dissipate more than eight hundred times the kinetic energy of any returning Apollo capsule. Her maneuver was correspondingly more dangerous, but since her designers could not equip her with a rocket powerful enough to decelerate her, it was the only option.

Now Ilse used her wits and every dyne in her tiny electric thrusters to arc herself about Able II at the proper attitude and altitude. The acceleration rose steadily toward five hundred gravities, or almost five kilometers per second in velocity lost every second. Beyond that Ilse knew that she would lose consciousness. Just centimeters away from her body the air glowed at fifty thousand degrees. The fireball that surrounded her lit the ocean seventy kilometers below as with daylight.

Four hundred and fifty gravities. She felt a cryostat shatter, and one branch of her brain short through. Still Ilse worked patiently and blindly to keep her body properly oriented. If she had calculated correctly, there were less than five seconds to go now.

She came within sixty kilometers of the surface, then rose steadily back into space. But now her velocity was only seven kilometers per second. The acceleration fell to a mere fifteen gravities, then to zero. She coasted back through a long ellipse to plunge, almost gently, into the depths of Able II's atmosphere.

At twenty thousand meters altitude, Ilse opened her eye and scanned the world below. Her lens had been cracked, and several of her gestalt programs damaged, but she saw green and knew her navigation hadn't been too bad.

It would have been a triumphant moment if only she could have remembered what she was supposed to do *after* she landed.

At ten thousand meters, Ilse popped her paraglider from the hull behind her eye. The tough plastic blossomed out above her, and her fall became a shallow glide. Ilse saw that she was flying over a prairie spotted here and there by forest. It was near sunset and the long shadows cast by trees and hills made it easy for her to gauge the topography.

Two thousand meters. With a glide ratio of one to four, she couldn't expect to fly more than another eight kilometers. Ilse looked ahead, saw a tiny forest, and a stream glinting through the trees. Then she saw a glade just inside the forest, and some vagrant memory told her this was an appropriate spot. She pulled in the paraglider's forward lines and slid more steeply downward. As she passed three or four meters over the trees surrounding the glade, Ilse pulled in the rear lines, stalled her glider, and fell into the deep, moist grass. Her dun and green paraglider collapsed over her charred body so that she might be mistaken for a large black boulder covered with vegetation.

The voyage that had crossed one hundred centuries and four light-years was ended.

❧

Ilse sat in the gathering twilight and listened. Sound was an undreamed-of dimension to her: tiny things burrowing in their holes, the stream gurgling nearby, a faint chirping in the distance. Twilight ended and a shallow fog rose in the dark glade. Ilse knew her voyaging was over. She would never move again. No matter. That had been planned, she was sure. She knew that much of her computing machinery—her mind—had been destroyed in the landing. She would not survive as a conscious being for more than another century or two. No matter.

What did matter was that she knew that her mission was not completed, and that the most important part remained, else the immense gamble her makers had undertaken would finally come to nothing. That possibility was the only thing which could frighten Ilse. It was part of her design.

She reviewed all the programmed memories that had survived the centuries and the planetary entry, but discovered nothing new. She investigated the rest of her body, testing her parts in a thorough, almost destructive, way she never would have dared while still centuries from her destination. She discovered nothing new. Finally she came to that load of ice she had carried so far. With one of her cryostats broken, she couldn't keep it at its proper temperature for more than a few years. She recalled the apparently useless leads that disappeared into that mass. There was only one thing left to try.

Ilse turned down her cryostats, and waited as the temperature within her climbed. The ice near her small fusion reactor warmed first. Somewhere in the frozen mass a tiny piece of metal expanded just far enough to complete a circuit, and Ilse discovered that her makers had taken one last precaution to insure her reliability. At the base of the icy hulk, next to the reactor, they had placed an auxiliary memory unit, and now Ilse had access to it. Her designers had realized that no matter what dangers they imagined, there would be others, and so they had decided to leave this backup cold and inactive till the very end. And the new memory unit was quite different from her old ones, Ilse vaguely realized. It used optical rather than magnetic storage.

Now Ilse knew what she must do. She warmed a cylindrical tank filled with frozen amniotic fluid to thirty-seven degrees centigrade. From the store next to the cylinder, she injected a single microorganism into the tank. In a few minutes she would begin to suffuse blood through the tank.

It was early morning now and the darkness was moist and cool. Ilse tried to probe her new memory further, but was balked. Apparently the instructions were delivered according to some schedule to avoid unnecessary use of the memory. Ilse reviewed what she had learned, and decided that she would know more in another nine months.

In the Hall of the Martian Kings

JOHN VARLEY

*John Varley appeared on the science-fiction scene in 1974, and by the end of
1976—in what was a meteoric rise to prominence even for a field known for
meteoric rises—he was already being recognized as one of the hottest new writers
of the seventies. His first story, "Picnic on Nearside," appeared in 1974 in the*
Magazine of Fantasy & Science Fiction *and was followed by as concentrated an
outpouring of first-rate stories as the genre has ever seen, stories such as "The
Phantom of Kansas," "Retrograde Summer," "In the Bowl," "Gotta Sing, Gotta
Dance," "Equinoctial," "The Black Hole Passes," "Overdrawn at the Memory
Bank," and many others, smart, bright, fresh, brash, audacious, effortlessly imag-
inative stories that seemed to suddenly shake the field out of its uneasy slumber
like a wake-up call from a brand-new trumpet. It's hard to think of a group of
short stories that has had a greater, more concentrated impact on the field, with
the exception of Robert Heinlein's early work for John W. Campbell's* Astounding
or perhaps Roger Zelazny's early stories in the mid-sixties.

*Varley was one of the first new writers to become interested in the solar system
again, after several years in which it had been largely abandoned as a setting for
stories because the space probes of the late sixties and early seventies had
"proved" that it was nothing but an "uninteresting" collection of balls of rock and
ice, with no available abodes for life. Instead, Varley seemed to find the solar
system lushly romantic just as it was, lifeless balls of rock and all (and this was
even before the later* Mariner *probes to the Jupiter and Saturn system had proved
the solar system to be a lot more surprising than people thought that it was), an
aesthetic shift in perception that will go ringing on down through the eighties and
nineties in the work of writers such as G. David Nordley, Stephen Baxter, and a
dozen others. Varley makes this obvious in the complex and inventive story that
follows which takes us along with a team of explorers to Mars—not Burroughs's
Mars, laced with canals, chockablock with giant green warriors, sword-wielding
heroes, and beautiful egg-laying princesses, but rather the bleak, oxidized, apparently lifeless Mars of the* Mariner *probes—for a strange tale about the different
kinds of rebirth . . . a tale that may well have served as the rebirth of the Martian
story as well, after long years of neglect.*

*Varley somehow never had as great an impact with his novels as he did with
his short fiction, with the possible exception of his first novel,* Ophiuchi Hotline.
His other novels include the somewhat disappointing Gaean *trilogy, consisting of*
Titan, Wizard, *and* Demon; *a novelization of one of his own short stories that was
also made into a movie,* Millennium; *and the collections* The Persistence of Vision, The Barbie Murders, Picnic on Nearside, *and* Blue Champagne.

*In the eighties Varley moved away from the print world to produce a number
of screenplays for Hollywood producers, most of which were never produced. He
produced one last significant story, 1984's "Press Enter □," which won him both*

the Hugo and the Nebula Award. (He also won a Hugo in 1982 for his story "The Pusher," and a Hugo and a Nebula in 1979 for his novella The Persistence of Vision.) *After "Press Enter ☐," little was heard from Varley in the genre until the publication of a major new novel,* Steel Beach, *in 1992, which was successful commercially but received a lukewarm reception from many critics. He was largely silent throughout most of the rest of the decade of the nineties but seems to be making something of a comeback here at the end of the century, publishing a major new novel,* The Golden Globe, *in 1998, with another new novel,* Irontown Blues, *coming up soon. He has won two Nebulas and two Hugos for his short fiction.*

It took perseverance, alertness and a willingness to break the rules to watch the sunrise in Tharsis Canyon. Matthew Crawford shivered in the dark, his suit heater turned to emergency setting, his eyes trained toward the east. He knew he had to be watchful. Yesterday he had missed it entirely, snatched away from him in the middle of a long, unavoidable yawn. His jaw muscles stretched, but he controlled it and kept his eyes firmly open.

And there it was. Like the lights in a theater after the show is over: just a quick brightening, a splash of localized bluish purple over the canyon rim, and he was surrounded by footlights. Day had come, the truncated Martian day that would never touch the blackness over his head.

This day, like the nine before it, illuminated a Tharsis radically changed from what it had been over the last sleepy ten thousand years. Wind erosion of rocks can create an infinity of shapes, but it never gets around to carving out a straight line or a perfect arc. The human encampment below him broke up the jagged lines of the rocks with regular angles and curves.

The camp was anything but orderly. No one would get the impression that any care had been taken in the haphazard arrangement of dome, lander, crawlers, crawler tracks, and scattered equipment. It had grown, as all human base camps seem to grow, without pattern. He was reminded of the footprints around Tranquility Base, though on a much larger scale.

Tharsis Base sat on a wide ledge about halfway up from the uneven bottom of the Tharsis arm of the Great Rift Valley. The site had been chosen because it was a smooth area, allowing easy access up a gentle slope to the flat plains of the Tharsis Plateau, while at the same time only a kilometer from the valley floor. No one could agree which area was more worthy of study: plains or canyon. So this site had been chosen as a compromise. What it meant was that the exploring parties had to either climb up or go down; because there wasn't a damn thing worth seeing near the camp. Even the exposed layering and its areological records could not be seen without a half-kilometer crawler ride up to the point where Crawford had climbed to watch the sunrise.

He examined the dome as he walked back to camp. There was a figure hazily visible through the plastic. At this distance he would have been unable to tell who it was if it weren't for the black face. He saw her step up to the dome wall and wipe a clear circle to look through. She spotted his bright red suit and pointed at him. She was suited except for her helmet, which contained her radio. He knew he was in trouble. He saw her turn away and bend to the ground to pick up her helmet, so she could tell him what she thought of people who disobeyed her orders, when the dome shuddered like a jellyfish.

An alarm started in his helmet, flat and strangely soothing coming from the tiny speaker. He stood there for a moment as a perfect smoke ring of dust billowed up around the rim of the dome. Then he was running.

He watched the disaster unfold before his eyes, silent except for the rhythmic beat of the alarm bell in his ears. The dome was dancing and straining, trying to fly. The floor heaved up in the center, throwing the black woman to her knees. In another second the interior was a whirling snowstorm. He skidded on the sand and fell forward, got up in time to see the fiberglass ropes on the side nearest him snap free from the steel spikes anchoring the dome to the rock.

The dome now looked like some fantastic Christmas ornament, filled with snowflakes and the flashing red and blue lights of the emergency alarms. The top of the dome heaved over away from him, and the floor raised itself high in the air, held down by the unbroken anchors on the side farthest from him. There was a gush of snow and dust; then the floor settled slowly back to the ground. There was no motion now but the leisurely folding of the depressurized dome roof as it settled over the structures inside.

◆

The crawler skidded to a stop, nearly rolling over, beside the deflated dome. Two pressure-suited figures got out. They started for the dome hesitantly, in fits and starts. One grabbed the other's arm and pointed to the ladder. The two of them changed course and scrambled up the rope ladder hanging over the side.

Crawford was the only one to look up when the lock started cycling. The two people almost tumbled over each other coming out of the lock. They wanted to *do* something, and quickly, but didn't know what. In the end, they just stood there silently twisting their hands and looking at the floor. One of them took off her helmet. She was a large woman in her thirties, with red hair shorn off close to the scalp.

"Matt, we got here as . . ." She stopped, realizing how obvious it was. "How's Lou?"

"Lou's not going to make it." He gestured to the bunk where a heavy-set man lay breathing raggedly into a clear plastic mask. He was on pure oxygen. There was blood seeping from his ears and nose.

"Brain damage?"

Crawford nodded. He looked around at the other occupants of the room. There was the Surface Mission Commander, Mary Lang, the black woman he had seen inside the dome just before the blowout. She was sitting on the edge of Lou Prager's cot, her head cradled in her hands.

In a way, she was a more shocking sight than Lou. No one who knew her would have thought she could be brought to this limp state of apathy. She had not moved for the last hour.

Sitting on the floor huddled in a blanket was Martin Ralston, the chemist. His shirt was bloody, and there was dried blood all over his face and hands from the nosebleed he'd only recently gotten under control, but his eyes were alert. He shivered, looking from Lang, his titular leader, to Crawford, the only one who seemed calm enough to deal with anything. He was a follower, reliable but unimaginative.

Crawford looked back to the newest arrivals. They were Lucy Stone McKillian, the redheaded ecologist, and Song Sue Lee, the exobiologist. They still stood numbly by the airlock, unable as yet to come to grips with the fact of fifteen dead men and women beneath the dome outside.

"What do they say on the *Burroughs?*" McKillian asked, tossing her helmet on the floor and squatting tiredly against the wall. The lander was not the most comfortable place to hold a meeting; all the couches were mounted horizontally since their purpose was cushioning the acceleration of landing and takeoff. With the ship sitting on its tail, this made ninety percent of the space in the lander useless. They were all gathered on the circular bulkhead at the rear of the life system, just forward of the fuel tank.

"We're waiting for a reply," Crawford said. "But I can sum up what they're going to say: not good. Unless one of you two has some experience in Mars-lander handling that you've been concealing from us."

Neither of them bothered to answer that. The radio in the nose sputtered, then clanged for their attention. Crawford looked over at Lang, who made no move to go answer it. He stood up and swarmed up the ladder to sit in the copilot's chair. He switched on the receiver.

"Commander Lang?"

"No, this is Crawford again. Commander Lang is . . . indisposed. She's busy with Lou, trying to do something."

"That's no use. The doctor says it's a miracle he's still breathing. If he wakes up at all, he won't be anything like you knew him. The telemetry shows nothing like the normal brain wave. Now I've got to talk to Mission Commander Lang. Have her come up." The voice of Mission Commander Weinstein was accustomed to command, and about as emotional as a weather report.

"Sir, I'll ask her, but I don't think she'll come. This is still her operation, you know." He didn't give Weinstein time to reply to that. Weinstein had been trapped by his own seniority into commanding the *Edgar Rice Burroughs*, the orbital ship that got them to Mars and had been intended to get them back. Command of the *Podkayne*, the disposable lander that would make the lion's share of the headlines, had gone to Lang. There was little friendship between the two especially when Weinstein fell to brooding about the very real financial benefits Lang stood to reap by being the first woman on Mars, rather than the lowly mission commander. He saw himself as another Michael Collins.

Crawford called down to Lang, who raised her head enough to mumble something.

"What'd she say?"

"She said take a message." McKillian had been crawling up the ladder as she said this. Now she reached him and said in a lower voice, "Matt, she's pretty broken up. You'd better take over for now."

"Right, I know." He turned back to the radio, and McKillian listened over his shoulder as Weinstein briefed them on the situation as he saw it. It pretty much jibed with Crawford's estimation, except at one crucial point. He signed off and they joined the other survivors.

He looked around at the faces of the others and decided it wasn't the time to speak of rescue possibilities. He didn't relish being a leader. He was hoping Lang would recover soon and take the burden from him. In the meantime he had to get them started on something. He touched McKillian gently on the shoulder and motioned her to the lock.

"Let's go get them buried," he said. She squeezed her eyes shut tight, forcing out tears, then nodded.

It wasn't a pretty job. Halfway through it, Song came down the ladder with the body of Lou Prager.

◆

"Let's go over what we've learned. First, now that Lou's dead there's very little chance of ever lifting off. That is, unless Mary thinks she can absorb everything she needs to know about piloting the *Podkayne* from those printouts Weinstein sent down. How about it, Mary?"

Mary Lang was lying sideways across the improvised cot that had recently held the *Podkayne* pilot, Lou Prager. Her head was nodding listlessly against the aluminum hull plate behind her, her chin was on her chest. Her eyes were half open.

Song had given her a sedative from the dead doctor's supplies on the advice of the medic aboard the *E.R.B.* It had enabled her to stop fighting so hard against the screaming panic she wanted to unleash. It hadn't improved her disposition. She had quit, she wasn't going to do anything for anybody.

When the blowout started, Lang had snapped on her helmet quickly. Then she had struggled against the blizzard and the undulating dome bottom, heading for the roofless framework where the other members of the expedition were sleeping. The blowout was over in ten seconds, and she then had the problem of coping with the collapsing roof, which promptly buried her in folds of clear plastic. It was far too much like one of those nightmares of running knee-deep in quicksand. She had to fight for every meter, but she made it.

She made it in time to see her shipmates of the last six months gasping soundlessly and spouting blood from all over their faces as they fought to get into their pressure suits. It was a hopeless task to choose which two or three to save in the time she had. She might have done better but for the freakish nature of her struggle to reach them; she was in shock and half believed it was only a nightmare. So she grabbed the nearest, who happened to be Doctor Ralston. He had nearly finished donning his suit; so she slapped his helmet on him and moved to the next one. It was Luther Nakamura, and he was not moving. Worse, he was only half suited. Pragmatically, she should have left him and moved onto save the ones who still had a chance. She knew it now but didn't like it any better than she had liked it then.

While she was stuffing Nakamura into his suit, Crawford arrived. He had walked over the folds of plastic until he reached the dormitory, then sliced through it with his laser normally used to vaporize rock samples.

And he had had time to think about the problem of whom to save. He went straight to Lou Prager and finished suiting him up. But it was already too late. He didn't know if it would have made any difference if Mary Lang had tried to save him first.

Now she lay on the bunk, her feet sprawled carelessly in front of her. She slowly shook her head back and forth.

"You sure?" Crawford prodded her, hoping to get a rise, a show of temper, *anything*.

"I'm sure," she mumbled. "You people know how long they trained Lou to fly this thing? And he almost cracked it up as it was. I . . . ah, nuts. It isn't possible."

"I refuse to accept that as a final answer," he said. "But in the meantime we should explore the possibilities if what Mary says is true."

Ralston laughed. It wasn't a bitter laugh; he sounded genuinely amused. Crawford plowed on.

"Here's what we know for sure. The *E.R.B.* is useless to us. Oh, they'll help us out with plenty of advice, maybe more than we want, but any rescue is out of the question."

"We know that," McKillian said. She was tired and sick from the sight of the faces of her dead friends. "What's the use of all this talk?"

"Wait a moment," Song broke in. "Why can't they . . . I mean they have plenty of time, don't they? They have to leave in six months, as I understand it, because of the orbital elements, but in that time . . ."

"Don't you know anything about spaceships?" McKillian shouted. Song went on, unperturbed.

"I do know enough to know the *Edgar* is not equipped for an atmosphere entry. My idea was, not to bring down the whole ship but only what's aboard the ship that we need. Which is a pilot. Might that be possible?"

Crawford ran his hands through his hair, wondering what to say. That possibility had been discussed, and was being studied. But it had to be classed as extremely remote.

"You're right," he said. "What we need is a pilot, and that pilot is Commander Weinstein. Which presents problems legally, if nothing else. He's the captain of a ship and should not leave it. That's what kept him on the *Edgar* in the first place. But he did have a lot of training on the lander simulator, back when he was so sure he'd be picked for the ground team. You know Winey, always the instinct to be the one-man show. So if he thought he could do it, he'd be down here in a minute to bail us out and grab the publicity. I understand they're trying to work out a heat-shield parachute system, from one of the drop capsules that were supposed to ferry down supplies to us during the stay here. But it's very risky. You don't modify an aerodynamic design lightly, not one that's supposed to hit the atmosphere at ten thousand-plus kilometers. So I think we can rule that out. They'll keep working on it, but when it's done. Winey won't step into the damn thing. He wants to be a hero, but he wants to live to enjoy it, too."

There had been a brief lifting of spirits among Song, Ralston, and McKillian at the thought of a possible rescue. The more they thought about it, the less happy they looked. They all seemed to agree with Craw-ford's assessment.

"So we'll put that one in the Fairy Godmother file and forget about it. If it happens, fine. But we'd better plan on the assumption that it won't. As you may know, the *E.R.B.* and the *Podkayne* are the only ships in existence that can reach Mars and land on it. One other pair is in the congressional funding stage. Winey talked to Earth and thinks there'll be a speedup in the preliminary paperwork and the thing'll start building in a year. The launch was scheduled for five years from now, but it might get as much as a year's boost. It's a rescue mission now, easier to sell. But the design will need modification, if only to include five more seats to bring us all back. You can bet on there being more modifications when we send in our report on the blowout. So we'd better add another six months to the schedule."

McKillian had had enough. "Matt, what the hell are you talking about? Rescue mission? Damn it, you know as well as I that if they find us here, we'll be long dead. We'll probably be dead in another year."

"That's where you're wrong. We'll survive."

"How?"

"I don't have the faintest idea." He looked her straight in the eye as he said this. She almost didn't bother to answer, but curiosity got the best of her.

"Is this just a morale session? Thanks, but I don't need it. I'd rather face the situation as it is. Or do you really have something?"

"Both. I don't have anything concrete except to say that we'll survive the same way humans have always survived: by staying warm, by eating, by drinking. To that list we have to add 'by breathing.' That's a hard one, but other than that, we're no different than any other group of survivors in a tough spot. I don't know what we'll have to do, specially, but I know we'll find the answers."

"Or die trying," Song said.

"Or die trying." He grinned at her. She at least had grasped the essence of the situation. Whether survival was possible or not, it was necessary to maintain the illusion that it was. Otherwise, you might as well cut your throat. You might as well not even be born, because life is an inevitably fatal struggle to survive.

"What about air?" McKillian asked, still unconvinced.

"I don't know," he told her cheerfully. "It's a tough problem, isn't it?"

"What about water?"

"Well, down in that valley there's a layer of permafrost about twenty meters down."

She laughed. "Wonderful. So that's what you want us to do? Dig down there and warm the ice with our pink little hands? It won't work, I tell you."

Crawford waited until she had run through a long list of reasons why they were doomed. Most of them made a great deal of sense. When she was through, he spoke softly.

"Lucy, listen to yourself."

"I'm just—"

"You're arguing on the side of death. Do you want to die? Are you so determined that you won't listen to someone who says you can live?"

She was quiet for a long time, then shuffled her feet awkwardly. She glanced at him, then at Song and Ralston. They were waiting, and she had to blush and smile slowly at them.

"You're right. What do we do first?"

"Just what we were doing. Taking stock of our situation. We need to make a list of what's available to us. We'll write it down on paper, but I can give you a general rundown." He counted off the points on his fingers.

"One, we have food for twenty people for three months. That comes to about a year for the five of us. With rationing, maybe a year and a half. That's assuming all the supply capsules reach us all right. In addition, the *Edgar* is going to clean the pantry to the bone and give us everything they can possibly spare and send it to us in the three spare capsules. That might come to two years or even three.

"Two, we have enough water to last us forever if the recyclers keep going. That'll be a problem, because our reactor will run out of power in two years. We'll need another power source, and maybe another water source.

"The oxygen problem is about the same. Two years at the outside. We'll have to find a way to conserve it a lot more than we're doing. Offhand, I don't know how. Song, do you have any ideas?"

She looked thoughtful, which produced two vertical punctuation marks between her slanted eyes.

"Possibly a culture of plants from the *Edgar*. If we could rig some way to grow plants in Martian sunlight and not have them killed by the ultraviolet . . ."

McKillian looked horrified, as any good ecologist would.

"What about contamination?" she asked. "What do you think that sterilization was for before we landed? Do you want to louse up the entire ecological balance of Mars? No one would ever be sure if samples in the future were real Martian plants or mutated Earth stock."

"What ecological balance?" Song shot back. "You know as well as I do that this trip has been nearly a zero. A few anaerobic bacteria, a patch of lichen, both barely distinguishable from Earth forms—"

"That's just what I mean. You import Earth forms now, and we'll never tell the difference."

"But it could be done, right? With the proper shielding so the plants won't be wiped out before they ever sprout, we could have a hydroponics plant functioning—"

"Oh, yes, it could be done. I can see three or four dodges right now. But you're not addressing the main question, which is—"

"Hold it," Crawford said. "I just wanted to know if you had any ideas." He was secretly pleased at the argument; it got them both thinking along the right lines, moved them from the deadly apathy they must guard against.

"I think this discussion has served its purpose, which was to convince everyone here that survival is possible." He glanced uneasily at Lang, still nodding, her eyes glassy as she saw her teammates die before her eyes.

"I just want to point out that instead of an expedition, we are now a colony. Not in the usual sense of planning to stay here forever, but all our planning will have to be geared to that fiction. What we're faced with is not a simple matter of stretching supplies until rescue comes. Stopgap measures are not likely to do us much good. The answers that will save us are the long-term ones, the sort of answers a colony would be looking for. About two years from now we're going to have to be in a position to survive with some sort of life-style that could support us forever. We'll have to fit into this environment where we can and adapt it to us where we can. For that, we're better off than most of the colonists of the past, at least for the short term. We have a large supply of everything a colony needs: food, water, tools, raw materials, energy, brains, and women. Without these things, no colony has much of a chance. All we lack is a regular resupply from the home country, but a really good group of colonists can get along without that. What do you say? Are you all with me?"

Something had caused Mary Lang's eyes to look up. It was a reflex by now, a survival reflex conditioned by a lifetime of fighting her way to the top. It took root in her again and pulled her erect on the bed, then to her feet. She fought off the effects of the drug and stood there, eyes bleary but aware.

"What makes you think that women are a natural resource, Crawford?" she said, slowly and deliberately.

"Why, what I meant was that without the morale uplift provided by members of the opposite sex, a colony will lack the push needed to make it."

"That's what you meant, all right. And you meant women, available to the *real* colonists as a reason to live. I've heard it before. That's a male-oriented way to look at it, Crawford." She was regaining her stature as they watched, seeming to grow until she dominated the group with the intangible power that marks a leader. She took a deep breath and came fully awake for the first time that day.

"We'll stop that sort of thinking right now. I'm the mission commander. I appreciate your taking over while I was . . . how did you say it? Indisposed. But you should pay more attention to the social aspects of our situation. If anyone is a commodity here, it's you and Ralston, by virtue of your scarcity. There will be some thorny questions to resolve there, but for the meantime we will function as a unit, under my command. We'll do all we can to minimize social competition among the women for the men. That's the way it must be. Clear?"

She was answered by quiet assent and nods of the head. She did not acknowledge it but plowed right on.

"I wondered from the start why you were along, Crawford." She was pacing slowly back and forth in the crowded space. The others got out of her way almost without thinking, except for Ralston, who still huddled under his blanket. "A historian? Sure, it's a fine idea, but pretty impractical. I have to admit that I've been thinking of you as a luxury, and about as useful as the nipples on a man's chest. But I was wrong. All the NASA people were wrong. The Astronaut Corps fought like crazy to keep you off this trip. Time enough for that on later flights. We were blinded by our loyalty to the test-pilot philosophy of space flight. We wanted as few scientists as possible and as many astronauts as we could manage. We don't like to think of ourselves as ferryboat pilots. I think we demonstrated during Apollo that we could handle science jobs as well as anyone. We saw you as a kind of insult, a slap in the face by the scientists in Houston to show us how low our stock has fallen."

"If I might be able to—"

"Shut up. But we were wrong. I read in your résumé that you were quite a student of survival. What's your honest assessment of our chances?"

Crawford shrugged, uneasy at the question. He didn't know if it was the right time to even postulate that they might fail.

"Tell me the truth."

"Pretty slim. Mostly the air problem. The people I've read about never sank so low that they had to worry about where their next breath was coming from."

"Have you ever heard of Apollo 13?"

He smiled at her. "Special circumstances. Short-term problems."

"You're right, of course. And in the only two other real space emergencies since that time, all hands were lost." She turned and scowled at each of them in turn.

"But we're *not* going to lose." She dared any of them to disagree, and no one was about to. She relaxed and resumed her stroll around the room. She turned to Crawford again.

"I can see I'll be drawing on your knowledge a lot in the years to come. What do you see as the next order of business?"

Crawford relaxed. The awful burden of responsibility, which he had never wanted, was gone. He was content to follow her lead.

"To tell you the truth, I was wondering what to say next. We have to make a thorough inventory. I guess we should start on that."

"That's fine, but there is an even more important order of business. We have to go out to the dome and find out what the hell caused the blowout. The damn thing should *not* have blown; it's the first of its type to do so. And from the *bottom*. But it did blow, and we should know why, or we're ignoring a fact about Mars that might still kill us. Let's do that first. Ralston, can you walk?"

When he nodded, she sealed her helmet and started into the lock. She turned and looked speculatively at Crawford.

"I swear, man, if you had touched me with a cattle prod you couldn't have got a bigger rise out of me than you did with what you said a few minutes ago. Do I dare ask?"

Crawford was not about to answer. He said, with a perfectly straight face, "Me? Maybe you should just assume I'm a chauvinist."

"We'll see, won't we?"

◆

"What is that stuff?"

Song Sue Lee was on her knees, examining one of the hundreds of short, stiff spikes extruding from the ground. She tried to scratch her head but was frustrated by her helmet.

"It looks like plastic. But I have a strong feeling it's the higher life-form Lucy and I were looking for yesterday."

"And you're telling me those little spikes are what poked holes in the dome bottom? I'm not buying that."

Song straightened up, moving stiffly. They had all worked hard to empty out the collapsed dome and peel back the whole, bulky mess to reveal the ground it had covered. She was tired and stepped out of character for a moment to snap at Mary Lang.

"I didn't tell you that. We pulled the dome back and found spikes. It was your inference that they poked holes in the bottom."

"I'm sorry," Lang said quietly. "Go on with what you were saying."

"Well," Song admitted, "it wasn't a bad inference, at that. But the holes I saw were not punched through. They were eaten away." She waited for Lang to protest that the dome bottom was about as chemically inert as any plastic yet devised. But Lang had learned her lesson. And she had a talent for facing facts.

"So. We have a thing here that eats plastic. And seems to be made of plastic, into the bargain. Any ideas why it picked this particular spot to grow, and no other?"

"I have an idea on that," McKillian said. "I've had it in mind to do some studies around the dome to see if the altered moisture content we've been creating here had any effect on the spores in the soil. See, we've been here nine days, spouting out water vapor, carbon dioxide, and quite a bit of oxygen into the atmosphere. Not much, but maybe more than it seems, considering the low concentrations that are naturally available. We've altered the biome. Does anyone know where the exhaust air from the dome was expelled?"

Lang raised her eyebrows. "Yes, it was under the dome. The air we exhausted was warm, you see, and it was thought it could be put to use one last time before we let it go, to warm the floor of the dome and decrease heat loss."

"And the water vapor collected on the underside of the dome when it hit the cold air. Right. Do you get the picture?"

"I think so," Lang said. "It was so little water, though. You know we didn't want to waste it; we condensed it out until the air we exhausted was dry as a bone."

"For Earth, maybe. Here it was a torrential rainfall. It reached seeds or spores in the ground and triggered them to start growing. We're going to have to watch it when we use anything containing plastic. What does that include?"

Lang groaned. "All the airlock seals, for one thing." There were grimaces from all of them at the thought of that. "For another, a good part of our suits. Song, watch it, don't step on that thing. We don't know how powerful it is or if it'll eat the plastic in your boots, but we'd better play it safe. How about it, Ralston? Think you can find out how bad it is?"

"You mean identify the solvent these things use? Probably, if we can get some sort of workspace and I can get to my equipment."

"Mary," McKillian said, "it occurs to me that I'd better start looking for airborne spores. If there are some, it could mean that the airlock on the *Podkayne* is vulnerable. Even thirty meters off the ground."

"Right. Get on that. Since we're sleeping in it until we can find out what we can do on the ground, we'd best be sure it's safe. Meantime, we'll all sleep in our suits." There were helpless groans at this, but no protests. McKillian and Ralston headed for the pile of salvaged equipment, hoping to rescue enough to get started on their analyses. Song knelt again and started digging around one of the ten-centimeter spikes.

Crawford followed Lang back toward the *Podkayne*.

"Mary, I wanted . . . is it all right if I call you Mary?"

"I guess so. I don't think 'Commander Lang' would wear well over five years. But you'd better still think commander."

He considered it. "All right, Commander Mary." She punched him playfully. She had barely known him before the disaster. He had been a name on a roster and a sore spot in the estimation of the Astronaut Corps. But she had borne him no personal malice and now found herself beginning to like him.

"What's on your mind?"

"Ah, several things. But maybe it isn't my place to bring them up now. First, I want to say that if you're . . . ah, concerned, or doubtful of my support or loyalty because I took over command for a while . . . earlier today, well . . ."

"Well?"

"I just wanted to tell you that I have no ambitions in that direction," he finished lamely.

She patted him on the back. "Sure, I know. You forget, I read your dossier. It mentioned several interesting episodes that I'd like you to tell me about someday, from your 'soldier-of-fortune' days—"

"Hell, those were grossly overblown. I just happened to get into some scrapes and managed to get out of them."

"Still, it got you picked for this mission out of hundreds of applicants. The thinking was that you'd be a wild card, a man of action with proven survivability. Maybe it worked out. But the other thing I remember on your card was that you're not a leader. No, that you're a loner who'll cooperate with a group and be no discipline problem, but you work better alone. Want to strike out on your own?"

He smiled at her. "No, thanks. But what you said is right. I have no hankering to take charge of anything. But I do have some knowledge that might prove useful."

"And we'll use it. You just speak up, I'll be listening." She started to say something, then thought of something else. "Say, what are your ideas on a woman bossing this project? I've had to fight that all the way from my Air Force days. So if you have any objections you might as well tell me up front."

He was genuinely surprised. "You didn't take that crack seriously, did you? I might as well admit it. It was intentional, like that cattle prod you mentioned. You looked like you needed a kick in the ass."

"And thank you. But you didn't answer my question."

"Those who lead, lead," he said, simply. "I'll follow you as long as you keep leading."

"As long as it's in the direction you want?" She laughed and poked him in the ribs. "I see you as my Grand Vizier, the man who holds the arcane knowledge and advises the regent. I think I'll have to watch out for you. I know a little history, myself."

Crawford couldn't tell how serious she was. He shrugged it off.

"What I really wanted to talk to you about is this: You said you couldn't fly this ship. But you were not yourself, you were depressed and feeling hopeless. Does that still stand?"

"It stands. Come on up and I'll show you why."

In the pilot's cabin, Crawford was ready to believe her. Like all flying machines since the days of the windsock and open cockpit, this one was a mad confusion of dials, switches, and lights designed to awe anyone who knew nothing about it. He sat in the copilot's chair and listened to her.

"We had a backup pilot, of course. You may be surprised to learn that it wasn't me. It was Dorothy Cantrell, and she's dead. Now I know what everything does on this board, and I can cope with most of it easily. What I don't know, I could learn. Some of the systems are computer driven; give it the right program and it'll fly itself in space." She looked longingly at the controls, and Crawford realized that, like Weinstein, she didn't relish giving up the fun of flying to boss a gang of explorers. She was a former test pilot, and above all things she loved flying. She patted an array of hand controls on her right side. There were more like them on the left.

"This is what would kill us, Crawford. What's your first name? Matt. Matt, this baby is a flyer for the first forty thousand meters. It doesn't have the juice to orbit on the jets alone. The wings are folded up now. You probably didn't see them on the way in, but you saw the models. They're very light, supercritical, and designed for this atmosphere. Lou said it was like flying a bathtub, but it flew. And it's a *skill*, almost an art. Lou practiced for three years on the best simulators we could build and still had to rely on things you can't learn in a simulator. And he barely got us down in one piece. We didn't noise it around, but it was a *damn* close thing. Lou was young; so was Cantrell. They were both fresh from flying. They flew every day, they had the *feel* for it. They were tops." She slumped back into her chair. "I haven't flown anything but trainers for eight years."

Crawford didn't know if he should let it drop.

"But you were one of the best, everyone knows that. You still don't think you could do it?"

She threw up her hands. "How can I make you understand? This is nothing like anything I've ever flown. You might as well . . ." She groped for a comparison, trying to coax it out with gestures in the air. "Listen. Does the fact that someone can fly a biplane, maybe even be the best goddamn biplane pilot that ever was, does that mean they're qualified to fly a helicopter?"

"I don't know."

"It doesn't. Believe me."

"All right. But the fact remains that you're the closest thing on Mars to a pilot for the *Podkayne*. I think you should consider that when you're deciding what we should do." He shut up, afraid to sound like he was pushing her.

She narrowed her eyes and gazed at nothing.

"I have thought about it." She waited for a long time. "I think the chances are about a thousand to one against us if I try to fly it. But I'll do it, if we come to that. And that's *your* job. Showing me some better odds. If you can't, let me know."

⊸

Three weeks later, the Tharsis Canyon had been transformed into a child's garden of toys. Crawford had thought of no better way to describe it. Each of the plastic spikes had blossomed into a fanciful windmill, no two of them just alike. There were tiny ones, with the vanes parallel to the ground and no more than ten centimeters tall. There were derricks of spidery plastic struts that would not have looked too out of place on a Kansas farm. Some of them were five meters high. They came in all colors and many configurations, but all had vanes covered with a transparent film like cellophane, and all were spinning into colorful blurs in the stiff Martian breeze. Crawford thought of an industrial park built by gnomes. He could almost see them trudging through the spinning wheels.

Song had taken one apart as well as she could. She was still shaking her head in disbelief. She had not been able to excavate the long insulated taproot, but she could infer how deep it went. It extended all the way to the layer of permafrost, twenty meters down.

The ground between the windmills was coated in shimmering plastic. This was the second part of the plants' ingenious solution to survival on Mars. The windmills utilized the energy in the wind, and the plastic coating on the ground was in reality two thin sheets of plastic with a space between for water to circulate. The water was heated by the sun then pumped down to the permafrost, melting a little more of it each time.

"There's still something missing from our picture," Song had told them the night before, when she delivered her summary of what she had learned. "Marty hasn't been able to find a mechanism that would permit these things to grow by ingesting sand and rock and turning it into plasticlike materials. So we assume there is a reservoir of something like crude oil down there, maybe frozen in with the water."

"Where would that have come from?" Lang had asked.

"You've heard of the long-period Martian seasonal theories? Well, part of it is more than a theory. The combination of the Martian polar inclination, the precessional cycle, and the eccentricity of the orbit produces seasons that are about twelve thousand years long. We're in the middle of winter, though we landed in the nominal 'summer.' It's been theorized that if there were any Martian life it would have adapted to these longer cycles. It hibernates in spores during the cold cycle, when the water and carbon dioxide freeze out at the poles, then comes out when enough ice melts to permit biological processes. We seem to have fooled these plants; they thought summer was here when the water vapor content went up around the camp."

"So what about the crude?" Ralston asked. He didn't completely believe that part of the model they had evolved. He was a laboratory chemist, specializing in inorganic compounds. The way these plants produced plastics without high heat, through purely catalytic interactions, had him confused and defensive. He wished the crazy windmills would go away.

"I think I can answer that," McKillian said. "These organisms barely scrape by in the best of times. The ones that have made it waste nothing. It stands to reason that any really ancient deposits of crude oil would have been exhausted in only a few of these cycles. So it must be that what we're thinking of as crude oil must be something a little different. It has to be the remains of the last generation."

"But how did the remains get so far below ground?" Ralston asked. "You'd expect them to be high up. The winds couldn't bury them that deep in only twelve thousand years."

"You're right," said McKillian. "I don't really know. But I have a theory. Since these plants waste nothing, why not conserve their bodies when they die? They sprouted from the ground; isn't it possible they could withdraw when things start to get tough again? They'd leave spores behind them as they retreated, distributing them all through the soil. That way, if the upper ones blew away or were sterilized by the ultraviolet, the ones just below them would still thrive when the right conditions returned. When they reached the permafrost, they'd decompose into this organic slush we've postulated, and . . . well, it does get a little involved, doesn't it?"

"Sounds all right to me," Lang assured her. "It'll do for a working theory. Now what about airborne spores?"

It turned out that they were safe from that imagined danger. There were spores in the air now, but they were not dangerous to the colonists. The plants attacked only certain kinds of plastics, and then only in certain stages of their lives. Since they were still changing, it bore watching, but the airlocks and suits were secure. The crew was enjoying the luxury of sleeping without their suits.

And there was much work to do. Most of the physical sort devolved on Crawford and, to some extent, on Lang. It threw them together a lot. The other three had to be free to pursue their researches, as it had been decided that only in knowing their environment would they stand a chance.

The two of them had managed to salvage most of the dome. Working with patching kits and lasers to cut the tough material, they had constructed a much smaller dome. They erected it on an outcropping of bare rock, rearranged the exhaust to prevent more condensation on the underside, and added more safety features. They now slept in a pressurized building inside the dome, and one of them stayed awake on watch at all times. In drills, they had come from a deep sleep to full pressure-integrity in thirty seconds. They were not going to get caught again.

Crawford looked away from the madly whirling rotors of the windmill farm. He was with the rest of the crew, sitting in the dome with his helmet off. That was as far as Lang would permit anyone to go except in the cramped sleeping quarters. Song Sue Lee was at the radio giving her report to the *Edgar Rice Burroughs*. In her hand was one of the pump modules she had dissected out of one of the plants. It consisted of a half-meter set of eight blades that turned freely on Teflon bearings. Below it were various tiny gears and the pump itself. She twirled it idly as she spoke.

"I don't really get it," Crawford admitted, talking quietly to Lucy McKillian. "What's so revolutionary about little windmills?"

"It's just a whole new area," McKillian whispered back. "Think about it. Back on Earth, nature never got around to inventing the wheel. I've sometimes wondered why not. There are limitations, of course, but it's such a good idea. Just look what *we've* done with it. But all motion in nature is confined to up and down, back and forth, in and out, or squeeze and relax. Nothing on Earth goes round and round, unless we built it. Think about it."

Crawford did, and began to see the novelty of it. He tried in vain to think of some mechanism in an animal or plant of earthly origin that turned and kept on turning forever. He could not.

Song finished her report and handed the mike to Lang. Before she could start, Weinstein came on the line.

"We've had a change in plan up here," he said, with no preface. "I hope this doesn't come as a shock. If you think about it, you'll see the logic in it. We're going back to Earth in seven days."

It didn't surprise them too much. The *Burroughs* had given them just about everything it could in the form of data and supplies. There was one more capsule load due; after that, its presence would only be a frustration to both groups. There was a great deal of irony in having two such powerful ships so close to each other and being so helpless to do anything concrete. It was telling on the crew of the *Burroughs*.

"We've recalculated everything based on the lower mass without the twenty of you and the six tons of samples we were allowing for. By using the fuel we would have ferried down to you for takeoff, we can make a faster orbit down toward Venus. The departure date for that orbit is seven days away. We'll rendezvous with a drone capsule full of supplies we hadn't counted on." And besides, Lang thought to herself, it's much more dramatic. *Plunging sunward on the chancy cometary orbit, their pantries stripped bare, heading for the fateful rendezvous. . . .*

"I'd like your comments," he went on. "This isn't absolutely final as yet."

They all looked at Lang. They were reassured to find her calm and unshaken.

"I think it's the best idea. One thing: you've given up on any thoughts of me flying the *Podkayne*?"

"No insult intended, Mary," Weinstein said, gently. "But, yes, we have. It's the opinion of the people Earthside that you couldn't do it. They've tried some experiments, coaching some very good pilots and putting them into the simulators. They can't do it, and we don't think you could, either."

"No need to sugarcoat it. I know it as well as anyone. But even a billion to one shot is better than nothing. I take it they think Crawford is right, that survival is at least theoretically possible?"

There was a long hesitation. "I guess that's correct. Mary, I'll be frank. I don't think it's possible. I hope I'm wrong, but I don't expect . . ."

"Thank you, Winey, for the encouraging words. You always did know what it takes to buck a person up. By the way, that other mission, the one where you were going to ride a meteorite down here to save our asses, that's scrubbed, too?"

The assembled crew smiled, and Song gave a high-pitched cheer. Weinstein was not the most popular man on Mars.

"Mary, I told you about that already," he complained. It was a gentle complaint, and, even more significant, he had not objected to the use of his nickname. He was being gentle with the condemned. "We worked on it around the clock. I even managed to get permission to turn over command temporarily. But the mock-ups they made Earthside didn't survive the re-entry. It was the best we could do. I couldn't risk the entire mission on a configuration the people back on Earth wouldn't certify."

"I know. I'll call you back tomorrow." She switched the set off and sat back on her heels. "I swear, if the Earthside tests on a roll of toilet paper didn't . . . he wouldn't . . ." She cut the air with her hands. "What am I saying? That's petty. I don't like him, but he's right." She stood up, puffing out her cheeks as she exhaled a pent-up breath.

"Come on, crew, we've got a lot of work."

☙

They named their colony New Amsterdam, because of the windmills. The name of whirligig was the one that stuck on the Martian plants, though Crawford held out for a long time in favor of spinnakers.

They worked all day and tried their best to ignore the *Burroughs* overhead. The messages back and forth were short and to the point. Helpless as the mother ship was to render them more air, they knew they would miss it when it was gone. So the day of departure was a stiff, determinedly nonchalant affair. They all made a big show of going to bed hours before the scheduled breakaway.

When he was sure the others were asleep, Crawford opened his eyes and looked around the darkened barracks. It wasn't much in the way of a home; they were crowded against each other on rough pads made of insulating material. The toilet facilities were behind a flimsy barrier against one wall, and smelled. But none of them would have wanted to sleep outside in the dome, even if Lang had allowed it.

The only light came from the illuminated dials that the guard was supposed to watch all night. There was no one sitting in front of them. Crawford assumed the guard had gone to sleep. He would have been upset, but there was no time. He had to suit up, and he welcomed the chance to sneak out. He began to furtively don his pressure suit.

As a historian, he felt he could not let such a moment slip by unobserved. Silly, but there it was. He had to be out there, watch it with his own eyes. It didn't matter if he never lived to tell about it, he must record it.

Someone sat up beside him. He froze, but it was too late. She rubbed her eyes and peered into the darkness.

"Matt?" she yawned. "What's . . . what is it? Is something—"

"Shh. I'm going out. Go back to sleep, Song."

"Um hmmm." She stretched, dug her knuckles fiercely into her eyes and smoothed her hair back from her face. She was dressed in a loose-fitting bottom of a ship suit, a gray piece of dirty cloth that badly needed washing, as did all their clothes. For a moment, as he watched her shadow stretch and stand up, he wasn't interested in the *Burroughs*. He forced his mind away from her.

"I'm going with you," she whispered.

"All right. Don't wake the others."

Standing just outside the airlock was Mary Lang. She turned as they came out, and did not seem surprised.

"Were you the one on duty?" Crawford asked her.

"Yeah. I broke my own rule. But so did you two. Consider yourselves on report." She laughed and beckoned them over to her. They linked arms and stood staring up at the sky.

"How much longer?" Song asked, after some time had passed.

"Just a few minutes. Hold tight." Crawford looked over to Lang and thought he saw tears, but he couldn't be sure in the dark.

There was a tiny new star, brighter than all the rest, brighter than Phobos. It hurt to look at it but none of them looked away. It was the fusion drive of the *Edgar Rice Burroughs*, heading sunward, away from the long winter on Mars. It stayed on for long minutes, then sputtered and was lost. Though it was warm in the dome, Crawford was shivering. It was ten minutes before any of them felt like facing the barracks.

They crowded into the airlock, carefully not looking at each other's faces as they waited for the automatic machinery. The inner door opened and Lang pushed forward—and right back into the airlock. Crawford had a glimpse of Ralston and Lucy McKillian; then Mary shut the door.

"Some people have no poetry in their souls," Mary said.

"Or too much," Song giggled.

"You people want to take a walk around the dome with me? Maybe we could discuss ways of giving people a little privacy."

The inner lock door was pulled open, and there was McKillian, squinting into the bare bulb that lighted the lock while she held her shirt in front of her with one hand.

"Come on in," she said, stepping back. "We might as well talk about this." They entered, and McKillian turned on the light and sat down on her mattress. Ralston was blinking, nervously tucked into his pile of blankets. Since the day of the blowout he never seemed to be warm enough.

Having called for a discussion, McKillian proceeded to clam up. Song and Crawford sat on their bunks, and eventually as the silence stretched tighter, they all found themselves looking to Lang.

She started stripping out of her suit. "Well, I guess that takes care of that. So glad to hear all your comments. Lucy, if you were expecting some sort of reprimand, forget it. We'll take steps first thing in the morning to provide some sort of privacy for that, but, no matter what, we'll all be pretty close in the years to come. I think we should all relax. Any objections?" She was half out of her suit when she paused to scan them for comments. There were none. She stripped to her skin and reached for the light.

"In a way it's about time," she said, tossing her clothes in a corner. "The only thing to do with these clothes is burn them. We'll all smell better for it. Song, you take the watch." She flicked out the lights and reclined heavily on her mattress.

There was much rustling and squirming for the next few minutes as they got out of their clothes. Song brushed against Crawford in the dark and they murmured apologies. Then they all bedded down in their own bunks. It was several tense, miserable hours before anyone got to sleep.

◆

The week following the departure of the *Burroughs* was one of hysterical overreaction by the New Amsterdamites. The atmosphere was forced and false; an eat-drink-and-be-merry feeling pervaded everything they did.

They built a separate shelter inside the dome, not really talking aloud about what it was for. But it did not lack for use. Productive work suffered as the five of them frantically ran through all the possible permutations of three women and two men. Animosities developed, flourished for a few hours, and dissolved in tearful reconciliations. Three ganged up on two, two on one, one declared war on all the other four. Ralston and Song announced an engagement, which lasted ten hours. Crawford nearly came to blows with Lang, aided by McKillian. McKillian renounced men forever and had a brief, tempestuous affair with Song. Then Song discovered McKillian with Ralston, and Crawford caught her on the rebound, only to be thrown over for Ralston.

Mary Lang let it work itself out, only interfering when it got violent. She herself was not immune to the frenzy but managed to stay aloof from most of it. She went to the shelter with whoever asked her, trying not to play favorites, and gently tried to prod them back to work. As she told McKillian toward the first of the week, "At least we're getting to know one another."

Things did settle down, as Lang had known they would. They entered their second week alone in virtually the same position they had started: no romantic entanglements firmly established. But they knew each other a lot better, were relaxed in the close company of each other, and were supported by a new framework of interlocking friendships. They were much closer to being a team. Rivalries never died out completely, but they no longer dominated the colony. Lang worked them harder than ever, making up for the lost time.

Crawford missed most of the interesting work, being more suited for the semiskilled manual labor that never seemed to be finished. So he and Lang had to learn about the new discoveries at the nightly briefings in the shelter. He remembered nothing about any animal life being discovered, and so when he saw something crawling through the whirligig garden, he dropped everything and started over to it.

At the edge of the garden he stopped, remembering the order from Lang to stay out unless collecting samples. He watched the thing—bug? turtle?—for a moment, satisfied himself that it wouldn't get too far away at its creeping pace, and hurried off to find Song.

"You've got to name it after me," he said as they hurried back to the garden. "That's my right, isn't it, as the discoverer?"

"Sure," Song said, peering along his pointed finger. "Just show me the damn thing and I'll immortalize you."

The thing was twenty centimeters long, almost round, and dome-shaped. It had a hard shell on top.

"I don't know quite what to do with it," Song admitted. "If it's the only one, I don't dare dissect it, and maybe I shouldn't even touch it."

"Don't worry, there's another over behind you." Now that they were looking for them, they quickly spied four of the creatures. Song took a sample bag from her pouch and held it open in front of the beast. It crawled halfway into the bag, then seemed to think something was wrong. It stopped, but Song nudged it in and picked it up. She peered at the underside and laughed in wonder.

"Wheels," she said. "The thing runs on wheels."

❧

"I don't know where it came from," Song told the group that night. "I don't even quite believe in it. It'd make a nice educational toy for a child, though. I took it apart into twenty or thirty pieces, put it back together, and it still runs. It has a high-impact polystyrene carapace, nontoxic paint on the outside—"

"Not really polystyrene," Ralston interjected.

"—and I guess if you kept changing the batteries it would run forever. And it's *nearly* polystyrene, that's what you said."

"Were you serious about the batteries?" Lang asked.

"I'm not sure. Marty thinks there's a chemical metabolism in the upper part of the shell, which I haven't explored yet. But I can't really say if it's alive in the sense we use. I mean, it runs on *wheels!* It has three wheels, suited for sand, and something that's a cross between a rubber-band drive and a mainspring. Energy is stored in a coiled muscle and released slowly. I don't think it could travel more than a hundred meters. Unless it can re-coil the muscle, and I can't tell how that might be done."

"It sounds very specialized," McKillian said thoughtfully. "Maybe we should be looking for the niche it occupies. The way you describe it, it couldn't function without help from a symbiote. Maybe it fertilizes the plants, like bees, and the plants either donate or are robbed of the power to wind the spring. Did you look for some mechanism the bug could use to steal energy from the rotating gears in the whirligigs?"

"That's what I want to do in the morning," Song said. "Unless Mary will let us take a look tonight?" She said it hopefully, but without real expectation. Mary Lang shook her head decisively.

"It'll keep. It's *cold* out there, baby."

●

A new exploration of the whirligig garden the next day revealed several new species, including one more thing that might be an animal. It was a flying creature, the size of a fruit fly, that managed to glide from plant to plant when the wind was down by means of a freely rotating set of blades, like an autogiro.

Crawford and Lang hung around as the scientists looked things over. They were not anxious to get back to the task that had occupied them for the last two weeks: that of bringing the *Podkayne* to a horizontal position without wrecking her. The ship had been rigged with stabilizing cables soon after landing, and provision had been made in the plans to lay the ship on its side in the event of a really big windstorm. But the plans had envisioned a work force of twenty, working all day with a maze of pulleys and gears. It was slow work and could not be rushed. If the ship were to tumble and lose pressure, they didn't have a prayer.

So they welcomed an opportunity to tour fairyland. The place was even more bountiful than the last time Crawford had taken a look. There were thick vines that Song assured him were running with water, both hot and cold, and various other fluids. There were more of the tall variety of derrick, making the place look like a pastel oilfield.

They had little trouble finding where the "matthews" came from. They found dozens of twenty-centimeter lumps on the sides of the large derricks. They evidently grew from them like tumors and were released when they were ripe. What they were for was another matter. As well as they could discover, the matthews simply crawled in a straight line until their power ran out. If they were wound up again, they would crawl farther. There were dozens of them lying motionless in the sand within a hundred-meter radius of the garden.

Two weeks of research left them knowing no more. They had to abandon the matthews for the time, as another enigma had cropped up which demanded their attention.

This time Crawford was the last to know. He was called on the radio and found the group all squatted in a circle around a growth in the grave-yard.

The graveyard, where they had buried their fifteen dead crewmates on the first day of the disaster, had sprouted with life during the week after the departure of the *Burroughs*. It was separated from the original site of the dome by three hundred meters of blowing sand. So McKillian assumed this second bloom was caused by the water in the bodies of the dead. What they couldn't figure out was why this patch should differ so radically from the first one.

There were whirligigs in the second patch, but they lacked the variety and disorder of the originals. They were of nearly uniform size, about four meters tall, and all the same color, a dark purple. They had pumped water for two weeks, then stopped. When Song examined them, she re-ported the bearings were frozen, dried out. They seemed to have lost the plasticizer that kept the structures fluid and living. The water in the pipes was frozen. Though she would not commit herself in the matter, she felt they were dead. In their place was a second network of pipes which wound around the derricks and spread transparent sheets of film to the sunlight, heating the water which circulated through them. The water was being pumped, but not by the now-familiar system of windmills. Spaced along each of the pipes were expansion-contraction pumps with valves very like those in a human heart.

The new marvel was a simple affair in the middle of that living pet-rochemical complex. It was a short plant that sprouted up half a meter, then extruded two stalks parallel to the ground. At the end of each stalk was a perfect globe, one gray, one blue. The blue one was much larger than the gray one.

Crawford looked at it briefly, then squatted down beside the rest, won-dering what all the fuss was about. Everyone looked very solemn, almost scared.

"You called me over to see this?"

Lang looked over at him, and something in her face made him nervous.

"Look at it, Matt. Really look at it." So he did, feeling foolish, won-dering what the joke was. He noticed a white patch near the top of the larger globe. It was streaked, like a glass marble with swirls of opaque material in it. It looked very familiar, he realized, with the hair on the back of his neck starting to stand up.

"It turns," Lang said quietly. "That's why Song noticed it. She came by here one day and it was in a different position than it had been."

"Let me guess," he said, much more calmly than he felt. "The little one goes around the big one, right?"

"Right. And the little one keeps one face turned to the big one. The big one rotates once in twenty-four hours. It has an axial tilt of twenty-three degrees."

"It's a . . . what's the word? Orrery. It's an orrery." Crawford had to stand up and shake his head to clear it.

"It's funny," Lang said, quietly. "I always thought it would be something flashy, or at least obvious. An alien artifact mixed in with caveman bones, or a spaceship entering the system. I guess I was thinking in terms of pottery shards and atom bombs."

"Well, that all sounds pretty ho-hum to me up against *this*," Song said. "Do you . . . do you *realize* . . . what are we talking about here? Evolution, or . . . or engineering? Is it the plants themselves that did this, or were they made to do it by whatever built them? Do you see what I'm talking about? I felt funny about those wheels for a long time. I just won't believe they'd evolve naturally."

"What do you mean?"

"I mean I think these plants we've been seeing were designed to be the way they are. They're *too* perfectly adapted, *too* ingenious to have just sprung up in response to the environment." Her eyes seemed to wander, and she stood up and gazed into the valley below them. It was as barren as anything that could be imagined: red and yellow and brown rock outcroppings and tumbled boulders. And in the foreground, the twirling colors of the whirligigs.

"But why this thing?" Crawford asked, pointing to the impossible artifact-plant. "Why a model of the Earth and Moon? And why right here, in the graveyard?"

"Because we were expected," Song said, still looking away from them. "They must have watched the Earth, during the last summer season. I don't know; maybe they even went there. If they did, they would have found men and women like us, hunting and living in caves. Building fires, using clubs, chipping arrowheads. You know more about it than I do, Matt."

"Who are *they*?" Ralston asked. "You think we're going to be meeting some Martians? People? I don't see how. I don't believe it."

"I'm afraid I'm skeptical, too," Lang said. "Surely there must be some other way to explain it."

"No! There's no other way. Oh, not people like us, maybe. Maybe we're seeing them right now, spinning like crazy." They all looked uneasily at the whirligigs. "But I think they're not here yet. I think we're going to see, over the next few years, increasing complexity in these plants and animals as they build up a biome here and get ready for the builders. Think about it. When summer comes, the conditions will be very different. The atmosphere will be almost as dense as ours, with about the same partial pressure of oxygen. By then, thousands of years from now, these early forms will have vanished. These things are adapted for low pressure, no oxygen, scarce water. The later ones will be adapted to an environment much like ours. And *that*'s when we'll see the makers, when the stage is properly set." She sounded almost religious when she said it.

Lang stood up and shook Song's shoulder. Song came slowly back to them and sat down, still blinded by a private vision. Crawford had a glimpse of it himself, and it scared him. And a glimpse of something else, something that could be important but kept eluding him.

"Don't you see?" she went on, calmer now. "It's too pat, too much of a coincidence. This thing is like a . . . a headstone, a monument. It's growing right here in the graveyard, from the bodies of our friends. Can you believe in that as just a coincidence?"

Evidently no one could. But likewise, Crawford could see no reason why it should have happened the way it did.

It was painful to leave the mystery for later, but there was nothing to be done about it. They could not bring themselves to uproot the thing, even when five more like it sprouted in the graveyard. There was a new consensus among them to leave the Martian plants and animals alone. Like nervous atheists, most of them didn't believe Song's theories but had an uneasy feeling of trespassing when they went through the gardens. They felt subconsciously that it might be better to leave them alone in case they turned out to be private property.

And for six months, nothing really new cropped up among the whirligigs. Song was not surprised. She said it supported her theory that these plants were there only as caretakers to prepare the way for the less hardy, air-breathing varieties to come. They would warm the soil and bring the water closer to the surface, then disappear when their function was over.

The three scientists allowed their studies to slide as it became more important to provide for the needs of the moment. The dome material was weakening as the temporary patches lost strength, and so a new home was badly needed. They were dealing daily with slow leaks, any of which could become a major blowout.

The *Podkayne* was lowered to the ground, and sadly decommissioned. It was a bad day for Mary Lang, the worst since the day of the blowout. She saw it as a necessary but infamous thing to do to a proud flying machine. She brooded about it for a week, becoming short-tempered and almost unapproachable. Then she asked Crawford to join her in the private shelter. It was the first time she had asked any of the other four. They lay in each other's arms for an hour, and Lang quietly sobbed on his chest. Crawford was proud that she had chosen him for her companion when she could no longer maintain her tough, competent show of strength. In a way, it was a strong thing to do, to expose weakness to the one person among the four who might possibly be her rival for leadership. He did not betray the trust. In the end, she was comforting him.

After that day Lang was ruthless in gutting the old *Podkayne*. She supervised the ripping out of the motors to provide more living space, and only Crawford saw what it was costing her. They drained the fuel tanks and stored the fuel in every available container they could scrounge. It would be useful later for heating, and for recharging batteries. They managed to convert plastic packing crates into fuel containers by lining them with sheets of the double-walled material the whirligigs used to heat water. They were nervous at this vandalism, but had no other choice. They kept looking nervously at the graveyard as they ripped up meter-square sheets of it.

They ended up with a long cylindrical home, divided into two small sleeping rooms, a community room, and a laboratory-storehouse-workshop in the old fuel tank. Crawford and Lang spent the first night together in the "penthouse," the former cockpit, the only room with windows.

Lying there wide awake on the rough mattress, side by side in the warm air with Mary Lang, whose black leg was a crooked line of shadow lying across his body, looking up through the port at the sharp, unwinking stars—with nothing done yet about the problems of oxygen, food, and water for the years ahead and no assurance he would live out the night on a planet determined to kill him—Crawford realized he had never been happier in his life.

➤

On a day exactly eight months after the disaster, two discoveries were made. One was in the whirligig garden and concerned a new plant that was bearing what might be fruit. They were clusters of grape-sized white balls, very hard and fairly heavy. The second discovery was made by Lucy McKillian and concerned the absence of an event that up to that time had been as regular as the full moon.

"I'm pregnant," she announced to them that night, causing Song to delay her examination of the white fruit.

It was not unexpected; Lang had been waiting for it to happen since the night the *Burroughs* left. But she had not worried about it. Now she must decide what to do.

"I was afraid that might happen," Crawford said. "What do we do, Mary?"

"Why don't you tell me what you think? You're the survival expert. Are babies a plus or a minus in our situation?"

"I'm afraid I have to say they're a liability. Lucy will be needing extra food during her pregnancy, and afterward, and it will be an extra mouth to feed. We can't afford the strain on our resources." Lang said nothing, waiting to hear from McKillian.

"Now wait a minute. What about all this line about 'colonists' you've been feeding us ever since we got stranded here? Who ever heard of a colony without babies? If we don't grow, we stagnate, right? We *have* to have children." She looked back and forth from Lang to Crawford, her face expressing formless doubts.

"We're in special circumstances, Lucy," Crawford explained. "Sure, I'd be all for it if we were better off. But we can't be sure we can even provide for ourselves, much less a child. I say we can't afford children until we're established."

"Do you want the child, Lucy?" Lang asked quietly.

McKillian didn't seem to know what she wanted. "No. I . . . but, yes. Yes, I guess I do." She looked at them, pleading for them to understand.

"Look, I've never had one, and never planned to. I'm thirty-four years old and never, never felt the lack. I've always wanted to go places, and you can't with a baby. But I never planned to become a colonist on Mars, either. I . . . things have changed, don't you see? I've been depressed."

She looked around, and Song and Ralston were nodding sympathetically. Relieved to see that she was not the only one feeling the oppression, she went on, more strongly. "I think if I go another day like yesterday and the day before—and today—I'll end up screaming. It seems so pointless, collecting all that information, for what?"

"I agree with Lucy," Ralston said, surprisingly. Crawford had thought he would be the only one immune to the inevitable despair of the castaway. Ralston in his laboratory was the picture of carefree detachment, existing only to observe.

"So do I," Lang said, ending the discussion. But she explained her reasons to them.

"Look at it this way, Matt. No matter how we stretch our supplies, they won't take us through the next four years. We either find a way of getting what we need from what's around us, or we all die. And if we find a way to do it, then what does it matter how many of us there are? At the most, this will push our deadline a few weeks or a month closer, the day we have to be self-supporting."

"I hadn't thought of it that way," Crawford admitted.

"But that's not important. The important thing is what you said from the first, and I'm surprised you didn't see it. If we're a colony, we expand. By definition. Historian, what happened to colonies that failed to expand?"

"Don't rub it in."

"They died out. I know that much. People, we're not intrepid space explorers anymore. We're not the career men and women we set out to be. Like it or not, and I suggest we start liking it, we're pioneers trying to live in a hostile environment. The odds are very much against us, and we're not going to be here forever, but like Matt said, we'd better plan as if we were. Comment?"

There was none, until Song spoke up, thoughtfully.

"I think a baby around here would be fun. Two should be twice as much fun. I think I'll start. Come on, Marty."

"Hold on, honey," Lang said, dryly. "If you conceive now, I'll be forced to order you to abort. We have the chemicals for it, you know."

"That's discrimination."

"Maybe so. But just because we're colonists doesn't mean we have to behave like rabbits. A pregnant woman will have to be removed from the work force at the end of her term, and we can only afford one at a time. After Lucy has hers, then come ask me again. But watch Lucy carefully, dear. Have you really thought what it's going to take? Have you tried to visualize her getting into her pressure suit in six or seven months?"

From their expressions, it was plain that neither Song nor McKillian had thought of it.

"Right," Lang went on. "It'll be literal confinement for her, right here in the *Poddy*. Unless we can rig something for her, which I seriously doubt. Still want to go through with it, Lucy?"

"Can I have a while to think it over?"

"Sure. You have about two months. After that, the chemicals aren't safe."

"I'd advise you to do it," Crawford said. "I know my opinion means nothing after shooting my mouth off. I know I'm a fine one to talk; I won't be cooped up in here. But the colony needs it. We've all felt it: the lack of a direction or a drive to keep going. I think we'd get it back if you went through with this."

McKillian tapped her teeth thoughtfully with the tip of a finger.

"You're right," she said. "Your opinion *doesn't* mean anything." She slapped his knee delightedly when she saw him blush. "I think it's yours, by the way. And I think I'll go ahead and have it."

☙

The penthouse seemed to have gone to Lang and Crawford as an unasked-for prerogative. It just became a habit, since they seemed to have developed a bond between them and none of the other three complained. Neither of the other women seemed to be suffering in any way. So Lang left it at that. What went on between the three of them was of no concern to her as long as it stayed happy.

Lang was leaning back in Crawford's arms, trying to decide if she wanted to make love again, when a gunshot rang out in the *Podkayne*.

She had given a lot of thought to the last emergency, which she still saw as partly a result of her lag in responding. This time she was through the door almost before the reverberations had died down, leaving Crawford to nurse the leg she had stepped on in her haste.

She was in time to see McKillian and Ralston hurrying into the lab at the back of the ship. There was a red light flashing, but she quickly saw it was not the worst it could be; the pressure light still glowed green. It was the smoke detector. The smoke was coming from the lab.

She took a deep breath and plunged in, only to collide with Ralston as he came out, dragging Song. Except for a dazed expression and a few cuts, Song seemed to be all right. Crawford and McKillian joined them as they laid her on the bunk.

"It was one of the fruit," she said, gasping for breath and coughing. "I was heating it in a beaker, turned away, and it blew. I guess it sort of stunned me. The next thing I knew, Marty was carrying me out here. Hey, I have to get back in there! There's another one . . . it could be dangerous, and the damage, I have to check on that—" She struggled to get up but Lang held her down.

"You take it easy. What's this about another one?"

"I had it clamped down, and the drill—did I turn it on, or not? I can't remember. I was after a core sample. You'd better take a look. If the drill hits whatever made the other one explode, it might go off."

"I'll get it," McKillian said, turning toward the lab.

"You'll stay right here," Lang barked. "We know there's not enough power in them to hurt the ship, but it could kill you if it hit you right. We stay right here until it goes off. The hell with the damage. And shut that door, quick!"

Before they could shut it they heard a whistling, like a teakettle coming to boil, then a rapid series of clangs. A tiny white ball came through the doorway and bounced off three walls. It moved almost faster than they could follow. It hit Crawford on the arm, then fell to the floor where it gradually skittered to a stop. The hissing died away, and Crawford picked it up. It was lighter than it had been. There was pinhole drilled in one side. The pinhole was cold when he touched it with his fingers. Startled, thinking he was burned, he stuck his finger in his mouth, then sucked on it absently long after he knew the truth.

"These 'fruit' are full of compressed gas," he told them. "We have to open up another, carefully this time. I'm afraid to say what gas I think it is, but I have a hunch that our problems are solved."

◆

By the time the rescue expedition arrived, no one was calling it that. There had been the little matter of a long, brutal war with the Palestinian Empire, and a growing conviction that the survivors of the first expedition had not had any chance in the first place. There had been no time for luxuries like space travel beyond the Moon and no billions of dollars to invest while the world's energy policies were being debated in the Arabian Desert with tactical nuclear weapons.

When the ship finally did show up, it was no longer a NASA ship. It was sponsored by the fledgling International Space Agency. Its crew came from all over Earth. Its drive was new, too, and a lot better than the old one. As usual, war had given research a kick in the pants. Its mission was to take up the Martian exploration where the first expedition had left off and, incidentally, to recover the remains of the twenty Americans for return to Earth.

The ship came down with an impressive show of flame and billowing sand, three kilometers from Tharsis Base.

The captain, an Indian named Singh, got his crew started on erecting the permanent buildings, then climbed into a crawler with three officers for the trip to Tharsis. It was almost exactly twelve Earth-years since the departure of the *Edgar Rice Burroughs*.

The *Podkayne* was barely visible behind a network of multicolored vines. The vines were tough enough to frustrate their efforts to push through and enter the old ship. But both lock doors were open, and sand had drifted in rippled waves through the opening. The stern of the ship was nearly buried.

Singh told his people to stop, and he stood back admiring the complexity of the life in such a barren place. There were whirligigs twenty meters tall scattered around him, with vanes broad as the wings of a cargo aircraft.

"We'll have to get cutting tools from the ship," he told his crew. "They're probably in there. What a place this is! I can see we're going to be busy." He walked along the edge of the dense growth, which now covered several acres. He came to a section where the predominant color was purple. It was strangely different from the rest of the garden. There were tall whirligig derricks but they were frozen, unmoving. And covering all the derricks was a translucent network of ten-centimeter-wide strips of plastic, which was thick enough to make an impenetrable barrier. It was like a cobweb made of flat, thin material instead of fibrous spider-silk. It bulged outward between all the crossbraces of the whirligigs.

"Hello, can you hear me now?"

Singh jumped, then turned around, looked at the three officers. They were looking as surprised as he was.

"Hello, hello, hello? No good on this one, Mary. Want me to try another channel?"

"Wait a moment. I can hear you. Where are you?"

"Hey, he hears me! Uh, that is, this is Song Sue Lee, and I'm right in front of you. If you look real hard into the webbing, you can just make me out. I'll wave my arms. See?"

Singh thought he saw some movement when he pressed his face to the translucent web. The web resisted his hands, pushing back like an inflated balloon.

"I think I see you." The enormity of it was just striking him. He kept his voice under tight control, as his officers rushed up around him, and managed not to stammer. "Are you well? Is there anything we can do?"

There was a pause. "Well, now that you mention it, you might have come on time. But that's water through the pipes, I guess. If you have some toys or something, it might be nice. The stories I've told little Billy of all the nice things you people were going to bring! There's going to be no living with him, let me tell you."

This was getting out of hand for Captain Singh.

"Ms. Song, how can we get in there with you?"

"Sorry. Go to your right about ten meters, where you see the steam coming from the web. There, see it?" They did, and as they looked, a section of the webbing was pulled open and a rush of warm air almost blew them over. Water condensed out of it in their faceplates, and suddenly they couldn't see very well.

"Hurry, hurry, step in! We can't keep it open too long." They groped their way in, scraping frost away with their hands. The web closed behind them, and they were standing in the center of a very complicated network made of single strands of the webbing material. Singh's pressure gauge read 30 millibars.

Another section opened up and they stepped through it. After three more gates were passed, the temperature and pressure were nearly Earth-normal. And they were standing beside a small oriental woman with skin tanned almost black. She had no clothes on, but seemed adequately dressed in a brilliant smile that dimpled her mouth and eyes. Her hair was streaked with gray. She would be—Singh stopped to consider—forty-one years old.

"This way," she said, beckoning them into a tunnel formed from more strips of plastic. They twisted around through a random maze, going through more gates that opened when they neared them, sometimes getting on their knees when the clearance lowered. They heard the sound of children's voices.

They reached what must have been the center of the maze and found the people everyone had given up on. Eighteen of them. The children became very quiet and stared solemnly at the new arrivals, while the other four adults . . .

The adults were standing separately around the space while tiny helicopters flew around them, wrapping them from head to toe in strips of webbing like human maypoles.

◆

"Of course we don't know if we would have made it without the assist from the Martians," Mary Lang was saying, from her perch on an orange thing that might have been a toadstool. "Once we figured out what was happening here in the graveyard, there was no need to explore alternative ways of getting food, water, and oxygen. The need just never arose. We were provided for."

She raised her feet so a group of three gawking women from the ship could get by. They were letting them come through in groups of five every hour. They didn't dare open the outer egress more often than that, and Lang was wondering if it was too often. The place was crowded, and the kids were nervous. But better to have the crew satisfy their curiosity in here where we can watch them, she reasoned, than have them messing things up outside.

The inner nest was free-form. The New Amsterdamites had allowed it to stay pretty much the way the whirlibirds had built it, only taking down an obstruction here and there to allow humans to move around. It was a maze of gauzy walls and plastic struts, with clear plastic pipes running all over and carrying fluids of pale blue, pink, gold, and wine. Metal spigots from the *Podkayne* had been inserted in some of the pipes. McKillian was kept busy refilling glasses for the visitors who wanted to sample the antifreeze solution that was fifty percent ethanol. It was good stuff, Captain Singh reflected as he drained his third glass, and that was what he still couldn't understand.

He was having trouble framing the questions he wanted to ask, and he realized he'd had too much to drink. The spirit of celebration, the rejoicing at finding these people here past any hope; one could hardly stay aloof from it. But he refused a fourth drink regretfully.

"I can understand the drink," he said, carefully. "Ethanol is a simple compound and could fit into many different chemistries. But it's hard to believe that you've survived eating the food these plants produced for you."

"Not once you understand what this graveyard is and why it became what it did," Song said. She was sitting cross-legged on the floor nursing her youngest, Ethan.

"First you have to understand that all this you see," she waved around at the meters of hanging soft-sculpture, causing Ethan to nearly lose the nipple, "was designed to contain beings who are no more adapted to *this* Mars than we are. They need warmth, oxygen at fairly high pressures, and free water. It isn't here now, but it can be created by properly designed plants. They engineered these plants to be triggered by the first signs of free water and to start building places for them to live while they waited for full summer to come. When it does, this whole planet will bloom. Then we can step outside without wearing suits or carrying airberries."

"Yes, I see," Singh said. "And it's all very wonderful, almost too much to believe." He was distracted for a moment, looking up to the ceiling where the airberries—white spheres about the size of bowling balls—hung in clusters from the pipes that supplied them with high-pressure oxygen.

"I'd like to see that process from the start," he said. "Where you suit up for the outside, I mean."

"We were suiting up when you got here. It takes about half an hour; so we couldn't get out in time to meet you."

"How long are those . . . suits good for?"

"About a day," Crawford said. "You have to destroy them to get out of them. The plastic strips don't cut well, but there's another specialized animal that eats that type of plastic. It's recycled into the system. If you want to suit up, you just grab a whirlibird and hold onto its tail and throw it. It starts spinning as it flies, and wraps the end product around you. It takes some practice, but it works. The stuff sticks to itself, but not to us. So you spin several layers, letting each one dry, then hook up an airberry, and you're inflated and insulated."

"Marvelous," Singh said, truly impressed. He had seen the tiny whirlibirds weaving the suits, and the other ones, like small slugs, eating them away when the colonists saw they wouldn't need them. "But without some sort of exhaust, you wouldn't last long. How is that accomplished?"

"We use the breather valves from our old suits," McKillian said. "Either the plants that grow valves haven't come up yet or we haven't been smart enough to recognize them. And the insulation isn't perfect. We only go out in the hottest part of the day, and our hands and feet tend to get cold. But we manage."

Singh realized he had strayed from his original question.

"But what about the food? Surely it's too much to expect for these Martians to eat the same things we do. Wouldn't you think so?"

"We sure did, and we were lucky to have Marty Ralston along. He kept telling us the fruits in the graveyard were edible by humans. Fats, starches, proteins; all identical to the ones we brought along. The clue was in the orrery, of course."

Lang pointed to the twin globes in the middle of the room, still keeping perfect Earth-time.

"It was a beacon. We figured that out when we saw they grew only in the graveyard. But what was it telling us? We felt it meant that we were expected. Song felt that from the start, and we all came to agree with her. But we didn't realize just how much they had prepared for us until Marty started analyzing the fruits and nutrients here.

"Listen, these Martians-and I can see from your look that you still don't really believe in them, but you will if you stay here long enough—they know genetics. They really know it. We have a thousand theories about what they may be like, and I won't bore you with them yet, but this is one thing we do know. They can build anything they need, make a blueprint in DNA, encapsulate it in a spore and bury it, knowing exactly what will come up in forty thousand years. When it starts to get cold here and they know the cycle's drawing to an end, they seed the planet with the spores and . . . do something. Maybe they die, or maybe they have some other way of passing the time. But they know they'll return.

"We can't say how long they've been prepared for a visit from us. Maybe only this cycle; maybe twenty cycles ago. Anyway, at the last cycle they buried the kind of spores that would produce these little gismos." She tapped the blue ball representing the Earth with one foot.

"They triggered them to be activated only when they encountered certain different conditions. Maybe they knew exactly what it would be; maybe they only provided for a likely range of possibilities. Song thinks they've visited us, back in the Stone Age. In some ways it's easier to believe than the alternative. That way they'd know our genetic structure and what kinds of food we'd eat, and could prepare.

" 'Cause if they didn't visit us, they must have prepared other spores. Spores that would analyze new proteins and be able to duplicate them. Further than that, some of the plants might have been able to copy certain genetic material if they encountered any. Take a look at that pipe behind you." Singh turned and saw a pipe about as thick as his arm. It was flexible, and had a swelling in it that continuously pulsed in expansion and contraction.

"Take that bulge apart and you'd be amazed at the resemblance to a human heart. So there's another significant fact; this place started out with whirligigs, but later modified itself to use human heart pumps from the genetic information *taken from the bodies of the men and women we buried*." She paused to let that sink in, then went on with a slightly bemused smile.

"The same thing for what we eat and drink. That liquor you drank, for instance. It's half alcohol, and that's probably what it would have been without the corpses. But the rest of it is very similar to hemoglobin. It's sort of like fermented blood. Human blood."

Singh was glad he had refused the fourth drink. One of his crew members quietly put his glass down.

"I've never eaten human flesh," Lang went on, "but I think I know what it must taste like. Those vines to your right; we strip off the outer part and eat the meat underneath. It tastes good. I wish we could cook it, but we have nothing to burn and couldn't risk it with the high oxygen count, anyway."

Singh and everyone else was silent for a while. He found he really was beginning to believe in the Martians. The theory seemed to cover a lot of otherwise inexplicable facts.

Mary Lang sighed, slapped her thighs, and stood up. Like all the others, she was nude and seemed totally at home with it. None of them had worn anything but a Martian pressure suit for eight years. She ran her hand lovingly over the gossamer wall, the wall that had provided her and her fellow colonists and their children protection from the cold and the thin air for so long. He was struck by her easy familiarity with what seemed to him outlandish surroundings. She looked at home. He couldn't imagine her anywhere else.

He looked at the children. One wide-eyed little girl of eight years was kneeling at his feet. As his eyes fell on her, she smiled tentatively and took his hand.

"Did you bring any bubblegum?" the girl asked.

He smiled at her. "No, honey, but maybe there's some in the ship." She seemed satisfied. She would wait to experience the wonders of earthly science.

"We were provided for," Mary Lang said, quietly. "They knew we were coming and they altered their plants to fit us in." She looked back to Singh. "It would have happened even without the blowout and the burials. The same sort of thing was happening around the *Podkayne*, too, triggered by our waste; urine and feces and such. I don't know if it would have tasted quite as good in the food department, but it would have sustained life."

Singh stood up. He was moved, but did not trust himself to show it adequately. So he sounded rather abrupt, though polite.

"I suppose you'll be anxious to go to the ship," he said. "You're going to be a tremendous help. You know so much of what we were sent here to find out. And you'll be quite famous when you get back to Earth. Your back pay should add up to quite a sum."

There was a silence, then it was ripped apart by Lang's huge laugh. She was joined by the others, and the children, who didn't know what they were laughing about but enjoyed the break in the tension.

"Sorry, Captain. That was rude. But we're not going back."

Singh looked at each of the adults and saw no trace of doubt. And he was mildly surprised to find that the statement did not startle him.

"I won't take that as your final decision," he said. "As you know, we'll be here six months. If at the end of that time any of you want to go, you're still citizens of Earth."

"We are? You'll have to brief us on the political situation back there. We were United States citizens when we left. But it doesn't matter. You won't get any takers, though we appreciate the fact that you came. It's nice to know we weren't forgotten." She said it with total assurance, and the others were nodding. Singh was uncomfortably aware that the idea of a rescue mission had died out only a few years after the initial tragedy. He and his ship were here now only to explore.

Lang sat back down and patted the ground around her, ground that was covered in a multiple layer of the Martian pressure-tight web, the kind of web that would have been made only by warm-blooded, oxygen-breathing, water-economy beings who needed protection for their bodies until the full bloom of summer.

"We *like* it here. It's a good place to raise a family, not like Earth the last time I was there. And it couldn't be much better now, right after another war. And we can't leave, even if we wanted to." She flashed him a dazzling smile and patted the ground again.

"The Martians should be showing up any time now. And we aim to thank them."

Ginungagap

MICHAEL SWANWICK

One of the most popular and respected of all the new writers who entered the field in the eighties, Michael Swanwick made his debut in 1980 with two strong and compelling stories, "The Feast of St. Janis" and "Ginungagap," both of which were Nebula Award finalists that year and both selected either for a Best of the Year anthology or for that year's annual Nebula Awards volume—as auspicious a debut as anyone has ever made.

He stayed in the public eye and on major award ballots throughout the rest of the eighties with intense and powerful stories such as "Mummer Kiss," "The Man Who Met Picasso," "Trojan Horse," "Dogfight" (written with William Gibson), "Covenant of Souls," "The Dragon Line," "Snow Angles," "A Midwinter's Tale," and many others, all of which earned him a reputation as one of the most powerful and consistently inventive short-story writers of his generation. Nor has his output of short fiction slackened noticeably in the nineties, in spite of a burgeoning career as a novelist, and recent years have seen the appearance of major Swanwick stories such as "The Edge of the World," "The Changeling's Tale," "Griffin's Egg," "Cold Iron," and "The Dead," which was on the final Hugo ballot in 1997 and on the Nebula final ballot in 1998; he remains one of science fiction's most prolific writers at short lengths. By the end of the nineties, his short work would have won him several Asimov's Reader's Awards (including, most recently, one in 1999 for his story "Radiant Doors"), a Sturgeon Award, the World Fantasy Award, and a Hugo Award.

At first, Swanwick's reputation as a novelist lagged behind his reputation as a short-story writer, with his first novel, In the Drift—published in 1985 as part of Terry Carr's resurrected Ace Specials line, along with first novels by William Gibson, Kim Stanley Robinson, and Lucius Shepard—largely ignored by the critics and panned by some of them. His second novel, though, the critically-acclaimed Vacuum Flowers, caused a stir, and with his third and perhaps best-known novel, Stations of the Tide, he established himself firmly as among the vanguard of the hot new novelists of the nineties; Stations of the Tide won him a Nebula Award in 1991. His next novel, The Iron Dragon's Daughter, a finalist for both the World Fantasy Award and the Arthur C. Clarke Award (a unique distinction!), explored new literary territory on the ambiguous borderland of science fiction and fantasy and has been hailed by some critics as the first example of an as-yet-still-nascent subgenre called hard fantasy (sort of a mix between the Dickensian sensibilities of "steampunk," high-tech science fiction, and traditional Tolkienesque fantasy). His most recent novel, Jack Faust, a sly reworking of the Faust legend that explores the unexpected impact of technology on society, blurs genre boundaries even more and has garnered rave reviews from nearly every source, from the Washington Post to Interzone. He's currently at work on another novel, featuring time travelers and hungry dinosaurs.

During the late eighties, Swanwick was sometimes, unfairly, judged to be derivative of William Gibson, although "Ginungagap" was published in 1980 and Gibson's "Burning Chrome" and Neuromancer *weren't published until 1982 and 1985, respectively—in fact, science fiction rarely evolves in such a straightforward way, and the resemblances between Swanwick and Gibson are better explained as convergent evolution, by both writers being influenced by people such as Samuel R. Delany, Alfred Bester, James Tiptree, Jr., and John Varley than by their influence on each other. (When it's steam engine time, somebody invents the steam engine.) For instance, the vivid and inventive adventure that follows clearly prefigures many of what would later come to be considered cyberpunk tropes, as well as a few post*cyberpunk *tropes, all wrapped up in the same package years before either "Movement" was identified by critics and all wrapped around the story of a young explorer who finds that the cost of achievement may ultimately turn out to be more than you wanted to spend.*

Swanwick's other books include the novella-length Griffin's Egg, *one of the most brilliant and compelling of modern-day Moon-colony stories. His short fiction has been assembled in* Gravity's Angels *and in a collection of his collaborative short work with other writers,* Slow Dancing through Time. *His most recent books are a collection of critical articles,* The Postmodern Archipelago, *and a new collection,* A Geography of Unknown Lands. *Swanwick lives in Philadelphia with his wife, Marianne Porter, and their son, Sean.*

Abigail checked out of Mother of Mercy and rode the translator web to Toledo Cylinder in Juno Industrial Park. Stars bloomed, dwindled, disappeared five times. It was a long trek, halfway around the sun.

Toledo was one of the older commercial cylinders, now given over almost entirely to bureaucrats, paper pushers, and free-lance professionals. It was not Abigail's favorite place to visit, but she needed work and 3M had already bought out of her contract.

The job broker had dyed his chest hairs blond and his leg hairs red. They clashed wildly with his green *cache-sexe* and turquoise jewelry. His fingers played on a key-out, bringing up an endless flow of career trivia. "Cute trick you played," he said.

Abigail flexed her new arm negligently. It was a good job, but pinker than the rest of her. And weak, of course, but exercise would correct that. "Thanks," she said. She laid the arm underneath one breast and compared the colors. It matched the nipple perfectly. Definitely too pink. "Work outlook any good?"

"Naw," the broker said. A hummingbird flew past his ear, a nearly undetectable parting of the air. "I see here that you applied for the Proxima colony."

"They were full up," Abigail said. "No openings for a gravity bum, hey?"

"I didn't say that," the broker grumbled. "I'll find—Hello! What's this?" Abigail craned her neck, couldn't get a clear look at the screen. "There's a tag on your employment record."

"What's that mean?"

"Let me read." A honeysuckle flower fell on Abigail's hair and she brushed it off impatiently. The broker had an open-air office, framed by hedges and roofed over with a trellis. Sometimes Abigail found the older Belt cylinders a little too lavish for her taste.

"Mmp." The broker looked up. "Bell-Sandia wants to hire you. Indefinite term one-shot contract." He swung the keyout around so she could see. "*Very* nice terms, but that's normal for a high risk contract."

"High risk? From B-S, the Friendly Communications People? What kind of risk?"

The broker scrolled up new material. "There." He tapped the screen with a finger. "The language is involved, but what it boils down to is they're looking for a test passenger for a device they've got that uses black holes for interstellar travel."

"Couldn't work," Abigail said. "The tidal forces—"

"Spare me. Presumably they've found a way around that problem. The question is, are you interested or not?"

Abigail stared up through the trellis at a stream meandering across the curved land overhead. Children were wading in it. She counted to a hundred very slowly, trying to look as if she needed to think it over.

◆

Abigail strapped herself into the translation harness and nodded to the technician outside the chamber. The tech touched her console and a light stasis field immobilized Abigail and the air about her while the chamber wall irised open. In a fluid bit of technological sleight of hand, the translator rechanneled her inertia and gifted her with a velocity almost, but not quite, that of the speed of light.

Stars bloomed about her and the sun dwindled. She breathed in deeply and—was in the receiver device. Relativity had cheated her of all but a fraction of the transit time. She shrugged out of harness and frog-kicked her way to the lip station's tug dock.

The tug pilot grinned at her as she entered, then turned his attention to his controls. He was young and wore streaks of brown makeup across his chest and thighs—only slightly darker than his skin. His mesh vest was almost in bad taste, but he wore it well and looked roguish rather than overdressed. Abigail found herself wishing she had more than a *cache-sexe* and nail polish on—some jewelry or makeup, perhaps. She felt drab in comparison.

The star-field wraparound held two inserts routed in by synchronous cameras. Alphanumerics flickered beneath them. One showed her immediate destination, the Bell-Sandia base *Arthur C. Clarke*. It consisted of five wheels, each set inside the other and rotating at slightly differing speeds. The base was done up in red-and-orange supergraphics. Considering its distance from the Belt factories, it was respectably sized.

Abigail latched herself into the passenger seat as the engines cut in. The second insert—

Ginungagap, the only known black hole in the sun's gravity field, was dis-

covered in 2023, a small voice murmured. *Its presence explained the long-puzzling variations in the orbits of the outer planets. The* Arthur C. Clarke *was* . . .

"Is this necessary?" Abigail asked.

"Absolutely," the pilot said. "We abandoned the tourist program a year or so ago, but somehow the rules never caught up. They're very strict about the regs here." He winked at Abigail's dismayed expression. "Hold tight a minute while—" His voice faded as he tinkered with the controls.

. . . *established forty years later and communications with the Proxima colony began shortly thereafter. Ginungagap* . . .

The voice cut off. She grinned thanks. "Abigail Vanderhoek."

"Cheyney," the pilot said. "You're the gravity bum, right?"

"Yeah."

"I used to be a vacuum bum myself. But I got tired of it, and grabbed the first semipermanent contract that came along."

"I kind of went the other way."

"Probably what I should have done," Cheyney said amiably. "Still, it's a rough road. I picked up three scars along the way." He pointed them out: a thick slash across his abdomen, a red splotch beside one nipple, and a white crescent half obscured by his scalp. "I could've had them cleaned up, but the way I figure, life is just a process of picking up scars and experience. So I kept 'em."

If she had thought he was trying to impress her, Abigail would have slapped him down. But it was clearly just part of an ongoing self-dramatization, possibly justified, probably not. Abigail suspected that, tour trips to Earth excepted, the *Clarke* was as far down a gravity well as Cheyney had ever been. Still he did have an irresponsible, boyish appeal. "Take me past the net?" she asked.

Cheyney looped the tug around the communications net trailing the *Clarke.* Kilometers of steel lace passed beneath them. He pointed out a small dish antenna on the edge and a cluster of antennae on the back. "The loner on the edge transmits into Ginungagap," he said. "The others relay information to and from Mother."

"Mother?"

"That's the traditional name for the *Arthur C. Clarke.*" He swung the tug about with a careless sweep of one arm, and launched into a long and scurrilous story about the origin of the nickname. Abigail laughed, and Cheyney pointed a finger. "There's Ginungagap."

Abigail peered intently. "Where? I don't see a thing." She glanced at the second wraparound insert, which displayed a magnified view of the black hole. It wasn't at all impressive: a red smear against black nothingness. In the star-field it was all but invisible.

"Disappointing, hey? But still dangerous. Even this far out, there's a lot of ionization from the accretion disk."

"Is that why there's a lip station?"

"Yeah. Particle concentration varies, but if the translator was right at the *Clarke,* we'd probably lose about a third of the passengers."

Cheyney dropped Abigail off at Mother's crew lock and looped the tug off and away. Abigail wondered where to go, what to do now.

"You're the gravity bum we're dumping down Ginungagap." The short, solid man was upon her before she saw him. His eyes were intense. His *cache-sexe* was a conservative orange. "I liked the stunt with the arm. It takes a lot of guts to do something like that." He pumped her arm. "I'm Paul Girard. Head of external security. In charge of your training. You play verbal Ping Pong?"

"Why do you ask?" she countered automatically.

"Don't you know?"

"Should I?"

"Do you mean now or later?"

"Will the answer be different later?"

A smile creased Paul's solid face. "You'll do." He took her arm, led her along a sloping corridor. "There isn't much prep time. The dry run is scheduled in two weeks. Things will move pretty quickly after that. You want to start your training now?"

"Do I have a choice?" Abigail asked, amused.

Paul came to a dead stop. "Listen," he said. "Rule number one: don't play games with *me*. You understand? Because I always win. Not sometimes, not usually—always."

Abigail yanked her arm free. "You maneuvered me into that," she said angrily.

"Consider it part of your training." He stared directly into her eyes. "No matter how many gravity wells you've climbed down, you're still the product of a near-space culture—protected, trusting, willing to take things at face value. This is a dangerous attitude, and I want you to realize it. I want you to learn to look behind the mask of events. I want you to grow up. And you will."

Don't be so sure. A small smile quirked Paul's face as if he could read her thoughts. Aloud, Abigail said, "That sounds a little excessive for a trip to Proxima."

"Lesson number two," Paul said: "don't make easy assumptions. You're not going to Proxima." He led her outward-down the ramp to the next wheel, pausing briefly at the juncture to acclimatize to the slower rate of revolution. "You're going to visit spiders." He gestured. "The crew room is this way."

◆

The crew room was vast and cavernous, twilight gloomy, Keyouts were set up along winding paths that wandered aimlessly through the work space. Puddles of light fell on each board and operator. Dark-loving foliage was set between the keyouts.

"This is the heart of the beast," Paul said. "The green keyouts handle all Proxima communications—pretty routine by now. But the blue . . ." His eyes glinting oddly, he pointed. Over the keyouts hung silvery screens with harsh, grainy images floating on their surfaces, black-and-white blobs that Abigail could not resolve into recognizable forms.

"Those," Paul said, "are the spiders. We're talking to them in real-time. Response delay is almost all due to machine translation."

In a sudden shift of perception, the blobs became arachnid forms. That mass of black fluttering across the screen was a spider leg and *that* was its thorax. Abigail felt an immediate, primal aversion, and then it was swept away by an all-encompassing wonder.

"Aliens?" she breathed.

"Aliens."

They actually looked no more like spiders than humans looked like apes. The eight legs had an extra joint each, and the mandible configuration was all wrong. But to an untrained eye they would do.

"But this is—How long have you—? Why in God's name are you keeping this a secret?" An indefinable joy arose in Abigail. This opened a universe of possibilities, as if after a lifetime of being confined in a box someone had removed the lid.

"Industrial security," Paul said. "The gadget that'll send you through Ginungagap to their black hole is a spider invention. We're trading optical data for it, but the law won't protect our rights until we've demonstrated its use. We don't want the other corporations cutting in." He nodded toward the nearest black-and-white screen. "As you can see, they're weak on optics."

"I'd love to talk . . ." Abigail's voice trailed off as she realized how little-girl hopeful she sounded.

"I'll arrange an introduction."

There was a rustling to Abigail's side. She turned and saw a large black tomcat with white boots and belly emerge from the bushes. "This is the esteemed head of Alien Communications," Paul said sourly.

Abigail started to laugh, then choked in embarrassment as she realized that he was not speaking of the cat. "Julio Dominguez, section chief for translation," Paul said. "Abigail Vanderhoek, gravity specialist."

The wizened old man smiled professorially. "I assume our resident gadfly has explained how the communications net works, has he not?"

"Well—" Abigail began.

Dominguez clucked his tongue. He wore a yellow *cache-sexe* and matching bow tie, just a little too garish for a man his age. "Quite simple, actually. Escape velocity from a black hole is greater than the speed of light. Therefore, within Ginungagap the speed of light is no longer the limit to the speed of communications."

He paused just long enough for Abigail to look baffled. "Which is just a stuffy way of saying that when we aim a stream of electrons into the boundary of the stationary limit, they emerge elsewhere—out of another black hole. And if we aim them just so"—his voice rose whimsically—"they'll emerge from the black hole of our choosing. The physics is simple. The finesse is in aiming the electrons."

The cat stalked up to Abigail, pushed its forehead against her leg, and mewed insistently. She bent over and picked it up. "But nothing can emerge from a black hole," she objected.

Dominguez chuckled. "Ah, but anything can fall in, hey? A positron falling into Ginungagap in positive time is only an electron falling out in negative time. Which means that a positron falling into a black hole in negative time is actually an electron falling out in positive time—exactly the effect we want. Think of Ginungagap as being the physical manifestation of an equivalence sign in mathematics."

"Oh," Abigail said, feeling very firmly put in her place. White moths flittered along the path. The cat watched, fascinated, while she stroked its head.

"At any rate, the electrons do emerge, and once the data are in, the theory has to follow along meekly."

"Tell me about the spiders," Abigail said before he could continue. The moths were darting up, sideward, down, a chance ballet in three dimensions.

"The *aliens*," Dominguez said, frowning at Paul, "are still a mystery to us. We exchange facts, descriptions, recipes for tools, but the important questions do not lend themselves to our clumsy mathematical codes. Do they know of love? Do they appreciate beauty? Do they believe in God, hey?"

"Do they want to eat us?" Paul threw in.

"Don't be ridiculous," Dominguez snapped. "Of course they don't."

The moths parted when they came to Abigail. Two went to either side; one flew over her shoulder. The cat batted at it with one paw. "The cat's name is Garble," Paul said. "The kids in Bio cloned him up."

Dominguez opened his mouth, closed it again.

Abigail scratched Garble under the chin. He arched his neck and purred all but noiselessly. "With your permission," Paul said. He stepped over to a keyout and waved its operator aside.

"Technically you're supposed to speak a convenience language, but if you keep it simple and non-idiomatic, there shouldn't be any difficulty." He touched the keyout. "Ritual greetings, spider." There was a blank pause. Then the spider moved, a hairy leg flickering across the screen.

"Hello, human."

"Introductions: Abigail Vanderhoek. She is our representative. She will ride the spinner." Another pause. More leg waving.

"Hello, Abigail Vanderhoek. Transition of vacuum garble resting garble commercial benefits garble still point in space."

"Tricky translation," Paul said. He signed to Abigail to take over.

Abigail hesitated, then said, "Will you come to visit us? The way we will visit you?"

"No, you see—" Dominguez began, but Paul waved him to silence.

"No, Abigail Vanderhoek. We are sulfur-based life."

"I do not understand."

"You can garble black hole through garble spinner because you are carbon-based life. Carbon forms chains easily but sulfur combines in lattices or rosettes. Our garble simple form garble. Sometimes sulfur forms short chains."

"We'll explain later," Paul said. "Go on, you're doing fine."

Abigail hesitated again. What do you say to a spider, anyway? Finally, she asked, "Do you want to eat us?"

"Oh, Christ, get her off that thing," Dominguez said, reaching for the keyout.

Paul blocked his arm. "No," he said. "I want to hear this."

Several of the spider legs wove intricate patterns. "The question is false. Sulfur-based life derives no benefit from eating carbon-based life."

"You see," Dominguez said.

"But if it were possible," Abigail persisted. "If you could eat us and derive benefit. Would you?"

"Yes, Abigail Vanderhoek. With great pleasure."

Dominguez pushed her aside. "We're terribly sorry," he said to the alien. "This is a horrible, horrible misunderstanding. You!" he shouted to the operator. "Get back on and clear this mess up."

Paul was grinning wickedly. "Come," he said to Abigail. "We've accomplished enough here for one day."

As they started to walk away, Garble twisted in Abigail's arms and leaped free. He hit the floor on all fours and disappeared into the greenery. "Would they really eat us?" Abigail asked. Then amended it to, "Does that mean they're hostile?"

Paul shrugged. "Maybe they thought we'd be insulted if they *didn't* offer to eat us." He led her to her quarters. "Tomorrow we start training for real. In the meantime, you might make up a list of all the ways the spiders could hurt us if we set up transportation and they are hostile. Then another list of all the reasons we shouldn't trust them." He paused. "I've done it myself. You'll find that the lists get rather extensive."

⬣

Abigail's quarters weren't flashy, but they fit her well. A full star field was routed to the walls, floor, and ceiling, only partially obscured by a trellis inner frame that supported fox-grape vines. Somebody had done research into her tastes.

"Hi." The cheery greeting startled her. She whirled, saw that her hammock was occupied.

Cheyney sat up, swung his legs over the edge of the hammock, causing it to rock lightly. "Come on in." He touched an invisible control and the star field blue-shifted down to a deep, erotic purple.

"Just what do you think you're doing here?" Abigail asked.

"I had a few hours free," Cheyney said, "so I thought I'd drop by and seduce you."

"Well, Cheyney, I appreciate your honesty," Abigail said. "So I won't say no."

"Thank you."

"I'll say maybe some other time. Now get lost. I'm tired."

"Okay." Cheyney hopped down, walked jauntily to the door. He paused. "You said 'Later,' right?"

"I said *maybe* later."

"Later. Gotcha." He winked and was gone.

Abigail threw herself into the hammock, red-shifted the star field until the universe was a sparse smattering of dying embers. Annoying creature! There was no hope for anything more than the most superficial of relationships with him. She closed her eyes, smiled. Fortunately, she wasn't currently in the market for a serious relationship.

She slept.

➻

She was falling . . .

Abigail had landed the ship an easy walk from 3M's robot laboratory. The lab's geodesic dome echoed white clouds to the north, where Nix Olympus peeked over the horizon. Otherwise all—land, sky, rocks—was standard issue Martian orange. She had clambered to the ground and shrugged on the supply backpack.

Resupplying 3M-RL stations was a gut contract, easy but dull. So perhaps she was less cautious than usual going down the steep, rock-strewn hillside, or perhaps the rock would have turned under her no matter how carefully she placed her feet. Her ankle twisted and she lurched sideways, but the backpack had shifted her center of gravity too much for her to be able to recover.

Arms windmilling, she fell.

The rock slide carried her downhill in a panicky flurry of dust and motion, tearing her flesh and splintering her bones. But before she could feel pain, her suit shot her full of a nerve synesthetic, translating sensation into colors—reds, russets, and browns, with staccato yellow spikes when a rock smashed into her ribs. So that she fell in a whirling rainbow of glorious light.

She came to rest in a burst of orange. The rocks were settling about her. A spume of dust drifted away, out toward the distant red horizon. A large, jagged slab of stone slid by, gently shearing off her backpack. Tools, supplies, airpacks flew up and softly rained down.

A spanner as long as her arm slammed down inches from Abigail's helmet. She flinched, and suddenly events became real. She kicked her legs and sand and dust fountained up. Drawing her feet under her body— the one ankle bright gold—she started to stand.

And was jerked to the ground by a sudden tug on one arm. Even as she turned her head, she became aware of a deep purple sensation in her left hand. It was pinioned to a rock not quite large enough to stake a claim to. There was no color in the fingers.

"Cute," she muttered. She tugged at the arm, pushed at the rock. Nothing budged.

Abigail nudged the radio switch with her chin. "Grounder to Lip Station," she said. She hesitated, feeling foolish, then said, "Mayday. Repeat, Mayday. Could you guys send a rescue party down for me?"

There was no reply. With a sick green feeling in the pit of her stomach, Abigail reached a gloved hand around the back of her helmet. She touched something jagged, a sensation of mottled rust, the broken remains of her radio.

"I think I'm in trouble." She said it aloud and listened to the sound of it. Flat, unemotional—probably true. But nothing to get panicky about.

She took quick stock of what she had to work with. One intact suit and helmet. One spanner. A worldful of rocks, many close at hand. Enough air for—she checked the helmet readout—almost an hour. Assuming the lip station ran its checks on schedule and was fast on the uptake, she had almost half the air she needed.

Most of the backpack's contents were scattered too far away to reach. One rectangular gaspack, however, had landed nearby. She reached for it but could not touch it, squinted but could not read the label on its nozzle. It was almost certainly liquid gas—either nitrogen or oxygen—for the robot lab. There was a slim chance it was the spare airpack. If it was, she might live to be rescued.

Abigail studied the landscape carefully, but there was nothing more. "Okay, then, it's an airpack." She reached as far as her tethered arm would allow. The gaspack remained a tantalizing centimeter out of reach.

For an instant she was stymied. Then, feeling like an idiot, she grabbed the spanner. She hooked it over the gaspack. Felt the gaspack move grudgingly. Slowly nudged it toward herself.

By the time Abigail could drop the spanner and draw in the gaspack, her good arm was blue with fatigue. Sweat running down her face, she juggled the gaspack to read its nozzle markings.

It was liquid oxygen—useless. She could hook it to her suit and feed in the contents, but the first breath would freeze her lungs. She released the gaspack and lay back, staring vacantly at the sky.

Up there was civilization: tens of thousands of human stations strung together by webs of communication and transportation. Messages flowed endlessly on laser cables. Translators borrowed and lent momentum, moving streams of travelers and cargo at almost (but not quite) the speed of light. A starship was being readied to carry a third load of colonists to Proxima. Up there, free from gravity's relentless clutch, people lived in luxury and ease. Here, however . . .

"I'm going to die." She said it softly and was filled with wondering awe. Because it was true. She was going to die.

Death was a black wall. It lay before her, extending to infinity in all directions, smooth and featureless and mysterious. She could almost reach out an arm and touch it. Soon she would come up against it and, if anything lay beyond, pass through. Soon, very soon, she would *know*.

She touched the seal to her helmet. It felt gray—smooth and inviting. Her fingers moved absently, tracing the seal about her neck. With sudden horror, Abigail realized that she was thinking about undoing it, releasing her air, throwing away the little time she had left. . . .

She shuddered. With sudden resolve, she reached out and unsealed the shoulder seam of her captive arm.

The seal clamped down, automatically cutting off air loss. The flesh of her damaged arm was exposed to the raw Martian atmosphere. Abigail took up the gaspack and cradled it in the pit of her good arm. Awkwardly, she opened the nozzle with the spanner.

She sprayed the exposed arm with liquid oxygen for over a minute before she was certain it had frozen solid. Then she dropped the gaspack, picked up the spanner, and swung.

Her arm shattered into a thousand fragments.

She stood up.

◆

Abigail awoke, tense and sweaty. She blue-shifted the walls up to normal light, and sat up. After a few minutes of clearing her head, she set the walls to cycle from red to blue in a rhythm matching her normal pulse. Eventually the womb-cycle lulled her back to sleep.

◆

"Not even close," Paul said. He ran the tape backward, froze it on a still shot of the spider twisting two legs about each other. "That's the morpheme for 'extreme disgust,' remember. It's easy to pick out, and the language kids say that any statement with this gesture should be reversed in meaning. Irony, see? So when the spider says that the strong should protect the weak, it means—"

"How long have we been doing this?"

"Practically forever," Paul said cheerfully. "You want to call it a day?"

"Only if it won't hurt my standing."

"Hah! Very good." He switched off the keyout. "Nicely thought out. You're absolutely right; it would have. However, as reward for realizing this, you can take off early *without* it being noted on your record."

"Thank you," Abigail said sourly.

Like most large installations, the *Clarke* had a dozen or so smaller structures tagging along after it in minimum maintenance orbits. When Abigail discovered that these included a small wheel gymnasium, she had taken to putting in an hour's exercise after each training shift. Today she put in two.

The first hour she spent shadowboxing and practicing *savate* in heavy-gee to work up a sweat. The second hour she spent in the axis room, performing free-fall gymnastics. After the first workout, it made her feel light and nimble and good about her body.

She returned from the wheel gym sweaty and cheerful to find Cheyney in her hammock again: "Cheyney," she said, "this is not the first time I've had to kick you out of there. Or even the third, for that matter."

Cheyney held his palms up in mock protest. "Hey, no," he said. "Nothing like that today. I just came by to watch the raft debate with you."

Abigail felt pleasantly weary, decidedly uncerebral. "Paul said something about it, but . . ."

"Turn it on, then. You don't want to miss it." Cheyney touched her wall, and a cluster of images sprang to life at the far end of the room.

"Just what is a raft debate anyway?" Abigail asked, giving in gracefully. She hoisted herself onto the hammock, sat beside him. They rocked gently for a moment.

"There's this raft, see? It's adrift and powerless and there's only enough oxygen on board to keep one person alive until rescue. Only there are three on board—two humans and a spider."

"Do spiders breathe oxygen?"

"It doesn't matter. This is a hypothetical situation." Two thirds of the image area was taken up by Dominguez and Paul, quietly waiting for the debate to begin. The remainder showed a flat spider image.

"Okay, what then?"

"They argue over who gets to survive. Dominguez argues that he should, since he's human and human culture is superior to spider culture. The spider argues for itself and its culture." He put an arm around her waist. "You smell nice."

"Thank you." She ignored the arm. "What does Paul argue?"

"He's the devil's advocate. He argues that no one deserves to live and they should dump the oxygen."

"Paul would enjoy that role," Abigail said. Then, "What's the point to this debate?"

"It's an entertainment. There isn't supposed to be a point."

Abigail doubted it was that simple. The debate could reveal a good deal about the spiders and how they thought, once the language types were done with it. Conversely, the spiders would doubtless be studying the human responses. *This could be interesting*, she thought. Cheyney was stroking her side now, lightly but with great authority. She postponed reaction, not sure whether she liked it or not.

Louise Chang, a vaguely high-placed administrator, blossomed in the center of the image cluster. "Welcome," she said, and explained the rules of the debate. "The winner will be decided by acclaim," she said, "with half the vote being human and half alien. Please remember not to base your vote on racial chauvinism, but on the strengths of the arguments and how well they are presented." Cheyney's hand brushed casually across her nipples; they stiffened. The hand lingered. "The debate will begin with the gentleman representing the aliens presenting his thesis."

The image flickered as the spider waved several legs. "Thank you, Ms. Chairman. I argue that I should survive. My culture is superior because of our technological advancement. Three examples. Humans have used translation travel only briefly, yet we have used it for sixteens of garble. Our black hole technology is superior. And our garble has garble for the duration of our society."

"Thank you. The gentleman representing humanity?"

"Thank you, Ms. Chairman." Dominguez adjusted an armlet. Cheyney leaned back and let Abigail rest against him. Her head fit comfortably against his shoulder. "My argument is that technology is neither the sole nor the most important measure of a culture. By these standards dolphins would be considered brute animals. The aesthetic considerations—the arts, theology, and the tradition of philosophy—are of greater import. As I shall endeavor to prove."

"He's chosen the wrong tactic," Cheyney whispered in Abigail's ear. "That must have come across as pure garble to the spiders."

"Thank you. Mr. Girard?"

Paul's image expanded. He theatrically swigged from a small flask and hoisted it high in the air. "Alcohol! There's the greatest achievement of the human race!" Abigail snorted. Cheyney laughed out loud. "But I hold that neither Mr. Dominguez nor the distinguished spider deserves to live, because of the disregard both cultures have for sentient life." Abigail looked at Cheyney, who shrugged. "As I shall endeavor to prove." His image dwindled.

Chang said, "The arguments will now proceed, beginning with the distinguished alien."

The spider and then Dominguez ran through their arguments, and to Abigail they seemed markedly lackluster. She didn't give them her full attention, because Cheyney's hands were moving most interestingly across unexpected parts of her body. He might not be too bright, but he was certainly good at some things. She nuzzled her face into his neck, gave him a small peck, returned her attention to the debate.

Paul blossomed again. He juggled something in his palm, held his hand open to reveal three ball bearings. "When I was a kid I used to short out the school module and sneak up to the axis room to play marbles." Abigail smiled, remembering similar stunts she had played. "For the sake of those of us who are spiders, I'll explain that marbles is a game played in free-fall for the purpose of developing coordination and spatial perception. You make a six-armed star of marbles in the center . . ."

One of the bearings fell from his hand, bounced noisily, and disappeared as it rolled out of camera range. "Well, obviously it can't be played here. But the point is that when you shoot the marble just right, it hits the end of one arm and its kinetic energy is transferred from marble to marble along that arm. So that the shooter stops and the marble at the far end of the arm flies away." Cheyney was stroking her absently now, engrossed in the argument.

"Now, we plan to send a courier into Ginungagap and out the spiders' black hole. At least, that's what we say we're going to do.

"But what exits from a black hole is not necessarily the same as what went into its partner hole. We throw an electron into Ginungagap and another one pops out elsewhere. It's identical. It's a direct causal relationship. But it's like the marbles—they're identical to each other and have the same kinetic force. It's simply not the same electron."

Cheyney's hand was still, motionless. Abigail prodded him gently, touching his inner thigh. "Anyone who's interested can see the equations. Now, when we send messages, this doesn't matter. The message is important, not the medium. However, when we send a human being in . . . what emerges from the other hole will be cell for cell, gene for gene, atom for atom identical. *But it will not be the same person.*" He paused a beat, smiled.

"I submit, then, that this is murder. And further, that by conspiring to commit murder, both the spider and human races display absolute disregard for intelligent life. In short, no one on the raft deserves to live. And I rest my case."

"Mr. Girard!" Dominguez objected, even before his image was restored to full size. "The simplest mathematical proof is an identity: that A equals A. Are you trying to deny this?"

Paul held up the two ball bearings he had left. "These marbles are identical too. But they are not the same marble."

"We know the phenomenon you speak of," the spider said. "It is as if garble the black hole bulges out simultaneously. There is no violation of continuity. The two entities are the same. There is no death."

Abigail pulled Cheyney down, so that they were both lying on their sides, still able to watch the images. "So long as you happen to be the second marble and not the first," Paul said. Abigail tentatively licked Cheyney's ear.

"He's right," Cheyney murmured.

"No he's not," Abigail retorted. She bit his earlobe.

"You mean that?"

"Of course I mean that. He's confusing semantics with reality." She engrossed herself in a study of the back of his neck.

"Okay."

Abigail suddenly sensed that she was missing something. "Why do you ask?" She struggled into a sitting position. Cheyney followed.

"No particular reason." Cheyney's hands began touching her again. But Abigail was sure something had been slipped past her.

They caressed each other lightly while the debate dragged to an end. Not paying much attention, Abigail voted for Dominguez, and Cheyney voted for Paul. As a result of a nearly undivided spider vote, the spider won. "I told you Dominguez was taking the wrong approach," Cheyney said. He hopped off the hammock. "Look, I've got to see somebody about something. I'll be right back."

"You're not leaving *now*?" Abigail protested, dumbfounded. The door irised shut.

Angry and hurt, she leaped down, determined to follow him. She couldn't remember ever feeling so insulted.

Cheyney didn't try to be evasive; it apparently did not occur to him that she might follow. Abigail stalked him down a corridor, up an in-ramp, and to a door that irised open for him. She recognized that door.

Thoughtfully she squatted on her heels behind an untrimmed boxwood and waited. A minute later, Garble wandered by, saw her, and demanded attention. "Scat!" she hissed. He butted his head against her knee. "Then be quiet, at least." She scooped him up. His expression was smug.

The door irised open and Cheyney exited, whistling. Abigail waited until he was gone, stood, went to the door, and entered. Fish darted between long fronds under a transparent floor. It was an austere room, almost featureless. Abigail looked, but did not see a hammock.

"So Cheyney's working for you now," she said coldly. Paul looked up from a corner keyout.

"As a matter of fact, I've just signed him to permanent contract in the crew room. He's bright enough. A bit green. Ought to do well."

"Then you admit that you put him up to grilling me about your puerile argument in the debate?" Garble struggled in her arms. She juggled him into a more comfortable position. "And that you staged the argument for my benefit in the first place?"

"Ah," Paul said. "I knew the training was going somewhere. You've become very wary in an extremely short time."

"Don't evade the question."

"I needed your honest reaction," Paul said. "Not the answer you would have given me, knowing your chances of crossing Ginungagap rode on it."

Garble made an angry noise. "You tell him, Garble!" she said. "That goes double for me." She stepped out the door. "You lost the debate," she snapped.

Long after the door had irised shut, she could feel Paul's amused smile burning into her back.

◆

Two days after she returned to kick Cheyney out of her hammock for the final time, Abigail was called to the crew room. "Dry run," Paul said. "Attendance is mandatory." And cut off.

The crew room was crowded with technicians, triple the number of keyouts. Small knots of them clustered before the screens, watching. Paul waved her to him.

"There," he motioned to one screen. "That's Clotho—the platform we built for the transmission device. It's a hundred kilometers off. I wanted more, but Dominguez overruled me. The device that'll unravel you and dump you down Ginungagap is that doohickey in the center." He tapped a keyout and the platform zoomed up to fill the screen. It was covered by a clear, transparent bubble. Inside, a space-suited figure was placing something into a machine that looked like nothing so much as a giant armor-clad clamshell. Abigail looked, blinked, looked again.

"That's Garble," she said indignantly.

"Complain to Dominguez. I wanted a baboon."

The clamshell device closed. The space-suited tech left in his tug, and alphanumerics flickered, indicating the device was in operation. As they watched, the spider-designed machinery immobilized Garble, transformed his molecules into one long continuous polymer chain, and spun it out an invisible opening at near light speed. The water in his body was separated out, piped away, and preserved. The electrolyte balances were recorded and simultaneously transmitted in a parallel stream of electrons. It would reach the spider receiver along with the lead end of the cat-polymer, to be used in the reconstruction.

Thirty seconds passed. Now Garble was only partially in Clotho. The polymer chain, invisible and incredibly long, was passing into Ginunga-gap. On the far side the spiders were beginning to knit it up.

If all was going well . . .

Ninety-two seconds after they flashed on, the alphanumerics stopped twinkling on the screen. Garble was gone from Clotho. The clamshell opened and the remote cameras showed it to be empty. A cheer arose.

Somebody boosted Dominguez atop a keyout. Intercom cameras swiveled to follow. He wavered fractionally, said "My friends," and launched into a speech. Abigail didn't listen.

Paul's hand fell on her shoulder. It was the first time he had touched her since their initial meeting. "He's only a scientist," he said. "He had no idea how close you are to that cat."

"Look, I *asked* to go. I knew the risks. But Garble's just an animal; he wasn't given the choice."

Paul groped for words. "In a way, this is what your training has been about—the reason you're going across instead of someone like Dominguez. He projects his own reactions onto other people. If—"

Then, seeing that she wasn't listening, he said, "Anyway, you'll have a cat to play with in a few hours. They're only keeping him long enough to test out the life systems."

⮞

There was a festive air to the second gathering. The spiders reported that Garble had translated flawlessly. A brief visual display showed him stalking about Clotho's sister platform, irritable but apparently unharmed.

"There," somebody said. The screen indicated that the receiver net had taken in the running end of the cat's polymer chain. They waited a minute and a half and the operation was over.

It was like a conjuring trick: the clamshell closed on emptiness. Water was piped in. Then it opened and Garble floated over its center, quietly licking one paw.

Abigail smiled at the homeliness of it. "Welcome back, Garble," she said quietly. "I'll get the guys in Bio to brew up some cream for you."

Paul's eyes flicked in her direction. They lingered for no time at all, long enough to file away another datum for future use, and then his attention was elsewhere. She waited until his back was turned and stuck out her tongue at him.

The tub docked with Clotho and a technician floated in. She removed her helmet self-consciously, aware of her audience. One hand extended, she bobbed toward the cat, calling softly.

"Get that jerk on the line," Paul snapped. "I want her helmet back on. That's sloppy. That's real—"

And in that instant Garble sprang.

Garble was a black-and-white streak that flashed past the astonished tech, through the air lock, and into the open tug. The cat pounced on the pilot panel. Its forelegs hit the controls. The hatch slammed shut, and the tug's motors burst into life.

Crew room techs grabbed wildly at their keyouts. The tech on Clotho frantically tried to fit her helmet back on. And the tug took off, blasting away half the protective dome and all the platform's air.

The screens showed a dozen different scenes, lenses shifting from close to distant and back. "Cheyney," Paul said quietly. Dominguez was frozen, looking bewildered. "Take it out."

"It's coming right at us!" somebody shouted.

Cheyney's fingers flicked: rap-tap-rap.

A bright nuclear flower blossomed.

There was silence, dead and complete, in the crew room. *I'm missing something*, Abigail thought. *We just blew up 5 percent of our tug fleet to kill a cat.*

"*Pull* that transmitter!" Paul strode through the crew room, scattering orders. "Nothing goes out! You, you, and you"—he yanked techs away from their keyouts—"*off* those things. I want the whole goddamned net shut *down*."

"Paul, . . ." an operator said.

"Keep on receiving." He didn't bother to look. "Whatever they want to send. Dump it all in storage and don't merge any of it with our data until we've gone over it."

Alone and useless in the center of the room, Dominguez stuttered, "What—what happened?"

"You blind idiot!" Paul turned on him viciously. "Your precious aliens have just made their first hostile move. The cat that came back was nothing like the one we sent. They made changes. They retransmitted it with instructions wet-wired into its brain."

"But why would they want to steal a tug?"

"*We don't know!*" Paul roared. "Get that through your head. We don't know their motives and we don't know how they think. But we would have known a lot more about their intentions than we wanted if I hadn't rigged that tug with an abort device."

"You didn't—" Dominguez began. He thought better of the statement.

"—have the authority to rig that device," Paul finished for him. "That's right. I didn't." His voice was heavy with sarcasm.

Dominguez seemed to shrivel. He stared bleakly, blankly, about him, then turned and left, slightly hunched over. Thoroughly discredited in front of the people who worked for him.

That was cold, Abigail thought. She marveled at Paul's cruelty. Not for an instant did she believe that the anger in his voice was real, that he was capable of losing control.

Which meant that in the midst of confusion and stress, Paul had found time to make a swift play for more power. To Abigail's newly suspicious eye, it looked like a successful one, too.

⬤

For five days Paul held the net shut by sheer willpower and force of personality. Information came in but did not go out. Bell-Sandia administration was not behind him; too much time and money had been sunk into Clotho to abandon the project. But Paul had the support of the tech crew, and he knew how to use it.

"Nothing as big as Bell-Sandia runs on popularity," Paul explained. "But I've got enough sympathy from above, and enough hesitation and official cowardice to keep this place shut down long enough to get a message across."

The incoming information flow fluctuated wildly, shifting from subject to subject. Data sequences were dropped halfway through and incomplete. Nonsense came in. The spiders were shifting through strategies in search of the key that would reopen the net.

"When they start repeating themselves," Paul said, "we can assume they understand the threat."

"But we *wouldn't* shut the net down permanently," Abigail pointed out.

Paul shrugged. "So it's a bluff."

They were sharing an after-shift drink in a fifth-level bar. Small red lizards scuttled about the rock wall behind the bartender. "And if your bluff doesn't work?" Abigail asked. "If it's all for nothing—what then?"

Paul's shoulders sagged, a minute shifting of tensions. "Then we trust in the goodwill of the spiders," he said. "We let them call the shots. And they will treat us benevolently or not, depending. In either case," his voice became dark, "I'll have played a lot of games and manipulated a lot of people for no reason at all." He took her hand. "If that happens, I'd like to apologize." His grip was tight, his knuckles pale.

◆

That night Abigail dreamed she was falling.

Light rainbowed all about her, in a violent splintering of bone and tearing of flesh. She flung out an arm and it bounced on something warm and yielding.

"Abigail."

She twisted and tumbled and something smashed into her ribs. Bright spikes of yellow darted up.

"Abigail!" Someone was shaking her, speaking loudly into her face. The rocks and sky went gray, were overlaid by unresolved images. Her eyelids struggled apart, fell together, opened.

"Oh," she said.

Paul rocked back on his heels. Fish darted about in the water beneath him. "There now," he said. Blue-green lights shifted gently underwater, moving in long, slow arcs. "Dream over?"

Abigail shivered, clutched his arm, let go of it almost immediately. She nodded.

"Good. Tell me about it."

"I—" Abigail began. "Are you asking me as a human being or in your official capacity?"

"I don't make that distinction."

She stretched out a leg and scratched her big toe, to gain time to think. She really didn't have any appropriate thoughts. "Okay," she said, and told him the entire dream.

Paul listened intently, rubbed a thumb across his chin thoughtfully when she was done. "We hired you on the basis of that incident, you know," he said. "Coolness under stress. Weak body image. There were a lot of gravity bums to choose from. But I figured you were just a hair tougher, a little bit grittier."

"What are you trying to tell me? That I'm replaceable?"

Paul shrugged. "Everybody's replaceable. I just wanted to be sure you knew that you could back out if you want. It wouldn't wreck our project."

"I don't want to back out." Abigail chose her words carefully, spoke them slowly, to avoid giving vent to the anger she felt building up inside. "Look, I've been on the gravity circuit for ten years. I've been everywhere in the system there is to go. Did you know that there are less than two thousand people alive who've set foot on Mercury *and* Pluto? We've got a little club; we get together once a year." Seaweed shifted about her; reflections of the floor lights formed nebulous swimming shapes on the walls. "I've spent my entire life going around and around and around the sun, and never really getting anywhere. I want to travel, and there's no-where left for me to go. So you offer me a way out and then ask if I want to back down. Like hell I do!"

"Why don't you believe that going through Ginungagap is death?" Paul asked quietly. She looked into his eyes, saw cool calculations going on behind them. It frightened her, almost. He was measuring her, passing judgment warping events into long logical chains that did not take human factors into account. He was an alien presence.

"It's—common sense, is all. I'll be the same when I exit as when I go in. There'll be no difference, not an atom's worth, not a scintilla."

"The *substance* will be different. Every atom will be different. Not a single electron in your body will be the same one you have now."

"Well, how does that differ so much from normal life?" Abigail de-manded. "All our bodies are in constant flux. Molecules come and go. Bit by bit, we're replaced. Does that make us different people from moment to moment? 'All that is body is as coursing vapors,' right?"

Paul's eyes narrowed. "Marcus Aurelius. Your quotation isn't complete, though. It goes on: 'All that is of the soul is dreams and vapors.' "

"What's that supposed to mean?"

"It means that the quotation doesn't say what you claimed it did. If you care to read it literally, it argues the opposite of what you're saying."

"Still, you can't have it both ways. Either the me that comes out of the spider black hole is the same as the one who went in, or I'm not the same person as I was an instant ago."

"I'd argue differently," Paul said. "But no matter. Let's go back to sleep."

He held out a hand, but Abigail felt no inclination to accept it. "Does this mean I've passed your test?"

Paul closed his eyes, stretched a little. "You're still reasonably afraid of dying, and you don't believe that you will," he said. "Yeah. You pass."

"Thanks a heap," Abigail said. They slept, not touching, for the rest of the night.

⬤

Three days later Abigail woke up, and Paul was gone. She touched the wall and spoke his name. A recording appeared. "Dominguez has been called up to Administration," it said. Paul appeared slightly distracted; he had not looked directly into the recorder and his image avoided Abigail's eyes. "I'm going to reopen the net before he returns. It's best we beat him to the punch." The recording clicked off.

Abigail routed an intercom call through to the crew room. A small chime notified him of her call, and he waved a hand in combined greeting and direction to remain silent. He was hunched over a keyout. The screen above it came to life.

"Ritual greetings, spider," he said.

"Hello, human. We wish to pursue our previous inquiry: the meaning of the term 'art' which was used by the human Dominguez six-sixteenths of the way through his major presentation."

"This is a difficult question. To understand a definition of art, you must first know the philosophy of aesthetics. This is a comprehensive field of knowledge comparable to the study of perception. In many ways it is related."

"What is the trade value of this field of knowledge?"

Dominguez appeared, looking upset. He opened his mouth, and Paul touched a finger to his own lips, nodding his head toward the screen.

"Significant. Our society considers art and science as being of roughly equal value."

"We will consider what to offer in exchange."

"Good. We also have a question for you. Please wait while we select the phrasing." He cut the translation lines, turned to Dominguez. "Looks like your raft gambit paid off. Though I'm surprised they bit at that particular piece of bait."

Dominguez looked weary. "Did they mention the incident with the cat?"

"No, nor the communications blackout."

The old man sighed. "I always felt close to the aliens," he said. "Now they seem—cold, inhuman." He attempted a chuckle. "That was almost a pun, wasn't it?"

"In a human, we'd call it a professional attitude. Don't let it spoil your accomplishment," Paul said. "This could be as big as optics." He opened the communications line again. "Our question is now phrased." Abigail noted he had not told Dominguez of her presence.

"Please go ahead."

"Why did you alter our test animal?"

Much leg waving. "We improved the ratios garble centers of perception garble wetware garble making the animal twelve-sixteenths as intelligent as a human. We thought you would be pleased."

"We were not. Why did the test animal behave in a hostile manner toward us?"

The spider's legs jerked quickly and it disappeared from the screen. Like an echo, the machine said, "Please wait."

Abigail watched Dominguez throw Paul a puzzled look. In the background, a man with a leather sack looped over one shoulder was walking slowly along the twisty access path. His hand dipped into the sack, came out, sprinkled fireflies among the greenery. Dipped in, came out again. Even in the midst of crisis the trivia of day-to-day existence went on.

The spider reappeared, accompanied by two of its own kind. Their legs interlaced and retreated rapidly, a visual pantomime of an excited conversation. Finally one of their number addressed the screen.

"We have discussed the matter."

"So I see."

"It is our conclusion that the experience of translation through Ginungagap had a negative effect on the test animal. This was not anticipated.

It is new knowledge. We know little of the psychology of carbon-based life."

"You're saying the test animal was driven mad?"

"Key word did not translate. We assume understanding. Steps must be taken to prevent a recurrence of this damage. Can you do this?"

Paul said nothing.

"Is this the reason why communications were interrupted?"

No reply.

"There is a cultural gap. Can you clarify?"

"Thank you for your cooperation," Paul said, and switched the screen off. "You can set your people to work," he told Dominguez. "No reason why they should answer the last few questions, though."

"Were they telling the truth?" Dominguez asked wonderingly.

"Probably not. But at least now they'll think twice before trying to jerk us around again." He winked at Abigail, and she switched off the intercom.

◆

They re-ran the test using a baboon shipped out from the Belt Zoological Gardens. Abigail watched it arrive from the lip station, crated and snarling.

"They're a lot stronger than we are," Paul said. "Very agile. If the spiders want to try any more tricks, we couldn't offer them better bait."

The test went smooth as silk. The baboon was shot through Ginungagap, held by the spiders for several hours, and returned. Exhaustive testing showed no tampering with the animal.

Abigail asked how accurate the tests were. Paul hooked his hands behind his back. "We're returning the baboon to the Belt. We wouldn't do that if we had any doubts. But—" He raised an eyebrow, asking Abigail to finish the thought.

"But if they're really hostile, they won't underestimate us twice. They'll wait for a human to tamper with."

Paul nodded.

◆

The night before Abigail's send-off they made love. It was a frenzied and desperate act, performed wordlessly and without tenderness. Afterward they lay together, Abigail idly playing with Paul's curls.

"Gail . . ." His head was hidden in her shoulder; she couldn't see his face. His voice was muffled.

"Mmmm?"

"Don't go."

She wanted to cry. Because as soon as he said it, she knew it was another test, the final one. And she also knew that Paul wanted her to fail it. That he honestly believed transversing Ginungagap would kill her, and that the woman who emerged from the spiders' black hole would not be herself.

His eyes were shut; she could tell by the creases in his forehead. He knew what her answer was. There was no way he could avoid knowing.

Abigail sensed that this was as close to a declaration of emotion as Paul was capable of. She felt how he despised himself for using his real emotions as yet another test, and how he could not even pretend to himself that there were circumstances under which he would *not* so test her. *This must be how it feels to think as he does,* she thought. *To constantly scrabble after every last implication, like eternally picking at a scab.*

"Oh, Paul," she said.

He wrenched about, turning his back to her. "Sometimes I wish"—his hands rose in front of his face like claws; they moved toward his eyes, closed into fists—"that for just ten goddamned minutes I could turn my mind off." His voice was bitter.

Abigail huddled against him, looped a hand over his side and onto his chest. "Hush," she said.

➾

The tug backed away from Clotho, dwindling until it was one of a ring of bright sparks pacing the platform. Mother was a point source lost in the star field. Abigail shivered, pulled off her arm bands and shoved them into a storage sack. She reached for her *cache-sexe,* hesitated.

The hell with it, she thought. *It's nothing they haven't seen before.* She shucked it off, stood naked. Gooseflesh rose on the backs of her legs. She swam to the transmittal device, feeling awkward under the distant watching eyes.

Abigail groped into the clamshell. "Go," she said.

The metal closed about her seamlessly, encasing her in darkness. She floated in a lotus position, bobbing slightly.

A light, gripping field touched her, stilling her motion. On cue, hypnotic commands took hold in her brain. Her breathing became shallow; her heart slowed. She felt her body ease into stasis. The final command took hold.

Abigail weighed 50 keys. Even though the water in her body would not be transmitted, the polymer chain she was to be transformed into would be 275 kilometers long. It would take 15 minutes and 17 seconds to unravel at light speed, negligibly longer at translation speed. She would still be sitting in Clotho when the spiders began knitting her up.

It was possible that Garble had gone mad from a relatively swift transit. Paul doubted it, but he wasn't taking any chances. To protect Abigail's sanity, the meds had wet-wired a travel fantasy into her brain. It would blind her to external reality while she traveled.

➾

She was an eagle. Great feathered wings extended out from her shoulders. Clotho was gone, leaving her alone in space. Her skin was red and leathery, her breasts hard and unyielding. Feathers covered her thighs, giving way at the knees to talons.

She moved her wings, bouncing lightly against the thin solar wind swirling down into Ginungagap. The vacuum felt like absolute freedom. She screamed a predator's exultant shrill. Nothing enclosed her; she was free of restrictions forever.

Below her lay Ginungagap, the primal chasm, and invisible challenge marked by a red smudge of glowing gases. It was inchoate madness, a gibbering, impersonal force that wanted to draw her in, to crush her in its embrace. Its hunger was fierce and insatiable.

Abigail held her place briefly, effortlessly. Then she folded her wings and dove.

A rain of X rays stung through her, the scattering of Ginungagap's accretion disk. They were molten iron passing through a ghost. Shrieking defiance, she attacked, scattering sparks in her wake.

Ginungagap grew, swelled until it swallowed up her vision. It was purest black, unseeable, unknowable, a thing of madness. It was Enemy.

A distant objective part of her knew that she was still in Clotho, the polymer chain being unraveled from her body, accelerated by a translator, passing through two black holes, and simultaneously being knit up by the spiders. It didn't matter.

She plunged into Ginungagap as effortlessly as if it were the film of a soap bubble.

In—

—And out.

It was like being reversed in a mirror, or watching an entertainment run backward. She was instantly flying out the way she came. The sky was a mottled mass of violet light.

The stars before her brightened from violet to blue. She craned her neck, looked back at Ginungagap, saw its disk-shaped nothingness recede, and screamed in frustration because it had escaped her. She spread her wings to slow her flight and—

—was sitting in a dark place. Her hand reached out, touched metal, recognized the inside of a clamshell device.

A hairline crack of light looped over her, widened. The clamshell opened.

Oceans of color bathed her face. Abigail straightened, and the act of doing so lifted her up gently. She stared through the transparent bubble at a phosphorescent foreverness of light.

My God, she thought. *The stars.*

The stars were thicker, more numerous than she was used to seeing them—large and bright and glittery rich. She was probably someplace significant, in a star cluster or the center of the galaxy; she couldn't guess. She felt irrationally happy to simply be; she took a deep breath, then laughed.

"Abigail Vanderhoek."

She turned to face the voice, and found that it came from a machine. Spiders crouched beside it, legs moving silently. Outside, in the hard vacuum, were more spiders.

"We regret any pain this may cause," the machine said.

Then the spiders rushed forward. She had no time to react. Sharp mandibles loomed before her, then dipped to her neck. Impossibly swift, they sliced through her throat, severed her spine. A sudden jerk and her head was separated from her body.

It happened in an instant. She felt brief pain, and the dissociation of actually *seeing* her decapitated body just beginning to react. And then she died.

◆

A spark. A light. *I'm alive*, she thought. Consciousness returned like an ancient cathode tube warming up. Abigail stretched slowly, bobbing gently in the air, collecting her thoughts. She was in the sister-Clotho again—not in pain, her head and neck firmly on her shoulders. There were spiders in the platform, and a few floating outside.

"Abigail Vanderhoek," the machine said. "We are ready to begin negotiations."

Abigail said nothing.

After a moment, the machine said, "Are you damaged? Are your thoughts impaired?" A pause, then, "Was your mind not protected during transit?"

"Is that you waving the legs there? Outside the platform?"

"Yes. It is important that you talk with the other humans. You must convey our questions. They will not communicate with us."

"I have a few questions of my own," Abigail said. "I won't cooperate until you answer them."

"We will answer any questions provided you neither garble nor garble."

"What do you take me for?" Abigail asked. "Of course I won't."

Long hours later she spoke to Paul and Dominguez. At her request the spiders had withdrawn, leaving her alone. Dominguez looked drawn and haggard. "I swear we had no idea the spiders would attack you," Dominguez said. "We saw it on the screens. I was certain you'd been killed. . . ." His voice trailed off.

"Well, I'm alive, no thanks to you guys. Just what is this crap about an explosive substance in my bones, anyway?"

"An explosive—I swear we know nothing of anything of the kind."

"A close relative to plastique," Paul said. "I had a small editing device attached to Clotho's translator. It altered roughly half the bone marrow in your sternum, pelvis, and femurs in transmission. I'd hoped the spiders wouldn't pick up on it so quickly."

"You actually did," Abigail marveled. "The spiders weren't lying; they decapitated me in self-defense. What the holy hell did you think you were *doing?*"

"Just a precaution," Paul said. "We wet-wired you to trigger the stuff on command. That way, we could have taken out the spider installation if they'd tried something funny."

"Um," Dominguez said, "this *is* being recorded. What I'd like to know, Ms. Vanderhoek, is how you escaped being destroyed."

"I didn't," Abigail said. "The spiders killed me. Fortunately, they anticipated the situation, and recorded the transmission. It was easy for them to recreate me—after they edited out the plastique."

Dominguez gave her a odd look. "You don't—feel anything particular about this?"

"Like what?"

"Well—" He turned to Paul helplessly.

"Like the real Abigail Vanderhoek died and you're simply a very realistic copy," Paul said.

"Look, we've been through this garbage before," Abigail began angrily.

Paul smiled formally at Dominguez. It was hard to adjust to seeing the two in flat black-and-white. "She doesn't believe a word of it."

"If you guys can pull yourselves up out of your navels for a minute," Abigail said, "I've got a line on something the spiders have that you want. They claim they've sent probes through their black hole."

"Probes?" Paul stiffened. Abigail could sense the thoughts coursing through his skull, of defenses and military applications.

"Carbon-hydrogen chain probes. Organic probes. Self-constructing transmitters. They've got a carbon-based secondary technology."

"Nonsense," Dominguez said. "How could they convert back to coherent matter with a receiver?"

Abigail shrugged. "They claim to have found a loophole."

"How does it work?" Paul snapped.

"They wouldn't say. They seemed to think you'd pay well for it."

"That's very true," Paul said slowly. "Oh, yes."

The conference took almost as long as her session with the spiders had. Abigail was bone weary when Dominguez finally said, "That ties up the official minutes. We now stop recording." A line tracked across the screen, was gone. "If you want to speak to anyone off the record, now's your chance. Perhaps there is someone close to you . . ."

"Close? No." Abigail almost laughed. "I'll speak to Paul alone, though."

A spider floated by outside Clotho II. It was a golden, crablike being, its body slightly opalescent. It skittered along unseen threads strung between the open platforms of the spider star-city. "I'm listening," Paul said.

"You turned me into a *bomb*, you freak."

"So?"

"I could have been killed."

"Am I supposed to care?"

"You damn well ought to, considering the liberties you've taken with my fair white body."

"Let's get one thing understood," Paul said. "The woman I slept with, the woman I cared for, is dead. I have no feelings toward or obligations to you whatsoever."

"Paul," Abigail said. "*I'm not dead*. Believe me, I'd know if I were."

"How could I possibly trust what you think or feel? It could all be attitudes the spiders wet-wired into you. We know they have the technology."

"How do you know that *your* attitudes aren't wet-wired in? For that matter, how do you know anything is real? I mean, these are the most sophomoric philosophic ideas there are. But I'm the same woman I was a few hours ago. My memories, opinions, feelings—they're all the same as they were. There's absolutely no difference between me and the woman you slept with on the *Clarke*."

"I know." Paul's eyes were cold. "That's the horror of it." He snapped off the screen.

Abigail found herself staring at the lifeless machinery. *God, that hurt*, she thought. *It shouldn't, but it hurt*. She went to her quarters.

The spiders had done a respectable job of preparing for her. There were no green plants, but otherwise the room was the same as the one she'd had on the *Clarke*. They'd even been able to spin the platform, giving her an adequate down-orientation. She sat in her hammock, determined to think pleasanter thoughts. About the offer the spiders had made, for example. The one she hadn't told Paul and Dominguez about.

Banned by their chemistry from using black holes to travel, the spiders needed a representative to see to their interests among the stars. They had offered her the job.

Or perhaps the plural would be more appropriate—they had offered her the jobs. Because there were too many places to go for one woman to handle them all. They needed a dozen—in time, perhaps, a hundred—Abigail Vanderhoeks.

In exchange for licensing rights to her personality, the right to make as many duplicates of her as were needed, they were willing to give her the rights to the self-reconstructing black hole platforms.

It would make her a rich woman—a hundred rich woman—back in human space. And it would open the universe. She hadn't committed herself yet, but there was no way she was going to turn down the offer. The chance to see a thousand stars? No, she would not pass it by.

When she got old, too, they could create another Abigail from their recording, burn her new memories into it, and destroy her old body.

I'm going to see the stars, she thought. I'm going to *live forever*. She couldn't understand why she didn't feel elated, wondered at the sudden rush of melancholy that ran through her like the precursor of tears.

Garble jumped into her lap, offered his belly to be scratched. The spiders had recorded him, too. They had been glad to restore him to his unaltered state when she made the request. She stroked his stomach and buried her face in his fur.

"Pretty little cat," she told him. "I thought you were dead."

Exploring Fossil Canyon

KIM STANLEY ROBINSON

Kim Stanley Robinson sold his first story in 1976 and quickly established himself as one of the most respected and critically acclaimed writers of his generation. His story "Black Air" won the World Fantasy Award in 1984, and his novella "The Blind Geometer," won the Nebula Award in 1987. His novel The Wild Shore was published in 1984 as the first title in the resurrected Ace Special line, along with first novels by other new writers such as William Gibson, Michael Swanwick, and Lucius Shepard, and was quickly followed up by other novels such as Icehenge, The Memory of Whiteness, A Short, Sharp Shock, The Gold Coast, and The Pacific Shore and by collections such as The Planet on the Table, Escape from Kathmandu, and Remaking History.

Robinson's already-distinguished literary reputation took a quantum jump in the decade of the nineties, however, with the publication of his acclaimed Mars trilogy, Red Mars, Green Mars, and Blue Mars. Red Mars won a Nebula Award, both Green Mars and Blue Mars won Hugo Awards, and the trilogy has come to be widely recognized as the genre's most accomplished, detailed, sustained, and substantial look at the colonization and terraforming of another world, rivaled only by Arthur C. Clarke's The Sands of Mars.

The Mars trilogy will probably associate Robinson's name forever with the Red Planet, but it was not the first time he would explore a fictional Mars; Robinson visited Mars in several stories of the eighties, including the memorable novella "Green Mars," and the evocative story of exploration that follows, during which occurs one of those perceptual shifts that come along every once in a while, one of the first appearances of the idea that, rather than terraforming Mars and re-shaping it into a mirror image of the Earth, we should leave it alone, leave it just as it is, rocks, rust, red dirt, and all.

Robinson's latest books are the novel Antarctica and a collection of stories and poems set on his fictional Mars, The Martians. He lives with his family in California.

Two hours before sunset their guide, Roger Clayborne, declared it was time to set camp, and the eight members of the tour trooped down from the ridges or up out of the side canyons they had been exploring that day as the group slowly progressed west, toward Olympus Mons. Eileen Monday, who had had her intercom switched off all day (the guide could override her deafness) turned to the common band and heard the voices of her companions, chattering. Dr. Mitsumu and Cheryl Martinez had pulled the equipment wagon all day, down a particularly narrow canyon bottom, and their vociferous complaints were making Mrs. Mitsumu laugh. John Nobleton was suggesting, as usual, that they camp farther down the ancient water-formed arroyo they were following; Eileen could not be sure which of the dusty-suited figures was him, but she guessed it was the one enthusiastically bounding up the wash, kicking up sand with every jump, and floating like an impala. Their guide, on the other hand, was unmistakable: tall even when sitting against a tall boulder, high on the spine flanking one side of the deep canyon. When the others spotted him, they groaned. The equipments wagon weighed less than seven hundred kilograms in Mars's gravity, but still it would take several of them to pull it up the slope to the spot Clayborne had in mind.

"Roger, why don't we just pull it down the road we've got here and camp around the corner?" John insisted.

"Well, we certainly could," Roger said—he spoke so quietly that the intercoms barely transmitted his dry voice—"but I haven't yet learned to sleep comfortably at a forty-five-degree angle."

Mrs. Mitsumu giggled. Eileen snicked in irritation, hoping Roger could identify the maker of the sound. His remark typified all she disliked about the guide; he was both taciturn and sarcastic, a combination Eileen did not like any more for considering it unusual. And his wide derisive grin was no help either.

"I found a good flat down there," John protested.

"I saw it. But I suspect out tent needs a little more room."

Eileen joined the crew hauling the wagon up the slope. "I suspect," she mimicked as she began to pant and sweat inside her suit.

"See?" came Roger's voice in her ear. "Ms. Monday agrees with me."

She snicked again, more annoyed than she cared to show. So far, in her opinion, this expedition was a flop. And their guide was a very significant factor in its failure, even if he was so quiet that she had barely noticed him for the first three or four days. But eventually his sharp tongue had caught her attention.

She slipped in some soft dirt and went to her knees; bounced back up and heaved again, but the contact reminded her that Mars itself shared the blame for her disappointment. She wasn't as willing to admit that as she was her dislike for Clayborne, but it was true, and it disturbed her. All through her many years at the University of Mars Burroughs, she had studied the planet—first in literature (she had read every Martian tale every written, she once boasted), then in areology, particularly seismology. But she had spent most of her twenty four years in Burroughs itself, and the big city was not like the canyons. Her previous exposure to the Martian landscape consisted visits to the magnificent domed section of Hephaestus Chasma called Lazuli Canyon, where icy water ran in rills and springs, in waterfalls and pools, and tundra grass grew on every wet red beach. Of course she knew that the virgin Martian landscape was not like Lazuli, but somewhere in her mind, when she had seen the advertisement for the hike—"Guaranteed to be terrain *never before trodden* by human feet"—she must have had an image of something similar to that green world. The thought made her curse herself a fool. The slope they were struggling up at that very moment was a perfect representative sample of the untrodden terrain they had been hiking over for the week: It was composed of dirt of every consistency and hue, so that it resembled an immense layered cake slowly melting, made of ingredients that looked like baking soda, sulfur, brick dust, curry powder, coal slag, and alum. And it was only one cake out of thousands of them, all stacked crazily for as far as the eye could see. Dirt piles.

Just short of Roger's flat campsite, they stopped to rest. Sweat was stinging in Eileen's left eye. "Let's get the wagon up here," Roger said, coming down to help. His clients stared at him mutinously, unmoving. The doctor leaned over to adjust his boot, and as he had been holding the wagon's handle, the others were caught off guard; a pebble gave way under the wagon's rear wheel, and suddenly it was out of their grasp and rolling down the slope—

In an explosion of dust Roger dived headfirst down the hill, chocking the rear wheel with a stone the size of a breadloaf. The wagon plowed the chock downhill a couple of meters and came to a halt. The group stood motionlessly, staring at the prone guide, Eileen as surprised as the rest of them; she had never seen him move so fast. He stood up at his usual lazy pace and started wiping dust from his face-plate. "Best to put the chock down before it starts rolling," he murmured, smiling to himself. They gathered to pull the wagon up the flat, chattering again. But Eileen considered it; if the wagon had careened all the way down to the canyon bottom, there would have been at least the possibility that it would have been damaged. And if it had been damaged badly enough, it could have killed them all. She pursed her lips and climbed up to the flat.

Roger and Ivan Corallton were pulling the base of the tent from the wagon. They stretched it out over the posts that kept it level and off the frozen soil; Ivan and Kevin Ottalini assembled the curved poles of the tension dome. The three of them and John carefully got the poles in place, and pulled the transparent tent material out of the base to stretch it under the framework. When they were done the others stood, a bit stiffly—they had traveled some twenty kilometers that day—and walked in through the flaccid airlock, hauling the wagon in behind them. Roger twisted valves on the side of the wagon, and compressed air pushed violently into their protective bag. Before it was full, Dr. Mitsumu and his wife were disengaging the bath and the latrine assemblies from the wagon. Roger switched on the heaters, and after a few minutes of gazing at the gauges, he nodded. "Home again home again," he said as always. Condensation was beading on the inside of their dome's clear skin. Eileen unclipped her helmet from her suit and pulled it off. "It's too hot." No one heard her. She walked to the wagon and turned down the heater, catching Roger's sardonic grin out of the corner of her eye; she always thought the tent's air was too hot. Dr. Mitsumu, regular as clockwork, ducked into the latrine as soon as his suit was off. The air was filled with the smells of sweat and urine, as everyone stripped their suits off and poured the contents of the runoffs into the water purifier on the wagon. Doran Stark got to the bath first as always—Eileen was amused by how quickly a group established its habits and customs—and stood in the ankle-deep water, sponging himself down and singing "I Met Her in a Phobos Restaurant." As she emptied her suit into the purifier Eileen found herself smiling at all their domestic routines, performed in a transparent bubble in the midst of an endless rust desolation.

She took her sponge bath last except for Roger. There was a shower curtain that could be pulled around the tiny tub at shoulder level, but nobody else used it, so Eileen didn't either, although she was made a bit uncomfortable by the surreptitious glances of John and the doctor. Nevertheless, she sponged down thoroughly, and in the constantly moving air her clean wet skin felt good. Besides it was rather a splendid sight, all the ruddy naked bodies standing about on the ledge of a spine extending thousands of meters above and below them, the convolutions of canyon after canyon scoring the titled landscape, Olympus Mons bulging to the west, rising out of the atmosphere so that it appeared to puncture the dome of the sky, and the blood-red sun about to set behind it. Roger did know how to pick a campsite, Eileen admitted to herself (he somehow sponged down with his back always to her, shower curtain partly pulled out, and dressed while still wet, signaling the gradual rehabiliment of the others). It was truly a sublime sight, as all of their campsite prospects had been. Sublime: to have your senses telling you you are in danger, when you know you are not; that was Burke's definition of the sublime, more or less, and it fit practically every moment of these days, from dawn to dusk. But that in itself could get wearing. The sublime is not the beautiful, after all, and one cannot live comfortably in a perpetual sense of danger. But at sunset, in the tent, it was an apprehension that could be enjoyed: the monstrous bare landscape, her bare skin; the utter serenity of the slow movement of Beethoven's last string quartet, which Ivan played every day during the sun's dying moments. . . . "Listen to this," Cheryl said, and read from her constant companion, the volume *If Wang Wei Lived on Mars:*

> Sitting out all night thinking.
> Sun half-born five miles to the east.
> Blood pulses through all this still air:
> The edge of a mountain, great distance away.
> Nothing moves but the sun,
> Blood to fire as it rises.
> How many, these dawns?
> How far, our home?
> Stars fade. Big rocks splinter
> The mind's great fear:
> Peace here. Peace, here.

It was a fine moment, Eileen thought, made so by what was specifically human in the landscape. She dressed with the rest of them, deliberately turning away from John Nobleton as she rooted around in her drawer of the wagon, and they fell to making dinner. For more than an hour after Olympus Mons blotted out the sun the sky stayed light; pink in the west, shading to brick-black in the east. They cooked and ate by this illumination. Their meal, planned by Roger, was a thick vegetable stew, seemingly fresh French bread, and coffee. Most of them kept off the common band during long stretches of the day, and now they discussed what they had seen, for they explored different side canyons as they went. The main canyon they were following was a dry outflow wash, formed by flash floods working down a small fault line in a large tilted plateau. It was relatively young, Roger said—meaning two billion years old, but younger than most of the water-carved canyons on Mars. Wind erosion and the marvelous erratics created by volcanic bombardment from Olympus Mons gave the expedition members a lot of features to discuss: beach terracing from long-lost lakes, meandering streambeds, lava bombs shaped like giant teardrops, or colored in a way that implied certain gases in copious quantities in the Hesperian atmosphere.... This last, plus the fact that these canyons had been carved by water, naturally provoked a lot of speculation about the possibilities of ancient Martian life. And the passing water, and the resiliencies of the rock, had created forms fantastical enough to seem the sculpture of some alien art. So they talked, with the enthusiasm and free speculation that only amateurs seem to bring to a subject: Sunday paper areologists, Eileen thought. There wasn't a proper scientist among them; she was the closest thing to it, and the only thing she knew was the rudiments of areology. Yet she listened to the talk with interest.

Roger, on the other hand, never contributed to these free-ranging discussions, and didn't even listen. At the moment he was engaged in setting up his cot and "bedroom" wall. There were panels provided so that each sleeper, or couple, could block off an area around their cot; no one took advantage of them but Roger, the rest preferring to lie out under the stars together. Roger set two panels against the sloping side of the dome, leaving just enough room for his cot under the clear low roof. It was yet another way that he set himself apart, and watching him, Eileen shook her head. Expedition guides were usually so amiable—how did he keep his job? Did he ever get repeat customers? She set out her cot, observing his particular preparations: He was one of the tall Martians, well over two meters (Lamarckianism was back in vogue, as it appeared that the more generations of ancestors you had on Mars, the taller you grew; it was true for Eileen herself, who was fourth-generation, or *yonsei*)—long-faced, long-nosed, homely as English royalty . . . long feet that were clumsy once out of their boots. . . . He rejoined them, however, this evening, which was not always his custom, and they lit a lantern as the wine-dark sky turned black and filled with stars. Bedding arranged, they sat down on cots and the floor around the lantern's dim light and talked some more. Kevin and Doran began a chess game.

For the first time, they asked Eileen questions about her area of expertise. Was it true that the southern highlands now held the crust of both primeval hemispheres? Did the straight line of the three great Tharsis volcanoes indicate a hot spot in the mantle? Sunday paper areology again, but Eileen answered as best she could. Roger appeared to be listening.

"Do you think there'll ever be a marsquake we can actually feel?" he asked with a grin.

The others laughed, and Eileen felt herself blush. It was a common jest; sure enough, he followed it up: "You sure you seismologists aren't just inventing these marsquakes to keep yourself in employment?"

"You're out here enough," she replied. "One of these days a fault will open up and swallow you."

"She hopes," Ivan said. The sniping between them had of course not gone unnoticed.

"So you think I might actually feel a quake someday," Roger said.

"Sure. There's thousands every day, you know."

"But that's because your seismographs register every footstep on the planet. I mean, a big one?"

"Of course. I can't think of anyone who deserves a shaking more."

"Might even have to use the Richter scale, eh?"

Now that was unfair, because the Harrow scale was necessary to make finer distinctions between low-intensity quakes. But later in the same conversation, she got hers back. Cheryl and Mrs. Mitsumu were asking Roger about where he had traveled before in his work, how many expeditions he had guided and the like. "I'm a canyon guide," he replied at one point.

"So when will you graduate to Marineris?" Eileen asked.

"Graduate?"

"Sure, isn't Marineris the ultimate goal of every canyon man?"

"Well, to a certain extent—"

"You'd better get assigned there in a hurry, hadn't you—I hear it takes a whole lifetime to learn those canyons." Roger looked to be about forty.

"Oh not for our Roger," Mrs. Mitsumu said, joining in the ribbing.

"No one ever learns Marineris," Roger protested. "It's eight thousand kilometers long, with hundreds of side canyons—"

"What about Gustafsen?" Eileen said. "I thought he and a couple others knew every inch of it."

"Well . . ."

"Better start working on that transfer."

"Well, I'm a Tharsis fan myself," he explained, in a tone so apologetic that the whole group burst out laughing. Eileen smiled at him and went to get some tea started.

After the tea was distributed, John and Ivan turned the conversation to another favorite topic, the terraforming of the canyons. "This system would be as beautiful as Lazuli," John said. "Can you imagine water running down the drops we took today? Tundra grass everywhere, finches in the air, little horned toads down in the cracks . . . alpine flowers to give it some color."

"Yes, it will be exquisite," Ivan agreed. With the same material that made their tent, several canyons and craters had been domed, and thin cold air pumped beneath, allowing arctic and alpine life to exist. Lazuli was the greatest of these terraria, but many more were springing up.

"Unnh," Roger muttered.

"You don't agree?" Ivan asked.

Roger shook his head. "The best you can do is make an imitation Earth. That's not what Mars is for. Since we're on Mars, we should adjust to what it is, and enjoy it for that."

"Oh but there will always be natural canyons and mountains," John said. "There's as much land surface on Mars as on Earth, right?"

"Just barely."

"So with all that land, it will take centuries for it all to be terraformed. In this gravity, maybe never. But centuries, at least."

"Yes, but that's the direction it's headed," Roger said. "If they start orbiting mirrors and blowing open volcanoes to provide gases, they'll change the whole surface."

"But wouldn't that be marvelous!" Ivan said.

"You don't seriously object to making life on the open surface possible, do you?" Mrs. Mitsumu asked.

Roger shrugged. "I like it the way it is."

John and the rest continued to discuss the considerable problems of terraforming, and after a bit Roger got up and went to bed. An hour later Eileen got up to do the same, and the others followed her, brushing teeth, visiting the latrine, talking more. . . . Long after the others had settled down, Eileen stood under one edge of the tent dome, looking up at the stars. There near Scorpio, as a high evening star, was the Earth, a distinctly bluish point, accompanied by its fainter companion the moon. A double planet of resonant beauty in the host of constellations. Tonight it gave her an inexplicable yearning to see it, to stand on it.

Suddenly John appeared at her side, standing too close to her, shoulder to shoulder, his arm rising, as if with a life of its own, to circle her waist. "Hike'll be over soon," he said. She didn't respond. He was a very handsome man; aquiline features, jet-black hair. He didn't know how tired Eileen was of handsome men. She had been as impetuous in her affairs as a pigeon in a park, and it had brought her a lot of grief. Her last three lovers had all been quite good-looking, and the last of them, Eric, had been rich as well. His house in Burroughs was made of rare stones, as all the rich new houses were: a veritable castle of dark purple chert, inlaid with chalcedony and jade, rose quartz and jasper, its floors intricately flagged patterns of polished yellow slate, coral, and bright turquoise. And the parties! Croquet picnics in the maze garden, dances in the ballroom, masques all about the extensive grounds. . . . But Eric himself, brilliant talker though he was, had turned out to be rather superficial, and promiscuous as well, a discovery that Eileen had been slow to make. It had hurt her feelings. And since that had been the third intimate relationship to go awry in four years, she felt tired and unsure of herself, unhappy, and particularly sick of that easy mutual attraction of the attractive which had gotten her into such painful trouble, and which was what John was relying on at that very moment.

Of course he knew nothing of all this, as his arm hugged her waist (he certainly didn't have Eric's way with words), but she wasn't inclined to excuse his ignorance. She mulled over methods of diplomatically slipping out of his grasp and back to a comfortable distance. This was certainly the most he had made so far in the way of a move. She decided on one of her feints—leaning into him to peck his cheek, then pulling away when his guard was down—and had started the maneuver, when with a bump one of Roger's panels knocked aside and Roger stumbled out, in his shorts, bleary-eyed. "Oh?" he said sleepily, as he noticed them; then saw who they were, and their position—"Ah," he said, and stumped away toward the latrine.

Eileen took advantage of the disturbance to slip away from John and go to bed, which was no-trespass territory, as John well knew. She lay down in some agitation. That smile, that "Ah"—the whole incident irritated her so much that she had trouble falling asleep. And the double star, one blue, one white, returned her stare all the while.

☙

The next day it was Eileen and Roger's turn to pull the wagon. This was the first time they had pulled together, and while the rest ranged ahead or to the sides, they solved the many small problems presented by the task of getting the wagon down the canyon. An occasional drop-off was high enough to require winch, block, and tackle—sometimes even one or two of the other travelers—but mostly it was a matter of guiding the flexible little cart down the center of the wash. They agreed on band 33 for their private communication, but aside from the business at hand, they conversed very little. "Look out for that rock." "How nice, that triangle of shards." To Eileen it seemed clear that Roger had very little interest in her or her observations. Or else, it occurred to her, he thought the same of her.

At one point she asked, "What if we let the wagon slip right now?" It was poised over the edge of a six-or seven-meter drop, and they were winching it down.

"It would fall," his voice replied solemnly in her ear, and through his faceplate she could see him smiling.

She kicked pebbles at him. "Come on, would it break? Are we in danger of our lives most every minute?"

"No way. These things are practically indestructible. Otherwise, it would be too dangerous to use them. They've dropped them off four-hundred-meter cliffs—not sheer you understand, but steep—and it doesn't even dent them."

"I see. So when you saved the wagon from slipping down that slope yesterday, you weren't actually saving our lives."

"Oh no. Did you think that? I just didn't want to climb down that hill and recover it."

"Ah." She let the wagon thump down, and they descended to it. After that there were no exchanges between them for a long time. Eileen contemplated the fact that she would be back in Burroughs in three or four days, with nothing in her life resolved, nothing different about it.

Still, it would be good to get back to the open air, the illusion of open air. Running water. Plants.

Roger clicked his tongue in distress.

"What?" Eileen asked.

"Sandstorm coming." He switched to the common band, which Eileen could now hear. "Everyone get back to the main canyon, please, there's a sandstorm on the way."

There were groans over the common band. No one was actually in sight. Roger bounced down the canyon with impeccable balance, bounced back up. "No good campsites around," he complained. Eileen watched him; he noticed and pointed at the western horizon. "See that feathering in the sky?"

All Eileen could see was a patch where the sky's pink was perhaps a bit yellow, but she said "Yes?"

"Dust storm. Coming our way, too. I think I feel the wind already." He put a hand up. Eileen thought that feeling the wind through a suit when the atmospheric pressure was thirty millibars was strictly a myth, a guide's boast, but she stuck her hand up as well, and thought that there might be a faint fluctuating pressure on it.

Ivan, Kevin, and the Mitsumus appeared far down the canyon. "Any campsites down there?" Roger asked.

"No, the canyon gets even narrower."

Then the sandstorm was upon them, sudden as a flash flood. Eileen could see fifty meters at the most; they were in a shifting dome of flying sand, it seemed, and it was as dark as their long twilights, or darker.

Over band 33, in her left ear, Eileen heard a long sigh. Then in her right ear, over the common band, Roger's voice: "You all down the canyon there, stick together and come on up to us. Doran, Cheryl, John, let's hear from you—where are you?"

"Roger?" It was Cheryl on the common band, sounding frightened.

"Yes, Cheryl, where are you?"

A sharp thunder roll of static: "We're in a sandstorm, Roger! I can just barely hear you."

"Are you with Doran and John?"

"I'm with Doran, and he's just over this ridge, I can hear him, but he says he can't hear you."

"Get together with him and start back for the main canyon. What about John?"

"I don't know, I haven't seen him in over an hour."

"All right. Stay with Doran—"

"Roger?"

"Yes?"

"Doran's here now."

"I can hear you again," Doran's voice said. He sounded more scared than Cheryl. "Over that ridge there was too much interference."

"Yeah, that's what's happening with John I expect," Roger said.

Eileen watched the dim form of their guide move up the canyon's side slope in the wavering amber dusk of the storm. The "sand" in the thin air was mostly dust, or fines even smaller than dust particles, like smoke; but occasional larger grains made a light *tik tik tik* against her faceplate.

"Roger, we can't seem to find the main canyon," Doran declared, scratchy in the interference.

"What do you mean?"

"Well, we've gone up the canyon we descended, but we must have taken a different fork, because we've run into a box canyon."

Eileen shivered in her warm suit. Each canyon system lay like a lightning bolt on the tilted land, a pattern of ever-branching forks and tributaries; in the storm's gloom it would be very easy to get lost; and they still hadn't heard from John.

"Well, drop back to the last fork and try the next one to the south. As I recall, you're over in the next canyon north of us."

"Right," Doran said. "We'll try that."

The four who had been farther down the main canyon appeared like ghosts in mist. "Here we are," Ivan said with satisfaction.

"Nobleton! John! Do you read me?"

No answer.

"He must be off a ways," Roger said. He approached the wagon. "Help me pull this up the slope."

"Why?" Dr. Mitsumu asked.

"We're setting the tent up there. Sleep on an angle tonight, you bet."

"But why up there?" Dr. Mitsumu persisted. "Couldn't we set up the tent here in the wash?"

"It's the old arroyo problem," Roger replied absently. "If the storm keeps up the canyon could start spilling sand as if it were water. We don't want to be buried."

They pulled it up the slope with little difficulty, and secured it with chock rocks under the wheels. Roger set up the tent mostly by himself, working too quickly for the others to help.

"Okay, you four get inside and get everything going. Eileen—"

"Roger?" It was Doran.

"Yes."

"We're still having trouble finding the main canyon."

"We thought we were in it," Cheryl said, "but when we descended we came to a big drop-off!"

"Okay. Hold on a minute where you are. Eileen, I want you to come up the main canyon with me and serve as a radio relay. You'll stay in the wash, so you'll be able to walk right back down to the tent if we get separated."

"Sure," Eileen said. The others were carefully rolling the wagon into the lock. Roger paused to oversee that operation, and then he gestured at Eileen through the tawny murk and took off upcanyon. Eileen followed.

They made rapid time. On band 33 Eileen heard the guide say, in an unworried conversational tone, "I hate it when this happens." It was as if he were referring to a shoelace breaking.

"I bet you do!" Eileen replied. "How are we going to find John?"

"Go high. Always go high when lost. I believe I told John that with the rest of you."

"Yes." Eileen had forgotten, however, and she wondered if John had too.

"Even if he's forgotten," Roger said, "when we get high enough, the radios will be less obstructed and we'll be able to talk to him. Or at the worst, we can bounce our signals off a satellite and back down. But I doubt we'll have to do that. Hey, Doran!" he said over the common band.

"Yeah?" Doran sounded very worried.

"What can you see now?"

"Um—we're on a spine—it's all we can see. The canyon to the right—"

"South?"

"Yeah, the south, is the one we were in. We thought the one here to the north would be the main one, but it's too little, and there's a drop-off in it."

"Okay, well, my APS has you still north of us, so cross back to the opposite spine and we'll talk from there. Can you do that?"

"Sure," Doran said, affronted. "It'll take a while, maybe."

"That's all right, take your time." The lack of concern in Roger's voice was almost catching, but Eileen felt that John was in danger; the suits would keep one alive for forty-eight hours at least, but these sandstorms often lasted a week, or more.

"Let's keep moving up," Roger said on band 33. "I don't think we have to worry about those two."

They climbed up the canyon floor, which rose at an average angle of about thirty degrees. Eileen noticed all the dust sliding loosely downhill, sand grains rolling, dust wafting down; sometimes she couldn't see her feet, or make out the ground, so that she had to step by feeling.

"How are you doing back in camp?" Roger asked on the common band.

"Just fine," Dr. Mitsumu answered. "It's on too much of a tilt to stand, so we're just sitting around and listening to the developments up there."

"Still in your suits?"

"Yes."

"Good. One of you stay suited for sure."

"Whatever you say."

Roger stopped where the main canyon was joined by two large tributary canyons, brancing in each direction. "Watch out, I'm going to turn up the gain on the radio," he warned Eileen and the others. She adjusted the controls on her wrist.

"JOHN! Hey, John! Oh, Jo-uhnnn! Come in, John! Respond on common band. Please."

The radio's static sounded like the hiss of flying sand grains. Nothing within it but crackling.

"Hmm," Roger said in Eileen's left ear.

"Hey Roger!"

"Cheryl! How are you doing?"

"Well, we're in what we think is the main canyon, but . . ."

Doran continued, embarrassed: "We really can't be sure, now. Everything looks the same."

"You're telling me," Roger replied. Eileen watched him bend over and,

apparently, inspect his feet. He moved around some in this jacknifed position. "Try going to the wash at the lowest point in the canyon you're
in."

"We're there."

"Okay, lean down and see if you find any boot prints. Make sure they
aren't yours. They'll be faint by now, but Eileen and I just went upcanyon,
so there should still be—"

"Hey! Here's some," Cheryl said.

"Where?" said Doran.

"Over here, look."

Radio hiss.

"Yeah, Roger, we've found some going upcanyon and down."

"Good. Now start downcanyon. Dr. M, are you still in your suit?"

"Just as you said, Roger."

"Good. Why don't you get out of the tent and go down to the wash.
Keep your bearing, count your steps and all. Wait for Cheryl and Doran.
That way they'll be able to find the tent as they come down."

"Sounds good."

After some chatter: "You all down there switch to band 5 to talk on,
and just listen to common. We need to hear up here." Then on band 33:
"Let's go up some more. I believe I remember a gendarme on the ridge
up here with a good vantage."

"Fine. Where do you think he could be?"

"You got me."

When Roger located the outcropping he had in mind, they called
again, and again got no response. Eileen then installed herself on top of
the rocky knob on the ridge: an eerie place with nothing to see but the
fine sand whipped about her, in a ghost wind barely felt on her back
like the lightest puff of an air conditioner, despite the visual resemblance to some awful typhoon. She called for John from time to time.
Roger ranged to north and south over difficult terrain, always staying
within radio distance of Eileen, although once he had a hard time re-
locating her.

Three hours passed that way, and Roger's easygoing tone changed—
not to worry, Eileen judged, but rather to boredom, and annoyance with
John. Eileen herself was extremely concerned. If John had mistaken north
for south, or fallen . . .

"I suppose we should go higher." Roger sighed. "Although I thought
I saw him back when we brought the wagon down here, and I doubt he'd
go back up."

Suddenly Eileen's earphones crackled. *"Pss flunk bdzz,"* and it was clear
again. *"Ckk ssss* ger, lo! *ckk."*

"Sounds like he may have indeed gone high," Roger said with satisfaction, and, Eileen noticed, just a touch of relief. "Hey, John Nobleton!
Do you read us?"

"Ckk sssssssss yeah, hey! *ssss kuh sssss."*

"We read you badly, John! Keep moving, keep talking! Are you all—"

"Roger! *ckk.* Hey, Roger!"

"John! We read you, are you all right?"

". . . *sssss* not exactly sure where I am."

"Are you all right?"

"Yes! Just lost."

"Well not anymore, we hope. Tell us what you see."

"Nothing!"

So began the long process of locating him and bringing him back. Eileen ranged left and right on her own, helping to get a fix on John, who had been instructed to stay still and keep talking.

"You won't believe it." John's voice was entirely free of fear; in fact, he sounded elated. "You won't believe it, Eileen, Roger. *crk!* Just before the storm hit I was way off down a tributary to the south, and I found . . ."

"Found what?"

"Well . . . I've found some things I'm sure must be fossils. I swear! A whole rock formation of them!"

"Oh yeah?"

"No seriously, I've got some with me. Very small shells, like little sea snails, or crustacea. Miniature nautiloids, like. They just couldn't be anything else. I have a couple in my pocket, but there's a whole wall of them back there! I figure if I just left I wouldn't be able to find the same canyon ever again, what with this storm, so I built a duck trail on the way back over to the main canyon, if that's where I am. So it took me a while to get back in radio clear."

"What color are they?" Ivan asked from below.

"You down there, be quiet," Roger ordered. "We're still trying to find him."

"We'll be able to get back to the site. Eileen, can you believe it? We'll all be—*Hey!*"

"It's just me," Roger said.

"Ah! You gave me a start, there."

Eileen smiled as she imagined John startled by the ghostlike appearance of the lanky, suited Roger. Soon enough Roger had led John down-canyon to Eileen, and after John hugged her, they proceeded down the canyon to Dr. Mitsumu, who again led them up the slope to the tent, which rested at a sharper angle than Eileen had recalled.

Once inside, the reunited group chattered for an hour concerning their adventure, while Roger showered and got the wagon on an even keel, and John revealed the objects he had brought back with him:

Small shell-shaped rocks, some held in crusts of sandstone. Each shell had a spiral swirl on its inside surface, and they were mottled red and black. By and large they were black.

They were unlike any rocks Eileen had ever seen; they looked exactly like the few Terran shells she had seen in school. Seeing them there in John's hand, she caught her breath. Life on Mars; even if only fossil traces of it, *life on Mars*. She took one of the shells from John and stared and stared at it. It very well could be. . . .

They had to arrange their cots across the slope of the tent floor and prop them level with clothes and other domestic objects from the wagon.

Long after they were settled they discussed John's discovery, and Eileen found herself more and more excited by the idea of it. The sand pelting the tent soundlessly only made its presence known by the complete absence of stars. She stared at the faint curved reflection of them all on the dome's surface, and thought of it. The Clayborne Expedition, in the history books. And Martian life . . . The others talked and talked.

"So we'll go there tomorrow, right?" John asked Roger. The tilt of the tent made it impossible for Roger to set up his bedroom.

"Or as soon as the storm ends, sure." Roger had only glanced at the shells, shaking his head and muttering, "I don't know, don't get your hopes up too high." Eileen wondered about that. "We'll follow that duck trail of yours, if we can." Perhaps he was jealous of John now?

On and on they talked. Yet the hunt had taken it out of Eileen; to the sound of their voices she suddenly fell asleep.

●

She woke up when her cot gave way and spilled her down the floor; before she could stop herself, she had rolled over Mrs. Mitsumu and John. She got off John quickly and saw Roger over at the wagon, smiling down at the gauges. Her cot had been by the wagon; had he yanked out some crucial item of clothing? There was something of the prankster in the man. . . .

The commotion woke the rest of the sleepers. Immediately the conversation returned to the matter of John's discovery, and Roger agreed that their supplies were sufficient to allow a trip back up-canyon. And the storm had stopped; dust coated their dome, and was piled half a centimeter high on its uphill side, but they could see that the sky was clear. So after breakfast they suited up, more awkward than ever on the tilted floor, and emerged from their shelter.

The distance back up to where they had met John was much shorter than it had seemed to Eileen in the storm. All of their tracks had been covered, even the sometimes deep treadmarks of the wagon. John led the way, leaping upward in giant bounds that were almost out of his control.

"There's the gendarme where we found you," Roger said from below, pointing to the spine on their right for John's benefit. John waited for them, talking nervously all the while. "There's the first duck," he told them. "I see it way over there, but with all the sand, it looks almost like any other mound. This could be hard."

"We'll find them," Roger assured him.

When they had all joined John, they began to traverse the canyons to the south, each one a deep multifingered trench in the slope of Mars facing Olympus Mons. John had very little sense of where he had been, except that he had not gone much above or below the level they were on. Some of the ducks were hard to spot, but Roger had quite a facility for it, and the others spotted some as well. More than once none of them saw it, and they had to trek off in nine slightly different directions, casting about in hopes of running into it. Each time someone would cry, "Here it is," as if they were children hunting Easter eggs, and they would convene and search again. Only once were they unable to locate the next duck, and then Roger pumped John's memory of his hike; after all, as Ivan pointed out, it had been the full light of day when he walked to the site. A crestfallen John admitted that, each little red canyon looking so much like the next one, he couldn't really recall where he had gone from there.

"Well, but there's the next duck," Roger said with surprise, pointing at a little niche indicating a side ravine. And after they had reached the niche John cried, "This is it! Right down this ravine, in the wall itself. And some of them have fallen."

The common band was a babble of voices as they dropped into the steep-sided ravine one by one. Eileen stepped down through the narrow entrance and confronted the nearly vertical south wall. There, embedded in hard sandstone, were thousands of tiny black stone snail shells. The bottom of the ravine was covered with them; all of them were close to the same size, with holes that opened into the hollow interior of the shells. Many of them were broken, and inspecting some fragments, Eileen saw the spiral ribbing that so often characterized life. Her earphones rang with the excited voices of her companions. Roger had climbed the canyon wall and was inspecting a particular section, his faceplate only centimeters from stone. "See what I mean?" John was asking. "Martian snails! It's like those fossil bacterial mats they talk about, only further advanced. Back when Mars had surface water and an atmosphere, life *did* begin. It just didn't have time to get very far."

"Nobleton snails," Cheryl said, and they laughed. Eileen picked up fragment after fragment, her excitement growing. They were all very similar. She was taxing her suit's cooling system, starting to sweat. She examined a well-preserved specimen carefully, pulling it out of the rock to do so. The common band was distractingly noisy, and she was about to turn it off when Roger's voice said slowly, "Uh-ohh. . . . Hey, people. Hey."

When it was silent he said hesitantly, "I hate to spoil the party, but . . . these little things aren't fossils."

"What?"

"What do you mean?" John and Ivan challenged. "How do you know?"

"Well, there are a couple reasons," Roger said. Everyone was still now, and watching him. "First, I believe that fossils are created by a process that requires millions of years of water seepage, and Mars never had that."

"So we think now," Ivan objected. "But it may not be so, because it's certain that there was water on Mars all along. And after all, here are these things."

"Well . . ." Eileen could tell he was deciding to let that argument pass. "Maybe you're right, but a better reason is, I think I know what these are. They're lava pellets—bubble pellets, I've heard them called—although I've never seen ones this small. Little lava bombs from one of the Olympus Mons eruptions. A sort of spray."

Everyone stared at the objects in their hands.

"See, when lava pellets land hot in a certain sort of sand, they sink right through it and melt the sand fast, releasing gas that forms the bubble, and these glassy interiors. When the pellet is spinning, you get these spiral chambers. So I've heard, anyway. It must have happened on a flat plain long ago, and when the whole plain tilted and started falling down this slope, these layers broke up and were buried by later deposits."

"I don't believe that's necessarily so," John declared, while the others looked at the wall. But even he sounded pretty convinced to Eileen.

"Of course we'll have to take some back to be sure," Roger agreed in a soothing tone.

"Why didn't you tell us this last night?" Eileen asked.

"Well, I couldn't tell till I had seen the rock they were in. But this is lava-sprayed sandstone, they call it. That's why it's so hard in its upper layers. But you're an areologist, right?" He wasn't mocking.

"Don't they look like they're made of lava?"

Eileen nodded, reluctantly. "Looks like it."

"Well, lava doesn't make fossils."

⮞

Half an hour later a dispirited group was stretched out over the duck trail, straggling along in silence. John and Ivan trailed far behind, weighted down by several kilos of lava pellets. Pseudofossils, as both areologists and geologists called them. Roger was ahead, talking with the Mitsumus, attempting to cheer them all up, Eileen guessed. She felt bad about not identifying the rock the previous night. She felt more depressed than she could easily account for, and it made her angry. Everything was so empty out here, so meaningless, so without form. . . .

"Once I thought I had found traces of aliens," Roger was saying. "I was off by myself around the other side of Olympus, hiking canyons as usual, except I was by myself. I was crossing really broken fretted terrain, when suddenly I came across a trail duck. Stones never stack up by themselves. Now the Explorer's Society keeps a record of every single hike and expedition, you know, and I had checked before and I knew I was in fresh territory, just like we are now. No humans had ever been in that part of the badlands, as far as the Society knew. Yet here was this duck. And I started finding other ones right away. Set not in a straight line, but zigzagging, tacking like. And little. Tiny piles of flat rock, four or five high. Like they were set up by little aliens who saw best out of the sides of their eyes."

"You must have been astounded," Mrs. Mitsumu said.

"Exactly. But, you know—there were three possibilities. It was a natural rock formation—extremely unlikely, but it could be that breadloaf formations had slid onto their sides and then been eroded into separate pieces, still stacked on each other. Or they were set up by aliens. Also unlikely, in my opinion. Or someone had hiked through there without reporting it, and had played a game, maybe, for someone later to find. To me, that was the most likely explanation. But for a while there . . ."

"You must have been disappointed," said Mrs. Mitsumu.

"Oh no," Roger replied easily. "More entertained than anything, I think."

Eileen stared at the form of their guide, far ahead with the others. He truly didn't care that John's discovery had not been the remnants of life, she judged. In that way he was different, unlike John or Ivan, unlike herself; for she felt his obviously correct explanation of the little shells as a loss larger than she ever would have guessed. She wanted life out there as badly as John or Ivan or any of the rest of them did, she realized. All those books she had read, when studying literature. . . . That was why she had not let herself remember that igneous rock would never be involved with fossilization. If only life had once existed here—snails, lichen, bacteria, anything—it would somehow take away some of this landscape's awful barrenness.

And if Mars itself could not provide, it became necessary to supply it—to do whatever was necessary to make life possible on its desolate surface, to transform it as soon as possible, to *give it life*. Now she understood the connection between the two main topics of evening conversation in their isolated camps: terraforming, and the discovery of extinct Martian lifeforms; and the conversations took place all over the planet, less intently than out here in the canyons, perhaps, but still, all her life Eileen had been hoping for this discovery, had *believed* in it.

She pulled the half dozen lava pellets she had saved from one of her suit pockets and stared at them. Abruptly, bitterly, she tossed them aside, and they floated out into the rust waste. They would never find remnants of Martian life; no one ever would. She knew that was true in every cell of her. All the so-called discoveries, all the Martians in her books—they were all part of a simple case of projection, nothing more. Humans wanted Martians, that was all there was to it. But there were not, and never had been, any canal-builders; no lamppost creatures with heat-beam eyes, no brilliant lizards or grasshoppers, no manta ray intelligences, no angels and no devils; there were no four-armed races battling in blue jungles, no big-headed skinny thirsty folk, no sloe-eyed dusky beauties dying for Terran sperm, no wise little Bleekmen wandering stunned in the desert, no golden-eyed golden-skinned telepaths, no doppelgänger race—not a fun-house mirror image of any kind; there weren't any ruined adobe palaces, no dried-oasis castles, no mysterious cliff dwellings packed like a museum, no hologrammatic towers waiting to drive humans mad, no intricate canal systems with their locks all filled with sand, no not a single canal; there were not even any mosses creeping down from the polar caps every summer, nor any rabbitlike animals living far underground; no plastic windmill-creatures, no lichen capable of casting dangerous electrical fields, no lichen of any kind; no algae in the hot springs, no microbes in the soil, no microbacteria in the regolith, no stromatolites, no nanobacteria in the deep bedrock . . . no primeval soup.

All so many dreams. Mars was a dead planet. Eileen scuffed the freeze-dried dirt and watched through damp eyes as the pinkish sand lofted away from her boot. All dead. That was her home: dead Mars. Not even dead, which implied a life and a dying. Just . . . nothing. A red void.

They turned down the main canyon. Far below was their tent, looking like it would slide down its slope any instant. Now there was a sign of life. Eileen grinned bleakly behind her faceplate. Outside her suit it was forty degrees below zero, and the air was not air.

Roger was hurrying down the canyon ahead of them, no doubt to turn on the air and heat in the tent, or pull the wagon out to move it all downcanyon. In the alien gravity she had lived in all her life, he dropped down the great trench as in a dream, not bounding gazelle-like in the manner of John or Doran, but just on the straightest line, the most efficient path, in a sort of boulder ballet all the more graceful for being so simple. Eileen liked that. Now there, she thought, is a man reconciled to the absolute deadness of Mars. It seemed his home, his landscape. An old line occurred to her: "We have met the enemy, and he is us." And then something from Bradbury: "The Martians were there . . . Timothy and Robert and Michael and Mom and Dad."

She pondered the idea as she followed Clayborne down their canyon trying to imitate that stride.

➤

"But there *was* life on Mars." That evening she watched him. Ivan and Doran talked to Cheryl; John sulked on his coat. Roger chatted with the Mitsumus, who liked him. At sunset when they showered (they had moved the tent to another fine flat site) he walked over to his paneled cubicle naked, and the flat onyx bracelet he wore around his left wrist suddenly seemed to Eileen the most beautiful ornamentation. She realized she was glancing at him in the same way John and the doctor looked at her—only differently—and she blushed.

After dinner the others were quiet, returning to their cots. Roger continued telling the Mitsumus and Eileen stories. She had never heard him talk so much. He was still sarcastic with her, but that wasn't what his smile was saying. She watched him move . . . and sighed, exasperated with herself; wasn't this just what she had come out here to get away from? Did she really need or want this feeling again, this quickening interest?

"They still can't decide if there's some ultrasmall nanobacteria down in the bedrock. The arguments go back and forth in the scientific journals all the time. Could be down there, so small we can't even see it. There's been reports of drilling contamination. . . . But I don't think so."

Yet he certainly was different from the men she had known in recent years. After everyone had gone to bed, she concentrated on that difference, that quality; he was . . . Martian. He was that alien life, and she wanted him in a way she had never wanted her other lovers. Mrs. Mitsumu had been smiling at them, as if she saw something going on, something she had seen developing long before, when the two of them were always at odds . . . Earth girl lusts for virile Martian; she laughed at herself, but there it was. Still constructing stories to populate this planet, still falling in love, despite herself. And she wanted to do something about it. She had always lived by Eulert's saying: If you don't act on it, it wasn't a true feeling. It had gotten her in trouble, too, but she was forgetting that. And tomorrow they would be at the little outpost that was their destination, and the chance would be gone. For an hour she thought about it, evaluating the looks he had given her that evening. How did you evaluate an alien's glances? Ah, but he was human—just adapted to Mars in a way she wished she could be—and there had been something in his eyes very human, very understandable. Around her the black hills loomed against the black sky, the double star hung overhead, that home she had never set foot on. It was a lonely place.

Well, she had never been particularly shy in these matters, but she had always favored a more inpulling approach, encouraging advances rather than making them (usually) so that when she quietly got off her cot and slipped into shorts and a shirt, her heart was knocking like a tympani roll. She tiptoed to the panels, thinking *Fortune favors the bold*, and slipped between them, went to his side.

He sat up; she put her hand to his mouth. She didn't know what to do next. Her heart was knocking harder than ever. That gave her an idea, and she leaned over and pulled his head around and placed it against her ribs, so he could hear her pulse. He looked up at her, pulled her down to the cot. They kissed. Some whispers. The cot was too narrow and creaky, and they moved to the floor, lay next to each other kissing. She could feel him, hard against her thigh; some sort of Martian stone, she reckoned, like that flesh jade. . . . They whispered to each other, lips to each other's ears like headpiece intercoms. She found it difficult to stay so quiet making love, exploring that Martian rock, being explored by it. . . . She lost her mind for a while then, and when she came to she was quivering now and again; an occasional aftershock, she thought to herself. A seismology of sex. He appeared to read her mind, for he whispered happily in her ear, "Your seismographs are probably picking us up right now."

She laughed softly, then made the joke current among literature majors at the university: "Yes, very nice . . . the Earth moved."

After a second he got it and stifled a laugh. "Several thousand kilometers."

Laughter is harder to suppress than the sounds of love.

◆

Of course it is impossible to conceal such activity in a group—not to mention a tent—of such small size, and the next morning Eileen got some pointed looks from John, some smiles from Mrs. M. It was a clear morning, and after they got the tent packed into the wagon and were on their way, Eileen hiked off whistling to herself. As they descended toward the broad plain at the bottom of the canyon mouth, she and Roger tuned in to their band 33 and talked.

"You really don't think this wash would look better with some cactus and sage in it, say? Or grasses?"

"Nope. I like it the way it is. See that pentagon of shards there?" He pointed. "How nice."

With the intercom they could wander far apart from each other and still converse, and no one could know they were talking, while each voice hung in the other's ear. So they talked and talked. Everyone has had conversations that have been crucial in their lives: clarity of expression,

quickness of feeling, attentiveness to the other's words, a belief in the
reality of the other's world—of these and other elements are such conversations made, and at the same time the words themselves can be concerned with the simplest, most ordinary things:

"Look at that rock."

"How nice that ridge is against the sky—it must be a hundred kilometers away, and it looks like you could touch it."

"Everything's so red."

"Yeah. Red Mars, I love it. I'm for red Mars."

She considered it. They hiked down the widening canyon ahead of the
others, on opposite slopes. Soon they would be back in the world of cities,
the big wide world. There were lots and lots of people out there, and
anyone you met you might never see again. On the other hand . . . she
looked across at the tall awkwardly proportioned man, striding with feline
Martian grace over the dunes, in the dream gravity. Like a dancer.

"How old are you?" she asked.

"Twenty-six."

"My God!" He was already quite wrinkled. More sun than most.

"What?"

"I thought you were older."

"No."

"How long have you been doing this?"

"Hiking canyons?"

"Yes."

"Since I was six."

"Oh." That explained how he knew all this world so well.

She crossed the canyon to walk by his side; seeing her doing it, he
descended his slope and they walked down the center of the wash.

"Can I come on another trip with you?"

He looked at her: behind the faceplate, a grin. "Oh yes. There are a
lot of canyons to see."

The canyon opened up, then flattened out, and its walls melted into
the broad boulder-studded plain on which the little outpost was set, some
kilometers away. Eileen could just see it in the distance, like a castle made
of glass: a tent like theirs, really, only much bigger. Behind it Olympus
Mons rose straight up out of the sky.

Promises to Keep

JACK McDEVITT

Born in Philadelphia, Jack McDevitt now lives in Brunswick, Georgia, with his family. He is a frequent contributor to Asimov's Science Fiction *and has also sold stories to* Analog, The Magazine of Fantasy & Science Fiction, Full Spectrum, Universe, The Twilight Zone Magazine, Chess Life *and elsewhere. An ex–naval officer, ex–English teacher, and ex–customs inspector, he retired in 1995 and now works full-time as a writer. His first novel,* The Hercules Text, *won a special citation for the Philip K. Dick award. His novels* Ancient Shores *and* Moonfall *have been Nebula finalists, and* The Engines of God *was a finalist for the Arthur C. Clarke Award. His other books include the story collection* Standard Candles *and most recently,* Infinity Beach.*

Here he takes us across the solar system to the moons of Jupiter, to the desolate frozen snowscapes of Callisto, for a very human drama of risk and exploration played out against the cold, inhuman immensity of space. . . .

I received a Christmas card last week from Ed Iseminger. The illustration was a rendering of the celebrated Christmas Eve telecast from Callisto: a lander stands serenely on a rubble-strewn plain, spilling warm yellow light through its windows. Needle-point peaks rise behind it, and the rim of a crater curves across the foreground. An enormous belted crescent dominates the sky.

In one window, someone has hung a wreath.

It is a moment preserved, a tableau literally created by Cathie Perth, extracted from her prop bag. Somewhere here, locked away among insurance papers and the deed to the house, is the tape of the original telecast, but I've never played it. In fact, I've seen it only once, on the night of the transmission. But I know the words, Cathie's words, read by Victor Landolfi in his rich baritone, blending the timeless values of the season with the spectral snows of another world. They appear in schoolbooks now, and on marble.

Inside the card, in large, block, defiant letters, Iseminger had printed "SEPTEMBER!" It is a word with which he hopes to conquer a world. Sometimes, at night, when the snow sparkles under the hard cold stars (the way it did on Callisto), I think about him, and his quest. And I am very afraid.

I can almost see Cathie's footprints on the frozen surface. It was a good time, and I wish there were a way to step into the picture, to toast the holidays once more with Victor Landolfi, to hold onto Cathie Perth (and not let go!), and somehow to save us all. It was the end of innocence, a final meeting place for old friends.

We made the Christmas tape over a period of about five days. Cathie took literally hours of visuals, but Callisto is a place of rock and ice and deadening sameness: there is little to soften the effect of cosmic indifference. Which is why all those shots of towering peaks and tumbled boulders were taken at long range, and in half-light. Things not quite seen, she said, are always charming.

Her biggest problem had been persuading Landolfi to do the voice-over. Victor was tall, lean, ascetic. He was equipped with laser eyes and a huge black mustache. His world was built solely of subatomic particles, and driven by electromagnetics. Those who did not share his passions excited his contempt; which meant that he understood the utility of Cathie's public relations function at the same time that he deplored its necessity. To participate was to compromise one's integrity. His sense of delicacy, however, prevented his expressing that view to Cathie: he begged off rather on the press of time, winked apologetically, and straightened his mustache. "Sawyer will read it for you," he said, waving me impatiently into the conversation.

Cathie sneered, and stared irritably out a window (it was the one with the wreath) at Jupiter, heavy in the fragile sky. We knew, by then, that it had a definable surface, that the big planet was a world sea of liquid hydrogen, wrapped around a rocky core. "It must be frustrating," she said, "to know you'll never see it." Her tone was casual, almost frivolous, but Landolfi was not easily baited.

"Do you really think," he asked, with the patience of the superior being (Landolfi had no illusions about his capabilities), "that these little pieces of theater will make any difference? Yes, Catherine, of course it's frustrating. Especially when one realizes that we have the technology to put vehicles down there. . . ."

"And scoop out some hydrogen," Cathie added.

He shrugged. "It may happen someday."

"Victor, it never will if we don't sell the Program. This is the last shot. These ships are old, and nobody's going to build any new ones. Unless things change radically at home."

Landolfi closed his eyes. I knew what he was thinking: Cathie Perth was an outsider, an ex-television journalist who had probably slept her way on board. She played bridge, knew the film library by heart, read John Donne (for style, she said), and showed no interest whatever in the scientific accomplishments of the mission. We'd made far-reaching discoveries in the fields of plate tectonics, planetary climatology, and a dozen other disciplines. We'd narrowed the creation date down inside a range of a few million years. And we finally understood how it had happened! But Cathie's televised reports had de-emphasized the implications, and virtually ignored the mechanics of such things. Instead, while a global audience watched, Marjorie Aubuchon peered inspirationally out of a cargo lock at Ganymede (much in the fashion that Cortez must have looked at the Pacific on that first bright morning), her shoulder flag patch resplendent in the sunlight. And while the camera moved in for a close-up (her features were illuminated by a lamp Cathie had placed for the occasion in her helmet), Herman Selma solemnly intoned Cathie's comments on breaking the umbilical.

That was her style: brooding alien vistas reduced to human terms. In one of her best-known sequences, there had been no narration whatever: two spacesuited figures, obviously male and female, stood together in the shadow of the monumental Cadmus Ice Fracture on Europa, beneath three moons.

"Cathie," Landolfi said, with his eyes still shut, "I don't wish to be offensive: but do you really care? For the Program, that is? When we get home, you will write a book, you will be famous, you will be at the top of your profession. Are you really concerned with where the Program will be in twenty years?"

It was a fair question: Cathie'd made no secret of her hopes for a Pulitzer. And she stood to get it, no matter what happened after this mission. Moreover, although she'd tried to conceal her opinions, we'd been together a long time by then, almost three years, and we could hardly misunderstand the dark view she took of people who voluntarily imprisoned themselves for substantial portions of their lives to go 'rock-collecting.'

"No," she said. "I'm not, because there won't be a Program in twenty years." She looked around at each of us, weighing the effect of her words. Iseminger, a blond giant with a reddish beard, allowed a smile of lazy tolerance to soften his granite features. "We're in the same class as the pyramids," she continued, in a tone that was unemotional and irritatingly condescending. "We're a hell of an expensive operation, and for what? Do you think the taxpayers give a good goddam about the weather on Jupiter? There's nothing out here but gas and boulders. Playthings for eggheads!"

I sat and thought about it while she smiled sweetly, and Victor smoldered. I had not heard the solar system ever before described in quite those terms; I'd heard people call it *vast, awesome, magnificent, serene,* stuff like that. But never *boring.*

◆

In the end, Landolfi read his lines. He did it, he said, to end the distraction.

Cathie was clearly pleased with the result. She spent three days editing the tapes, commenting frequently (and with good-natured malice) on the *resonance* and tonal qualities of the voice-over. She finished on the morning of the 24th (ship time, of course), and transmitted the report to *Greenswallow* for relay to Houston. "It'll make the evening newscasts," she said with satisfaction.

It was our third Christmas out. Except for a couple of experiments-in-progress, we were finished on Callisto and, in fact, in the Jovian system. Everybody was feeling good about that, and we passed an uneventful afternoon, playing bridge and talking about what we'd do when we got back. (Cathie had described a deserted beach near Tillamook, Oregon, where she'd grown up. "It would be nice to walk on it again, under a *blue* sky," she said. Landolfi had startled everyone at that point: he looked up from the computer console at which he'd been working, and his eyes grew very distant. "I think," he said, "when the time comes, I would like very much to walk with you. . . .")

For the most part, Victor kept busy that afternoon with his hobby: he was designing a fusion engine that would be capable, he thought, of carrying ships to Jupiter within a few weeks, and, possibly, would eventually open the stars to direct exploration. But I watched him: he turned away periodically from the display screen, to glance at Cathie. Yes (I thought), she would indeed be lovely against the rocks and the spume, her black hair free in the wind.

Just before dinner, we watched the transmission of Cathie's tape. It was very strong, and when it was finished we sat silently looking at one another. By then, Herman Selma and Esther Crowley had joined us. (Although two landers were down, Cathie had been careful to give the impression in her report that there had only been one. When I asked why, she said, "In a place like this, one lander is the Spirit of Man. Two landers is just two landers.") We toasted Victor, and we toasted Cathie. Almost everyone, it turned out, had brought down a bottle for the occasion. We sang and laughed, and somebody turned up the music. We'd long since discovered the effect of low-gravity dancing in cramped quarters, and I guess we made the most of it.

Marj Aubuchon, overhead in the linkup, called to wish us season's greetings, and called again later to tell us that the telecast, according to Houston, had been "well-received." That was government talk, of course, and it meant only that no one in authority could find anything to object to. Actually, somebody high up had considerable confidence in her: in order to promote the illusion of spontaneity, the tapes were being broadcast directly to the commercial networks.

Cathie, who by then had had a little too much to drink, gloated openly. "It's the best we've done," she said. "Nobody'll ever do it better."

We shared that sentiment. Landolfi raised his glass, winked at Cathie, and drained it.

We had to cut the evening short, because a lander's life-support system isn't designed to handle six people. (For that matter, neither was an Athena's.) But before we broke it up, Cathie surprised us all by proposing a final toast: "To Frank Steinitz," she said quietly. "And his crew."

Steinitz: there was a name, as they say, to conjure with. He had led the first deep-space mission, five Athenas to Saturn, fifteen years before. It had been the first attempt to capture the public imagination for a dying program: an investigation of a peculiar object filmed by a Voyager on Iapetus. But nothing much had come of it, and the mission had taken almost seven years. Steinitz and his people had begun as heroes, but in the end they'd become symbols of futility. The press had portrayed them mercilessly as personifications of outworn virtues. Someone had compared them to the Japanese soldiers found as late as the 1970s on Pacific islands, still defending a world long since vanished.

The Steinitz group bore permanent reminders of their folly: prolonged weightlessness had loosened ligaments and tendons, and weakened muscles. Several had developed heart problems, and all suffered from assorted neuroses. As one syndicated columnist had observed, they walked like a bunch of retired big-league catchers.

"That's a good way to end the evening," said Selma, beaming benevolently.

Landolfi looked puzzled. "Cathie," he rumbled, "you've questioned Steinitz's good sense any number of times. And ours, by the way. Isn't it a little hypocritical to drink to him?"

"I'm not impressed by his intelligence," she said, ignoring the obvious parallel. "But he and his people went all the way out to Saturn in those damned things—" she waved in the general direction of the three Athenas orbiting overhead in linkup "—hanging onto baling wire and wing struts. I have to admire that."

"Hell," I said, feeling the effects a little myself, "we've got the same ships he had."

"Yes, you do," said Cathie pointedly.

◆

I had trouble sleeping that night. For a long time, I lay listening to Landolfi's soft snore, and the electronic fidgeting of the operations computer. Cathie was bundled inside a gray blanket, barely visible in her padded chair.

She was right, of course. I knew that rubber boots would never again cross that white landscape, which had waited a billion years for us. The peaks glowed in the reflection of the giant planet: fragile crystalline beauty, on a world of terrifying stillness. Except for an occasional incoming rock, nothing more would ever happen here. Callisto's entire history was encapsuled within twelve days.

Pity there hadn't been something to those early notions about Venusian rain forests and canals on Mars. The Program might have had easier going had Burroughs or Bradbury been right. My God: how many grim surprises had disrupted fictional voyages to Mars? But the truth had been far worse than anything Wells or the others had ever committed to paper: the red planet was so dull that we hadn't even gone there.

Instead, we'd lumbered out to the giants. In ships that drained our lives and our health.

We could have done better; our ships could have been better. The computer beside which Landolfi slept contained his design for the fusion engine. And at JPL, an Army team had demonstrated that artificial gravity was possible: a real gravity field, not the pathetic fraction created on the Athenas by spinning the inner hull. There were other possibilities as well: infrared ranging could be adapted to replace our elderly scanning system; new alloys were under development. But it would cost billions to build a second-generation vehicle. And unless there were an incentive, unless Cathie Perth carried off a miracle, it would not happen.

Immediately overhead, a bright new star glittered, moving visibly (though slowly) from west to east. That was the linkup, three ships connected nose to nose by umbilicals and a magnetic docking system. Like the Saturn mission, we were a multiple vehicle operation. We were more flexible that way, and we had a safety factor: two ships would be adequate to get the nine-man mission home. Conditions might become a little stuffy, but we'd make it.

I watched it drift through the icy starfield.

Cathie had pulled the plug on the Christmas lights. But it struck me that Callisto would only have one Christmas, so I put them back on.

◆

Victor was on board *Tolstoi* when we lost it. No one ever really knew precisely what happened. We'd begun our long fall toward Jupiter, gaining the acceleration which we'd need on the flight home. Cathie, Herman Selma (the mission commander), and I were riding *Greenswallow*. The ships had separated, and would not rejoin until we'd rounded Jupiter, and settled into our course for home. (The Athenas are really individually-powered modular units which travel, except when maneuvering, as a single vessel. They're connected bow-to-bow by electromagnets. Coils of segmented tubing, called "umbilicals" even though the term does not accurately describe their function, provide ready access among the forward areas of the ships. As many as six Athenas can be linked in this fashion, although only five have ever been built. The resulting structure would resemble a wheel.)

Between Callisto and Ganymede, we hit something: a drifting cloud of fine particles, a belt of granular material stretched so thin it never appeared on the LGD, before or after. Cathie later called it a cosmic sandbar; Iseminger thought it an unformed moon. It didn't matter: whatever it was, the mission plowed into it at almost 50,000 kilometers per hour. Alarms clattered, and red lamps blinked on.

In those first moments, I thought the ship was going to come apart. Herman was thrown across a bank of consoles and through an open hatch. I couldn't see Cathie, but a quick burst of profanity came from her direction. Things were being ripped off the hull. Deep within her walls, *Greenswallow* sighed. The lights dipped, came back, and went out. Emergency lamps cut in, and something big glanced off the side of the ship. More alarms howled, and I waited for the clamor of the throaty klaxon which would warn of a holing, and which consequently would be the last sound I could expect to hear in this life.

The sudden deceleration snapped my head back on the pads. (The collision had occurred at the worst possible time: *Greenswallow* was caught in the middle of an attitude alignment. We were flying backwards.)

The exterior monitors were blank: that meant the cameras were gone. Cathie's voice: "Rob, you okay?"

"Yes."

"Can you see Herman?"

My angle was bad, and I was pinned in my chair. "No. He's back in cargo."

"Is there any way you can close the hatch?"

"Herman's in there," I protested, thinking she'd misunderstood.

"If something tears a hole out back there, we're all going to go. Keeping the door open won't help him."

I hesitated. Sealing up seemed to be the wrong thing to do. (Of course, the fact that the hatch had been open in the first place constituted a safety violation.) "It's on your console," I told her. "Hit the numerics on your upper right."

"Which one?"

"Hit them all." She was seated at the status board, and I could see a row of red lights: several other hatches were open. They should have closed automatically when the first alarms sounded.

We got hit again, this time in front. *Greenswallow* trembled, and loose pieces of metal rattled around inside the walls like broken teeth.

"Rob," she said. "I don't think it's working."

The baleful lights still glowed across the top of her board.

◆

It lasted about three minutes.

When it was over, we hurried back to look at Herman. We were no longer rotating, and gravity had consequently dropped to zero. Selma, gasping, pale, his skin damp, was floating grotesquely over a pallet of ore-sample canisters. We got him to a couch and applied compresses. His eyes rolled shut, opened, closed again. "Inside," he said, gently fingering an area just off his sternum. "I think I've been chewed up a little." He raised his head slightly. "What kind of shape are we in?"

I left Cathie with him. Then I restored power, put on a suit and went outside.

The hull was a disaster: antennas were down, housings scored, lenses shattered. The lander was gone, ripped from its web. The port cargo area had buckled, and an auxiliary hatch was sprung. On the bow, the magnetic dock was hammered into slag. Travel between the ships was going to be a little tougher.

Greenswallow looked as if she had been sandblasted. I scraped particles out of her thruster nozzles, replaced cable, and bolted down mounts. I caught a glimpse of Amity's lights, sliding diagonally across the sky. As were the constellations.

"Cathie," I said. "I see Mac. But I think we're tumbling."

"Okay."

Iseminger was also on board Amity. And, fortunately, Marj Aubuchon, our surgeon. Herman's voice broke in, thick with effort. "Rob, we got no radio contact with anyone. Any sign of Victor?"

Ganymede was close enough that its craters lay exposed in harsh solar light. Halfway round the sky, the Pleiades glittered. *Tolstoi*'s green and red running lights should have been visible among, or near, the six silver stars. But the sky was empty. I stood a long time and looked, wondering how many other navigators on other oceans had sought lost friends in that constellation. What had they called it in antiquity? The rainy Pleiades. . . . "Only Amity," I said.

I tore out some cable and lobbed it in the general direction of Ganymede. Jupiter's enormous arc was pushing above the maintenance pods, spraying October light across the wreckage. I improvised a couple of antennas, replaced some black boxes, and then decided to correct the tumble, if I could.

"Try it now," I said.

Cathie acknowledged.

Two of the thrusters were useless. I went inside for spares, and replaced the faulty units. While I was finishing up, Cathie came back on. "Rob," she said, "radio's working, more or less. We have no long-range transmit, though."

"Okay. I'm not going to try to do anything about that right now."

"Are you almost finished?"

"Why?"

"Something occurred to me. Maybe the cloud, whatever that damned thing was that we passed through: maybe it's U-shaped."

"Thanks," I said. "I needed something to worry about."

"Maybe you should come back inside."

"Soon as I can. How's the patient doing?"

"Out," she said. "He was a little delirious when he was talking to you. Anyhow, I'm worried: I think something's broken internally. He never got his color back, and he's beginning to bring up blood. Rob, we need Marj."

"You hear anything from *Amity* yet?"

"Just a carrier wave." She did not mention *Tolstoi*. "How bad is it out there?"

From where I was tethered, about halfway back on the buckled beam, I could see a crack in the main plates that appeared to run the length of the port tube. I climbed out onto the exhaust assembly, and pointed my flashlight into the combustion chamber. Something glittered where the reflection should have been subdued. I got in and looked: silicon. Sand, and steel, had fused in the white heat of passage. The exhaust was blocked.

Cathie came back on. "What about it, Rob?" she asked. "Any serious problems?"

"Cathie," I said, "*Greenswallow*'s going to Pluto."

●

Herman thought I was Landolfi: he kept assuring me that everything was going to be okay. His pulse was weak and rapid, and he alternated between sweating and shivering. Cathie had got a blanket under him and buckled him down so he wouldn't hurt himself. She bunched some pillows under his feet, and held a damp compress to his head.

"That's not going to help much. Raising his legs, I mean."

She looked at me, momentarily puzzled. "Oh," she said. "Not enough gravity."

I nodded.

"Oh, Rob." Her eyes swept the cases and cannisters, all neatly tagged, silicates from Pasiphae, sulfur from Himalia, assorted carbon compounds from Callisto. We had evidence now that Io had formed elsewhere in the solar system, and been well along in middle age when it was captured. We'd all but eliminated the possibility that life existed in Jupiter's atmosphere. We understood why rings formed around gas giants, and we had a new clue to the cause of terrestrial ice ages. And I could see that Cathie was thinking about trading lives to satisfy the curiosity of a few academics. "We don't belong out here," she said, softly. "Not in these primitive shells."

I said nothing.

"I got a question for you," she continued. "We're not going to find *Tolstoi*, right?"

"Is that your question?"

"No. I wish it were. But the LGD can't see them. That means they're just not there." Her eyes filled with tears, but she shook her head impatiently. "And we can't steer this thing. Can *Amity* carry six people?"

"It might have to."

"That wasn't what I asked."

"Food and water would be tight. Especially since we're running out of time, and wouldn't be able to transfer much over. If any. So we'd all be a little thinner when we got back. But yes, I think we could survive."

We stared at one another, and then she turned away. I became conscious of the ship: the throb of power deep in her bulkheads (power now permanently bridled by conditions in the combustion chambers), the soft amber glow of the navigation lamps in the cockpit.

McGuire's nasal voice, from *Amity*, broke the uneasy silence. "Herman, you okay?"

Cathie looked at me, and I nodded. "Mac," she said, "this is Perth. Herman's hurt. We need Marj."

"Okay," he said. "How bad?"

"We don't know. Internal injuries, looks like. He appears to be in shock."

We heard him talking to someone else. Then he came back. "We're on our way. I'll put Marj on in a minute; maybe she can help from here. How's the ship?"

"Not good: the dock's gone, and the engine might as well be."

He asked me to be specific. "If we try a burn, the rear end'll fall off."

McGuire delivered a soft, venomous epithet. And then: "Do what you can for Herman. Marj'll be right here."

Cathie was looking at me strangely. "He's worried," she said.

"Yes. He's in charge now. . . ."

"Rob, you say you *think* we'll be okay. What's the problem?"

"We might," I said, "run a little short of air."

⬩

Greenswallow continued her plunge toward Jupiter at a steadily increasing rate and a sharp angle of approach: we would pass within about 60,000 kilometers, and then drop completely out of the plane of the solar system. We appeared to be heading in the general direction of the Southern Cross.

Cathie worked on Herman. His breathing steadied, and he slipped in and out of his delirium. We sat beside him, not talking much. After awhile, Cathie asked, "What happens now?"

"In a few hours," I said, "we'll reach our insertion point. By then, we have to be ready to change course." She frowned, and I shrugged. "That's it," I said. "It's all the time we have to get over to *Amity*. If we don't make the insertion on time, *Amity* won't have the fuel to throw a U-turn later."

"Rob, how are we going to get Herman over there?"

That was an uncomfortable question. The prospect of jamming him down into a suit was less than appealing, but there was no other way. "We'll just have to float him over," I said. "Marj won't like it much."

"Neither will Herman."

"You wanted a little high drama," I said, unnecessarily. "The next show should be a barnburner."

Her mouth tightened, and she turned away from me.

One of the TV cameras had picked up the approach of *Amity*. Some of her lights were out, and she too looked a bit bent. The Athena is a homely vessel in the best of times, whale-shaped and snub-nosed, with a midship flare that suggests middle-age spread. But I was glad to see her.

Cathie snuffled at the monitor, and blew her nose. "Your Program's dead, Rob." Her eyes blazed momentarily, like a dying fire into which one has flung a few drops of water. "We're leaving three of our people out here; and if you're right about the air, we'll get home with a ship-load of detectives, or worse. Won't that look good on the six o'clock news?" She gazed vacantly at *Amity*'s image. "I'd hoped," she said, "that if things went well, Victor would have lived to see a ship carry his fusion engine. And maybe his name, as well. Ain't gonna happen, though. Not ever."

I had not allowed myself to think about the oxygen problem we were going to face. The Athenas recycle their air supply: the converters in a single ship can maintain a crew of three, or even four, indefinitely. But six?

I was not looking forward to the ride home.

A few minutes later, a tiny figure detached itself from the shadow of the Athena and started across: Marj Aubuchon on a maintenance sled. McGuire's voice erupted from the ship's speakers. "Rob, we've taken a long look at your engines, and we agree with your assessment. The damage complicates things." Mac had a talent for understatement. It derived, not from a sophisticated sense of humor, but from a genuine conviction of his own inferiority. He preferred to solve problems by denying their existence. He was the only one of the nine astronauts who could have been accurately described as passive: other people's opinions carried great weight with him. His prime value to the mission was his grasp of Athena systems. But he'd been a reluctant crewman, a man who periodically reminded us that he wanted only to retire to his farm in Indiana. He wouldn't have been along at all except that one guy died and somebody else came down with an unexpected (but thoroughly earned) disease. Now, with Selma incapacitated and Landolfi gone, McGuire was in command. It must have been disconcerting for him. "We've got about five hours," he continued. "Don't let Marj get involved in major surgery. She's already been complaining to me that it doesn't sound as if it'll be possible to move him. *We have no alternative.* She knows that, but you know how she is. Okay?"

One of the monitors had picked him up. He looked rumpled, and nervous. Not an attitude to elicit confidence. "Mac," said Cathie, "we may kill him trying to get him over there."

"You'll kill him if you don't," he snapped. "Get your personal stuff together, and bring it with you. You won't be going back."

"What about trying to transfer some food?" I asked.

"We can't dock," he said. "And there isn't time to float it across."

"Mac," said Cathie, "is *Amity* going to be able to support six people?"

I listened to McGuire breathing. He turned away to issue some trivial instructions to Iseminger. When he came back he said, simply and tonelessly, "Probably not." And then, coldbloodedly (I thought), "How's Herman doing?"

Maybe it was my imagination. Certainly there was nothing malicious in his tone, but Cathie caught it too, and turned sharply round. "McGuire is a son-of-a-bitch," she hissed. I don't know whether Mac heard it.

∽

Marjorie Aubuchon was short, blond, and irritable. When I relayed McGuire's concerns about time, she said, "God knows, that's all I've heard for the last half-hour." She observed that McGuire was a jerk, and bent over Herman. The blood was pink and frothy on his lips. After a few minutes she said, to no one in particular, "Probably a punctured lung." She waved Cathie over, and began filling a hypo; I went for a walk.

At sea, there's a long tradition of sentiment between mariners and their ships. Enlisted men identify with them, engineers baby them, and captains go down with them. No similar attitude has developed in space flight. We've never had an *Endeavor*, or a *Golden Hind*. Always, off Earth, it has been the mission, rather than the ship. Friendship VII and Apollo XI were far more than vehicles. I'm not sure why that is; maybe it reflects Cathie's view that travel between the worlds is still in its Kon-Tiki phase: the voyage itself is of such epic proportions that everything else is overwhelmed.

But I'd lived almost three years on *Greenswallow*. It was a long time to be confined to her narrow spaces. Nevertheless, she was shield and provider against that enormous abyss, and I discovered (while standing in the doorway of my cabin) a previously unfelt affection for her.

A few clothes were scattered round the room, a shirt was hung over my terminal, and two pictures were mounted on the plastic wall. One was a Casnavan print of a covered bridge in New Hampshire; the other was a telecopy of an editorial cartoon that had appeared in the *Washington Post*. The biggest human problem we had, of course, was sheer boredom. And Cathie had tried to capture the dimensions of the difficulty by showing crewmembers filling the long days on the outbound journey with bridge. ("It would be nice," Cathie's narrator had said at one point, "if we could take everybody out to an Italian restaurant now and then.") The *Post* cartoon had appeared several days later: it depicted four astronauts holding cards. (We could recognize Selma, Landolfi, and Marj. The fourth, whose back was turned, was exceedingly feminine, and appeared to be Esther Crowley.) An enormous bloodshot eye is looking in through one window; a tentacle and a UFO are visible through another. The "Selma" character, his glasses characteristically down on his nose, is examining his hand, and delivering the caption. *Dummy looks out the window and checks the alien.*

I packed the New Hampshire bridge, and left the cartoon. If someone comes by, in 20 million years or so, he might need a laugh. I went up to the cockpit with my bag.

McGuire checked with me to see how we were progressing. "Fine," I told him. I was still sitting there four hours later when Cathie appeared behind me.

"Rob," she said, "we're ready to move him." She smiled wearily. "Marj says he should be okay if we can get him over there without breaking anything else."

We cut the spin on the inner module to about point-oh-five. Then we lifted Herman onto a stretcher, and carried him carefully down to the airlock.

Cathie stared straight ahead, saying nothing. Her fine-boned cheeks were pale, and her eyes seemed focused far away. These, I thought, were her first moments to herself, unhampered by other duties. The impact of events was taking hold.

Marj called McGuire and told him we were starting over, and that she would need a sizable pair of shears when we got there to cut Herman's suit open. "Please have them ready," she said. "We may be in a hurry."

I had laid out his suit earlier: we pulled it up over his legs. That was easy, but the rest of it was slow, frustrating work. "We need a special kind of unit for this," Marj said. "Probably a large bag, without arms or legs. If we're ever dumb enough to do anything like this again, I'll recommend it."

McGuire urged us to hurry.

Once or twice, Cathie's eyes met mine. Something passed between us, but I was too distracted to define it. Then we were securing his helmet, and adjusting the oxygen mixture.

"I think we're okay," Marj observed, her hand pressed against Selma's chest. "Let's get him over there . . ."

I opened the inner airlock, and pulled my own helmet into place. Then we guided Herman in, and secured him to *Greenswallow*'s maintenance sled. (The sled was little more than a toolshed with jet nozzles.) I recovered my bag and stowed it on board.

"I'd better get my stuff," Cathie said. "You can get Herman over all right?"

"Of course," said Marj. "*Amity*'s sled is secured outside the lock. Use that."

She hesitated in the open hatchway, raised her left hand, and spread the fingers wide. Her eyes grew very round, and she formed two syllables that I was desperately slow to understand: in fact, I don't think I translated the gesture, the word, until we were halfway across to *Amity*, and the lock was irrevocably closed behind us.

"Good-bye."

Cathie's green eyes sparkled with barely controlled emotion across a dozen or so monitors. Her black hair, which had been tied back earlier, now framed her angular features and fell to her shoulders. It was precisely in that partial state of disarray that tends to be most appealing. She looked as if she'd been crying, but her jaw was set, and she stood erect. Beneath the gray tunic, her breast rose and fell.

"What the hell are you doing, Perth?" demanded McGuire. He looked tired, almost ill. He'd gained weight since we'd left the Cape, his hair had whitened and retreated, his flesh had grown blotchy, and he'd developed jowls. The contrast with his dapper image in the mission photo was sobering. "Get moving!" he said, striving to keep his voice from rising. "We're not going to make our burn!"

"I'm staying where I am," she said. "I couldn't make it over there now anyway. I wouldn't even have time to put on the suit."

McGuire's puffy eyelids slid slowly closed. "Why?" he asked.

She looked out of the cluster of screens, a segmented Cathie, a group Cathie. "Your ship won't support six people, Mac."

"Dammit!" His voice was a harsh rasp. "It would have just meant we'd cut down activity. Sleep a lot." He waved a hand in front of his eyes, as though his vision were blurred. "Cathie, we've lost you. There's no way we can get you back!"

"I know."

No one said anything. Iseminger stared at her.

"Is Herman okay?" she asked.

"Marj is still working on him," I said. "She thinks we got him across okay."

"Good."

A series of yellow lamps blinked on across the pilot's console. We had two minutes. "Damn," I said, suddenly aware of another danger: *Amity* was rotating, turning toward its new course. Would *Greenswallow* even survive the ignition? I looked at McGuire, who understood. His fingers flicked over press pads, and rows of numbers flashed across the navigation monitor. I could see muscles working in Cathie's jaws; she looked down at Mac's station as though she could read the result.

"It's all right," he said. "She'll be clear."

"Cathie . . ." Iseminger's voice was almost strangled. "If I'd known you intended anything like this . . ."

"I know, Ed." Her tone was gentle, a lover's voice, perhaps. Her eyes were wet: she smiled anyway, full face, up close.

Deep in the systems, pumps began to whine. "I wish," said Iseminger, absolutely without expression, "that we could do something."

She turned her back, strode with unbearable grace across the command center, away from us, and passed into the shadowy interior of the cockpit. Another camera picked her up there, and we got a profile: she was achingly lovely in the soft glow of the navigation lamps.

"There is something . . . you can do," she said. "Build Landolfi's engine. And come back for me."

For a brief moment, I thought Mac was going to abort the burn. But he sat frozen, fists clenched, and did the right thing, which is to say, nothing. It struck me that McGuire was incapable of intervening.

And I knew also that the woman in the cockpit was terrified of what she had done. It had been a good performance, but she'd utterly failed to conceal the fear that looked out of her eyes. And I realized with shock that she'd acted, not to prolong her life, but to save the Program. I watched her face as *Amity*'s engines ignited, and we began to draw away. Like McGuire, she seemed paralyzed, as though the nature of the calamity which she'd embraced was just becoming clear to her. Then it—she—was gone.

"What happened to the picture?" snapped Iseminger.

"She turned it off," I said. "I don't think she wants us to see her just now."

He glared at me, and spoke to Mac. "Why the hell," he demanded, "couldn't he have brought her back with him?" His fists were knotted.

"I didn't know," I said. "How could I know?" And I wondered, how could I not?

When the burn ended, the distance between the two ships had opened to only a few kilometers. But it was a gulf, I thought, wider than any across which men had before looked at each other.

Iseminger called her name relentlessly. (We knew she could hear us.) But we got only the carrier wave.

Then her voice crackled across the command center. "Good," she said. "Excellent. Check the recorders: make sure you got everything on tape." Her image was back. She was in full light again, tying up her hair. Her eyes were hooded, and her lips pursed thoughtfully. "Rob," she continued, "fade it out during Ed's response, when he's calling my name. Probably, you'll want to reduce the background noise at that point. Cut all the business about who's responsible. We want a sacrifice, not an oversight."

"My God, Cathie," I said. I stared at her, trying to understand. "What have you done?"

She took a deep breath. "I meant what I said. I have enough food to get by here for eight years or so. More if I stretch it. *And plenty of fresh air*. Well, relatively fresh. I'm better off than any of us would be if six people were trying to survive on *Amity*."

"Cathie!" howled McGuire. He sounded in physical agony. "Cathie, we didn't know for sure about life support. The converters might have kept up. There might have been enough air! It was just an estimate!"

"This is a hell of a time to tell me," she said. "Well, it doesn't matter now. Listen, I'll be fine. I've got books to read, and maybe one to write. My long-range communications are *kaput*, Rob knows that, so you'll have to come back for the book, too." She smiled. "You'll like it, Mac." The command center got very still. "And on nights when things really get boring, I can play bridge with the computer."

McGuire shook his head. "You're sure you'll be all right? You seemed pretty upset a few minutes ago."

She looked at me and winked.

"The first Cathie was staged, Mac," I said.

"I give up," McGuire sighed. "Why?" He swiveled round to face the image on his screen. "Why would you do that?"

"That young woman," she replied, "was committing an act of uncommon valor, as they say in the Marines. And she had to be vulnerable." And compellingly lovely, I thought. In those last moments, I was realizing what it might mean to love Cathie Perth. "This Cathie," she grinned, "is doing the only sensible thing. And taking a sabbatical as well. Do what you can to get the ship built. I'll be waiting." She paused. "Somebody should suggest they name it after Victor."

☞

This is the fifth Christmas since that one on Callisto. It's a long time by any human measure. We drifted out of radio contact during the first week. There was some talk of broadcasting instructions to her for repairing her long-range transmission equipment. But she'd have to go outside to do it, so the idea was prudently tabled.

She was right about that tape. In my lifetime, I've never seen people so singlemindedly aroused. It created a global surge of sympathy and demands for action that seem to grow in intensity with each passing year. Funded partially by contributions and technical assistance from abroad, NASA has been pushing the construction of the fusion vessel that Victor Landolfi dreamed of.

Iseminger was assigned to help with the computer systems, and he's kept me informed of progress. The most recent public estimates had anticipated a spring launch. But that single word *September* in Iseminger's card suggests that one more obstacle has been encountered; and it means still another year before we can hope to reach her.

We broadcast to her on a regular basis. I volunteered to help, and I sit sometimes and talk to her for hours. She gets a regular schedule of news, entertainment, sports, whatever. And, if she's listening, she knows that we're coming.

And she also knows that her wish that the fusion ship be named for Victor Landolfi has been disregarded. The rescue vehicle will be the *Catherine Perth*.

If she's listening: we have no way of knowing. And I worry a lot. Can a human being survive six years of absolute solitude? Iseminger was here for a few days last summer, and he tells me he is confident. "She's a tough lady," he said, any number of times. "Nothing bothers her. She even gave us a little theater at the end."

And that's what scares me: Cathie's theatrical technique. I've thought about it, on the long ride home, and here. I kept a copy of the complete tape of that final conversation, despite McGuire's instructions to the contrary, and I've watched it a few times. It's locked downstairs in a file cabinet now, and I don't look at it anymore. I'm afraid to. There are two Cathie Perths on the recording: the frightened, courageous one who galvanized a global public; and our Cathie, preoccupied with her job, flexible, almost indifferent to her situation. A survivor.

And, God help me, I can't tell which one was staged.

Lieserl

STEPHEN BAXTER

Like many of his colleagues here at the end of the nineties—Greg Egan comes to mind, as do people like Paul J. McAuley, Michael Swanwick, Iain M. Banks, Bruce Sterling, Pat Cadigan, Brian Stableford, Gregory Benford, Ian McDonald, Gwyneth Jones, Vernor Vinge, Greg Bear, David Marusek, Geoff Ryman, and a half-dozen others—British writer Stephen Baxter has been engaged for the last ten years or so with the task of revitalizing and reinventing the hard-science story for a new generation of readers, producing work on the cutting edge of science that bristles with weird new ideas and often takes place against vistas of almost outrageously cosmic scope.

Arthur C. Clarke's work has clearly been a strong influence on Baxter's own (he's even written a story in collaboration with Clarke), and, like Clarke, Baxter seems to have a special fascination with the theme of exploration, delighting in taking us to places never visited by anyone before, including ice caverns deep inside Mercury, the core of the Moon, the surface of a sentient Venus, an artificial planet made of dark matter, and many other outré locations. Like Clarke, however, and like his colleagues named earlier, Baxter rarely loses track of the human side of the equation—as amply demonstrated by "Lieserl," which introduces us to one of the strangest and most haunting characters you're ever likely to meet and shows us that sometimes explorers aren't born; they're made.

Baxter made his first sale to Interzone *in 1987 and since then has become one of that magazine's most frequent contributors, as well as making sales to* Asimov's Science Fiction, Science Fiction Age, Zenith, *and* New Worlds *and elsewhere. He's one of the most prolific of the new writers of the nineties and is rapidly becoming one of the most popular and acclaimed of them as well. Baxter's first novel,* Raft, *was released in 1991 to wide and enthusiastic response and was rapidly followed by other well-received novels such as* Timelike Infinity, Anti-Ice, Flux, *and the H. G. Wells homage—a sequel to* The Time Machine—The Time Ships, *which won both the Arthur C. Clarke Award and the Philip K. Dick Award. Baxter's other books include the novels* Voyage, Titan, *and* Moonseed *and the collections* Vacuum Diagrams: Stories of the Xeelee Sequence *and* Traces. *His most recent book is the novel* Mammoth, Book One: Silverhair. *Upcoming is a new novel,* Manifold: Time *and a collaboration with Sir Arthur C. Clarke,* The Light of Other Days.*

Lieserl was suspended inside the body of the Sun.

She spread her arms wide and lifted up her face. She was deep within the Sun's convective zone, the broad mantle of turbulent material beneath the glowing photosphere; convective cells larger than the Earth, tangled with ropes of magnetic flux, filled the world around her. She could hear the roar of the great convective founts, smell the stale photons diffusing out towards space from the remote fusing core.

She felt as if she were inside some huge cavern. Looking up she could see how the photosphere formed a glowing roof over her world perhaps fifty thousand miles above her, and the boundary of the inner radiative zone was a shining, impenetrable floor another fifty thousand miles beneath.

Lieserl? Can you hear me? Are you all right?

Kevan Scholes. It sounded like her mother's voice, she thought.

She thrust her arms down by her sides and swooped up, letting the floor and roof of the cavern-world wheel around her. She opened up her senses, so that she could feel the turbulence as a whisper against her skin, the glow of hard photons from the core as a gentle warmth against her face.

Lieserl? Lieserl?

She remembered how her mother had enfolded her in her arms. 'The Sun, Lieserl. *The Sun . . .*'

⬯

Even at the moment she was born she knew something was wrong.

A face loomed over her: wide, smooth, smiling. The cheeks were damp, the glistening eyes huge. 'Lieserl. Oh, Lieserl . . .'

Lieserl. My name, then.

She explored the face before her, studying the lines around the eyes, the humorous upturn of the mouth, the strong nose. It was an intelligent, lived-in face. *This is a good human being,* she thought. *Good stock . . .*

Good stock? What am I thinking of?

This was impossible. She felt terrified of her own explosive consciousness. She shouldn't even be able to focus her eyes yet . . .

She tried to touch her mother's face. Her own hand was still moist with amniotic fluid—*but it was growing visibly*, the bones extending and broadening, filling out the loose skin like a glove.

She opened her mouth. It was dry, her gums already sore with budding teeth.

She tried to speak.

Her mother's eyes brimmed with tears. 'Oh, Lieserl. My impossible baby.'

Strong arms reached beneath her. She felt weak, helpless, consumed by growth. Her mother lifted her up, high in the air. Bony adult fingers dug into the aching flesh of her back; her head lolled backwards, the expanding muscles still too weak to support the burgeoning weight of her head. She could sense other adults surrounding her, the bed in which she'd been born, the outlines of a room.

She was held before a window, with her body tipped forward. Her head lolled; spittle laced across her chin.

An immense light flooded her eyes.

She cried out.

Her mother enfolded her in her arms. 'The Sun, Lieserl. *The Sun . . .*'

☞

The first few days were the worst. Her parents—impossibly tall, looming figures—took her through brightly lit rooms, a garden always flooded with sunlight. She learned to sit up. The muscles in her back fanned out, pulsing as they grew. To distract her from the unending pain, clowns tumbled over the grass before her, chortling through their huge red lips, then popping out of existence in clouds of pixels.

She grew explosively, feeding all the time, a million impressions crowding into her soft sensorium.

There seemed to be no limit to the number of rooms in this place, this House. Slowly she began to understand that some of the rooms were Virtual chambers—blank screens against which any number of images could be projected. But even so, the House must comprise hundreds of rooms. And she—with her parents—wasn't alone here, she slowly realized. There were other people, but at first they kept away, out of sight, apparent only by their actions: the meals they prepared, the toys they left her.

On the third day her parents took her on a trip by flitter. It was the first time she'd been away from the House, its grounds. She stared through the bulbous windows, pressing her nose to heated glass. The journey was an arc over a toylike landscape; a breast of blue ocean curved away from the land, all around her. This was the island of Skiros, her mother told her, and the sea was called Aegean. The House was the largest construct on the island; it was a jumble of white, cube-shaped buildings, linked by corridors and surrounded by garden-grass, trees. Further out there were bridges and roads looping through the air above the ground, houses like a child's bricks sprinkled across glowing hillsides.

Everything was drenched in heavy, liquid sunlight.

The flitter snuggled at last against a grassy sward close to the shore of an ocean. Lieserl's mother lifted her out and placed her—on her stretching, unsteady legs—on the rough, sandy grass.

Hand in hand, the little family walked down a short slope to the beach.

The Sun burned through thinned air from an unbearably blue sky. Her vision seemed telescopic. She looked at distant groups of children and adults playing—far away, half-way to the horizon—and it was as if she was among them herself. Her feet, still uncertain, pressed into gritty, moist sand. She could taste the brine salt on the air; it seemed to permeate her very skin.

She found mussels clinging to a ruined pier. She prised them away with a toy spade, and gazed, fascinated, at their slime-dripping feet.

She sat on the sand with her parents, feeling her light costume stretch over her still-stretching limbs. They played a simple game, of counters moving over a floating Virtual board, pictures of ladders and hissing snakes. There was laughter, mock complaints by her father, elaborate pantomimes of cheating.

Her senses were electric. It was a wonderful day, full of light and joy, extraordinarily vivid sensations. Her parents loved her—she could see that in the way they moved with each other, came to her, played with her.

They must know she was different; but they didn't seem to care.

She didn't want to be different—to be *wrong*. She closed her mind against the thoughts, and concentrated on the snakes, the ladders, the sparkling counters.

Every morning she woke up in a bed that felt too small.

Lieserl liked the garden. She liked to watch the flowers straining their tiny, pretty faces towards the Sun, as the great light climbed patiently across the sky. The sunlight made the flowers grow, her father told her. Maybe she was like a flower, she thought, growing too quickly in all this sunlight.

On the fifth day she was taken to a wide, irregularly shaped, colourful classroom. This room was full of children—*other children!*—and toys, drawings, books. Sunlight flooded the room; perhaps there was some clear dome stretched over the open walls.

The children sat on the floor and played with paints and dolls, or talked earnestly to brilliantly-coloured Virtual figures—smiling birds, tiny clowns. The children turned to watch as she came in with her mother, their faces round and bright, like dapples of sunlight through leaves. She'd never been so close to other children before. Were these children *different* too?

One small girl scowled at her, and Lieserl quailed against her mother's legs. But her mother's familiar warm hands pressed into her back. 'Go ahead. It's all right.'

As she stared at the unknown girl's scowling face, Lieserl's questions, her too-adult, too-sophisticated doubts, seemed to evaporate. Suddenly, all that mattered to her—all that mattered in the world—was that she should be accepted by these children—that they wouldn't know she was *different*.

An adult approached her: a man, young, thin, his features bland with youth. He wore a jumpsuit coloured a ludicrous orange; in the sunlight, the glow of it shone up over his chin. He smiled at her. 'Lieserl, isn't it? My name's Michael. We're glad you're here.' In a louder, exaggerated voice, he said, 'Aren't we, people?'

He was answered by a rehearsed, chorused 'Yes'.

'Now come and we'll find something for you to do,' Michael said. He led her across the child-littered floor to a space beside a small boy. The boy—red-haired, with startling blue eyes—was staring at a Virtual puppet which endlessly formed and reformed: the figure two, collapsing into two snowflakes, two swans, two dancing children; the figure three, followed by three bears, three fish swimming in the air, three cakes. The boy mouthed the numbers, following the tinny voice of the Virtual. 'Two. One. Two and one is three.'

Michael introduced her to the boy—Tommy—and she sat down with him. Tommy, she was relieved to find, was so fascinated by his virtual that he scarcely seemed aware that Lieserl was present—let alone *different*.

The number Virtual ran through its cycle and winked out of existence. 'Bye-bye, Tommy! Goodbye, Lieserl!'

Tommy was resting on his stomach, his chin cupped in his palms. Lieserl, awkwardly, copied his posture. Now Tommy turned to her—without appraisal, merely looking at her, with unconscious acceptance.

Lieserl said, 'Can we see it again?'

He yawned and poked a finger into one nostril. 'No. Let's see another. There's a great one about the pre-Cambrian explosion—'

'The what?'

He waved a hand dismissively. 'You know, the Burgess Shale and all that. Wait till you see *Hallucigenia* crawling over your neck . . .'

The children played, and learned, and napped. Later, the girl who'd scowled at Lieserl—Ginnie—started some trouble. She poked fun at the way Lieserl's bony wrists stuck out of her sleeves (Lieserl's growth rate was slowing, but she was still growing out of her clothes during a day). Then—unexpectedly, astonishingly—Ginnie started to bawl, claiming that Lieserl had walked through her Virtual. When Michael came over Lieserl started to explain, calmly and rationally, that Ginnie must be mistaken; but Michael told her not to cause such distress, and for punishment she was forced to sit away from the other children for ten minutes, without stimulation.

It was all desperately, savagely unfair. It was the longest ten minutes of Lieserl's life. She glowered at Ginnie, filled with resentment.

The next day she found herself looking forward to going to the room with the children again. She set off with her mother through sunlit corridors. They reached the room Lieserl remembered—there was Michael, smiling a little wistfully to her, and Tommy, and the girl Ginnie—but Ginnie seemed different: childlike, unformed . . .

At least a head shorter than Lieserl.

Lieserl tried to recapture that delicious enmity of the day before, but it vanished even as she conjured it. Ginnie was just a kid.

She felt as if something had been stolen from her.

Her mother squeezed her hand. 'Come on. Let's find a new room for you to play in.'

☙

Every day was unique. Every day Lieserl spent in a new place, with new people.

The world glowed with sunlight. Shining points trailed endlessly across the sky: low-orbit habitats and comet nuclei, tethered for power and fuel. People walked through a sea of information, with access to the Virtual libraries available anywhere in the world, at a subvocalized command. Lieserl learned quickly. She read about her parents. They were scientists, studying the Sun. They weren't alone; there were many people, huge resources, devoted to the Sun.

In the libraries there was a lot of material about the Sun, little of which she could follow. But she sensed some common threads.

Once, people had taken the Sun for granted. No longer. Now—for some reason—they *feared* it.

On the ninth day Lieserl studied herself in a Virtual holo-mirror. She had the image turn around, so she could see the shape of her skull, the lie of her hair. There was still some childish softness in her face, she thought, but the woman inside her was emerging already, as if her childhood was a receding tide. She would look like her mother—Phillida—in the strong-nosed set of her face, her large, vulnerable eyes; but she would have the sandy colouring of her father, George.

Lieserl looked about nine years old. But she was just nine *days* old.

She bade the Virtual break up; it shattered into a million tiny images of her face which drifted away like flies in the sunlit air.

Phillida and George were fine parents, she thought. They spent their time away from her working through technical papers—which scrolled through the air like falling leaves—and exploring elaborate, onion-ring Virtual models of stars. Although they were both clearly busy they gave themselves to her without hesitation. She moved in a happy world of smiles, sympathy and support.

Her parents loved her unreservedly. But that wasn't always enough.

She started to come up with more complicated, detailed questions. Like, what was the mechanism by which she was growing so rapidly? She didn't seem to eat more than the other children she encountered; what could be fuelling her absurd growth rates?

How did she *know* so much? She'd been born self-aware, with even the rudiments of language in her head. The Virtuals she interacted with in the classrooms were fun, and she always seemed to learn something new; but she absorbed no more than scraps of knowledge through them compared to the feast of insight with which she awoke each morning.

What had taught her, in the womb? What was teaching her now?

She had no answers. But perhaps—somehow—it was all connected with this strange, global obsession with the Sun. She remembered her childish fantasy—that she might be like a flower, straining up too quickly to the Sun. Maybe, she wondered now, there was some grain of truth in that insight.

The strange little family had worked up some simple, homely rituals together. Lieserl's favourite was the game, each evening, of snakes and ladders. George brought home an old set—a *real* board made of card, and wooden counters. Already Lieserl was too old for the game; but she loved the company of her parents, her father's elaborate jokes, the simple challenge of the game, the feel of the worn, antique counters.

Phillida showed her how to use Virtuals to produce her own game boards. Her first efforts, on her eleventh day, were plain, neat forms, little more than copies of the commercial boards she'd seen. But soon she began to experiment. She drew a huge board of a million squares, which covered a whole room—she could walk through the board, a planar sheet of light at about waist-height. She crammed the board with intricate, curling snakes, vast ladders, vibrantly glowing squares—detail piled on detail.

The next morning she walked with eagerness to the room where she'd built her board—and was immediately disappointed. Her efforts seemed pale, static, derivative—obviously the work of a child, despite the assistance of the Virtual software.

She wiped the board clean, leaving a grid of pale squares floating in the air. Then she started to populate it again—but this time with animated half-human snakes, slithering 'ladders' of a hundred forms. She'd learned to access the Virtual libraries, and she plundered the art and history of a hundred centuries to populate her board.

Of course it was no longer possible to play games on the board, but that didn't matter. The board was the thing, a little world in itself. She withdrew a little from her parents, spending long hours in deep searches through the libraries. She gave up her classes. Her parents didn't seem to mind; they came to speak to her regularly, and showed an interest in her projects, and respected her privacy.

The board kept her interest the next day. But now she evolved elaborate games, dividing the board into countries and empires with arbitrary bands of glowing light. Armies of ladder-folk joined with legions of snakes in crude reproductions of the great events of human history.

She watched the symbols flicker across the Virtual board, shimmering, coalescing; she dictated lengthy chronicles of the histories of her imaginary countries.

By the end of the day, though, she was starting to grow more interested in the history texts she was plundering than in her own elaborations on them. She went to bed, eager for the next morning to come.

☙

She awoke in darkness, doubled in agony.

She called for light, which flooded the room, sourceless. She sat up in bed.

Blood spotted the sheets. She screamed.

☙

Phillida sat with her, cradling her head. Lieserl pressed herself against her mother's warmth, trying to still her trembling.

'I think it's time you asked me your questions.'

Lieserl sniffed. 'What questions?'

'The ones you've carried around with you since the moment you were born.' Phillida smiled. 'I could see it in your eyes, even at that moment. You poor thing . . . to be burdened with so much *awareness*. I'm sorry, Lieserl.'

Lieserl pulled away. Suddenly she felt cold, vulnerable.

'Tell me why you're sorry,' she said at last.

'You're my daughter.' Phillida placed her hands on Lieserl's shoulders and pushed her face close; Lieserl could feel the warmth of her breath, and the soft room light caught the grey in her mother's blonde hair, making it seem to shine. 'Never forget that. You're as human as I am. But—' She hesitated.

'But what?'

'But you're being—*engineered*.'

Nanobots swarmed through Lieserl's body, Phillida said. They plated calcium over her bones, stimulated the generation of new cells, force-growing her body like some absurd human sunflower—they even implanted memories, artificial learning, directly into her cortex.

Lieserl felt like scraping at her skin, gouging out this artificial infection. '*Why?* Why did you let this be done to me?'

Phillida pulled her close, but Lieserl stayed stiff, resisting mutely. Phillida buried her face in Lieserl's hair; Lieserl felt the soft weight of her mother's cheek on the crown of her head. 'Not yet,' Phillida said. 'Not yet. A few more days, my love. That's all . . .'

Phillida's cheeks grew warmer, as if she was crying, silently, into her daughter's hair.

◆

Lieserl returned to her snakes-and-ladders board. She found herself looking on her creation with affection, but also nostalgic sadness; she felt distant from this elaborate, slightly obsessive concoction.

Already she'd outgrown it.

She walked into the middle of the sparkling board and bade a Sun, a foot wide, rise out from the center of her body. Light swamped the board, shattering it.

She wasn't the only adolescent who had constructed fantasy worlds like this. She read about the Brontes, in their lonely parsonage in the north of England, and their elaborate shared world of kings and princes and empires. And she read about the history of the humble game of snakes and ladders. The game had come from India, where it was a morality teaching aid called *Moksha-Patamu*. There were twelve vices and four virtues, and the objective was to get to Nirvana. It was easier to fail than to succeed . . . The British in the nineteenth century had adopted it as an instructional guide for children called *Kismet*; Lieserl stared at images of claustrophobic boards, forbidding snakes. Thirteen snakes and eight ladders showed children that if they were good and obedient their life would be rewarded.

But by a few decades later the game had lost its moral subtexts. Lieserl found images from the early twentieth century of a sad-looking little clown; he slithered haplessly down snakes and heroically clambered up ladders. Lieserl stared at him, trying to understand the appeal of his baggy trousers, walking cane and little moustache.

The game, with its charm and simplicity, had survived through the twenty centuries which had worn away since the death of that forgotten clown.

She grew interested in the *numbers* embedded in the various versions of the game. The twelve-to-four ratio of *Moksha-Patamu* clearly made it a harder game to win than *Kismet's* thirteen-to-eight—but how much harder?

She began to draw new boards in the air. But these boards were abstractions—clean, colourless, little more than sketches. She ran through high-speed simulated games, studying their outcomes. She experimented with ratios of snakes to ladders, with their placement. Phillida sat with her and introduced her to combinatorial mathematics, the theory of games—to different forms of wonder.

On her fifteenth day she tired of her own company and started to attend classes again. She found the perceptions of others a refreshing counterpoint to her own, high-speed learning.

The world seemed to open up around her like a flower; it was a world full of sunlight, of endless avenues of information, of stimulating people.

She read up on nanobots.

Body cells were programmed to commit suicide. A cell itself manufactured enzymes which cut its DNA into neat pieces, and quietly closed down. The suicide of cells was a guard against uncontrolled growth—tumours—and a tool to sculpt the developing body: in the womb, the withering of unwanted cells carved fingers and toes from blunt tissue buds. Death was the default state of a cell. Chemical signals were sent by the body, to instruct cells to remain alive.

The nanotechnological manipulation of this process made immortality simple.

It also made the manufacture of a Lieserl simple.

Lieserl studied this, scratching absently at her inhabited, engineered arms. She still didn't know *why*.

◆

With a boy called Matthew, from her class, she took a trip away from the House—without her parents for the first time. They rode a flitter to the shore where she'd played as a child, twelve days earlier. She found the broken pier where she'd discovered mussels. The place seemed less vivid—less magical—and she felt a sad nostalgia for the loss of the freshness of her childish senses.

But there were other compensations. Her body was strong, lithe, and the sunlight was like warm oil on her skin. She ran and swam, relishing the sparkle of the ozone-laden air in her lungs. She and Matthew mock-wrestled and chased in the surf, clambering over each other like young apes—like children, she thought, but not quite with complete innocence . . .

As sunset approached they allowed the flitter to return them to the House. They agreed to meet the next day, perhaps take another trip somewhere. Matthew kissed her lightly, on the lips, as they parted.

That night she could barely sleep. She lay in the dark of her room, the scent of salt still strong in her nostrils, the image of Matthew alive in her mind. Her body seemed to pulse with hot blood, with its endless, continuing growth.

The next day—her sixteenth—Lieserl rose quickly. She'd never felt so alive; her skin still glowed from the salt and sunlight of the shore, and there was a hot tension inside her, an ache deep in her belly, a tightness.

When she reached the flitter bay at the front of the House, Matthew was waiting for her. His back was turned, the low sunlight causing the fine hairs at the base of his neck to glow.

He turned to face her.

He reached out to her, uncertainly, then allowed his hands to drop to his sides. He didn't seem to know what to say; his posture changed, subtly, his shoulders slumping slightly; before her eyes he was becoming shy of her.

She was taller than him. Visibly *older*. She became abruptly aware of the still-childlike roundness of his face, the awkwardness of his manner. The thought of *touching* him—the memory of her feverish dreams during the night—seemed absurd, impossibly adolescent.

She felt the muscles in her neck tighten; she felt as if she must scream. Matthew seemed to recede from her, as if she was viewing him through a tunnel.

Once again the labouring nanobots—the damned, unceasing nano-technological infection of her body—had taken away part of her life.

This time, though, it was too much to bear.

●

'Why? *Why?*' She wanted to scream abuse at her mother—to *hurt* her.

Phillida had never looked so old. Her skin seemed drawn tight across the bones of her face, the lines etched deep. 'I'm sorry,' she said. 'Believe me. When we—George and I—volunteered for this programme, we knew it would be painful. But we never dreamed how much. Neither of us had had children before. Perhaps if we had, we'd have been able to anticipate how this would feel.'

'I'm a freak—an absurd experiment,' Lieserl shouted. 'A *construct*. Why did you make me human? Why not some insentient animal? Why not a Virtual?'

'Oh, you had to be human. As human as possible . . .' Phillida seemed to come to a decision. 'I'd hoped to give you a few more days of—life, normality—before it had to end. You seemed to be finding some happiness—'

'In fragments,' Lieserl said bitterly. 'This is no life, Phillida. It's *grotesque.*'

'I know. I'm sorry, my love. Come with me.'

'Where?'

'Outside. To the garden. I want to show you something.'

Suspicious, hostile, Lieserl allowed her mother to take her hand; but she made her fingers lie lifeless, cold in Phillida's warm grasp.

It was mid-morning now. The Sun's light flooded the garden; flowers—white and yellow—strained up towards the sky.

Lieserl looked around; the garden was empty. 'What am I supposed to be seeing?'

Phillida, solemnly, pointed upwards.

Lieserl tilted back her head, shading her eyes to block out the light. The sky was a searing blue dome, marked only by a high vapour trail and the lights of habitats.

'No.' Gently, Phillida pulled Lieserl's hand down from her face, and, cupping her chin, tipped her face flower-like towards the Sun.

The star's light seemed to fill her head. Dazzled, she dropped her eyes, stared at Phillida through a haze of blurred, streaked retinal images.

The Sun. Of course . . .

●

Kevan Scholes said, *Damn it, Lieserl, you're going to have to respond properly. Things are difficult enough without—*

'I know. I'm sorry. How are you feeling, anyway?'

Me? I'm fine. But that's hardly the point, is it? Now come on, Lieserl, the team here are getting on my back; let's run through the tests.

'You mean I'm not down here to enjoy myself?'

Scholes, speaking from his safe habitat far beyond the photosphere, didn't respond.

'Yeah. The tests. Okay, electromagnetic first.' She adjusted her sensorium. 'I'm plunged into darkness,' she said drily. 'There's very little free radiation at any frequency—perhaps an X-ray glow from the photosphere; it looks a little like a late evening sky. And—'

We know the systems are functioning. I need to know what you see, what you feel.

'What I feel?'

She spread her arms and sailed backwards through the 'air' of the cavern. The huge convective cells buffeted and merged like living things, whales in this insubstantial sea of gas.

'I see convection fountains,' she said. 'A cave full of them.'

She rolled over onto her belly, so that she was gliding face down, surveying the plasma sea below her. She *opened* her eyes, changing her mode of perception. The convective honeycomb faded into the background of her senses, and the magnetic flux tubes came into prominence, solidifying out of the air; beyond them the convective pattern was a sketchy framework, overlaid. The tubes were each a hundred yards broad, channels cutting through the air; they were thousands of miles long, and they filled the air around her, all the way down to the plasma sea.

Lieserl dipped into a tube; she felt the tingle of enhanced magnetic strength. Its walls rushed past her, curving gracefully. 'It's wonderful,' she said. 'I'm inside a flux tube. It's an immense tunnel; it's like a fairground ride. I could follow this path all the way round the Sun.'

Maybe. I don't know if we need the poetry, Lieserl. Kevan Scholes hesitated, and when he spoke again he sounded severely encouraging, as if he'd been instructed to be nice to her. *We're glad you're feeling—ah—happy in yourself, Lieserl.*

'My new self. Maybe. Well, it was an improvement on the old; you have to admit that.'

Yes. I want you to think back to the downloading. Can you do that?

'The downloading? Why?'

Come on, Lieserl. It's another test, obviously.

'A test of what?'

Your trace functions. We want to know if—

'My trace functions. You mean my memory.'

. . . *Yes.* He had the grace to sound embarrassed. *Think back, Lieserl. Can you remember?*

Downloading . . .

◆

It was her ninetieth day, her ninetieth physical-year. She was impossibly frail—unable even to walk, or feed herself, or clean herself.

They'd taken her to a habitat close to the Sun. They'd almost left the download too late; they'd had one scare when an infection had somehow got through to her and settled into her lungs, nearly killing her.

She wanted to die.

Physically she was the oldest human in the System. She felt as if she were underwater: she could barely feel, or taste, or see anything, as if she was encased in some deadening, vicious fluid. And she knew her mind was failing.

It was so fast she could *feel* it. It was like a ghastly reverse run of her accelerated childhood. She woke every day to a new diminution of her self. She had come to dread sleep, yet could not avoid it.

She couldn't bear the indignity of it. Everybody else was immortal, and young; and the AS technology which had made them so was being used to kill Lieserl. She hated those who had put her in this position.

Her mother visited her for the last time, a few days before the download. Lieserl, through her ruined, rheumy old eyes, was barely able to recognize Phillida—this young, weeping woman, only a few months older than when she had held up her baby girl to the Sun.

Lieserl cursed her, sent her away.

At last she was taken, in her bed, to a downloading chamber at the heart of the habitat.

◆

Do you remember, Lieserl? Was it—continuous?

'. . . No.'

It was a sensory explosion.

In an instant she was young again, with every sense alive and vivid. Her vision was sharp, her hearing impossibly precise. And slowly, slowly, she had become aware of new senses—senses beyond the human. She could see the dull infra-red glow of the bellies and heads of the people working around the shell of her own abandoned body, the sparkle of X-ray photons from the Solar photosphere as they leaked through the habitat's shielding.

She'd retained her human memories, but they were qualitatively different from the experiences she was accumulating now. Limited, partial, subjective, imperfectly recorded: like fading paintings, she thought.

. . . Except, perhaps, for that single, golden, day at the beach.

She studied the husk of her body. It was almost visibly imploding now, empty . . .

'I remember,' she told Kevan Scholes. 'Yes, I remember.'

◆

Now the flux tube curved away to the right; and, in following it, she became aware that she was tracing out a spiral path. She let herself relax into the motion, and watched the cave-world beyond the tube wheel around her. The flux tubes neighbouring her own had become twisted into spirals too, she realized; she was following one strand in a rope of twisted-together flux tubes.

Lieserl, what's happening? We can see your trajectory's altering, fast.

'I'm fine. I've got myself into a flux rope, that's all . . .'

Lieserl, you should get out of there . . .

She let the tube sweep her around. 'Why? This is fun.'

Maybe. But it isn't a good idea for you to break the surface; we're concerned about the stability of the wormhole—

Lieserl sighed and let herself slow. 'Oh, damn it, you're just no fun. I would have enjoyed bursting out through the middle of a sunspot. What a great way to go.'

We're not done with the tests yet, Lieserl.

'What do you want me to do?'

One more . . .

'Just tell me.'

Run a full self-check, Lieserl. Just for a few minutes . . . Drop the Virtual constructs.

She hesitated. 'Why? The systems are obviously functioning to specification.'

Lieserl, you don't need to make this difficult for me. Scholes sounded defensive. *This is a standard suite of tests for any AI which—*

'All right, damn it.'

She closed her eyes, and with a sudden, impulsive stab of will, let her Virtual image of herself-the illusion of a human body around her-crumble.

◡

It was like waking from a dream: a soft, comfortable dream of childhood, waking to find herself entombed in a machine, a crude construct of bolts and cords and gears.

She considered herself.

The tetrahedral Interface of the wormhole was suspended in the body of the Sun. The thin, searing-hot gas of the convective zone poured into its four triangular faces, so that the Interface was surrounded by a sculpture of inflowing gas, a flower carved dynamically from the Sun's flesh, almost obscuring the Interface itself. The solar material was, she knew, being pumped through the wormhole to the second Interface in orbit around the Sun; convection zone gases emerged, blazing, from the drifting tetrahedron, making it into a second, miniature Sun around which human habitats could cluster.

By pumping away the gas, and the heat it carried, the Interface refrigerated itself, enabling it to survive—with its precious, fragile cargo of datastores . . .

The stores which sustained the awareness of herself, Lieserl.

She inspected herself, at many levels, simultaneously.

At the physical level she studied crisp matrices of data, shifting, coalescing. And overlaid on that was the logical structure of data storage and access paths which represented the components of her mind.

Good . . . Good, Lieserl. You're sending us good data. How are you feeling?

'You keep asking me that, damn it. I feel—'

Enhanced . . .

No longer trapped in a single point, in a box of bone behind eyes made of jelly.

What made her conscious? It was the ability to be aware of what was happening in her mind, and in the world around her, and what had happened in the past.

By any test, she was more conscious than any other human—because she had more of the *machinery* of consciousness.

She was supremely conscious—the most conscious human who had ever lived.

If, she thought uneasily, she was still human.

Good. Good. All right, Lieserl. We have work to do.

She let her awareness implode, once more, into a Virtual-human form. Her perception was immediately simplified. To be seeing through apparently-human eyes was comforting . . . and yet, she thought, restrictive.

Perhaps it wouldn't be much longer before she felt ready to abandon even this last vestige of humanity. And then what?

Lieserl?

'I hear you.'

She turned her face towards the core.

←

'There is a *purpose*, Lieserl,' her mother said. 'A justification. You aren't simply an experiment. You have a mission.' She waved her hand at the sprawling, friendly buildings that comprised the House. 'Most of the people here, particularly the children, don't know anything about you. They have jobs, goals—lives of their own to follow. But they're here for *you*.

'Lieserl, your experiences have been designed—George and I were selected, even—to ensure that the first few days of your existence would *imprint* you with humanity.'

'The first few days?' Suddenly the unknowable future was like a black wall, looming towards her; she felt as out of control of her life as if she was a counter on some immense, invisible snakes-and-ladders board.

'I don't want this. I want to be me. I want my freedom, Phillida.'

'No, Lieserl. You're not free, I'm afraid; you never can be. You have a goal.'

'What goal?'

'Listen to me. The Sun gave us life. Without it—without the other stars—we couldn't survive.

'We're a strong species. We believe we can live as long as the stars— for tens of billions of years. And perhaps even beyond that. But we've had—glimpses—of the future, the far distant future . . . Disturbing glimpses. People are starting to plan for that future—to work on projects which will take millions of years to come to fruition . . .

'Lieserl, you're one of those projects.'

'I don't understand.'

Phillida took her hand, squeezed it gently; the simple human contact seemed incongruous, the garden around them transient, a chimera, before this talk of megayears and the future of the species.

'Lieserl, something is wrong with the Sun. *You* have to find out what. The Sun is dying; something—or someone—is *killing* it.'

Phillida's eyes were huge before her, staring, probing for understanding. 'Don't be afraid. My dear, you will live forever. If you want to. You are a new form of human. And you will see wonders of which I—and everyone else who has ever lived—can only dream.'

Lieserl listened to her tone, coldly, analysing it. 'But you don't *envy* me. Do you, Phillida?'

Phillida's smile crumbled. 'No,' she said quietly.

Lieserl tipped back her head. An immense light flooded her eyes. She cried out.

Her mother enfolded her in her arms. 'The Sun, Lieserl. *The Sun* . . .'

Crossing Chao Meng Fu

G. DAVID NORDLEY

Like John Varley, Michael Swanwick, Stephen Baxter, Kim Stanley Robinson, and others, G. David Nordley is a writer who finds the solar system an exotic-enough setting for adventures just as it is, as he's demonstrated with stories of exploration and conflict on a grand scale, such as "Into the Miranda Rift," "Out of the Quiet Years," "Dawn Venus," "Comet Gypsies," "Alice's Asteroid," "The Day of Their Coming," "Messengers of Chaos," and others. Many of these stories make effective use of the latest data from the Voyager *space probes, data that show just how bizarre, complex, surprising, and mysterious a place our solar system really is, a far cry from the conception of the solar system as a dull collection of rock, ice, and cinders that was common in the seventies.*

In the suspenseful tale that follows, Nordley shows us that while the determination to stick to a task until you complete it, to push through no matter what the odds or how overwhelming the problems you face, can be a positive quality, particularly in an explorer, on the airless, sun-blasted surface of Mercury, with death only inches away at any moment, sometimes it may not be such a good idea . . .

G. David Nordley is a retired air force officer and physicist who has become a frequent contributor to Analog *in the last couple of years, winning that magazine's Analytical Laboratory readers poll in 1992 for his story "Poles Apart"; he also won the same award for his story "Into the Miranda Rift," to which the story that follows "Crossing Chao Meng Fu" is a "prequel." He has also sold stories to* Asimov's Science Fiction, Tomorrow, *and* Mindsparks *and elsewhere. Although fairly prolific at short lengths, Nordley has yet to publish a novel—even though he has several series in progress that could be worked up into novels without too much difficulty. Until then, you'll just have to look for him in the science fiction magazines, where he appears with pleasing frequency. Nordley lives in Sunnyvale, California.*

Begin a ghostly plain
Dim white in pale starlight.
Flat as far as you can see
To where a distant black ridge
Divides reality.
Above the stars shine
Below the ground crunches;
Hillary, Byrd, Peary and Amundsen,
Are your guides. It is beautiful.
But you cannot stop long;
The plain is life itself;
Move on now, trod onward,
Or stand and freeze, they say.
—W.B.

I am in the middle of a line of people walking determinedly across the most everything-forsaken boring waste in the Solar System. I am so sore and tired I could scream—if there were a warm bed around somewhere, I'd crawl in it to shudder. My attitude has hit rock bottom, but it is time to file my report and if I want anything good out of this pain, I'd best sound positive:

"I am Wojciech Bubka, college teacher, occasional poet and now your . . ." I take a breath of sterile suit air, ". . . guide to the natural universe, courtesy of the Solar System Astrographic Society and its many sponsors and members. Welcome to my personal journey through exotic, dangerous, and unusual places of the Solar System." I take another deep breath—got to keep up with everyone else. "Come with me while there are still such places to explore—for as we approach the twenty-third century, this frontier, too, is receding."

I try to gain a little ground to stop briefly and pan my helmet cam over the dirty ice field. Despite the exertion, the change of pace lifts my spirits a bit. But not even a ten-to-one vertical exaggeration will make this landscape interesting. Come on, Bubka. You're a poet? Find meaning.

"These are not robot explorations to be experienced in a video display, but personal ones. I seek authentic, not virtual, reality. I seek the *go there*, *see there*, and *be there* experience of the human explorer, not sterile pixels." Breathe deep. "There is nothing between me and the crunch of crampon spikes on this frozen mud, the strike of an axe into virgin scarps, the strain of muscles, the hiss of sliding ropes, and the sight of wonders. Such is the dream and the experience I seek to share with you here, today, on the frozen wastes of Chao Meng Fu crater on Mercury."

Said strain of muscles gets my attention as I start walking again, and I groan involuntarily. I am tired from the almost week of walking under a pack that brought my weight close to Earth normal—when what is normal for me is Mars. I wiggle my toes as hard as I can—despite vacuum insulation, thermistor environmental control and loose, fluffy socks, I think my feet are beginning to get cold.

"Come on, mate. Another hour will get us there." That is Ed Blake, a gentleman adventurer from New Zealand with Antarctic experience. Ed is my tent-mate, lanky, mostly bald and prematurely gray, confident, competent, and reserved—unless he gets that kind of twinkle in his eye. Then beware a terrible pun. He's cheerful enough to me, but I sense a certain condescension.

Understandable, I think. What the frozen hell am I doing here?

⬤

I had been getting bored at Jovis Tholis University. Poetry, these days, includes video as well as text—something which would have delighted Will Shakespeare, I assure you—and has blended with drama so much that we distinguish the two by picking nits over length and symbolic content. But even in its media-inflated majesty, a dozen years of going over the same basic stuff while fighting battles with New Reformation censors and left-wing nihilists—neither of whom take kindly to the display of material contrary to their philosophies—has me well on my way to burnout.

JTU is in a dome over an ostensibly extinct volcano on Tharsis, roughly halfway to Olympus Mons from the tether tube terminal on Ascraeus. The location worked, and it became the biggest university on Mars—of which I was an increasingly small and out-of-step part.

As the politics of being an important academic became increasingly burdensome, my dreams of "out there" grew. I might teach at Saturn High Station with its magnificent view of the rings. Or I could compose random meter verse at Hyperion institute, the lonely retreat of mathematical philosophers set on a detached mountain peak that careens about Saturn as metaphor of an uncertain future. Or I could volunteer to ride a comet and watch robots turn it into Martian air while writing my epics in the freedom of isolation as the comet fell for a decade into the inner Solar System. Or, and this was my most favorite, I might become a journalist in the old sense on the first expedition to Pluto and Charon.

Thus did I dream. But so, of course, dream millions of others. Only a chosen few can go anywhere the first time or do anything the first time. I dabbled at trail writing; journals of hikes and visits to parts of the vanishing "Red" Mars, but got little notice beyond a reasonably nice "been there, done that" rejection from the Solar System Astrographic Society. I needed an entree, a contact, an idea, something to lift me out of the background.

Then, last year (Martian year, everyone; almost two standard years ago), Miranda Lotati, the daughter of the man in charge of Solar System Astrographic Society's expeditions division, walked into my literature class at Jovis Tholis University, a junior transfer from Stanford on Earth. She looked to be a hard, vigorous, and exciting person but could barely choke two words out in succession—about as contrary to stereotype as one could be and still have breasts.

She was not really beautiful—too muscular, too thin in the face, too boyish a figure, but I saw the possibilities in that. Less competition, and perhaps a complement to my esthetic, well, softness, I told myself. I saw the romance of an attraction of opposites who themselves were opposites of conventionality, and I was looking for some romance somewhere—the women of my normal circles were hopeless and helpless in anything but words, and even seemed to take pride in that. I saw in her an invitation to beyond and away from here. If I played it right—and I resolved to do so.

It wasn't easy. Miranda was a rough-edged, prickly student, and her essays were condensed dullness, never more than the required length. A spoken sentence of more than a half dozen words was a rarity from her, and she sometimes seemed to speak a language so far evolved from today's English in its lack of articles and verbs that, had it been deliberate, would have been considered art in some circles. Nonetheless I was intent. I persisted in bringing her along. I bided my time.

I had to expend some moral capital, but convinced myself that she covered the ground on her final well enough to let me pass her. She liked me, I think. But I said nothing unethical to her, nor hinted at anything romantic while she was my student—I have my standards.

I saw her on the last day of classes of the winter semester, after the final grades were in.

"You're off to Mercury, I hear, to be along on your father's attempt to walk across Chao Meng Fu Crater?" Shielded from the Sun, that huge crater was an ice field—Mercury's Antarctica.

She nodded.

"Have you set the expedition membership?"

She shook her head, confirming what was known publicly.

"Will you have any journalists along? It would make a very exciting nature piece."

She smiled a bit. "Like your Aseraeus Mons hike piece? Dad liked that and sent me here."

He'd seen that? I tried to remember the rejection letter. I was flattered but a bit worried that it was a little light for a Lotati expedition. Then the alarm bells rang in my head. My competition for the position of expedition bard was standing in front of me.

I reached for a tone of professional authority. "Randi, uh. You've come a long way in your composition . . ."

She shrugged. "Yeah. Thanks to you. Someone's got to do the article. Someone who fits on the team. Wish I wrote better."

"Randi, I suppose I shouldn't be obscure. Is there any chance I might come myself?"

Her eyes lit up for a moment, then she frowned. "Rough business, exploring."

"Then my accounts of it should draw interest, maybe enough to push Solar System Astrographic's allocation priorities a little further up." Not to mention that a single Astrographic article could bring in the equivalent in allocations of my entire Jovis Tholus University stipend for a year. A *Martian* year.

"Uh, huh." A doubtful assent on her part.

"Might even help you get to your namesake, out by Uranus. Now there would be an angle that people would notice!"

That got her attention. "Dad's idea too. My name. Not that easy, though. No place for amateurs, out there."

I smiled at her. "I bet I'll make a good explorer. I'm observant, handy, and in reasonably good shape."

She gave me a somewhat skeptical look and a sigh. "Mercury first. Chao Meng Fu. Hundred fifty kilometer-wide. Never sees the Sun. Covered with granite-hard permafrost. Probably take us two, three weeks to walk it."

"Walk?"

She nodded. "Unassisted. Carry everything. Vacuum suits, tents, supplies, samples."

"Walk it? Uh, why?"

She looked at me as if I was born in some other cosmos. "Because we can."

There is this recklessness about me that allows me to throw words around without fully considering the consequences. "Well, I think I can too. I've done enough hiking around Tharsis—I even have a cinder cone named after me."

She looked skeptically at me. "Oh? How high?"

She had me there. I grinned sheepishly. "Well, 'Bubka Mons' is only a hundred meters above local mean. But it's kind of impressive because there's nothing else around it." And I knew someone in the Martian Geology Institute that was laying out the local real estate.

She giggled.

"It *is* registered, Randi. Anyway, my Ascraeus trip was solo, and by a new route."

She looked judiciously at me and sighed. "Lose ten kilos. Do fifty kilometers a day." We stood silent for a couple of seconds as I tried to digest that.

She turned away. "Physics final—see you." And she was gone, gliding easily down the hall.

Dreams are free; but realizing them has a price. And I resolved to pay it.

❦

By the end of last semester. I had walked up a few Martian mountains and lost the ten kilos. I talked to her again and we arranged a checkout hike down to the base of Jovis Tholis and back up to the town again with full packs, breather gear, and by the most difficult route she could pick. She watched every move I made, and seemed satisfied enough to make another "date."

As this went on, I grew utterly fascinated with her. She was a busy woman. Reporters called her, outfitters called her. She was always meeting young women explorers who knew her reputation as a companion of her father, and old men explorers who had been somewhere with her father. My metaphor for Randi was a black hole; people and things seem to swirl around and accrete to her without any significant verbal effort on her part, as if her presence distorts space so that all roads simply lead to her and none away.

The week she was to leave Mars for Mercury she called me.

"You're in, Professor Bubka. Can you make the Shannon inbound? Friday?"

By moving heaven and Mars, I could, and did. I had, it seemed, been within her event horizon for some time now.

❦

So, Mercury. Mercury gravity is the same as Mars gravity, which some say is more than a coincidence, but a coincidence as yet unexplained. The gravity here is exactly the same as on Mars, but I'm carrying three times my mass in supplies and vacuum survival equipment. I might as well be hiking in Antarctica with a light pack. Indeed, I could use the conditioning to visit Earth! Despite the extra mass, we try to keep up the fifty kilometers a day—a pace I must maintain.

There are eight of us strung out along the Chao Meng Fu crater floor, Dr. Lotati in the lead. Dr. Juanita Tierzo, a Harvard-trained geologist, follows him. Juanita is actually on the JTU faculty—in the Martian Geology Institute—but I had to come to Mercury to meet her. Randi follows her. Then come Ed, myself, and one of Dr. Tierzo's graduate students, Eloni Wakhweya, a slight Kenyan woman with a big grin. Solar System Astrographic expedition staffers Mike and Karen Svenson come last, pulling an equipment pallet on two large wire wheels.

They meant it; no robots, no powered vehicles, and in my now humbled opinion, no sense. If Mercury had a breathable atmosphere, they'd have done without the spacesuits and all their built-in communications and amenities, too. I'm exhausted, uncomfortable, and increasingly uneasy with this exercise in cosmic hubris.

The view is simple, unrelieved flatness, the kind of view that should reach one's soul in the way of all great expanses. The crater's stark lines go its namesake's art one spareness better; the vertical dimension is almost absent. It too is painted in an ink of five colors, all gray. It is Aldrin's magnificent desolation, without relief. I appreciate it more in intellectual abstract than in person.

There is light to see: the tips of the peaks behind us blaze like distant arc lamps, and fill the bowl of Chao Meng Fu with a ghostly kind of moonlight. Small, rounded crater rims dot this frozen plane—very few higher than a man, for ice flows in time. The brighter stars shine down on us hard and free. Brilliant Earth hangs just over the horizon, a tiny dazzling blue-white star. Luna lies well away from it, a faint gray dot lost in Sagittarius.

Invisible to us in the Earth's glare is the beginning of Earth's Sunshield. This mammoth project will partly shade the heat-polluted atmosphere from the fires of Apollo's chariot someday. It is taking form at the Earth-Sun L-l point, balanced there with the help of reflected light—they plan to reduce insolation by 1 percent. But more relevant to our endeavor is that it is the home of Solar System Astrographic's solar radio antenna, which we use to apprise the rest of the Solar System of the status of this madcap adventure. I look that way wondering why I ever left.

"Another five kilometers to the crevasse," Dr. Lotati tells us on the comnet.

This desolate flat sameness is an illusion; we have real work ahead. The crevasse is a major obstacle, or a major objective if you are a geologist. Halfway between the rim of Chao Meng Fu crater and its central peaks lies a huge crack in the permafrost caused, they think, by an almost infinitely slow lifting of the crater floor, still rebounding from the billion-year-old impact that formed the crater. To this poet, overhead views make the crevasse look like the mouth of the planet—and I worry about being devoured.

—

By noon, universal time, the mouth of Mercury yawns directly in front of us, an ugly black crack that makes the dark gray plain around us look silvery by comparison. We halt to plan our crossing. Juanita proposes that we simply go down into this thing, down into a darkness that has never known the Sun, and out again on the other side. That idea creates enough interest to scare me. But not now. A descent will take planning, and, in the meantime, I luxuriate in not having to move my body.

Yet, standing still, I forget my pain and become curious. The crevasse seems to run to the horizon to my right and left. The other side is the length of a football field away. I shudder—it is impossible to repress the thought that such darkness is not meant for human beings, that the laws of physics will become conscious and punish us for trying it. Perversely, the challenge of that danger attracts me.

Yet, there are reasons to go down beyond the simple thrill of it. Solar Astrographic's expedition is half stunt, half science—and here is where the other half gets its due. There is a mystery here and the root of it lies in a contrary mysticism of celestial dynamics. Here, a mere sixty million kilometers from its fiery photosphere, are surfaces that have not seen the Sun since the Caloris impact defined Mercury's final orientation.

This same counterintuitive magic then decrees that the ices of comets that orbit impossibly far—beyond even Pluto, Charon, and Persephone—are actually closer to the Sun, and Mercury, in the *energy* of their motion than anything in the inner Solar System. Something on Venus would have to be kicked at almost 11 km/s to reach Mercury, best case—but merely nudge a pair of Oort belt comets together and parts of them may fall into Mercury, decades hence. Sometimes these collisions *give* the planet a very temporary, tenuous atmosphere, which condenses in the deep freeze of Chao Meng Fu. Blame this on Kepler and Newton, not Ptolemy.

So near is far, and far is near, and the crevasse yawns from 'ere to 'ere. Does it have teeth? Do its open jaws reveal molecules from the beginning of time, such as measured in the Solar System? Lotati confers with his daughter, and Ed. Randi and Ed have a thing, I've found, and spend a fair amount of time touching helmets.

What great ideas I have! I despair of ever being able to itch again, let alone going to Miranda with its namesake. My rented vacuum gear fits like the skin of a hundred-year-old man; stretched taut digging into my flesh here, loose and bulging there. Randi says there's an art to it and I should take more time getting in. Next time I will.

I edge closer to the brink, attracted to the danger perhaps, or perhaps wanting to demonstrate courage to Randi. I gaze down. Here and there the dust has fallen from the sheer ice walls, and the layered structure is clear. There are Mercury's sediments. Each comet or meteor creates a temporary atmosphere for Mercury, and that which is not boiled away by the Sun condenses in the polar craters, mixed with ejecta dust. The bedrock lies perhaps a kilometer below us. After three days of the most physical labor I've done in decades, I now contemplate a rappel down to the bottom of a bottomless crevasse and the climb back up again.

I look away as though by not observing it, I can create the possibility that it does not exist.

But I have my journalist's duty. At my command, my helmet camera plays back the view, and it floats, reflected off my face plate, against the stars. It doesn't fit in the standard field of view, I realize, so I look over the edge again and slowly turn my head from horizon to horizon. An object of professional interest now, it begins to lose some of its scariness for me.

Bubka's prescription for fear of something—study the hell out of it.

How long and wide! Then I turn off all my lights, let my eyes relax, and turn back to see the solar corona, a peacock's tail of icy fire spreading from the Sun that sits just under those utterly black mountains that ring our horizon. If Chao Meng Fu did not flatten Mercury's globe here, we would not be able to see those mountains this far into the trek, so close is Mercury's horizon—but we have been heading ever so slightly inward, downhill, as well as south.

The furthest streamers of the corona glow far above that rim behind, looking almost like the aurora borealis back on Earth. Awed, I step back, and back again to catch my balance.

I happen to glance down—my boot is barely centimeters from the edge of the chasm.

"Bubka, freeze." Randi's voice echoes in my helmet.

I am already frozen.

"Now. Raise right hand," she continues.

I am carrying a strobe lamp in my right hand so I automatically start to raise my left—

"Your other right!" she snaps, instantly.

This time I get it right, raising both my arms and the strobe lamp.

"Now lean *that* way. Walk slowly. Away from edge."

I understand now: if I teeter, she wants me to teeter in the direction of safety. I walk away from the edge with as much dignity as I can muster, as if there were nothing at all wrong, knowing that anyone monitoring my heartbeat will know that I am anything but calm.

She detaches herself from the management group and strides toward me, ghostly dust glittering in my helmet light behind her footsteps. She halts in a cloud of fairy sparkles, grabs my hand, and leads me well away from the edge of the crevasse.

"Professor Bubka, near crevasses, tether. Always, always, tether."

"Professor" hangs in my mind dripping with irony. On Mars, I taught her literature. Here, I am her student—and I had just come close to failing a test where failure is judged somewhat more harshly than at Jovis Tholis University.

Nodding ruefully, I pull a piton gun from my pack and harpoon the planet. A test pull shows that it's secure, and I clip the line to my belt. Randi fires a piton in too, clips on, then clips another line between her belt and mine. "Ed, some baby-sitter you'd make! Going to take a look."

"Sorry, mate. Watching, Randi."

Baby-sitter?

"Now, Professor Bubka. Let's go look." Dark eyes, on a tanned face with a snub nose, twinkle at me behind the clear, non-reflecting visor.

We retrace my footprints together. We walk to the edge together. This time. I think to clip my strobe light to my belt as well.

One of the things I see is half a footprint at the edge of the crevasse. The toe half. Mine.

What I had done was, I realize, foolish, but I think I am forgiven. She pulls on her line, then actually leans out over the cut, to inspect its near side.

"Light." The word is a request and a command. Crystals from far down glitter in response.

Nervously, wrapping my line around my left hand and playing it out through a "smart slot" belay device, centimeter by centimeter, I lean out with her and shine my strobe on the wall under us. On a clean vertical, the layering resembles a diffraction grating—fine thin grooves, perfectly horizontal, broken occasionally by what must be the sections of ancient buried craters.

The strobe light looks continuous, but contains off-pulses for range—it times a journey of the absence of light. So. The crack goes down, a hundred meters, two hundred, three hundred. At five hundred, I can no longer see the light returning, but it can. I swing it slowly from side to side, as my helmet display paints a graph of angle and range. The walls seem to almost converge about twelve hundred meters below us here, with some flatness between them. I move the beam a bit to the left.

There is something across the chasm at eight hundred meters, just to our left. "Randi?"

"I see it. Bridge. Dad, channel seven."

"I have it, Randi! I'll think that is a billion years down if it's a day! What do you say, Juanita, my Randi's found a bridge!"

There seemed no point in immediately explaining that I'd found it.

"Eight hundred meters down and all the way across! Can we do it?" Juanita answers, thrill in her voice. "Do we have enough line?"

"Yes and yes," Randi's father answers after a moment of thought. Then he points to a slight dip almost above the bridge. "Probably half of an old crater, broken by the crack. That will get us a few meters closer. We could rappel down from there. Perhaps two billion years down, if the crevasse goes to the bottom of Chao Meng Fu. Do you want the bottom, Juanita?"

"God, yes, Emilio, if it isn't too dangerous."

Dr. Lotati shrugs. "It has been this way for millions of years of impacts; the walls should tolerate a few ants crawling on them. We'll go ourselves, instead of waiting for some robots to do it."

I look across the chasm for the other half of the ancient crater, but, like the other half of my footprint, there is no sign of it. Where did it go? I feel a curiosity as powerful as any hunger. What formed the bridge? What lies at the bottom? We shall find out, if the Laws of the Universe let us.

◆

We all have some climbing experience, but only the Lotatis and Ed have very much. It is, however, a very easy climb down in 38 percent gravity. The ropes are well secured to the plain above, the slope is usually less than vertical. Mike and Karen Svenson will remain on the rim with the bulk of the equipment until we are all safely down. They call themselves the "human robots" and have been in excellent humor. When Randi and Dr. Lotati scale the other wall, they will fire a rope across. The Lotatis will then pull over a larger rope on which a tram will carry the equipment. Meanwhile, at the bottom, Dr. Tierzo will supervise sample gathering by the rest of us. That is the plan.

It becomes dark quickly as we descend. The sky contracts to a starry band overhead, one edge of which glows a faint, frozen, shadowy pearl, a reflection lit by a reflection of sunlight on distant peaks. We turn on our helmet lights, and their glare banishes any other source of illumination. They spread sparkly pools of light on the wall—tiny crystals everywhere. I am conscious of a fine mist or fog, just on the edge of the perceivable. Our suits allow the skin's waste gases to diffuse slowly outward, our footsteps create microscopic dust clouds on which it may condense, our helmet lights evaporate hydrogen gas that has condensed on the wall. Our progress appears tinged with the ethereal.

◆

We are three hundred meters down: a football field on end. The descent is easy, simple, routine. You ease rope out under friction, take a pair of steps down, and ease out some more. This descent is demanding and terrifying. You dare not lose concentration. Pitons can pull out, crampons can slip, and you will be just as dead from a fall of a kilometer in Mercury's gravity as Earth's. Yes, it will take a few seconds longer and an academic might note that you hit with less velocity—only about five times instead of fifteen times what is needed to smash your helmet and the skull within it.

You dare not cause problems for everyone else. One foot after another.

A person in fear of his or her life needs no more excitement—but if you want it, you glance at the wall in front of you, at layers of ice laid down when dinosaurs were young. This is not on a screen, not a simulation, but never-seen-before reality that puts ice hard in front of your own eyes.

"Ed," I ask, "do you wonder if anyone might have been here a billion years ago?"

"Eh? Interesting thought, that. The feature would attract someone with enough curiosity to build spaceships, I should think. But the crack itself wouldn't be that old, now, would it?"

"No, I guess not." When the layers were laid down, of course, this had been a part of the plain.

Still, my eyes scan every layer, hoping.

"Has everyone got positive pressure in their suits?" Dr. Lotati asks, and receives chuckles. "There is," he continues, "a significant build-up of nitrogen gas, and a bare trace of nitrogen tri-flouride, which I would not recommend breathing."

I call up a temp display and find that it is cold in the crack—about eighty kelvins, versus a hundred twenty at the surface. As I think about it, I notice traces of frost on the outside of my gloves: our insulation is that good. I have no idea what the biological implications of nitrogen trifluoride are, but I would rather someone else perform the experiments. A drop rolls down my face plate.

"Watch your footing, Juanita," Dr. Lotati says. "It's slippery here."

So far, my crampons dig into the dirty clathrate walls with ease, but I can tell it is wet. The wall is mostly ice, but ice that is heavily mixed with crater ejecta, pocked with more volatile ices, and stiffened far harder than anything on Earth by cryogenic temperatures. Dr. Lotati says it's something like sandstone, but if it weren't for the gas in the ice, it would be like concrete. There are few cracks, but the piton gun works well, as does the ax.

"Nitrogen trifluoride data," I ask. Floating in the wall, by virtue of my helmet display hardware, are glowing numbers telling me that nitrogen tri-fluoride is liquid over a range of about 80 kelvins—from about 77 up to 145—which is over 120 Celsius degrees below the freezing point of water. Somehow, stating such temperatures in kelvins above absolute zero is less scary than using negative Celsius degrees below freezing. The vapor pressure of this big, heavy molecule is almost nil at the low end of this temperature range—a wet vacuum.

A hundred meters to go, and I can see the bridge clearly in the shifting pools of our helmet lights.

"A sliver of wall appears to have detached itself and slid down until it jammed," Dr. Tierzo tells us. "The top is a jumble with, here and there, flat spaces that may have been part of the original surface, including part of a crater. I wonder if that's what knocked it down?"

"Hello down there," Karen Svenson calls. "Yes, that crater would explain what looks like a ray network around where you went down. Now that I know what I'm looking at, this spiderweb network of cracks is a real giveaway."

I hadn't remembered any cracks. I ask my suit to play back my recording of our approach to the side. The surface in the depression was smooth. My pulse races. "Playback two hours ago," I command. In a ghostly video window, my suit shows me almost falling in to the crevasse, but . . .

"Hey, everyone!" I shout. "Those cracks weren't there before. Dr. Lotati, I've got it on channel six."

There is a moment of silence.

"Quickly now," Dr. Lotati speaks briefly and very businesslike. "Those of you still on the wall come down as quickly as possible without panic and without yanking on anything. Mike and Karen, set another belay well back of the cracked area."

I have my full attention on climbing down, gingerly as possible. Dr. Tierzo is off belay just below me. I remember to lock my crampon spikes *out*—the bridge is slippery.

Meanwhile, Dr. Lotati has set an ice bolt in at the far end of our bridge. Dr. Tierzo sets another one in the biggest hunk of bridge she can find at our end and pulls the line tight.

Then I am off the wall. I quickly clip my line to the bridge line and release myself from the wall ropes. "Off belay."

Miranda Lotati and the grad student, Eloni, are still on the wall.

I hear, I think, at very low frequency, a kind of groan.

"We have the protection in," Karen says. "The cracks are larger!"

"Wojciech can get your line, Ed," Dr. Lotati says, "release from the wall immediately!"

"No worry. Here." He tosses me the end of his spare line and I hit it with the loop of a smart 'biner, which opens, takes the line, and shuts faster than I can see—like that old magic trick with hoops. I take up the slack.

Ed releases and scrambles off the wall, holding the taut line for balance until he reaches me. We move further down the bridge.

"Come on, Eloni," Ed says encouragingly. The young Kenyan woman is the least experienced of our group—she descends slowly, but flawlessly, a few meters right of where Ed came down. "Toss me the end of your spare line."

She stops to find it. Miranda Lotati's feet are but a few meters above her. I hear another groan.

"Come on . . ." Ed says again.

Finally, Eloni tosses a coiled line toward Ed. It jerks short and dangles below her, a hopeless tangle.

"Sorry, I try to do this too fast."

"That's OK, mate," Ed says. "Just come on down now. We'll improvise."

We feel a slight tremor. She freezes.

"Down, Eloni. Fast," Randi says.

Eloni starts moving again. I can see her tremble.

"Ice!" Karen shouts. Our radios level amplitude, magnifying whispers and buffering shouts—that shout was well buffered.

Eloni freezes.

"Go," Randi snaps, and clips Eloni's helmet with the side of her boot. "Get going!"

Galvanized, Eloni half scrambles and half falls the remaining fifty meters, landing on her seat where the bridge butts against the wall. She starts fumbling with the 'biner holding her line to the wall belay line. Ed, clipped to a line, moves to help her—I think he has a knife in his hand. Needless, I follow him using crampons and ax. Ed reaches Eloni.

I look up and see the sky falling.

Randi releases and leaps from almost twenty meters up on the wall, unbelayed, right at me. "Catch," she shouts.

I have time to set my crampon spikes and open my arms. She hits hard, and various pieces of her gear dig into my chest. I grab her as the boots tear free and we skitter together down the side of the bridge. My line stops us after a three-meter slide.

Ten meters from us, with a roar clearly conducted through the ice we lie against, an avalanche of clathrate pours down. There is no sign of Ed and Eloni.

Randi clips a line to my belt, rolls off, and starts to scramble back to the top of the bridge, ice dust streaming around her.

"Ed!" she shouts. "Eloni!"

The fall increases, becoming a white wall. Randi scrambles into it. I follow and am enveloped in a stream of pulverized clathrate, and I can see nothing. It flows over me, not like sand or water, but something in between—not dense, but still exerting pressure.

I wait. My helmet is filled with the sound of my breathing.

"Ed!" Randi shouts again.

"We're alive." Ed's voice is hoarse and strained. "Trapped next to the wall. The fall created a bit of a pocket. No injuries, but it's getting somewhat cold."

In spacesuits with rebreathers and plenty of energy, we are in no danger of suffocating. But under our coveralls we wear skintight vacuum suits that depend on a surrounding vacuum for much of their thermal control and the fabric of the vacuum suits, while smart and extremely tough, is necessarily thin. Conduction of heat could quickly freeze Ed and Eloni. But, clinging to the side of the bridge with the landslide still in progress, there is nothing I can do to reach them.

"Got you on locator. Can move." That is Randi Lotati, for me. Move? How?

I roll over prone to the face of the bridge, reach forward into the flow with my hands, and find purchase. With both arms and legs, I find I can edge forward, too.

"Solid piece—here," Randi says. "Ice boulder. Think you're on other side."

"S—sounds that w—way," Ed replies.

"Line charge. My side. Push like hell when I say."

"No, Randi," Ed pleads, "too dangerous—"

"Push, damn it! Now!"

I hear the crack of the detonation.

"Randi?" I call, and claw my way toward the signals, white sand and occasional rocks still streaming by me. Somehow, though, it seems a bit easier. "Randi, Ed?"

"Wojciech, Ed. We—we're free. At—at least the rock's split. Need help with Eloni."

"I'm trying." I pant. "Where's Randi?" I am exhausted struggling against the continuing stream of material from above. I reach forward with my hand and hit flesh. Someone there. The world is gray in my helmet lamp; I can see nothing. "Ed, is that you?"

"Not me, mate. It's slackening a little. I've got some space."

The someone moans. The groan is female.

"Eloni?" I push the person in front of me again, harder.

"She's with me, Wojciech," Ed says.

"Randi?"

She grunts. "Wojciech. I'm OK, I'm just . . . stuck. Legs won't move." I feel a hand brush mine, then lock with mine. "Drag me back."

"I'll try." Trusting the precarious hand link, I sit up into the flow of clathrate mud. It tries to take me away with tremendous force, but my line holds me. Slowly I get my legs around in front of me and pull as hard as I dare. She doesn't move.

"It's no good. I'll hurt you if I pull any harder."

"Freezing's worse. Hurt me. Pull."

God knows how much force I put on her arm, but something seems to unstick, and she comes toward me, slowly at first; then something breaks free and we scoot back about four meters. I can see through whirls of snow here. I can see my clip still on the bridge line, see Randi strung out at the end of my arm.

"Dr. Lotati, she's out. Over here."

"What? Wojciech? Where? . . . There, I have you! I'll be right over."

He is there in a moment. "Had you on the other side of the bridge for a moment—propagation freak, I think. Randi, will you be all right for a few minutes?"

"Hurts like hell, Dad, but yes. Thanks, Wojciech."

Dr. Lotati gives her a pat and plunges into the remains of the ice fall. Minutes later, he and Ed emerge, carrying Eloni between them. "Mike, Karen, this is Emilio," he says. "We're all out of the avalanche. I don't know in what shape yet, but we're all out."

"Roger. We suggest all of you rest a bit until this plays itself out."

"Mike . . ." He pauses, catching his breath. "We'll consider that."

There are several rueful chuckles, and we spend the next five minutes or so watching the river of white dust slowly come to a halt.

Finally the ice fall abates entirely and we take stock. Randi reports a severe sprain in her right shoulder. Ed is recovering from hypothermia and is severely bruised as well. Eloni is better, physically, but appears to be in some kind of psychological shock. The rest of us have minor bruises.

The side of the crevasse looks like a giant took a huge, semicircular bite out of it. Karen and Mark wave at us from an edge that is now at least fifty meters back from where it was. We lost two long lines, buried in the debris. The avalanche has buried half the bridge and I worry that it could start again at any time and bury us along with the other half. I try to do some mental calculations on how long it would take a suborbital hopper to get here and pull us out.

"I think we are here for a while," Dr. Lotati says, "at least until we're all up to climbing out again. We might overnight on the bridge." If he's worried about the avalanche restarting, he isn't saying so.

"We'll need to revise the schedule a bit," Ed adds. "Another five kilometers per day would do it, I should think. Now, how do we get the gear down here?"

"Toboggan the big tent down to us," Randi says. "Meantime, collect data." I stare at Randi, stupefied.

"Are you OK, Eloni?" I ask, mainly out of concern but perhaps with a secondary agenda of reminding people of something.

Eloni raises her head and looks around in wonder. If she expects a chewing out, it seems she is in the wrong group. I lay a hand very on her shoulder, and, as if I touched some kind of hidden button, she leans into me and lets out a very long sigh, which I hear clearly where my helmet touches her. Randi is looking right at us, but in the glare of our headlights, her face is unreadable. Warning bells ring in my head.

"My mistake, Eloni," Ed says, "pressuring you like that for something that's not automatic. You needed to think it through, and with me talking at you like that, you couldn't. My mistake."

"Eloni," Dr. Lotati asks, "can you help Juanita get her samples tomorrow?"

Eloni takes a breath and slips away from me. "I—I can do that." A smile of relief creases the young woman's features.

"That a way!"

"Randi?" I ask, dumbfounded. "Your arm?"

"I'll live. Still go for the bottom, Juanita?"

"There may be a pond of liquid nitrogen trifluoride down there—it's unprecedented."

"Ed?"

He looks down, then at the crevasse sides. "Why don't I help Randi with the camp and prepare for climbing out of here?"

Apparently, we *will* sleep here—under the sword of Damocles.

"Wojciech?" Dr. Lotati asks.

I am at a loss for words. I am more tired and sore than I have ever been. How much more tired and sore can I be before I am a danger, I wonder? Everyone has been pummeled and challenged. But these people, these comrades of mine, will not admit disaster. They will press on. It is a collective decision—a spontaneous informal vote of voices that is already a majority. Voicing misgivings on my part would do no good at all, and my fate is tied to theirs. But I wonder that such things can still be in this age of robots. May the ghosts of Byrd, Amundsen, Lewis and Clark, and Bering fill my mind with whatever it is that gets one through. I came here to prove myself worthy and now the question is upon me. I look at the crevasse sides and down into its deep.

"Three climbers would be best," Dr. Lotati says.

"I'm . . . I can go with a little rest."

Dr. Lotati nods. "We can all use some. It's only 1100. We'll set up on the bridge. Mike and Karen, we'll take the big tent—you can probably slide it down on ropes."

This only takes a few minutes. We anchor the large vacuum tent to the bridge. It fits with about a meter to spare in width—with the door toward the intact wall. Room in the tent is limited. It was meant to sleep four and it is crowded with six of us. Our body odors again mingle in a forgettable stew of smells, and the drop curtain for its tiny commode is woefully inadequate for privacy. But we are relieved and happy—we have been through a memorable adventure and nobody has gotten killed.

Ed is quiet, eats quickly, and is asleep in his sack, fully clothed, in minutes. He says nothing. We will take a very real risk shortly far, far, from help—for the sake of samples that could easily be gathered by robots a month from now.

As a certified—and some might say certifiable—poet, suicidal undertakings are perhaps in my nature. But the milieu of the Gentleman Adventurer requires that one return from the adventure to recount it. While Ed was gallant in the crisis, the closeness of his brush with death might only now be sinking into him. I, with far less experience, accepted a challenge he did not—does he resent this? No, I tell myself, he is just exhausted.

I have to make myself eat—I'm hungry, but more tired. A warm sleepsack never felt so good, I realize. It seems I have barely closed my eyes when Dr. Lotati is gently rocking me awake.

"It's 1400," he says. "Time to go."

●

The trip to the bottom of the crevasse is a straightforward rappel. With Randi resting her arm, Eloni and I head for the bottom with Juanita in the lead.

"This could be Calorian clathrate—proof that Chao Meng Fu is older."

"But doesn't its flatness mean it's young?" I ask. Old surfaces are heavily cratered.

"Watch for a hollow to your left. No, the surface is young due to deposition—the crater itself is ancient. I'd guess we're about 3.8 billion years down, below the original crater floor. The walls are shock-fractured rock, not exposed sediment layers. No strata—" a swing of her ax tears a rough section of about a square meter from the wall "—underneath."

"Look, more signs of erosion," she adds later.

"Erosion?" The wall is a rough breccia, a compressed clathrate and gravel mixture. The larger stones are sharp, not rounded.

"There is evidence of atmosphere all around us—you can see icicles in the hollows, and a cold glistening wetness on the walls."

I turn off my radio. "Can you hear me?" I shout.

There is no answer—the vapor is still too thin, even at the bottom, to conduct sound.

We hang from the wall and gaze into the utterly still pool of nitrogen trifluoride in the circles of our helmet lamps below us. Unable to resist the temptation. I reach into one of Mercury's nostrils and break off an icicle and toss it into the pool. It ripples like oily water.

"Wojciech," Eloni says in a mildly scolding voice, "have some respect! That pool has been built up, molecule by molecule, probably over billions of years."

"How?" Juanita asks, gently. "Even if the crater is that old, the crevasse isn't."

Eloni is silent, then says, "Oh, of course. But where does it come from then?"

"The pool is a mystery, for now," Juanita says. "Perhaps some comet with an unusual concentration of fluorine ices struck not too long ago. Or something else." She laughs. "Fortunately, not all mysteries can be solved now. We would run out of things to do!"

I envision tentacles reaching out of that deep to pluck us from the crevasse wall. "Could something have evolved to base its blood on that, the way we use seawater?"

"Not my field," Juanita answers. "But let's take a sample."

She is closest, and deftly dips a sample capsule into the liquid. Nothing emerges to bite her hand off—so much for that fantasy. I might not have had the nerve. Then I have a moment of insight, to do this requires the right balance of imagination and nerve.

"I do not think," Eloni offers, "that there would be enough energy for life. If there were, the liquid would boil away. Hydrocarbons at these temperatures would be frozen solid, so what could one use to build life molecules? How could anything that would work at these temperatures get here without being destroyed by the Sun first? Still, it is an interesting thought, Wojciech."

"If the crack could go down a hundred kilometers or so," Juanita remarks, "it would be warm enough to evaporate everything, possibly warm enough to walk around with the right atmosphere. But Mercury would close a crack that deep; its crust is surprisingly thin, even now. This is not Mars."

She sounds like my fifth-year teacher back in Krakow. I suddenly feel far, far over my head. These people understand where they are and what they are doing: it holds no terror for them, no fear of sticking a hand where it might not come back. But for me, my overripe literary imagination haunts my mind like the tale of the bogeyman that kept me out of grandfather's basement until I was seven. I am not comfortable here—but, I tell myself, I will enjoy having been here more when, and if—always if—we get back.

"It's time to go back," Juanita says, her vials filled. "Climbing."

"Climbing," we all say.

"Belay on," Dr. Lotati says, from far above us.

The climb back up to the bridge is slow. Once we hit the layered material, we stop to take half-meter cores, drilled slantwise, at those layers which Juanita estimates to have been laid down during the great events of the inner Solar System: layers that may contain glass beads from the Imbrium impact on Luna, Caloris here, Hellas on Mars, and, just possibly, a few grains with the right isotope ratios to be from the K-T impact on Earth. If we find these, we can bring the geological history of the planets together. If, the paradigm goes, we understand better why the Solar System is the way it is, we will understand better why we are the way we are—the forces that have shaped our evolution and those of other sentient races. But we won't know if the samples contain what we suspect for many months, by which time we will have scattered to the nether ends of the Solar System.

We are tired and bruises remind us of yesterday's avalanche with each bump, but there is a sense of elation about us. We are the first people to see a pool of liquid on an alien planet in its natural state. And no machine saw it first.

When we arrive back at the ice bridge, Juanita sees me staring nervously at the slide.

"I've calculated the slope and the coefficient of friction, Wojciech—I think it's fully relaxed. It may stay that way for a billion years."

"Now you tell me!" But would the trip have been as thrilling if she had? "What caused it to go in the first place?"

"Our weight, I think, plus an accumulation of stresses. I'm beginning to think the crevasse is fairly young—otherwise a meteor impact would have caused the slump before we did."

"There could be more than physical tension," Eloni says. "Near the surface, over many years, radiation will cause chemical changes and produce unstable molecules in crystalline ice. A physical shock, such as an ax, might release these energies."

"Possibly," Juanita says.

I look down at the ice bridge under me. If the crevasse is fairly recent, this would be even more recent—and not, I hope, have had time to accumulate radiation "energies."

We are physically tired but the midday nap and the feeling of accomplishment leave us too hyper to sleep immediately. After rations, I suggest the idea that had led me to join their expedition in the first place.

"Randi?" I ask. "Dr. Lotati?"

They turn their heads to me.

"Are you aware of the theories of a Dr. Nikhil Ray?"

Dr. Lotati purses his lips as if he had something to say, then thought better of it.

Juanita answers. "He tries to explain the low density of Miranda and some other outer satellites, by making them a sponge of caverns. It is an innovative idea, but, I'm afraid, not well accepted."

Dr. Lotati grunts. "I've met the man. His theories are unorthodox and he has this infuriatingly superior manner about him. . . . Well, we'll know soon enough anyway. The IPA is finally getting around to dropping sonography stations on the major Uranian satellites."

As "free" robot-produced resources grew exponentially, so did the Interplanetary Association's influence on who goes where and does what. The IPA, whose main members are the United Nations of Earth, the Mars Council, and the Cislunar Republic, responds, in large measure, to politicians. They in turn respond to the media and the public—I am counting on this.

"I was," I venture, "thinking that it might be time to visit Miranda—and that, with the coincidence in their names, Randi might be the one to do it. It would certainly be an interesting angle. Especially if Dr. Ray could be persuaded to come."

Dr. Lotati frowns. "That would be rather commercial, wouldn't it?" Ed contributes with a wink in my direction. He is not taking this too seriously.

"Finish school," Randi says, "do some low g work in the asteroids, Saturn, then maybe." She grins at me. "My world. Caves?"

"There are certainly caves there," Juanita says with a grin, "but if they are big ones, you might be sorry about taking Nikhil. He's already insufferable with the issue in doubt. God help us if he's right!"

Dr. Lotati and Ed laugh heartily. Randi shrugs, and a flicker of pain crosses her face at the gesture. The shoulder hurts more than she wants us to know, I suspect.

"You can make too much of that," Ed says. "He's not a monster, Juanita. He can be very much the gentleman, and his conversation is always interesting. I sometimes wonder if the personality conflicts don't have more to do with his peer review problems than the merits of his work."

Dr. Lotati turns and tugs on his beard. "Uranus is the frontier," he finally says. "There's only one small inhabited scientific station in the Uranus system, in its outer satellite, Mustardseed. Within the Uranian magnetosphere, radiation is a concern." He stares briefly at me, then Randi. "Also, I don't want to associate the Society with Ray's claims just yet. Let's see what happens with the seismic study. And let's see how well Wojciech's presentation of this expedition is received."

I glance at Randi. She stares back at me, intently, and the ghost of a smile crosses her face as she wrinkles her nose.

"I could use a shower," I say—humorously. There will be no showers for several days yet.

But Randi hands me a silver foil wrapper. Her nose has decided that it's bath time—understandable in view of our exertions. The foil contains a light towelette soaked in a cleaning solution that does not have to be rinsed. She offers them to the others, removes her coveralls, and then releases the seam of her vacuum suit. Her father turns his back to us and, facing the wall of the tent, does the same. Eloni also turns to the wall of the tent. Ed watches Randi, and they exchange a brief smile.

We are a cross section of the Solar System, and a cross section of attitudes about our bodies. I still feel a slight twinge, as if in nostalgia for an old cultural taboo, but the observer of people in me rejoices in the passing of taboos. Ed, surprisingly, seems the one uncomfortable with communal bathing.

Juanita, whose family left Earth a century ago, is already sponging, oblivious to anything else. She is a well-endowed woman in excellent condition, as is everyone on this kind of endeavor. Her hair, unbound, hangs to her shoulders. It is almost all white and makes her skin look darker than it is in contrast. Her only other concessions to her fifty standard years are a slight gut and a bit of looseness on her neck and under her arms.

Randi is still watching Ed watch her, as if she enjoys it. She is a rangy young woman of jet-black hair and well defined, though not exaggerated muscles. Her female features seem like the afterthoughts of a god who in making an athlete decided at the last minute to make a woman, too. There is an intriguing hardness about the rest of her, including an untouched scar on her side. But her face, her smile, and her manner are womanly.

Embarrassed at myself for staring, I turn around like Dr. Lotati and finish undressing—applying the cleaning cloth to my body. But I love women too much to resist another look. When I do, both Eloni and Juanita are looking at me. Our eyes meet, we smile and I relax. My feelings as they watch me bathe are hard to describe—would it make sense to say that I felt first forgiven? I feel something of a sense of camaraderie.

Then Eloni reaches with both hands and turns me to the side of the tent. Its drum-tight bulge instantly reminds me of the vacuum, just beyond that millimeter of tough, impervious fabric.

I feel a damp cloth on my back, up and down, hitting every needful spot. When she is done, I return the favor. She sighs just on the edge of audibility. Almost like a purr.

I feel suddenly very good, and useful—should poetry and nature writing fail me completely, I could do this for a living. Well, maybe.

Dr. Lotati turns to crawl into his sleeping bag, and I accidentally get a brief glimpse of injuries he has chosen not to show the rest of us. Gunshot wounds? Before he can seal the side, Juanita touches his shoulder and crawls in with him.

Eloni turns from the wall then and sees Randi and me, not yet in our sleeping bags. She looks down, then looks up again, then crawls into her sleeping bag. I can't read the expression on her face.

I get into my bag, pull my suit and helmet in with me, and seal the hood behind me. Its flaps will close and hold pressure if there is an accident while I sleep.

"Lights off," Randi says, and the tent complies. It is utterly, totally dark. There is movement. As my eyes adapt, I glance in her direction, but her sleeping bag is empty. She is probably not sleeping with Eloni, which leaves Ed. I feel a twinge of jealousy, though I know Ed has known the Lotatis for many years, and gone on several expeditions with them.

The exhaustion of this day does not permit sexual regrets, however. It seems like only a moment, and then I awake to light, discussions about the ascent, and the smell of freshly opened breakfast bars. The discussion is between Ed and Emilio, and it concerns who is to go up the wall with Randi, to set the ropes for the rest of us.

"We need to make time," Dr. Lotati says.

"All the more reason for you to go with Randi. You're a team."

"Thank you, friend, but I am sixty-two years old and you are thirty-eight. You and Randi climb well together." There is a slight hint of humor in Emilio's voice to suggest to my perhaps oversensitive mind that he knows they do more than climb well together.

"It's only a kilometer, mate. You're as good as ever."

"I'll second that," Juanita says.

Dr. Lotati smiles and shakes his head. "The group comes first."

Randi embraces her father, wordlessly, but I can see her eyes glisten. Then Dr. Lotati reaches over to Ed and they grasp hands.

Something has passed, I realize, and who am I to witness such a passing? More than ever, I feel an ambitious interloper. I look over at Eloni. She is looking at me. Wistfully? I smile back.

We pack quickly and efficiently, filling the soft pressure packs first with the things that can stand vacuum, then the hard ones. When the tent is bare, the last pack is sealed and we take it down to a tenth of an atmosphere. We check each other's seals and fit. Randi frowns at mine, and has me depressurize to readjust my fit. If the pressure were much lower, I think, my blood would boil. We normally breathe a fifty-fifty oxygen-nitrogen mix at four-tenths atmosphere, so I still have a quarter of Earth normal oxygen partial pressure. I try not to get excited.

Randi treats this like an everyday event. She tugs, pulls, and smooths all my joint areas. She is utterly clinical about this, but happens to glance up with a wink when she adjusts my leg seams. "It's all in the family," her look seems to say.

I find myself slipping as if to an event horizon. Do I want to befriend this woman to pursue fame and fortune on her distant namesake moon, or has my idea for an expedition to the moon become an excuse to be near the woman? I suddenly realize that I am very, very taken by her.

She reseals my suit and I tell it to bring its pressure up again. She has indeed worked wonders, and I am much more comfortable than I was the day before. She apparently likes what she sees, grins, and squeezes my arm, then turns to the business at hand.

The tent finishes taking itself down to near vacuum. When the sides are noticeably softer, we open the main seal, and the tent ripples as the remaining millibar or so of air escapes. We turn our helmet lights on and emerge into the crevasse again.

The wall is suddenly lit with flood-lights—Mike and Karen have seen us emerge. It is one kilometer of gray-banded dirty clathrate, vertical, except for the parts that are more than vertical.

Randi leads; if she falls, she is less weight on the bolts and pitons that hold our ropes.

"This stuff is like soft sandstone," Ed says. "I can almost push a piton in by hand, here and there."

"Use more," Randi says. "Angle down."

"OK." He is silent for a while. "There. I suggest we do this before I lose my nerve. Belay on."

"Climbing," Randi answers. They proceed upward carefully but steadily, taking turns.

☞

I happen to be looking up when it happens. Randi is climbing when her foothold crumbles. She grabs for a line, says, "Damn!" then, "Falling." Her effort to grab has pushed her out from the wall, and when the rope goes taut, one of the pitons pops out of the wall with a shower of dust and ice. After a brief hesitation, the other two follow, and Ed yells, "Slack!"

Desperately, Randi tries to slow her fall by digging her hands and crampons into the wall beside her, throwing up a wake of dust. The smoothness of the wall helps; it is not completely vertical, and there are no bumps to throw her out.

The next set of pitons catches her rope, and for half a second it looks like it might hold. But before she comes to a complete halt, they pull out too and she starts to slide down again. Now, only Ed's own precarious hold on the wall stands between them and a five-hundred-meter fall. He is furiously trying to hammer in more pitons, but there is little rope left between him and Randi.

They need another secure line. Why, with six other more experienced explorers present, I am the one to think of something is a mystery. Perhaps it has something to do with creativity, or with not having a mind full of the knowledge of things that wouldn't work.

"Mike, Wojciech. Can you fire a rocket line right into the wall above them? It ought to penetrate that stuff and anchor itself."

He doesn't take time to answer me. There is a flash from overhead and an impact ten meters above Ed. The line it carries is much thinner than climbing rope, but drapes down beside them quickly in the vacuum. It continues to play out, draping all the way down to our little camp.

The line between Randi and Ed snaps tight, and his foot and arm come free in a shower of ice. He should hit the release, I think. Better one death than two, but he tries to hold on to the wall. He doesn't dare let go and reach for the new, untested line, hanging less than a meter away.

It almost works. Randi, caught short, manages to reach her ax and digs into the wall like a desperate fly. Working with her right hand, she sets one piton and then another, hammering them in with her fist.

Above her, the rest of the ice holding Ed begins to give way as he tries to regain his handhold. "Can't hold, falling!" He flails for the new line as he starts to slip, but it is out of reach.

They would, I think, be dead on Earth—but Mercury gravity is more forgiving. Working as Ed slides, Randi reaches the new line and yanks hard on it. She yanks hard again—it must not have been firmly set. Another hard pull and she seems satisfied. Ed slides down beside her in a plume of dust and ice, barely in contact with the wall.

Quickly Randi connects the new line to the line that still connects them, slack now, and loops it around the piton she has just set. "Protection in!"

Thirty meters below her, Ed bounces as the line pulls taut and pops the piton out of the wall in another shower of debris. Ed's weight pulls Randi free of her holds as well.

They both slide another ten meters, but now the slack in the line from the rocket has been taken up. They slide some more as it stretches, then, finally, stop. All told, Randi has fallen about a hundred meters and Ed perhaps fifty.

"Jupiter!" Karen, on the crevasse rim, exclaims. "Randi, Ed, set yourselves if you can. I can see the rocket: it's wedged itself vertically in the hole it made when it hit the wall, only about ten centimeters from the face. Try to hold tight while we think of something."

"OK," Ed says. "But don't take too long. I think I'm about at the end of my rope about this."

The laughter, fueled by relief, is perhaps a little too loud for the quality of the pun. Ed quickly starts hammering in additional protection. Randi, however, is simply hanging passively in her harness.

"Randi?" Mike calls.

"Injured. Both arms." Her voice attempts calm, but I can hear the pain in it.

"Can you climb?" Mike asks.

Randi tries to lift an arm up to her rope and gasps. "Not now."

"Descending," Ed says. "I'd like another belay if you can think of something."

What we think of is setting our remaining line rocket for maximum range and steering it about six meters under the far edge of the crevasse. It slams in hard, burying itself too far in for Karen to see. "Ice," Mike says, instantly, as a patch of icy regolith loosened by the rocket impact snows down left of the climbers. The upper layers, as we know, are softer. They pull the line from the far edge until it sets hard—ten kilonewtons tension, Mike estimates. Then they let the line drape down to us, and we walk it over to where Ed can reach it.

He connects the lines, and continues down.

Randi tries to descend. We hear the slightest hint of a cry of pain over the radio, then a loud "Damn! Dad, I can't lift my hands over my shoulders. Both shoulders shot."

"That's all right, Randi, I'm coming." Dr. Lotati turns and looks at me. "Come on, Wojciech. I want your head on that wall."

Juanita gives me a pat on the rear, and surprisingly, Eloni gives me a silent hug. Inside her visor, her dark eyes are glistening. I think of how frightened the Kenyan student must be, but she has just contributed in the only way she could think of.

"Thanks, team," I say, and squeeze her hand.

I clip my ascent ratchet on and start climbing. There are no problems and we reach Randi and Ed in half an hour.

Randi is calm. "Right arm. Won't go above shoulder. Maybe dislocated. Left arm works, sort of. But hurts too much. Might faint. OK as long as I keep my hands down."

"I'll take you down, papoose-style," Ed offers. "Then we'll ride the elevator up."

Dr. Lotati touches Randi. "OK?"

"I'll make it, Dad."

"Good, Wojciech and I will go up then, and set the anchor," Dr. Lotati decides. His voice crackles with leadership and confidence. I smile. Everyone, including him, has forgotten about his age. It won't be obvious on this climb; if anything, I will slow *him* down.

We replace Ed's backpack with Randi, tying her to his shoulder harness, and help guide them down. When they are safe below, Dr. Lotati nods to me, and says, "We have to consider everything we put into this surface to be hazardous, no?"

I nod. We are leaning out from a wall almost half a kilometer above a bridge about half a kilometer above a pool of cryogenic nitrogen trifluoride, talking about how the various things that hold our ropes to said wall may give way at any time.

"OK. We use four pitons, or bolts, or a combination, on each belay, and arrange the ropes like so." He demonstrates, creating what looks at first glance to be a cat's cradle of ropes between carabiners and pitons. "This equalizes forces among the pitons and minimizes the shock if one lets go." It takes me a couple of tries to get it right. He finally pats me on the shoulder, and without further ado says, "Climbing."

"On belay," I answer, wondering about people who seem to come alive only when staring death in the face. He ascends deliberately, and deceptively fast.

Actually, I keep up, but exhaust myself in the process. Dr. Lotati is only a centimeter or two taller than his daughter, and hardly much heavier. He is wiry strong; occasional rest stops are the only concession he makes to age—and I need them more than he does. We stop where the second line-bearing rocket buried itself in the fragile clathrate, six meters below the crater floor. The ledge is overhung by about a meter, more where the rocket impact dislodged a large hunk of wall.

"Can you stand a short fall?" he asks me. "I think we'll need several tries to get around that edge." I've never fallen on a belay line before. I want to impress Emilio; my Mirandas, moon and woman, are at stake. But the idea of trying to scramble almost upside down and free-falling six to ten meters, with only a questionable anchor to stop me if I slip, scares the crap out me. If there were any other way . . .

"Wojciech?"

"Yes." Then, perhaps because my mind works best in an emergency, or under a deadline, the idea comes to me. "Dr. Lotati—this is fairly soft stuff. You don't suppose we could just tunnel through it, up to the surface?"

He looks down at me. "Perhaps! I wouldn't consider desecrating an Earth climb like that, but I think we will be forgiven here. I knew your head would be good for something!" Then he takes an ax from his belt and swings it into the ice overhead. A good sized hunk falls and shatters into tiny chips on my helmet.

"Ice!" He looks at his handiwork, says, "Si," and swings again, and again, cutting a notch more than a tunnel as it turns out. We are through and up to the crater floor in less than an hour.

There is a round of cheers when we say, "On top!" Mike and Karen wave from the other side of the crevasse—only a hundred meters away. It has taken us two days to go that hundred meters.

I help set the next set of anchors a hundred meters back from the edge, in firm regolith. The rest is ropes, ascenders and pulleys. Mike and Karen send the remaining gear, and themselves, across in an ersatz tram, and help us hoist the rest of the party. Juanita is the last one to emerge from the crevasse and we all cheer, intoxicated with our close call and our final victory. By the time everything is up or over, we have been awake for thirty hours. Dr. Lotati decides to set up camp immediately.

We have four two-person tents in addition to the large one. They can be independent or their entrances can be sealed to connecting ports in the large tent, forming a mini-base looking something like an inflated starfish minus an arm. That way, early risers can let others sleep.

Randi's left shoulder is bad—a possible separation—and we have at least three days' march ahead of us to our pickup point. We discuss an evacuation, but she won't hear of it. Mike and Ed both have field medical training but Mike has more practice, so he is the closest thing to a doctor we have, and he consults with Earth. It turns out that our optical scattering imager is good enough to build up a picture of the injury; Randi's humerus is not quite in its socket.

Earth recommends evacuation. Randi says no. Dr. Lotati supports her—we are in an age where injuries can be healed if they can be endured, but the opportunities to do something more significant than entertain oneself and collect one's automation stipend are few and far between.

Randi, Ed told me several nights ago, is Dr. Lotati's only son. I laughed and asked Ed what that made him. "The gayest man on Mercury," he answered—and threw such a convincing leer at me that it took me an unsettling second to get the joke. But the humor disguises a poignant situation—a young woman trying to be, for her father, the son he could never have. How much was from her nature, how much was from her love? Or was there a difference? And what of her mother? Randi's mother was never mentioned by anyone, and the only public biographical info was that Emilio had divorced her when Randi was six and never married again.

Following instructions from the doctors on Earth, Mike resets the shoulder. It takes him two tries. Randi shuts her eyes and gasps—that is all. Then it is in. Painkillers, anti-inflammatory drugs, and reconstructive stimulants we have—she will be sore, but as good as new in a few months. Climbing is out, but she can walk the rest of the way.

Ed and Randi retire together, her arm immobilized to her body with tape.

Juanita decides to sleep with Emilio. Mike and Karen are a given.

Eloni is looking at me with dark pools of eyes and what could be a hopeful smile on her face. I look at the shy graduate student who had given me a hug to send me up a treacherous wall that had just come within the width of an idea of killing two people. I shrug and reach a hand out to her and she comes and sits by me with the widest grin on her face I have ever seen.

"You wish I were Randi, don't you?" Eloni asks me.

"That's not your fault."

Her smile fades. "I almost got us all killed by being too slow. That was my fault."

There are times when sympathy can do things lust cannot. I have my arms around her in a second. "No one blames you. You're part of us, now. Time to enjoy it."

She kind of melts into me and gently pushes me down onto my back on my sleepsack. She has a low, incredibly sexy voice. "That is about as much as I can enjoy. I hope I do not disappoint you."

Tired as I am, I'm relieved; and confused. "Eloni, I write about the male and female thing, more from reading than experience, I'm afraid. I may sigh, but disappointment would be putting things a bit strong. But I'm curious. Do you believe in abstinence, and if so, can you tell me why?"

No contraception, I speculate? In this day, I find that hard to believe—but she is studying at Jovis Tholis on Mars, I remind myself, in the middle of the New Reformation.

A certain hardness comes over her face. "You want to know? I spoke literal truth. Abstinence has nothing to do with it. I was mutilated so I cannot enjoy what most women can enjoy. So I hike across glaciers and climb mountains instead," she smiles wryly. "That is how I get high. Try to understand. I am not Kenyan by birth. Kenya is a civilized nation."

I have it then. Female circumcision. Back on Earth, the villages all have nice premanufactured houses, with bathrooms, electricity, diagnostic comm ports, and regular food deliveries. But here and there, otherwise gentle people protect primitive cultures from "western interference," and so we still permit this to be done to children.

"How old were you?"

"Ten. They were very thorough. But in a few years, doctors will be able to fix it, I think. Regenerate the tissue that was taken from me. That's a spin-off from the interstellar project. They needed to solve tissue regeneration to do cold sleep reliably. For now, I must enjoy giving and being enjoyed while I fantasize what it might really be like."

What can one say? I take her hand and she squeezes it.

"Oh, yes." Her voice is low and throaty. "They mutilated me, they tried to keep me barefoot and stupid to carry on their primitive culture. They even tried to keep me from school. But they could not shut off my mind. And here I am, yes, here I am where they thought I could never go doing what they thought to keep from me forever. So I am a space person now, part of another tribe."

Eloni and I are both, I realize, refugees from cultures that do not want who we are. Hers a primitive one, mine too sophisticated to see itself. I only want to hold her, smother her hurt, and bring a smile to her face. I try to kiss her.

She holds me off. "Someday I have to go back there and try to change what the people do to each other there. I cannot be a space person forever. Do you understand?" She buries her face in my shoulder. "For now. Just for now."

I understand. This is for now—and whatever our feelings for each other now, our destinies lie in different directions. I nod and she is in my arms. Our lips touch again and the future vanishes. "What do you want me to do?" I ask.

In answer, she releases the seal of my tight suit.

We remove each other's remaining clothes and slip into my sleep sack. She wriggles against me and we do kiss, and our hands do stroke and caress, and begin to defy the cold dead gray cruelty outside our bubble with yet another act of life.

But there really isn't very much room and we are both very tired. So, in each other's arms, we fall asleep, content with a mostly symbolic defiance.

◆

The remaining walk toward the center of Chao Meng Fu is two by two, the time filled mostly with conversations that share what we are and what we know, but sometimes with those comfortable silences in which your mind digests what you have learned, playing this way and that with it. There are more crevasses to cross, but we do so expeditiously.

During one of these crossings, I say, "On belay, Dr. Lotati."

"Climbing. Wojciech, call me Emilio, it's quicker."

A small thing, but it suggests to me a future more interesting than correcting undergraduate papers.

Juanita suggests we share a piece of music for our final approach to the central depot. It is by a twentieth-century composer named Alan Hovhaness, a symphony called "City of Light." She says it is his symphony number twenty-two.

"Twenty-two?" I ask. "Did I hear you right? I know Haydn wrote over a hundred, but that was when they were short and highly formatted. Beethoven wrote only nine. Tchaikovsky, six. I thought they'd pretty much stopped doing symphonies by the twenty-first century."

Juanita laughed. "We geologists call Hovhaness our patron composer because he actually wrote a symphony about a volcano—and that was number *fifty*. By the mid-twenty-first century, they were calling him 'the American Haydn.' Now let's just listen."

As we approach the brilliant peaks of the Chao Meng Fu central crown—great massive round Sun-gilded domes that speak of power and eternity—I am incapable of understanding why I once thought of this expedition as a stunt. I feel like a piece of steel, bent, hammered, bent and hammered again in the fire with greater strength and balance than I have ever known before.

It is a feeling I want to have again, if I must pursue it to the ends of the Solar System. Perhaps I am not in a class with Ed Blake and perhaps any fantasies I had of a match with Randi must remain fantasies, but I have found in my own backyard a delicate and precious union with Eloni and a friend and colleague in Juanita. And I think I have succeeded in my main objective—I have, I think, the friendship and respect of the people who could bring me out to the frontier which calls my spirit.

As I walk I feel the voices of a more broad-shouldered century calling me; Stanley, Peary, Scott, Teddy Roosevelt, and among poets, of course, Kipling. As I trudge, I amuse myself with a doggerel:

> *Perhaps those prudent people*
> *Who never risk the pit,*
> *Also never know the joy*
> *Of coming out of it.*

Not prize material, perhaps, but sums my experience, and in my present state of deranged ecstasy, I am no critic!

And if my words fail you—as they fail many others of highly educated tastes—then listen to the finale of Hovhaness' symphony. For if you cannot understand after hearing that, you have left the human race. What I learned, in the crossing of Chao Meng Fu, was that such things still can be, in any age, for anyone who will do them.

Wang's Carpets

GREG EGAN

As the new century approaches, it's obvious that Australian writer Greg Egan is one of the Big New Names to emerge in science fiction in the nineties, probably the best new hard-science writer to enter the field since Greg Bear, and already one of the most widely known of all Australian genre writers. In the last few years, Egan has become a frequent contributor to Interzone *and* Asimov's Science Fiction *and has made sales as well as to* Pulphouse, Analog, Aurealis, Eidolon *and elsewhere; many of his stories have also appeared in various "Best of the Year" series, and he was on the final Hugo ballot in 1995 for his story "Cocoon," which won the Ditmar Award and the* Asimov's Readers' Award. *His novella "Oceanic" won another* Asimov's Readers' Award *and is on this year's final Hugo ballot as I type these words. His first novel,* Quarantine, *appeared in 1992, to wide critical acclaim, and was followed by a second novel in 1994,* Permutation City, *which won the John W. Campbell Memorial Award. His most recent books are two new novels,* Distress *and* Diaspora, *and three collections of his short fiction,* Axiomatic, Luminous, *and* Our Lady of Chernobyl. *Upcoming is a new novel,* Teranesia. *He has a Web site at http://www.netspace.netau/^gregegan/.*

Although he often writes incisive studies of near-future sociological problems and the way they are complicated (for both better and worse) by technological change, such as "Cocoon," "Tap," "Yeyuka," "Silver Fire," and many others, Egan has also written his share of stories about explorers of one kind or another, including "Luminous," in which scientists explore congruent mathematical realms with a computer made of light, "Dust," in which a hacker investigates firsthand what "life" as a program running inside a virtual construct would be like, and one of 1997's two stories about explorers who plunge into a black hole, "The Planck Dive" (the other is Geoffrey A. Landis's "Approaching Perimelasma," reprinted later in this book). In the brilliant story that follows, though—one of those seminal stories that come along only every once in a long while, where the conceptualization is so original that it persuades other writers to change their own thinking about what the future is going to be like—Egan succeeded in reinventing the space travel/space exploration tale for a new generation, and I suspect that you'll be seeing the mark of "Wang's Carpet" on many such stories for long years to come.

Waiting to be cloned one thousand times and scattered across ten million cubic light-years, Paolo Venetti relaxed in his favorite ceremonial bathtub: a tiered hexagonal pool set in a courtyard of black marble flecked with gold. Paolo wore full traditional anatomy, uncomfortable garb at first, but the warm currents flowing across his back and shoulders slowly eased him into a pleasant torpor. He could have reached the same state in an instant, by decree—but the occasion seemed to demand the complete ritual of verisimilitude, the ornate curlicued longhand of imitation physical cause and effect.

As the moment of diaspora approached, a small gray lizard darted across the courtyard, claws scrabbling. It halted by the far edge of the pool, and Paolo marveled at the delicate pulse of its breathing, and watched the lizard watching him, until it moved again, disappearing into the surrounding vineyards. The environment was full of birds and insects, rodents and small reptiles—decorative in appearance, but also satisfying a more abstract aesthetic: softening the harsh radial symmetry of the lone observer; anchoring the simulation by perceiving it from a multitude of viewpoints. Ontological guy lines. No one had asked the lizards if they wanted to be cloned, though. They were coming along for the ride, like it or not.

The sky above the courtyard was warm and blue, cloudless and sunless, isotropic. Paolo waited calmly, prepared for every one of half a dozen possible fates.

An invisible bell chimed softly, three times. Paolo laughed, delighted.

One chime would have meant that he was still on Earth: an anti-climax, certainly—but there would have been advantages to compensate for that. Everyone who really mattered to him lived in the Carter-Zimmerman polis, but not all of them had chosen to take part in the diaspora to the same degree; his Earth-self would have lost no one. Helping to ensure that the thousand ships were safely dispatched would have been satisfying, too. And remaining a member of the wider Earth-based community, plugged into the entire global culture in real-time, would have been an attraction in itself.

Two chimes would have meant that this clone of Carter-Zimmerman had reached a planetary system devoid of life. Paolo had run a sophisticated—but non-sapient—self-predictive model before deciding to wake under those conditions. Exploring a handful of alien worlds, however barren, had seemed likely to be an enriching experience for him—with the distinct advantage that the whole endeavor would be untrammeled by the kind of elaborate precautions necessary in the presence of alien life. C-Z's population would have fallen by more than half—and many of his closest friends would have been absent—but he would have forged new friendships, he was sure.

Four chimes would have signaled the discovery of intelligent aliens. Five, a technological civilization. Six, spacefarers.

Three chimes, though, meant that the scout probes had detected unambiguous signs of life—and that was reason enough for jubilation. Up until the moment of the pre-launch cloning—a subjective instant before the chimes had sounded—no reports of alien life had ever reached Earth. There'd been no guarantee that any part of the diaspora would find it.

Paolo willed the polis library to brief him; it promptly rewired the declarative memory of his simulated traditional brain with all the information he was likely to need to satisfy his immediate curiosity. This clone of C-Z had arrived at Vega, the second closest of the thousand target stars, twenty-seven light-years from Earth. Paolo closed his eyes and visualized a star map with a thousand lines-radiating out from the sun, then zoomed in on the trajectory which described his own journey. It had taken three centuries to reach Vega—but the vast majority of the polis's twenty thousand inhabitants had programmed their exoselves to suspend them prior to the cloning, and to wake them only if and when they arrived at a suitable destination. Ninety-two citizens had chosen the alternative: experiencing every voyage of the diaspora from start to finish, risking disappointment, and even death. Paolo now knew that the ship aimed at Fomalhaut, the target nearest Earth, had been struck by debris and annihilated *en route*. He mourned the ninety-two, briefly. He hadn't been close to any of them, prior to the cloning, and the particular versions who'd willfully perished two centuries ago in interstellar space seemed as remote as the victims of some ancient calamity from the era of flesh.

Paolo examined his new home star through the cameras of one of the scout probes—and the strange filters of the ancestral visual system. In traditional colors, Vega was a fierce blue-white disk, laced with prominences. Three times the mass of the sun, twice the size and twice as hot, sixty times as luminous. Burning hydrogen fast—and already halfway through its allotted five hundred million years on the main sequence.

Vega's sole planet, Orpheus, had been a featureless blip to the best lunar interferometers; now Paolo gazed down on its blue-green crescent, ten thousand kilometers below Carter-Zimmerman itself. Orpheus was terrestrial, a nickel-iron-silicate world; slightly larger than Earth, slightly warmer—a billion kilometers took the edge off Vega's heat—and almost drowning in liquid water. Impatient to see the whole surface firsthand, Paolo slowed his clock rate a thousandfold, allowing C-Z to circumnavigate the planet in twenty subjective seconds, daylight unshrouding a broad new swath with each pass. Two slender ocher-colored continents with mountainous spines bracketed hemispheric oceans, and dazzling expanses of pack ice covered both poles—far more so in the north, where jagged white peninsulas radiated out from the midwinter arctic darkness.

The Orphean atmosphere was mostly nitrogen—six times as much as on Earth; probably split by UV from primordial ammonia—with traces of water vapor and carbon dioxide, but not enough of either for a runaway greenhouse effect. The high atmospheric pressure meant reduced evaporation—Paolo saw not a wisp of cloud—and the large, warm oceans in turn helped feed carbon dioxide back into the crust, locking it up in limestone sediments destined for subduction.

The whole system was young, by Earth standards, but Vega's greater mass, and a denser protostellar cloud, would have meant swifter passage through most of the traumas of birth: nuclear ignition and early luminosity fluctuations; planetary coalescence and the age of bombardments. The library estimated that Orpheus had enjoyed a relatively stable climate, and freedom from major impacts, for at least the past hundred million years.

Long enough for primitive life to appear—

A hand seized Paolo firmly by the ankle and tugged him beneath the water. He offered no resistance, and let the vision of the planet slip away. Only two other people in C-Z had free access to this environment—and his father didn't play games with his now-twelve-hundred-year-old son.

Elena dragged him all the way to the bottom of the pool, before releasing his foot and hovering above him, a triumphant silhouette against the bright surface. She was ancestor-shaped, but obviously cheating; she spoke with perfect clarity, and no air bubbles at all.

"Late sleeper! I've been waiting seven weeks for this!"

Paolo feigned indifference, but he was fast running out of breath. He had his exoself convert him into an amphibious human variant—biologically and historically authentic, if no longer the definitive ancestral phenotype. Water flooded into his modified lungs, and his modified brain welcomed it.

He said, "Why would I want to waste consciousness, sitting around waiting for the scout probes to refine their observations? I woke as soon as the data was unambiguous."

She pummeled his chest; he reached up and pulled her down, instinctively reducing his buoyancy to compensate, and they rolled across the bottom of the pool, kissing.

Elena said, "You know we're the first C-Z to arrive, anywhere? The Fomalhaut ship was destroyed. So there's only one other pair of us. Back on Earth."

"So?" Then he remembered. Elena had chosen not to wake if any other version of her had already encountered life. Whatever fate befell each of the remaining ships, every other version of him would have to live without her.

He nodded soberly, and kissed her again. "What am I meant to say? You're a thousand times more precious to me, now?"

"Yes."

"Ah, but what about the you-and-I on Earth? Five hundred times would be closer to the truth."

"There's no poetry in five hundred."

"Don't be so defeatist. Rewire your language centers."

She ran her hands along the sides of his ribcage, down to his hips. They made love with their almost-traditional bodies—and brains; Paolo was amused to the point of distraction when his limbic system went into overdrive, but he remembered enough from the last occasion to bury his self-consciousness and surrender to the strange hijacker. It wasn't like making love in any civilized fashion—the rate of information exchange between them was minuscule, for a start—but it had the raw insistent quality of most ancestral pleasures.

Then they drifted up to the surface of the pool and lay beneath the radiant sunless sky.

Paolo thought: *I've crossed twenty-seven light-years in an instant. I'm orbiting the first planet ever found to hold alien life. And I've sacrificed nothing— left nothing I truly value behind. This is too good, too good.* He felt a pang of regret for his other selves—it was hard to imagine them faring as well, without Elena, without Orpheus—but there was nothing he could do about that, now. Although there'd be time to confer with Earth before any more ships reached their destinations, he'd decided—prior to the cloning—not to allow the unfolding of his manifold future to be swayed by any change of heart. Whether or not his Earth-self agreed, the two of them were powerless to alter the criteria for waking. The self with the right to choose for the thousand had passed away.

No matter, Paolo decided. The others would find—or construct—their own reasons for happiness. And there was still the chance that one of them would wake to the sound of *four chimes*.

Elena said, "If you'd slept much longer, you would have missed the vote."

The vote? The scouts in low orbit had gathered what data they could about Orphean biology. To proceed any further, it would be necessary to send microprobes into the ocean itself—an escalation of contact which required the approval of two-thirds of the polis. There was no compelling reason to believe that the presence of a few million tiny robots could do any harm; all they'd leave behind in the water was a few kilojoules of waste heat. Nevertheless, a faction had arisen which advocated caution. The citizens of Carter-Zimmerman, they argued, could continue to observe from a distance for another decade, or another millennium, refining their observations and hypotheses before intruding . . . and those who disagreed could always sleep away the time, or find other interests to pursue.

Paolo delved into his library-fresh knowledge of the "carpets"—the single Orphean lifeform detected so far. They were free-floating creatures living in the equatorial ocean depths—apparently destroyed by UV if they drifted too close to the surface. They grew to a size of hundreds of meters, then fissioned into dozens of fragments, each of which continued to grow. It was tempting to assume that they were colonies of single-celled organisms, something like giant kelp—but there was no real evidence yet to back that up. It was difficult enough for the scout probes to discern the carpets' gross appearance and behavior through a kilometer of water, even with Vega's copious neutrinos lighting the way; remote observations on a microscopic scale, let alone biochemical analyses, were out of the question. Spectroscopy revealed that the surface water was full of intriguing molecular debris—but guessing the relationship of any of it to the living carpets was like trying to reconstruct human biochemistry by studying human ashes.

Paolo turned to Elena. "What do you think?"

She moaned theatrically; the topic must have been argued to death while he slept. "The microprobes are harmless. They could tell us exactly what the carpets are made of, without removing a single molecule. What's the risk? *Culture shock?*"

Paolo flicked water onto her face, affectionately; the impulse seemed to come with the amphibian body. "You can't be sure that they're not intelligent."

"Do you know what was living on Earth, two hundred million years after it was formed?"

"Maybe cyanobacteria. Maybe nothing. This isn't Earth, though."

"True. But even in the unlikely event that the carpets are intelligent, do you think they'd notice the presence of robots a millionth their size? If they're unified organisms, they don't appear to react to anything in their environment—they have no predators, they don't pursue food, they just drift with the currents—so there's no reason for them to possess elaborate sense organs at all, let alone anything working on a sub-millimeter scale. And if they're colonies of single-celled creatures, one of which happens to collide with a microprobe and register its presence with surface receptors . . . what conceivable harm could that do?"

"I have no idea. But my ignorance is no guarantee of safety."

Elena splashed him back. "The only way to deal with your *ignorance* is to vote to send down the microprobes. We have to be cautious, I agree—but there's no point *being here* if we don't find out what's happening in the oceans, right now. I don't want to wait for this planet to evolve something smart enough to broadcast biochemistry lessons into space. If we're not willing to take a few infinitesimal risks, Vega will turn red giant before we learn anything."

It was a throwaway line—but Paolo tried to imagine witnessing the event. In a quarter of a billion years, would the citizens of Carter-Zimmerman be debating the ethics of intervening to rescue the Or-pheans—or would they all have lost interest, and departed for other stars, or modified themselves into beings entirely devoid of nostalgic compassion for organic life?

Grandiose visions for a twelve-hundred-year-old. The Fomalhaut clone had been obliterated by one tiny piece of rock. There was far more junk in the Vegan system than in interstellar space; even ringed by defenses, its data backed up to all the far-flung scout probes, this C-Z was not invulnerable just because it had arrived intact. Elena was right; they had to seize the moment—or they might as well retreat into their own hermetic worlds and forget that they'd ever made the journey.

Paolo recalled the honest puzzlement of a friend from Ashton-Laval: *Why go looking for aliens? Our polis has a thousand ecologies, a trillion species of evolved life. What do you hope to find, out there, that you couldn't have grown at home?*

What had he hoped to find? Just the answers to a few simple questions. Did human consciousness bootstrap all of space-time into existence, in order to explain itself? Or had a neutral, pre-existing universe given birth to a billion varieties of conscious life, all capable of harboring the same delusions of grandeur—until they collided with each other? Anthrocos-mology was used to justify the inward-looking stance of most polises: if the physical universe was created by human thought, it had no special status which placed it above virtual reality. It might have come first—and every virtual reality might need to run on a physical computing device, subject to physical laws—but it occupied no privileged position in terms of "truth" versus "illusion." If the ACs were right, then it was no more *honest* to value the physical universe over more recent artificial realities than it was honest to remain flesh instead of software, or ape instead of human, or bacterium instead of ape.

Elena said, "We can't lie here forever; the gang's all waiting to see you."

"Where?" Paolo felt his first pang of homesickness; on Earth, his circle of friends had always met in a real-time image of the Mount Pinatubo crater, plucked straight from the observation satellites. A recording wouldn't be the same.

"I'll show you."

Paolo reached over and took her hand. The pool, the sky, the courtyard vanished—and he found himself gazing down on Orpheus again . . . nightside, but far from dark, with his full mental palette now encoding everything from the pale wash of ground-current long-wave radio, to the multi-colored shimmer of isotopic gamma rays and back-scattered cosmic-ray bremsstrahlung. Half the abstract knowledge the library had fed him about the planet was obvious at a glance, now. The ocean's smoothly tapered thermal glow spelt *three-hundred Kelvin* instantly—as well as backlighting the atmosphere's telltale infrared silhouette.

He was standing on a long, metallic-looking girder, one edge of a vast geodesic sphere, open to the blazing cathedral of space. He glanced up and saw the star-rich dust-clogged band of the Milky Way, encircling him from zenith to nadir; aware of the glow of every gas cloud, discerning each absorption and emission line, Paolo could almost feel the plane of the galactic disk transect him. Some constellations were distorted, but the view was more familiar than strange—and he recognized most of the old signposts by color. He had his bearings, now. Twenty degrees away from Sirius—south, by parochial Earth reckoning—faint but unmistakable: the sun.

Elena was beside him—superficially unchanged, although they'd both shrugged off the constraints of biology. The conventions of this environment mimicked the physics of real macroscopic objects in free-fall and vacuum, but it wasn't set up to model any kind of chemistry, let alone that of flesh and blood. Their new bodies were human-shaped, but devoid of elaborate microstructure—and their minds weren't embedded in the physics at all, but were running directly on the processor web.

Paolo was relieved to be back to normal; ceremonial regression to the ancestral form was a venerable C-Z tradition—and being human was largely self-affirming, while it lasted—but every time he emerged from the experience, he felt as if he'd broken free of billion-year-old shackles. There were polises on Earth where the citizens would have found his present structure almost as archaic: a consciousness dominated by sensory perception, an illusion of possessing solid form, a single time coordinate. The last flesh human had died long before Paolo was constructed, and apart from the communities of Gleisner robots, Carter-Zimmerman was about as conservative as a transhuman society could be. The balance seemed right to Paolo, though—acknowledging the flexibility of software, without abandoning interest in the physical world—and although the stubbornly corporeal Gleisners had been first to the stars, the C-Z diaspora would soon overtake them.

Their friends gathered round, showing off their effortless free-fall acrobatics, greeting Paolo and chiding him for not arranging to wake sooner; he was the last of the gang to emerge from hibernation.

"Do you like our humble new meeting place?" Hermann floated by Paolo's shoulder, a chimeric cluster of limbs and sense-organs, speaking through the vacuum in modulated infrared. "We call it Satellite Pinatubo. It's desolate up here, I know—but we were afraid it might violate the spirit of caution if we dared pretend to walk the Orphean surface."

Paolo glanced mentally at a scout probe's close-up of a typical stretch of dry land, an expanse of fissured red rock. "More desolate down there, I think." He was tempted to touch the ground—to let the private vision become tactile—but he resisted. Being elsewhere in the middle of a conversation was bad etiquette.

"Ignore Hermann," Liesl advised. "He wants to flood Orpheus with our alien machinery before we have any idea what the effects might be." Liesl was a green-and-turquoise butterfly, with a stylized human face stippled in gold on each wing.

Paolo was surprised; from the way Elena had spoken, he'd assumed that his friends must have come to a consensus in favor of the microprobes—and only a late sleeper, new to the issues, would bother to argue the point. "What effects? The carpets—"

"Forget the carpets! Even if the carpets are as simple as they look, we don't know what else is down there." As Liesl's wings fluttered, her mirror-image faces seemed to glance at each other for support. "With neutrino imaging, we barely achieve spatial resolution in meters, time resolution in seconds. We don't know anything about smaller lifeforms."

"And we never will, if you have your way." Karpal—an ex-Gleisner, human-shaped as ever—had been Liesl's lover, last time Paolo was awake.

"We've only been here for a fraction of an Orphean year! There's still a wealth of data we could gather non-intrusively, with a little patience. There might be rare beachings of ocean life—"

Elena said dryly, "Rare indeed. Orpheus has negligible tides, shallow waves, very few storms. And anything beached would be fried by UV before we glimpsed anything more instructive than we're already seeing in the surface water."

"Not necessarily. The carpets seem to be vulnerable—but other species might be better protected, if they live nearer to the surface. And Orpheus is seismically active; we should at least wait for a tsunami to dump a few cubic kilometers of ocean onto a shoreline, and see what it reveals."

Paolo smiled; he hadn't thought of that. A tsunami might be worth waiting for.

Liesl continued, "What is there to lose, by waiting a few hundred Orphean years? At the very least, we could gather baseline data on seasonal climate patterns—and we could watch for anomalies, storms and quakes, hoping for some revelatory glimpses."

A few hundred Orphean years? *A few terrestrial millennia?* Paolo's ambivalence waned. If he'd wanted to inhabit geological time, he would have migrated to the Lokhande polis, where the Order of Contemplative Observers watched Earth's mountains erode in subjective seconds. Orpheus hung in the sky beneath them, a beautiful puzzle waiting to be decoded, demanding to be understood.

He said, "But what if there *are* no 'revelatory glimpses'? How long do we wait? We don't know how rare life is—in time, or in space. If this planet is precious, *so is the epoch it's passing through*. We don't know how rapidly Orphean biology is evolving; species might appear and vanish while we agonize over the risks of gathering better data. The carpets— and whatever else—could die out before we'd learnt the first thing about them. What a waste that would be!"

Liesl stood her ground.

"And if we damage the Orphean ecology—or culture—by rushing in? That wouldn't be a waste. It would be a tragedy."

🙰

Paolo assimilated all the stored transmissions from his Earth-self—almost three hundred years' worth—before composing a reply. The early communications included detailed mind grafts—and it was good to share the excitement of the diaspora's launch; to watch—very nearly firsthand—the thousand ships, nanomachine-carved from asteroids, depart in a blaze of fusion fire from beyond the orbit of Mars. Then things settled down to the usual prosaic matters: Elena, the gang, shameless gossip, Carter-Zimmerman's ongoing research projects, the buzz of interpolis cultural tensions, the not-quite-cyclic convulsions of the arts (the perceptual aesthetic overthrows the emotional, again . . . although Valladas in Konishi polis claims to have constructed a new synthesis of the two).

After the first fifty years, his Earth-self had begun to hold things back; by the time news reached Earth of the Fomalhaut clone's demise, the messages had become pure audiovisual linear monologues. Paolo understood. It was only right; they'd diverged, and you didn't send mind grafts to strangers.

Most of the transmissions had been broadcast to all of the ships, indiscriminately. Forty-three years ago, though, his Earth-self had sent a special message to the Vega-bound clone.

"The new lunar spectroscope we finished last year has just picked up clear signs of water on Orpheus. There should be large temperate oceans waiting for you, if the models are right. So . . . good luck." Vision showed the instrument's domes growing out of the rock of the lunar farside; plots of the Orphean spectral data; an ensemble of planetary models. "Maybe it seems strange to you—all the trouble we're taking to catch a glimpse of what you're going to see in close-up, so soon. It's hard to explain: I don't think it's jealousy, or even impatience. Just a need for independence.

"There's been a revival of the old debate: should we consider redesigning our minds to encompass interstellar distances? One self spanning thousands of stars, not via cloning, but through acceptance of the natural time scale of the light-speed lag. Millennia passing between mental events. Local contingencies dealt with by non-conscious systems." Essays, pro and con, were appended; Paolo ingested summaries. "I don't think the idea will gain much support, though—and the new astronomical projects are something of an antidote. We have to make peace with the fact that we've stayed behind . . . so we cling to the Earth—looking outwards, but remaining firmly anchored.

"I keep asking myself, though: where do we go from here? History can't guide us. Evolution can't guide us. The C-Z charter says *understand and respect the universe* . . . but in what form? On what scale? With what kind of senses, what kind of minds? We can become anything at all—and that space of possible futures dwarfs the galaxy. Can we explore it without losing our way? Flesh humans used to spin fantasies about aliens arriving to 'conquer' Earth, to steal their 'precious' physical resources, to wipe them out for fear of 'competition' . . . as if a species capable of making the journey wouldn't have had the power, or the wit, or the imagination, to rid itself of obsolete biological imperatives. *Conquering the galaxy* is what bacteria with spaceships would do—knowing no better, having no choice.

"Our condition is the opposite of that: we have no end of choices. That's why we need to find alien life—not just to break the spell of the anthrocosmologists. We need to find aliens who've faced the same decisions—and discovered how to live, what to become. We need to understand what it means to inhabit the universe."

●

Paolo watched the crude neutrino images of the carpets moving in staccato jerks around his dodecahedral room. Twenty-four ragged oblongs drifted above him, daughters of a larger ragged oblong which had just fissioned. Models suggested that shear forces from ocean currents could explain the whole process, triggered by nothing more than the parent reaching a critical size. The purely mechanical break-up of a colony—if that was what it was—might have little to do with the life cycle of the constituent organisms. It was frustrating. Paolo was accustomed to a torrent of data on anything which caught his interest; for the diaspora's great discovery to remain nothing more than a sequence of coarse monochrome snapshots was intolerable.

He glanced at a schematic of the scout probes' neutrino detectors, but there was no obvious scope for improvement. Nuclei in the detectors were excited into unstable high-energy states, then kept there by fine-tuned gamma-ray lasers picking off lower-energy eigenstates faster than they could creep into existence and attract a transition. Changes in neutrino flux of one part in ten-to-the-fifteenth could shift the energy levels far enough to disrupt the balancing act. The carpets cast a shadow so faint, though, that even this near-perfect vision could barely resolve it.

Orlando Venetti said, "You're awake."

Paolo turned. His father stood an arm's length away, presenting as an ornately clad human of indeterminate age. Definitely older than Paolo, though; Orlando never ceased to play up his seniority—even if the age difference was only twenty-five percent now, and falling.

Paolo banished the carpets from the room to the space behind one pentagonal window, and took his father's hand. The portions of Orlando's mind which meshed with his own expressed pleasure at Paolo's emergence from hibernation, fondly dwelt on past shared experiences, and entertained hopes of continued harmony between father and son. Paolo's greeting was similar, a carefully contrived "revelation" of his own emotional state. It was more of a ritual than an act of communication—but then, even with Elena, he set up barriers. No one was totally honest with another person—unless the two of them intended to permanently fuse.

Orlando nodded at the carpets. "I hope you appreciate how important they are."

"You know I do." He hadn't included that in his greeting, though. "First alien life." *C-Z humiliates the Gleisner robots, at last*—that was probably how his father saw it. The robots had been first to Alpha Centauri, and first to an extrasolar planet—but first life was Apollo to their Sputniks, for anyone who chose to think in those terms.

Orlando said, "This is the hook we need, to catch the citizens of the marginal polises. The ones who haven't quite imploded into solipsism. This will shake them up—don't you think?"

Paolo shrugged. Earth's transhumans were free to implode into anything they liked; it didn't stop Carter-Zimmerman from exploring the physical universe. But thrashing the Gleisners wouldn't be enough for Orlando; he lived for the day when C-Z would become the cultural mainstream. Any polis could multiply its population a billionfold in a microsecond, if it wanted the vacuous honor of outnumbering the rest. Luring other citizens to migrate was harder—and persuading them to rewrite their own local charters was harder still. Orlando had a missionary streak: he wanted every other polis to see the error of its ways, and follow C-Z to the stars.

Paolo said, "Ashton-Laval has intelligent aliens. I wouldn't be so sure that news of giant seaweed is going to take Earth by storm."

Orlando was venomous. "Ashton-Laval intervened in its so-called 'evolutionary' simulations so many times that they might as well have built the end products in an act of creation lasting six days. They wanted talking reptiles, and—*mirabile dictu!*—they got talking reptiles. There are self-modified transhumans in *this polis* more alien than the aliens in Ashton-Laval."

Paolo smiled. "All right. Forget Ashton-Laval. But forget the marginal polises, too. We choose to value the physical world. That's what defines us—but it's as arbitrary as any other choice of values. Why can't you accept that? It's not the One True Path which the infidels have to be bludgeoned into following." He knew he was arguing half for the sake of it—he desperately wanted to refute the anthrocosmologists, himself—but Orlando always drove him into taking the opposite position. Out of fear of being nothing but his father's clone? Despite the total absence of inherited episodic memories, the stochastic input into his ontogenesis, the chaotically divergent nature of the iterative mind-building algorithms.

Orlando made a beckoning gesture, dragging the image of the carpets halfway back into the room. "You'll vote for the microprobes?"

"Of course."

"Everything depends on that, now. It's good to start with a tantalizing glimpse—but if we don't follow up with details soon, they'll lose interest back on Earth very rapidly."

"Lose interest? It'll be fifty-four years before we know if anyone paid the slightest attention in the first place."

Orlando eyed him with disappointment, and resignation. "If you don't care about the other polises, think about C-Z. This helps us, it strengthens us. We have to make the most of that."

Paolo was bemused. "The charter is the charter. What needs to be strengthened? You make it sound like there's something at risk."

"What do you think a thousand lifeless worlds would have done to us? Do you think the charter would have remained intact?"

Paolo had never considered the scenario. "Maybe not. But in every C-Z where the charter was rewritten, there would have been citizens who'd have gone off and founded new polises on the old lines. You and I, for a start. We could have called it Venetti-Venetti."

"While half your friends turned their backs on the physical world? While Carter Zimmerman, after two thousand years, went solipsist? You'd be happy with that?"

Paolo laughed. "No—but it's not going to happen, is it? *We've found life.* All right, I agree with you: this strengthens C-Z. The diaspora might have 'failed' . . . but it didn't. We've been lucky. I'm glad, I'm grateful. Is that what you wanted to hear?"

Orlando said sourly, "You take too much for granted."

"And you care too much what I think! I'm not your . . . heir." Orlando was first-generation, scanned from flesh—and there were times when he seemed unable to accept that the whole concept of generation had lost its archaic significance. "You don't need me to safeguard the future of Carter-Zimmerman on your behalf. Or the future of transhumanity. You can do it in person."

Orlando looked wounded—a conscious choice, but it still encoded something. Paolo felt a pang of regret—but he'd said nothing he could honestly retract.

His father gathered up the sleeves of his gold and crimson robes—the only citizen of C-Z who could make Paolo uncomfortable to be naked—and repeated as he vanished from the room: "You take too much for granted."

➤

The gang watched the launch of the microprobes together—even Liesl, though she came in mourning, as a giant dark bird. Karpal stroked her feathers nervously. Hermann appeared as a creature out of Escher, a segmented worm with six human-shaped feet—on legs with elbows—given to curling up into a disk and rolling along the girders of Satellite Pinatubo. Paolo and Elena kept saying the same thing simultaneously; they'd just made love.

Hermann had moved the satellite to a notional orbit just below one of the scout probes—and changed the environment's scale, so that the probe's lower surface, an intricate landscape of detector modules and attitude-control jets, blotted out half the sky. The atmospheric-entry capsules—ceramic teardrops three centimeters wide—burst from their launch tube and hurtled past like boulders, vanishing from sight before they'd fallen so much as ten meters closer to Orpheus. It was all scrupulously accurate, although it was part real-time imagery, part extrapolation, part *faux*. Paolo thought: *We might as well have run a pure simulation . . . and pretended to follow the capsules down*. Elena gave him a guilty/admonishing look. *Yeah—and then why bother actually launching them at all? Why not just simulate a plausible Orphean ocean full of plausible Orphean lifeforms? Why not simulate the whole diaspora?* There was no crime of heresy in C-Z; no one had ever been exiled for breaking the charter. At times it still felt like a tightrope walk, though, trying to classify every act of simulation into those which contributed to an understanding of the physical universe (good), those which were merely convenient, recreational, aesthetic (acceptable) . . . and those which constituted a denial of the primacy of real phenomena (time to think about emigration).

The vote on the microprobes had been close: seventy-two percent in favor, just over the required two-thirds majority, with five percent abstaining. (Citizens created since the arrival at Vega were excluded . . . not that anyone in Carter-Zimmerman would have dreamt of stacking the ballot, perish the thought.) Paolo had been surprised at the narrow margin; he'd yet to hear a single plausible scenario for the microprobes doing harm. He wondered if there was another, unspoken reason which had nothing to do with fears for the Orphean ecology, or hypothetical culture. *A wish to prolong the pleasure of unraveling the planet's mysteries?* Paolo had some sympathy with that impulse—but the launch of the microprobes would do nothing to undermine the greater long-term pleasure of watching, and understanding, as Orphean life evolved.

Liesl said forlornly, "Coastline erosion models show that the northwestern shore of Lambda is inundated by tsunami every ninety Orphean years, on average." She offered the data to them; Paolo glanced at it, and it looked convincing—but the point was academic now. "We could have waited."

Hermann waved his eye-stalks at her. "Beaches covered in fossils, are they?"

"No, but the conditions hardly—"

"No excuses!" He wound his body around a girder, kicking his legs gleefully. Hermann was first-generation, even older than Orlando; he'd been scanned in the twenty-first century, before Carter-Zimmerman existed. Over the centuries, though, he'd wiped most of his episodic memories, and rewritten his personality a dozen times. He'd once told Paolo, "I think of myself as my own great-great-grandson. Death's not so bad, if you do it incrementally. Ditto for immortality."

Elena said, "I keep trying to imagine how it will feel if another C-Z clone stumbles on something infinitely better—like aliens with wormhole drives—while we're back here studying rafts of algae." The body she wore was more stylized than usual—still humanoid, but sexless, hairless and smooth, the face inexpressive and androgynous.

"If they have wormhole drives, they might visit us. Or share the technology, so we can link up the whole diaspora."

"If they have wormhole drives, where have they been for the last two thousand years?"

Paolo laughed. "Exactly. But I know what you mean: *first alien life* . . . and it's likely to be about as sophisticated as seaweed. It breaks the jinx, though. Seaweed every twenty-seven light-years. Nervous systems every fifty? Intelligence every hundred?" He fell silent, abruptly realizing what she was feeling: electing not to wake again after first life was beginning to seem like the wrong choice, a waste of the opportunities the diaspora had created. Paolo offered her a mind graft expressing empathy and support, but she declined.

She said, "I want sharp borders, right now. I want to deal with this myself."

"I understand." He let the partial model of her which he'd acquired as they'd made love fade from his mind. It was non-sapient, and no longer linked to her—but to retain it any longer when she felt this way would have seemed like a transgression. Paolo took the responsibilities of intimacy seriously. His lover before Elena had asked him to erase all his knowledge of her, and he'd more or less complied—the only thing he still knew about her was the fact that she'd made the request.

Hermann announced, "Planetfall!" Paolo glanced at a replay of a scout probe view which showed the first few entry capsules breaking up above the ocean and releasing their microprobes. Nanomachines transformed the ceramic shields (and then themselves) into carbon dioxide and a few simple minerals—nothing the micrometeorites constantly raining down onto Orpheus didn't contain—before the fragments could strike the water. The microprobes would broadcast nothing; when they'd finished gathering data, they'd float to the surface and modulate their UV reflectivity. It would be up to the scout probes to locate these specks, and read their messages, before they self-destructed as thoroughly as the entry capsules.

Hermann said, "This calls for a celebration. I'm heading for the Heart. Who'll join me?"

Paolo glanced at Elena. She shook her head. "You go."

"Are you sure?"

"Yes! Go on." Her skin had taken on a mirrored sheen; her expressionless face reflected the planet below. "I'm all right. I just want some time to think things through, on my own."

Hermann coiled around the satellite's frame, stretching his pale body as he went, gaining segments, gaining legs. "Come on, come on! Karpal? Liesl? Come and celebrate!"

Elena was gone. Liesl made a derisive sound and flapped off into the distance, mocking the environment's airlessness. Paolo and Karpal watched as Hermann grew longer and faster—and then in a blur of speed and change stretched out to wrap the entire geodesic frame. Paolo demagnetized his feet and moved away, laughing; Karpal did the same.

Then Hermann constricted like a boa, and snapped the whole satellite apart.

They floated for a while, two human-shaped machines and a giant worm in a cloud of spinning metal fragments, an absurd collection of imaginary debris, glinting by the light of the true stars.

◆

The Heart was always crowded, but it was larger than Paolo had seen it—even though Hermann had shrunk back to his original size, so as not to make a scene. The huge muscular chamber arched above them, pulsating wetly in time to the music, as they searched for the perfect location to soak up the atmosphere. Paolo had visited public environments in other polises, back on Earth; many were designed to be nothing more than a perceptual framework for group emotion-sharing. He'd never understood the attraction of becoming intimate with large numbers of strangers. Ancestral social hierarchies might have had their faults—and it was absurd to try to make a virtue of the limitations imposed by minds confined to wetware—but the whole idea of mass telepathy as an end in itself seemed bizarre to Paolo . . . and even old-fashioned, in a way. Humans, clearly, would have benefited from a good strong dose of each other's inner life, to keep them from slaughtering each other—but any civilized transhuman could respect and value other citizens without the need to have *been them*, firsthand.

They found a good spot and made some furniture, a table and two chairs—Hermann preferred to stand—and the floor expanded to make room. Paolo looked around, shouting greetings at the people he recognized by sight, but not bothering to check for identity broadcasts from the rest. Chances were he'd met everyone here, but he didn't want to spend the next hour exchanging pleasantries with casual acquaintances.

Hermann said, "I've been monitoring our modest stellar observatory's data stream—my antidote to Vegan parochialism. Odd things are going on around Sirius. We're seeing electron-positron annihilation gamma rays, gravity waves . . . and some unexplained hot spots on Sirius B." He turned to Karpal and asked innocently, "What do you think those robots are up to? There's a rumor that they're planning to drag the white dwarf out of orbit, and use it as part of a giant spaceship."

"I never listen to rumors." Karpal always presented as a faithful reproduction of his old human-shaped Gleisner body—and his mind, Paolo gathered, always took the form of a physiological model, even though he was five generations removed from flesh. Leaving his people and coming into C-Z must have taken considerable courage; they'd never welcome him back.

Paolo said, "Does it matter what they do? Where they go, how they get there? There's more than enough room for both of us. Even if they shadowed the diaspora—even if they came to Vega—we could study the Orpheans together, couldn't we?"

Hermann's cartoon insect face showed mock alarm, eyes growing wider, and wider apart. "Not if they dragged along a white dwarf! Next thing they'd want to start building a Dyson sphere." He turned back to Karpal. "You don't still suffer the urge, do you, for . . . *astrophysical* engineering?"

"Nothing C-Z's exploitation of a few megatons of Vegan asteroid material hasn't satisfied."

Paolo tried to change the subject. "Has anyone heard from Earth, lately? I'm beginning to feel unplugged." His own most recent message was a decade older than the time lag.

Karpal said, "You're not missing much; all they're talking about is Orpheus . . . ever since the new lunar observations, the signs of water. They seem more excited by the mere possibility of life than we are by the certainty. And they have very high hopes."

Paolo laughed. "They do. My Earth-self seems to be counting on the diaspora to find an advanced civilization with the answers to all of transhumanity's existential problems. I don't think he'll get much cosmic guidance from kelp."

"You know there was a big rise in emigration from C-Z after the launch? Emigration, and suicides." Hermann had stopped wriggling and gyrating, becoming almost still, a sign of rare seriousness. "I suspect that's what triggered the astronomy program in the first place. And it seems to have stanched the flow, at least in the short term. Earth C-Z detected water before any clone in the diaspora—and when they hear that we've found life, they'll feel more like collaborators in the discovery because of it."

Paolo felt a stirring of unease. *Emigration and suicides? Was that why Orlando had been so gloomy?* After three hundred years of waiting, how high had expectations become?

A buzz of excitement crossed the floor, a sudden shift in the tone of the conversation. Hermann whispered reverently, "First microprobe has surfaced. And the data is coming in now."

The non-sapient Heart was intelligent enough to guess its patrons' wishes. Although everyone could tap the library for results, privately, the music cut out and a giant public image of the summary data appeared, high in the chamber. Pado had to crane his neck to view it, a novel experience.

The microprobe had mapped one of the carpets in high resolution. The image showed the expected rough oblong, some hundred meters wide—but the two- or three-meter-thick slab of the neutrino tomographs was revealed now as a delicate convoluted surface—fine as a single layer of skin, but folded into an elaborate space-filling curve. Paolo checked the full data: the topology was strictly planar, despite the pathological appearance. No holes, no joins—just a surface which meandered wildly enough to look ten thousand times thicker from a distance than it really was.

An inset showed the microstructure, at a point which started at the rim of the carpet and then—slowly—moved toward the center. Paolo stared at the flowing molecular diagram for several seconds before he grasped what it meant.

The carpet was not a colony of single-celled creatures. Nor was it a multi-cellular organism. It was a *single molecule*, a two-dimensional polymer weighing twenty-five million kilograms. A giant sheet of folded polysaccharide, a complex mesh of interlinked pentose and hexose sugars hung with alkyl and amide side chains. A bit like a plant cell wall—except that this polymer was far stronger than cellulose, and the surface area was twenty orders of magnitude greater.

Karpal said, "I hope those entry capsules were perfectly sterile. Earth bacteria would gorge themselves on this. One big floating carbohydrate dinner, with no defenses."

Hermann thought it over. "Maybe. If they had enzymes capable of breaking off a piece—which I doubt. No chance we'll find out, though: even if there'd been bacterial spores lingering in the asteroid belt from early human expeditions, every ship in the diaspora was double-checked for contamination *en route*. We haven't brought smallpox to the Americas."

Paolo was still dazed. "But how does it assemble? How does it . . . grow?" Hermann consulted the library and replied, before Paolo could do the same.

"The edge of the carpet catalyzes its own growth. The polymer is irregular, aperiodic—there's no single component which simply repeats. But there seem to be about twenty thousand basic structural units—twenty thousand different polysaccharide building blocks." Paolo saw them: long bundles of cross-linked chains running the whole two-hundred-micron thickness of the carpet, each with a roughly square cross-section, bonded at several thousand points to the four neighboring units. "Even at this depth, the ocean's full of UV-generated radicals which filter down from the surface. Any structural unit exposed to the water converts those radicals into more polysaccharide—and builds another structural unit."

Paolo glanced at the library again, for a simulation of the process. Catalytic sites strewn along the sides of each unit trapped the radicals in place, long enough for new bonds to form between them. Some simple sugars were incorporated straight into the polymer as they were created; others were set free to drift in solution for a microsecond or two, until they were needed. At that level, there were only a few basic chemical tricks being used . . . but molecular evolution must have worked its way up from a few small autocatalytic fragments, first formed by chance, to this elaborate system of twenty thousand mutually self-replicating structures. If the "structural units" had floated free in the ocean as independent molecules, the "lifeform" they comprised would have been virtually invisible. By bonding together, though, they became twenty thousand colors in a giant mosaic.

It was astonishing. Paolo hoped Elena was tapping the library, wherever she was. A colony of algae would have been more "advanced"—but this incredible primordial creature revealed infinitely more about the possibilities for the genesis of life. Carbohydrate, here, played every biochemical role: information carrier, enzyme, energy source, structural material. Nothing like it could have survived on Earth, once there were organisms capable of feeding on it—and if there were ever intelligent Orpheans, they'd be unlikely to find any trace of this bizarre ancestor.

Karpal wore a secretive smile.

Paolo said, "What?"

"Wang tiles. The carpets are made out of Wang tiles."

Hermann beat him to the library, again.

"*Wang* as in twentieth-century flesh mathematician, Hao Wang. *Tiles* as in any set of shapes which can cover the plane. Wang tiles are squares with various shaped edges, which have to fit complementary shapes on adjacent squares. You can cover the plane with a set of Wang tiles, as long as you choose the right one every step of the way. Or in the case of the carpets, grow the right one."

Karpal said, "We should call them Wang's Carpets, in honor of Hao Wang. After twenty-three hundred years, his mathematics has come to life."

Paolo liked the idea, but he was doubtful. "We may have trouble getting a two-thirds majority on that. It's a bit obscure . . ."

Hermann laughed. "Who needs a two-thirds majority? If we want to call them Wang's Carpets, we can call them Wang's Carpets. There are ninety-seven languages in current use in C-Z—half of them invented since the polis was founded. I don't think we'll be exiled for coining one private name."

Paolo concurred, slightly embarrassed. The truth was, he'd completely forgotten that Hermann and Karpal weren't actually speaking Modern Roman.

The three of them instructed their exoselves to consider the name adopted: henceforth, they'd hear "carpet" as "Wang's Carpet"—but if they used the term with anyone else, the reverse translation would apply.

Paolo sat and drank in the image of the giant alien: the first lifeform encountered by human or transhuman which was not a biological cousin. The death, at last, of the possibility that Earth might be unique.

They hadn't refuted the anthrocosmologists yet, though. Not quite. If, as the ACs claimed, human consciousness was the seed around which all of space-time had crystallized—if the universe was nothing but the simplest orderly explanation for human thought—then there was, strictly speaking, no need for a single alien to exist, anywhere. But the physics which justified human existence couldn't help generating a billion other worlds where life could arise. The ACs would be unmoved by Wang's Carpets; they'd insist that these creatures were physical, if not biological cousins—merely an unavoidable by-product of anthropogenic, life-enabling physical laws.

The real test wouldn't come until the diaspora—or the Gleisner robots—finally encountered conscious aliens: minds entirely unrelated to humanity, observing and explaining the universe which human thought had supposedly built. Most ACs had come right out and declared such a find impossible; it was the sole falsifiable prediction of their hypothesis. Alien consciousness, as opposed to mere alien life would always build itself a separate universe—because the chance of two unrelated forms of self-awareness concocting exactly the same physics and the same cosmology was infinitesimal—and any alien biosphere which seemed capable of evolving consciousness would simply never do so.

Paolo glanced at the map of the diaspora, and took heart. *Alien life already*—and the search had barely started; there were nine hundred and ninety-eight target systems yet to be explored. And even if every one of them proved no more conclusive than Orpheus . . . he was prepared to send clones out farther—and prepared to wait. Consciousness had taken far longer to appear on Earth than the quarter-of-a-billion years remaining before Vega left the main sequence—but the whole point of being here, after all, was that Orpheus wasn't Earth.

Orlando's celebration of the microprobe discoveries was a very first-generation affair. The environment was an endless sunlit garden strewn with tables covered in *food*, and the invitation had politely suggested attendance in fully human form. Paolo politely faked it—simulating most of the physiology, but running the body as a puppet, leaving his mind unshackled.

Orlando introduced his new lover, Catherine, who presented as a tall, dark-skinned woman. Paolo didn't recognize her on sight, but checked the identity code she broadcast. It was a small polis, he'd met her once before—as a man called Samuel, one of the physicists who'd worked on the main interstellar fusion drive employed by all the ships of the diaspora. Paolo was amused to think that many of the people here would be seeing his father as a woman. The majority of the citizens of C-Z still practiced the conventions of relative gender which had come into fashion in the twenty-third century—and Orlando had wired them into his own son too deeply for Paolo to wish to abandon them—but whenever the paradoxes were revealed so starkly, he wondered how much longer the conventions would endure. Paolo was same-sex to Orlando, and hence saw his father's lover as a woman, the two close relationships taking precedence over his casual knowledge of Catherine as Samuel. Orlando perceived himself as being male and heterosexual, as his flesh original had been . . . while Samuel saw himself the same way . . . and each perceived the other to be a heterosexual woman. If certain third parties ended up with mixed signals, so be it. It was a typical C-Z compromise: nobody could bear to overturn the old order and do away with gender entirely (as most other polises had done) . . . but nobody could resist the flexibility which being software, not flesh, provided.

Paolo drifted from table to table, sampling the food to keep up appearances, wishing Elena had come. There was little conversation about the biology of Wang's Carpets; most of the people here were simply celebrating their win against the opponents of the microprobes—and the humiliation that faction would suffer, now that it was clearer than ever that the "invasive" observations could have done no harm. Liesl's fears had proved unfounded; there was no other life in the ocean, just Wang's Carpets of various sizes. Paolo, feeling perversely even-handed after the fact, kept wanting to remind these smug movers and shakers: *There might have been anything down there. Strange creatures, delicate and vulnerable in ways we could never have anticipated. We were lucky, that's all.*

He ended up alone with Orlando almost by chance; they were both fleeing different groups of appalling guests when their paths crossed on the lawn.

Paolo asked, "How do you think they'll take this, back home?"

"It's first life, isn't it? Primitive or not. It should at least maintain interest in the diaspora, until the next alien biosphere is discovered." Orlando seemed subdued; perhaps he was finally coming to terms with the gulf between their modest discovery, and Earth's longing for world-shaking results. "And at least the chemistry is novel. If it had turned out to be based on DNA and protein, I think half of Earth C-Z would have died of boredom on the spot. Let's face it, the possibilities of DNA have been simulated to death."

Paolo smiled at the heresy. "You think if nature hadn't managed a little originality, it would have dented people's faith in the charter? If the solipsist polises had begun to look more inventive than the universe itself . . ."

"Exactly."

They walked on in silence, then Orlando halted, and turned to face him.

He said, "There's something I've been wanting to tell you. My Earth-self is dead."

"*What?*"

"Please, don't make a fuss."

"But . . . why? Why would he—?" *Dead* meant suicide; there was no other cause—unless the sun had turned red giant and swallowed everything out to the orbit of Mars.

"I don't know why. Whether it was a vote of confidence in the diaspora"—Orlando had chosen to wake only in the presence of alien life—"or whether he despaired of us sending back good news, and couldn't face the waiting, and the risk of disappointment. He didn't give a reason. He just had his exoself send a message, stating what he'd done."

Paolo was shaken. If a clone of *Orlando* had succumbed to pessimism, he couldn't begin to imagine the state of mind of the rest of Earth C-Z.

"When did this happen?"

"About fifty years after the launch."

"My Earth-self said nothing."

"It was up to me to tell you, not him."

"I wouldn't have seen it that way."

"Apparently, you would have."

Paolo fell silent, confused. How was he supposed to mourn a distant version of Orlando, in the presence of the one he thought of as real? Death of one clone was a strange half-death, a hard thing to come to terms with. His Earth-self had lost a father; his father had lost an Earth-self. What exactly did that mean to *him*?

What Orlando cared most about was Earth C-Z. Paolo said carefully, "Hermann told me there'd been a rise in emigration and suicide—until the spectroscope picked up the Orphean water. Morale has improved a lot since then—and when they hear that it's more than just water . . ."

Orlando cut him off sharply. "You don't have to talk things up for me. I'm in no danger of repeating the act."

They stood on the lawn, facing each other. Paolo composed a dozen different combinations of mood to communicate, but none of them felt right. He could have granted his father perfect knowledge of everything he was feeling—but what exactly would that knowledge have conveyed? In the end, there was fusion, or separateness. There was nothing in between.

Orlando said, "Kill myself—and leave the fate of transhumanity in your hands? You must be out of your fucking mind."

They walked on together, laughing.

➡

Karpal seemed barely able to gather his thoughts enough to speak. Paolo would have offered him a mind graft promoting tranquillity and concentration—distilled from his own most focused moments—but he was sure that Karpal would never have accepted it. He said, "Why don't you just start wherever you want to? I'll stop you if you're not making sense."

Karpal looked around the white dodecahedron with an expression of disbelief. "You live here?"

"Some of the time."

"But this is your base environment? No trees? No sky? No *furniture*?"

Paolo refrained from repeating any of Hermann's naive-robot jokes. "I add them when I want them. You know, like . . . music. Look, don't let my taste in decor distract you."

Karpal made a chair and sat down heavily.

He said, "Hao Wang proved a powerful theorem, twenty-three hundred years ago. Think of a row of Wang Tiles as being like the data tape of a Turing Machine." Paolo had the library grant him knowledge of the term; it was the original conceptual form of a generalized computing device, an imaginary machine which moved back and forth along a limitless one-dimensional data tape, reading and writing symbols according to a given set of rules.

"With the right set of tiles, to force the right pattern, the next row of the tiling will look like the data tape after the Turing Machine has performed one step of its computation. And the row after that will be the data tape after two steps, and so on. For any given Turing Machine, there's a set of Wang Tiles which can imitate it."

Paolo nodded amiably. He hadn't heard of this particular quaint result, but it was hardly surprising. "The carpets must be carrying out billions of acts of computation every second . . . but then, so are the water molecules around them. There are no physical processes which don't perform arithmetic of some kind."

"True. But with the carpets, it's not quite the same as random molecular motion."

"Maybe not."

Karpal smiled, but said nothing.

"What? You've found a pattern? Don't tell me: our set of twenty thousand polysaccharide Wang Tiles just happens to form the Turing Machine for calculating pi."

"No. What they form is a universal Turing Machine. They can calculate anything at all—depending on the data they start with. Every daughter fragment is like a program being fed to a chemical computer. Growth executes the program."

"Ah." Paolo's curiosity was roused—but he was having some trouble picturing where the hypothetical Turing Machine put its read/write head. "Are you telling me only one tile changes between any two rows, where the 'machine' leaves its mark on the 'data tape'...?" The mosaics he'd seen were a riot of complexity, with no two rows remotely the same.

Karpal said, "No, no. Wang's original example worked exactly like a standard Turing Machine, to simplify the argument . . . but the carpets are more like an arbitrary number of different computers with overlapping data, all working in parallel. This is biology, not a designed machine—it's as messy and wild as, say . . . a mammalian genome. In fact, there are mathematical similarities with gene regulation: I've identified Kauffman networks at every level, from the tiling rules up; the whole system's poised on the hyperadaptive edge between frozen and chaotic behavior."

Paolo absorbed that, with the library's help. Like Earth life, the carpets seemed to have evolved a combination of robustness and flexibility which would have maximized their power to take advantage of natural selection. Thousands of different autocatalytic chemical networks must have arisen soon after the formation of Orpheus—but as the ocean chemistry and the climate changed in the Vegan system's early traumatic millennia, the ability to respond to selection pressure had itself been selected for, and the carpets were the result. Their complexity seemed redundant, now, after a hundred million years of relative stability—and no predators or competition in sight—but the legacy remained.

"So if the carpets have ended up as universal computers . . . with no real need anymore to respond to their surroundings . . . what are they *doing* with all that computing power?"

Karpal said solemnly, "I'll show you."

Paolo followed him into an environment where they drifted above a schematic of a carpet, an abstract landscape stretching far into the distance, elaborately wrinkled like the real thing, but otherwise heavily stylized, with each of the polysaccharide building blocks portrayed as a square tile with four different colored edges. The adjoining edges of neighboring tiles bore complementary colors—to represent the complementary, interlocking shapes of the borders of the building blocks.

"One group of microprobes finally managed to sequence an entire daughter fragment," Karpal explained, "although the exact edges it started life with are largely guesswork, since the thing was growing while they were trying to map it." He gestured impatiently, and all the wrinkles and folds were smoothed away, an irrelevant distraction. They moved to one border of the ragged-edged carpet, and Karpal started the simulation running.

Paolo watched the mosaic extending itself, following the tiling rules perfectly—an orderly mathematical process, here: no chance collisions of radicals with catalytic sites, no mismatched borders between two new-grown neighboring "tiles" triggering the disintegration of both. Just the distillation of the higher-level consequences of all that random motion.

Karpal led Paolo up to a height where he could see subtle patterns being woven, overlapping multiplexed periodicities drifting across the growing edge, meeting and sometimes interacting, sometimes passing right through each other. Mobile pseudo-attractors, quasi-stable wave-forms in a one-dimensional universe. The carpet's second dimension was more like time than space, a permanent record of the history of the edge.

Karpal seemed to read his mind. "One dimensional. Worse than flat-land. No connectivity, no complexity. What can possibly happen in a system like that? Nothing of interest, right?"

He clapped his hands and the environment exploded around Paolo. Trails of color streaked across his sensorium, entwining, then disinte-grating into luminous smoke.

"Wrong. Everything goes on in a multidimensional frequency space. I've Fourier-transformed the edge into over a thousand components, and there's independent information in all of them. We're only in a narrow cross-section here, a sixteen-dimensional slice—but it's oriented to show the principal components, the maximum detail."

Paolo spun in a blur of meaningless color, utterly lost, his surroundings beyond comprehension. "You're a *Gleisner robot*, Karpal! *Only* sixteen di-mensions! How can you have done this?"

Karpal sounded hurt, wherever he was. "Why do you think I came to C-Z? I thought you people were flexible!"

"What you're doing is . . ." *What*? Heresy? There was no such thing. Officially. "Have you shown this to anyone else?"

"Of course not. Who did you have in mind? Liesl? *Hermann*?"

"Good. I know how to keep my mouth shut." Paolo invoked his exoself and moved back into the dodecahedron. He addressed the empty room. "How can I put this? The physical universe has three spatial dimensions, plus time. Citizens of Carter-Zimmerman inhabit the physical universe. Higher dimensional mind games are for the solipsists." Even as he said it, he realized how pompous he sounded. It was an arbitrary doctrine, not some great moral principle.

But it was the doctrine he'd lived with for twelve hundred years.

Karpal replied, more bemused than offended, "It's the only way to see what's going on. The only sensible way to apprehend it. Don't you want to know what the carpets are *actually like*?"

Paolo felt himself being tempted. Inhabit a *sixteen-dimensional slice of a thousand-dimensional frequency space*? But it was in the service of under-standing a real physical system—not a novel experience for its own sake.

And nobody had to find out.

He ran a quick—non-sapient—self-predictive model. There was a ninety-three percent chance that he'd give in, after fifteen subjective minutes of agonizing over the decision. It hardly seemed fair to keep Karpal waiting that long.

He said, "You'll have to loan me your mind-shaping algorithm. My exoself wouldn't know where to begin."

When it was done, he steeled himself, and moved back into Karpal's environment. For a moment, there was nothing but the same meaningless blur as before.

Then everything suddenly crystallized.

Creatures swam around them, elaborately branched tubes like mobile coral, vividly colored in all the hues of Paolo's mental palette—Karpal's attempt to cram in some of the information that a mere sixteen dimensions couldn't show? Paolo glanced down at his own body—nothing was missing, but he could see *around* it in all the thirteen dimensions in which it was nothing but a pin-prick; he quickly looked away. The "coral" seemed far more natural to his altered sensory map, occupying sixteen-space in all directions, and shaded with hints that it occupied much more. And Paolo had no doubt that it was "alive"—it looked more organic than the carpets themselves, by far.

Karpal said, "Every point in this space encodes some kind of quasi-periodic pattern in the tiles. Each dimension represents a different characteristic size—like a wavelength, although the analogy's not precise. The position in each dimension represents other attributes of the pattern, relating to the particular tiles it employs. So the localized systems you see around you are clusters of a few billion pattern, all with broadly similar attributes at similar wavelengths."

They moved away from the swimming coral, into a swarm of something like jellyfish: floppy hyperspheres waving wispy tendrils (each one of them more substantial than Paolo). Tiny jewel-like creatures darted among them. Paolo was just beginning to notice that nothing moved here like a solid object drifting through normal space; motion seemed to entail a shimmering deformation at the leading hypersurface, a visible process of disassembly and reconstruction.

Karpal led him on through the secret ocean. There were helical worms, coiled together in groups of indeterminate number—each single creature breaking up into a dozen or more wriggling slivers, and then recombining . . . although not always from the same parts. There were dazzling multicolored stemless flowers, intricate hypercones of "gossamer-thin" fifteen-dimensional petals—each one a hypnotic fractal labyrinth of crevices and capillaries. There were clawed monstrosities, writhing knots of sharp insectile parts like an orgy of decapitated scorpions.

Paolo said, uncertainly, "You could give people a glimpse of this in just three dimensions. Enough to make it clear that there's . . . *life* in here. This is going to shake them up badly, though." Life—embedded in the accidental computations of Wang's Carpets, with no possibility of ever relating to the world outside. This was an affront to Carter-Zimmerman's whole philosophy: if nature had evolved "organisms" as divorced from reality as the inhabitants of the most inward-looking polis, where was the privileged status of the physical universe, the clear distinction between truth and illusion?

And after three hundred years of waiting for good news from the diaspora, how would they respond to this back on Earth?

Karpal said, "There's one more thing I have to show you."

He'd named the creatures squids, for obvious reasons. *Distant cousins of the jellyfish, perhaps?* They were prodding each other with their tentacles in a way which looked thoroughly carnal—but Karpal explained, "There's no analog of light here. We're viewing all this according to ad hoc rules which have nothing to do with the native physics. All the creatures here gather information about each other by contact alone—which is actually quite a rich means of exchanging data, with so many dimensions. What you're seeing is communication by touch."

"Communication about what?"

"Just gossip, I expect. Social relationships."

Paolo stared at the writhing mass of tentacles.

"You think they're *conscious?*"

Karpal, point-like, grinned broadly. "They have a central control structure with more connectivity than the human brain—and which correlates data gathered from the skin. I've mapped that organ, and I've started to analyze its function."

He led Paolo into another environment, a representation of the data structures in the "brain" of one of the squids. It was—mercifully—three-dimensional, and highly stylized, built of translucent colored blocks marked with icons, representing mental symbols, linked by broad lines indicating the major connections between them. Paolo had seen similar diagrams of transhuman minds; this was far less elaborate, but eerily familiar nonetheless.

Karpal said, "Here's the sensory map of its surroundings. Full of other squids' bodies, and vague data on the last known positions of a few smaller creatures. But you'll see that the symbols activated by the physical presence of the other squids are linked to these"—he traced the connection with one finger—"representations. Which are crude miniatures of *this whole structure* here."

"This whole structure" was an assembly labeled with icons for memory retrieval, simple tropisms, short-term goals. The general business of being and doing.

"The squid has maps, not just of other squids' bodies, but their minds as well. Right or wrong, it certainly tries to know what the others are thinking about. And"—he pointed out another set of links, leading to another, less crude, miniature squid mind—"it thinks about its own thoughts as well. I'd call that *consciousness*, wouldn't you?"

Paolo said weakly, "You've kept all this to yourself? You came this far, without saying a word—?"

Karpal was chastened. "I know it was selfish—but once I'd decoded the interactions of the tile patterns, I couldn't tear myself away long enough to start explaining it to anyone else. And I came to you first because I wanted your advice on the best way to break the news."

Paolo laughed bitterly. "The best way to break the news that *first alien consciousness* is hidden deep inside a biological computer? That everything the diaspora was trying to prove has been turned on its head? The best way to explain to the citizens of Carter-Zimmerman that after a three-hundred-year journey, they might as well have stayed on Earth running simulations with as little resemblance to the physical universe as possible?"

Karpal took the outburst in good humor. "I was thinking more along the lines of the *best way to point out* that if we hadn't traveled to Orpheus and studied Wang's Carpets, we'd never have had the chance to tell the solipsists of Ashton-Laval that all their elaborate invented lifeforms and exotic imaginary universes pale into insignificance compared to what's really out here—and which only the Carter-Zimmerman diaspora could have found."

●

Paolo and Elena stood together on the edge of Satellite Pinatubo, watching one of the scout probes aim its maser at a distant point in space. Paolo thought he saw a faint scatter of microwaves from the beam as it collided with iron-rich meteor dust. *Elena's mind being diffracted all over the cosmos?* Best not think about that.

He said, "When you meet the other versions of me who haven't experienced Orpheus, I hope you'll offer them mind grafts so they won't be jealous."

She frowned. "Ah. Will I or won't I? I can't be bothered modeling it. I expect I will. You should have asked me before I cloned myself. No need for jealousy, though. There'll be worlds far stranger than Orpheus."

"I doubt it. You really think so?"

"I wouldn't be doing this if I didn't believe that." Elena had no power to change the fate of the frozen clones of her previous self—but everyone had the right to emigrate.

Paolo took her hand. The beam had been aimed almost at Regulus, UV—hot and bright, but as he looked away, the cool yellow light of the sun caught his eye.

Vega C-Z was taking the news of the squids surprisingly well, so far. Karpal's way of putting it had cushioned the blow: it was only by traveling all this distance across the real, physical universe that they could have made such a discovery—and it was amazing how pragmatic even the most doctrinaire citizens had turned out to be. Before the launch, "alien solipsists" would have been the most unpalatable idea imaginable, the most abhorrent thing the diaspora could have stumbled upon—but now that they were here, and stuck with the fact of it, people were finding ways to view it in a better light. Orlando had even proclaimed, "This will be the perfect hook for the marginal polises. 'Travel through real space to witness a truly alien virtual reality.' We can sell it as a synthesis of the two world views."

Paolo still feared for Earth, though—where his Earth-self and others were waiting in hope of alien guidance. Would they take the message of Wang's Carpets to heart, and retreat into their own hermetic worlds, oblivious to physical reality?

And he wondered if the anthrocosmologists had finally been refuted . . . or not. Karpal had discovered alien consciousness—but it was sealed inside a cosmos of its own, its perceptions of itself and its surroundings neither reinforcing nor conflicting with human and transhuman explanations of reality. It would be millennia before C-Z could untangle the ethical problems of daring to try to make contact . . . assuming that both Wang's Carpets, and the inherited data patterns of the squids, survived that long.

Paolo looked around at the wild splendor of the star-choked galaxy, felt the disk reach in and cut right through him. *Could all this strange haphazard beauty be nothing but an excuse for those who beheld it to exist? Nothing but the sum of all the answers to all the questions humans and transhumans had ever asked the universe—answers created in the asking?*

He couldn't believe that—but the question remained unanswered.

So far.

A Dance to Strange Musics

GREGORY BENFORD

Gregory Benford is one of the modern giants of the field. His 1980 novel Timescape *won the Nebula Award, the John W. Campbell Memorial Award, the British Science Fiction Association Award, and the Australian Ditmar Award and is widely considered to be one of the classic novels of the last two decades. His other novels include* The Stars in Shroud, In the Ocean of Night, Against Infinity, Artifact, Across the Sea of Suns, Great Sky River, Tides of Light, Furious Gulf, *and* Sailing Bright Eternity. *His short work has been collected in* Matter's End. *His most recent books are a new addition to Isaac Asimov's* Foundation *series,* Foundation's Fear; *a new solo novel,* Cosm; *and a nonfiction collection,* Deep Time. *Coming up is a new novel, about the exploration of Mars,* The Martian Race. *Benford is a professor of physics at the University of California, Irvine, and is one of the regular science columnists for* The Magazine of Fantasy & Science Fiction.

Benford has written almost as much about explorers and exploration as Arthur C. Clarke, certainly as much or more than any other writer of his generation. His most popular series, the Galactic Center *series of novels and stories (the latest of which is* Sailing Bright Eternity), *takes us tens of thousand of years into the future and into the core of the galaxy itself, where imical machine civilizations relentlessly hunt down the few remaining survivors of the organic societies they've destroyed, including that of Earth; he's also given us vivid glimpses of the tribulations of the first astronauts to explore Mars, in stories such as "All the Beer on Mars" and (with Elisabeth Malartre) "A Cold, Dry Cradle."*

Here he takes us along with the first Earth expedition to leave the solar system and attempt to explore the planets of another star . . . explorers who soon learn that you shouldn't look into the abyss if you don't want the abyss to look back.

I

The first crewed starship, the *Adventurer*, hung like a gleaming metallic moon among the gyre of strange worlds. Alpha Centauri was a triple-star system. A tiny flare star dogged the two big suns. At this moment in its eternal dance, the brilliant mote swung slightly toward Sol. Even though it was far from the two bright stars it was the nearest star to Earth: Proxima.

The two rich, yellow stars defined the Centauri system. Still prosaically termed A and B, they swam about each other, ignoring far Proxima.

The *Adventurer*'s astronomer, John, dopplered in on both stars, refreshing memories that were lodged deep. The climax of his career loomed before him. He felt apprehension, excitement, and a thin note of something like fear.

Sun B had an orbital eccentricity of 0.52 about its near-twin, with the extended axis of its ellipse 23.2 astronomical units long. This meant that the closest approach between A and B was a bit farther than the distance of Saturn from Sol.

A was a hard yellow-white glare, a G star with 1.08 the Sun's mass. Its companion, B, was a K-class star that glowed a reddish yellow, since it had 0.88 times the Sun's mass. B orbited with a period of 80 years around A. These two were about 4.8 billion years of age, slightly older than Sol. Promising.

Sun A's planetary children had stirred *Adventurer*'s expedition forth from Earth. From Luna, the system's single Earth-class planet was a mere mote, first detected by an oxygen absorption line in its spectrum. Only a wobbly image could be resolved by Earth's kilometer-sized interferometric telescope, a long bar with mirror-eyes peering in the spaces between A and B. Just enough of an image to entice.

A new Earth? John peered at its shrouded majesty, feeling the slight hum and surge of their ship beneath him. They were steadily moving inward, exploring the Newtonian gavotte of worlds in this two-sunned ballroom of the skies. Proxima was so far away, it was not even a wall-flower.

The Captain had named the fresh planet Shiva. It hung close to A, wreathed in water cirrus, a cloudball dazzling beneath A's simmering yellow-white glare. Shimmering with promise, it had beckoned to John for years during their approach.

Like Venus, but the gases don't match, he thought. The complex tides of the star system massaged Shiva's depths, releasing gases and rippling the crust. John's many-frequency probings had told him a lot, but how to stitch data into a weave of a world? He was the first astronomer to try out centuries of speculative thinking on a real planet.

Shiva was drier than Earth, oceans taking only 40 percent of the surface. Its air was heavy in nitrogen, with giveaway tags of 18 percent oxygen and traces of carbon dioxide; remarkably Earth-like Shiva was too warm for comfort, in human terms, but not fatally so; no Venusian runaway greenhouse had developed here. How had Shiva escaped that fate?

Long before, the lunar telescopes had made one great fact clear: The atmosphere here was far, far out of chemical equilibrium. Biological theory held that this was inevitably the signature of life. And indeed, the expedition's first mapping had shown that green, abundant life clung to two well-separated habitable belts, each beginning about 30 degrees from the equator.

Apparently the weird tidal effects of the Centauri system had stolen Shiva's initial polar tilt. Such steady workings had now made its spin align to within a single degree with its orbital angular momentum, so that conditions were steady and calm. The equatorial belt was a pale, arid waste of perpetual tornadoes and blistering gales.

John close-upped in all available bands, peering at the planet's crescent. Large blue-green seas, but no great oceans. Particularly, no water links between the two milder zones, so no marine life could migrate between them. Land migrations, calculations showed, were effectively blocked by the great equatorial desert. Birds might make the long flight, John considered, but what evolutionary factor would condition them for such hardship? And what would be the reward? Why fight the jagged mountain chains? Better to lounge about in the many placid lakes.

A strange world, well worth the decades of grinding, slow, starship flight, John thought. He asked for the full display and the observing bowl opened like a flower around him. He swam above the entire disk of the Centauri system now, the images sharp and rich.

To be here at last! *Adventurer* was only a mote among many—yet *here*, in the lap of strangeness. Far Centauri.

It did not occur to him that humanity had anything truly vital to lose here. The doctrine of expansion and greater knowledge had begun seven centuries before, making European cultures the inheritors of Earth. Although science had found unsettling truths, even those revelations had not blunted the agenda of ever-greater knowledge. After all, what harm could come from merely looking?

◆

The truth about Shiva's elevated ocean only slowly emerged. Its very existence was plainly impossible, and therefore was not at first believed.

Odis was the first to notice the clues. Long days of sensory immersion in the data-streams repaid her. She was rather proud of having plucked such exotica from the bath of measurements their expedition got from their probes—the tiny speeding, smart spindle-eyes that now cruised all over the double-stars realm.

The Centauri system was odd, but even its strong tides could not explain this anomaly. Planets should be spherical, or nearly so; Earth bulged but a fraction of a percent at its equator, due to its spin. Not Shiva, though.

Odis found aberrations in this world's shape. The anomalies were far away from the equator, principally at the 1,694-kilometer-wide deep blue sea, immediately dubbed the Circular Ocean. It sat in the southern hemisphere, its nearly perfect ring hinting at an origin as a vast crater. Odis could not take her gaze from it, a blue eye peeking coyly at them through the clouds: a planet looking back.

Odis made her ranging measurements, gathering in her data like number-clouds, inhaling their cottony wealth. Beneath her, *Adventurer* prepared to go into orbit about Shiva.

She breathed in the banks of data-vapor, translated by her kinesthetic programming into intricate scent-inventories. Tangy complex.

At first she did not believe the radar reflections. Contours leap into view, artfully sketched by the mapping radars. Calibratio checked, though, so she tried other methods: slow, analytic tedious hard to do in her excitement. They gave the same result.

The Circular Ocean stood a full 10 kilometers higher than the continent upon which it rested.

No mountains surrounded it. It sat like some cosmic magic trick, insolently demanding an explanation.

Odis presented her discovery at the daily Oversight Group meeting. There was outright skepticism, even curled lips of derision, snorts of disbelief. "The range of methods is considerable," she said adamantly. "These results cannot be wrong."

"Only thing to resolve this," a lanky geologist said, "is get an edge-on view."

"I hoped someone would say that." Odis smiled. "Do I have the authorized observing time?"

They gave it reluctantly. *Adventurer* was orbiting in a severe ellipse about Shiva's cloud-wrack. Her long swing brought her into a side view of the target area two days later. Odis used the full panoply optical, IR, UV, and microwave instruments to peer at the Circular Ocean's perimeter, probing for the basin that supported the round slab of azure water.

There was none. No land supported the hanging sea.

This result was utterly clear. The Circular Ocean was 1.36 kilometers thick and a brilliant blue. Spectral evidence suggested water rich in salt, veined by thick currents. It looked exactly like an enormous, troubled mountain lake, with the mountain subtracted.

Beneath that layer there was nothing but the thick atmosphere. No rocky mountain range to support the ocean-in-air. Just a many-Kilometer gap.

All other observations halted. The incontrovertible pictures showed an immense layer of unimaginable weight, blissfully poised above mere thin gases, contradicting all known mechanics. Until this moment Odis had been a lesser figure in the expedition. Now her work captivated everyone and she was the center of every conversation. The concrete impossibility yawned like an inviting abyss.

☞

Lissa found the answer to Shiva's mystery, but no one was happy with it.

An atmospheric chemist, Lissa's job was mostly done well before they achieved orbit around Shiva. She had already probed and labeled the gasses, shown clearly that they implied a thriving biology below. After that, she had thought, the excitement would shift elsewhere, to the surface observers.

Not so. Lissa took a deep breath and began speaking to the Oversight Group. She had to show that she was not wasting their time. With all eyes on the Circular Ocean, few cared for mere air.

Yet it was the key, Lissa told them. The Circular Ocean had intrigued her, too: so she looked at the mixture of oxygen, nitrogen, and carbon dioxide that apparently supported the floating sea. These proved perfectly ordinary, almost Earth-standard, except for one oddity. Their spectral lines were slightly split, so that she found two small spikes to the right and left of where each line should be.

Lissa turned from the images she projected before the Oversight Group. "The only possible interpretation," she said crisply, "is that an immensely strong electric field is inducing the tiny electric dipoles of these molecules to move. That splits the lines."

"An *electric* shift?" a grizzled skeptic called. "In a charge-neutral atmosphere? Sure, maybe when lightning flashes you could get momentary effect, but—"

"It is steady."

"You looked for lightning?" a shrewd woman demanded.

"It's there, sure. We see if forking between the clouds below the Circular Ocean. But that's not what causes the electric fields."

"What does?" This from the grave captain, who never spoke in scientific disputes. All heads turned to him, then to Lissa.

She shrugged. "Nothing reasonable." It pained her to admit it, but ignorance was getting to be a common currency.

A voice called, "So there must be an impossibly strong electric field *everywhere* in that 10 kilometers of air below the ocean?" Murmurs of agreement. Worried frowns.

"Everywhere, yes." The bald truth of it stirred the audience. "Everywhere."

◆

Tagore was in a hurry. Too much so.

He caromed off a stanchion but did not let that stop him from rebounding from the opposite wall, absorbing his momentum with his knees, and springing off with a full push. Rasters streaked his augmented vision, then flickered and faded.

He coasted by a full-view showing Shiva and the world below, a blazing crescent transcendent in its cloud-wrapped beauty. Tagore ignored the spectacle; marvels of the mind preoccupied him.

He was carrying the answer to it all, he was sure of that. In his haste he did not even glance at how blue-tinged sunlight glinted from the Circular Ocean. The thick disk of open air below it made a clear line under the blue wedge. At this angle the floating water refracted sunlight around the still-darkened limb of the planet. The glittering azure jewel heralded dawn, serene in its impudent impossibility.

The youngest of the entire expedition, Tagore was a mere theorist. He had specialized in planetary formation at university, but managed to snag a berth on this expedition by developing a ready, quick facility at explaining vexing problems the observers turned up. That, and a willingness to do scutwork.

"Cap'n, I've got it," he blurted as he came through the hatch. The captain greeted him, sitting at small oak desk, the only wood on the whole ship—then got to business. Tagore had asked for this audience because he knew the effect his theory could have on the others; so the captain should see first.

"The Circular Ocean is held up by electric field pressure," he announced. The captain's reaction was less than he had hoped: unblinking calm, waiting for more information.

"See, electromagnetic fields exert forces on the electrons in atoms," Tagore persisted, going through the numbers, talking fast. "The fields down there are so strong—I got that measurement out of Lissa's data— they can act like a steady support."

He went on to make comparisons: the energy density of a hand grenade, contained in every suitcase-sized volume of air. Even though the fields could simply stand there, as trapped waves, they had to suffer some losses. The power demands were *huge*. Plus, how the hell did such a gargantuan construction *work*?

By now Tagore was thoroughly pumped, oblivious to his audience.

Finally the captain blinked and said, "Anything like this ever seen on Earth?"

"Nossir, not that I've ever heard."

"No natural process can do the stunt?"

"Nossir, not that I can imagine."

"Well, we came looking for something different."

Tagore did not know whether to laugh or not; the captain was unreadable. Was this what exploration was like—the slow anxiety of not knowing? On Earth such work had an abstract distance, but here . . .

He would rather have some other role. Bringing uncomfortable truths to those in power put him more in the spotlight than he wished.

━

Captain Badquor let the Tagore kid go on a bit longer before he said anything more. It was best to let these technical types sing their songs first. So few of them ever thought about anything beyond their own warblings.

He gave Tagore a captainly smile. Why did they all look so young? "So this whole big thing on Shiva is artificial."

"Well, yeah, I suppose so . . ."

Plainly Tagore hadn't actually thought about that part very much; the wonder of such strong fields had stunned him. Well, it was stunning. "And all that energy, just used to hold up a lake?"

"I'm sure of it, sir. The numbers work out, see? I equated the pressure exerted by those electric fields, assuming they're trapped in the volume under the Circular Ocean, the way waves can get caught if they're inside a conducting box—"

"You think that ocean's conductor?" Might as well show the kid that even the captain knew a little physics. In fact, though he never mentioned it, he had a doctorate from MIT Not that he had learned much about command there.

"Uh, well, no. I mean, it is a fairly good conductor, but for my model, it's only a way of speaking—"

"It has salt currents, true? They could carry electrical currents." The captain rubbed his chin, the machinery of his mind trying to grasp how such a thing could be. "Still, that doesn't explain why the thing doesn't evaporate away, at those altitudes."

"Uh, I really hadn't thought . . ."

The captain waved a hand. "Go on." *Sing for me.*

"Then the waves exert an upward force on the water every time they reflect from the underside of the ocean—"

"And transfer that weight down, on invisible waves, to the rock that's 10 kilometers below."

"Uh, yessir."

Tagore looked a bit constipated, bursting with enthusiasm, with the experience of the puzzle, but not knowing how to express it. The captain decided to have mercy on the kid. "Sounds good. Not anything impossible about it."

"Except the *size* of it, sir."

"That's one way to put it."

"Sir?"

A curious, powerful feeling washed over the captain. Long decades of anticipation had steeled him, made him steady in the presence of the crew. But now he felt his sense of the room tilt, as though he were losing control of his status-space. The mind could go whirling off, out here in the inky immensities between twin alien suns. He frowned. "This thing is bigger than anything humanity ever built. And there's not a clue what it's for. The majesty of it, son, that's what strikes me. Grandeur."

●

John slipped into his helmet and Shiva enclosed him. *To be wrapped in a world*—His pov shifted, strummed, arced with busy fretworks—then snapped into solidity, stabilized.

Astronomy had become intensely interactive in the past century, the spectral sensoria blanketing the viewer. Through *Adventurer*'s long voyage he had tuned the system to his every whim. Now it gave him a nuanced experience like a true, full-bodied immersion.

He was eager to immerse himself in the *feel* of Shiva, in full 3-D wrap-around. Its crescent swelled below like a ripe, mottled fruit. He plunged toward it. A planet, fat in bandwidth.

For effect—decades before he had been a sky-diver—John had arranged the data-fields so that he accelerated into it. From their arcing orbit he shot directly toward Shiva's disk. Each mapping rushed toward him, exploding upward in finer detail. *There*—

The effect showed up first in the grasslands of the southern habitable belt. He slewed toward the plains, where patterns emerged in quilted confusions. After Tagore's astonishing theory about the Circular Ocean—odd, so audacious, and coming from a nonscientist—John had to be ready for anything. Somewhere in the data-fields must lurk the clue to who or what had made the ocean.

Below, the great grassy shelves swelled. But in places the grass was thin. Soon he saw why. The natural grass was only peeking out across plains covered with curious orderly patterns—hexagonals folding into triangles where necessary to cover hills and valleys, right up to the muddy banks of the slow-moving brown rivers.

Reflection in the UV showed that the tiles making this pattern were often small, but with some the size of houses, meters thick . . . and moving. They all jostled and worked with restless energy to no obvious purpose.

Alive? The UV spectrum broke down into a description of a complex polymer. Cross-linked chains bonded at many oblique angles to each other, flexing like sleek micro-muscles.

John brought in chemists, biologists in an ensemble suite: Odis and Lissa chimed in the scientific choir. In the wraparound display he felt them by the shadings they gave the data.

The tiles, Lissa found, fed on their own sky. Simple sugars rained from the clotted air, the fruit of an atmosphere that resembled an airy chicken soup. *Atmospheric electro-chemistry seems responsible, somehow*, Lissa sent. Floating microbial nuggets moderated the process.

The tiles were prime eaters. Oxidizing radicals the size of golf balls patroled their sharp linear perimeters. These pack-like rollers attacked invader chemicals, ejecting most, harvesting those they could use.

Lissa brought in two more biologists, who of course had many questions. *Are these tiles like great turtles?* one ventured, then chuckled uneasily. They yearned to flip one over.

Diurnal or nocturnal? *Some are, most aren't.*

Are there any small one? *A few.*

Do they divide by fission? *No, but. . . .* Nobody understood the complicated process the biologists witnessed. Reproduction seems a tricky matter.

There is some periodicity to their movements, some slow rhythms, and particularly a fast Fourier-spectrum spike at 1.27 seconds—but again, no clear reason for it.

Could they be all one life form?—could that be?

A whole planet taken over by a tiling-thing that co-opts all resources? The senior biologists scoffed. How could a species evolve to have only one member? And an ecosystem—a whole world!—with so few parts?

Evolution ruled that out. Bio-evolution, that is. But not social evolution.

John plunged further into the intricate matrices of analysis. The endless tile-seas cloaking mountains and valleys shifted and nuilled, fidgety, only occasionally leaving bare ground visible as a square fissioned into triangles. Oblongs met and butted with fevered energy.

Each hemisphere of the world was similar, though the tiles in the north had different shapes—pentagonals, mostly. Nowhere did the tiles cross rivers but they could ford streams. A Centauri variant of chlorophyll was everywhere, in the oceans and rivers, but not in the Circular Ocean.

The ground was covered with a thin grass, the sprigs living off the momentary sunlight that slipped between the edges in the jostling, jiggling, bumping, and shaking. Tiles that moved over the grass sometimes cropped it, sometimes not, leaving stubs that seemed to have been burned off.

The tiles' fevered dance ran incessantly, without sleep. Could these things be performing some agitated discourse, a lust-fest without end?

John slowed his descent. The tiles were a shock. Could these be the builders of the Circular Ocean? Time for the biologists to get to work.

◆

The computer folk thought one way, the biologists—after an initial rout, when they rejected the very possibility of a single entity filling an entire biosphere—quite another.

After some friction, their views converged somewhat. A biologist remarked that the larger tiles came together like dwarf houses making love . . . gingerly, always presenting the same angles and edges.

Adventurer had scattered micro-landers all over the world. These showed only weak electromagnetic fringing fields among the tiles. Their deft collisions seemed almost like neurons in a two-dimensional plan.

The analogy stirred the theorists. Over the usual after-shift menu of beer, soy nuts, and friendly insults, one maven of the digital realm ventured an absurd idea: Could the planet have become a computer?

Everybody laughed. They kidded the advocate of this notion . . . and then lapsed into frowning silence. Specialists find quite unsettling those ideas that cross disciplines.

Could a species turn itself into a biological computer? The tiles did rub and caress each other in systematic ways. Rather than carrying information in digital fashion, maybe they used a more complex language of position and angle, exploiting their planar geometry. If so, the information density flowing among them was immense. Every collision carried a sort of Euclidean talk, possibly rich in nuance.

The computer analogy brought up a next question—not that some big ones weren't left behind, perhaps lying in wait to bite them on their conceptual tail. Could the tiles know anything more than themselves? Or were they strange, geometroid solipsists? Should they call the tiles a single. It?

Sealed inside a cosmos of Its own making, was It even in principle interested in the outside world? Alpha Centauri fed It gratuitous energy, the very soupy air fueled It: the last standing power on the globe. What reason did it have to converse with the great Outside?

Curiosity, perhaps? The biologists frowned at the prospect. Curiosity in early prehumans was rewarded in the environment. The evolving ape learned new tricks, found fresh water, killed a new kind of game, invented a better way to locate those delicious roots—and the world duly paid it back.

Apparently—*but don't ask us why just yet!* the biologists cried—the game was different here. What reward came from the tiles' endless smacking together?

So even if the visiting humans rang the conceptual doorbell on the tile-things, maybe nobody would answer. Maybe nobody was home.

Should they try?

John and Odis and Lissa, Tagore and the captain, over a hundred other crew—they all pondered.

II

While they wrestled with the issue, exploration continued.

A flitter craft flew near the elevated ocean and inspected its supporting volume with distant sensors and probing telescopes. Even Shiva's weather patterns seemed wary of the Circular Ocean. Thunderclouds veered away from the gap between the ocean and the rugged land below. In the yawning height clouds formed but quickly dispersed, as if dissolved by unseen forces.

Birds flew through the space, birds like feathery kites.

Somehow they had missed noticing this class of life. Even the micro-landers had not had the speed to capture their darting lives. And while the kite-birds did seem to live mostly on tiny floating balloon-creatures that hovered in the murky air of the valleys, they were unusually common beneath the Circular Ocean.

John proposed that he send in a robo-craft of bird size, to measure physical parameters in the heart of the gap. Captain Badquor approved. The shops fabricated a convincing fake. Jet-powered and featuring fake feathers, it was reasonably convincing.

John flew escort in a rocket-plane. The bird-probe got 17 kilometers inside and then disappeared in a dazzling blue-white electrical discharge. Telemetry showed why: The Circular Ocean's support was a complex weave of electrical fields, supplying an upward pressure. These fields never exceeded the breakdown level of a megavolt per meter, above which Shiva's atmosphere would ionize. Field strength was about a million volts per meter.

The robo-craft had hit a critical peak in the field geometry. A conductor, it caused a flashover that dumped millions of watts into the bird within a millisecond.

As the cinder fell, John banked away from his monitoring position five kilometers beyond the gap perimeter. There was no particular reason to believe a discharge that deep within the gap would somehow spread, engulfing the region in a spontaneous discharge of the enormous stored energies. Surely whoever—no, whatever—had designed the Circular Ocean's supports would not allow the electromagnetic struts to collapse from the frying of a mere bird.

But something like that happened. The system responded.

The burned brown husk of the pseudo-bird turned lazily as it fell and sparks jumped from it. These formed a thin orange discharge that fed on the energy coursing through the now-atomized bird. The discharging line snaked away, following unerringly the bird's prior path. It raced at close to the speed of light back along the arc.

The system had *memory*, John realized. He saw a tendril of light at the corner of his vision as he turned his flitter craft. He had time only to think that it was like a huge, fast finger jabbing at him. An apt analogy, though he had no time to consider ironies. The orange discharge touched the flitter. John's hair stood on end as charge flooded into the interior.

Ideally, electrons move to the outer skin of a conductor. But when antennae connect deep into the interior, circuits can close.

Something had intended to dump an immense charge on the flitter, the origin of the pseudo-bird. Onboard instruments momentarily reported a charge exceeding 17 coulombs. By then John had, for all intents and purposes, ceased to exist as an organized bundle of electrical information.

◦

John's death did yield a harvest of data. Soon enough Lissa saw the true function of the Circular Ocean. It was but an ornament, perhaps an artwork.

Ozone fizzed all around it. Completely natural-seeming, the lake crowned a huge cavity that functioned like a steady, standing laser.

The electrical fields both supported ohe Ocean and primed the atoms of the entire atmosphere they permeated. Upon stimulus—from the same system that had fried John—the entire gap could release the stored energy into an outgoing electromagnetic wave. It was an optical bolt, powerful and complex in structure—triggered by John.

Twice more the ocean's gap discharged naturally as the humans orbited Shiva. The flash lasted but a second, not enough to rob the entire ocean structure of its stability. The emission sizzled out through the atmosphere and off into space.

Laser beams are tight, and this one gave away few of its secrets. The humans, viewing it from a wide angle, caught little of the complex structure and understood less.

Puzzled, mourning John, they returned to a careful study of the Shiva surface. Morale was low. The captain felt that a dramatic gesture could lift their spirits. He would have to do it himself.

◆

To Captain Badquor fell the honor of the first landing. A show of bravery would overcome the crew's confusions, surely. He would direct the complex exploring machines in real-time, up close.

He left the landing craft fully suited up, impervious to the complex biochem mix of the atmosphere.

The tiles jostled downhill from him. Only in the steep flanks of this equatorial mountain range did the tiles not endlessly surge. Badquor's boots crunched on a dry, crusty soil. He took samples, sent them back by runner-robo.

A warning signal from orbit: The tiles in his area seemed more agitated than usual. A reaction to his landing?

The tile polygons were leathery, with no obvious way to sense him. No eyes or ears. They seemed to caress the ground lovingly, though Badquor knew that they tread upon big crabbed feet.

He went forward cautiously. Below, the valley seemed alive with rippling turf, long waves sweeping to the horizon in the twinkling of an instant. He got an impression of incessant pace, of enthusiasm unspoken but plainly endless.

His boots were well insulated thermally, but not electrically; thus, when his headphones crackled he thought he was receiving noise in his transmission lines. The dry sizzle began to make his skin tingle.

Only when the frying noise rose and buried all other signals did he blink, alarmed. By then it was too late.

◆

Piezoelectric energy arises when mechanical stress massages rock. Pressure on an electrically neutral stone polarizes it at the lattice level by slightly separating the center of positive charge from the negative. The lattice moves, the shielding electron cloud does not. This happens whenever the rock crystal structure does not have a center of structural symmetry, and so occurs in nearly all bedrock.

The effect was well known on Earth, though weak. Stressed strata sometimes discharged, sending glow discharges into the air. Such plays of light were now a standard precursor warning of earthquakes. But Earth was a mild case.

Tides stressed the stony mantle of Shiva, driven by the eternal gravitational gavotte of both stars, A and B. Periodic alignments of the two stars stored enormous energy in the full body of the planet. Evolution favored life that could harness these electrical currents that rippled through the planetary crust. This, far more than the kilowatt per square meter of sunlight, drove the tile-forms.

All this explanation came after the fact, and seemed obvious in retrospect. The piezoelectric energy source was naturally dispersed and easily harvested. A sizzle of electric micro-fields fed the tiles' large, crusted footpads. After all, on Earth fish and eels routinely use electrical fields as both sensors and weapons.

This highly organized ecology sensed Badquor's intrusion immediately. To them, he probably had many of the signatures of a power-parasite. These were small creatures like stick insects that Badquor himself had noticed after landing; they lived by stealing electrical charge from the tile polygons.

Only later analysis made it clear what had happened. The inter-linked commonality of piezo-driven life moved to expel the intruder by overpowering it—literally.

Badquor probably had no inkling of how strange a fate he had met, for the several hundreds of amperes caused his muscles to seize up, his heart to freeze in a clamped frenzy, and his synapses to discharge in a last vision that burned into his eyes a vision of an incandescent rainbow.

➤

Lissa blinked. The spindly trees looked artificial, but weren't.

Groves of them spiraled around hills, zigzagged up razor-backed ridges and shot down the flanks of denuded rock piles. Hostile terrain for any sort of tree that earthly biologists understood. The trees, she noted, had growing patterns that bore no discernible relation to water flow, sunlight exposure, or wind patterns.

That was why Lissa went in to see. Her team of four had already sent the smart-eyes, rugged robots, and quasi-intelligent processors. Lightweight, patient, durable, these ambassadors had discovered little. Time for something a bit more interactive on the ground.

That is, a person. Captain Badquor's sacrifice had to mean something, and his death had strengthened his crew's resolve.

Lissa landed with electrically insulated boots. They now understood the piezoelectric ecology in broad outline, or thought they did. Courageous caution prevailed.

The odd beanpole trees made no sense. Their gnarled branches followed a fractal pattern and had no leaves. Still, there was ample fossil evidence—gathered by automatic prospectors sent down earlier—that the bristly trees had evolved from more traditional trees within the past few million years. But they had come so quickly into the geological record that Lissa suspected they were "driven" evolution—biological technology.

She carefully pressed her instruments against the sleek black sides of the trees. Their surfaces seethed with electric currents, but none strong enough to be a danger.

On Earth, the natural potential difference between the surface and the upper atmosphere provides a voltage drop of a hundred volts for each meter in height. A woman two meters tall could be at a significantly higher potential than her feet, especially if her feet had picked up extra electrons by walking across a thick carpet.

On Shiva this effect was much larger. The trees, Lissa realized, were harvesting the large potentials available between Shiva's rocky surface and the charged layers skating across the upper reaches of the atmosphere.

The "trees" were part of yet another way to reap the planetary energies—whose origin was ultimately the blunt forces of gravity, mass and torque—all for the use of life.

The potential-trees felt Lissa's presence quickly enough. They had evolved defenses against poachers who would garner stray voltages and currents from the unwary.

In concert—for the true living entity was the grove, comprising perhaps a million trees—they reacted.

Staggering back to her lander, pursued by vagrant electrical surges through both ground and the thick air, she shouted into her suit mike her conclusions. These proved useful in later analysis.

She survived, barely.

III

When the sum of these incidents sank in, the full import become clear. The entire Shiva ecology was electrically driven. From the planet's rotation and strong magnetosphere, from the tidal stretching of the Centauri system, from geological rumblings and compressions, came far more energy than mere sunlight could ever provide.

Seen this way, all biology was an afterthought. The geologists, who had been feeling rather neglected lately, liked this turn of events quite a bit. They gave lectures on Shiva seismology which, for once, everybody attended.

To be sure, vestigial chemical processes still ran alongside the vastly larger stores of charges and potentials; these were important for understanding the ancient biosphere that had once governed here.

Much could be learned from classic, old-style biology: from samples of the bushes and wiry trees and leafy plants, from the small insect-like creatures of 10 legs each, from the kite-birds, from the spiny, knife-like fish that prowled the lakes.

All these forms were ancient, unchanging. Something had fixed them in evolutionary amber. Their forms had not changed for many hundreds of millions of years.

There had once been higher forms, the fossil record showed. Something like mammals, even large tubular things that might have resembled reptiles.

But millions of years ago they had abruptly ceased. Not due to some trauma, either—they all ended together, but without the slightest sign of a shift in the biosphere, of disease or accident.

The suspicion arose that something had simply erased them, having no further need.

The highest form of life—defined as that with the highest brain/body volume ratio—had vanished slightly later than the others. It had begun as a predator wider than it was tall, and shaped like a turtle, though without a shell.

It had the leathery look of the tile-polygons, though.

Apparently it had not followed the classic mode of pursuit, but rather had outwitted its prey, boxing it in by pack-animal tactics. Later, it had arranged deadfalls and traps. Or so the sociobiologists suspected, from narrow evidence.

These later creatures had characteristic bony structures around the large, calculating brain. Subsequent forms were plainly intelligent, and had been engaged in a strange manipulation of their surroundings. Apparently without their inventing cities or agriculture, they had domesticated many other species.

Then, the other high life forms vanished from the fossil record. The scheme of the biosphere shifted. Electrical plant forms, like the spindly trees and those species that fed upon piezoelectric energy, came to the fore.

Next, the dominant, turtle-like predators vanished as well. Had they been dispatched?

On Shiva, all the forms humans thought of as life, plant and animal alike, were now in fact mere . . . well, maintenance workers. They served docilely in a far more complex ecology. They were as vital and as unnoticeable and as ignorable as the mitochondria in the stomach linings of *Adventurer*'s crew.

Of the immensely more complex electrical ecology, they were only beginning to learn even the rudiments. If Shiva was in a sense a single interdependent, colonial organism, what were its deep rules?

By focusing on the traditional elements of the organic biosphere they had quite missed the point.

Then the Circular Ocean's laser discharged again. The starship was nearer the lancing packet of emission, and picked up a side lobe. They learned more in a millisecond than they had in a month.

◆

A human brain has about 10 billion neurons, each connected with about 100,000 of its neighbors. A firing neuron carries one bit of information. But the signal depends upon the path it follows, and in the labyrinth of the brain there are 1,015 pathways. This torrent of information flows through the brain in machine-gun packets of electrical impulses, coursing through myriad synapses. Since a single book has about a million bits in it, a single human carries the equivalent of a billion books of information—all riding around in a two-kilogram lump of electrically wired jelly.

Only one to 10 percent of a human brain's connections are firing at any one time. A neuron can charge and discharge at best a hundred times in a second. Human brains, then, can carry roughly 1,010 bits of information in a second.

Thus, to read out a brain containing 1,015 bits would take 100,000 seconds, or about a day.

The turtle-predators had approximately the same capacity. Indeed, there were theoretical arguments that a mobile, intelligent species would carry roughly the same load of stored information as a human could. For all its limitations, the human brain has an impressive datastore capability, even if, in many, it frequently went unused.

The Circular Ocean had sent discrete packets of information of about this size, 1015 bits compressed into its powerful millisecond pulse. The packets within it were distinct, well bordered by banks of marker code. The representation was digital, an outcome mandated by the fact that any number enjoys a unique representation only in base 2.

Within the laser's millisecond burst were fully a thousand brain-equivalent transmissions. A trove. What the packets actually said was quite undecipherable.

The target was equally clear: a star 347 light years away. Targeting was precise; there could be no mistake. Far cheaper, if one knows the recipient, to send a focused message, rather than to broadcast wastefully in the low-grade, narrow bandwidth radio frequencies.

Earth had never heard such powerful signals, of course, not because humans were not straining to hear, but because Shiva was ignoring them.

◆

After Badquor's death and Lissa's narrow escape, *Adventurer* studied the surface with elaborately planned robot expeditions. The machines skirted the edge of a vast tile-plain, observing the incessant jiggling, fed on the piezoelectric feast welling from the crusted rocks.

After some days, they came upon a small tile lying still. The others had forced it out of the eternal jostling jam. It lay stiff and discolored, baking in the double suns' glare. Scarcely a meter across and thin, it looked like construction material for a patio in Arizona.

The robots carried it off. Nothing pursued them. The tile-thing was dead, apparently left for mere chemical processes to harvest its body.

This bonanza kept the ship's biologists sleepless for weeks as they dissected it. Gray-green, hard of carapace, and extraordinarily complex in its nervous system—these they had expected. But the dead alien devoted fully a quarter of its body volume to a brain that was broken into compact, separate segments.

The tile-creatures were indeed part of an ecology driven by electrical harvesting of the planetary energies. The tiles alone used a far higher percentage of the total energetic wealth than did Earth's entire sluggish, chemically driven biosphere.

And deep within the tile-thing was the same bone structure as they had seen in the turtle-like predator. The dominant, apparently intelligent species had not gone to the stars. Instead, they had formed the basis of an intricate ecology of the mind.

Then the engineers had a chance to study the tile-thing, and found even more.

As a manifestation of their world, the tiles were impressive. Their neurological system fashioned a skein of interpretations, of lived scenarios, of expressive renderings—all apparently for communication outward in well-sculpted bunches of electrical information, intricately coded. They had large computing capacity and ceaselessly exchanged great gouts of information with each other. This explained their rough skins, which maximized piezo connections when they rubbed against each other. And they "spoke" to each other through the ground, as well, where their big, crabbed feet carried currents, too.

Slowly it dawned that Shiva was an unimaginably huge computational complex, operating in a state of information flux many orders of magnitude greater than the entire sum of human culture. Shiva was to Earth as humans are to beetles.

◆

The first transmissions about Shiva's biosphere reached Earth four years later. Already, in a culture more than a century into the dual evolution of society and computers, there were disturbing parallels.

Some communities in the advanced regions of Earth felt that real-time itself was a pallid, ephemeral experience. After all, one could not archive it for replay, savor it, return until it became a true part of oneself. Real-time was for one time only, then lost.

So increasingly, some people lived instead in worlds made totally volitional—truncated, chopped, governed by technologies they could barely sense as ghostlike constraints on an otherwise wide compass.

"Disposable realities," some sneered—but the fascination of such lives was clear.

Shiva's implication was extreme: An entire world could give itself over to life-as-computation.

Could the intelligent species of Shiva have executed a huge fraction of their fellow inhabitants? And then themselves gone extinct? For what? Could they have fled—perhaps from the enormity of their own deeds?

Or had those original predators become the tile-polygons?

The *Adventurer* crew decided to return to Shiva's surface in force, to crack the puzzles. They notified Earth and descended.

◆

Shortly after, the Shiva teams ceased reporting back to Earth. Through the hiss of interstellar static there came no signal.

After years of anxious waiting, Earth launched the second expedition. They too survived the passage. Cautiously they approached Shiva.

Adventurer still orbited the planet, but was vacant.

This time they were wary. Further years of hard thinking and careful study passed before the truth began to come.

IV

—John/Odis/Lissa/Tagore/Cap'n—
  —all assembled/congealed/thickened—
  —into a composite veneer persona—
  —on the central deck of their old starship,
  —to greet the second expedition.
Or so they seemed to intend.
They came up from the Shiva surface in a craft not of human construction. The sleek, webbed thing seemed to ride upon electromagnetic winds.

They entered through the main lock, after using proper hailing protocols.

But what came through the lock was an ordered array of people no one could recognize as being from the *Adventurer* crew.

They seemed younger, unworn. Smooth, bland features looked out at the bewildered second expedition. The party moved together, maintaining a hexagonal array with a constant spacing of four centimeters. Fifty-six pairs of eyes surveyed the new Earth ship, each momentarily gazing at a different portion of the field of view, as if to memorize only a portion, for later integration.

To convey a sentence, each person spoke a separate word. The effect was jarring, with no clue to how an individual knew what to say, or when, for the lines were not rehearsed. The group reacted to questions in a blur of scattershot talk, words like volleys.

Sentences ricocheted and bounced around the assembly deck where the survivors of the first expedition all stood, erect and clothed in a shapeless gray garment. Their phrases made sense when isolated, but the experience of hearing them was unsettling. Long minutes stretched out before the second expedition realized that these hexagonally spaced humans were trying to greet them, to induct them into something they termed the Being Suite.

This offer made, the faces within the hexagonal array began to show separate expressions. Tapes of this encounter show regular facial alterations with a fixed periodicity of 1.27 seconds. Each separate face racheted, jerking among a menu of finely graduated countenances—anger, sympathy, laughter, rage, curiosity, shock, puzzlement, ecstasy—flickering, flickering, endlessly flickering.

A witness later said that it were as if the hexagonals (as they came to be called) knew that human expressiveness centered on the face, and so had slipped into a kind of language of facial aspects. This seemed natural to them, and yet the 1.27 second pace quickly gave the witnesses a sense of creeping horror.

High-speed tapes of the event showed more. Beneath the 1.27 frequency there was a higher harmonic, barely perceptible to the human eye, in which other expressions shot across the hexagonals' faces. These were like waves, muscular twitches that washed over the skin like tidal pulls.

This periodicity was the same as the tile-polygons had displayed. The subliminal aspects were faster than the conscious human optical processor can manage, yet research showed that they were decipherable in the target audience.

Researchers later concluded that this rapid display was the origin of the growing unease felt by the second expedition. The hexagonals said nothing throughout all this.

The second expedition crew described the experience as uncanny, racking, unbearable. Their distinct impression was that the first expedition now manifested as like the *tile-things*. Such testimony was often followed by an involuntary twitch.

Tapes do not yield such an impression upon similar audiences: they have become the classic example of having to be in a place and time to sense the meaning of an event. Still, the tapes are disturbing, and access is controlled. Some Earth audiences experienced breakdowns after viewing them.

But the second expedition agreed even more strongly upon a second conclusion. Plainly, the *Adventurer* expedition had joined the computational labyrinth that was Shiva. How they were seduced was never clear, the second expedition feared finding out.

Indeed, their sole, momentary brush with {—John/Odis/Lissa/Tagore/ Cap'n . . . —} convinced the second expedition that there was no point in pursuing the maze of Shiva.

The hostility radiating from the second expedition soon drove the hexagonals back into their ship and away. The fresh humans from Earth felt something gut-level and instinctive, a reaction beyond words. The hexagonals retreated without showing a coherent reaction. They simply turned and walked away, holding to the four centimeter spacing. The 1.27 second flicker stopped and they returned to a bland expression, alert but giving nothing away.

The vision these hexagonals conveyed was austere, jarring . . . and yet, plainly intended to be inviting.

The magnitude of their failure was a measure of the abyss that separated the two parties. The hexagonals were now both more and less than human.

The hexagonals left recurrent patterns that told much, though only in retrospect. Behind the second expedition's revulsion lay a revelation: of a galaxy spanned by intelligences formal and remote, far developed beyond the organic stage. Such intelligences had been born variously, of early organic forms, or of later machine civilizations which had arisen upon the ashes of extinct organic societies. The gleam of the stars was in fact a metallic glitter.

This vision was daunting enough: of minds so distant and strange, hosted in bodies free of sinew and skin. But there was something more, an inexpressible repulsion in the manifestation of {—John/Odis/Lissa/Tagore/Cap'n . . . —}.

A 19th century philosopher, Goethe, had once remarked that if one stared into the abyss long enough, it stared back. This proved true. A mere moment's lingering look, quiet and almost casual, was enough. The second expedition panicked. It is not good to stare into a pit that has no bottom.

They had sensed the final implication of Shiva's evolution. To alight upon such interior worlds of deep, terrible exotica exacted a high cost: the body itself. Yet all those diverse people had joined the *syntony* of Shiva—an electrical harmony that danced to unheard musics. Whether they had been seduced, or even raped, would forever be unclear.

Out of the raw data-stream the second expedition could sample transmissions from the tile-things, as well. The second expedition caught a link-locked sense of repulsive grandeur. Still organic in their basic organization, still tied to the eternal wheel of birth and death, the tiles had once been lords of their own world, holding dominion over all they knew.

Now they were patient, willing drones in a hive they could not comprehend. But—and here human terms undoubtedly fail they loved their immersion.

Where was their consciousness housed? Partially in each, or in some displaced, additive sense? There was no clear way to test either idea.

The tile-things were like durable, patient machines that could best carry forward the first stages of a grand computation. Some biologists compared them with insects, but no evolutionary mechanism seemed capable of yielding a reason why a species would give itself over to computation. The insect analogy died, unable to predict the response of the polygons to stimulus, or even why they existed.

Or was their unending jostling only in the service of calculation? The tile-polygons would not say. They never responded to overtures.

The Circular Ocean's enormous atmospheric laser pulsed regularly, as the planet's orbit and rotation carried the laser's field of targeting onto a fresh partner-star system. Only then did the system send its rich messages out into the galaxy. The pulses carried mind-packets of unimaginable data, bound on expeditions of the intellect.

The second expedition reported, studied. Slowly at first, and then accelerating, the terror overcame them.

They could not fathom Shiva, and steadily they lost crew members to its clasp. Confronting the truly, irreducibly exotic, there is no end of ways to perish.

In the end they studied Shiva from a distance, no more. Try as they could, they always met a barrier in their understanding. Theories came and went, fruitlessly. Finally, they fled.

It is one thing to speak of embracing the new, the fresh, the strange. It is another to feel that one is an insect, crawling across a page of the *Encyclopedia Britannica*, knowing only that something vast is passing by beneath, all without your sensing more than a yawning vacancy. Worse, the lack was clearly in oneself, and was irredeemable.

This was the first contact humanity had with the true nature of the galaxy. It would not be the last. But the sense of utter and complete diminishment never left the species, in all the strange millennia that rolled on thereafter.

Approaching Perimelasma

GEOFFREY A. LANDIS

A physicist who works for NASA and who has recently been working on the Martian Lander program, Geoffrey A. Landis is a frequent contributor to Analog and to Asimov's Science Fiction and has also sold stories to markets such as Interzone, Amazing, and Pulphouse. Landis is not a prolific writer by the high-production standards of the genre, but he is popular. His story "A Walk in the Sun" won him a Hugo Award in 1992, his story "Ripples in the Dirac Sea" won him a Nebula Award in 1990, and his story "Elemental" was on the final Hugo ballot a few years back. His first book was the collection Myths, Legends, and True History, and he has just sold his first novel, Mars Crossing. He lives in Berea, Ohio.

Here he takes us along on a suspenseful and hair-raising cosmic ride unlike any you've ever taken before, in company with an intrepid future adventurer bound for someplace nobody has ever gone before: a headlong plunge into a black hole and out of it again—if he can figure a way to get out of it, that is, with all the forces of the universe against him. . . .

There is a sudden frisson of adrenaline, a surge of something approaching terror (if I could still feel terror), and I realize that this is it, this time I am the one who is doing it.

I'm the one who is going to drop into a black hole.

Oh, my god. This time I'm not you.

This is real.

Of course, I have experienced this exact feeling before. We both know exactly what it feels like.

    ▬

My body seems weird, too big and at once too small. The feel of my muscles, my vision, my kinesthetic sense, everything is wrong. Everything is strange. My vision is fuzzy, and colors are oddly distorted. When I move, my body moves unexpectedly fast. But there seems to be nothing wrong with it. Already I am getting used to it. "It will do," I say.

There is too much to know, too much to be all at once. I slowly coalesce the fragments of your personality. None of them are you. All of them are you.

A pilot, of course, you must have, you must be, a pilot. I integrate your pilot persona, and he is me. I will fly to the heart of a darkness far darker than any mere unexplored continent. A scientist, somebody to understand your experience, yes. I synthesize a persona. You are him, too, and I understand.

And someone to simply *experience* it, to tell the tale (if any of me will survive to tell the tale) of how you dropped into a black hole, and how you survived. If you survive. Me. I will call myself Wolf, naming myself after a nearby star, for no reason whatsoever, except maybe to claim, if only to myself, that I am not you.

All of we are me are you. But in a real sense, you're not here at all. None of me are you. You are far away. Safe.

➤

Some black holes, my scientist persona whispers, are decorated with an accretion disk, shining like a gaudy signal in the sky. Dust and gas from the interstellar medium fall toward the hungry singularity, accelerating to nearly the speed of light in their descent, swirling madly as they fall. It collides; compresses; ionizes. Friction heats the plasma millions of degrees, to emit a brilliant glow of hard X-rays. Such black holes are anything but black; the incandescence of the infalling gas may be the most brilliantly glowing thing in a galaxy. Nobody and nothing would be able to get near it; nothing would be able to survive the radiation.

The Virgo hole is not one of these. It is ancient, dating from the very first burst of star-formation when the universe was new, and has long ago swallowed or ejected all the interstellar gas in its region, carving an emptiness far into the interstellar medium around it.

The black hole is fifty-seven light years from Earth. Ten billion years ago, it had been a supermassive star, and exploded in a supernova that for a brief moment had shone brighter than the galaxy, in the process tossing away half its mass. Now there is nothing left of the star. The burned-out remnant, some thirty times the mass of the sun, has pulled in space itself around it, leaving nothing behind but gravity.

➤

Before the download, the psychologist investigated my—your—mental soundness. We must have passed the test, obviously, since I'm here. What type of man would allow himself to fall into a black hole? That is my question maybe if I can answer that, I would understand ourself.

But this did not seem to interest the psychologist. She did not, in fact, even look directly at me. Her face had the focusless abstract gaze characteristic of somebody hotlinked by the optic nerve to a computer system. Her talk was perfunctory. To be fair, the object of her study was not the flesh me, but my computed reflection, the digital maps of my soul. I remember the last thing she said.

"We are fascinated with black holes because of their depth of metaphor," she said, looking nowhere. "A black hole is, literally, the place of no return. We see it as a metaphor for how we, ourselves, are hurled blindly into a place from which no information ever reaches us, the place from which no one ever returns. We live our lives falling into the future, and we will all inevitably meet the singularity." She paused, expecting, no doubt, some comment. But I remained silent.

"Just remember this," she said, and for the first time her eyes returned to the outside world and focused on me. "This is a real black hole, not a metaphor. Don't treat it like a metaphor. Expect reality." She paused, and finally added, "Trust the math. It's all we really know, and all that we have to trust."

Little help.

⬥

Wolf versus the black hole! One might think that such a contest is an unequal one, that the black hole has an overwhelming advantage.

Not quite so unequal.

On my side, I have technology. To start with, the wormhole, the technological sleight-of-space which got you fifty-seven light years from Earth in the first place.

The wormhole is a monster of relativity no less than the black hole, a trick of curved space allowed by the theory of general relativity. After the Virgo black hole was discovered, a wormhole mouth was laboriously dragged to it, slower than light, a project that took over a century. Once the wormhole was here, though, the trip became only a short one, barely a meter of travel. Anybody could come here and drop into it.

A wormhole—a far too cute name, but one we seem to be stuck with—is a shortcut from one place to another. Physically, it is nothing more than a loop of exotic matter. If you move through the hoop on this side of the wormhole, you emerge out the hoop on that side. Topologically, the two sides of the wormhole are pasted together, a piece cut out of space glued together elsewhere.

Exhibiting an excessive sense of caution, the proctors of Earthspace refused to allow the other end of the Virgo wormhole to exit at the usual transportation nexus, the wormhole swarm at Neptune-Trojan 4. The far end of the wormhole opens instead to an orbit around Wolf-562, an undistinguished red dwarf sun circled by two airless planets that are little more than frozen rocks, twenty-one light-years from Earthspace. To get here we had to take a double wormhole hop: Wolf, Virgo.

The black hole is a hundred kilometers across. The wormhole is only a few meters across. I would think that they were overly cautious.

The first lesson of relativity is that time and space are one. For a long time after the theoretical prediction that such a thing as a traversable wormhole ought to be possible, it was believed that a wormhole could also be made to traverse time as well. It was only much later, when wormhole travel was tested, that it was found that the Cauchy instability makes it impossible to form a wormhole that leads backward in time. The theory was correct—space and time are indeed just aspects of the same reality, spacetime—but any attempt to move a wormhole in such a way that it becomes a timehole produces a vacuum polarization to cancel out the time effect.

After we—the spaceship I am to pilot, and myself/yourself—come through the wormhole, the wormhole engineers go to work. I have never seen this process close up, so I stay nearby to watch. This is going to be interesting.

A wormhole looks like nothing more than a circular loop of string. It is, in fact, a loop of exotic material, negative-mass cosmic string. The engineers, working telerobotically via vacuum manipulator pods, spray charge onto the string. They charge it until it literally glows with Paschen discharge, like a neon light in the dirty vacuum, and then use the electric charge to manipulate the shape. With the application of invisible electromagnetic fields, the string starts to twist. This is a slow process. Only a few meters across, the wormhole loop has a mass roughly equal to that of Jupiter. Negative to that of Jupiter, to be precise, my scientist persona reminds me, but either way, it is a slow thing to move.

Ponderously, then, it twists further and further, until at last it becomes a lemniscate, a figure of eight. The instant the string touches itself, it shimmers for a moment, and then suddenly there are two glowing circles before us, twisting and oscillating in shape like jellyfish.

The engineers spray more charge onto the two wormholes, and the two wormholes, arcing lightning into space, slowly repel each other. The vibrations of the cosmic string are spraying out gravitational radiation like a dog shaking off water—even where I am, floating ten kilometers distant, I can feel it, like the swaying of invisible tides—and as they radiate energy, the loops enlarge. The radiation represents a serious danger. If the engineers lose control of the string for even a brief instant, it might enter the instability known as "squiggle mode," and catastrophically enlarge. The engineers damp out the radiation before it gets critical, though— they are, after all, well practiced at this—and the loops stabilize into two perfect circles. On the other side, at Wolf, precisely the same scene has played out, and two loops of exotic string now circle Wolf-562 as well. The wormhole has been cloned.

All wormholes are daughters of the original wormhole, found floating in the depths of interstellar space eleven hundred years ago, a natural loop of negative cosmic string as ancient as the Big Bang, invisible to the eyes save for the distortion of spacetime. That first one led from nowhere interesting to nowhere exciting, but from that one we bred hundreds, and now we casually move wormhole mouths from star to star, breeding new wormholes as it suits us, to form an ever-expanding network of connections.

I should not have been so close. Angry red lights have been flashing in my peripheral vision, warning blinkers that I have been ignoring. The energy radiated in the form of gravitational waves had been prodigious, and would have, to a lesser person, been dangerous. But in my new body, I am nearly invulnerable, and if I can't stand a mere wormhole cloning, there is no way I will be able to stand a black hole. So I ignore the warnings, wave briefly to the engineers—though I doubt that they can even see me, floating kilometers away—and use my reaction jets to scoot over to my ship.

◄►

The ship I will pilot is docked to the research station, where the scientists have their instruments and the biological humans have their living quarters. The wormhole station is huge compared to my ship, which is a tiny ovoid occupying a berth almost invisible against the hull. There is no hurry for me to get to it.

I'm surprised that any of the technicians can even see me, tiny as I am in the void, but a few of them apparently do, because in my radio I hear casual greetings called out: how's it, *ohayo gozaimasu*, hey glad you made it, how's the bod? It's hard to tell from the radio voices which ones are people I know, and which are only casual acquaintances. I answer back: how's it, *ohayo*, yo, surpassing spec. None of them seem inclined to chat, but then, they're busy with their own work.

They are dropping things into the black hole.

Throwing things in, more to say. The wormhole station orbits a tenth of an astronomical unit from the Virgo black hole, closer to the black hole than Mercury is to the sun. This is an orbit with a period of a little over two days, but, even so close to the black hole, there is nothing to see. A rock, released to fall straight downward, takes almost a day to reach the horizon.

One of the scientists supervising, a biological human named Sue, takes the time to talk with me a bit, explaining what they are measuring. What interests me most is that they are measuring whether the fall deviates from a straight line. This will let them know whether the black hole is rotating. Even a slight rotation would mess up the intricate dance of the trajectory required for my ship. However, the best current theories predict that an old black hole will have shed its angular momentum long ago, and, as far as the technicians can determine, their results show that the conjecture holds.

The black hole, or the absence in space where it is located, is utterly invisible from here. I follow the pointing finger of the scientist, but there is nothing to see. Even if I had a telescope, it is unlikely that I would be able to pick out the tiny region of utter blackness against the irregular darkness of an unfamiliar sky.

My ship is not so different from the drop probes. The main difference is that I will be on it.

Before boarding the station, I jet over in close to inspect my ship, a miniature egg of perfectly reflective material. The hull is made of a single crystal of a synthetic material so strong that no earthly force could even dent it.

A black hole, though, is no earthly force.

☙

Wolf versus the black hole! The second technological trick I have in my duel against the black hole is my body.

I am no longer a fragile, fluid-filled biological human. The tidal forces at the horizon of a black hole would rip a true human apart in mere instants; the accelerations required to hover would squash one into liquid. To make this journey, I have downloaded your fragile biological mind into a body of more robust material. As important as the strength of my new body is the fact that it is tiny. The force produced by the curvature of gravity is proportional to the size of the object. My new body, a millimeter tall, is millions of times more resistant to being stretched to spaghetti.

The new body has another advantage as well. With my mind operating as software on a computer the size of a pinpoint, my thinking and my reflexes are thousands of times faster than biological. In fact, I have already chosen to slow my thinking down, so that I can still interact with the biologicals. At full speed, my microsecondreactions are lightning compared to the molasses of neuron speeds in biological humans. I see far in the ultraviolet now, a necessary compensation for the fact that my vision would consist of nothing but a blur if I tried to see by visible light.

You could have made my body any shape, of course, a tiny cube or even a featureless sphere. But you followed the dictates of social convention. A right human should be recognizably a human, even if I am to be smaller than an ant, and so my body mimics a human body, although no part of it is organic, and my brain faithfully executes your own human brain software. From what I see and feel, externally and internally, I am completely, perfectly human.

As is right and proper. What is the value of experience to a machine?

Later, after I return—*if* I return—I can upload back. I can become you.

But return is, as they say, still somewhat problematical.

➤

You, my original, what do you feel? Why did I think I would do it? I imagine you laughing hysterically about the trick you've played, sending me to drop into the black hole while you sit back in perfect comfort, in no danger. Imagining your laughter comforts me, for all that I know that it is false. I've been in the other place before, and never laughed.

I remember the first time I fell into a star.

➤

We were hotlinked together, that time, united in online-realtime, our separate brains reacting as one brain. I remember what I thought, the incredible electric feel: ohmigod, am I really going to do this? Is it too late to back out?

The idea had been nothing more than a whim, a crazy idea, at first. We had been dropping probes into a star, Groombridge 1830B, studying the dynamics of a flare star. We were done, just about, and the last-day-of-project party was just getting in swing. We were all fuzzed with neurotransmitter randomizers, creativity spinning wild and critical thinking nearly zeroed. Somebody, I think it was Jenna, said, we could ride one down, you know. Wait for a flare, and then plunge through the middle of it. Helluva ride!

Helluva *splash* at the end, too, somebody said, and laughed.

Sure, somebody said. It might have been me. What do you figure? Download yourself to temp storage and then uplink frames from yourself as you drop?

That works, Jenna said. Better: we copy our bodies first, then link the two brains. One body drops; the other copy hotlinks to it.

Somehow, I don't remember when, the word "we" had grown to include me.

"Sure," I said. "And the copy on top is in null-input suspension; experiences the whole thing realtime!"

In the morning, when we were focused again, I might have dismissed the idea as a whim of the fuzz, but for Jenna the decision was already immovable as a droplet of neutronium. *Sure* we're dropping, let's start now.

We made a few changes. It takes a long time to fall into a star, even a small one like Bee, so the copy was reengineered to a slower thought-rate, and the original body in null-input was frame-synched to the drop copy with impulse-echoers. Since the two brains were molecule by molecule identical, the uplink bandwidth required was minimal.

The probes were reworked to take a biological, which meant mostly that a cooling system had to be added to hold the interior temperature within the liquidus range of water. We did that by the simplest method possible: we surrounded the probes with a huge block of cometary ice. As it sublimated, the ionized gas would carry away heat. A secondary advantage of the ice was that our friends, watching from orbit, would have a blazing cometary trail to cheer on. When the ice was used up, of course, the body would slowly vaporize. None of us would actually survive to hit the star.

But that was no particular concern. If the experience turned out to be too undesirable, we could always edit the pain part of it out of the memory later.

It would have made more sense, perhaps, to have simply recorded the brain-uplink from the copy onto a local high-temp buffer, squirted it back, and linked to it as a memory upload. But Jenna would have none of that. She wanted to experience it in realtime, or at least in as close to realtime as speed-of-light delays allow.

Three of us—Jenna, Martha, and me—dropped. Something seems to be missing from my memory here; I can't remember the reason I decided to do it. It must have been something about a biological body, some a-rational consideration that seemed normal to my then-body, that I could never back down from a crazy whim of Jenna's.

And I had the same experience, the same feeling then, as I, you, did, always do, the feeling that my god *I* am the copy and I am going to die. But that time, of course, thinking every thought in synchrony, there was no way at all to tell the copy from the original, to split the me from you.

It is, in its way, a glorious feeling.

I dropped.

You felt it, you remember it. Boring at first, the long drop with nothing but freefall and the chatter of friends over the radio-link. Then the ice shell slowly flaking away, ionizing and beginning to glow, a diaphanous cocoon of pale violet, and below the red star getting larger and larger, the surface mottled and wrinkled, and then suddenly we fell into and through the flare, a huge luminous vault above us, dwarfing our bodies in the immensity of creation.

An unguessable distance beneath me, the curvature of the star vanished, and, still falling at three hundred kilometers per second, I was hanging motionless over an infinite plane stretching from horizon to horizon.

And then the last of the ice vaporized, and I was suddenly suspended in nothing, hanging nailed to the burning sky over endless crimson horizons of infinity, and pain came like the inevitability of mountains—I didn't edit it—pain like infinite oceans, like continents, like a vast, airless world.

Jenna, now I remember. The odd thing is, I never did really connect in any significant way with Jenna. She was already in a quadrad of her own, a quadrad she was fiercely loyal to, one that was solid and accepting to her chameleon character, neither needing nor wanting a fifth for completion.

Long after, maybe a century or two later, I found out that Jenna had disassembled herself. After her quadrad split apart, she'd downloaded her character to a mainframe, and then painstakingly cataloged everything that made her Jenna: all her various skills and insights, everything she had experienced, no matter how minor, each facet of her character, every memory and dream and longing: the myriad subroutines of personality. She indexed her soul, and she put the ten thousand pieces of it into the public domain for download. A thousand people, maybe a million people, maybe even more, have pieces of Jenna, her cleverness, her insight, her skill at playing antique instruments.

But nobody has her sense of self. After she copied her subroutines, she deleted herself.

❧

And who am I?

❧

Two of the technicians who fit me into my spaceship and who assist in the ten thousand elements of the preflight check are the same friends from that drop, long ago; one of them even still in the same biological body as he had then, although eight hundred years older, his vigor undiminished by biological reconstruction. My survival, if I am to survive, will be dependent on microsecond timing, and I'm embarrassed not to be able to remember his name.

He was, I recall, rather stodgy and conservative even back then.

We joke and trade small talk as the checkout proceeds. I'm still distracted by my self-questioning, the implications of my growing realization that I have no understanding of why I'm doing this.

Exploring a black hole would be no adventure if only we had faster-than-light travel, but of the thousand technological miracles of the third and fourth millennia, this one miracle was never realized. If I had the mythical FTL motor, I could simply drive out of the black hole. At the event horizon, space falls into the black hole at the speed of light; the mythical motor would make that no barrier.

But such a motor we do not have. One of the reasons I'm taking the plunge—not the only one, not the main one, but one—is in the hope that scientific measurements of the warped space inside the black hole will elucidate the nature of space and time, and so I myself will make one of the innumerable small steps to bring us closer to an FTL drive.

The spaceship I am to pilot has a drive nearly—but not quite—as good. It contains a microscopic twist of spacetime inside an impervious housing, a twist that will parity-reverse ordinary matter into mirror-matter. This total conversion engine gives my ship truly ferocious levels of thrust. The gentlest nudge of my steering rockets will give me thousands of gravities of acceleration. Unthinkable acceleration for a biological body, no matter how well cushioned. The engine will allow the rocket to dare the unthinkable, to hover at the very edge of the event horizon, to maneuver where space itself is accelerating at nearly light-speed. This vehicle, no larger than a peanut, contains the engines of an interstellar probe.

Even with such an engine, most of the ship is reaction mass.

The preflight checks are all green. I am ready to go. I power up my instruments, check everything out for myself, verify what has already been checked three times, and then check once again. My pilot persona is very thorough. Green.

"You still haven't named your ship," comes a voice to me. It is the technician, the one whose name I have forgotten. "What is your call sign?"

One way journey, I think. Maybe something from Dante? No, Sartre said it better: no exit. "*Huis Clos,*" I say, and drop free.

Let them look it up.

☜

Alone.

The laws of orbital mechanics have not been suspended, and I do not drop into the black hole. Not yet. With the slightest touch of my steering engines—I do not dare use the main engine this close to the station—I drop into an elliptical orbit, one with a perimelasma closer to, but still well outside, the dangerous zone of the black hole. The black hole is still invisible, but inside my tiny kingdom I have enhanced senses of exquisite sensitivity, spreading across the entire spectrum from radio to gamma radiation. I look with my new eyes to see if I can detect an X-ray glow of interstellar hydrogen being ripped apart, but if there is any such, it is too faint to be visible with even my sensitive instruments. The interstellar medium is so thin here as to be essentially nonexistent. The black hole is invisible.

I smile. This makes it better, somehow. The black hole is pure, unsullied by any outside matter. It consists of gravity and nothing else, as close to pure mathematical abstraction as anything in the universe can ever be.

It is not too late to back away. If I were to choose to accelerate at a million gravities, I would reach relativistic velocities in about thirty seconds. No wormholes would be needed for me to run away; I would barely even need to slow down my brain to cruise at nearly the speed of light to anywhere in the colonized galaxy.

But I know I won't. The psychologist knew it, too, damn her, or she would never have approved me for the mission. Why? What is it about me?

As I worry about this with part of my attention, while the pilot persona flies the ship, I flash onto a realization, and at this realization another

memory hits. It is the psychologist, and in the memory I'm attracted to
her sexually, so much so that you are distracted from what she is saying.

I feel no sexual attraction now, of course. I can barely remember what
it is. That part of the memory is odd, alien.

"We can't copy the whole brain to the simulation, but we can copy
enough that, to yourself, you will still feel like yourself," she said. She is
talking to the air, not to you. "You won't notice any gaps."

I'm brain-damaged. This is the explanation.

You frowned. "How could I not notice that some of my memories are
missing?"

"The brain makes adjustments. Remember, at any given time, you
never even use 1 percent of 1 percent of your memories. What we'll be
leaving out will be stuff that you will never have any reason to think about.
The memory of the taste of strawberries, for example; the floor-plan of
the house you lived in as a teenager. Your first kiss."

This bothered you somewhat—you want to remain yourself. I concentrate, hard. What do strawberries taste like? I can't remember. I'm not
even certain what color they are. Round fruits, like apples, I think, only
smaller. And the same color as apples, or something similar, I'm sure,
except I don't remember what color that is.

You decided that you can live with the editing, as long as it doesn't
change the essential you. You smiled. "Leave in the first kiss."

So I can never possibly solve the riddle: what kind of a man is it that
would deliberately allow himself to drop into a black hole. I cannot, because I don't have the memories of you. In a real sense, I am not you at
all.

But I do remember the kiss. The walk in the darkness, the grass wet
with dew, the moon a silver sliver on the horizon, turning to her, and her
face already turned up to meet my lips. The taste indescribable, more
feeling than taste (not like strawberries at all), the small hardness of her
teeth behind the lips—all there. Except the one critical detail: I don't
have any idea at all who she *was*.

What else am I missing? Do I even know what I don't know?

I was a child, maybe nine, and there was no tree in the neighborhood
that you could not climb. I was a careful, meticulous, methodical climber.
On the tallest of the trees, when you reached toward the top, you were
above the forest canopy (did I live in a forest?) and, out of the dimness
of the forest floor, emerged into brilliant sunshine. Nobody else could
climb like you; nobody ever suspected how high I climbed. It was your
private hiding place, so high that the world was nothing but a sea of green
waves in the valley between the mountains.

It was my own stupidity, really. At the very limit of the altitude needed
to emerge into sunlight, the branches were skinny, narrow as your little
finger. They bent alarmingly with your weight, but I knew exactly how
much they would take. The bending was a thrill, but I was cautious, and
knew exactly what I was doing.

It was further down, where the branches were thick and safe, that I got careless. Three points of support, that was the rule of safety; but I was reaching for one branch, not paying attention, when one in my other hand broke, and I was off balance. I slipped. For a prolonged instant I was suspended in space, branches all about me, I reached out and grasped only leaves, and I fell and fell, and all I could think as leaves and branches fell upward past me was, oh my, I made a miscalculation; I was really stupid.

The flash memory ends with no conclusion. I must have hit the ground but I cannot remember it. Somebody must have found me, or else I wandered or crawled back, perhaps in a daze, and found somebody, but I cannot remember it.

❧

Half a million kilometers from the hole. If my elliptical orbit were around the sun instead of a black hole, I would already have penetrated the surface. I now hold the record for the closest human approach. There is still nothing to see with unmagnified senses. It seems surreal that I'm in the grip of something so powerful that is utterly invisible. With my augmented eyes used as a telescope, I can detect the black hole by what isn't there, a tiny place of blackness nearly indistinguishable from any other patch of darkness except for an odd motion of the stars near it.

My ship is sending a continuous stream of telemetry back to the station. I have an urge to add a verbal commentary—there is plenty of bandwidth—but I have nothing to say. There is only one person I have any interest in talking to, and you are cocooned at absolute zero, waiting for me to upload myself and become you.

My ellipse takes me inward, moving faster and faster. I am still in Newton's grip, far from the sphere where Einstein takes hold.

A tenth of a solar radius. The blackness I orbit is now large enough to see without a telescope, as large as the sun seen from Earth, and swells as I watch with time-distorted senses. Due to its gravity, the blackness in front of the star pattern is a bit larger than the disk of the black hole itself. Square root of twenty-seven over two—about two and a half times larger, the physicist persona notes. I watch in fascination.

What I see is a bubble of purest blackness. The bubble pushes the distant stars away from it as it swells. My orbital motion makes the background stars appear to sweep across the sky, and I watch them approach the black hole and then, smoothly pushed by the gravity, move off to the side, a river of stars flowing past an invisible obstacle. It is a gravitational lensing effect, I know, but the view of flowing stars is so spectacular that I cannot help but watch it. The gravity pushes each star to one side or the other. If a star were to pass directly behind the hole, it would appear to split and for an instant become a perfect circle of light, an Einstein ring. But this precise alignment is too rare to see by accident.

Closer, I notice an even odder effect. The sweeping stars detour smoothly around the bubble of blackness, but very close to the bubble, there are other stars, stars that actually move in the opposite direction, a counterflowing river of stars. It takes me a long time (microseconds perhaps) before my physicist persona tells me that I am seeing the image of the stars in the Einstein mirror. The entire external universe is mirrored in a narrow ring outside the black hole, and the mirror image flows along with a mirror of my own motion.

In the center of the ring there is nothing at all.

Five thousand kilometers, and I am moving fast. The gravitational acceleration here is over ten million gees, and I am still fifty times the Schwarzschild radius from the black hole. Einstein's correction is still tiny, though, and if I were to do nothing, my orbit would whip around the black hole and still escape into the outside world.

One thousand kilometers. Perimelasma, the closest point of my elliptical orbit. Ten times the Schwarzschild radius, close enough that Einstein's correction to Newton now makes a small difference to the geometry of space. I fire my engines. My speed is so tremendous that it takes over a second of my engine firing at a million gravities to circularize my orbit.

My time sense has long since speeded up back to normal, and then faster than normal. I orbit the black hole about ten times per second.

My god, this is why I exist, this is why I'm here!

All my doubts are gone in the rush of naked power. No biological could have survived this far; no biological could have even survived the million-gee circularization burn, and I am only at the very beginning! I grin like a maniac, throb with a most unscientific excitement that must be the electronic equivalent of an adrenaline high.

Oh, this ship is good. This ship is sweet. A million-gee burn, smooth as magnetic levitation, and I barely cracked the throttle. I should have taken it for a spin before dropping in, should have hot-rodded *Huis Clos* around the stellar neighborhood. But it had been absolutely out of the question to fire the main engine close to the wormhole station. Even with the incredible efficiency of the engine, that million-gee perimelasma burn must have lit up the research station like an unexpected sun.

I can't wait to take *Huis Clos* in and see what it will *really* do.

My orbital velocity is a quarter of the speed of light.

The orbit at nine hundred kilometers is only a parking orbit, a chance for me to configure my equipment, make final measurements, and, in principle, a last chance for me to change my mind. There is nothing to reconnoiter that the probes have not already measured, though, and there is no chance that I will change my mind, however sensible that may seem.

The river of stars swirls in a dance of counterflow around the blackness below me. The horizon awaits.

The horizon below is invisible, but real. There is no barrier at the horizon, nothing to see, nothing to feel. I will even be unable to detect it, except for my calculations.

An event horizon is a one-way membrane, a place you can pass into but neither you nor your radio signals can pass out of. According to the mathematics, as I pass through the event horizon, the directions of space and time change identity. Space rotates into time; time rotates into space. What this means is that the direction to the center of the black hole, after I pass the event horizon, will be the future. The direction out of the black hole will be the past. This is the reason that no one and nothing can ever leave a black hole; the way inward is the one direction we always must go, whether we will it or not: into the future.

Or so the mathematics says.

The future, inside a black hole, is a very short one.

So far the mathematics has been right on. Nevertheless, I go on. With infinitesimal blasts from my engine, I inch my orbit lower.

The bubble of blackness gets larger, and the counterflow of stars around it becomes more complex. As I approach three times the Schwarzschild radius, 180 kilometers, I check all my systems. This is the point of no rescue: inside three Schwarzschild radii, no orbits are stable, and my automatic systems will be constantly thrusting to adjust my orbital parameters to keep me from falling into the black hole or being flung away to infinity. My systems are all functional, in perfect form for the dangerous drop. My orbital velocity is already half the speed of light. Below this point, centrifugal force will decrease toward zero as I lower my orbit, and I must use my thrusters to increase my velocity as I descend, or else plunge into the hole.

When I grew up, in the last years of the second millennium, nobody thought that they would live forever. Nobody would have believed me if I told them that by my thousandth birthday, I would have no concept of truly dying.

Even if all our clever tricks fail, even if I plunge through the event horizon and am stretched into spaghetti and crushed by the singularity, I will not die. You, my original, will live on, and if *you* were to die, we have made dozens of back-ups and spin-off copies of myselves in the past, some versions of which must surely still be living on. My individual life has little importance. I can, if I chose, uplink my brain-state to the orbiting station right at this instant, and reawake, whole, continuing this exact thought, unaware (except on an abstract intellectual level) that I and you are not the same.

But we are not the same, you and I. I am an edited-down version of you, and the memories that have been edited out, even if I never happen to think them, make me different, a new individual. Not *you*.

On a metaphorical level, a black hole stands for death, the blackness that is sucking us all in. But what meaning does death have in a world of matrix backups and modular personality? Is my plunge a death wish? Is it thumbing my nose at death? Because I intend to survive. Not you. *Me*.

I orbit the black hole over a hundred times a second now, but I have revved my brain processing speed accordingly, so that my orbit seems to me leisurely enough. The view here is odd. The black hole has swollen to the size of a small world below me, a world of perfect velvet darkness, surrounded by a belt of madly rotating stars.

No engine, no matter how energetic, can put a ship into an orbit at 1.5 times the Schwarzschild radius; at this distance, the orbital velocity is the speed of light, and not even my total-conversion engine can accelerate me to that speed. Below that, there are no orbits at all. I stop my descent at an orbit just sixty kilometers from the event horizon, when my orbital velocity reaches 85 percent of the speed of light. Here I can coast, ignoring the constant small adjustments of the thrusters that keep my orbit from sliding off the knife-edge. The velvet blackness of the black hole is almost half of the universe now, and if I were to trust the outside view, I am diving at a slant downward into the black hole. I ignore my pilot's urge to override the automated navigation and manually even out the trajectory. The downward slant is only relativistic aberration, nothing more, an illusion of my velocity.

And 85 percent of the speed of light is as fast as I dare orbit; I must conserve my fuel for the difficult part of the plunge to come.

In my unsteady orbit sixty kilometers above the black hole, I let my ship's computer chat with the computer of the wormhole station, updating and downloading my sensors' observations.

At this point, according to the mission plan, I am supposed to uplink my brain state, so that should anything go wrong further down the well, you, my original, will be able to download my state and experiences to this point. To hell with that, I think, a tiny bit of rebellion. I am not you. If you awaken with my memories, I will be no less dead.

Nobody at the wormhole station questions my decision not to upload.

I remember one other thing now. "You're a type N personality," the psychologist had said, twitching her thumb to leaf through invisible pages of test results. The gesture marked her era; only a person who had grown up before computer hotlinks would move a physical muscle in commanding a virtual. She was twenty-first century, possibly even twentieth. "But I suppose you already know that."

"Type N?" you asked.

"Novelty-seeking," she said. "Most particularly, one not prone to panic at new situations."

"Oh," you said. You did already know that. "Speaking of novelty seeking, how do you feel about going to bed with a type N personality?"

"That would be unprofessional." She frowned. "I think."

"Not even one who is about to jump down a black hole?"

She terminated the computer link with a flick of her wrist, and turned to look at you. "Well—"

◆

From this point onward, microsecond timing is necessary for the dance we have planned to succeed. My computer and the station computer meticulously compare clocks, measuring Doppler shifts to exquisite precision. My clocks are running slow, as expected, but half of the slowness is relativistic time dilation due to my velocity. The gravitational redshift is still modest. After some milliseconds—a long wait for me, in my hyped-up state—they declare that they agree. The station has already done their part, and I begin the next phase of my descent.

The first thing I do is fire my engine to stop my orbit. I crack the throttle to fifty million gees of acceleration, and the burn takes nearly a second, a veritable eternity, to slow my flight.

For a moment I hover, and start to drop. I dare not drop too fast, and I ramp my throttle up, to a hundred megagee, five hundred, a billion gravities. At forty billion gravities of acceleration, my engine thrust equals the gravity of the black hole, and I hover.

The blackness has now swallowed half of the universe. Everything beneath me is black. Between the black below and the starry sky above, a spectacularly bright line exactly bisects the sky. I have reached the altitude at which orbital velocity is just equal to the speed of light, and the light from my rocket exhaust is in orbit around the black hole. The line I see around the sky is my view of my own rocket, seen by light that has traveled all the way around the black hole. All I can see is the exhaust, far brighter than anything else in the sky.

The second brightest thing is the laser beacon from the wormhole station above me, shifted from the original red laser color to a greenish blue. The laser marks the exact line between the station and the black hole, and I maneuver carefully until I am directly beneath the orbiting station.

At forty billion gravities, even my ultrastrong body is at its limits. I cannot move, and even my smallest finger is pressed against the form-fitting acceleration couch. But the controls, hardware-interfaced to my brain, do not require me to lift a finger to command the spacecraft. The command I give *Huis Clos* is: down.

My engine throttles down slightly, and I drop inward from the photon sphere, the bright line of my exhaust vanishes. Every stray photon from my drive is now sucked downward.

Now my view of the universe has changed. The black hole has become the universe around me, and the universe itself, all the galaxies and stars and the wormhole station, is a shrinking sphere of sparkling dust above me.

Sixty billion gravities. Seventy. Eighty.

Eighty billion gravities is full throttle. I am burning fuel at an incredible rate, and only barely hold steady. I am still twenty kilometers above the horizon.

There is an unbreakable law of physics: incredible accelerations require incredible fuel consumption. Even though my spaceship is, by mass, comprised mostly of fuel, I can maintain less than a millisecond worth of thrust at this acceleration. I cut my engine and drop.

It will not be long now. This is my last chance to uplink a copy of my mind back to the wormhole station to wake in your body, with my last memory the decision to upload my mind.

I do not.

The stars are blueshifted by a factor of two, which does not make them noticeably bluer. Now that I have stopped accelerating, the starlight is falling into the hole along with me, and the stars do not blueshift any further. My instruments probe the vacuum around me. The theorists say that the vacuum close to the horizon of a black hole is an exotic vacuum, abristle with secret energy. Only a ship plunging through the event horizon would be able to measure this. I do, recording the results carefully on my ship's on-board recorders, since it is now far too late to send anything back by radio.

There is no sign to mark the event horizon, and there is no indication at all when I cross it. If it were not for my computer, there would be no way for me to tell that I have passed the point of no return.

Nothing is different. I look around the tiny cabin, and can see no change. The blackness below me continues to grow, but is otherwise not changed. The outside universe continues to shrink above me; the brightness beginning to concentrate into a belt around the edge of the glowing sphere of stars, but this is only an effect of my motion. The only difference is that I have only a few hundred microseconds left.

From the viewpoint of the outside world, the light from my spacecraft has slowed down and stopped at the horizon. But I have far outstripped my lagging image, and am falling toward the center at incredible speed. At the exact center is the singularity, far smaller than an atom, a mathematical point of infinite gravity and infinite mystery.

Whoever I am, whether or not I survive, I am now the first person to penetrate the event horizon of a black hole. That's worth a cheer, even with nobody to hear. Now I have to count on the hope that the microsecond timing of the technicians above me had been perfect for the second part of my intricate dance, the part that might, if all goes well, allow me to survive.

Above me, according to theory, the stars have already burned out, and even the most miserly red dwarf has sputtered the last of its hydrogen fuel and grown cold. The universe has already ended, and the stars have gone out. I still see a steady glow of starlight from the universe above me, but this is fossil light, light that has been falling down into the black hole with me for eons, trapped in the infinitely stretched time of the black hole.

For me, time has rotated into space, and space into time. Nothing feels different to me, but I cannot avoid the singularity at the center of the black hole any more than I can avoid the future. Unless, that is, I have a trick.

Of course, I have a trick.

At the center of the spherical universe above me is a dot of bright blue-violet; the fossil light of the laser beacon from the orbiting station. My reaction jets have kept on adjusting my trajectory to keep me centered in the guidance beam, so I am directly below the station. Anything dropped from the station will, if everything works right, drop directly on the path I follow.

I am approaching close to the center now, and the tidal forces stretching my body are creeping swiftly toward a billion gees per millimeter. Much higher, and even my tremendously strong body will be ripped to spaghetti. There are only microseconds left for me. It is time.

I hammer my engine, full throttle. Far away, and long ago, my friends at the wormhole station above dropped a wormhole into the event horizon. If their timing was perfect—

From a universe that has already died, the wormhole cometh.

Even with my enhanced time sense, things happen fast. The laser beacon blinks out, and the wormhole sweeps down around me like the vengeance of God, far faster than I can react. The sparkle-filled sphere of the universe blinks out like a light, and the black hole—and the tidal forces stretching my body—abruptly disappears. For a single instant I see a black disk below me, and then the wormhole rotates, twists, stretches, and then silently vanishes.

Ripped apart by the black hole.

My ship is vibrating like a bell from the abrupt release of tidal stretching. "I did it," I shout. "It worked! God damn it, it really worked!"

This was what was predicted by the theorists, that I would be able to pass through the wormhole before it was shredded by the singularity at the center. The other possibility, that the singularity itself, infinitesimally small and infinitely powerful, might follow me through the wormhole, was laughed at by everyone who had any claim to understand wormhole physics. This time, the theorists were right.

But where am I?

There should be congratulations pouring into my radio by now, teams of friends and technicians swarming over to greet me, cheering and shouting.

"*Huis Clos,*" I say, over the radio. "I made it! *Huis Clos* here. Is anybody there?"

In theory, I should have reemerged at Wolf-562. But I do not see it. In fact, what I see is not recognizably the universe at all.

There are no stars.

Instead of stars, the sky is filled with lines, parallel lines of white light by the uncountable thousands. Dominating the sky, where the star Wolf-562 should have been, is a glowing red cylinder, perfectly straight, stretching to infinity in both directions.

Have I been transported into some other universe? Could the black hole's gravity sever the wormhole, cutting it loose from our universe entirely, and connect it into this strange new one?

If so, it has doomed me. The wormhole behind me, my only exit from this strange universe, is already destroyed. Not that escaping through it could have done me any good—it would only have brought me back to the place I escaped, to be crushed by the singularity of the black hole.

I could just turn my brain off, and I will have lost nothing, in a sense. They will bring you out of your suspended state, tell you that the edition of you that dropped into the black hole failed to upload, and they lost contact after it passed the event horizon. The experiment failed, but you had never been in danger.

But, however much you think we are the same, *I am not you*. I am a unique individual. When they revive you, without your expected new memories, I will still be gone.

I want to survive, I want to return.

A universe of tubes of light! Brilliant bars of an infinite cage. The bright lines in the sky have slight variations in color, from pale red to plasma-arc blue. They must be similar to the red cylinder near me, I figure, but light-years away. How could a universe have lines of light instead of stars?

I am amazingly well equipped to investigate that question, with senses that range from radio through X-ray, and I have nothing else to do for the next thousand years or so. So I take a spectrum of the light from the glowing red cylinder.

I have no expectation that the spectrum will reveal anything I can interpret, but oddly, it looks normal. Impossibly, it looks like the spectrum of a star.

The computer can even identify, from its data of millions of spectra, precisely which star. The light from the cylinder has the spectral signature of Wolf-562.

Coincidence? It cannot possibly be coincidence, out of billions of possible spectra, that this glowing sword in the sky has exactly the spectrum of the star that should have been there. There can be no other conclusion but that the cylinder *is* Wolf-562.

I take a few more spectra, this time picking at random three of the lines of light in the sky, and the computer analyzes them for me. A bright one: the spectrum of 61 Virginis. A dimmer one: a match to Wolf-1061. A blue-white streak: Vega.

The lines in the sky are stars.

What does this mean?

I'm not in another universe. I am in *our* universe, but the universe has been transformed. Could the collision of a wormhole with a black hole destroy our entire universe, stretching suns like taffy into infinite straight lines? Impossible. Even if it had, I would still see far-away stars as dots, since the light from them has been traveling for hundreds of years.

The universe cannot have changed. Therefore, by logic, it must be *me* who has been transformed.

Having figured out this much, the only possible answer is obvious.

When the mathematicians describe the passage across the event horizon of a black hole, they say that the space and time directions switch identity. I had always thought this only a mathematical oddity, but if it were true, if I had rotated when I passed the event horizon, and was now perceiving time as a direction in space, and one of the space axes as time—this would explain everything. Stars extend from billions of years into the past to long into the future; perceiving time as space, I see lines of light. If I were to come closer and find one of the rocky planets of Wolf-562, it would look like a braid around the star, a helix of solid rock. Could I land on it? How would I interact with a world where what I perceive as time is a direction in space?

My physicist persona doesn't like this explanation, but is at a loss to find a better one. In this strange sideways existence, I must be violating the conservation laws of physics like mad, but the persona could find no other hypothesis and must reluctantly agree: time is rotated into space.

To anybody outside, I must look like a string, a knobby long rope with one end at the wormhole and the other at my death, wherever that might be. But nobody could see me fast enough, since with no extension in time I must only be a transient event that bursts everywhere into existence and vanishes at the same instant. There is no way I can signal, no way I can communicate—

Or? Time, to me, is now a direction I can travel in as simply as using my rocket. I could find a planet, travel parallel to the direction of the surface—

But, no, all I could do would be to appear to the inhabitants briefly as a disk, a cross-section of myself, infinitely thin. There is no way I could communicate.

But I can travel in time, if I want. Is there any way I can use this?

Wait. If I have rotated from space into time, then there is one direction in space that I cannot travel. Which direction is that? The direction that used to be away from the black hole.

Interesting thoughts, but not ones which help me much. To return, I need to once again flip space and time. I could dive into a black hole. This would again rotate space and time, but it wouldn't do me any good: once I left the black hole—if I could leave the black hole—nothing would change.

Unless there were a wormhole inside the black hole, falling inward to destruction just at the same instant I was there? But the only wormhole that has fallen into a black hole was already destroyed. Unless, could I travel forward in time? Surely some day the research team would drop a new wormhole into the black hole—

Idiot. Of course there's a solution. Time is a spacelike dimension to me, so I can travel either direction in time now, forward or back. I need only to move back to an instant just after the wormhole passed through the event horizon, and, applying full thrust, shoot through. The very moment that my original self shoots through the wormhole to escape the singularity, I can pass through the opposite direction, and rotate myself back into the real universe.

The station at Virgo black hole is forty light years away, and I don't dare use the original wormhole to reach it. My spacetime-rotated body must be an elongated snake in this version of space-time, and I do not wish to find out what a wormhole passage will do to it until I have no other choice. Still, that is no problem for me. Even with barely enough fuel to thrust for a few microseconds, I can reach an appreciable fraction of light-speed, and I can slow down my brain to make the trip appear only an instant.

To an outside observer, it takes literally no time at all.

●

"No," says the psych tech, when I ask her. "There's no law that compels you to uplink back into your original. You're a free human being. Your original can't force you."

"Great," I say. Soon I'm going to have to arrange to get a biological body built for myself. This one is superb, but it's a disadvantage in social intercourse being only a millimeter tall.

The transition back to real space worked perfectly. Once I figured out how to navigate in time-rotated space, it had been easy enough to find the wormhole and the exact instant it had penetrated the event horizon.

"Are you going to link your experiences to public domain?" the tech asks. "I think he would like to see what you experienced. Musta been pretty incredible."

"Maybe," I said.

"For that matter," the psych tech added, "I'd like to link it, too."

"I'll think about it."

So I am a real human being now, independent of you, my original.

There had been cheers and celebrations when I had emerged from the wormhole, but nobody had an inkling quite how strange my trip had been until I told them. Even then, I doubt that I was quite believed until the sensor readings and computer logs of *Huis Clos* confirmed my story with hard data.

The physicists had been ecstatic. A new tool to probe time and space. The ability to rotate space into time will open up incredible capabilities. They were already planning new expeditions, not the least of which was a trip to probe right to the singularity itself.

They had been duly impressed with my solution to the problem, although, after an hour of thinking it over, they all agreed it had been quite obvious. "It was lucky," one of them remarked, "that you decided to go through the wormhole from the opposite side, that second time."

"Why?" I asked.

"If you'd gone through the same direction, you'd have rotated an additional ninety degrees, instead of going back."

"So?"

"Reversed the time vector. Turns you into antimatter. First touch of the interstellar medium—Poof."

"Oh," I said. I hadn't thought of that. It made me feel a little less clever.

Now that the mission is over, I have no purpose, no direction for my existence. The future is empty, the black hole that we all must travel into. I will get a biological body, yes, and embark on the process of finding out who I am. Maybe, I think, this is a task that everybody has to do.

And then I will meet you. With luck, perhaps I'll even like you.

And maybe, if I should like you enough, and I feel confident, I'll decide to upload you into myself, and once more, we will again be one.